PRAISE FOR
GUNS
& SMOKE

"Guns & Smoke is a triumph of a book with characters who face real & dark internal struggles & who must learn to accept & face their demons."
-Independent Book Review

"Sevier & Smith have balanced a dark world with a bright romance. This fresh look at the western genre that grapples with questions of redemption, trauma, & the many wounds of life that love both can & cannot heal . . . We can trust these authors with our hearts."
-Michelle Cavalier, Cavalier House Books

"This high-octane dystopian thriller from Lauren Sevier & Abbie Lynn Smith takes readers on an exhilarating journey into a ruined world..."
-Prairies Book Review

PRAISE FOR

LEATHER & LACE

"A western-dystopian filled with the kind of angst, drama, and swoonworthy romance that readers will wish every sequel delivered."
-Independent Book Review

"Sevier and Smith are masters of their craft, queens of writing concise beautiful prose that manages to weave plotlines together without feeling jumbled or confusing."
-Emily S Hurricane, Author

"A genre-bending take on the classic western, this wonderfully satisfying, superbly crafted tale is hard to beat."
-Prairies Book Review

THE FOOL'S ADVENTURE SERIES

Guns & Smoke
Leather & Lace
Chains & Reckoning

LEATHER & LACE

The Fool's Adventure Series
Volume 2

LAUREN SEVIER
ABBIE LYNN SMITH

This is a work of fiction. Similarities to real people, places, or events are entirely coincidental.

LEATHER & LACE

First Edition

Copyright © 2022 by Lauren Sevier & Abbie Lynn Smith

Written by Lauren Sevier & Abbie Lynn Smith

TRIGGER WARNING

Please be aware that *Leather & Lace* contains dark and possibly triggering themes including graphic violence, language, sexual violence, infant/pregnancy loss, depictions of human trafficking, and substance use disorder.
Remember that your mental health matters.

To the people who have forgotten, love remembers . . .

And for Paw Paw Wayne, the best outlaw of us all.

JESSE

FUCK THE SILENCE.

Anything was better than the all-consuming, yawning darkness of my mind. The silence was filled with too many memories. Her beautiful voice twisted into wails. Bones cracking. How she pleaded for my life. My brother's life. For help.

Beyond the steel door of the old service station bathroom, a riot of clashing voices echoed and drowned out the commentator. The vibration of stomping feet and screaming voices shook the ground. Apparently, my opening act was just getting good. The thunderous roar soothed me, dragging me away from that insidious silence.

I wound the bandage around my bicep once, twice, a third time. The fresh ink had barely dried, and I wasn't about to mess it up. I split the bandage with my teeth, tossing the roll into my bag.

No doubt my opponent tonight would be bigger than me. They usually were.

After all, everyone wanted a shot at beating me, and I was only in town for one night.

Mickey and I had arrived in Little Rock with the sunrise this morning, and we'd be gone by first light. We had places to go, things to do.

We had to find Bonnie.

I'd spent a month at the bottom of a tequila bottle after Jones's men stole her from me. It was only when my kid brother gave me a swift kick in the ass that I sobered up and made plans. Even now, three years later, the temptation to get lost in a bottle was strong. I shoved off the bench and paced the small room, forcing back the hopelessness at the edge of my mind.

We would find her. It was just a matter of when. If I didn't hold onto that hope, I'd have died three years ago.

1

LAUREN SEVIER & ABBIE LYNN SMITH

A fist pounded against the door as the crowd roared. An unstable calm stole over me, as it often did before a fight. My breathing steadied, and the pounding in my chest steeled me as I pulled open the door.

"C'mon, Jess," Mickey said a couple weeks after Sixgun stole Bonnie. I sat alone on the back patio of my uncle's house, trying not to think about the last time we were back here. I tried not to imagine Bonnie teaching The Kid to properly aim a knife at a target. I tried not to think about Will's attempt to teach Clara to shoot a gun. I tried not to think about Bonnie draped across my lap.

Thinking about what I lost hurt too much.

"I'm good." I tipped back the bottle of tequila I'd swiped from his kitchen. I didn't like the liquor, but it was all Mickey had.

My uncle sat across from me, blue eyes bright beneath furrowed brows. "I know what you're feeling—"

"You don't know a fucking thing." My nostrils flared as I shoved down my anger. But it was always there, just beneath my skin.

Mickey ran a hand over his face. "I know more than you think, Jess." Something unreadable passed through his eyes as he looked at his fingers and picked his nails. "You aren't the only person that's ever lost the woman he loves."

"No shit."

"So quit acting like the world is over."

"And do what?" I leaned forward, plunking the bottle on the glass table. "The Kid can't keep his eyes open for more than a few minutes because of the drugs. I can't go after Bonnie until he's okay. There's nothing else here for me."

I averted my gaze as hurt passed across his face. Guilt coiled like a snake in my throat, choking back the other harsh words threatening to spill forward.

"Why do you even care?" I asked after a tense silence.

"Because until you came along, I'd forgotten."

"Forgotten what?"

"What it's like to give a shit about anyone other than myself," Mickey said plainly. "We're family, Jess, and we take care of family."

The stinging burn of grief snuck up in my chest. I'd said that to him. Right before Bonnie was taken. I inhaled sharply, eyes slamming shut as I forced the emotion back. I couldn't lose my shit. Not now. Not in front of Mickey. Maybe not ever.

"C'mon," he said again, rising.

"Where are we going?"

"You'll see." He swiped the tequila from the table as he moved past me.

After I changed my clothes, Mickey led me down the main drag of the base. We walked in silence until he turned off the road toward a giant metal building. A long strip of aged asphalt spread out across the ground for what could have been a mile.

To the west, the sun dipped behind the horizon, its rays painting the clouds in bright reds and oranges. My breath caught as an image of Bonnie straddling me in the bed of the truck flashed through my mind. The bright hues of sunset caressing the lines of her face, making love to the soft slope of her nose and angle of her eyes just as I was making love to her. As if the whole world wanted to see the pleasure soaked in the depths of her eyes. And I was the only bastard lucky enough to witness it.

It was all we had. Those two nights.

Shouting sounded as we approached the building. My uncle grinned over his shoulder and led me into the open building. Most of the cavernous space was empty. Sound reverberated off the metal, making the place seem fuller than it actually was. A small bar lined the wall to my right. Several tables were arranged around an open square marked by orange cones. Barbed wire was slung between the cones. A man edged backward into the wire, cursing loudly as the barbs dug into the bare skin of his calf. Another man approached him with a menacing grin, taking advantage of the distraction. He delivered a swift uppercut to the man's chin, sending him reeling backward, his legs tangling in the barbed wire.

"What is this?"

"Fighting pits." Mickey grinned.

He introduced me to some of his friends, men and women who traveled the fighting circuit. After procuring a glass of tequila, Mickey chatted up his friends. But me? I watched the battle in the ring. I caught myself lurching forward with each desperate blow. Before long, I shouted alongside the other spectators.

"You good, Jess?" Mickey asked warily. I didn't realize I'd jumped to my feet as another round ended.

"Yep." I lowered into my seat.

As the night wore on, unspent energy tingled in my fingers. A guy twice my size had just knocked out his opponent. Blood tinged his teeth as he grinned at the crowd.

"Who's next?" he called.

An image of Bonnie's head lolling to the side filled my mind. I thought of my brother, just a sweet kid who may never fully regain control of his shooting arm. Guilt at not being able to protect them rose up in my throat.

I practically jumped into the ring.

Screaming voices and a high-pitched whistle drowned out my thoughts as I walked through the smoky, pulsing crowd. The walls of the old service station were littered with graffiti and signs depicting a rather familiar likeness. A sly smile found its way to my mouth. They never could get Bonnie's eyes right on those old wanted posters. Though I focused on the rough-hewn ring, more than one person recognized me.

"Montana?"

"Is that *him?*"

"Oh my God, he's sexier than the posters!"

Ignoring the hands that reached out and the voices that shouted for my attention, I focused on breathing. A sick sense of relief coursed through me at the thought I would get a good night's sleep tonight. I'd found out after that first fight that my nightmares disappeared when I was too exhausted to think.

Fighting was my drug; I fell into it with reckless abandon. It was the remedy to my nightmares, the means to find Bonnie.

Heat radiated from the crowd as I climbed onto the platform made from an old highway sign. I unbuckled my holster, pausing to grip the ivory handle of Selene—the .22 pistol Bonnie'd given me for safekeeping. With deft fingers, I unbuttoned my shirt, to the excitement of the crowd. Wolf whistles and eager screams mingled with the electricity in the air.

"Give it up for Montana!" The already pulsing crowd exploded. A mixture of roars and jeers drowned out any coherent thoughts. I faced my opponent. He was only a few inches taller, his hair cropped close to his scalp. An ugly shadow blossomed on his cheek; yellow tinted the bruise, hinting it wasn't fresh.

Between us, a spotlight shone down on the aluminum sign, worn down over the years. The man sized me up as hecklers cursed my name.

You didn't become a well-known fighter without gaining a few enemies along the way.

Light flashed across my opponent's face as he stalked nearer. The tip of his nose hooked to the a little to the left, no doubt from too many breaks. In the crowd behind him, I caught sight of a man wearing a pair of aviators beneath a black cowboy hat. Panic gripped my heart.

Sixgun. The monster who stole Bonnie.

LEATHER & LACE

I lunged toward him, not bothering to retrieve Selene. I'd murder the motherfucker with my bare hands.

"Hey!"

The announcer moved in front of me, momentarily distracting me from my mark. I shoved him out of the way, eyes flashing to the crowd, searching for the cowboy hat. A calloused hand gripped my bicep, twisting hard enough to elicit a hiss from between my lips. *My fucking tattoo.* I bared my teeth at my opponent and ripped my arm from his grip, punching his throat. He staggered backward.

The crowd exploded.

Desperation clawed up my throat as I wheeled around. Aviators. Black hat. Where the hell was he?

"Montana!" the announcer shouted. I sidestepped him again. There were only a handful of cowboy hats in the crowd, and none of them were the dusty black I was so familiar with. "Get back to your position or forfeit!"

I clenched my jaw against the helplessness that coiled in my belly and spread outward. Maybe I'd imagined Sixgun. It wouldn't be the first time.

The announcer lifted his eyebrows, silently questioning whether I intended on throwing the fight. I ducked my head and moved back into place outside the ring of light. My opponent wrapped his fingers around his throat, glaring as he squared off. Fire coursed in his eyes; veins bulged in his neck.

"Sorry 'bout that," I said, my words barely registering above the crowd.

The man merely smirked at me, lips pulling away from his yellow-stained teeth. "I'm gonna murder you."

A cocky grin crossed my lips, and I lifted an eyebrow at him. We'd just have to see.

"There ain't no rules," the announcer said, having regained some semblance of control over the crowd. "First to yield, knock out, or die loses." His hard eyes darted between us. "Good luck."

"Fuck luck," I murmured.

A siren wailed. The man charged, surprising me with his speed.

Most of the fighters I faced underestimated me, and I used it to my advantage. My farm-toned muscles had changed. With targeted training over the last three years, I'd gained enough mass that I needed an entirely new wardrobe. Softness that might have layered my body hardened over time. Though I was just over six feet tall, most of the people I fought were taller, broader, maybe even stronger.

5

But strength didn't always win.

Texas fighters were ruthless and swift on their feet. They taught me to use my added bulk to my advantage, to trick my opponents with misdirection.

As the man advanced, I dodged his meaty fist and ducked beneath his arm. The crowd screamed as I delivered a swift punch to his kidney. A choked sound came from between his lips as he wheeled around. Sweat and fury lined his face. I shrugged, unable to help my smirk. Maybe if he'd listened to what people said about me, he could have been better prepared. I didn't fight for money or glory. I fought for something more. Something harder to achieve.

I fought to free my mind from chaos, left behind in Bonnie's wake.

From the moment I'd seen Bonnie's dark, pin-straight hair whipping around her beautiful face, I was done. I fell into her trap and kept falling.

A malicious grimace flashed across the man's face as I split my stance. I lifted my fists to protect as satisfaction warmed my chest. I'd angered him. I wouldn't feel bad about kicking his ass. My opponent circled the light, and I mirrored him, waiting for his strike. It was always easier to let the brutes tire themselves before knocking them out.

Anticipation tingled along my skin as predator and prey sized one another up.

Fuck this.

I wanted his skin to split beneath my knuckles. I wanted to distract myself from the dark blue eyes that haunted me night after night. If only for a moment, I wanted to remember what it was like to be worthy of someone like her.

Losing her was my fault. That fact rattled me all the way to my core. I'd struggled when The Kid and I left Montana, never quite feeling like I could take care of him. Somehow, I'd reached a place of peace within myself, a place he would be safe. Because he had Bonnie and me. Now all he had was me.

And I was a massive fuck-up.

I motioned for my opponent to come at me. He rounded his shoulders to make himself look bigger. I shifted my weight back and forth, feeling the bounce of the metal ring. The movement caught his attention, which gave me an opening to punch him in his left eye.

I'm no angel, and I don't pretend to be. I'll do whatever it takes.

If Bonnie taught me anything, it was that we did whatever it took to survive. I would do whatever I had to in order to get her back.

Jesse had been an honorable man; he'd tried to do the right thing.

But Montana? Montana didn't give a fuck.

As the man's hand reflexively reached for his face, I drove my knee into his gut. A whoosh of air spilled out of his lungs; I bit back a gag at the decay on his breath. He hunched over, but I caught him easily, letting him rest against my shoulder for a single breath. I shoved him away, satisfaction blossoming inside me as he stumbled. My chest heaved with the adrenaline coursing through my veins.

I motioned for him to come at me again. He staggered forward, movements sluggish as he attempted recovery. With a sweep of my leg, he crashed to the metal highway sign, a resonant *crack* snapping above the crowd. As the spectators roared, I drove my knee into his gut and covered his body with my own.

My knuckles ached as they bashed against the man's cheekbone. The pain was familiar, soothing in a way that it shouldn't have been. I reveled in it. In feeling something visceral and real before me, something I could touch, instead of the things that haunted me.

Damnit, Bonnie, trust me! I've got you!

Hesitant, dark blue eyes flashed through my mind. I could almost feel her delicate hand grasping mine as we jumped onto a moving train. What would my life look like now if Bonnie hadn't taken my hand?

I drove my fist into the man's nose. The crunch beneath my hands gave a sick sense of pleasure. Satisfaction roared in my chest. I reared my arm back, readying for another blow to his face. I wasn't even close to being done.

Rough hands grabbed me, dragging me bodily back from my opponent's form. I bared my teeth as another man wrapped his arms around me to secure my arms at my sides. I bashed my head forward against the first man, pain blasting behind my eyes as I made contact with his nose. He released me, hands immediately going to his nose.

Blood dripped down my forehead, sticky and warm.

I drove my elbow backward into the gut of the man holding me and delivered a swift right hook to his jaw, enjoying how he fell into the crowd.

"Montana's dirty!" a voice bellowed. I turned toward it. A man about half my size stood near the edge of the ring, holding what looked like an old bullhorn. His eyes widened as I lifted my brows in challenge. I lurched toward him, and he flinched backward, dropping the plastic thing to the floor. He staggered away and fled.

I grinned at the raucous crowd, extending my arms to beckon the next challenger.

A drunk stumbled into the ring. Their long hair was tied back with a leather strap. They drained the drink in their hand and slammed it to the ground. Shards of glass shattered against the floor of the ring; light bounced off of them, and dancing colors filled my vision.

A small, blue glass bead flashed through my mind. It had delicate whorls of silver carved into it.

Something to remember me, or trade. If you're ever in a pinch.

I'd carried that bead with me every day since. A year ago, when hope of finding Bonnie dwindled, I took some of my winnings to a jeweler outside of Dallas. He fashioned that bead into a ring.

It became a promise. To myself. That I'd find Bonnie and give her that damn ring if it killed me.

A cocky grin curled across the drunk's face as he staggered toward me. I landed a single punch to his face, and he went down. As I scanned the room for any other challengers, pain exploded in the back of my knee. I landed heavily on the aluminum, an ache lancing up my spine. I turned in time to see my original opponent, red staining his chin, as he lifted a booted foot.

Son of a bitch wanted to play dirty?

So be it.

I hooked my arm around his boot and yanked him toward me. The man's massive bulk couldn't keep up. He crashed to the floor of the ring. I flipped him over and delivered a swift kick to his ribs, barely registering the crack of the bone.

Instead of the satisfaction of breaking him with my strength, all I saw was The Kid, writhing on the ground after one of Jones's men had shattered his arm.

He has The Kid, Jesse. My *Kid.* Our *Kid.*

Stumbling backward, I suddenly remembered the crowd watching this display.

"Montana, damnit, you won. C'mon!" the announcer said. I turned toward the man, finding two bouncers on either side of him.

I swiped beneath my nose, nodding.

I won.

So why didn't I feel like a winner?

I still didn't have Bonnie.

After scooping up my shirt and holster, I staggered away from the ring. People patted me on the shoulder as I passed, but I ignored them all. Instead,

I focused on re-dressing and securing the holster and Selene at my side. My fingers wrapped around the cool, comforting handle of Bonnie's gun. I ignored the shouts of *fuck you!* from people who'd lost money by betting against me. Time slowed nearly to a stop as the bar slipped into my sight. I sidled up to it, ignoring the patrons that either gaped or jeered at me.

The bartender was at the far end, grinning at a woman wearing a red ribbon who leaned on top of the bar with a low-cut top. As I contemplated whether I should climb over the bar and get my own drink, a warm hand slid across my lower back. A pretty blonde woman shimmied up beside me, tucking her hand into my back pocket.

"Hey sugar," she said around the pop of chewing gum in her mouth. "I can help you clean all that blood off back at my place." Her eyebrows lifted suggestively.

I clenched her wrist, yanking her hand out of my pocket. I shrugged her off. "Go find some other dumb asshole."

The woman scoffed. I ignored her, whistling louder to get the bartender's attention. The man reached toward the whore, tugging on the end of the red ribbon around the woman's throat. He wasn't worried about anything but getting that whore alone.

Leveraging my weight, I jumped the bar, feet hitting the concrete floor lightly. Voices rose in dissension, but I didn't give a shit. I rifled through half-empty bottles arrayed on a cart. Because of Gabriela's family in the Borderlands, Fort Hood was rife with tequila. I couldn't remember the last time I'd had good whiskey.

Amber liquid caught my sight, and I plucked the bottle. The cap clattered to the floor as I upended it; the whiskey's bite made me grimace. It burned away the hazed edges of my vision. The room snapped into startling clarity. My gaze moved about as I hopped the bar a second time, whiskey still in hand.

Shouts erupted nearby. Someone slammed into my side, knocking me off-kilter. The bottle slipped and crashed to the floor, whiskey sloshing across my boots. The fighting pit around me faded, replaced instead by a landing at some inn in a nondescript town in the desert. Bonnie's hands tangled in my hair, teeth grazed across my mouth. I could feel her ass in those short fucking shorts as she moaned against me.

We have to get to the room.

Desperate kisses filled my senses. I could smell the sand on her skin.

My heart ached. Three years. Three long years dreaming of stolen moments like that, when it was just Bonnie and me and our undeniable attraction. It was more than just physical. I missed her body, but I missed her sharp tongue and clever mind. I missed how she called me out when I was being an asshole.

I missed her in a way I never thought I could miss anyone. As though my entire body seized with a helplessness that left me frozen, teetering on the edge of shattering into a million pieces and being blown away on a breeze.

Could I last another three years without her? Hell, another day?

A fight broke out in earnest, snapping me back to the bar. I stalked away, gripping Selene as I shoved through the crowd. A familiar form hovered near the exit. I stopped short.

My uncle tipped his head up. Blue eyes like mine, sandy hair graying near the edges, and gray stubble lining his chin greeted me.

"Mickey," I said by way of greeting. His eyes were clearer than my own, the expression in them determined, a glint I hadn't seen in months.

"What?" I asked. "Is it The Kid?"

"No, he's fine," Mickey said. "It's Bonnie."

My heart stuttered in my rib cage. I reached for the front of his shirt, eyes widening as panic revealed the cracks in my controlled facade. He wouldn't say anything about her unless he had news. Mickey wouldn't mess with me. Not when it came to her.

"We know where she is."

We found her.

Hot relief coursed through my veins, heating my skin and inflating my chest. It spilled out through my extremities. My vision wavered, eyes slamming shut.

We found her.

Three years of searching, of fighting, of reliving the best and worst moments of my life culminated in this single, solitary moment.

We found her.

Now it was time to get the woman I loved back.

CHAPTER ONE

BONNIE

S OMETIMES IT FELT LIKE a war raged inside of me. I recalled being told a story about two wolves living within you: one white, the other dark. They constantly battled, each trying to gain the upper hand. Rabid beasts like the ones that grew twisted in the craters left by bombs dropped years ago.

The thing was, I couldn't remember who'd told me that story. Or what the point was supposed to be. Because my wolves were scarred and bloody, and both of them were pitch fucking black.

There were nights I woke up covered in sweat with the snapping of fangs clanging in my ears loud enough to force my pulse into my throat. Certainty lingered on my tongue like a dark film informing me something vital was missing. Other nights, like tonight, I woke screaming so loud it rattled my bones. My head split open, like it was going to cleave in two. Loss hit me like a freight car on a runaway train. I was unmade by it.

Then I realized the screaming was mine.

"Open your eyes." A whisper across my consciousness, a deep voice soothing the ragged edges of mania. *"I want to see you."*

Hard hands dug into my wrists, pulling my nails away from my face and hair. My eyes flew open, panic flooding my veins as shapes and voices overwhelmed me with sensation.

"Calm down!" It wasn't the same voice from before, but definitely masculine. And terrified. *"Babe*, you're going to wake the whole house!"

"Savannah!" The name dragged from the pit of my gut, reverberating along glass windows and keening down dark corridors. A wail from so deep inside me that no amount of fear or logic could quiet it. No, this scream rattled the foundation of my sanity and let it seep from wounds I couldn't name or heal.

11

Panicked eyes locked on a stranger's face in the dim light; his eyes were wide, and he was so *very* naked. Tears of desperation tracked down my cheeks, making his image wobble and blur. He had dark eyes, like the muddy waters of the Mississippi River, but I had the distinct impression they were supposed to be blue. He held me down tighter, his grip punishing as he tried to stop my frantic thrashing.

"What are you doing? Let her go!" This voice *was* familiar. Savannah, my friend and salvation, come to wrest me from the darkness that took hold inside my head. The hands that'd clamped me down disappeared, and with a gasp of desperation, I gathered my sweat-soaked sheet around my body and scrambled toward the headboard. "Find things you remember."

I'll come for you.

A terror-soaked promise echoed dully where my mind used to be.

My gaze tracked the room, catching on objects that grounded me to reality. A stack of books on the desk in the corner, the bindings tattered and pages yellowed with age. Hairpins glinted in the scant light, sticking from the center of my closet door from furious throwing sessions and fits of anger. Thick blue drapes framed wide plantation windows fitted securely with iron bars welded from outside, allowing gray morning light to spill in.

"Breathe." Another command I obeyed instinctually, my ragged breaths shuddering to a stop as I focused on the syncopated rhythm that would stitch me back together again.

In . . . two . . . three . . . four . . . out . . . two . . . three . . . four . . .

Long, familiar arms wrapped around me and held tight. The hard squeeze shocked me back to this moment. Until the fading adrenaline made me tremble and shake, my brain catching up to what the rest of me had already accepted.

There was no danger here. Just the monsters clawing at me from inside my skull.

"You're safe," Savannah said, her husky voice a gentle hush infused with calm affection. When she said I was safe, logic told me it was true, but her lack of conviction left me strangely unnerved regardless.

"Are you alright, babe?" Peering over Savannah's shoulder, I stared at the naked man on the edge of my bed. *Shit.* I'd completely forgotten his name. He looked exactly like the last few guys I'd invited to bed, and all of them blurred together. Close-cropped hair, broad-shouldered, dumb, and completely unremarkable in every way. Unfortunately, I meant *every* way. But they were a good distraction that helped me sleep before the nightmares sank their dark claws into my shattered mind.

Staring blankly at the man, I slid from the mattress and the relative comfort of Savannah's arms. There would be no peace for me today, not even the flimsy approximation of it, and I wasn't in the mood to deal with an overly sentimental one-night stand.

"Get rid of him," I rasped, my throat ravaged by my inhuman keening. Savannah sighed deeply, weary of my unhealthy coping mechanisms. With a sidelong glance and a dark scowl, between us passed the grim reminder that *this* was not as bad as my coping got.

Even now, I felt the unnatural pull to numb my turmoil with glowing blue radiation.

Savannah stood rigidly, gathering his crumpled clothes forgotten around the room. His pants were by the legs of the chaise, boots near the foot of the bed, but his shirt and jacket were near the door. They hadn't made it much farther past the threshold. The night before came back to me in fits and starts, shards of shame and weakness hidden by the night and dulled with alcohol.

In the darkness of my room, I could pretend that he was *anyone* and that I was someone else. Someone who believed the lies of happily ever after. Someone worthy of being loved.

In the harsh light of day, there was no escaping the fact that bad things happened to good people all the time. So, really, what the fuck was the point in trying?

"What do you mean? Babe! Don't do this. We have something special, and last night—"

I shuffled to the door of my en-suite bathroom, ignoring the half-whined protests from the mostly naked man being shoved from my rooms. Dropping the sheet to the floor, I twisted the taps and slid into the clawfoot tub, erasing the night's horror from my mind.

It was harder than normal this morning. Those whispered words in my consciousness were a stark reminder of everything I'd lost. As the scalding water rose, I sank beneath the surface, begging that voice to drag me further. Until everything just stopped hurting.

Instead, I broke through the surface of the water, gasping and spluttering as I tried to reorder my mind. My fingers curled over the lip of the clawfoot tub and clenched tight, until the knuckles stood taut against my skin, when Savannah appeared. She was already buttoned into her conservative dress for the day, this one a dull gray starched until the seams were so straight it was any wonder it fell against her skin at all.

"Don't say it." I groaned, leaning my head against the tub to stare at the ceiling. But, like usual, Savannah didn't listen. The best friends usually didn't.

"I mean, he wasn't even that attractive." She crossed to the linen cabinet and pulled out a couple of fluffy white towels.

"Oh yeah?" I flicked water from the tub onto her starched cotton dress. "What would you know about it?"

She gasped and rubbed at the wet spot, wrinkling her nose and making her warm brown eyes stand out against her high cheekbones and full pink lips. "Whatever, *babe*."

I groaned again and she cracked a smile, kneeling beside the tub and resting her arms next to me.

"He was enthusiastic, okay?" A grin cracked through my bad mood to lessen the tension simmering between us.

"Oh, I just bet he was." She giggled. "You've *got* to stop screwing the guards."

"—*Ex-guard*, technically."

She rolled her eyes. "They're all dumb meatheads with no imagination."

"I screw some of the maids too." A smile lit up my face at her scandalized expression. Her ochre skin radiated this morning, like she'd swallowed sunshine. Jealousy roiled in my gut when I looked upon her sweet naivete. Her easy smile fell, and her sunny expression darkened with concern.

"How bad is it?" she asked without preamble. It felt like something was caving in near the center of my chest. Another piece of me crumbling into dust and nothing.

Explaining it would be impossible. So instead, I said, "Bad."

"Do you want to talk about it?" Pity made her graceful eyes impossibly wide and doe-like. I couldn't look at them, so I scrubbed vigorously at my skin to rid myself of last night's sins.

"What's there to talk about? Just another nightmare," I said in a falsely neutral voice. One that Savannah saw through easily, like she always had.

"Well, maybe if you told me what they were about, I could help you work through them," she replied kindly, reaching out to still my scrubbing hand, which was raking the skin of my collarbone raw.

Swallowing the bitter taste of fear in my mouth, I dropped the hand towel into the rapidly cooling water by my legs.

"There's nothing to work out," I told her honestly. "It's a jumble of things, all out of place. When I wake, all I remember is the impression left behind. Blood and pain, fear and loss. Nothing tangible. No monster to slay."

Only that was a lie. *I'll come for you.* I still heard the echo of that deep voice, ringing clear with a conviction that could sink blades deep between my ribs and lodge there.

"Loss?" she asked in a small voice. My screaming from another bloody night filled my mind as memories assaulted me.

"Not *that.*" I stood abruptly from the water and watched it slosh violently as I stepped out, completely unashamed of my nakedness.

"Then what?" She handed me a towel that I wrapped haphazardly around my body. I turned my back on her, walking into my room and grabbing whatever hung nearest from my wardrobe to toss onto the bed. She followed slowly, giving me time and space like a spooked horse. She knew I would confide in her; I always did. Sometimes, it felt like I had no one else to talk to. Like because she knew all my broken pieces so intimately, there was no use explaining the jagged bits to anyone new. Quickly, I put on my underthings, ignoring my reflection in the mirror as I chewed on my thumbnail.

"Do you remember when we put that god-awful puzzle together during the hurricane blackout last year?" I asked, watching carefully as she nodded. Her brows were drawn low in contemplation, honeyed eyes dark with worry. I hadn't been this fidgety in a while, and she saw the urge inside me to numb myself to it all. The craving for sweet blue oblivion written in my frantic eyes.

"It took us two days to finish the damned thing because we couldn't find the corner piece. It's a lot like that. Like my nightmares are telling me I'm missing something that will make all those other pieces fit together." I scoured her features to see if she understood.

But all she offered me was confusion.

"Never mind." I ducked my head to keep my reflection out of sight as I pulled on the pristinely-laundered cotton blouse and stretchy pants. There would be no peace today. No long hours in my favorite window seat with a book or mischievous rule-breaking that ended in laughter.

I needed pain. Enough to beat the yearning ache for glowroot right out of my chest. If Savannah's clear disapproval was any indication, she knew exactly where I was heading. I tied my hair back tightly from my face, the ends still dripping from my quick dip in the tub. Savannah crossed her arms and scowled.

"He won't be up for hours, you know," she said, her voice so scathing it hardly sounded like her. "He might not even be in the house."

Her warning echoed behind me down the hallway, an ominous portrayal of my own thoughts. Only, I didn't have a choice. So, as the sun peaked higher in the sky and the light grew golden, I marched purposefully to the staircase. No one was about yet, no staff members making their rounds, no friendly morning greetings.

Good.

I wasn't in the mood to fake a polite smile and a sweet temperament; I needed to make someone bleed. Badly. On nimble feet, I navigated the sweeping oak staircase, avoiding each squeaky spot on the well-worn steps that had somehow miraculously survived the end of the world.

As I descended, the house opened up to me, as if it'd been waiting for me all along. White columns with carved pedestals held up walls with ornately trimmed wainscoting; they guided me forward and into the body of the sprawling home. Wings of finely appointed rooms veered off from the main hallway, enticing newcomers to explore. This house, with all its lavish embellishment, was like me. A beautiful prison filled with dark secrets clawing their way out.

But, ultimately, empty inside.

I didn't slow down to feel the weight of the manor crushing me as I did sometimes when I felt reckless. The need to run burned in my blood, pounded in my pulse. It chased me down the hallways as I entered the courtyard and kept thudding on. Each step banged through my body like the frantic beat of a drum, urging me faster.

Too soon, I found myself in the stables near the backhouse where the live-in staff resided. The warm animal scent of hay, horses, and leather assaulted my senses and forced my vision clear. Soft nickering and the clipping of impatient hooves were the only sounds that broke the peaceful morning silence. That was, until I reached the stall at the end, where a massive towering creature made of nightmares and shadow stomped in agitation at my presence.

"Don't try me today, hell horse, or I'll make you into fuckin' glue." He slammed his hooves against the stall door in response. Chuffing in annoyance, the massive beast turned, ducking to nudge a dirty heap of long bronze limbs and wrinkled, bourbon-soaked clothes in the corner.

An arm sluggishly raised to scratch the horse's nose with a grunt. Good, he wasn't dead. Yet.

"Wake up, asshole." My loud voice forced the man to sit up and drag his black cowboy hat from covering his scarred face. "Time to train."

It took longer than I wanted for him to struggle clumsily to his feet, slapping off hay and dirt from black clothes that had suspicious stains.

"I don't have all day, Ellis."

He turned to regard me carefully for a few long moments, as if lost deep in memory. Will Ellis was the most infuriating man on staff in the household. Trouble stalked after him like a dark portent of death on the horizon. Unfortunately, he was exactly what I needed right now.

"That bad, huh?" Sleep clung to the vowels of his words and dragged them from his mouth. He wasn't wrong, though; it was bad. Bad enough that I needed him to *hurry*.

"You don't get paid to ask me personal questions." Some of the venom had inevitably leeched from my words, making them sound petulant and childish instead.

"I don't get paid to deal with *putas* at the ass-crack of dawn, either." The Spanish rolled off his tongue. His horse ducked his head, nudging insistently against the front of his shirt.

"Bad enough." I crossed my arms defensively.

"Cravings?" He took his sweet time unbuttoning the front pocket of his shirt and holding a sugar cube for his mount to nudge off his palm with clumsy lips.

"Yes." The word was forced out from between clenched teeth on a hot breath. That admission cost me. Even more when Will turned dark, intelligent eyes on me, raking over every inch of my strung-tight body.

"I'll get the guards." He pet his horse before settling his hat low enough to hide the wicked scar curving from his hairline to the corner of his eye. "How many will I need today?"

"Six." I turned to avoid whatever expression might cross his stern face. I didn't care what he thought anyway. I just needed to feel in control again, more than I needed to breathe.

I met him in the courtyard, with six burly guards stretching out muscles slow to respond from the last vestiges of sleep. He'd cleaned up, his long curly hair raked into a semi-neat leather strap and face splashed with water. With a whistle, the guards moved into position around me.

"Don't hold back," he commanded darkly. The guards shifted nervously and shared hesitant glances. "If you do, she'll kill you."

For the next few hours, my body was punished by Will's cruel lessons until there was no room to think or feel or *crave*. His voice barking in my ear was the only thing I could clearly remember.

Don't hesitate. If you hesitate you'll be—

Dead.

There are two kinds of people in this world—

The killers and the killed.

There is no room for honor in a fight, no rules, there is only—

Escape or murder.

You fight to—

Incapacitate or kill.

An enemy left alive is an enemy—

Who'll come for you later.

Every muscle in my body screamed and sweat drenched my clothes, but other than Will's fucked-up life lessons, there was nothing in my mind but blissful silence. No ominous voice promising retribution. No tangled fear knotting in my throat and stealing my breath. No ache for the numbing blue drug to drag me into oblivion.

"We're done," Will said, earning grateful glances from my sparring partners. Most of them looked like they might fall over at any moment.

"What?" I walked on quaking legs. "Not yet, I can still—"

"It's past noon and you haven't eaten," he said, cutting me off abruptly. "Besides, I have shit to do, *mi cielo.*"

He turned his attention to his pockets, patting them down until he pulled out a scuffed cigarette case and a match.

"What does that mean? *Mi cielo.* You call me that a lot." I stretched an arm behind my back to pull on a particularly sore shoulder muscle. A puff of smoke obscured his face then faded on the slight breeze. Before he could stamp it down, I noted the deep sorrow etched into the tight expression around his eyes.

"It means *pain in my ass,*" he mumbled. Then he turned his back and walked away.

Liar, I thought viciously but kept the accusation lodged inside as I shuffled toward the kitchens on heavy legs. The scent of roasted meat permeated the air all the way down the hall and incited a riot of grumbles from my empty stomach. Hunger tore through my thrashing gut. Maybe Will hadn't been wrong to call the training session to an end, not that I would admit it.

As I pushed the plain wooden door open from the quiet hallway, the world was suddenly thrust into delicious chaos. Kitchen staff scrambled around hot fire burning stoves, serving staff in pristine black pinafores polished silver and stacked porcelain plates and bowls, red-faced cooks clanged pots and pans, and in the midst of it all was Etty in all her glory, shouting orders above the clamorous din like a general at war.

Savannah stood at a countertop, whisk in hand, a soft smile on her face as she tried to take up as little space and notice as possible in the midst of the unruly fray. I snuck up behind her carefully, tugging the tie of her apron until it fell around her ankles. Confused, she looked at her feet and noticed me grinning over her shoulder.

"You are such a *brat.*" She rolled her eyes. I smiled wider, until it almost reached my eyes.

"Bravo, Savannah." I clapped mockingly. "I think that's the worst word I've ever heard you say."

"You smell worse than you look." She gave a prim sniff.

"I'm hungry." I rested my chin on her shoulder until she shook me off with a disgusted scoff. "You think Etty has something layin' around?"

"I *always* have somethin' on standby, darlin'," Etty said from the other side of the room, startling me. "C'mon, sugar, you know I got eyes in the back of my head."

With a sheepish smile, I turned to see her crossing the room with a jovial sway in her apron-clad hips. A plate with a sandwich rested on her palm as she leaned in for a hug. Etty was goodness and motherly love all wrapped up in one, and she never ceased to make me smile. Even though Savannah wasn't part of the kitchen's staff, if she wasn't with me, I could usually find her down here or on an errand for Etty.

Before Etty's warm arms and distinct flour-and-honey scent could envelop me, she reared back, nearly knocking over the plate in her haste. Nose scrunched and eyes watering, she shoved it into my hands before taking a tentative step back.

"Child, I think you need to burn those clothes; no way the smell is coming out of 'em." She whistled low. I rolled my eyes as she and Savannah exchanged grins. No doubt this was only the beginning of the teasing.

"I hate it when you both gang up on me," I muttered with a scowl. Etty snickered and retied her apron around her generous waist. Taking a bite of the sandwich, I groaned, relishing the feel of a full belly. I couldn't quite remember the last time I'd eaten, maybe yesterday morning, and it was made abundantly clear when I shoved more of the sandwich into my mouth. Alcohol was nothing but empty calories, after all. Or so Etty reminded me when she felt particularly petty.

Before long, I finished the sandwich and licked my fingers of the excess drippings. Savannah and Etty stared at me with mirrored expressions of disgust.

"I don't think she breathed," Etty said, earning a glare from me.

"I don't think she *chewed*," Savannah corrected, still whisking whatever sweet confection was in her bowl while bumping me with her hip.

"What can I say? Etty makes the best food in the city." I grinned, hugging her against her protestations. "I could kiss you, it was that good."

She arched a brow, and suddenly I felt like all my secrets were bare before her. Uncanny how she could do that so easily.

"From what I hear, you need to stop kissin' the staff before you wind up in more trouble than you bargained for." Her chastisement made my face burn. "That young guard came back to the side door an hour ago, beggin' to see you. Said what you had was *special*."

I groaned. Special? Hell, I didn't even remember most of the night. Just that I'd been unsatisfied and blissfully exhausted by the end of it.

"Speakin' of which," Etty said, pulling a mug down from a cabinet. A few moments later she slid a piping hot cup of herbal tea across the counter with a dark expression in her eyes. "Down the hatch, girl. You've already had your fair share of trouble."

She wasn't wrong there.

Wrinkling my nose, I choked down the first swallow of the bitter liquid. It raked down my throat like musty weeds steeped in river water. Savannah smiled cruelly at me, and in retaliation, I scooped a white glob of her mixture onto my finger and swallowed it. Whipped cream with *real* vanilla. That made the rest barely tolerable, at the very least.

The next hour passed easily, in the kind of companionable coexistence that only true friends could embody. When the conversation went quiet, there was no awkward need to fill the space. When we did speak or tease, laughter followed right behind. It was *this*, these moments, strung together like pearls on a string, painstakingly collected, that'd pieced me back together when I'd shattered.

LEATHER & LACE

"It's gettin' late, girls, and Mr. Lee was very clear he wanted to have dinner tonight," Etty said as the sun sank low in the sky. My eyebrows pinched together in confusion.

"I thought he was working tonight?"

"He is." She nodded as she stirred a pot on the stove, moving it out of the direct heat. "Asked to have it in the study."

My eyes nearly bulged out of my head at the news. In all the years I'd been here, I could count on one hand how many times I'd been allowed in his study.

"Damnit, Etty! I smell like an outhouse. He'll have my hide." My pulse hammered a frantic beat in my ears.

"That's what you get for lollygaggin' around down here." She gave an unconcerned sniff. Her eyes never left the pot in front of her. Savannah's hand gripped my arm as she led me toward the back stairs that would take me up to my rooms.

"That old *witch*," I grumbled after a couple steps before a sharp "I heard that!" echoed from below.

Savannah tugged on my arm more insistently, until we were both nearly sprinting to my room. As soon as the door slammed shut, I stripped out of my sweat-soaked clothes and Savannah turned on the taps to the bath.

"I'm going to dump all the lavender oil in, and then maybe he won't notice your . . . *aroma* as much?"

My only response was a grunt as I flung a shoe across the room.

"I swear, if it were anyone but Etty, they'd have a black eye." I struggled with my pants at my ankles.

"Stop griping and hurry," she said from the bathroom. I turned quickly, catching sight of myself in the mirror across the room.

My spine snapped straight, and a sick churning started in my gut. Eyes riveted on my reflection like a horror scene I couldn't unsee. *Wrong.* Everything I saw was wrong. A stranger stared back at me, and suddenly my skin felt too tight. As if someone else's features wrapped around me, trapping me in a prison of flesh and sinew.

Many people called me beautiful. I wasn't. Not really. They only saw the pretty, polished pieces I allowed to show. If they saw this, the patchwork of scars raised along my flesh, they'd shut the hell up.

I studied the angles and planes of my face in morbid fascination. Deep blue eyes that slanted upward at the corners accentuated high cheekbones and the delicate slope of my nose. My dark eyebrows cut a swath across the pale

21

expanse of my face and full lips pinkened by my teeth worrying them. If I was beautiful, it was a fearsome sort of beauty. A far cry from the soft, fresh-faced debutantes that frequented the lavish parties here. The kind of beauty that could wound with a glance, intoxicating but dangerous.

"We don't have *time!*" Savannah shouted from the bathroom, breaking my stare.

I didn't feel the heat of the water on my skin. Couldn't recall how many pins it took Savannah to force my hair up into a sleek, tight bun, just the way it was preferred. I slid the sundress on numbly, slipping my feet into soft shoes. On stilted legs, I walked across the house until I stood staring at the dark oak door before me.

I'll come for you.

The dark promise in those words reverberated through my skin. Sucking a shuddered breath between my teeth, I knocked. The door swung open, held by a woman with cinnamon-colored hair in a black pinafore, her eyes carefully averted.

Stepping into this room was like being blanketed with secrets, as if it were forbidden to speak in anything but whispers. This was where plans were made, deals negotiated, and the fate of the entire city determined each day.

The dark wood paneling and wall of hand-carved bookcases were beautiful, but the real fascination came in the form of a map framed along the wall behind a massive desk. It showed our country in its current state. Each crater site, gang territory, borderland, or free state clearly marked.

This was what waited for me outside the walls and bars of this house: a whole world ready to greet me. Not that I'd ever be allowed to see it.

He sat behind his desk, hunched over a familiar red leather ledger, scribbling in his tiny block lettering. Neither I nor the woman in the pinafore made a sound, too afraid to break his deep concentration. Finally, he noticed me there and waved an impatient hand for me to sit across from him. The cinnamon-haired woman set a place for me atop his desk, complete with pristine porcelain plates, silver cutlery, and a crystal wine glass.

I knew better than to ask the questions burning at the tip of my tongue. In this house, you didn't speak until spoken to. Instead, as he finished his work, I studied his features intently.

Iron gray streaks of hair faded into the deepest black, his figure imposing in his signature all-black suit. All save for the tie pin; *that* was a gold fleur-de-lis with a large diamond in the center, winking at me as if it were in my confidence.

The lines of his face were severe, skin folded deep above his brows and around his mouth. As if he hadn't laughed or smiled his entire life.

There was no part of him that was not intimidating, save for his height. Though taller than me, when he stood straight, he couldn't have been more than five-and-a-half feet tall. Despite that, I'd witnessed him silence men of all shapes and sizes with a glance.

He finished writing, stretching his hand from the strain before closing the ledger and tucking it safely in a drawer next to him. As soon as his work was done and his dark eyes, bottomless voids that were impossible to read, focused on my face, he changed.

His stern expression, displaying his advanced age, softened. Those dark pools went from the cold blackness of deepest night to the warmth of blackberries in summer, swollen with a sweetness that he reserved only for me. Subtle, but significant in a way I couldn't explain.

"I've been looking forward to this all day," he admitted, which coaxed an affectionate smile onto my mouth.

"I was surprised, since you said the deal with Manhattan wasn't finalized. I thought you'd be working all night." I unfolded the linen napkin and rested it gently in my lap as his place was set and dinner was served. He peered at me across the desk. "*Again*," I added pointedly.

He acknowledged the observation with a short grunt of affirmation. "It's actually the Manhattan Island deal I wanted to discuss tonight." He tracked the woman as she poured our wine and left the bottle on the corner of the desk.

"You're dismissed."

Ignoring the command and steeling myself, I tried to keep my face composed. Years I'd wanted him to allow me into this room, into the discussions about his business. I'd studied history, philosophy, economics, and business strategy as if my life depended on it. Countless days of finding myself floundering with no purpose beyond the obvious. He'd *never* wanted to discuss business with me before tonight. If there were ever a time to prove my worth, it was now.

"It's no secret that you've had your fair share of bad luck—"

I snorted. My first mistake, it would seem, since not only did he lack any tolerance for sarcasm, he abhorred any hint of impropriety. His hardening glare dried up any smart-ass reply that had drifted through my mind, however briefly.

23

"The Governor of Manhattan Island is reluctant to finalize any contracts without a formal meeting. After *many* failed negotiations, we've decided to take a more personal approach."

Whatever *personal approach* was decided, it was clearly not one I would like. Why else would he dangle the opportunity to be useful in the business when he never had before? The hair on the back of my neck rose at the open implication of his too-logical words, carefully devoid of emotion. As if he were preparing me for a hard blow.

"As you know, many business partnerships are guaranteed with more than just signed contracts—"

"No," I ground between my clenched teeth.

"Paper doesn't mean anything to the roaming bands of outlaws beyond this city—"

"I didn't stutter. My answer is *no,*" I said firmly, barely keeping the violence from seeping into my words.

He slammed his fist against the desk loud enough to clatter the plates and force my eyes shut with the shock. As intimidating as he could be, there'd never been a hint of violence in him before. Just cold apathy that ordered violence to sully other hands.

"Goddamnit! You've squandered every opportunity here. What's going to happen to you when I'm gone?" The question was rhetorical, but his wide eyes and how he leaned in almost demanded an answer. "Hmm?"

Gaping in dumbfounded silence, I tried to speak and failed. Once. Twice.

"Marriage is the *only* way to protect you," he said, those angry edges blunting as he stared at me.

"I have more to offer than just spreading my legs for some rich asshole," I spat between heaving breaths. "If you'd let me in, let me help you with the business, you'd see I could—"

"We *need* this contract, or it'll be disastrous. I've run the numbers a thousand times," he said, his tone fractured. His dark brows furrowed deep with worry that'd been plaguing him for weeks now. It felt like an admission. One that only someone he trusted deeply could have earned. "I thought, considering your *accident*—"

Accident. I hated that word. How many accidents left a man's name carved into someone's skin? How many accidents happened with so many unanswered questions left behind?

"—how hard it's been for you to acclimate. There's no one of substance left in this city who will consider you as a match. The rumors alone have made you damn near untouchable—"

Anger, hot and bitter, clawed up my throat and begged to be set free. To rend and rage against what my mind couldn't contextualize.

"So you're selling me for a shipping contract?" I asked. Blunt. Sharp. Like the edge of a blade slicing against skin and settling deep between muscle and bone.

He took a moment, then another, to hold my stare and prove to me exactly how little say I had in this matter. The warmth seeped from his eyes, until they were those fathomless pools of black, completely devoid of human emotion. His jaw hardened into stone, no hint of softness to be found in his expression.

"The governor's son, Lucas Rutherford, will be here soon, and you are expected to give him *every* reason to partner with our shipping company," he stated as a matter of fact, not a hint of consideration for me included. This was, after all, business. If there was one thing I'd learned these past few years, it was that morals didn't matter as long as the money kept coming in.

I stood, stomach thrashing as what few freedoms I'd enjoyed bled from me while the man before me issued ultimatums and barely veiled threats. The walls of this house seemed to shrink, the tons of brick, mortar, and wood crushing down around me.

"—besides, once you're married, you'll be able to travel to Manhattan Island."

"What?" I asked. The numbness spreading from the center of my chest stuttered to a stop.

"Lucas isn't the governor, sweetheart. I'm sure he'll want to travel. Especially after being newly wed."

"I'll get to *leave*?" I asked, breathless, feeling the prickle of desperate tears at the corners of my eyes. He nodded, face as stern as I'd ever seen it. No hint of the machinations that were no doubt turning in his mind.

After a silence that seemed to fracture with unspoken arguments rose between us, I took a steadying breath. If there was anything I'd learned in the last few years, it was that *nothing was free*. Was my hand in marriage worth escaping this beautiful prison?

"I won't marry a man I don't love." I swallowed down the doubt that crept up the back of my throat. "But I won't turn him away without trying."

The satisfied smile he gifted me settled heavily on my shoulders. As if I'd agreed to something against my will, even though it was clearly my choice.

"I expect you to represent us well. That means *no more training* while Lucas is here." He took his first bite of dinner from his plate. I grumbled but understood it was important for me to make a good impression. "He'll be here tomorrow."

"Tomorrow?" I questioned, strangled. All he offered was a nod. Silence descended between us, the kind that made it impossible to talk. Instead, I moved my food around my plate. Cutting things into smaller and smaller pieces and pretending he didn't notice. Finally, he gave me leave to stand on stiff legs. He stood as well, his few inches hovering above me like floors of a building. Separating us in space and station. I should have drained the bottle of wine while it was available at the table.

He wrapped me in his arms, cocooning me in his peppermint and coffee scent. As if I were something precious to him, not just a commodity. Loathing and comfort warred for control inside me as I sank into that embrace. I closed my eyes against hateful tears that threatened to surface against my will. He pressed his lips into my hair, smoothing it back as he separated us to rake assessing eyes over me.

"Never forget how much I love you, Audrey," he said, his voice tender and calm.

"I love you, too," I said softly as he walked me to the door. "Dad."

CHAPTER TWO

JESSE

THE MIGHTY MISSISSIPPI: AN expansive body of water that cleaved the east from the west. I'd seen it once before when I fought in St. Louis. This time, however, it felt different. As if the knowledge that Bonnie was just on the other side of it made it more dangerous.

Deep reds and purples streaked across the cloudy sky behind the hulking mass of concrete and metal that loomed ahead. Mickey eased his mount into a walk. Brows furrowed, I tugged on No Name's reins, eyeing my uncle suspiciously.

"Why are we slowing down?"

My uncle's blue eyes were clearer than they'd ever been. Aside from the salt-and-pepper stubble on his chin, he looked like a completely new man from the one I first met three years ago in Fort Hood. Then, he'd been haunted and lost to the bottle; now, he sat straighter in the saddle and spoke with the quiet assurance I'd expected to find when we first made it to Fort Hood.

"I need to make sure you're not gonna do something stupid, Jess," Mickey said. The lines of his face softened. "We haven't come this far to screw it up now."

The simmering anger that kept me on this path flared bright in my belly. The leather reins creaked in my hands as I coiled that fury into a tight ball and stamped it down. He had good reason to worry I'd lose my shit. We hadn't stopped in the weeks since my fight in Little Rock, other than breaking to sleep a few hours or give the horses a breather.

I hadn't spent three fucking years looking for the woman that I loved to slow now.

And she was just across that river.

"I'm not." I forced the bitter edge from my voice.

Mickey fixed me with a curious stare, his brows lifted and mouth threatening to curve upward. "Do I look stupid?"

"No." I clenched my jaw. If I weren't holding No Name's reins, I'd have crossed my arms over my chest like a petulant child.

"I'm not your pop, but I know you, Jess." He shook his head. "We've got no idea what's happening on the other side of that bridge." He motioned toward the hulking mass of metal and concrete. "This isn't some backwoods fighting pit. If I can't trust you to keep a cool head, tell me now."

"Good to see you have such faith in me," I mumbled.

"I do have faith in you. But you have a short goddamned temper."

"What do you know?"

Mickey scowled in my direction. "I know a hell of a lot more than you think."

"What does that mean?"

"That means," Mickey said, a harsh edge to his voice, "I watch your fights. I see how little it takes to set you off. We can't afford that. Not here."

"I can control myself."

"You sure?" he asked. "What makes this any different than Little Rock? Or any of the dozen towns you've fought in the last year?"

What made New Orleans different?

"Bonnie," I said, her name like a prayer on my tongue. "Bonnie's here."

Mickey's eyes darkened, and his lips pulled downward. An echo of the drunk, desperate man I'd first met years ago flickered across his face, as if the ghosts of his past still stalked him, even if he'd managed to achieve some semblance of normalcy.

"Promise me, Jess. Promise that you won't fuck this up—" He pointed at me as I opened my mouth to bark bitter words at him. "And! If you do, I get to throw you on No Name and send your ass back to Fort Hood."

My mouth snapped shut. I couldn't go back. Not now that we were so close. I couldn't sit at the base, waiting and watching the world pass, living on scraps of information. It drove The Kid crazy. He was angry at me for leaving him behind, but that was the only way I could safely do what I needed.

I couldn't go back there. Not when she was so close.

"I give you my word," I said, turning my gaze to the bridge.

"Good," Mickey said, then clicked his tongue. "Let's go."

We set off down the cracked remnants of the highway. The bridge loomed ahead, growing larger as time passed. The sun rose in front of us, the first rays of light warming my face. Anticipation crept up from my belly. I gripped the reins tight to keep my hands from shaking.

Three years. Three years of focusing only on my promise.

I'll come for you and bring you home.

Home. A place I hadn't known in so long. Before the fire, Montana had been home. Then I found Bonnie. *She* and The Kid were home.

I clenched my thighs around No Name as we began the ascent at the base of the bridge looming ominously ahead of us. Dark clouds moved behind the sprawling beams of steel ahead.

My gaze shifted to my left. I hadn't seen it at first, but the highway had split some time ago. The ruins of a second steel structure jutted from the river bank. Wind whipped up so hard, Mickey had to slap a hand to his head to keep his hat.

"I forgot how windy it could be," he said, more to himself than me. "You know, your parents and I came down for Mardi Gras one year."

"Mardi Gras?" The unfamiliar word felt foreign on my tongue.

"Fat Tuesday."

I stared at him dumbly, brows lifted.

"Carnival?" He cursed beneath his breath. "I forget how much you still don't know." A lazy smile crossed his lips as he relaxed into his saddle. "I forget how it started, but Mardi Gras was the day before Lent."

I didn't know what Lent was, either. Honestly, I didn't really care.

"It was a time for parties, parades, and too much alcohol." Mickey's eyes lit like they always did when he was lost to a good memory. "Your mom wasn't too crazy about it, but I loved it. There's something about New Orleans. Like the city never settled." He prattled on, but I tuned him out, instead focusing on the path ahead.

The bridge structure swayed as a particularly brusque wind kicked up. Dark figures swung on the breeze. My brows furrowed as the path flattened and we reached the top. I stared at the figures, confused. Dark shadows hung from long ropes.

A bitter tang rose in my throat as one of the dark figures turned in a circle. I grabbed Mickey's arm and yanked my reins to still No Name. Mottled flesh covered some of the swinging skeletons. By the look of them, they couldn't be too old. A black crow darted down from the steel rafters above, landing on the shoulder of one. I fought the urge to retch as it plucked one of the eyes from the body. The crow flapped its wings and flew off. My brows furrowed as I noted a fleur-de-lis carved into the corpse's forehead.

"Well, that's different," Mickey said, letting out a low whistle.

"What the fuck?"

My uncle shook his head and moved his mount forward. I veered No Name to the other side of Mickey, closer to the metal railing that overlooked the river below. Hulking masses of rusty metal broke its muddy surface. I stared as we began our descent down the far side of the bridge. Something seemed almost familiar.

"Are those ships?"

Mickey steered his mount closer. "Yep. People used to take cruises from the Port of New Orleans. They'd sail all over the place."

The old ships spanned the entire river. Near the far bank, men lined metal platforms on either side of a gap in the river, armed with assault rifles. A line of boats waited. One of the armed soldiers waved a hand, and a small tug boat moved through the canal-like passage.

"State your names and your purpose," a bored voice said.

I hadn't noticed the men in uniforms. Mickey's back straightened, eyes narrowing as he scrutinized them. "Name's Kincaid." He glanced at me. "This is my boy. We're just passing through."

"Through to where?" one of the men questioned, hands tightening on their assault rifle.

"There's a glowroot harvest in Biloxi in a few weeks," he said, the lie rolling easily from his tongue.

"You should cross farther north then. You'll be adding a week trying to get around the Pontchartrain."

Mickey leaned forward to rest an elbow on his saddle horn. "I'm aware," he remarked. "But, see, my boy's never been to New Orleans."

A grin crossed one of the guard's faces as he shared a glance with the other. They parted as the guard said, "Be sure to take him down Bourbon."

Mickey tipped his hat and steered his horse around the barricades made from giant tires. I followed, eyes low. As we passed, I stole a glimpse at their uniforms, or, more specifically, the patches on their breast pockets.

It was the same crooked flower design that'd been on Sixgun's neck. The *fleur-de-lis*, as Mickey called it.

"Mickey," I said.

"Hush," he whispered.

The city opened up around us as we descended. Sprawling concrete bridges splayed out, creating wide tributaries, like a river, interspersed between towering buildings. Mickey motioned to our right.

"That was the Riverwalk," he said. "Do you see that painted wall?" I squinted against the morning light. A brick facade painted with streaks of white and blue caught my attention. "That was an aquarium." I opened my mouth to question, but he cut me off. "That's where they kept marine animals. Sharks. Whales. Exotic fish. You paid to go inside and see them."

"Why would you need to pay to see animals you could see in the wild?"

Mickey let out an uneasy chuckle. "If only there were time to explain." He dug in his heels and took off at a trot, murmuring something beneath his breath that sounded oddly like *naive kid.*

We followed looping concrete highways, eventually veering off at one near an odd, dome-shaped building. It towered above us as we rode by, its rusty shell giving way to smooth, polished steel in patches. Crumbling concrete sidewalks were littered with metal baskets and makeshift tents. Barrels lit from within by fire were surrounded by people wrapped in threadbare clothing. They looked up at us with disinterest and exhaustion lining their features.

"Best not to look too close," Mickey said. "This isn't all that different from what it looked like before."

Buildings made of concrete and glass lined either side of a four-lane boulevard as we continued onward. Many of the old windows were broken. Lights flickered within some of the rooms. We saw very few faces. The lost souls wandering the gray streets took one look at us and veered away onto a side street or into an alley between buildings.

We turned onto a narrow side street made of a single lane. The brick buildings were much closer together, crowding us in a way that made me sit straighter in the saddle. I wasn't used to the city. Not being able to see around every corner and crevice left me feeling vulnerable, as though danger lurked just out of sight.

If Jones and his men were staked out in New Orleans, as Mickey suspected, no doubt they'd be lying in wait for us.

My only hope was that after three years, the man who'd raised Bonnie would have given up on me rescuing her. That was the only good thing that could come from all of this time apart.

Rusted-out cars lined either side of the street, leaving a narrow pathway that we had to ride single-file through. First the guards on the bridge and the blockade on the river. Now this?

I couldn't reconcile the image of the outlaw in my mind that Bonnie'd warned me about with an operation of this size. Jones couldn't have had a large enough operation to control an entire city.

Could he?

Eventually, the street widened, spilling out into a larger avenue. The city seemed to be waking up finally. Women sauntered down the street in long dresses with skirts flowing whimsically around their legs, holding lace parasols even though the sun hadn't quite gotten high enough to need them. Perhaps it was some strange fashion statement I'd never understand.

After all, the southern heat would wage war enough on them in those dresses before the sun ever did.

A man in a starched linen shirt and vest escorted a young woman wearing an airy dress and lace gloves. It almost felt like something out of a picture book I'd seen once. Pop had been obsessed with the Old West and had given me a book on trains. I hadn't thought about it then, but women wore frilly gowns similar to these in the illustrations.

"The square is coming up on the left," Mickey said quietly beside me.

As we passed a four-story building with an old-style balcony running across the second floor, I saw it. Trees towered above a black iron fence. Foot traffic was far busier here. People glanced at me or Mickey, then turned their attention away as if our presence wasn't unusual.

There were more guards in uniforms with the patches on the breast pockets. One of them turned his head, revealing a fleur-de-lis tattooed on their neck. An image of Sixgun with that same mark passed through my mind. The reins creaked against my hands.

We were so close to Bonnie, I could taste it.

"Easy," Mickey warned.

I attempted to school my features but failed the moment I turned to my uncle. He gave me a stern look, then motioned with his head to the right. Within minutes, he climbed down from his horse.

"What are you doing?"

"This," he said, jerking a thumb over his shoulder, "is a stable. We walk from here." I turned my head to the white concrete building that looked more like a bank than a stable. *Jackson Brewing Company*. I blew out a long breath, then climbed down from No Name and followed my uncle.

After twenty minutes of haggling with the stablemaster, we left our mounts and ventured back into the city.

"Jackson Square once overlooked the Mississippi River," Mickey said, eyes wide. "Until the city started sinking and they had to build up the levee system to protect from flooding. Not that it did much good." He eyed my hands, balled into fists at my side. "Maybe you should take a sip from your flask. Steel your nerves a bit." I shook my head. It was too early for a drink, even though my fingers shook with the lack of alcohol. I had to stay focused.

And when I saw Bonnie again, the last thing I wanted was for her to smell tequila on me.

"For all the talk you've done about this city, it's not exactly what I imagined." We crossed the busy street that led to the square.

"I guess you had to be here." He shrugged as we passed the iron fencing and a shiny, horse-drawn carriage.

"Care for a romantic ride, gentlemen?" a man in a pinstriped suit asked. He had a thick mustache and pointed beard.

"No thanks," Mickey said.

Clacking sounded ahead of us. As I lifted my head, I caught sight of a young man with obsidian skin, his feet moving in rhythm with the clacking. I slowed as we neared him, noting the metal weights attached to the bottom of his shined shoes. He tapped against a metal board. People dropped brass and copper bits in a hat near his feet.

Mickey tapped my shoulder and led me between iron columns into the square. Patches of grass lined a pebble walkway. Directly ahead of it, in the center of the square, was an iron statue of a man seated on a rearing horse. Only, something seemed off.

"That's different," Mickey said under his breath.

People brushed past us on either side as I looked over at him.

"What is?"

"That's not Jackson." He pointed at the statue. "Looks like they lopped Jackson's head off and replaced it with some . . . other guy." He shook his head.

Sure enough, when I looked closer at the statue, the original metal ended at the neck. A haphazard job had been done to attach the new piece to the old. There was something odd in the replacement's features.

"Huh," Mickey said. He'd moved several feet away. I followed his line of sight to where an inscription had been carved into the side.

"Major General—" I cut off, unable to make out the carving below. Someone had chiseled the original part of the inscription off.

"Andrew Jackson," Mickey finished. "But that's not Jackson."

"Clearly." I crossed my arms. "Look, I don't mean to be an insensitive prick when it comes to your love affair with old shit—"

"Don't be an asshole."

"We don't have time for this." My fingers twitched at my sides. While my uncle was lost to the past, Bonnie was in danger. If Mickey hadn't kept the location from me, I'd have come straight here the moment we arrived.

"Make time," he grumbled. He turned from the statue, moving farther into the square. Gravel crunched beneath our boots. We passed artisans set up with makeshift tables, displaying painted canvases and ones that had what looked like toys made out of old door hinges, bottle caps, and broken glass.

Eventually, I dragged Mickey away from a table with small clay figurines. He tucked something in his pocket as we ventured toward the far end.

"There." He gripped my wrist and dragged me to one side of the exit. Mickey's gaze shot out around us, gauging the faces nearby. I lifted an eyebrow at him.

"What?"

"Hush." He led me toward the iron fence and motioned to the metal bars with his head.

"What? Bars?"

"The other side," Mickey said.

Then, I saw it.

A three-story mansion. Stone archways lined the ground floor. Shadowy figures milled about. My eyes adjusted: guards on patrol. Most of them had assault rifles strapped to their backs and knives sheathed at their sides. Bars covered the arched windows on the second floor. An alleyway between the house and a cathedral beside it was rife with people coming to and fro.

"Those don't look like Hanged Men."

Mickey cursed beneath his breath. "It's not," he said. "Sixgun must have been working for someone else."

"Who?" I asked, the word coming out on a sharp breath.

An echo of a past conversation filled my mind.

My dad took a job up north . . . he had to burn it all down . . . somewhere in Montana . . .

"I don't know, Jess," Mickey said. "But whoever it is, I think they killed your mom and pop."

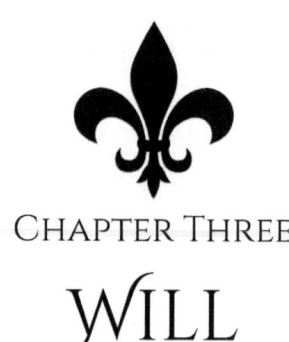

CHAPTER THREE

WILL

I couldn't remember the sound of my own laugh anymore. Or what it felt like before the weight of my sins, instead of my father's, weighed down my shoulders. In fact, there were very few moments when I felt alive at all. But being cock-deep inside an enthusiastic lover muted the sting of loneliness long enough to get me through another day.

Although, that usually came with its own problems.

Shifting on the mattress in my tangled sheets, I plucked a cigarette from my case on the nightstand and lit it quickly. The earthy aroma of burning tobacco did nothing to hide the scent of sex heavy in the humid air.

The nicotine buzz combined with adrenaline rushed in my blood like a goddamned drug. More potent than glowroot. Harder to quit, I imagined. Flopping bonelessly against the headboard, I sucked in another greedy drag as my pounding heart slowed.

The mattress dipped, causing ash to rain down on my sweat-soaked chest. When I turned, Clara pulled her skirt up over her trim hips. Just like that, the high I'd been riding faded into emptiness.

"Callin' it quits already?" I stubbed the cigarette out on my nightstand and sat upright. Resting an arm on my knee, I leaned forward and wrapped a lazy arm around her waist, dragging her back if only for a moment. Her blonde hair was nearly translucent in the places where the light fell on the messy waves. She patted me on the forearm like she was comforting a child before she twisted out of my embrace.

"I have a train to catch, but this was fun," she said primly, breasts still bare as she scooped her lacy panties off the floor. "It always is."

"Right." *This* was less complicated than the alternative. Even if it left me lying here feeling used. No messy, emotional pleas. No broken hearts or hidden resentments. Just the flare of cheap pleasure and then back to work. Running my hands through my hair and down my face, I tried to flush the dark thoughts from my mind without success.

"Train?" I scratched at my stubble. I needed a shave and a shower. Badly. Clara never stayed around for long, but she'd only gotten in yesterday. It was unusual for her to leave so soon.

"Yeah." She sighed, clipping her bra behind her back and pulling a strap over her shoulder. "Off to Dallas this time."

Though I didn't acknowledge her, she slipped her shirt back on then turned to me with narrowed eyes as if I'd said something revealing. Instead, I leaned back against the headboard and focused on anything but her stare. She didn't relent, and finally, with a long-suffering sigh, I asked.

"How long will you be gone this time?"

A triumphant smile broke across her lips. "A few weeks, maybe a couple of months," she teased, tucking her shirt in before pulling her sex-mussed hair into a bun at the nape of her neck. "There have been some *supply chain* issues I need to handle."

Even though I knew better and tried biting back the grumble rising in my throat, I still mumbled a swift, "That shit'll get you killed."

Anger flashed bright in her dark eyes, playfulness evaporating swiftly. She'd never listened to me before. I didn't know why I thought she would now. It didn't matter that dealing glowroot was a ruthless business that left more people dead than the *Beast of the Bridge*. Clara Higgins did whatever the fuck she wanted, and she didn't care what anyone had to say.

Least of all me.

"Don't look at me like that." She pinned me with a stare that promised retribution.

"Like what?" I asked, quickly growing bored with her hysterics. *This* was the part of Clara that I forgot about. As cunning and cruel as she could be, Clara was always logical. Until she felt judged.

"Like you *care* about me," she said, surprising me. The shock made me feel numb for a few seconds that felt like years. I scowled, dark and ugly. I didn't have the luxury of caring about anyone anymore. Myself included.

"The only thing I *care about*," I said slowly, drawing out the words while she shoved one of her feet into a boot, "is getting my dick wet. Which you're always more than eager to help me with. Thanks for that, but I think we're done here."

I didn't feel the sting as the sound of her slap echoed in my ears, but my head snapped to the side all the same. There was no question I deserved it. I deserved *so much more* for worse crimes than hurting a woman's feelings. Nevertheless, my stomach recoiled in disgust.

"You're absolutely right, *we're done here*." She turned on her heel and marched to the sun-scorched door. Her hand hesitated on the doorknob for a moment before she whirled to face me, with all the fires of hell in her eyes.

"You don't fool anyone, Will Ellis. You can bury yourself in all the booze and whores your money can buy and it won't stop you from hating yourself. Because the truth is, you are *fundamentally* broken, and there's nothing you can do to fix the fact that you're a failure." Her words rang with a truth that echoed deep in my chest. Then, with the slam of the door shaking the frame, she was gone. Along with the last remnants of hope I had left.

I sat there for long enough that the sun rose markedly higher in the sky, burning down more cigarettes than I should. Until the only thing left to do was untwist myself from my rumpled sheets and let the tepid but clean water wash away the filth on my skin. The water reminded me of things long lost, people that only lived in my memories now. I heard the pounding of a violent desert storm lashing against the thick, waterproofed tarp of the tent my mother and I shared. I saw Bonnie's pale face in a flash of lightning, blue eyes wide in the darkness, gripping my hand as if her life depended on it.

Even at ten years old, protecting her had given me a purpose that acted as a lens to focus my life. My hands slapped against the wet, filmy tile of my shower as my head hung low and water sluiced around my face. Grinding my teeth together, I forced my thoughts anywhere but the past. But the silence was oppressive, heightening my loneliness as my eyes burned. It was moments like these that it was impossible not to think of Bonnie, of how I failed her. And *exactly* how fucking pathetic I was.

I barely reached the beam with the dull kitchen knife, my sobs blurring my vision until I couldn't see. No matter how much my arms and shoulders ached, I didn't stop sawing at the barely frayed rope.

It took hours to cut her down as she swung, lifeless, in the middle of the home we'd shared. Swinging softly, like she was being lifted by a gentle summer breeze. Hours or days later, Bonnie found me, huddled in a mess of long limbs, the knife clutched so tightly in my hand I couldn't feel my fingers anymore.

"I'm here," she said, loosening it from my grip. "I'm here, Will."

All I saw was my mother's face, drained of blood, lips pale, with mottled blue-black bruises around her neck. Her eyelids were shut so gently she could have been sleeping. Only sleeping. My tears had dried hours ago, but horror remained lodged in my throat.

Bonnie was barely more than a girl, not quite a woman but no longer childish in any respect. She'd been on too many cons for there to be any lingering innocence left inside her. I opened and closed my mouth wordlessly, unable to articulate anything. She stroked her fingers through my hair, jaw clenched tight, letting my fingers dig into her arms until I thought I would break skin.

She never once complained.

"I'm alone now."

Her eyes hardened at my words, and like a slap to the face, I remembered that Bonnie had been alone all this time. Instead of harsh criticism, she scooted closer on her knees, the warmth of her skin a shock to my senses.

"You'll never be alone." Her words didn't register. She gripped the sides of my face and pulled my eyes away from my mother's lifeless body until all I saw were the blue shadows deep in her eyes. "I won't ever let you be alone. Do you hear me?" she said, with enough violence in her voice that I'd clung to her strength in desperation.

Then she pressed her lips to mine. A hard push against my mouth that both shocked and ignited something inside of me. My first kiss. Anchoring me to something real. Someone real.

I slammed the heel of my hand against the tile, the water long since grown cold. Not that I felt it. Not that I felt much of anything anymore. Squeezing my hand into a fist, I slammed the side of it into the tile. Again. And again. And again.

What does that mean? Mi cielo. *You call me that a lot.*

She looked right through me yesterday. Like she did all the time now. Bonnie was the only person who saw me for exactly who I was and loved me in spite of it. It didn't matter how lazy or reckless or offensive I could be. It never mattered. Not to her.

But Bonnie was gone.

I screamed. Jaw so wide my saliva and the shower water ran together, neck straining as an inhuman howl ripped through me. Maybe the things they whispered about me were true. Born of the devil. Soulless. Soaked in blood.

I twisted the taps until the water abruptly stopped and yanked the worn towel from its hook. After ruffling my hair and patting myself dry, I went about gearing up for the day. Settling a black shirt around my shoulders and dark jeans over my thighs, I tried not to remember why I preferred dark colors. How well it could hide me in the shadows.

Or bloodstains, a wicked voice reminded me, echoing through my thoughts. Scratching at the stubble on my jaw, I realized I should have shaved but couldn't find the energy to care about damn near anything anymore. Much less my appearance. With a couple of heavy thunks, my boots tightened around my ankles. It wasn't until I reached for the gun belt that I paused.

A dark six-chamber Colt revolver that fit in my hand like I'd been born with it taunted me from my leather holster. I fucking hated guns. But I strapped it low on my hip just the same.

An insistent rapping at the door sounded through the small space, setting my nerves on edge. In a couple long strides, I tossed the door open, not bothering to spare the black-and-gold-clad boy much notice. I felt more than saw how nervous he was, not that I could blame him. The rustling of his uniform as he shifted his weight grated on my nerves.

"Well?" I asked, still not bothering to look at the kid. "Do you speak?"

Crossing to the nightstand, I pulled out one of my cigarettes from my case, lighting the end with the quick flick of a match. When the messenger still said nothing, I faced him, tucking the case into the front pocket of my shirt. *Mierda.* Tall, gangly, mop of messy dark hair, and freckles. He reminded me of another cheeky kid I'd known once upon a time.

"Spit it out." I took another long drag and let the bite of nicotine drag deep into my lungs.

"Mr. Lee needs you at the house immediately," he spat out so quickly that it almost sounded like one long word. I felt the dark tilt of my lips as I settled my black cowboy hat low over my eyes. Time to get to work. The messenger boy scurried down the hall before the thud of my boots crossed the room.

There was no reason to bother locking my apartment, since there wasn't a person alive in New Orleans brave enough to steal from me. Perks of chipping away pieces of your soul until there was nothing left, I guessed. I'd forgotten the leather strap to tie my hair back with, and as a result, the long curls swung in front of my eyes as I loped down the dark staircase and into the bustle of the bar at the ground floor. A large chalkboard had been drilled into the wall behind the bar with betting odds on everything from dog fights to bare-knuckle brawls and horse races. The bookie who ran the betting was a good enough landlord. As long as I paid on time for my room, he didn't care about anything else.

Besides a few sidelong glances, no one bothered me. Or took note of my comings and goings. Just how I liked it.

The path to Lee's expansive manor was so familiar that my mind wandered, mostly to musings about what Lee could possibly want from me now. There was little that I wasn't privy to when it came to his underhanded business dealings. If there was a loan that hadn't been paid, or a shipment of something unsavory that had gone amiss, I was there. In the middle of it all.

Sullying my hands so that Zachary Lee could keep his pristine in the eyes of New Orleans high society. The few families that managed to retain their good fortune or wrest enough money and power in the chaos of the end of the world climbed to the top of the social ladder here. All of them fat rats stuck in a cage together, tearing each other limb from limb with smiles on their faces as they desperately grasped for more. More money, more power, more control over their own lives.

Fucking fools, the lot of them. Zachary controlled it all.

"Ellis!" A shout rose from behind me, but I didn't acknowledge it. Lee Manor was just ahead, and I didn't have time for whatever fresh hell this was. "Turn and face me like a man!"

Another stranger with a grudge. Seeking revenge. This happened too often lately. Just as I neared the front steps of the manor, a pair of familiar dark eyes caught mine beneath the brim of my hat. *Great.* Just what I needed. A witness to this shit-show.

Shame and loneliness weighed my shoulders down as Sebastian gazed at me in clear disappointment. *Failure.* I'd failed Seb too, breaking his heart a thousand times over the last couple years. He was convinced I was a better man than I was capable of being, and all that those lofty expectations did was hurt us both. Time and again.

"You fuckin' coward!" the voice shouted again from behind me. Closing my eyes for a moment, I sucked in a steadying breath before turning to find a stranger shouting at me across the distance until his face was red and ruddy. I didn't pay attention to what he said. There were any number of reasons he confronted me now. All I focused on was the gun in his hand. Instead of arguing,

LAUREN SEVIER & ABBIE LYNN SMITH

I unclipped my Colt from its holster. There were plenty of people spectating, still meandering down the stretch of cobblestone street, but that didn't matter.

The weight of the Colt in my hand didn't register, or the kick; just as quickly as I'd pulled the gun, I secured it at my side. The square went silent, horrified eyes tracking the fall of the man; he was dead before collapsing to the ground, a hole blasted cleanly through one of his eye sockets. Before the crowd grew rowdy, I turned my back and took the stairs two at a time. Even though I paused at Seb's shoulder for half a breath, I didn't look at him.

I already knew what I'd see written in his dark, expressive eyes.

"I see what it costs you." He ran desperate hands into my hair. "There's nothing keeping you here. Keeping us here. We can leave anytime, Will."

"I can't." I tried not to crack beneath his hurt expression. His mouth ran over my jaw, trying to change my mind. But he didn't understand the stakes for me, because I couldn't confide in him. Not how I wanted to. When he realized I wouldn't be swayed, his pleading turned into stony silence.

"You have a choice," he said, words hot with anger. "You act like you don't, but you always have a choice."

"I know," I said, my words quietly resigned. "I've made it, Seb."

Every broken promise and deep regret was mapped in lines stretched tight around the corners of his mouth. I sighed deeply, continuing up the front steps and across the threshold into Lee's manor. I was immune to the expensive furnishings by now, not sparing a second glance. The guards didn't give me a moment of consideration as I marched through the middle of the expansive home, practically a permanent fixture here.

Dread unfurled in my gut as I stopped outside Lee's study. My blood ran cold as I thought of the next job and how it might take more of my soul than I had left. Instead of knocking, I flung the door open and didn't bother acknowledging Lee behind his desk. He was finishing a letter, and I was uncapping the decanter of scotch in the corner of his room.

On the drink tray was a list of names in Zachary's neat handwriting. Curious, I picked it up and flipped it over as I drained the scotch in my glass. Columns of figures and betting odds much like the figures my landlord kept for his gambling business. Eyebrows furrowing in confusion, I turned to see Zachary watching me.

It struck me then, as it often did, how similar he and Bonnie looked. Sometimes, depending on his expression, it almost hurt to see the resemblance. Today, however, he looked more like the devil than my lost friend.

"I didn't think you were a gamblin' man." I handed him the list before pouring myself another splash of liquor. I needed to be appropriately numb for whatever he asked of me next. Zachary Lee wasn't the kind of man who threw his money away; if he bet on a fight, he'd rigged it beforehand.

"I'm not," he offered dully. "I've been researching the return on investments for sponsoring a fighter. I'm going to the pits tonight to scout some potential candidates."

That made sense. Anything that could earn him a couple more bits to line his pockets. I grunted in acknowledgment, not wanting to prolong this meeting unless it was absolutely necessary.

"What's the job this time?" I swallowed the earthy burn of scotch as he laced his fingers together and rested his chin on top.

"I have a guest arriving shortly from Manhattan Island," he said matter-of-factly. No need to mince words or beat around the bush. That wasn't what we did. I was here for one thing, and it wasn't the fucking conversation.

"How badly do you want him hurt?" I set the cut crystal glass down on the oversized, solid-oak desk. Did Lee realize that he looked like a child sitting behind a desk that large? Or did he even care, since he owned the whole goddamned city?

"No." Dark eyes settled sternly on my face. "Not this time. I'm trying to secure a lucrative trade deal with his father, so he isn't to be touched."

A tight knot of tension relaxed at the base of my spine, and I leaned back in my chair, hooking my ankle on my knee as I settled into the leather. After the confrontation with Clara earlier and how hopeless I'd been the last few months, I didn't think I could handle a violent job. At least not well. Lee pulled out a folded page of thick, off-white paper, sliding it across the top of the desk.

"A list of his known associates in the area," he explained. Not that he needed to. I knew the way Zachary Lee thought by now. He didn't take risks, didn't gamble, and he sure as shit didn't ask twice. If he was securing a trade deal, that meant he wanted leverage. Enough blackmail that would ensure the negotiations veered steeply in his favor.

I picked up the paper, saluting him with it mockingly before tucking it behind my cigarette case in my front pocket. With a groan, I lumbered onto my feet, rolling my shoulders to relieve some of the tension that'd gathered there.

"Oh, and Ellis?" he called as I crossed to the door. I peered over my shoulder, he was still comfortably seated, never having bothered to stand and acknowledge me. "No more lessons with Audrey while he's here."

Of course. There was no way he would let me leave without giving more of myself away. Even the small moments of peace or connection I'd painstakingly cultivated. Instead of arguing, though, I dipped my head so that he couldn't read my violent thoughts.

Without another word, I left. What was I still doing here? Bonnie didn't know me. Everything I sacrificed was for *nothing.* Turning a corner, I stopped short, leaning heavily against the doorframe leading to the kitchens. I dragged my hat off my head as laughter trilled in the air, feminine and delicate.

Savannah Beauregard was so pretty it fuckin' hurt.

Etty was trying to shoo her out on some errand, and Savannah's normally too-polite face was lit in an expression of real joy. A rare occurrence, especially if I happened to be around. I was content to watch her from the shadows, tracking the swish of her skirt as she untied her apron. Tearing my eyes away from her was physically painful.

There was nothing as good in this world as her.

Sometimes, I hated how unaffected she was by the kind of darkness I drowned in. Other times, like today, I clung to the reminder that not everyone was as broken as me.

Before I could escape, Etty caught sight of me over Savannah's shoulder. Her face fell and her eyes grew distrustful in my presence. Savannah turned to see what could have possibly dulled Etty's lively expression. Realization dawned on her face a moment later. Her smile disappeared.

"William," she said by way of greeting. She was the only one who called me that. I cleared my throat, gripping the brim of my hat a little tighter.

"I didn't mean to bother you," I started, ignoring the pointed glare that clearly said I'd accomplished the exact opposite. "Just wanted to check on Audrey."

Savannah's animosity faded before she offered a deep sigh.

"She was in pretty rough shape yesterday," I said gruffly. I watched Savannah's dark curls bounce with her nod. She pressed her lips firmly together, the way she often did when she spoke to me about Bonnie. As if she didn't like betraying her friend's confidence but couldn't help herself.

"All I know," she said softly, eyes bright, "is that whatever she discussed with her father at dinner last night has her refusing to see anyone today. Including me."

I sighed, stifling the urge to bury my hands in her hair. To pull her forward and kiss her until she begged me to stop. Instead, I settled my hat back on my head and offered a low, "Thanks."

The unnatural compulsion toward Savannah had grown more acute the longer I'd been here, nearly shattering me with the force of my yearning. My desire to desecrate her goodness could bring me to my knees if I let it. But I wouldn't.

"Savannah, honey," Etty said firmly, glaring at me. "You should head to the bakery before it gets late."

A clear warning away from me.

Clara was right. I was a fucked-up piece of shit. One that only wanted Savannah so ravenously because I wanted to defile that goodness I hated so much. Until she was just as corrupt and rotten as me. Until none of her immaculate grace remained and her judgmental looks were nothing more than distant, hypocritical memories. She shifted on her feet, and I caught the delicate scent of cinnamon on her skin. No doubt from the baking she enjoyed so much.

My mouth watered, and before I could do something about that, I walked across the courtyard toward the side entrance of the house. *Don't fucking do it, Ellis.* I wanted to tug at my scalp, wanted to feel something other than the overwhelming urges dragging toward this woman who clearly hated me. My thoughts lingered on all the things I could do to make her gasp my name in delight or horror.

Goddamnit! Stop, Will.

This would be the last time. I swore it. Though, I'd done that hundreds of times before over the years. My feet carried me around the side of the house, waiting until she walked past before slinking from the shadows, my path a way to trail her swishing skirts into the city. *It's just to keep her safe.*

I was really good at lying to myself.

She never looked back as I stalked her through the crowds. Not once. Instead, she tilted her chin toward the sunlight, a pretty smile on her mouth. Contented. Peaceful. Happy.

I needed to taste that mouth. Feel how soft her skin was beneath my fingertips. Drink down her sweetness. Then maybe some of that happiness could be mine, if only for a moment. Her gait changed, from a purposeful march into a lazy stroll as she looked through windows of different shops on this side of the street. She didn't linger long on anything, perusing fabrics, items in a leather shop, a pre-Culling boutique filled with oddities from the world before.

Then she stopped short in front of the bookstore. It was her favorite one. She always paused here when running errands. They had a display in front of the open door, meant to entice customers inside. Savannah's fingers trailed reverently down the spine of a book, and I shuddered as if she'd trailed that finger down my chest. She angled herself, plucking the book from the cart, and I ducked beneath the awning of another store to hide as I watched her through the dirty glass. A small grin curled on her mouth, her eyes filled with regret as she placed the book back in the cart.

The bakery was next door, and she disappeared inside before I left my perch, striding purposefully into the bookstore before I reminded myself this wasn't a good idea. The owner behind the counter was talking to another customer until he caught sight of me. His face paled, eyes widening in terror as he abandoned his patron to scramble toward me.

"C-can I help you with—"

"The books on display. Deliver them all to Lee's house, for the library." I grunted as he followed me outside. My gaze darted toward the bakery, where Savannah spoke with her hands, gesturing to a king cake on display in the window. She and the owner seemed to be haggling over the price. I plucked the book she'd chosen from the cart, scanning the cover. A half-naked man with dark olive skin and a black cowboy hat graced the cover. Scanning the description on the back, a wicked grin slid over my lips.

"Put this one on top," I instructed gruffly as the shop owner nodded vigorously.

"O-of course, Mr. . . . uh, sir. Half price for the lot, naturally." He was sweating into the collar of his shirt. I shoved two gold bits into his hand, eyes sliding back to Savannah briefly.

"Keep the change, but *don't be late.*"

He whimpered but began tugging the cart into the shop to pack up for delivery. Savannah headed toward the door, so I ducked my head and walked across the street, leaning with my back to her until she passed me again. Sick satisfaction curled through me as I followed her back to the house, knowing that she would be cradling that book in her elegant hands later tonight. Even if she never knew where it came from, a part of me would be with her, giving her pleasure in whatever limited way I could.

As we arrived back at Lee Manor, I dragged my eyes away from her. She was back safely now, unharmed, and it settled something ragged inside of me. I had to stop fucking doing this. It was driving me insane.

Because the truth is, you are fundamentally *broken, and there's nothing you can do to fix the fact that you're a failure.*

I hated that Clara was right, but I hated myself more.

I ducked into an alley that ran alongside the house. Secluded, I kicked over a trash bin as my absolute uselessness rattled through me, shaking my resolve. What the fuck was I doing anymore? Why was I still here, keeping a promise to a dead woman? That's what Bonnie was, when it came down to it. Dead.

A stranger walked around in her skin, torturing me with every interaction. Reminding me of my failure with every conversation. Every memory I held onto with both hands slipped through her mind like water through a sieve.

It unraveled me a little more each day.

I adjusted my hat, sucking in a sharp breath before pulling out my cigarette case to light one. I struck the match on the brick at my side and inhaled deeply, watching the smoke disappear on the faint breeze before me.

"Ellis," a voice said behind me. Familiar and haunting.

The deep timbre sent equal parts panic and disbelief running down my shoulders like frigid water. The cigarette dropped from my fingertips, forgotten. I turned slowly, taking in the tall, fearsome sight of him with the sun at his back.

"Jesse?" I couldn't reconcile the man before me with the person I once knew. He shifted on his feet, and a shaft of light spilled over the harsh lines of his face, his blue eyes sharp in the dim alley. He looked different. His hair was shorn close on the sides, the top kept long and slicked back. Once, I'd thought he was too weak to keep Bonnie safe, too naïve. Looking at him now, I only saw the barest echo of that man standing before me.

Hope, like a flame, sparked to life inside me. Rushing toward him in long, loping strides. My loneliness and grief hollowed me out, and with just a word, he'd somehow managed to blunt the edges of that deep-rooted pain.

Before I could say anything, his fist thudded hard against my jaw, the strike coming so fast I'd barely seen it before I lurched to the side. I slammed against the wall of the alley, clutching my jaw.

"Not the face, *pendejo*." I worked my jaw back and forth to ease the pain radiating from the blow. My hat fell unceremoniously to the ground, and he had an unimpeded view of my entire face now. And the jagged scar that graced my left side, spanning from my temple to the corner of my eye. His eyes caught there and held, some of the hardness wavering at the sight.

"Three years," he ground out between his teeth. "It's been three goddamn years, Will."

"Okay." I offered a shrug by way of non-apology. "I deserved that one."

"I'm here for Bonnie." He looked past me to the door at the end of the alley. Nodding, I ignored the sick feeling twisting in the pit of my stomach. There was a part of me that had known this day might come. One that ignored the probability as stringently as possible.

"Yeah, I figured as much." I ignored the deadly intention that flashed in his eyes. That was new. But three years could change a lot about a person. I knew that firsthand. I maneuvered my way around his broad shoulders and started down the street, farther away from the house.

"Where do you think you're going?" He forced out the question through clenched teeth. I paused to look at him from over my shoulder, shoving my hands deep into my jean pockets.

"Feel free to force your way in that door and get yourself killed if you prefer." I offered him a dull glance. "Otherwise, this conversation calls for a drink."

He narrowed his eyes, clearly pissed off at my lackadaisical attitude. From the corner of my eye, I noticed another familiar face. Mickey Kincaid, in all his fifty-some-odd years, leaning casually against the brick wall. He stared at me in a way that forced the air to shift wrong in my throat. Too familiar. As if he saw just how fucked-up and broken I was after all this time.

I didn't like that.

"Fine," Jesse said. I continued on as my past and present clanged together in a dizzying mess. More than likely, I'd need several drinks to get through this night unscathed.

CHAPTER FOUR

SAVANNAH

W ILLIAM ELLIS ALWAYS ATTRACTED the worst kind of trouble. Probably because the man himself was sin incarnate.

I'd gone out to the bakery to pick up an out-of-season king cake for Mr. Lee's
guests from Manhattan Island. His assistant had been aghast when I offered
to make it for the occasion. At her horrified expression, I rattled off a list
of ingredients and explained to her, step-by-step in excruciating detail, the
exact process of baking a king cake. The woman, exasperated with my sarcasm,
demanded I make arrangements to pick it up.

So there I was, making my way back to the manor house in the square, a
cardboard box painted with Mardi Gras masks on the outside and the bakery's
name emblazoned across the top, when who did I see but William Ellis himself,
moments after a man with blonde hair punched him in the jaw. I snorted
derisively.

Probably another lover. At least this one wasn't on staff.

I straightened my shoulders, letting out a sharp huff, and walked beneath
one of the arches that led to the front breezeway lined with armed guards. I
kept my eyes low, as I always did, and headed toward the double doors of the
entrance. A shadowed figure moved in front of me. I clutched the box tighter.
One heartbeat passed, then another. When the guard didn't budge, I lifted my
eyes to theirs.

The warmth of his brown skin contrasted so starkly with the chilly expression in Sebastian's eyes. He'd been a guard in the household nearly as long as
I'd been here. Once, I might have called us acquaintances, if not friendly.

Then, a certain *troublemaker* showed up in the dead of night.

"Where have you been?" Sebastian asked as he blocked my entry to the manor.

"I had an errand to run." I glanced down at the box in my hands.

His brows lifted. "Smells oddly like a king cake."

"Mr. Lee requested it for his guests."

Sebastian stared at me with an unnatural calmness. His cold demeanor made little sense. In fact, if anyone had a right to be angry, it was me, but I wasn't. I'd had enough to deal with when it came to the other staff members in the house.

"I'd like to try it," he said.

I stepped back. "No. This was ordered specially for Mr. Lee's guests."

Sebastian shrugged and adjusted the rifle over his shoulder. With one broad arm, he jerked the box from my hands. I let out a muffled cry. My blood ran cold as he opened the top and reached inside with his bare hands. A moment later, he shoved a large piece of the cake in his mouth, moaning in pleasure as he chewed.

"This is good. Boys?" He handed the box off to the next guard: his right hand, Jimmy, a man with a cross tattooed on his hand who, despite Lee's orders I be left alone, never hesitated to join in on Sebastian's harassment.

I stared at him, wide-eyed, shaking my head slowly back and forth. Even if they didn't eat it all, it was ruined. There was no way I'd be able to have another cake made by the bakery in time.

"Thanks, Savannah. The crew sure enjoys sweets." Sebastian flashed a cruel smile.

I wanted to demand a reason for his treatment. But it didn't matter. He hated me, and that wasn't going to change any time soon. I strangled back the cry threatening to tear from my throat and shoved past him, forcing my way through the front door of the manor. The guards' laughter was barely muffled by the doors as I slammed them shut.

What was I going to do?

My knees threatened to give out. I gripped the staircase banister, digging my nails into the wooden surface until they ached. My bottom lip quivered. I clenched my jaw, forcing the rising emotion down as deep as it would go.

I allowed myself this moment. I breathed, acknowledged their unfair treatment, and released the banister. I couldn't change what any of the other staff thought of me. All I could do was better prepare myself to avoid such interactions in the future.

Minutes later, I stomped into an already-clean kitchen. Etty sat at the island, drinking something out of a glass. She took one look at me and was on her feet.

"What's wrong, baby?"

I shook my head, averting my gaze from hers. She had a way of ripping the truth from me if I let her look too long. "I need your help."

"With what?"

"I need to make a king cake before tomorrow."

Etty's expression hardened. She opened her mouth to question me, but I shook my head. Instead, I yanked my apron from its hook and tied it around my waist. As I allowed myself to get lost in flour and sugar, my mind drifted to that fateful night three years ago. A night that had felt like a beginning and an ending wrapped together.

"They won't cool if you're watching them," Etty said beside me at the kitchen island. I jumped, surprised by her sudden appearance. I'd been waiting for the last batch of cupcakes to cool so I could go to bed.

"I need to ice them," I remarked half-heartedly, even as my eyelids drooped and my feet ached from standing all day.

"It's late. You're exhausted, child." Etty brushed some of my dark hair back. When it'd fallen from the careful bun I'd pinned my hair in that morning, I couldn't be sure. I smoothed it down, gaze darting about the kitchen in case there were any wandering eyes.

"Really, it won't be long." I forced my spine to straighten.

"Go. Rest."

How many times in the last seven years had we had this argument? The stern look she gave me silenced the protests on my tongue. I untied my apron, yawning as I folded it and hung it up next to the door.

"Keep the guards out of those." I pointed to the tower of brightly decorated cupcakes.

With a grin, Etty said, "You know how they are about your sweets. I don't think I could stop them."

I shook my head and pushed open the door into the courtyard. Gentle raindrops kissed my cheeks as I padded across the cobblestones. The coolness brought relief to my hot, flour-coated face.

Lightning flashed, illuminating the stone benches and fountain in the courtyard. Silently, I counted the seconds. One Mississippi ... two Mississippi ... three— Thunder rumbled long and low behind it.

My mother taught me to count the seconds between lightning and thunder when I was young. It was a game of sorts on nights when we had no oil for our lamps or wood for heat, a way to tell if the storm was getting closer or moving away.

Before I reached the far side of the corridor, the rain began in earnest, dousing my hair and shoulders. I dashed the rest of the way, careful to keep from skittering across the smooth stone. Thunder rumbled as soon as I reached the front house. My bedroom beckoned me. A hot bath and a nice book would help me decompress before bed. I imagined sinking into the heated depths, allowing it to work out my sore muscles. Heaven. Or as close to it as I could get.

As I pressed forward, my mind lost to the claw-foot tub in my rooms on the second floor, something more than thunder registered. Shouting? Who in the world would be making such a ruckus at this hour? I quickened my pace, heading toward the main entry. The double doors were wide open. Rain poured just beyond the stone archways.

Men flowed inside, water cascading off of their clothes and onto the polished wood floors. Mr. Lee would be horrified at such a sight. The maids would be even worse.

Guards milled about, their faces full of confusion and fear. I clutched the skirts of my gown and walked toward them. A man broke away from the crowd, and I froze. I knew that man, had known him for years. A shiver ran up my spine.

Sixgun. Lee's personal assassin.

Why was he here? I hadn't seen him in more than a year.

"You!" he barked, pointing at me. I bit back the squeak that threatened to worm its way from between my lips. "Where's Lee?"

Behind him, a younger man with bronze skin walked forward, clutching a child-like form in his arms.

"He's out for the evening." I turned my attention to the younger man or, rather, the thing—the person—*he carried. I tried to move past Sixgun, but he extended an arm to block me. "What's going on?"*

"I've found his daughter," the man said in a gravelly voice.

His daughter? Audrey?

"I've brought her home, as requested. I wanna see Lee." The man's rancid breath sent me a step backward.

"Retrieve Mr. Lee," I said to the nearest guard. When he didn't move, I snapped my fingers. "Now!"

"She needs a doctor," the younger man said, panic edging his voice.

Somehow, I found the strength to push past Sixgun. Panic and fear laced the younger man's face, shoulders hiked up almost to his ears. His brows were low, brown eyes wide as he begged for my help. He adjusted the woman in his arms, quivering as he exhaled. I moved closer, inspecting the young woman's face. Her pale skin was clammy to the touch, and her coloring was a mottled gray.

Audrey was young. Younger than I expected. Water matted her hair and . . . blood. Blood caked the dark strands. I glanced up at the younger man, who stared bleakly at me.

"Get Dr. Moreau," I snapped at the nearest guard. Once again, hesitation. "Tell him Mr. Lee has called for him." The guard eyed the limp woman. "Jesus Christ! Now!" The guard jumped into action, and I turned from them all. "Bring her this way."

Footsteps reverberated off of the empty hallway as I led them down the main corridor. The dining room was closest. As I shoved open the pocket doors, I barked out an order for fresh linens, hot water, and whatever alcohol they could find. I pulled the crystal candlesticks from the table and swiped the remaining items to the floor.

The young man didn't hesitate. He laid the woman down on its surface. While I barked orders, he focused on the woman, smoothing her hair down and inspecting the wound to her head. He spoke soft words in Spanish as I shoved the dining room chairs out of the way.

A red-haired maid arrived with supplies: a single washing bowl of steaming water and a few hand towels. I shook my head at her.

"More." She scowled at me before turning on her heel and exiting the room. I couldn't handle the staff's distaste for me right now, not when a woman's life was in danger.

As I soaked a towel in water and moved toward Audrey's limp body, I noted the young man's hands quaking beside her head. I wiped some of the blood away from her scalp. The best I could tell, the gash extended several inches across the back of her head and was at least an inch wide.

"What happened to her?" I barely managed to keep my voice at a normal level.

"Head trauma," Sixgun grunted.

"Maybe they should have specified 'alive and undamaged' on the goddamned posters," the younger man said. He retrieved a metal case from his pocket and

53

pulled out a cigarette. I stared at him, mouth open as he lit a match and brought it to the tip.

"There's no smoking in here," I grumbled. With a shake of my head, I turned back to the patient. "Miss Audrey? I'm Savannah. We're going to help you." The words sounded more confident than I felt.

Audrey only moaned, eyes shut tight.

The doctor arrived moments before Zachary Lee charged into the room. As I followed the doctor's instructions to shear off Audrey's hair, Mr. Lee commanded the room. I kept my head low, focused on my task and not getting noticed. My movements stilled as he moved beside me, his eyes narrowing as he inspected the wound.

"What did you do?" he asked in a low growl. I didn't dare lift my gaze.

"It was an accident," Sixgun said emotionlessly.

The doctor spoke with the younger man, who'd removed his hat and pinched the brim of it with his fingers. I tried to focus, but it was hard to do while trying to make sense of words like cerebral *and* edema *as the two conferred. Anything I might have gleaned from the conversation whooshed out of my mind a moment later.*

"Savannah," Mr. Lee ordered. I stilled at his sharp tone.

"Yes, sir," I said, lowering the shears beside Audrey's head.

"I need you to get the maids to prepare Audrey's chambers." He fixed me with a stare so hard that my stomach ached. "I want you with her at all times. Help the doctor with whatever he needs."

I'd known the man for seven years. I'd seen him angry. I'd seen him happy. But tonight . . . I'd never seen fear in his eyes before. I gave a curt nod and went off in search of the staff to pass along orders.

A new kind of hell had broken by the time I returned.

"You can't just drill *into my daughter's skull," Lee said, tense as he glared between the doctor and the young man. Guards milled about the hallway just beyond the entrance. Sixgun had disappeared altogether.*

"We have to relieve the pressure. Her brain is swelling, and it'll only get worse if we do nothing," the doctor said, panic tinging his words. He slumped beneath Mr. Lee's stare.

Audrey whimpered as the doctor instructed the hands around him. He retrieved a strange metal gadget from his bag, shouting for alcohol to sterilize it. I crossed to the credenza, making quick work with a bottle of Mr. Lee's favorite scotch.

"We need as many hands as possible to hold her down," the doctor said.

The younger man was on his feet. He let out a long breath, as if steeling himself for what was about to happen. It was the first chance I'd had to really look at him. His clothes were caked with dirt and blood, but his hands were clean as he ran them through his damp hair. It flopped across his forehead, drawing my eyes to the gnarled scar at his temple. The skin was angry and red, blood crusting the sutures keeping his skin together. Beneath the dirt and blood, though, I noticed his angular jaw and sloping nose. Sensuous lips that pursed together as he crossed to the table. He was actually quite beautiful for a man.

As if sensing my gaze, his eyes met mine. I pivoted toward the doctor instead of acknowledging him.

The men got into position around the table. Cold rushed over me, my eyes widening as I realized they were actually going to drill into her head. I froze, horror striking me deep in the chest. As the room continued moving forward around me, time slowed. The man moved to the table, an unwavering steadiness coming over him as he clutched Audrey's head. His fingers dug into her temples and cheeks. The moment he pressed down, she convulsed beneath him. He clenched his jaw, and sweat beaded across his blood-stained skin.

Audrey thrashed as hands pushed her down against the surface.

I didn't move. All I could do was stand there, horrified. Helpless.

Help. I wanted to help. I didn't know this woman. Only her name. Only that she was the reason I was here in the first place.

The young man's eyes found mine, a silent plea in them that I didn't even think he knew was there, and I knew what I had to do.

As the doctor began his work, drilling into Audrey's skull, I darted toward the door.

"Where are you going?" Mr. Lee demanded. I froze just inside the entryway and turned toward him.

"She needs something to calm her." My words came out in a hot rush. "Glowroot. That will help. I need money."

The man's hard expression wavered. His eyes darted toward the woman's prone form on the table. "How much?"

"Whatever you have."

I didn't know the going rate for glowroot these days, but it didn't matter. Mr. Lee handed over five gold bits and retreated back into the room.

It took me ten minutes to run through the pouring rain from the square to Bourbon Street. Another five to find a glowroot den amongst the bars, brothels, and other seedy enterprises. I shoved three gold bits into the hands of a man who looked at me like I was crazy. He shoved his supply into a bag.

Then I sprinted as fast as my feet would carry me.

Audrey's screams filled the air.

Blood soaked the towels beneath Audrey's head. The doctor's sleeves were at his elbows, and his hands were red. He stood at the head of the table, maneuvering his tool around the man who held her head still. An ear-piercing shriek sounded as the doctor cranked the tool.

"Wait!" I skittered to a stop beside them, stumbling as my slick feet hit the carpet. I yanked a vial of glowroot from the bag. As I uncorked it, the men attempted to pry Audrey's mouth open. Instead, the woman's jaw clenched tighter. I pinched her nose shut, not thinking. Her lips parted and she gasped in a breath.

"Please forgive me." I poured the blue liquid into her mouth.

Tense silence filled the room. Rain pounded against the windows as everyone waited for a long moment.

Then, the woman relaxed. Her body went limp. I let out a breath, not realizing that I'd been holding it while praying to whatever God might be watching that it would work. I stumbled away as they resumed their work. My knees quivered, and I settled on one of the forgotten dining room chairs, hands shaking as I set the bag on the floor.

Hours later, once the doctor deemed Audrey stable enough, we moved her upstairs to her room. They peppered me with questions about glowroot, and I answered as best I could.

No, I didn't know how long the effects would last. Yes, it could kill her if I gave her too much. No, I lived in the house and I would make sure she was dosed long enough to heal.

"Ellis," Lee said in a low voice as we stood vigil in Audrey's opulent chambers. The young man who'd brought Audrey in left the room with Lee and Sixgun. I settled in the chair next to the bed.

For the past seven years, I'd been educated in this household with one purpose: to be Audrey's companion. If I were honest, until tonight, I thought she didn't exist. After all, why hadn't she shown up yet?

I stared at her porcelain skin. Finally clean of the blood, I noticed that her eyes held the same shape as her father's. Her round face looked oddly similar.

Where had she been all of this time?

Anytime I asked, Mr. Lee said the same thing about Audrey's arrival: soon.

Soon turned into months, into years, and now . . . I stared down at her still form, brows furrowed as I tried to make sense of it. I shoved my hands into the pockets of my dress, eyes widening as my fingers brushed against the cool metal of the remaining gold bits. I didn't dare pull them from my pocket, should Lee return.

My mind strayed to the small purse hidden beneath a floorboard in my room. I finally had enough.

Slowly, I'd been saving money to get back to St. Louis, to my mother. There was only one steamboat in New Orleans without Lee's fleur-de-lis, and they wanted an exorbitant amount to transport me. For all intents and purposes, I'd be a fugitive the moment I left without permission. The brand on my neck made me dangerous goods.

The door creaked, and I stood swiftly, trying my best to erase the guilt from my face as I tugged my hand from my pocket. Lee surveyed the room, eyes landing on Audrey's soiled clothing on top of her vanity.

"Burn those," he said to me.

With merely a nod, I exited with the clothing through the bathroom that connected to my room. After locking the door, I dug up the floorboard and tossed the two gold bits into my purse.

Soon, Mama. Soon.

I leaned back on my knees, eyes falling to the blood and dirt caked clothing. I glanced over my shoulder to double check the door. Then I tossed the clothes into a box and beneath the floorboard.

If I had the chance to keep something of my life before I came here, I would.

After wiping my skin down with a warm washcloth, I changed into a night-gown and prepared myself to finally sink into my feather mattress. The sky was beginning to lighten just beyond my barred windows. The adrenaline faded, and it was time for me to rest.

As I pulled the comforter back, a crash sounded from the hallway.

What now?

I snatched my robe, secured it swiftly, and opened the door to my bedroom, peering into the hallway.

The young man, the one who'd carried Audrey in, sat with his back against the wall and his head in his hands. Pieces of an expensive vase littered the floor around him.

I should have just gone to bed.

The man ran his fingers through his hair, swearing to himself.

I shouldn't get involved.

But I'd recognized pain in him earlier. Grief.

I padded across the polished floors. He didn't hear me as I knelt before him. I reached out, barely touching his shoulder. He stilled, then lifted his head, grief-stricken eyes finding mine.

"Are you okay?" His brown eyes wavered between me and Audrey's door. His mouth hung open, like he wanted to say something but couldn't. I frowned. I knew what that was like. I rose and extended a hand. "Come with me."

He hesitated for a long moment, eyeing my hand as though I might hit him or something. But then, he clasped his large fingers around mine and climbed to his feet. He towered over me. How I hadn't realized just how tall he was surprised me. Beneath the dirt and blood was a younger face than I'd anticipated. Staring at him up close like this, though, his beauty struck me all over again.

Beautiful really was the only way to describe him. From his too-long lashes to his strong nose and his full lips. It was unfair for a man to have such features.

I realized I was staring again and averted my eyes. I started toward the staircase, registering his footsteps behind me. We descended silently. In fact, neither of us spoke the entire way to the kitchen.

Once there, I grabbed a kettle and filled it with water. He sat on one of the barstools on the far side of the island. His eyes felt like a gentle caress to my bare neck as I lit the stove and set the water to boil. When I finally dared to look at him, he still stared. Blatantly. Without any trepidation or shame. I lowered my gaze, catching sight of his still-bloodied hands as they rested on the kitchen island.

Without a word, I crossed to the sink with a hand towel and soaked it with warm water. He stared at me as I sat beside him. I took one of his oversized hands in mine. They were covered in calluses; his long fingers splayed out as I swiped his palm with the damp rag. His hands were different than any of the men I'd touched before, not that there had been many. Absently, I wondered what it would feel like for those calluses to brush across my cheek.

"I'm Savannah," I said quietly, switching to his other hand. When I dared to peek up at him through my eyelashes, he looked at me with a wide stare, his mouth open like he wanted to say something. His fingers twitched around mine.

"Will." His eyes followed the curve of my cheek, down along my jaw, and rested on my lips. My skin heated beneath his inspection.

"Nice to meet you," I said, the words too airy.

Flecks of silver highlighted the brown of his eyes. They were a curious shade, something I'd never seen. Almost like the bark from a hickory tree. Deep and dark, but soft. He let out a sharp breath from between sensuous lips, and I couldn't help but stare and wonder.

The kettle whistled, and I made a hasty exit. Because the way I felt looking at him was troublesome.

I didn't do trouble.

I retrieved the tea service and, within minutes, set a full cup before him, avoiding his stare.

"Tea?" he asked, incredulous.

The corners of my mouth drew up as I crossed to Etty's liquor cabinet and pulled out a bottle of bourbon. I set it down on the island with a thunk.

"If you so choose," I remarked and poured myself a cup of tea and settled beside him once more. I lifted the cup to my mouth, trying my best not to watch as he unscrewed the bottle and dumped a heaping dose into his cup. He upended the bottle and took a long pull. He turned to me, offering the alcohol. I shook my head.

"Have it your way," he remarked, some of the hoarseness gone from his voice.

We stayed that way for a while, drinking in silence. I didn't know what to say to him, and I doubt he felt like talking uselessly after tonight.

"What exactly is your role here?" he asked. "Are you a maid?"

My eyes fluttered shut at the common misconception. "No," I said, reminding myself that Will had no clue about the hierarchy of Lee Manor. "I was brought here to be a companion for Miss Audrey."

"Companion?" he asked, lifting an eyebrow.

"Sort of like a friend?" I shrugged. "To be honest, I didn't think she was real. My job is simple. Make sure Audrey follows whatever lessons Mr. Lee expects, attends important events, and that she's happy."

"He hired someone for that?"

"Are you really hired if you don't get paid?"

Will didn't respond. Instead, he fixed me with an intense stare. I shifted on my seat, focusing far too intently on sipping the dregs of my tea. "How long have you been here?"

"Seven years," I said. His eyes widened, and he took a sip from his cup.

"And where were you before?"

"So many questions." The corners of my mouth quirked up. "Where were you before?" Before he could respond, I said, "Doesn't really matter, does it? This is where I am now."

I drained my cup, skin tingling beneath his heavy gaze and nonstop questioning. By the time I set down my cup, he was staring at me again. I placed my hands together in my lap and swiveled to face him.

"What?"

"You're beautiful."

Skin heating, I averted my gaze from him altogether. I wasn't sure how to take such a blatant compliment from anyone, let alone a stranger. I'd had men hit on me before, but they never sounded so sincere.

Then again, Will had been drinking bourbon. I doubted he'd slept much. He probably didn't mean it.

"Thank you."

Suddenly, warm, calloused fingers touched my chin. He tugged on it enough to turn my head toward him. "Why do you do that?"

"Do what?"

"Turn away when I look at you." His words were so gentle, it made my heart squeeze in my chest.

With a shrug, I said, "It makes me uncomfortable."

"What? Me looking at you?"

"Anyone looking at me like that," I said too quickly. My cheeks heated with shame. Why did I tell him that?

"Like what?"

"Like you . . . Like I . . ." I blew out a frustrated breath. "I don't know, like that!"

"You're very articulate, Savvy." A grin crossed his face, and my heart stuttered. The wound at his temple pulled tight as his lips tugged upward. Even the gnarled patch of skin didn't diminish his beauty. And he was *beautiful.*

"My name *is Savannah." I picked up my cup and began to move from the stool.*

"Wait," he said, his warm fingertips brushing against my forearm. I stilled at the gentle touch, eyes falling to the place where our skin met. He reached up, cupping my cheek with warm, calloused fingers. His thumb brushed against my jawline, sending a shiver down my spine. He tangled his fingers in my hair. I took in a sharp breath as he leaned toward me.

Will's lips were warm and smooth, soft, like velvet. My heart faltered, then sped up at the sudden kiss. I softened into the contact, warmth spreading to my extremities as my eyes fluttered closed. I rested a hand against his chest, just above his pounding heartbeat.

When Will's tongue brushed against my bottom lip, I stilled. It would be all too easy to curl my fingers into the fabric of his shirt. To melt into this kiss and this man. To forget all that happened tonight and get lost in someone I barely knew.

Instead, I pulled back, my hand still flat against his chest. I blinked, lips curling into a smile as his brown eyes flickered open.

"Why did you do that?"

"Because I wanted to," Will said, without a shred of dishonesty.

Just like that? Huh. My hand dropped to my side, and I gathered up my forgotten teacup. I rose from the stool and crossed to the kitchen sink. The room wobbled on the edge of my vision. I set the cup in the sink and turned toward the door. My gaze flickered to Will, whose warm eyes caressed my cheek.

"Well." I shifted my weight from one foot to the other. "Goodnight."

His lips curled around the rim of his cup. "Night, Savvy."

A smile rose unbidden to my lips, and I rolled my eyes before leaving him alone in the kitchen.

The day after he kissed me, Will slept with Sebastian. And he wasn't exactly shy about people knowing.

CHAPTER FIVE

JESSE

WHY WERE WE WALKING away from Bonnie when she was *right* there?

As people in the square parted to let Will pass, Mickey fixed me with hard eyes. I released my clenched jaw and let my arms swing at my sides, if only to give my uncle the appearance that I was under control.

Because controlled was the furthest from what I felt.

White hot rage built inside of me, as though the madness of these years away from her had only kept the ember burning. Now, the flames threatened to burn out of control.

Will wended through the crowded streets of the French Quarter, not bothering to check that I was still there. He knew he had me on a string. I could only hope he wouldn't fuck with me. I lacked patience and time. Judging by his dull eyes, Bonnie needed me. Now.

A woman in a frilly, powder-pink dress paused as we walked by. She whispered something to her companion. I narrowed my eyes at her, sneering when she dared meet my eye. They turned quickly, hurrying in the other direction. I focused on Will's shoulders, how they bunched and released as he led us onto an overrun thoroughfare. People spilled onto the street. Jazz music floated in the air above them.

"Ahh," Mickey remarked, a grin lighting up his eyes. "I can't believe it."

As we pushed into the thronging crowd, I asked, "Can't believe what?"

"It even smells the same."

"Of what? Piss and vomit?" My features tightened in disgust.

Ahead of us, the crowd seemed to give way. I picked up my pace to match Will's long strides as he ducked beneath an awning and through an open door.

Will led the way to a table bracketed by a wall on one side and the window on the other.

"Nothing like it," Mickey said, grinning as he settled into one of the chairs.

"Bourbon Street?" Will asked as he signaled to the bartender.

"Hasn't changed one bit."

I stared between them, incredulous as I took the chair nearest the wall. A waiter delivered a bottle and three glasses as Will settled his hat on the tabletop. I stared at the man I'd begrudgingly considered a friend back in Fort Hood. He purposefully avoided my glare, instead taking his time to pour hefty fingers of whiskey into the glasses.

Will was different. The easy smile permanently attached to his face back in the desert was gone. My gaze traveled to the scar on the left side of his face. The tissue had clearly healed a long time ago. The gnarled skin was darker than his usual bronze, jagged as it reached from his eye to his hairline. The leaden suspicion of who had given him that scar settled deep within my gut, stilling some of my nervous energy. I flexed my hand before grabbing the glass, the ache in my knuckles soothing my raw edges.

Will had seen some shit, just as I had, since our parting in Fort Hood. The least I could do was let him explain. For Bonnie. She'd want me to.

After draining his drink, Will poured a second, avoiding my gaze for so long that it felt uncomfortable. Even Mickey's usually casual mood seemed bleaker as he leaned back in his chair.

"You're different," Will finally said. My eyebrows shot up. He said it as though the changes I'd undergone were news to me. As if all of us hadn't been forever altered by what had happened in Fort Hood. I opened my mouth to call him a smartass, but he cut me off, his eyes meeting mine for the first time. "I'm not stalling. I just . . . don't know where to start."

"The beginning. I want to know everything." The man steeled himself by taking a deep pull of his glass and releasing a long, whiskey-tinged breath.

"After that Crimson Fist asshole hit her over the head, my dad dragged us into the back of slavers' wagons." He stared at the surface of the table as he leaned forward. "Turns out, he didn't really need the cages. He hit her. Hard." His knuckles blanched as his fingers tightened on the edge of the table. "Hard enough that she didn't wake up. Not for a long time. When she did, her eyes were black."

Will shook his head, some of his unruly locks falling into his face. When I'd first spied him outside of the house, I almost didn't notice him. The long hair and stubbled chin made him nearly unrecognizable from a distance.

"Her pupils were so dilated that you couldn't see the blue anymore. When she tried to talk, her words were nonsense. She couldn't keep anything down. Then her breathing—"

Will's jaw clenched, and he gripped his glass so hard it might crack. He took in a ragged breath. The helplessness that'd haunted me for three years . . . Somehow, I knew he'd understood it. I recognized the expression on his face. It was one I'd worn countless times when there was no news.

"I did everything I could, but she needed a *real* doctor." He took another large swallow from his glass, eyes closing as if he were reveling in the burn. I recognized that, too.

Everything in me wanted to push him forward, to ask questions about Bonnie, but I couldn't. I couldn't do that to him any more than I could to myself. I didn't realize through my anger that they'd been with a band of fucking outlaws who would do worse than murder you. Because I was selfish. Just like I'd been with Bonnie.

When he finally looked at me, Will seemed steadier. "I'm not proud to say that I didn't realize my dad was bringing us here instead of Tent City, where Jones's crew is stationed, until we arrived. I only cared about Bonnie. About keeping her alive. But I was failing at that, too."

I should have never let her walk back into this. I should have been stronger. I should have been faster. I should have been braver.

"Is she alive?" I finally asked, my voice tight. If she was dead . . . If the last three years were for *nothing*—

"They said her brain was swollen inside of her skull," he said instead. "The doctor drilled into it to relieve the pressure. I had to hold her still while they did it."

My jaw clenched as I fought the raging fire inside of me. It wasn't Will's fault; I knew that. But he was the closest thing I had to the person who *was* responsible.

"She's alive, mostly."

"What does that mean?" I ground out through clenched teeth.

Will exhaled as he poured another drink. "They gave her glowroot while she recovered." Glowroot? Jesus. "We had to keep her sedated, to keep her from thrashing in pain or trying to get up." He fixed me with red-rimmed eyes. My gaze dropped to my drink. I couldn't imagine having to make that decision. "For weeks, she didn't leave that bed. She wasn't aware of anything other than the high. When they finally weaned her down enough . . ." He pulled the cigarette case from his pocket and struck a match. He took his precious time lighting it and inhaling deeply.

As the smoke settled in the air, the scent of tobacco and whiskey numbing my panicked heart, he said, "She doesn't remember who she was. She doesn't remember me. She sure as hell doesn't remember you." Tension snapped my spine straight. "She doesn't remember anything before she woke up in that house." He shook his head.

"So," he said, lifting his gaze to mine. "Ask me again if Bonnie is alive. Because, her body is . . . but she isn't Bonnie anymore. She goes by Audrey now; she doesn't even know who Bonnie is."

A thousand questions rose in my mind. Surely the woman I loved couldn't just be gone? Because of a head wound and a drug? That wasn't Bonnie. Bonnie was strong and resilient. Immovable. I didn't buy it.

Because if Bonnie was gone . . . what was the fucking point?

"You didn't try hard enough," I said, barely veiling the fire in my words.

"Jess," Mickey admonished. I spared a single glance at my uncle, whose brows lifted to make his point. In all honesty, I'd been so wrapped in Will's words, I'd forgotten he was here at all.

Will chuckled darkly. "I sold my soul to the fuckin' devil to stay by her side, *pendejo*," he said. "Sixgun owed Lee a debt. Something big. I took it on, agreed to work for him. I've tried to jog her memory so many times. You don't *get* it." He drove his finger into the hard surface of the table, rattling the glasses. "She's my best friend. I've known her my entire motherfuckin' life. I try. Every. Single. Day. Still, when she looks at me, all she sees is another employee. Nothing works."

"Three fucking years, Will," I said. "In three years, did it never cross your mind to, I don't know, write a goddamn letter?"

"I couldn't." He stubbed his cigarette out on the table.

"Why the fuck not?"

"Well, for one, how do you write a letter like that? *By the way, Bonnie's gone.* I didn't know how to do that." He sat straighter in his chair. "And secondly, her father told her she was *raped*. That her head injury was the result of an attack, one in which she was brutally assaulted." He let out another dark laugh. "You'd

LAUREN SEVIER & ABBIE LYNN SMITH

have come running the second you found out, and it wouldn't have helped her. Or you."

"He'd have run here half-cocked and gotten himself killed." I glared at my uncle. He wasn't wrong, though.

"Wait," I said as Will's words passed beyond the angry barrier in my chest. "Her father?"

"Yup," he said, leaning back in his chair as he lit another cigarette. "Zachary Lee."

"Fuck." Mickey's eyes widened. Some of the color leached from his normally-rosy cheeks.

"Who's Zachary Lee?"

"He owns New Orleans. If there's an unsavory business going on, his hands are in it. Glowroot. Slave trade. Brothels. Smuggling. All of it," Will said.

"And Bonnie's father," my uncle said. *No shit, asshole.* "What reinforcements do you have in the city?"

"Reinforcements?" Will asked, his eyebrows disappearing beneath his hair. "None, *hombre*. I work for Lee." He pointed to the branded fleur-de-lis on his neck. Mickey swore and rose from his seat.

"Where are you going?" I asked as he stuffed his hat on his head.

"To send word to Fort Hood."

"And let that word get handed directly to Lee's guards on its way across the bridge?" Will asked.

I depended on my uncle, on his unwavering optimism when it came to finding Bonnie. Seeing his shoulders deflate as he sat down sent a bolt of panic through me.

You always need someone to tell you what to do. First it was Mom, then Bonnie. Now, it's me.

The Kid's voice reverberated through my mind, reminding me of the swift kick in the ass he'd given me after Bonnie was taken. He was right. I let others dictate what I did too often. Whatever my uncle knew about Zachary Lee, it was enough to throw him. He was speechless as he reached across the table to grab the bottle.

Mickey hadn't had a sip of liquor in three years. *Fuck.* We didn't know what we were up against. Even my uncle seemed at a loss.

It was up to me.

"Mickey," I said. "You'll leave first thing tomorrow for Fort Hood." He opened his mouth to question me, but I barreled forward. "The only way to be sure Lee doesn't see us coming is for you to deliver the message yourself. Get The Kid. Get everyone you can and bring them back here. I'll be in touch."

"And what are you gonna do?"

I turned to Will, a grim smile crossing my face. "My good friend here is going to figure out a way to get me into that household," I said. "He knows the ins and outs of the house. He's established. He can put in a good word for me."

"How the hell am I supposed to do that, *pendejo?*"

I shrugged. "We'll figure it out." I turned back to Mickey. "On your way out of the city, scout out where we can hide an army."

"How are you going to get word out to me?"

"There's gotta be some way to smuggle letters out of the city. We just have to figure it out," I said.

"Bonnie *did* say Jesse was better at the con than me," Will remarked as he stubbed his cigarette out beside the first.

"Goddamn it. I bet a hundred on that guy in Little Rock," a man said loudly from the bar. "Fucking Montana." My ears perked up as I turned my attention toward the patrons at the bar.

"That guy's insane. I heard he knocked Wainwright on his ass in five minutes. I wouldn't bet against him next time," another said.

A smirk crossed my face. Will's head cocked to the side, and he narrowed his eyes at me.

"Wait." He leaned forward, a glint flickering in his eyes. "No." My smirk widened into a grin. "What the fuck?"

"You did always say I had violent tendencies," I said, lifting my glass and taking a swig.

Will's eyes illuminated, as they had in Fort Hood, when he talked about joining the med team at the base and helping people. Hope flared in my chest at the sight. We could do this. We could get her back. A grin crossed his face, reminding me more of the smartass gunslinger I'd befriended three years ago. "How do you feel about brands?"

I sputtered on my whiskey. "What?"

"Lee's gonna to be at the fighting pits tonight," he explained. "He's looking to get into the business, hiring his own fighter." He looked me up and down, then relaxed back against his chair. "I know just the man for the job."

Looking far too pleased with himself, Will outlined his plan for securing a spot for me in Lee's household. And, hopefully, for helping Bonnie find a way back to herself.

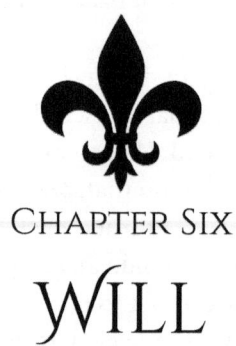

CHAPTER SIX

WILL

J ESSE'S PLAN WAS INSANE, at best, but what else did I have left to lose at this point? After we'd finished most of the whiskey—save for Mickey, who'd sat in stoic silence the entire time—and nursing a healthy buzz, I led the way across town to the pits. As we pushed through crowds that were thickening as night fell and the city came to life, Jesse's eyes darted back and forth as he watched people move out of our way on the busy streets.

"Why do they do that?" he asked, and I couldn't find the words to explain. Perhaps I'd become too accustomed to how people in the city regarded me. In fact, I hardly noticed it anymore. Mickey's gray-blue gaze settled on me, and I just shrugged, offering an easy smile that didn't reach my eyes. Instead of answering or lying outright to him, I changed the subject.

"So, *Montana*, huh?" I stifled a grin at the thought of Jesse's fighting moniker being a nickname I'd mockingly coined forever ago in the desert. He didn't acknowledge me for a long moment; then he looked at me from the corner of his eye.

"It's where I'm from," he said dully, but I didn't believe him. After all, if he'd been going by the name for this long, there was a chance he'd missed my companionship almost as much as I'd missed his. Not that I'd admit it.

"I told him it was fucking stupid, but he insisted," Mickey piped up, making my grin widen. Jesse grumbled incoherently for a moment, avoiding my gaze. I slapped his shoulder and leaned in close to him.

"I missed you too, Jess."

He twisted from beneath my grip and shoved me away on the street. I lost my balance and knocked bodily into a man walking the opposite way. My hat fell to the ground, and the man's vehement swearing filled the air as I retrieved it. Slowly I stood to my full height, dragging my eyes up to his face. At first, it was screwed up in anger and offense, until he recognized who stared down at him. The ruddy red hue faded into a ghostly white pallor. He scrambled back and apologized profusely, the words a jumbled mess. Settling my hat back on my head, being careful to tilt the brim down, I ignored Jesse's pointed stare.

"P-please," he stammered louder as I slapped some dust from my jeans.

"It's fine." Relief melted the haggard, stricken lines off his face. "It was an accident."

"Thank you," he breathed, as if I'd pardoned him of all his sins and opened the pearly gates for him myself. He didn't wait around to watch my mood sour and disappeared around a corner.

"What was *that?*" Jesse asked, eyes piercing through the haze of bullshit I was usually so good at using to shift focus.

"Nothing." I watched a muscle feather in his jaw. It was a lie, clearly, but he didn't press the issue . . . yet. Mickey came to my rescue, reminding us all that the fights were going to start soon.

When we arrived at the pits, they were exactly as expected. Excited screams billowed up into the night sky from the sinkhole-turned-gambling den. Jesse and Mickey peered over the edge to see the different fights two stories below. With a grin, I jerked my head to the right, showing them the narrow staircase leading into the uncovered tunnel system. The cacophony of the crowd was muffled as we descended in single file, with me at the helm, so I took this opportunity to try to prepare my wayward friends for what to expect.

"When you meet Lee, keep things short and simple. More talking means more opportunities for him to find out who you are. Steer away from personal information, and for fuck's sake, don't argue with him." I finished just as we reached the end of the dank staircase. When I turned, Jesse was already searching the room for Lee. *Too eager.* Warning bells clanged in my ears.

The crowd was rowdy tonight, a crater beast cage match dragging most of the patrons into the lower level of the rings. An otherworldly screeching made my ears ring as Jesse stared down at the four well-armed men circling the creature. Claws scrabbled against the concrete, scoring ridges deep in the earth as its armored beak snapped threateningly.

"What the hell is that?" Morbid curiosity leaked into his voice.

"That, *my friend,*" I said, clapping a hand on his shoulder, "is an eagle-lion. The crater beast matches are a big draw. Twenty men per creature. Anyone surviving at the end of the round or killing the creature wins the pot."

He shook his head, incredulous as he stared at the remaining men standing. After a moment, he dragged his eyes away and tried to shove past me, but I gripped his shirt and pulled him closer as Mickey crowded in.

"This isn't a quick con in a town you'll only be in for a few hours, Montana." I pointedly neglected to use his name now that there were prying ears around every corner. "It's a long con, with multiple opportunities every hour of every day for you to fuck it up and get killed. Are you sure you're ready for this?"

"Of course I am," he said through a haze of trepidation he couldn't hide. Though it was obvious that he *wasn't*, in fact, ready for this . . . he was willing to try. For her.

"Alright then, last tip: if you have to lie to him, keep it as close to the truth as possible. He's Bonnie's father, and he can smell bullshit from a mile away." I caught sight of Lee's starched black suit across the space as he leaned toward someone in a dress shirt and expensive shoes taking notes on the fighters. "If all else fails, I have your back."

I turned to tell Mickey to make himself scarce, but he'd already disappeared into the crowd. Steering Jesse forward as crowds parted for us, I adopted my usual dark scowl.

"Mr. Lee." I clasped his hand quickly in greeting. He didn't look too surprised to see me, but that was to be expected. I always knew where he was, who he was meeting with, and how long he would be gone, just in case there was ever a need to find him in a hurry. Perks of being trusted by the devil, I guess.

"You have news for me already?" He raised a surprised eyebrow. Right. The blackmail on the rich guy. Chuckling swiftly, I shook my head before motioning to Jesse at my side.

"I'm good, but I'm not *that* good," I said, watching as an easy smile accompanied shrewd glances towards Jesse's stiff shoulders. Before he could question why I was bothering him, I turned to make introductions. "Actually, Mr. Lee, I think my friend here could help you with finding a sponsored fighter."

He assessed Jesse quickly, clearly finding him lacking, if the imperious curl to his upper lip was any indication. The unfamiliar man next to him dragged his eyes away from the fight then, rejoining the conversation. The affable smile on his face unnerved me, like he genuinely enjoyed being down here in the crush of sweaty, screaming bodies. As if anyone could enjoy this desperate shit.

"Is that so?" Mr. Lee asked disbelievingly. Facing Jesse fully, I clapped him on the shoulder with a shit-eating grin on my face.

"Mr. Lee, meet *Montana*." The second his fighting moniker fell from my mouth, all disinterest bled from Lee's face. Instead, he peered curiously between us and extended a hand for Jesse to shake. His smiling guest shook Jesse's hand the moment Lee dropped it.

"I saw you fight in Louisville," he gushed excitedly.

"Surely you can't mean *the* Montana," Mr. Lee said to me quietly, but all I did was raise my eyebrows and purse my lips in Jesse's direction. At this point, it would be up to him to prove himself.

"Ellis, Montana, this is Lucas Rutherford. He's come from Manhattan Island to convince me to marry off my daughter," Lee said with a sharp laugh, one that fell on stale air and stilted silence. I could practically hear Jesse's teeth grinding together. Clearing my throat, I tried to distract Lee from the dangerous glint that appeared in Jesse's eyes.

Lee regarded him carefully, and I was proud to see my friend wrestle himself into a semblance of control. Even though I hadn't seen Jesse for years, his control was hanging on by a quickly fraying thread. He shifted onto the balls of his feet, readying himself for a fight as he clenched his fists at his sides. I tried to catch his eye over Lee's shoulder, but he ignored me like it was his purpose in life.

"And you're what? Getting into training now? You have a fighter you want me to sponsor?" Lee crossed his arms and assessed Jesse.

"I'm the one looking for a sponsor, Mr. Lee," Jesse said firmly and more confidently than I thought possible.

"I might not have a fighter on my roster yet, but I do my due diligence. You've never *been* sponsored before. Why the sudden change of heart?"

"Easy. Money," Jesse said, but Lee's body language was off. He didn't like the turn of events, or maybe this deal felt too good to be true. In fact, he'd probably only entertained Jesse thus far because of me. But, if we couldn't convince him of Jesse's legitimacy fast, we were going to lose his only opportunity to get hired onto the household staff.

They kept talking, but I scanned the room, looking for anything to bolster Jesse's case. Something that might alleviate the bunching tension in his shoulders and soften his murderous glares. A fight ended in front of us, and the victor waved the crowd forward with blood-soaked teeth.

There.

I shoved Jesse hard into the cleared-out ring, watching as Rutherford and Lee tracked him. When he straightened, he glared at me before I tipped my

71

head and offered a grim smile. Understanding passed between us then. He needed to get his aggression out and show Lee *exactly* why he should hire him.

Lee glared at me, but I shrugged. "He's a fighter. I thought you'd want to see him fight." Rutherford laughed, entertained enough that Lee didn't question the strange turn of events. I only watched until Jesse peeled his shirt off, revealing a *ton* of tattoos spanning the length of his torso. Huh. That was unexpected. Shaking off the appreciation of his body art, I made myself scarce until Mickey found me slinking into the dark shadows of the room.

Crowds of people like this could be problematic for me with my *reputation*, and I didn't exactly feel like having to shoot anyone or cause pandemonium in this small, enclosed space.

"How'd he do?"

"Almost lost his shit." I sighed. "But, surprisingly, he kept it together long enough for me to toss him in the ring. Is he always on such a short goddamn fuse?"

Mickey laughed darkly, making the hair on the back of my neck stand up. "You have no fuckin' clue."

Our conversation faded into thick silence. I grew increasingly more uncomfortable the longer it stretched, but Mickey wasn't bothered in the slightest. There was something unnerving about how Mickey had stared at me since we'd met up. Just when I felt like the silence might strangle me, he finally said, "You do what you have to, son."

I couldn't breathe. The air in my lungs burned away as scorching hot shame filled my chest. I wanted to let my knees buckle from the weight of my sins, wanted to deny every horrible thing I'd done until I was blue in the face from lying.

But he'd called me *son*.

"I know what men look like when they've been to war." His voice was quiet beneath the crowd's roar of excitement at whatever was happening in the fight. "I know what they look like when they've seen the worst of humanity. When they've *been* the worst of humanity."

I opened my mouth. To do what, I didn't know. There was nothing in my mind but a myriad of faces, some crying, some pleading, all afraid. Then there was Bonnie in my mind's eye, bloody and pale, when we didn't know if she would make it through the night. It was the first time I'd ever prayed, not that anyone listened to a sorry sack of shit like me.

"I've been the worst of humanity, too." His gray-blue eyes slid to mine. I blinked hard, seeing Jesse elbow one man in his teeth before knocking another out with one swift uppercut.

"How did you come back from it?" The barely whispered words fell unbidden from my tongue. A shadow of the real questions roiled in my mind. *Is there any coming back from this at all? Will I ever start to feel alive again? Am I worthy of redemption?*

He offered a knowing smile and grasped the back of my neck, as if anchoring me to the ground at my feet and his steady presence at my side.

"One day at a time." It wasn't a perfect answer, but if his clear eyes, devoid of the sheen of alcohol, were any indication, it was working well enough for him. "Jesse'll probably never thank you for what you've lost. What you've *sacrificed* for Bonnie. So I'll do it for him."

He held his hand out to me, respect and pride bright in his eyes. It'd been so long since anyone had looked at me like I was more than a disappointment; the air shifted wrong in my throat as I shook his hand.

Another roar from the crowd made it clear that not only was Jesse winning, but he was winning by a *lot*. Enough that he should have worked off most of his aggression by now.

"At least he looks more in control than he did in Little Rock," Mickey said, peering through the crush of bodies. "Thought he was gonna kill a guy out there and wind up in a noose for it."

Just as Mickey finished speaking, Jesse's boot slammed against his opponent's chest as he kicked him halfway across the space. With a swift forearm to the throat, the man went down hard and didn't get back up again. A bell rang, and Jesse barreled forward, sweat dripping down his neck and nostrils flared as he caught sight of me.

"Alright," I said when he got close enough. "You calmer now?"

"You heard what that fucker said?" I nodded, not a hint of levity in my expression.

"It just means we have to get you into that house. Fast. Are you ready to pass back by Lee?" He nodded, jaw set with purpose. But before we found them, Lee and Rutherford strolled toward us. Lee stopped, peering up at Jesse as if looking at an interesting puzzle waiting to be solved.

"You've got yourself a sponsor, Mr. . . ." Lee trailed off, but Jesse took the question in stride, offering a wide, honest smile.

"Montana is fine, Mr. Lee. I look forward to working for you."

I saw what Bonnie had all that time ago. At first, I couldn't understand why she thought the farm boy with little experience and too much trust in his eyes could be good at deception. Now, seeing how easily he turned on that affable charm and those honorable, forthright expressions, I understood exactly how manipulative he could be given the right circumstances.

"Ellis will bring you up to speed on standard operating procedure, and he'll arrange a time tomorrow for you to come to the house to get *situated.*" Lee tipped his chin in my direction, and I nodded obediently, like the lapdog I was. With a few more pleasantries, they departed and we met back up with Mickey, letting him know that against all odds, Jesse's crazy plan had worked.

"I think this calls for drinks." I led the way back to my apartment and the bar underneath. "*Lots* of drinks." The rest of the night passed in a haze of booze and booming laughter. Trading wild stories with friends and not feeling lonely for the first time in longer than I could remember.

Then I realized the laughter was mine.

CHAPTER SEVEN

JESSE

*T*HE BLAZING SUN FLARED *from above. I lifted my hand to block the light, squinting to make sense of my surroundings. Expansive yellow sand stretched as far as I could see. I wheeled around, not understanding. Mountains lined the horizon. Jagged peaks jutted starkly against the harsh white sky. With the exception of cacti dotting the scenery, there was nothing.*

Only the dust. Only the sun. Only me.

Heat licked my calf. I spun, hissing at the bite of flame erupting from nowhere. Fire whipped out, coiling around me like a snake. Before I could escape, it surrounded me. My lungs struggled to keep up as the flames shot higher.

"Jesse!"

I whirled toward the voice. "Bonnie?"

There she was. On the other side of the fire, the woman I loved stood, a circle of fire caging her in, too. Wind gusted, whipping her long locks into the air. Shoulders tense, she turned panicked eyes on me.

"You said you'd come for me!"

"I am!" I forced down my panic. I had to be strong. For her. I had to save her. My gaze dropped to the flames, searching for any weakness in the line.

"What are you doing, Jesse?" Another voice. This time, younger, masculine. The Kid. I spun toward him, unable to do anything as the flames crept closer. "Save Bonnie!"

"I'm trying!" I glanced between them, heart racing faster than I could keep up. I had no water. The ground at my feet was dry. Too dry.

"It's been years, Jesse." Bonnie's voice wavered as flames consumed her.

"You're never getting her back," a third voice said.

75

Will, this time. He stood just out of reach on the other side of the fire, twisting the brim of his hat in his hands. "You failed, Jess. You didn't fight for her. Not nearly hard enough." I clenched my jaw against his harsh words. "Now she's gone."

Brows furrowed, I whirled around. But he was right. The flames shot higher into the sky, devouring her image, stealing her away from me.

"Where's your brother?" Will asked.

I whipped toward The Kid. He was gone, too.

"If you aren't careful," he said. When I turned toward him, something was different. Off. It wasn't Will. Not really. His eyes were jet black, not even a hint of light penetrating them. "You're gonna end up just like me."

A swift blow from a steel-toe boot startled me awake. A freshly shaved man stood in place of my friend. Will tied his hair back with a leather strap and washed his face. Even his cowboy hat looked like it'd been scrubbed. He handed me a mug, the liquid steaming from within.

"We've got work to do." His eyes were clear, and a grin tugged at his mouth.

I groaned, averting my eyes to shake his image from my nightmare, and leaned back against the cushion as my head ached in time with my pulse. I hadn't drunk that much in a single night in forever. How the hell did Will recover so quickly?

By the time I finished my coffee, the drunken haze dissipated, even if the terror from my dream lingered.

"Want to talk about it?" he asked as I stood in his small bathroom. I splashed cool water over my face. I looked terrible.

"Talk about what?" I swished water in my mouth.

Will leaned against the doorframe, staring at me in the mirror from over my shoulder. He lifted an eyebrow as he crossed his arms over his chest. "You were whimperin' in your sleep."

Fuck. I spit in the sink, twisted the handle off, and shoved him out of the doorway.

"There's nothing to talk about." I studied the small apartment with sober eyes.

A large bed bucked up to one wall, bracketed on either side by mismatched tables. Cigarette butts stuck out of them. The dilapidated couch I'd slept on might have been blue, or green, but its color had faded to a mottled gray. I didn't want to think about the species of insects I slept with last night. Dingy light filtered in through the lone window; its panes either painted a shade of off-white or just too damn dirty. Beside the couch, a bookshelf leaned hard into the corner.

As I moved toward it, he said, "Sure there isn't."

I exhaled loudly. "I have nightmares sometimes. It's nothing."

Will's brows lifted, and though I saw doubt in his eyes, amusement brightened their color. "I just wonder what in the world could scare big, bad Montana."

I let out a dark laugh. "We need to stop off at the stables across from the square."

"Why?"

"Because when I see Bonnie again, I don't plan on smelling like I came from a bar."

As if on cue, a sharp knock sounded, and Mickey entered. He, like Will, appeared fresh and ready to take on the day.

"Good," he said. "You're awake. I need to get going."

"I'll come with you," I said. "I'll meet you at the house in an hour?" Without waiting for Will's confirmation, we left. Fresh cigarette smoke filled my nostrils as we descended the staircase into the bar. I hesitated as we neared the door. Part of me itched for a glass of whiskey or tequila. Anything, really, that might steady me for today.

"C'mon, Jess, I need to get on the road." Mickey settled his hat on his head, lingering at the door.

The bright morning sun slanted between the buildings of Bourbon Street. While it wasn't empty, as I might have expected, the streets were markedly quieter than last night. I shoved my hands into my pockets, walking silently.

"I hope you know what you've gotten yourself into, Jess." Mickey guided me off of Bourbon and into a quieter alleyway.

"Do I ever?" A smartass grin crossed my face.

"That's why I'm worried."

Within minutes, we neared the square. As I veered right, my uncle grabbed my arm and motioned for us to keep walking. With the iron fence on my right and buildings on my left, I took a long breath.

"You shouldn't worry about me." Though I felt anything but confident, the least I could do was convince Mickey.

"It's not even your hothead." We passed a gaggle of giggling children in uniforms. He shuffled to one side of the cobblestones, nodding grimly to the woman chasing after the kids. Once they passed, he continued forward. "It's Lee."

"You act like I haven't faced bad people before." We reached the main road. The stable waited on the far side of the square. Instead of steering us that way, he headed directly across the street.

The bitter scent of coffee mingled with a sugary sweetness that reminded me of home. *Montana*. People walked to and fro before us, but the cafe behind them caught my attention. As we filed into a line, I searched the tables on the open patio.

"What is this?"

Mickey flashed a grin. "Cafe du Monde." As though that explained it. When he glanced at me again, he shrugged. "Anna may have loved this place so much that she made beignets every Sunday. Or at least that's what your pop told me."

Beignets. I hadn't heard the word in so long.

Every Sunday, I'd awoken to the aromas of pastries and coffee. Even though we never took a day off, Mom would have the doughy pastries made. Sometimes, she added a dusting of powdered sugar. My mouth watered the closer to the front of the line we got.

"You okay?" Mickey's voice snapped me from the memory. I cleared my throat, nodding.

"She did."

His brows rose in question.

"Mom. She made beignets almost every Sunday."

My stomach growled while my heart plummeted. I wished The Kid were here. He'd appreciate this just as much as I did. A wistful expression passed over my uncle's face, and I knew he was lost to memory and grief, just like me.

Within minutes, we headed toward the stable. The moment the beignet touched my lips, my eyes fluttered shut, and I was back at the dining table my father had built. Only, this memory made warmth spread from my chest. I hadn't appreciated those mornings with my family.

I swore once we got Bonnie back, once this was all over, I would do better with The Kid. He deserved that. I'd failed him too often.

"Jess." Mickey stopped on the corner next to the stable. "I want you to be careful."

"I will be."

He shook his head, fixing me with hard blue eyes. "You don't get it. Zachary Lee is dangerous." I'd never seen fear in my uncle. Not fear that ran so deep I thought I was staring into my mother's eyes the night she died. "If he finds out who you are, he won't hesitate."

"How would he know anything about me?"

Mickey balled up the white paper bag in his hands, knuckles blanching. "Who do you think introduced Emma to Lee?"

How should I know?

I kept silent. Mickey was tight-lipped about a lot of things. He wasn't the type to sit around and reminisce about the past, like the loss of his sister, my mother.

"We were all friends, remember?" Mickey lowered his gaze and exhaled sharply. "Anna introduced them. Before." The *Culling*. The nuclear event that ended civilization. "I'll never understand how it happened. Lee and your mother worked together. He *hated* Anna. And if he finds out you're her kid, you're gonna be up shit creek without a paddle. The only person I ever saw him care about was Bonnie's mom." His throat bobbed. "But it was easy to love Emma."

I had more questions than Mickey would, or could, really answer.

"Did he hate her enough to kill her?"

"I don't know—" He blew out a breath and clapped a hand on my shoulder. "Listen, focus on Bonnie, okay? Don't go sniffing out what may or may not be related to your mom. Not until I get back."

I swallowed around the lump in my throat, nodding as we entered the stables. Mickey passed a few bits over to the groom. As he saddled his mount, I found No Name's stall and rifled through my bags. I changed swiftly, then grabbed an apple from the next stall, sliced it, and fed the pieces to him. He huffed in displeasure as I locked his stall door. I tucked a small black box into my pocket.

Once outside in the crisp, morning air, Mickey stared at me. "I don't like this, for the record."

"Noted." I grinned. "For the record, I'm glad you're leaving."

"Wow. Maybe you're more like your pop than I realized." A grin broke across his face. He clapped me on the shoulder. "Be careful, Jess." I nodded.

Mickey had been with me every day for the last three years. Could I handle this without him?

I had no choice. We needed backup, and I wasn't leaving without Bonnie.

Instead of acknowledging the emotion, I tugged the box from my pocket. "Give this to The Kid for me?"

"What is it?"

"A promise I made a long time ago." I handed it to him. "Tell The Kid I don't trust anyone but him to bring that back to me."

Mickey nodded and tucked the box into his saddlebag. The next time I saw it, I wanted The Kid to hand it over. Because it would mean my family was whole again. I needed that.

My uncle stared at me, a mixture of dread and determination on his face. I wrapped him in a quick one-armed hug and held tight for a moment. Then I shoved away from him.

"Ride fast."

"As the wind." Mickey grinned, even through the sadness in his eyes.

As he swung into the saddle, I forced my rising panic down. The Kid had been right. I couldn't let other people fix my problems. I had to take ownership. I had to be the man my parents always wanted me to be.

Mickey couldn't save Bonnie. The Kid couldn't. Not even Will. It had to be me.

And I would do whatever it took. Because that was what you did for the people you loved.

As he receded in the distance, I inhaled deeply to steel myself. With one final look, I headed back to the square.

Meeting Lee last night had been nerve-wracking. If he hadn't agreed to give me a shot, then the plan to infiltrate his household wouldn't have worked. Now I had a chance. I crossed the street, keeping my eyes low as I navigated the foot traffic of the square. I passed by the statue Mickey'd said was so different.

I'd missed the fleur-de-lis carved into the stone.

Sixgun had been looking for Bonnie when he went to Montana. It hadn't been on Jones's orders.

What did it have to do with my parents?

I was so lost in my thoughts I didn't realize I was near the house until I bumped into a branded guard. I murmured an apology and brushed past him, heading for the side alley.

Will leaned against a stone wall, a grin on his lips as he spoke to a man in a different sort of uniform, also marked with the fleur-de-lis.

"I told you, you gotta watch out for him."

"That hellbeast bit me." They turned to me as I walked up.

"Ah!" Will said, dropping his cigarette and stomping it out. "There he is."

My eyebrows lifted at my friend's overly enthusiastic greeting. He introduced me to the groom, then steered me into a stable.

"What took so long?" Will asked. "You and Mickey start cryin' over your goodbyes?"

I punched him in the arm. "Fuck you."

"Listen, that was possible, once. But that ship has long since sailed." Will grinned. "You ready?"

"Ready for what?"

Will stepped back, and the groom lifted an iron rod from flames. The fleur-de-lis tip glowed red. The groom set it back into the fire.

"You need to get your brand."

"Do I have to?" I eyed the poker, nose scrunching in disdain.

"It hurts more if you let it cool," he teased. "Look, I'm supposed to round up the guards and get you wasted. Then give you shit all night. But we don't have time for that."

"Fucking fine." I unbuttoned my shirt and peeled it off of one side. The groom handed me a thick leather strap. I eyed it, confused.

"To keep you from cracking your jaw, *pendejo*." Will took the iron from the flames.

"Get it over with." I shoved the strap into my mouth, clenching it between my teeth.

"One . . . two . . ."

"Fucking do it—" White-hot pain lanced up my neck. I flinched, the taste of leather on my tongue. My eyes watered, blurring my vision. I tensed, teeth and fists clenching as I fought back a scream. The heat receded, leaving behind the hot sting of iron. I spit out the strap and faced Will. "Asshole."

"Yeah, yeah." Will headed through a door on the other end of the stable. I followed him into a long corridor, clenching and unclenching my fists.

"Jesus, that hurt." I resisted touching the marred skin of my neck.

"I've got some stuff at my apartment that'll help." Will lifted a match to the tip of his cigarette. "I'll bring it to you tomorrow."

I lifted an eyebrow. It was barely the middle of the afternoon. "Tomorrow?"

"Yeah, I've got a job for Lee," he said, exhaling a stream of smoke in my face. I swatted the air.

"How about tonight? I'm fighting at the pits again."

Will gave me a quick introduction to the house, mentioning the front versus the back, how we weren't supposed to be in the front house, even though that was where Bonnie was. I tuned him out after that, gaze drifting to the front house even as Will showed me my room and where to find the communal bath.

Not long after, Will left.

Even though he'd *told* me I wasn't supposed to be in the front house, I could easily feign ignorance under the guise of being a new employee.

I needed to see her. Just once.

Turning back the way we came, I stalked silently down the long hall, boots echoing in the eerily silent air. The ugly wallpaper and opulent furnishings somehow fit what I'd seen of the city. Over the top, extravagant, and pointless. As long as a person had four walls, why did they need crystal candlestick holders?

The first floor was devoid of people. I took the wide staircase up to the second. Paintings in gilded frames, garish light fixtures, and overly plush rugs lined this corridor. It felt like I was in some strange nightmare.

Feminine voices caught my attention. My heart stuttered, and I wheeled around, hoping to see Bonnie. Instead, two women toting stacks of folded laundry headed in my direction. They wore uniforms with the brand stitched across the breast. They froze the moment they saw me. I adopted an easy, disarming grin.

"Hi, I think I'm lost."

"What are you looking for?" one asked. My gaze barely marked her features as I turned around in the corridor.

"I'm looking for the staff's quarters," I said. "This doesn't look like it."

The women chuckled. "You're in the front house," the other said.

"Easiest way is to take the breezeway to the far side of the manor."

"On the *first* floor."

"Thanks." My grin fell the moment I turned my back. I followed the hall around a corner, spying said breezeway just beyond a door propped open by a wooden crate.

A framed portrait captured my attention. I slowed, boots skimming across the too-thick rug. It wasn't the portrait of the man holding a pitchfork and the woman beside him that caught my eye. It was the frame. Thus far, everything in this house had a garish, gaudy feel to it. The frame was made of simple wood. Oak or cedar, maybe. Plain. Far too plain for the tastes of Lee, if I had to guess.

What made this painting so important?

Zachary Lee didn't strike me as the type to keep things around that didn't have some sort of value.

A sharp intake of breath made my spine straighten. Even after three years, I knew the sound of her breathing, heard it in my sleep. I remained frozen, focusing solely on the hall around me, isolating my sense of sound to identify its source. Soft rustling. Like the brush of tree limbs against one another on a summer breeze or the swish of layered skirts. I turned, focused intently on my periphery. Light spilled from an open door. A large garden window let in the bright afternoon sunshine. But against the window, there was a shadow. The hair on the back of my neck lifted. Keeping my focus razor sharp, I pivoted slowly, the rug muffling my steps. All at once, the room beyond the open door snapped into focus, and my heart plummeted.

Bonnie.

Bonnie.

I braced myself against the doorframe, unable to look away. She rested on the window seat, leaning against a large, velvety plush cushion, one leg tucked beneath her and the other pulled up. In her hands, she held a book. A *book*. My throat became like sandpaper, and breath escaped me.

Bonnie was *reading*.

Dark brows low on her forehead, blue eyes glued to the text, she didn't notice me. Her dark hair, styled into long ringlets, coiled over her shoulder. Her porcelain skin appeared smoother than I remembered. My fingers twitched, and I fought against every ounce of self-control I had. Her mouth pursed intently as she scanned the page. *Soft lips pressing against my throat in the truck.* I shivered at the memory of her touch.

She was right *there*.

She sure as hell doesn't remember you.

How was it possible I could know the woman before me so well? Know all of the ins and outs of her mind, her body, her soul . . . but she didn't know me?

Grief sliced me anew. I clenched my jaw, refusing to let it break me. Ever since that day in Fort Hood, I'd fractured, teetered on the edge of shattering altogether. But I hadn't.

But having her here . . .

So close.

But so far.

I swallowed around the lump in my throat, gaze trailing the length of her ornate bodice. The dark blue fabric glinted beneath the afternoon sunlight. The ring I'd handed off to Mickey passed through my mind.

If I had it with me, no doubt I'd have already gotten down on one knee.

Layers of skirts bunched together around her; one side slid up to reveal the smooth skin of her leg. My hands clenched as I remembered running my fingertips along her thighs, pressing my lips to the sensitive skin there, tasting her everywhere.

A faint line ran down the center of her thigh. My eyes narrowed. That wasn't there before. I'd mapped every inch of Bonnie's body in my memory. That scar was new.

My hand lifted as if of its own volition, aching to reach out and run my thumb over it. To ask what happened. To remind her what it felt like when I touched her.

But I didn't do any of it.

I knew Bonnie well enough to know that the moment she got spooked, she'd run. Would that be the same for Audrey?

Instead of giving in to my devilish needs, I shifted my weight, balancing fully. I leaned against the doorframe, crossing my arms over my chest and adopting a casual smile.

God, she was so fucking beautiful it hurt.

I cleared my throat, a weak attempt to capture her attention. I expected her to turn to me, disdain on her face at my interruption.

Instead, she let out a shriek, and the book flew from her hands.

It thumped to the floor at her feet. For an infinitesimal moment, the world suspended as wide, shocked blue eyes met mine. Her body went ramrod straight, her hand flat against her breast. Her chest heaved with ragged breaths as she climbed to her feet. Shock slipped, followed quickly by curiosity. Her eyes trailed the length of my body.

I felt her appraising look all the way to my gut.

I was used to women openly staring at me, ogling like I was something to be devoured. But when *she* did it ... when Bonnie's eyes were on me, my soul was bare. She saw every mangled, bitter, fractured piece of me.

Curiosity shifted to confrontation. The line between her brows was as familiar to me as the lash of her tongue when she'd called me farm *boy* back in Vegas.

"Who the fuck are you?" She recovered quickly, shoulders straightening.

"Who do you want me to be?" The corners of my mouth curled upward. A pretty flush crossed her cheeks. I shouldn't have felt the satisfaction that I did at her speechlessness. I crossed the room—a library—in quick strides and retrieved her book from the floor. I scanned the cover quickly, my brows lifting at the very bare, very masculine chest on it. "From the way you were biting your lip, maybe you'd like me to be him?"

As I brandished the cover in her direction, the pretty flush on her cheeks deepened. I forgot how satisfying it was to push her buttons.

"Good book?"

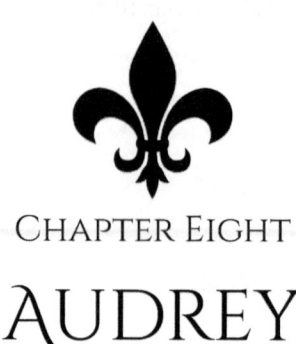

CHAPTER EIGHT

AUDREY

A ROUSAL, HEADY AND CLOYING, thudded deeper with every ragged beat of my heart. My skin felt too tight, and the room was suddenly stifling, the air too hot and thick to drag into my lungs. I couldn't be sure if it was the book I'd been reading, the devastating smile this strange man leveled me with, or some combination of both. Whatever the cause, I'd been thrown off balance, and decided I *hated* it.

Padding on bare feet, I tried not to notice the near-desperate edge sharpening his eyes into lapis blades as he raked his gaze over my form. It would be easy to order him to leave me alone, as I had to everyone the last two days, avoiding Mr. Lucas Rutherford. Instead, some insistent pull had me shuffling even closer.

"Yes," I answered him honestly. The skin on the side of his neck was angry and red, the same place my father branded his staff. Even as I stared, the red irritation crept farther up his neck. "I was enjoying it a lot before you interrupted me."

The hopeful waver in his breath was masked in an instant, and a falsely charming smile spread wide on his face. It was beautiful, *he* was beautiful, and perhaps it was because I'd used my own beauty to disarm and manipulate in the past that I saw through his cocky facade.

He faced me fully, the tall broad bulk of him taking up all the oxygen in the room. I tipped my head back to keep him in my sight. He handed the book back to me, and I grasped the worn cover with clumsy fingers.

"By all means," he said, sinking into a leather armchair directly in front of my window seat. "Carry on."

Running my thumb over the worn spine of my book, I stifled a chuckle that feathered from my lips. With a half-hearted shrug, I sat gingerly on the window seat and stared straight ahead at him with the book resting in my lap. For longer than I wanted to acknowledge, we sat in silence, staring. As my eyes tracked down the long aquiline ridge of his nose and across his jaw, his lingered on my face and the full pout of my bottom lip. I felt every glance like the whisper of a caress, forcing a shiver of delight down my spine. He swallowed hard, and my eyes caught on the nervous bob of his Adam's apple.

"You aren't reading." He tried to appear calm and self-assured. My eyes ticked up to his as a wicked grin curled on my mouth.

"Oh yes I am." I placed the book beside me as I stood. In the back corner of the room was a tray Savannah had left with fruit, cheese, and a glass of iced tea. I'd left it untouched, too engrossed in the romance. He tracked me across the room, gaze lingering on my hands as I pulled the fine linen napkin off the tray and shook it open.

"I assume you already know who I am." I didn't bother to look at him as I plunged my fingers into the glass of tea, fishing out shards of ice that cost my father more bits than I cared to think about. "But it's still pretty rude not to introduce yourself."

I paused to glance over my shoulder at him, and his spine stiffened and his knuckles strained as he clenched his fingers around the arm of his chair. Dropping the last shard of ice onto the napkin, I gathered the corners together and waded through the tension-thick air toward him.

"Here, I'll demonstrate." I couldn't keep the sarcastic edge from my voice. "I'm Audrey Lee, your boss's daughter, and you are . . . ?"

"Montana."

I blinked at his answer, pausing before I continued toward him. Instead of stopping an appropriate distance away, as he probably expected, I walked straight between his splayed legs, putting my weight on my knee and leaning into the leather seat between his thighs. His inhalation was deafening as I used my thumb and forefinger to tilt his chin, brandishing his neck to my hungry eyes.

"Montana, huh?" I unbuttoned the top button of his shirt with a deft flick of my fingers before pulling his collar out of the way.

"It's what my friends call me."

My breasts were eye-level with him, but he didn't gape the way I'd come to expect of men. The blonde stubble beneath my fingertips was nearly translucent in the bright light, but rough enough to remind me he wasn't a figment of my imagination.

"Is that what you want us to be? Friends?" A playful smile stretched on my mouth.

"We could be." His voice was low and sensual. "If that's what you wanted."

My gaze dropped to the red, angry wound swelling on his raw skin. A horrified hiss of air sucked between my teeth. Pulling harder on his collar, I lifted the fabric away from the inflamed area.

"Fuckin' hell." My brows pinched together in concern. "This still looks fresh. How long has it been since they branded you? Have you felt feverish?" He glanced up at me before looking sheepishly away.

"About twenty minutes," he muttered, stunning me into silence. An incredulous chuckle escaped my mouth before I could press my lips together to stop it. The sound made him lift his head to regard me expectantly.

"You just had a hot branding iron on your neck and your first thought afterwards was *gee, I'd really like to wander the house and annoy a woman hiding in the library?*" I liked how his eyes crinkled at the corners and warmed into a soft, cornflower blue. "My first thought would have been: *that hurts. Where's the liquor?*"

We settled into a companionable quiet as I raised the napkin full of ice, and he nodded. He groaned, eyes screwing painfully shut as I pressed it to the angry wound. One of his hands splayed on the small of my back, fingers spread nearly to my sides, and his arm banded around my waist. Clenching me tight, like holding me somehow made the pain easier to bear.

"Breathe through it." He struggled with the initial shock of pain before stilling once more. Eventually he cracked his eyes open, and for a moment, our faces were impossibly close together. I thought he might lean forward and kiss me. It was an insane notion, considering he was a complete stranger, but I had the distinct impression he was holding himself back.

Suddenly, the gentle brush of his fingertips on my knee stole my focus. My heart slammed against my ribs, a ragged gasp heaving from my chest. His touch jolted me into a painful awareness of every inch of space between our bodies.

"I saw a scar earlier when you were sitting in the window." The tip of his forefinger found the very bottom of the raised flesh. It was an innocent touch, one that shouldn't have unnerved me. Especially considering I'd practically crawled into his lap moments before. "What's it from?"

I shoved his arm off and, with a firm grip on his wrist, guided his palm to cover the ice at his neck before putting much-needed distance between us. All at once, my past appeared in the room, suffocating me with the burden of my grief and the crushing weight of my father's expectations. Swallowing down my trepidation and picking up the worn romance novel, I brought the pages to my nose and inhaled deeply. The musty smell of aged paper with a hint of vanilla and ink filled my senses. It might be my favorite scent in the world.

"It's what happens when you're too weak to stand the pain, a consequence of numbing it." My words were sharp enough to wound, the ache for blue glowing warmth roiling in my gut. The cravings hibernated, for a time. When things were good, and life didn't feel so heavy, they became so nonexistent I wondered why it was hard to fight them at all.

Then one tiny inconvenience upset my day, some stupid reminder of the past, and they raged back to the surface. More violent and potent than was humanly possible to withstand. A tidal wave of need that buckled my knees.

My thoughts circled and coalesced on that insistent ache until he spoke again, dragging my attention back to my surroundings.

"What?" I asked, not registering his words.

"I asked what you were hiding from in here. You mentioned it earlier." Water droplets seeped through the napkin and dripped between his clenched fingers.

Fuck.

I hadn't meant to let that slip.

"Have you ever been on a farm?"

He stood abruptly, dropping the ice-laden napkin on the side table and whirling to face me. The motion was so sudden that instinctively I backed away until my shoulders were flush against the bookshelves.

His blue eyes were merciless as they appraised me, scouring every line and hollow of my face, lingering around my shoulders, skimming the rapid pulse at my throat. As if he were searching for an answer to some question he'd never even asked.

"I only ask to see if you know why they use brands on the livestock," I said, clearly attempting to smooth over whatever offense I'd made.

"So they don't lose them."

I nodded, searching the shelves for the space where the novel had come from. Once, there'd been lots of empty spaces to fill with pretty trinkets, books being such a valuable commodity. Now, the shelves were so packed that it'd be impossible to shove the novel anywhere new.

"Yeah, because they're considered *property*," I pressed. "So, what did you trade your freedom for?"

"Love." No hesitation. I snorted derisively, cruelly, without thought or concern. He raised an eyebrow, but all I did was roll my eyes and search the next shelf. I didn't know why I was even still conversing with him. If my father saw me acting so friendly with the staff while I'd been pointedly avoiding his guest of honor, he'd skin me alive.

"I get it now." I glanced at him swiftly over my shoulder. "You're an idiot."

"You don't believe in love?"

"Nope." My eyes found a space on a shelf just out of reach. "I don't believe in magic, or fairy tales, or that your friends really call you *Montana* either."

I stretched up, high on my tiptoes, inching the book closer to the gap in the shelves. The hair on the back of my neck stood on end, gooseflesh raising on my arms in an otherworldly awareness of this man who'd forced his way into my focus. I knew he was behind me without looking, so this time I didn't startle when he gently pulled the book from my hands and slid it into place.

"I'm going to make you fall in love with me." The words tumbled hot against my ear. "I'm going to ruin you for everyone but me."

I whirled, and my eyes locked squarely on his very broad chest. For a moment, panic clawed up my throat. But as quickly as he'd loomed over to help me shelve the book, he backed away, the picture of the perfect gentleman.

This man was no gentleman. There was power in his stance and rolling off his shoulders. Tattoos peeked up from his collar and down one arm where his sleeve ended. He shifted, raising one eyebrow in question as a sinful grin tugged at his mouth. A thrill raced up my spine in response. Instead of being wary, I was *enticed.*

His gaze dropped from mine and landed heavily on my lips. The air in my lungs suddenly evaporated. *Don't do it.* Every tiny piece of me screamed to stop this. *This* wasn't how I did things. Getting caught up in a beautiful lie from an even more beautiful stranger.

He gripped the shelf behind me, wood groaning beneath the crush of his fingers. The heat from his skin rolled over me, leaving me raw and too vulnerable. I tasted the humid sweetness of spun sugar and earthiness of chicory coffee on his breath. My lips fell open to drag his breath down into my lungs. This close, I realized his eyes weren't blue. Not really.

They were dark, with streaks of light akin to lightning fracturing from his pupil, and it was that indefinable in-between place that made them seem blue. Something about his eyes tugged at a shadowy corner in my mind.

Just as I opened my mouth to ask him if it was possible we'd met before, Savannah entered, wringing nervous hands in front of her. Snapping my jaw shut with an audible click of my teeth, I twisted beneath his arm to see what had my friend so distressed.

"Audrey!" She peered from me to Montana as she gripped my wrist tight enough to force a grunt of discomfort from between my lips. She craned her neck to peer at him until settling her eyes on the brand at his neck.

"What is it? What happened?" I asked quietly.

"He's *looking for you*!"

"Who is?" I asked dumbly. "My dad?"

"No." Her teeth clenched. Rolling my eyes a bit petulantly, I twisted my wrist from her grip.

"If it's that Lucas Rutherford guy, then—"

"I don't know his name!"

I gripped her shoulders and stared calmly into her eyes. "Slow down and tell me who it was."

"The one I chased out of your room the other morning!"

My first thought was of the absolutely disastrous impression I was making on one of our newest staff members in the house. And the second was *oh fuck*, because it was at that moment that the one-night stand I couldn't get rid of walked into the cramped room.

"Breaking hearts all over the place today," Montana said with a grin. I glared daggers at him in response.

"It's not funny," I muttered spitefully.

"Babe!" It was all I could do to keep myself from physically cringing as the guard crossed the room with arms open wide.

"How the fuck did you get into the house?" I dodged his embrace and tried not to feel remorse when his face crumpled.

"Savannah—" I implored, but she shook her head vigorously, palms outstretched like she was trying to push away the whole dramatic debacle.

"Uh uh." She backed toward the exit. "You got yourself into this mess, you clean it up."

With a disdainful swish of her skirts, she left me alone to face the consequences of my actions. I squeezed my eyes shut, pinching the bridge of my nose in a last-ditch effort to stave off a growing headache. Unclenching my jaw and taking in a long, calming breath, I set my shoulders and turned to see both men staring expectantly at me.

"Huh." My gaze tracked between them a few times, and I noted several similarities. General height and build, something angular in their jaws. Did I have a type or what? Shaking off the strange observation, I focused on the man presenting me with the biggest problem right now. The one I'd slept with, not the one I currently *wanted* to sleep with.

"Listen—" I kept my words gentle and my demeanor kind. "I know that you think what we shared was special, Eric—"

"That's not my name." His dark eyes dimmed. I shut my mouth, brows furrowing as I desperately reached for his name.

"Andrew?" My shoulders hiked up with discomfort. He shook his head again. *Well, shit.*

Montana snorted, trying to contain his laughter. I ground my teeth together to stop from screaming profanities in his direction.

"Everyone keeps telling me it didn't mean anything—"

I opened my mouth to confirm the night we'd spent together didn't *in fact* mean anything, at least not to me, when his next words knocked the breath from my chest.

"But I remember how scared you were, how desperate for me to hold you." An echo of that night flickered in my mind, like a candle at the end of the wick, barely there and gone again. He was right; I *had* been scared. Alone, in the darkness, I couldn't keep the dark memory at bay. "I know we have somethin'—"

"I don't even know your fuckin' name," I said spitefully. "I was letting you down easy, because you seem . . . clingy, if I'm honest—" Shoving his arms away, I put some distance between us, his expression crestfallen. "Clearly, that's not working here."

Pressing my lips together, I tried and failed to ignore how Montana's eyes bore into me. *Too interested.* "My father is going to make you *beg* for death if you don't get out of here. Right now."

He just stared dumbly, and helpless rage welled within me.

"Don't you understand? You can't *be* here, saying stupid shit in front of Lucas Rutherford—"

"Who can't say stupid shit in front of me?" a smooth voice said behind my left shoulder. My breath hitched, my heart pounding in my throat. *No. No, no, no. Fuck. Fuck, fuck, fuck.*

My gaze locked on the man I'd spent a reckless night with, the hard edges of heartbreak written into his dark eyes. I saw every vicious thought before it even passed through his mind. *And I still can't remember his goddamn name.* Time stood still, lurching one way and the next as I struggled to compose my horrified expression.

Why did Mr. Lucas Rutherford pick this moment to stumble into what was already an impossibly awkward situation?

"Montana, I wanted to talk to you about—" As he crossed into my periphery, panic lanced down my spine, snapping it straight. Warm hazel eyes slid over to me and caught on my face, widening imperceptibly in surprise.

"Miss Lee!" His shocked exclamation was oddly thrilling. There was a subtle catch in his breath as he tried, and failed, not to allow his gaze to roam over me freely. Everything about Lucas Rutherford was exactly what I'd expected. Average height, average build, perfectly pressed clothes, and hair artfully swept over his forehead. Nothing out of place. Nothing messy or harried in his mannerisms.

After all, he was one of the richest, most privileged men in the world . . . It wasn't like anyone kept him waiting or complained if he wasn't on schedule.

"Mr. Rutherford." I dipped my chin in acknowledgment. He opened his mouth but shut it again, swallowing heavily as he wavered toward me on his feet. Seeing him so speechless at the sudden introduction was oddly endearing. I bit my bottom lip to keep a smile from curling on my mouth.

"You wanted to ask me something," Montana asked gruffly, his face an unreadable mask. Rutherford blinked a few times as the mountainous man walked closer, angling himself between us.

"R-right, yes. I had an idea for an exhibition match and—"

Happy to let Montana distract him, I took the opportunity to slink a few steps away. My one-night stand, however, saw my desire to escape the room. He gripped my wrist and pressed in tight to my side.

"Maybe your fancy guest would like to learn *exactly* what kind of cold-hearted slut you are," he whispered hatefully in my ear. I tugged at his punishing grip, unable to shake his hold without being noticed. "I bet *Daddy* would pay an exorbitant amount for my silence."

Cold fury made me tremble with involuntary shudders as I wrestled with my self-control. *Don't kill him. Get a grip!* What was meant to be a fun but ultimately meaningless sexual encounter soured into blackmail and extortion. If I hadn't already been aware of how close I was to rock bottom, this would be a glaring reminder.

"Jersey's a big name in our district, and I think it could open up more opportunities to—" Rutherford prattled on, talking with his hands at Montana, who glared at my wrist and the man's hold on it.

"Yes," Montana said swiftly, fists clenching at his sides.

"Really?" Rutherford asked, skeptical. "I thought you'd be a harder sell, considering you've never participated in an exhibition match."

Montana's jaw worked with frustration, a muscle jumping as he clenched his teeth together. He dragged his eyes away from my wrist to face Rutherford once more. *Think, damnit, think.* There had to be a way to extricate myself without embarrassing my father with my bad decisions.

"Maybe ruining your reputation will make me a little more *memorable* to you."

I wanted to tell him to go fuck himself. Or make him quake beneath the threats poised on the tip of my tongue. Instead, I was trapped, a false smile stitched onto my mouth and bloodlust barely caged inside my ribs.

"Honestly, I can't agree to anything without Mr. Lee's consent now that he's my sponsor," Montana said, clapping a friendly hand on Rutherford's shoulder. "But, if you'll ask him to meet us in his study before lunch, I'm sure we could pin down the details."

He guided Mr. Rutherford toward the door when, surprisingly, Rutherford turned back to regard me. "I hope I'll see you at lunch, Miss Lee."

I smiled against my better judgment, and my fling crushed my wrist in his grip.

Then they were gone. Warm relief nearly buckled my knees, and before my captor could issue any more threats, I twisted my wrist and drove my palm hard against his solar plexus. He crumpled against the bookshelves, coughing and sputtering unattractively.

"Listen, whoever the hell you are." I narrowed my eyes into a hateful glare. He struggled onto his feet, and I rubbed my wrist absentmindedly. "The next time you threaten me—"

But I didn't get the chance to finish my statement.

Everything happened so fast, *too* fast for my eyes to track fully. One moment, my unsatisfying sexual partner scowled at me, and the next, he struggled to breathe around an iron fist closed around his windpipe. His head cracked against the shelves, and several books toppled to the floor. I flinched at the thought of them damaged, since it wasn't guaranteed that I could replace them.

"The next time you fucking touch her," Montana growled, voice deadly, "I'll kill you."

The nameless man's face flushed, his mouth opening and closing without sound, but Montana didn't release him. Not yet. My heartbeat pounded in my chest, my stomach swooping in a rush when I realized that he was *defending* me.

"I didn't need your help." I wasn't some debutante in distress waiting for a brute of a man to rescue me.

"I know." He dropped the man, and I stepped up to rest at Montana's side. We watched as the man sprawled on the floor choked and raked in ragged breath, face slowly returning to its normal hue.

"Thanks anyway." I didn't look at him. I couldn't, for some reason. "But I'm still completely fucked."

Calloused fingers brushed along my wrist, the tender touch almost shy and questioning. My gaze dropped to our hands, watching as the tip of his finger traced along the red skin of my wrist like the whisper of wind on my cheeks. I didn't know why, but instead of pulling away, I leaned into that touch. Until he turned my wrist over in his large, calloused palm.

Those hands could inflict pain, I realized. They were instruments of work and violence, but the way he held me reminded me of the people who passed by my windows every Sunday on their way to the cathedral next door. Their reverent expressions were half awe and half hope, like they were waiting to witness a miracle.

He touched me like that. Like I was a miracle.

"Why?"

I pulled my wrist from his grasp. "Why am I fucked? Because *he* made it very clear he was going to ruin my reputation with Rutherford unless my dad pays him off." I half-heartedly kicked him in the leg. "My dad made it clear I was supposed to impress Rutherford while he's here."

"Ah." Understanding and amusement warred for control in his bright, expressive eyes. "You're kind of a mess, aren't you?"

I snorted unattractively. "Kind of?"

"I could help you." The timbre of his voice deepened, sending a shiver down my spine.

"Why would you do that? You barely know me." My voice was too breathless for him not to notice.

"I never said I'd do it for free."

My stomach bottomed out, brows pinching together in disapproval. *Of course.* What did I expect? Decency from one of my father's hired thugs?

"Forget it." I turned my back to him. "I'm not going to trade one blackmailer for another."

"One hour a day of your time, that's all I ask," he said in a rush.

"What?" My curiosity piqued. When I glanced over at him, towering in the corner, I realized there was something in his expression that made him seem *small.*

"I told you, I'm going to make you fall in love with me."

Rolling my eyes, I crossed my arms defensively.

"I can't do that if I never see you."

My gaze flicked to the still-nameless man sitting up on the floor. I had no idea how I would get him out of the manor without help. I couldn't ask Savannah to put her neck on the line any more than I already had. And my father's words about how much this shipping contract meant to our family business, how it could be a way out of this place for me, made me feel a little reckless.

"No expectations. I won't pressure you. I just want the pleasure of your company. Six hours a week." With each amendment, he stepped toward me until I felt the heat of his skin like a living thing struggling towards me, clawing at my skin, enveloping me until I was dizzy with the feel of him.

"I have a lot of great qualities, but good decision-making is *apparently* not one of them." I waved lackadaisically at the man on the floor. "Why in the hell would you want to spend time with someone like me?"

He shrugged, a grin playing on his mouth. "Maybe I don't make good decisions either."

"Clearly." I laughed, sucking my bottom lip between my teeth. "I'll do two hours a week."

"Five," he said, not budging an inch.

"Three is my final offer."

"Five."

Pausing to glance between my anonymous lover and the tall, mysterious stranger before me, I weighed my options.

"I'll do four, if you make it hurt when you kick his ass out of town. Final offer, or I'll deal with the consequences of my actions and I won't look back."

He crossed his strong arms over his chest, forearms bared and flexing in the afternoon light. He stared at me, testing my resolve, but I wouldn't waver.

"Fine," he said, flippant. "Hope you have fun explaining all this to Mr. Lee."

The headache I'd been trying to stave off pounded through my temples until my eyes felt like they would cross. Truthfully, headaches were commonplace for me these days, but sometimes, they got bad enough to turn my stomach. I didn't relish the thought of explaining all of this and wrestling the urge to spill my breakfast. With a weary, defeated sigh, I waved him over and offered him my hand. Then, like the sun breaking out from behind dark clouds, a smile illuminated his face.

"Fine, it's a deal." He gripped my hand, shook it once, then pressed the back of it to his lips. I didn't think anyone had ever kissed my hand before. The soft swell of his lips and his rough palms made me dizzy.

"I'll see you tomorrow then." His fingers lingered as if reluctant to let go.

"How will I know where to go?"

"Meet me in the courtyard." His voice dipped into that deep timbre that sent an involuntary shiver down my spine. "I'll come for you there."

I'll come for you.

Fear unfurled within me, an echo of the nightmare I couldn't quite shake resounding through my mind. I snatched my hand away, as if his touch burned me.

"What did you say?" I asked, throat suddenly ashen.

"I asked you to meet me in the courtyard." His brows furrowed in concern. I nodded stiffly, shuffling closer to the door.

"Right, well . . . tomorrow then." Clumsily, I fled, padding down the corridor as fast as my bare feet could take me. When I returned to my bedroom, I slammed the door and pressed my back to the solid oak surface in an attempt to slow my racing heart.

It was official. I was losing my goddamn mind.

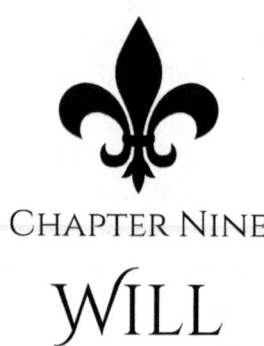

CHAPTER NINE

WILL

THE SOUND OF CRACKING bones echoed in my ears. It reminded me of branches snapping while tending to a campfire. Only thicker, and meatier, the sound muffled by layers of muscle and sinew. I'd heard enough of it after leaving Jesse to track down leads on this Rutherford guy.

So why couldn't I get the sound out of my head?

I didn't bother looking where I was going as I loped along the busy sidewalk. Everyone parted in front of me as if I were as radioactive as the crater sites. It'd been nice to forget the constant fear that haunted me with Jesse. If only for a little while.

But it returned, strong enough to choke the humanity right out of me.

The sun dipped low in the sky, the light hazy and dim as night fell in earnest. I might have thought it was beautiful, if I could see anything other than the tear-filled eyes of a man's wife as I dropped him in a crumpled heap of blood and limbs. He'd been a source of information, an *unwilling* one.

By the time I made it back to Lee Manor, my mind spiraled and my hands wouldn't still, fingers twitching with an overabundance of guilt and energy. I pulled out a cigarette to keep them busy. I didn't even want one . . . Well, that was a lie. There was hardly a time I *didn't* want bracing, addictive smoke filling my lungs to bursting.

It took everything to force away the day's work. Without thought, my feet carried me inside and to the kitchen, my eyes scanning the nearly empty room. Etty sat at the counter, sipping on a glass filled with amber liquid. Otherwise, the room was as hollow as I felt.

Sighing and running a hand wearily down my face before realizing it was speckled in blood, I forced myself to keep walking. Not long until I'd be reporting to Mr. Lee, then *finally* I could drink myself into oblivion in the relative peace of my shitty apartment, where the only thing watching me fall apart was peeling wallpaper.

"Sure, she's hot, but she's *crazy*. They call her *insane Audrey*. If Luke thinks he can handle that, more power to him, but you wouldn't catch me within spitting distance of that one." I was too tired to deal with this shit right now. After my day, I'd learned all about Lucas Rutherford and his friends that journeyed from Manhattan Island. Hearing them casually insulting Bonnie rankled my nerves, but it didn't seem out of character for them.

"Ha! The crazy ones are the best in bed, my friend. I've got my eyes set on her sweet little friend," another said. Something inside me snapped, and before I could blink, I was slinking around the corner, eyes locking on an attractive, ebony-skinned man with a bright smile that infuriated me. "She seems a little naive. You know how I like the innocent ones—"

His words were cut off by laughter, the men shaking their heads and clapping him on the shoulder. As if casually marking his territory on an independent, free-thinking woman was an *admirable* trait and not at all predatory. My fingers twitched toward my pistol, palm sliding over the butt in a motion that was as natural as breathing.

They gathered around a credenza set into an alcove with glasses clenched in their hands. The glaze of drink made their eyes glassy and their cheeks red. The thought of any of them touching Savannah made something dark and violent rear its head within my chest. A staff member in a black dress that contrasted starkly against her white skin announced dinner through the doors, head bowed.

They filed in without even looking back. I flicked the safety on and off of my pistol. *Don't do it.* I tried to talk myself out of the reckless thought but found myself marching toward the formal dining room regardless.

Never in the three-plus years I'd been employed by Lee had I disrupted or challenged this false gentile bullshit he seemed so fond of. All the manners and restrictions were a façade: desperate people at the end of the world trying in vain to recapture some semblance of society. Where things made sense and there were rules, punishments, rewards.

They didn't realize they were fighting against the inevitable.

The world ended. Society collapsed. And none of us would find redemption for the lengths we went to in order to survive. Me, least of all.

My spurs clanged against the parquet floor, and the door to the dining room banged open loudly enough to stop the conversation. Several pairs of eyes fell on me, and though a cocky grin curled on my mouth, my stomach dropped to my ankles. Fear presented in several faces, aversion or indifference in others. Lee seemed confused as I took in the formally appointed room with the polished oak table and took an empty seat. The chair creaked as I dropped heavily across from Savannah.

Ignoring the contrast of my bloodstained, dirty clothes and the delicate lace edges of the table runner or the clear, pristine angles of the cut crystal glasses, I leaned back in my chair and swept my eyes across the guests. Mr. Lee at the head of the table, naturally. Audrey sat stiffly at his right, with Lucas Rutherford sweating profusely across from her. Several of Rutherford's *associates*, thugs, mostly, befriended during his misspent youth, sat at the mid-section of the table.

Then, there she was at the very end, like an afterthought. Glaring at me with an ugly scowl.

Her anger was a welcome relief from the fear, familiar and comfortable, a reminder that I was *alive*. Currently, making an ass out of myself.

"Am I late?" I grinned wider as Savannah scoffed in my direction. The man from earlier, who'd spoken about Savannah, sat close enough to her that my hackles rose and I shifted in my chair. I shouldn't have worn my gun belt here.

It only tempted me to scare him off.

Of course, I wouldn't. It wasn't my place, even if I felt protective over Savannah in a way I hadn't about anyone other than Bonnie. She would only resent me, of that I was sure. But I also couldn't trust myself to know where the *line* was. I was too far gone to understand when enough was actually enough.

"Mr. Ellis is one of my high-ranking employees," Mr. Lee said, dark eyes promising retribution for my interruption. I sat a little straighter, shoulders back in an approximation of pride. Though, nothing I'd done in Zachary Lee's employ made me anything close to *proud.*

The man who'd referenced Savannah earlier leaned close to her and said something low that I couldn't hear. I tracked the movement of his lips and measured the exact space between his mouth and her flesh.

"So why exactly did *you* decide to travel all the way from Manhattan Island?" I asked through gritted teeth, snapping impatiently at one of the ladies in the corner of the room to serve me. I wasn't going *anywhere*. Not until I knew that the flush on Savannah's cheeks was from the familiarity with which he'd spoken to her and not some misplaced notion of *attraction.*

No. She deserved more than the barest pieces of my ragged soul. She sure as shit deserved better than this asshole, with his fancy suit and pretty lies. Savannah's expression hardened as I addressed the man, almost in warning. *Adorable.*

While he prattled on about wanting to see *more of the world* and started listing the south's many desirable travel traits, her eyes never wavered from mine. I could drown in the molten honey depths of them, too sweet for a fuck-up like me. I raised a mocking eyebrow at his lackluster answer.

"It sure wasn't because of that charm you're always bragging about," she muttered.

All of a sudden, I couldn't remember the darkness that had clouded my mind before I barged in. My entire world focused on her stiff posture and the strength with which she gripped her fingers together in her lap.

"Have you fallen for the Ellis charm, Savvy?" My eyes crinkled at the corners with my smile.

"In your dreams, William," she retorted swiftly, barely a moment's hesitation.

"Better an Ellis than a Manhattanite, from what I hear." I lifted a glass of water to take a few swallows before setting it down. It wasn't until I saw Savvy's horrified expression that I realized it belonged to the place setting to my right. Oh well. The table went silent at my comment, several eyes falling on me once more, much to my chagrin.

"What do you mean, about Manhattanites?" Rutherford asked, the shadow of offense darkening his expression.

"Ah, you know," I said with a congenial smile that *no one* believed. "That old rumor about Manhattanites only dating based on neighborhood."

His eyes slid from mine, shoulders relaxing, but his friend looked at me more shrewdly than before. Clearly, he didn't buy my line of bullshit and knew I wasn't happy about the attention he was paying Savannah. Which was *exactly* why he leaned over to her, careful to keep eye contact with me, and said something that made her look at me with an amused glimmer in her eyes. One I hadn't seen in *years.*

My teeth creaked as they ground together.

"Don't you have a bridge to keep watch over?" Savannah asked, eyes narrowed and tone dismissive. *Bones cracking. Families pleading. The sniveling suck of tears as men came to terms with their mortality.*

"Don't you have a companion to keep company? Or is she sick of your hovering?" The words were hot as they fell from my tongue. As soon as I thought *perhaps* I'd gone too far, Savannah responded with more sarcasm and vitriol than I'd thought possible.

"I'm sorry, I think you have us confused." She cocked her head to the side and quirked an eyebrow. "See, I'm *delightful*; it's *you* people find obnoxious. I was actually *invited* to this dinner."

I leaned forward on my elbows until I loomed closer to Savannah's fire, to her *warmth*, the comfort her anger and her compassion always instilled in me, despite her best efforts.

"You don't know what you'd do without me." A thrill raced down my spine when she scowled again. "Ruining your careful plans, getting under your skin." If nothing else, I wanted these people to know *damn* well to keep their thoughts *off* of Savvy. Even if the flirtatiousness between us was contrived. Though, I had to admit, it felt *really* good to let a part of me free.

"Believe it or not, I'd much rather spend my time doing things I enjoy, instead of damage control from whatever trouble you've gotten yourself into on any given day." She rolled her eyes. My answering grin was feral, and I could taste the heat from her furious blush. It made me imagine her in ways I shouldn't: her neat hair falling down around her face, skirts crumpled, those eyes of hers glazed in passion, pupils blown wide and mindless with desire.

Fuck. Now I was hard at the goddamned dinner table. My cock pressed painfully against the front seam of my jeans, and I shifted until the pressure eased. Not only was it embarrassing that I had as little control of myself as a lusty teenage boy, it infuriated me that it was *Savannah* who had this effect on me.

She'd had a front row seat to more of my failures than I was comfortable with. Although she didn't care enough about me to judge, her perfectionism grated against every fucked-up, broken part of me. It scraped at vulnerable places I didn't even know existed. I ached to destroy her sanctimonious view of the world, which was why I tried to stay as far away from her as possible.

It was *never* far enough.

"All that anger is foreplay, Savvy," I said, my voice a deep purr of sensuality. I never could leave well enough alone. "One day we'll tell our kids about how much *damage control* you did before you finally fell for my charm."

Even though it was meant to be playful, to rankle her steadfastness, there was a thread of promise in my voice. One day, I would have her. When the last bits of my conscience chipped away and I no longer cared enough to protect her from myself. Perhaps when I finally lost the last shred of my humanity. But it wouldn't be today.

Today, I felt alive.

Her face slackened in horror. Then I remembered that we were in a room full of people. Everything was too quiet, no clinking cutlery or soft murmur of conversation. *Well, shit.*

Rutherford's friend glared between us, jaw set in challenge. Like he could compete with me for anything. He was a sniveling, boastful coward who didn't have a sincere bone in his body or the balls to back up his arrogance. Besides, Savannah had forgotten him completely. Instead, she gaped at me, snapping her mouth shut in righteous fury.

"I pity the woman who has your *litter* of children. No doubt they'll all be beastly little hellions like *you!*"

"One can only hope, *mi sol.*" A rapacious grin curled on my mouth. I shouldn't have liked the stunned expression in her honeyed eyes. It made me want to shock her in ways that elicited that little gasping noise in the back of her throat again.

"What is it exactly that Mr. Ellis does for you, Mr. Lee?" Rutherford asked, eyes sliding from Audrey's bored expression to me. Reluctantly, I turned from my study of Savannah's expressive face to lean back into the antique chair with a perilous-sounding groan from the wood.

My smile turned murderous then.

Lee cleared his throat in warning, though the thought of detailing my duties in front of Rutherford and his asshole friend who still glared at me was almost too good to pass up. Instead, I sniffed loudly, fishing in my front shirt pocket for my cigarette case.

"I'm a man of many talents; whatever Mr. Lee needs done, I do it." Crossing one of my ankles over my knee, I struck a match on the bottom of my boot and, with a few short inhalations, felt the sweet relief of nicotine flood my lungs.

"So, a valet then? Or a personal assistant? My father has several similar paid staff positions," Rutherford asked shrewdly.

"Yeah," I agreed with a cynical laugh. "Something like that, *gringo.*"

"You must have worked here for a long time then." He lifted his spoon to his mouth. "Valets are usually long-term positions. I've never seen one so young. It's a little strange, isn't it? Don't you want to . . . I don't know, *sow your wild oats?*"

"He asked about the riverboats, security in and out of the city, storage facilities near the gulf! I swear! That's all. P-please, please don't kill me." The crunch of bone preceded a nearly inhuman wail of pain.

"I've never been to Manhattan Island, but here in the south, even protected behind Mr. Lee's security measures, we've all seen our fair share of adventure." I tried to ignore how Audrey white-knuckled her fork like she wanted to stab someone.

"Very well spoken," Lee interrupted, trying to earn Rutherford's attention back. "We've had our fair share of difficulty with some of the local criminal elements. Which is precisely why New Orleans is perfectly positioned for our shipping endeavors. Access to the river and the gulf is key to directing trade—"

"What kind of adventures have *you* had, Miss Audrey?" Rutherford asked, having noticed her clear discomfort. I glanced at Savannah, and she leveled me with a worried stare that had me putting my cigarette out in a half-full wine glass with a hiss and curl of smoke.

The room went deathly still. Even the staff members serving at the table refused to move or speak or, hell, even breathe. Audrey laughed, setting down her fork too forcefully before crossing her arms over her chest and narrowing her eyes at Rutherford. If she hadn't lost her memories, I would have warned Rutherford to duck from her assessing gaze. Now, as Audrey, I could never predict what she would do or say.

Lee gripped her forearm tightly, shaking his head slowly, another warning. It seemed Lee couldn't quite predict her reactions either. She brushed him off roughly and cleared her throat.

"You're asking because you already know, don't you?" She raised an eyebrow at Rutherford. To his credit, he didn't so much as breathe too deeply, his features an unreadable mask.

"Audrey—"

"It's fine, Daddy. He'll find out soon enough if he hasn't already." She gave Lee a patronizing pat on the wrist. He deflated in the face of her determination, and something warm twisted in my chest at the sight. Only Bonnie could order Zachary Lee like she was born to do it. "Go ahead, Mr. Rutherford, ask your questions."

"As I was exploring the city and meeting some of your neighbors—"

Audrey chuckled darkly, blue eyes flashing dangerously across the table at the esteemed guest. Rutherford hesitated, putting his cutlery down and leveling Audrey with an appraising stare. I hated to admit they were well matched, but, looking at them now, I couldn't deny it. At least Rutherford and *Audrey* were. If he met Bonnie, she would've already broken his nose.

"I'm not schlepping around town stirring up gossip, but you have to admit it's a little strange." Rutherford's shoulders hiked up to his ears as Audrey raised an eyebrow derisively in his direction. "You just forgot your whole life? Everything?"

Audrey let out a weary sigh, leaning back in her chair before sweeping her eyes around the room. They settled on me for a second, and I didn't know what she saw in my expression. If she noticed the flicker of reluctant hope that Jesse'd reignited some of Bonnie's fire within her. That my best friend would wake up and help me figure out how to salvage the last slivers of my soul.

Then the second ended, and she smiled mischievously.

"Look at all of you!" She bit her bottom lip in amusement. "You all look so *serious.*"

Rutherford's shoulders dropped incrementally, the tightness at the corners of his eyes relaxing slightly. "What *do* you remember?"

"Lots of things." She spoke casually, but she hadn't eaten anything on her plate. "I just *know* stuff. Like an instinct. My favorite color is blue. I love strawberries and *hate* peas. Clowns freak me out and rain makes me happy."

Laughter trilled in the dry morning air as Bonnie and Jesse emerged from the bathroom with wide smiles and wet hair. I grinned at her. She scrunched her nose but didn't hide the mirth in her blue eyes. Eyes as familiar as my own, maybe even more so. As they walked past, I waggled my brows mockingly.

"Shut up," she said, smile widening. "The shower reminds me of rain."

Something twisted painfully in my chest as I realized that there were shadows of Bonnie lingering, reminding me of a girl I loved and hated in equal measure. Someone I'd given up on between the head injury, the glowroot addiction, and the worst night of my life.

"But events, people, experiences, they're gone. It's like I have the impression of them, the wisdom that comes from making bad choices when you're young. I'm not naive to the world, but I'm also not jaded into submission." She twirled her fork on her plate. Rutherford cleared his throat, straightening somewhat in his chair. She leveled him with a look I knew too well. The one that lured in marks, made them helpless to her charm.

Lucas Rutherford was a lost cause now.

The discomfort at the table was stifling, so when Lee clapped his hands, everyone was relieved to refocus. He called for dessert, and the hum of conversation started again. The prick next to Savvy recaptured her attention before I could, which was probably for the best. I hated it anyway.

When the king cake was brought out on a cypress cake stand, the crowd gasped in delight. My gaze skimmed the confection, recognizing the pristine lines of colored sugar and the bright white icing. It wasn't the same as the one she'd gone to the bakery for. This one was neater, more precise, perfectly risen. I'd watched Savannah make so many sweets over the years, I saw her perfectionism on perfect display now. The loneliness of Bonnie's incomplete memory faded into something warm and welcoming when I thought about Savvy in her stained linen apron with flour in her dark hair.

"You've really outdone yourself this time, Savvy." My voice echoed above the din of appreciation. She turned to me, eyes wide and horrified at my compliment.

Suddenly, the warmth I'd languored in slipped away, and I was left cold. Feeling like more of a fuck-up than ever when Lee said, "I thought I told you to buy the cake from the bakery on the other side of the square."

His voice split the air in the room. Savannah's shoulders turned in on themselves as she dipped her eyes to the table in front of her. Rage, hot and insistent, roiled in my gut at the sight.

"I-I did get a cake from the bakery, but—"

"It's just a cake—" I tried to come to her defense. Apparently whatever goodwill I'd scrabbled together had dissipated, because Lee stood abruptly, glaring at us.

"In my office, the both of you," he commanded. "Now."

Fuck me. Settling my hat on my head and taking care with how I rose from my seat, I followed Savvy out of the room and into the corridor. I didn't want that prick to watch her skirts swish as she stomped from the room. As soon as we were alone, however, she whirled on me, her honey eyes flashing like a viper's in the dim light.

"You just couldn't help yourself, could you?" She was careful to keep her volume low even as she hurled more accusation at me than I thought possible. "The *one* time you could have kept your stupid comments to yourself and you just *had* to say something!"

"It was a cake!" I argued, but she wasn't listening.

"It wasn't *just* a cake, and you aren't that stupid, William." She turned and strode confidently away from me. It was like she *knew* I wouldn't be able to let her have the last word, that I'd be reduced to chasing after her like a dog.

Which was, of course, *exactly* what I did. In long loping strides, I caught up to her easily, and before I could open my mouth to speak, she glared at me. "Why were you even there? And the things you said—"

"I was there to eat, *princesa.*" I forced the mocking words through clenched teeth. "And what's wrong with the things I said? I'm sure you didn't mind whatever that asshole whispered in your ear."

"What does that have to do with—" She stopped abruptly. Her eyes went wide and her mouth parted in a way that had me clenching my hands as my sides to keep from reaching out to her. *Mierda, I want to kiss her.* "You're jealous!"

The exclamation washed over her, a revelation, one that terrified me because it was true. I was so goddamn jealous. The violent thoughts I had as I counted each millimeter between that man's mouth and her ear would have terrified her. If Savvy knew that, though, if she suspected the ways I wanted her, it would change things between us. She would see me for who I was. There was nothing that scared me more than that.

Slipping into a comfortable, mocking grin, I leaned close enough to her that I felt the flush on her skin heating the air between us. "Is that what you want, Savvy? You want me to be jealous?"

She made a startled, squeaking noise, high-pitched and adorable, in the base of her throat before her back pressed firmly against the door.

"Let me guess." I breathed a laugh as I reached down near her hip. "You dream about *taming* the beast."

"I dream about stabbing you."

But we both knew it was a breathless, empty threat. Her pupils were blown wide, making her eyes dark with desire. I wanted to drown in her expression, wanted to push her further, wanted to see her completely unraveled.

Goddamnit.

"Don't threaten me with a good time." I leaned close enough that her eyes fluttered shut. It would be so easy to kiss her, to lean down and take a taste of her. Just a taste, one that would linger for years, if my experience was any indication. Instead, with a grin and a swift turn of my wrist, the door to the study opened behind her.

She stumbled in clumsily, scowling and calling me names. Giving her a wide berth, I slipped into the study before crossing to Lee's decanter and pouring myself a glass of his pretentious fake scotch. It wasn't anything more than rot-gut whiskey in a fancy bottle, but he paid a premium for it anyway.

Leaning against Lee's bookcase, I peered at her from beneath the brim of my hat. She was tall and athletic for a woman. Though compared to my height and bulk, she was still small and delicate. The high arches of her brows led down her aristocratic nose and guided my eyes directly to her full, pillowy, pink lips once more. Lips I wanted to part, to taste, to see swollen from the crush of my mouth on hers. Everything about her was inviting, like a personal lure made *just* for me. My eyes skimmed the ebony corkscrew curls near her ears and temples that'd escaped from her tight hairstyle.

Pieces of chaos escaping the strict strangle of control she exerted over every piece of herself. She didn't acknowledge my study of her, but she felt it. I could tell by the nervous way she averted her eyes and shifted her weight back and forth on her feet. I couldn't stop, I *wouldn't*. Fuck, even the color of her skin called to me like a siren song. A golden tawny shade that reminded me of childhood. Of long days in the prairie, baking beneath an autumn sun, where the land and the sky lived in a dark golden haze. The days before I became a monster, when I'd just been a broken boy finding beauty in quiet moments between living nightmares.

Lee barged in before I could do anything stupid, and I'd been closer than I wanted to think about to doing exactly that.

"You," he said, pointing directly at me, "better have a real good explanation of why you made a spectacle of yourself tonight."

I tipped the glass to him before draining it and setting it on a nearby shelf. He grunted as his attention shifted to Savannah standing stiffly in front of him, and he unbuttoned his dinner jacket before sitting behind his massive oak desk.

"Yes, well," he said, clearing his throat. "I'm sure you had your reasons, Ellis. I will need a de-briefing once I'm finished with Miss Beauregard."

Crossing my arms over my chest, I stayed silent and made no indication that I'd even heard him. He knew he had me by the balls. I was *his* monster, and there was nothing to be done about that. He'd stripped me of my humanity and used it as a shackle to bind me into his service.

"You, however, had strict instructions, Savannah." He leveled cruel eyes on her submissive form. All the fire and warmth that Savvy embodied turned dim and cold. I hated it. So I clenched my teeth together to keep from saying something really fucking stupid. "Yet you disobeyed."

She opened her mouth in a rush to defend herself, and I stared hard at the side of her face. Slowly I shook my head back and forth, hoping she'd see the slight motion from the corner of her eye. Lee hadn't asked a question. Speaking out of turn would only piss him off more. Her jaw snapped shut again, and she swallowed heavily, nodding as her gaze dropped to the floor.

"I'll let this grievance go," he said, and a relieved breath rattled from my lungs. "For now."

Running a weary hand down my face, I shifted on my feet, and Lee seemed to remember I was in the room. "Before I dismiss you, there's another matter I wish to discuss."

I crossed back to the decanter of "scotch" and poured myself another generous glass. I didn't ask for permission, but I didn't need it. Lee depended on me to do all the unspeakable things he couldn't afford to be associated with. His level of trust in me after three years of loyal service, doing the kinds of things I had, earned me a lot more freedom than I usually bothered exercising.

"Mr. Rutherford and his associates are here to secure a shipping deal between his father, the Governor of Manhattan Island, and my company. But I asked Lucas and his companions here for another reason as well." Lee snapped his fingers at me. I poured another glass and crossed to the desk, handing it to him swiftly. "It's my intention to arrange a marriage between Audrey and Lucas Rutherford. She's aware of this, of course, and it's her responsibility to charm him."

I bit back a frustrated sigh. Feeling pressure in my temples.

"You're aware of her difficulties with social interactions," he said to Savannah, who was looking at Mr. Lee with renewed interest at the news. "So I'm charging you with making sure that this match happens."

Savannah gaped, nearly choking on the air in shock. All I could do was drink, so I drained my glass and tried not to slam it down in fury. Jesse was *here* in this house, close enough to jog her memory. To get Bonnie back. To bring my best friend back to me.

"If Lucas Rutherford or his companions need anything, you make it happen. If they want drugs, you find them. Alcohol, ship it in. They want to fuck the women on staff, arrange it. I don't care what it takes to make them happy; it's your responsibility to ensure they stay satisfied. Long enough, at least, for Audrey and Lucas to form a connection." Lee stood, glaring cruelly at Savannah.

"Even if they want *you*," he said casually. "Am I clear?"

A click sounded loudly throughout the room.

It wasn't until Lee and Savannah's eyes turned to me that I realized I'd clicked off the safety on my pistol and was resting my palm on the handle as if to

LAUREN SEVIER & ABBIE LYNN SMITH

draw it. Savannah's eyes went wide, shaking her head slightly to admonish me. Lee smiled, clearly thinking I was reinforcing his threat. Pompous ass. The thought that it was so easy for him to expect blind loyalty churned my stomach violently.

The next few moments blurred together, possibly an effect of the fake scotch I'd guzzled settling into my bloodstream. Lee called for guards to escort Savannah away, and it took everything in my power to pull my hand away from the gun, fingers shaking. When she was gone, I sat in front of Lee's desk, clumsy hands rifling for a cigarette to settle my nerves.

Had it only been this morning when I'd branded Jesse? I felt like I'd lived a thousand years since. Weariness sank deep into my muscles and weighed my shoulders down, anchoring me in this room. Staring across from the devil.

"You want to tell me what that show was earlier?" Lee asked. I inhaled a ragged, smoke-filled breath.

"I learned a lot about Rutherford and his *friends* today," I said on an exhale that filled the space with curling puffs of smoke. "I wanted to get the measure of them myself."

I watched as Zachary's fury dimmed, savoring the taste of nicotine on the tip of my tongue. To his credit, he waited until I finished my smoke, expectation clear in his black eyes. The grin that crossed my face was absolutely feral. As much as I hated the work I did for Zachary, I knew without a doubt I was *good* at it. A fact that made me too much like my father for me to process without several drinks in hand.

"Rutherford's father is known for his public stance against the slave trade." I pulled a pocket knife from my jeans and dug some of the dirt from beneath my nails as I gave my report. "He's closed Manhattan Island off, claiming it as a sanctuary state, which has made him *very* rich over the last few years." Zachary didn't seem amused by my report thus far, considering these were facts he was already aware of.

"However, *Lucas* doesn't seem to have the same noble intentions," I said, dangling the information I'd gleaned before him. He crossed his arms and leaned forward on his elbows, attention rapt.

"I'm listening."

"Manhattan has been struggling in several industries over the last few years. Textiles mainly, as the rest of New York has been buying slave labor for their factories and seen enormous growth. Lucas is primed to take over for his father in the next few years but needs a solid platform to earn public support. After

LEATHER & LACE

applying pressure to a few of his *associates* and their family members, I found out he's making inquiries about smuggling slaves into Manhattan. A way to win back some of the textile business from the factories in New York with free labor." I stubbed my cigarette out in the dregs of the liquor lingering at the bottom of my glass.

"There are several businessmen he could approach in the slave trade who are better connected to the larger auction sites and markets. How does this serve me?" Lee asked.

"Simple: you're respectable. Involved in enough *above reproach* shipping needs that he can get slaves in without undermining his father's public stance or challenging Manhattan's sanctuary status, *and . . .*" I held up a finger to emphasize my point.

"You hold New Orleans. The Mississippi is the easiest way to smuggle slaves in," I finished, leaning back to watch Lee's mind whirring, the same way Bonnie's did when she was plotting a con.

A familiar tug of loneliness stretched wide within me, banished only by the thin hope that Jesse could help her remember soon. Lee smiled wide as he sipped on the amber liquid in his own glass and gazed at me, exhaling for a long moment.

"I wish I had ten of you, Ellis." His lips pulled too far back from his teeth. A predatory glint illuminated the dark pits of his eyes. Another long moment passed between us.

"Sometimes I wish I knew her before you delivered her here." His words shocked me from my dark thoughts.

"No," I said confidently. "You don't."

He raised one dark eyebrow in question. I rose, standing taller than I had in what seemed like forever.

"If she knew half of your *business enterprises*, she'd kill you without thinking twice." I strode out of his study. I didn't bother looking for his reaction. Didn't bother to wait for dismissal. If he wanted to talk about Bonnie, he could have kept my father under his thumb. I wouldn't sit here and comfort a man who had erased everything his daughter had been for his own comfort. There wasn't enough money in the world for me to do that.

My feet brought me into the stables even though my mind raced with all the events of the day. The groom made some sarcastic comment about my horse as I walked by, but I didn't acknowledge him. Instead, I opened the stall door and folded inside, reaching out to his snout and scratching him under the chin

111

the way he liked. He tossed his head before shuffling forward and knocking my hat off.

Chuffing near my ear, he nosed my shoulder, trying to get at the front pocket where I kept sugar cubes for him. "Greedy tonight," I murmured, unbuttoning the pocket and letting him lift a cube from my palm. While he pranced in place, content, I retrieved a brush and started on his coat. No one else would take care of him. He was too large and mean-spirited to everyone but me. These menial tasks were good for distracting me from things I'd rather not think about.

Time faded as I tended to him. Like it always did.

"Will?" a familiar voice called a while later, and I turned to see Sebastian in his primly starched guard's uniform, sweeping his eyes around the stalls. I leaned on the lip of the door and sighed loudly. He regarded me, dark eyes filled with pity as he walked closer.

We had been on-again off-again lovers since I'd arrived in New Orleans. He wanted things that I couldn't give him, pieces of me that had long since been stripped away. He couldn't understand why I couldn't give him what he wanted, but no matter how many times we tried, it never worked out.

He shuffled closer, his hands rubbing my forearms and shoulders until there was only the door between us. I needed his familiarity to ground my chaotic thoughts, and his touch reminded me that there were still people who saw *Will* when they looked at me. Not just the *Beast*.

Savannah's hateful eyes clouded my soul, twisting inside of me like a cancer, eating away all the goodness that I'd clung to with white knuckles. Seb ran his hands into my hair, and I dropped my face into the crook of his shoulder, inhaling the familiar peppermint soap on his skin.

"I miss you," he whispered. Then he pulled away and opened the door, the last obstacle between us. When it latched shut behind him, I slung an arm around his shoulders and dragged him flush to me. I'd been so cold. So numb. My mouth found his, and, with desperation, I crushed our lips together. He folded against the onslaught of me, letting me take and take and take to fill up those dark places inside. Pulling back long enough for our hot breaths to mingle together, I leaned my forehead against his.

"I need to forget." The words broke something inside of me.

"I know," he said softly, pressing his swollen mouth to my neck as his hands gripped my belt. He lowered to his knees, and I leaned my head back against the stall, trying to stay present in this moment. Seb deserved that much.

Only I was a piece of shit and couldn't even manage that.

My eyes shut as my fingers tangled in his hair, and his mouth wrapped around me like so many times before. As he wrung pleasure out of me, all I saw were Savannah's desire-soaked eyes. And when, with a cry of release, I sucked in shaky breaths to still my racing heart, the way she smiled at that guy came back with a vengeance. I felt even worse than before.

I thumped my head heavily against the wall, hoping the short blast of pain could straighten out my fucked-up mind. It didn't work. No surprises there.

I tugged my pants up and buckled my belt as Seb stood, smiling like the world was right again. How could I explain myself to him? He must have seen it in my expression, though, because his smile faltered and faded into nothing.

"Seb—"

"I don't understand why we can't just try again," he said, ripping my heart to pieces.

"It's *never* worked—"

"That's because you won't let it!" He opened the stall door, making me chase after him.

"That's not fair. You want me to be something I'm *not*." I gripped his arm to stop him from leaving like this. I just needed to *explain*.

"We could leave." Tears thickened his words. "We could be together. You wouldn't have to torture yourself every time *he* gives you an order. We could be *happy*. You know we could."

I turned to him slowly, cupping his jaw and hating the desperate sorrow in his eyes as he studied me for a long, silent moment.

"We could be," I said softly. "But I can't leave."

"Hey!" At the sound of another voice, I dropped my hands and found Jesse walking up from the alleyway entrance. "Where were you? I thought you were coming to my fight tonight."

Seb glared at me in betrayal. *Fuck*. He shoved me back, pointing an accusing finger at Jesse. "*Can't*," he spat, eyes shifting between Jesse and me. "Or won't?"

"Seb, it's not—" But he turned before I could explain and marched from the stables. "Like that," I finished lamely, even though he was already gone. Running frustrated hands through my hair, I turned to Jesse, who stopped short, confusion heavy on his brows.

"Did I interrupt something?" Jesse asked, concern lacing his question.

"Yeah," I said gruffly, retrieving my hat and settling it back on my head. "He thinks I'm screwing you."

Jesse choked, eyes widening in shock.

"Don't worry about it." I wasn't going to talk about Seb with Jesse tonight. Maybe ever. A long, awkward silence stretched between us as I locked the stall door and returned the brushes and tack where they belonged.

"Alright then," he responded after a while. "Who the fuck is this Lucas Rutherford guy and why is he trying to marry Bonnie?"

The blunt change in topic made me chuckle. I was so sick of talking about Lucas Rutherford today. When did I become the authority on that *pendejo*? "He's a potential business partner of Lee's. He's trying to secure a lucrative shipping contract with a more *permanent* kind of partnership between him and Audrey."

"I've gathered that much. Will she fall for it?"

I ran weary fingers down my face and pressed the heels of my hands against my eyes before fixing my stare on his.

"Can we talk about this tomorrow? I've had a long day, and I really just want to drink the shit whiskey on my nightstand and fall asleep."

"Your nightstand?" He crossed his arms over his chest. "At your apartment?"

"Yeah, where the fuck else would my nightstand be?"

"Fuck that. You got me into this mess. You're staying right here to help me through it." Jesse's rumbling voice indicated that he was annoyed enough to hit me. He'd done it enough by now for me to recognize the signs.

"I'm not exactly *welcome* here, if you couldn't tell." I hoped he'd leave it alone and let me go so I didn't have to deal with frightened staff members or explain why they looked at me like I was the grim fucking reaper.

"I don't give a shit." He clapped a hand on my shoulder and led me out of the stalls and toward the room Zachary had assigned him. "Besides, they already think we're fucking, so no one will think twice about you staying with me."

We walked in silence until we arrived at his sparsely furnished room. Staff members hung out on their balconies, chatting after a long day's work. Gossiping about the dinner I'd crashed and the goings-on of the house. Too many ears to talk safely. At least, until the door clicked shut and we were alone.

"Rutherford." Jesse sat on the edge of his bed and leaned forward. "How big of a threat is he?"

"You want the truth?"

He nodded.

"If she were *Bonnie*, she wouldn't have looked at him twice. But—"

"She's not." His blue eyes darkened at the thought of competing for Bonnie's affection.

"He's rich, not bad looking, and intelligent. He also doesn't spook easily, which I think will intrigue her." I didn't want to discourage Jesse, but he needed to know exactly what he was up against. Especially if I had *any chance* of getting my friend back. "Jess, I'm gonna be honest with you. When you and Bonnie traveled together three years ago, you were alone, and you had the time to win her trust and her heart. Time we *don't* have now."

Jesse dropped his head into his hands, sighing in grim resignation. I sank onto the spindly chair in the corner. When he looked up, the helplessness in his expression caught me off guard. I guess I'd never considered Jesse having a breaking point, especially after a three-year crusade built on hope and whispers. But if he had one, he was teetering dangerously on the edge of it now.

"What do I do, Will?"

"If you don't remind her of who she is, and soon, you might lose her for good." I wouldn't lie to him. Not now. Not about *her.* "If I know Bonnie, and I do, she'd never choose a pompous ass from Manhattan when there's a perfectly *bad* outlaw in front of her." A spark of hope brightened his eyes. "Now, I need to find the bottom of a bottle in the worst way."

I stood from my chair and crossed to the door, intent on finding something strong enough to strip paint to help me forget for a while. Forget about failing Bonnie, Savannah, Seb, and now Jesse, too.

"Where do you think you're going?"

"Like I said, to drink myself stupid."

"No." He shook his head. "I need you with a clear head. Get comfortable. I'm not letting you out of my sight until we have a plan to get Bonnie back."

"Oh, you want me *close.*" I waggled my eyebrows. He only glared in return and threw a pillow at my face.

"You sleep on the floor."

I laughed.

How long had it been since I'd laughed like that?

CHAPTER TEN

JESSE

A VERY WARM, VERY solid body pressed against mine, the warmth a welcome change to the frigid sheets that normally greeted me each morning. I tried to remember what I'd been doing before I fell asleep. Maybe Bonnie would know. I ran my fingers along her arm, tugging her back against my chest.

The body grunted. There was a *maleness* to it. That wasn't Bonnie.

Bonnie wasn't Bonnie. Bonnie was Audrey. And Will Ellis was in my bed.

"*Will.*" I shoved him hard. He rolled away, muttering a Spanish curse.

Bonnie. Her name was a prayer as I remembered our brief interlude in the library yesterday. It'd been more fun than I remembered, getting her flustered. The flush of her cheeks made me keenly aware of my cock as it pressed against my jeans.

Fuck. I needed to get up. My eyes slammed open, and I set my feet on the floor.

"That a pistol in your pocket, Jess, or are you just happy to see me?" Will grinned as he rolled to his back. He lifted his eyebrows. I yanked the pillow from beneath his head and smacked him in the face. I stumbled blearily from the bed, seeking my boots across the room as I readjusted my cock. I needed some goddamn privacy. I glanced at my friend as I sat in the rickety chair and worked the laces of my boots.

"Don't get in too much of a hurry." Will reached over to the small table beside the bed for his cigarette case. "You'll ruin my reputation. None of the people I screw do the walk of shame at dawn. They usually can't walk yet."

I'd forced Will to stay, sure, but I'd also told him he would sleep on the floor. As if reading my mind, my friend took a long drag from his freshly lit cigarette and smirked.

A hint of the man I'd known in Fort Hood returned. The lines of his face weren't so hard, and a glimmer of light twinkled in them.

"What's your plan, Jess?" Will reclined against the mattress.

"I blackmailed Audrey into spending five hours a week with me."

"Wait . . . you saw her?" He sat up, more alert than before. "Why the fuck didn't you mention it?"

I finished tying my laces, shrugging as I thought back to the library. It'd been entirely too fun pushing her buttons, teasing and testing the limits of *Audrey*. Seeing the flush on her porcelain skin had reminded me of the rare moments on our travels when I managed to knock the sense from her. A glint of triumph ran through me. Along with the contemplation on her face when I'd negotiated our time together.

Bonnie was still there somewhere. I knew it with every piece of my battered, weary soul.

All I had to do was fight in the sewers of New Orleans, outshine a rich asshole from Manhattan, make Audrey fall in love with me, and somehow bring Bonnie back.

Easy.

"It didn't seem important," I said. "Did you know she could read?"

Will looked at me like I was crazy. "Yeah?"

Bonnie had asked me to tell her what her scar said. Because she couldn't read it. Now she could.

"She couldn't . . . before."

"That was Savvy's doing," Will said. My brows lifted.

"Savvy?"

"Not important." He shifted to the edge of the mattress. "Did she remember you?"

"No."

Will's shoulders slumped.

"But I saw a spark of . . . something in her eyes." My brow furrowed as I remembered the glint of recognition when I told her I'd come for her in the courtyard. "I don't know. I'm meeting her this morning."

"How'd you blackmail her?"

I barely contained a breathy laugh. "Some guy was harassing her. Talking about how they had something special." I rolled my eyes. "I told her I'd make her a deal. I'd get rid of the guy if she spent time with me."

A measure of respect filled his eyes.

"Might have dosed him with glowroot and dumped him on a riverboat heading out of the city."

"Didn't think you had it in you," Will said, then, narrowing his eyes in curiosity.

"Does she do this often?" I looked to the floor. A shred of betrayal flared up in my chest.

"Do you want me to lie to you?"

"Would I be a dumbass if I said yes?"

Will chuckled and cocked his head to the side, eyeing me with curiosity. "Huh."

"What?" I asked, suddenly defensive beneath his scrutiny.

"You really haven't gotten laid in three years."

How did he do that? It was like he could read my mind.

"No."

"You're saving yourself. How adorable." He grinned.

"It's not—" Anger flared bright in my chest. "Listen, I take my promises seriously. I made a promise to Bonnie."

He lifted his hands in surrender.

"Besides, I take a lot of showers."

Will reclined, perching his hat on his head. "So *that's* why you fell for the Ellis charm. I knew it was only a matter of time." He blew out a smoke ring and winked at me. "I mean, after all, what are friends for?"

With a shake of my head, I crossed to the small table where I'd left Selene. I secured her in my holster, noticing a flinch from Will.

"What?"

He let out a bracing breath. "Thought you were gonna shoot me again."

I grinned and rifled through the desk, finding a piece of paper and a pen. I sat at the small side table and started scribbling on the page.

"What are you doing?"

"Letting The Kid know I've got Bonnie."

"How is the little fucker?" Will asked. I glared at him. "What?"

"That's my brother you're talking about."

"And?"

I rolled my eyes and, instead, focused on the letter. Just in case it was intercepted, I had to be careful.

Kid,

Found her. Working on getting her back. Let M know I'm safe. Miss you. Take care of yourself.

J

Once secured in an envelope, I tucked it into my pocket. "How can I get this out of the city without it being intercepted?"

A half smile crept across my friend's face. "Etty."

"What's an Etty?"

"A tornado in an apron." Will hopped up from the mattress. He buttoned his shirt and stamped his cigarette out before retrieving his boots. I followed as he strolled out the door. While I secured the lock, movement from the far end of the breezeway caught my attention. A man in a guard's uniform stood stoically at the end, jaw working while he glared at me. It was the man from last night.

The guard's gaze shot past me to Will's receding form.

Yikes. That wasn't good. I strolled off behind my friend, skin buzzing as I thought of spending time with Bonnie. The open breezeway gave a perfect view of a courtyard. On the level below, a fountain was carved into the center. People milled about. Staff carried heavy bundles or walked by one another with a sense of self-importance.

The corridor spilled into a staircase. As we approached a woman dressed in a uniform at the bottom, her eyes darted to Will. She froze, then backed away slowly. That terrified expression eased as she turned her gaze to me. Will walked past without acknowledging her.

There was something decidedly strange in how people treated Will here. From the way they avoided him when we went to his apartment, to the man who'd crashed into him on the street, fear permeated the air around him.

Will led the way into the kitchen. "Hey, Etty," he said to a rotund woman with a warm smile.

"Will Ellis, you better not cause any trouble in my kitchen." When she caught sight of me, her eyes lit up. "You must be the new hire."

As she studied me, Will snagged the letter from my pocket.

"That's Montana."

I turned, coming face-to-face with the younger woman who'd come to the library yesterday to warn Audrey about her . . . little problem. The younger woman fixed me with an intense stare, distrust making the brown of her eyes duller. Her nostrils flared as she let out a heavy sigh. Her gaze flickered to Will. The expression shifted then, from disinterest to fury. She scowled at Will, headed through a doorway, and tossed over her shoulder, "I'm done, Etty. I'll see you later."

"Wait a second." I touched the woman's forearm. She wheeled around to look at me, eyes full of accusation. I dropped my hand, hackles rising at the rage in her eyes. A shiver slipped down my spine. The warning was clear: this woman wasn't to be fucked with. "You're Miss Audrey's maid, aren't you?"

"Companion," she corrected. "Com. Pan. Yon." She pinched the bridge of her nose and let out an exasperated sigh. "Who are you anyway, *Montana?*"

"He's the newest fighter in New Orleans, Savvy." Will slung an arm around her shoulders. She stiffened beneath his touch.

"It's *Savannah.*" She almost violently shrugged his arm off. She stared at me once more with simmering anger. "You don't look like much of a fighter to me." With a blatant scoff, Savannah stalked off.

"That neckline is mighty high, isn't it, Savvy!" Will called after her. "You should drop a button or two!" The woman tossed a vulgar gesture over her shoulder before disappearing from sight. A loud smack filled the kitchen. When I turned, Will was rubbing the back of his head. Etty glared at him as he smiled sheepishly. "Hey, Etty. I need to get this out of the city." He flashed her that typical Ellis grin. The woman crossed her arms over her chest and eyed him with suspicion. "It's for Montana."

The woman's gaze found me, and she smiled, the hard lines easing in her expression. "I'll get it out." She snatched the letter, tucked it into her apron, and handed me a biscuit. "You look like you need this, sugar." She pointed a finger in Will's face. "Keep this one in line. He's bound to get into some sort of trouble." I grinned as the woman turned her back, then bit into the biscuit.

Will scowled. "I didn't get a biscuit." We exited into the courtyard. "Give me that—" He tried to snatch it from my hand, but I shoved him in the chest.

"Fuck you," I said. "I didn't insult the *companion.*"

"I was defending you, asshole," Will said, playful betrayal on his face.

"Yeah, well, I'm a fighter. You're not. Stick to what you're good at." I shoved his shoulder and set off to the far side of the courtyard, gaze darting to the open breezeway of the second floor.

"Where are we going?"

"I'm going to teach you how to fight."

"You're gonna teach *me* how to fight?" A dark chuckle bubbled up from his chest. "Okay."

"Come on, anyone can learn." I unbuttoned my shirt as we neared the fountain.

After swallowing the last bite of my biscuit, I tore my shirt off, folding it quickly and setting it on the lip of the fountain. My white undershirt did little to cover my tattoos. Morning heat filtered down on us from above, slicking my skin. This heat was worse than the desert. The air hovered, sticking to me like a second skin. The damn desert didn't kill me, but this humidity just might.

Figures stood on the open breezeway of the second floor. I glanced up and found several female members of the staff feigning disinterest. I flashed a grin before turning back to Will.

"What?" he asked.

"Fight me." I lifted my hands, balancing my weight from one foot to the other. My friend shrugged, not wanting to engage. I circled him. "Or are you a coward?"

"I just don't wanna hurt you, *pendejo*," he said, a hint of darkness flickering through his eyes.

If he wasn't going to jump in, I would have to make him. Light on my feet, I bridged the space, throwing a right hook at his jaw. He ducked, faster than I'd anticipated.

"Shit, Montana, not the face."

While his shoulders slackened, he lifted his fists and circled me as well. Good.

Movement across the courtyard stole my gaze. The guard from earlier stood near an open doorway, watching with anger in his eyes. He wasn't the only spectator. We'd somehow garnered the attention of a dozen different staff members. Maybe if word got out that I was nearly shirtless in the courtyard, Miss *Audrey* would join me sooner rather than later.

"Your boyfriend saw us leaving my room." I ducked as Will swiped his long arm at me.

"He's *not* my boyfriend." Will's gaze darted toward the guard.

"For someone who's not your boyfriend, he looks pretty pissed." Taking advantage of his distraction, I delivered a blow to his ribs. He groaned, curling inward.

"Really?" Will took in a sharp breath. I paused so he could regain his breath. "Oh, hey, Miss Audrey—"

"Huh?" I turned, following his gaze. Instead of the woman I loved, there was only the same staff spectating over this sparring match. When I wheeled around, Will threw an elbow at me, catching my shoulder and sending me reeling. I staggered backward, calves hitting the stone lip of the fountain.

My arms shot out as I tried to maintain my balance. Instead, I toppled directly into the frigid water, head banging against the marble sculpture on my way down. I inhaled water before coming up sputtering. My slickened hair fell across my forehead, sticking up at odd angles as Will approached.

"It's been entirely too long since someone knocked you on your ass." He offered me a hand. I took it and climbed from the water. "Can we be done with the fighting?"

"We just got started," I said, my jeans sticking to my skin. The white shirt was now completely see-through. Thankfully, the warm summer sun cast across the courtyard, keeping me from shivering too hard.

"That was quite the exhibition," an amused female voice said.

I turned slowly, confidence wavering as I came face to face with Bonnie.

She wore a dress in a deep shade of olive, which accentuated the smooth line of her pale neck and shoulders. My mouth went dry at the sight of her. Her hair was halfway pinned back, the long, dark locks resting over one shoulder. A silver chain hung from her neck, a large opal perched precariously between the swell of her breasts. The neckline was lower than the dress she'd worn yesterday. Almost as if she chose it because of me.

Not Bonnie. *Audrey.*

My cock twitched against my saturated jeans. An ache surged deep in my gut and expanded through the rest of my body, heating my skin faster than the sun glaring down. She looked so sexy, so damn put together. So unlike Bonnie yet perfectly her just the same. I ached to run my fingers through her precariously pinned hair. I wanted to mess up the flawless image of a high-born lady and bring her back to who she truly was.

My Bonnie. *Mine.*

It had taken every ounce of my self-control to *not* kiss her in that library. That attraction didn't lessen when seeing her again. I wanted to rip her bodice open, shove her against the nearest wall, and smother myself between her thighs.

Will cleared his throat. "Morning, Miss Audrey."

"I didn't realize you were training this morning, Ellis." She crossed her arms over her chest. Her blue eyes traveled to me, a flash of aggravation. A shock of recognition coursed through me as I remembered another time I'd squared off against her in the desert. Her hair had been pulled back then, and she'd worn those shorts. Those *fucking* shorts.

"I'm not," he said, motioning to me with his thumb. "Montana was."

Audrey's blue eyes darkened as they trailed down the expanse of my shoulders and along my left arm. Heady desire filled them as they slid across the ink staining my skin. Her tongue darted out to wet her bottom lip, and my knees quivered.

"Good. I could use a new sparring partner." Audrey tipped her chin defiantly.

I grinned and crossed my arms over my chest, chuckling. "I'm not fighting you."

Dark brows lifted on her forehead. The thrill of a challenge passed through her gaze, and, for a moment, I thought Bonnie stood before me.

Until I took in her perfectly styled hair, the flawless lines of her skirt, and her pink painted lips. She wasn't Bonnie. But she affected me the same.

"I didn't take you for a coward, Montana." Her words were breathless and low. My cock strained against my jeans, aching at her nearness, at the banter I so desperately missed.

"I doubt your father would appreciate it." I shifted my weight, hoping to relieve some of the goddamn pressure.

"My father isn't here, is he?" She glanced around the courtyard pointedly.

"Out of respect, Miss Audrey, I can't." I gathered my discarded shirt from the lip of the fountain.

"Your father forbade training while your guests are here," Will added.

Audrey's mouth pursed into a thin line as she rolled her eyes.

I stripped out of the undershirt slowly, acutely aware of every spot her eyes lingered. She was lucky we weren't alone. I'd have already shoved her skirts over her hips. *Fuck.* That thinking would do me no good. After replacing my button-down and securing it with quick fingers, I turned to face her.

"We should go." I strolled past, forcing my gaze ahead so I didn't trip over my own feet. One moment, my only worry was the soggy jeans hugging my ass. The next, something caught my ankle and the world upended. I slammed against the stone courtyard, air whooshing from my lungs.

Audrey loomed over me, fisting her skirts in her hands enough to show her pale thigh. She pressed a booted heel to my throat.

"Respectfully, *Montana*, you leave yourself open when you go on the attack." My body tightened beneath her harsh voice. She dropped her skirts and extended a hand, lips quirked up at the edges. "It's a wonder that you've won so many fights with a tell like that."

An image of her beside me in the truck flashed through my mind.

You love me? she'd asked, a mixture of suspicion and relief and joy. *I love you so much it hurts.*

It hurt. Staring up at her, seeing the woman I loved and knowing she didn't love me back. My chest tightened as I gripped her hand. Even as I schooled my features, my heart squeezed tight, grief threatening to drown me.

This was only the first day, and I was a goddamn mess.

As if sensing it, Will clapped me on the shoulder. "Well, *Montana*, I'm off." He tipped his hat toward her. "Audrey." Then he was gone, not that I noticed.

A pretty flush stained Bonnie's cheeks as she turned blue eyes on me. "Well?"

"Well what?"

Another memory rushed forward from our time in the desert. I'd been staring at Bonnie all morning. So lost in my thoughts, I'd missed my brother's question about what to name her horse. Amusement had sparkled in her eyes.

That same amusement greeted me now.

"Did you take care of it?"

I blinked, for a moment not understanding. As the glimmer faded from her expression and shifted into aggravation, I suddenly remembered our deal.

Right. The deal. The one that forced her to spend time with me. Because I was a fucking stranger to her now.

I shoved my shoulders back, adopting a boyish grin. "Yep. Put him on a riverboat last night."

"A riverboat? He could just come back." Her gaze darted around the court-yard as if anticipating the man to appear suddenly.

"I took care of it," I said. "Trust me. I've got you."

Audrey blinked, a crease forming on her brow as her features shifted toward confusion. It was better than the fear in her eyes when she'd questioned me in the library yesterday. Still, it unnerved me.

"You okay, Miss Audrey?" I clenched and unclenched my hands to keep myself from touching her. She blinked once more and turned on me with narrowed eyes.

"It's just Audrey." The harsh edge to her voice sent a shiver down my spine. I couldn't help the boyish grin that crossed my face.

There she was.

"Shall we?" I offered my arm, but she rolled her eyes and started toward the front house, leaving me to trail behind. We walked silently from the courtyard, much to the chagrin of the staff who'd been enjoying the show. Tension set her shoulders as we entered the front house.

"Where are we going?"

How the hell should I know? It wasn't *my* house. "The library," I said, more confident than I felt. I knew Bonnie. She didn't like indecision. If I waffled on this, I could lose her before I even had a chance.

Part of me expected her to argue, but she didn't. Instead, she headed for the staircase, and once again, I followed. We made it to the second floor and took a sharp left, following the path I'd taken the day before when I first saw her.

"You're on the clock," she said the moment our feet hit the carpet. She faced me, crossing her arms over her chest and fixing me with a hard stare.

Shit. She didn't know how much that stare brought me back to days left frustrated and lonely after enduring her endless taunts while we traversed the wide-open desert with no end in sight.

I crossed to the bookshelves, scouring the spines of the aged tomes. Most of them weren't like the naughty novel I'd caught her with before. Instead, there were books about battle strategy, history, even a few medical tomes. I was acutely aware of her stare on my face, even as she moved to the window seat and sat obstinately. She crossed one leg over the other, something Bonnie would have never done.

I had no idea how to do this.

If you don't remind her of who she is, and soon, you might lose her for good.

Will's warning rang clear as day. I had to reach Bonnie through the haze of Audrey.

But how could I do that if I didn't know Audrey first?

"Have you read all of these?" I asked, glancing over my shoulder.

With a shrug, Audrey said, "Mostly." My brows shot up. It was still so strange that she could read. What did she know about the scar on her arm? The one that spelled Jones's name? What had Lee told her? I tugged a book from the shelf, barely glancing over the half-naked cowboy on the cover.

"What about this one?"

Audrey's expression hardened, aggravation evident in her tense shoulders. Clearly, she thought this was a waste of her time.

"Humor me." I crossed the room and handed the novel to her. Blue eyes glossed across the cover. Her fingertips trailed along the cowboy hat hiding the figure's face.

"You got a thing for cowboys?" A hint of a smile appeared on her lips. With a shrug, I moved to the plush leather chair across from her and sat, not giving a shit that my clothes were still soggy. "I haven't, actually. I think this is one of Savannah's."

I settled back against the cushions. "Good."

Audrey lifted her head to stare at me. "Good?"

"You haven't read it yet." I crossed an ankle over my knee. "I'd like you to."

She let out an incredulous laugh, but my expression never faltered. "You're serious."

"There are worse ways to spend your hour." I tossed another disarming grin at her. Her cheeks flushed, but some of the tension in her eased. She settled back on the window seat, tucking her legs up like yesterday.

"Okay, then," she said, folding open the front cover of the book.

Time. I didn't have nearly enough, but if I was going to make this work, I needed to make the most of whatever time I had.

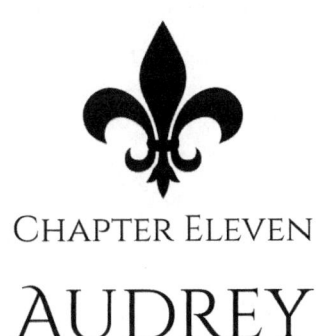

Chapter Eleven

AUDREY

H E WAS STARING. AGAIN.

I didn't realize time could decide how quickly or slowly to move, but after the last three days, trapped in stifling silence with a man who had some strange fondness for *watching me read*, an hour became an eternity. The first day he'd planted himself in an armchair, and I spent the entire hour trying to ignore the steady dripping of his wet clothes onto the floor. The second, he actually plucked a book from the shelves and made an attempt to act normally, turning a page once every so often even though his eyes never dipped towards the book.

Today, like the last two, he stared at me. In silence. I felt every furious thump of my heart and each individual breath he took across the room. The slide of his gaze along my skin was dizzying, a type of instinctual awareness heightened by close proximity. My skin felt too hot and too tight, like I would burst. A headache throbbed in my temples, the pressure building until I couldn't take it anymore.

"What!" I slammed the book down. His eyes didn't even widen at my outburst, as if he'd expected my temper. That unnerved me. So did the familiar way he spoke to me and the hint of expectation in his eyes when he thought I wasn't looking. "For the love of God and liquor, would you just *say something* already!"

"God and liquor?" That infuriating grin of his pulled at his mouth and lit up his bright eyes.

"I said what I said."

He chuckled softly, the sound deep and rumbling, unsettling me on my favored window seat. It used to make me feel less trapped, looking out on the gardens and the people below. Now, after three days stranded with this stranger, I felt exposed. Like I was on display for more than just his ravenous gaze, but completely transparent to everyone I used to look down at. He took his time before responding, forcing my pulse into my throat.

"I'm just trying to figure you out." As if that wasn't the most ridiculous thing he could possibly say. Normally, I would've insulted his intelligence at the very least. Not this time.

I'm just tryin' to figure you out.

The words roared through my mind, familiar and strange, mingling into a cocktail of confusion that made my temples throb. My chest squeezed in a painful crush, and suddenly I couldn't breathe properly. I stood swiftly, pinching the bridge of my nose in a desperate last attempt to stave off a full-blown migraine.

How did he *do* that?

The first time, when he'd coincidentally echoed the words that'd been replaying in my mind from my nightmare, I let my imagination run wild. *Montana* was obviously a nickname. One used prominently in the fighting circuits, if rumors could be believed. So really, when I thought about it, I knew exactly *nothing* about him and had somehow felt comfortable enough to agree to be alone with him multiple times a week.

So fucking stupid.

My head throbbed, and I squeezed my eyes tight against the glare of the afternoon sun. Either I hadn't realized I'd wobbled on my feet or this mountain of a man was surprisingly stealthy, because unexpectedly, his calloused hands gripped me tight. One slid surely beneath my elbow and the other clutched above my forearm, as if to steady me. What he couldn't have known was how my entire world narrowed to the friction of his hands on my skin. Or how it felt like the ground beneath my feet was being upended more now than it had before.

"Are you alright?" His deep voice fell softly against the crook of my neck. I nodded abruptly, motioning toward the window with an impatient flick of my fingers.

"The light—" I said, eyes screwed shut against the glare.

"Hold on." He kept his voice low. Then his hands were gone and it felt too cold in the room, too empty. The scraping screech of the curtains struck through the pressure building behind my eyes, and I hissed, covering my ears.

Then his hands were on me again, each touch innocent and unsure, asking permission as he slid his arms securely around me and led me to the small settee in the darkest corner. I finally cracked my eyes open as I slumped into the seat next to him, and before my vision cleared, something about his face tugged at my heart. Like I should know him.

But that was ridiculous.

Then the blurriness faded. As I blinked my throbbing eyes open, a concerned expression settled into the lines of his face. Stony and unmoving, folded deep into the corners of his eyes and the tightness around his mouth.

"It's fine. I just get headaches sometimes." Why did I feel the need to soften the edges of his concern?

"Is it from . . ." He trailed off, but his meaning was clear. *The accident.* The infamous accident. The one that defined me, since I couldn't remember anything and neither could anyone else. Instead of responding, I shrugged. There was no way to know if my headaches were from stress or my head trauma.

"I'm sure drilling my skull open didn't *help*," I drawled caustically. Unlike others, who found my penchant for sarcasm and dark cynicism off-putting, he smiled. He smiled like it was one of his favorite things about me. Another curiosity. "I guess you've heard all about that, since you've known me more than five minutes."

"Come here." He motioned for me to turn my back to him. We were already so close on the small settee that I couldn't imagine coming any closer. I was practically on his lap as it was. But, without question, I turned as requested. His fingers, strong and calloused, gripped the top of my neck and rubbed towards the base of my skull. His fingers were strong, and the pressure was steady and rhythmic. Tension I didn't realize I'd been holding eased instinctually.

"You think the staff gossips about you?" he asked, like I was capable of forming words as his hands worked the tension free. His big fingers barely dipped into my hair, and I wanted him to sink them in deep. I nodded slightly, so as not to discourage his steady strokes.

What would those hands feel like on my breasts, or between my thighs?

The thought startled me enough that my eyes snapped open, and I cleared my throat to remind myself that I'd been *blackmailed* into being here with him. This wasn't some hot forbidden tryst beneath my father's nose.

Then his fingers did sink into my hair, and I melted into his touch. Melted. I became pliant as they traveled up and his palm clenched, pulling my hair gently and expertly. My mouth dropped open, and a needy gasp that sounded downright erotic spilled forth.

"Where did you learn how to do that?" I asked, breathless as his hand fell and I realized my headache was gone.

A grin illuminated his words as he said, "Just one of my tricks." Facing him once more, I shuffled back, biting my bottom lip hard to stop the string of things I wanted to say. Instead, I squirmed on the settee, trying to get comfortable in his nearness.

"Why do you think the staff gossips about you?" He leaned against the back of the small settee and propped his angular jaw on his fist.

I snorted derisively.

"The only thing the staff does more than gossip about me is spend my dad's money," I replied dryly. "They're not the only ones. I'm an oddity after . . . everything." I didn't know why I suddenly felt embarrassed, as if he hadn't heard about my glowroot addiction or memory loss. These were parts of me now, and trying to separate *me* from them would be as impossible as changing the color of my eyes.

I stared at him expectantly, waiting for the inevitable questions. *What do you remember? How did it happen? Where were you before?*

Just like with Lucas Rutherford the other night, I was a curiosity, like some strange object on display behind a glass case. Fragile and alluring. Easy to look at but too easy to break. Because I'd been broken before, hurt before, and there was no hiding it. The cracks were all anyone saw. Not the strength it'd taken to piece myself back together.

"That must be really hard for you."

We fell into silence. Stunned silence. No questions came forth. No morbid fascination with my apparent tragedy.

"It was." I blinked away my surprise. "It still is."

He didn't press for more details, didn't push me to share, and because of his consideration, I felt safe to do just that. I opened my mouth, then shut it, wondering if I'd lost my mind. This man was a *stranger*. I didn't even know his real name. Yet, here I was, almost confiding in him.

"My mom used to get headaches when she spent too long reading by candle-light," he offered, clearing his throat. "My pop would do that to comfort her."

It wasn't much. Barely anything, really, but he confessed with such earnest-ness that it made him seem *boyish*. This hard, violent bulk of man wasn't as tough as he wanted people to think. That much was suddenly clear to me.

"The worst part of not remembering is knowing that I'm missing important pieces of myself," I whispered. "Like my mother. Or what happened in the attack."

Unconsciously, my fingers drifted toward the jagged scar hidden beneath the fashionable sleeve of my blouse. His eyes tracked the motion hungrily, and I let my fingertips fall away. The image of him in the courtyard had been seared into the backs of my eyes for days. Black ink crawling over his skin and down his left arm like warning signs, failing to scare me away from him. I could still see the way his white shirt had turned translucent when wet and clung to every line and ridge of his muscled torso.

I'd thought of it often in quiet moments, toying with the idea of asking him to my bed. But his words from the first time I'd met him stopped those wayward thoughts.

I'm going to make you fall in love with me.

The kind of fling I wanted, the detachment I craved, was a far cry from his challenge of more. More wasn't possible. Not from me. You had to have a heart to fall in love, and mine died one bloody night over two years ago.

But the image remained, and I reached toward his left arm, the one he leaned against the back of the settee. "Who's Bonnie?" The name swept down from his shoulder to nearly his forearm. The font was jagged, an artistic mirror of my scar and a tenuous thread of connection between us.

His eyes dimmed and shuttered, and suddenly his face was an unreadable mask instead of his usual open expression. The change was subtle and startling, reminding me that I didn't know him as well as I thought I did. Pulling my hand back, I settled it in my lap and forced myself not to twist my fingers together.

"You don't have to—" I started to say, but he cut me off.

"No." The word was harsh. It was clearly a painful topic, but before I could insist that he didn't need to confide anything in me, he said, "She's the love of my life."

My mind whirled, stomach churning as jealousy and confusion pounded through me in dizzying intervals. Didn't he say he wanted to make *me* fall in love with him?

"Oh." The word felt stupid even as I said it. I wanted to ask him what this was all for then. Why he'd tried so hard to get me to spend time with him, making declarations and using blackmail when I'd resisted his flirtation.

"She's *gone* now." His arm fell to his side, and I realized what he'd been trying to hide from me: sorrow. Deep and dark, a fathomless pit with no end in sight. I knew because there was a well of my own, overfull with the same insidious pain. People liked to believe that pain was something to be endured or overcome. It comforted them to know that once you suffered, it ended. The truth was that pain—real, lasting, the kind that stems from loss—doesn't end. It was the stone you broke against over and over. Just when you thought you'd weathered the worst, a wave crashed forth to drive you back into a million shattered pieces.

I didn't know when I reached for him, but my fingers tangled with his and gripped tight, holding on for dear life. Because it seemed we were both adrift in the midst of the same grasping monster, lost to its immensity, and for the first time, I didn't feel so alone.

"I know what that's like." My voice wavered. "To lose someone."

His jaw worked, words poised on his mouth that he battled against. I saw his struggle in the restless desperation tensing his shoulders. He didn't know me well either. Still, he gripped my hand, and neither of us pulled away.

Slowly, I dragged the sleeve of my blouse up my arm to show him the scar he'd probably already heard about. My eyes fell from his as I bunched the fabric around my shoulder. The jagged name carved into my skin, a horrifying echo of his tattoo. *Jones.*

"It's the name of the man who hurt me," I said quietly. "My father and the staff call it an *accident*, what happened to my head, but how many accidents come with scars like this?" I scoffed. "No, *this* is personal."

Leaning my head against the settee, I let the fabric fall, covering my gnarled flesh. "It took me an embarrassing amount of time to ask my father about it," I admitted. "And he's really good at answering questions without giving any *real* answers, but I understood enough to fill in the blanks."

He was so still I didn't think he even breathed, so still it felt like I was alone in the room and my secrets, whispered between us in the darkness, would remain forever. That it would be alright to admit them. So I raised my eyes to the ceiling and blinked away the heat rising and wobbling in my vision.

"Jones abducted me, raped me, and nearly killed me," I said. "And I'm pretty sure it was my dad's fault."

Helpless. Weak. Used.

Self-loathing, thick and cloying, filled my mind with the thoughts I buried beneath my bravado. I blinked hard to contain my sorrow. Montana didn't say anything; he didn't have to. He was there, listening to something I needed to say out loud for longer than I remembered, and that was enough.

"I think—" I cleared my throat, forcing the emotion behind a shaky mask of indifference. "I think that's why he's so protective, you know? He feels like he failed me before." If Montana hadn't been watching me so closely, he might not have noticed as I stealthily wiped the moisture from my eyes.

Now that I'd said it, a weight lifted. Like the pressure of keeping the truth locked inside released and I could finally breathe. "Rethinking your arrangement with me now, aren't you?" Playful cynicism laced my words. But when I looked over at him, his blue eyes were oceans of yearning, and being caught by them was like being sucked into a tornado.

"What do I have to do to get another hour with you this week?"

"You want to spend *six* hours with me?" My head snapped up, and my spine straightened. He squeezed my hand, reminding me our fingers were still entwined.

"I want to spend all my time with you." That boyish honesty rang clear between us.

Instead of answering him, I took a steadying breath and asked, "How long has it been since Bonnie . . . ?"

"Years," he croaked, as if acknowledging the time reminded him of the lingering ache of losing her. That was familiar too. There were days I almost forgot my loss. Days that felt normal or hopeful or good. Days when I smiled and laughed, like grief had never touched me. Then I saw pity in one of the maid's eyes and remembered every second like an eternity.

Looking at Montana now, how young and hale he was, his strength prominent in the lines of his battle-hardened body, it was impossible to think he'd suffered for years. How young had he been when he lost her? Had he buried her memory as I had, in drink and nights of pleasure? There was so much I didn't know about him yet. Too much. That I wanted to shocked me.

"You shouldn't feel guilty." I slid my fingers from his steady grasp. "I understand needing to distract yourself. You didn't have to blackmail me, you know. If you'd just asked me to fuck you, I wouldn't have said no."

His eyes widened, shock flitting through them quickly. Desire flared in his wide pupils before fading into a stony sorrow I didn't understand. Had I gotten it wrong? Every time I tried to wrap my mind around his motivations for this foolhardy entrapment, I came up empty. If he didn't want to use me to forget his grief, then what was this for?

"You have a low opinion of me." He dropped his arm and straightened.

"I have a realistic opinion of men and what little I have to offer them," I retorted sharply.

"Little?" he asked, but it wasn't a serious question. Not really. His voice was laced with anger, his intent clear. He wanted to prove me wrong.

"Yes. *Little*," I said waspishly. "I've studied business, economics, history, and industry. Could probably balance my father's books better than the geriatric asshole he pays a fortune to, but do you think anyone cares about that? Of course not. The first time he brought me into his study wasn't to let me in on the family business, it was to tell me I had to charm a potential business client."

His silence cleaved into me, though he did nothing malicious; these truths tangled deep into my existence. Insecurities that haunted me into fitful nights of sleep. Not good enough. *Never* good enough.

"Since you've actually spoken to me for more than five minutes, you know that all my *charm* is located between my thighs. I'm notoriously bad at . . ." I waved a hand between us impatiently. "People."

His stony expression broke, gifting me with a small grin that felt like a ray of sunlight breaking through thick cloud cover.

"I like how bad you are at people."

An incredulous scoff escaped my lips.

"What?" he asked, chuckling. "I do."

"So." I leveled my eyes on him once more. "You're saying you *don't* want to fuck me?"

"No," he replied quickly, leaning close enough that I could feel the heat from his skin. "What I'm saying is that I don't *just* want to fuck you."

I felt like screaming in frustration. He was maddening. Talking in circles, giving so little of himself, making me crave more.

"Is it me? I mean, I'm sure you've been with plenty of—"

"No one." The depth of his voice rumbled through my skin. "Not since Bonnie."

The admission had me hissing a shocked breath through my teeth, and the room became stifling. My mind buzzed with the knowledge that a man who looked like an outlaw god, chiseled to inhuman perfection, could spend *years* with no one to warm his bed. I gaped openly, and it amused him to no end.

Pressing two fingers to my forehead, I opened my mouth but snapped my jaw shut shortly afterwards.

My speechlessness broke through the last of his clouded expression, until the blue of his eyes was as bright as a summer sky.

"No one?" I asked. He shook his head. "Alright, no sex, but surely you've let a woman..." I made a few vague motions near my mouth to indicate my intention without spelling it out. Again, he shook his head.

My brow furrowed and my eyebrows knit together as I thought of the nights I'd barely felt human. When losing myself to the bottom of a bottle and the heat of a stranger's skin kept me from destroying the last shred of my humanity. Of the times I'd felt so lonely and hollow that even that feeble connection kept me grounded in reality.

Montana hadn't had that. Not the fleeting comfort, or the swirl of shame and self-loathing that came with the temporary relief. He'd borne the heaviness of his sorrow on those broad shoulders. For who knew how long. It made me sad for him.

"Then you haven't had the comfort of a woman's touch either, have you?" I asked, barely above a whisper. He held my gaze for so long my lungs ached, all the air burned out beneath the intensity of his gaze. Slowly, he shook his head, and my heart broke for him.

"That's cruel," I whispered, even though the words felt loud between us. "She wouldn't have wanted that."

I probably shouldn't have said anything. It wasn't my place to pass judgment on how he coped with his pain. But being robbed of human touch, of comfort, made my chest ache uncomfortably.

"I'm going to touch you," I said, more confidently this time. Then I reached out to him. I half-expected him to pull away. Uncertainty wavered in his expression, so maybe he wasn't sure if he would either.

Then my fingertips met his hot, stubbled jaw, and both of us went still. Not for long, though. His mouth parted and his chest heaved, urging me on. My lips were dry and ashen, barren of words as I watched the layers of distrust fall away to bare his loneliness.

Gently, I traced the curve of his upper lip, a chiseled bow that reminded me so much of the only person I'd ever love. The slide of my skin against his abrasive jaw, hard as granite, sent a ripple of sensation down my spine. He reached for my hand, guiding me until I cupped his cheek. He trembled, eyelids fluttering shut at the contact. His body released tension like the wire holding him upright had finally been cut. His shoulders slumped forward, the crease between his eyes smoothed. It made him so beautiful it was painful to look at him.

Sad, lonely, and achingly beautiful.

Maybe that was why I shuffled closer, until my thigh pressed tight against his on the small settee. Here, in the shadows of my sanctuary, I could be anyone I wanted. I could be the broken woman who had arrived here in pieces all those years ago, or the high-handed daughter of a powerful man.

Montana made me want to be someone different. Someone strong and kind, a safe place for heart-sore souls like him. With careful slowness, I lowered my hand, drowning in the anguish and confusion shimmering in the depths of his eyes as he blinked them open. Instead of explaining, I wrapped my arms around him. Turning my cheek, I pressed my ear to a spot on his shoulder that seemed like it was made to cradle me. He was so large compared to me, it must have seemed like a child embracing him. One of my arms slid over his shoulder, the other snaked around his waist, and I held him tight.

His breath shuddered in my ear as his head fell between my neck and shoulder, hiding those expressive eyes. Then he crushed me to him, fingers tangling in my hair, squeezing so tightly I couldn't breathe.

His heart thundered beneath my jaw, thumping so hard it was a wonder it hadn't leapt from his chest. My legs were slung over his now as he clutched me closer, as if he could cage me completely in his body if he gripped tight enough. He inhaled, drinking in the scent of my hair, a loud ragged breath, filling his lungs with me.

When he finally exhaled, I felt his jaggedness in hot puffs against my neck as he admitted, "I miss her."

As he'd done for me before, I stayed there, silent and steady, allowing him enough space to say what he needed. Because a man this torn apart was one I *wanted* to know. I wanted to ease those old wounds, give him the comfort I denied myself with my self-imposed detachment.

"I couldn't protect her," he croaked against my throat.

"If she loved you," I said, pressing my lips into his hair, "then she forgave you."

He lifted his head, eyes wet, staring like I'd just given him salvation. His lips parted, and my eyes dropped to them, hot with need. I wanted to taste his sorrow. I wanted to devour it until it gave way to pleasure. My nose brushed against his, and I cupped his jaw again, giving him permission, begging him to close the space.

"Our hour is up." His teeth clenched around his words until I felt a muscle jump beneath my hand.

Gulping in a few steadying breaths, I nodded and cleared my throat. "Right. Of course," I stammered like an idiot.

Stupid. So fucking stupid.

I'd pushed too far. He'd been open and vulnerable, and I was no better than a cat in heat, practically crawling into his lap. Pulling my arms back, I wriggled on the seat until there was enough distance between us that I could stand comfortably. The air was clearer the farther I retreated. Without looking back, I headed for the door until his voice stopped me.

"Next time, I want to draw you." Arrogant confidence returned to his voice. I whirled to face him, watching as he rose to his towering height.

"Draw me?" I asked. "You and your weird kinks." His grin was familiar and playful, softening the awkwardness from moments before. I rolled my eyes and flipped my hair over my shoulder as I headed for the exit.

"Sure," I said, a smile tilting on my lips. "You can draw me."

Once I'd gone far enough from sight, I pressed my back against the dark oak-paneled walls and bit my bottom lip so hard I tasted the metallic tang of blood. *Holy shit.*

Montana made me feel more in that hug, those innocent touches, than I had with any person I'd fucked. My skin buzzed and my mind raced, like my body was waking up from a deep sleep.

"Miss Audrey, are you alright?" A familiar voice had my eyes refocusing swiftly. Lucas Rutherford stood before me in a starched shirt, his chestnut waves flopped too perfectly over his forehead.

"Y-yes, I just—" I sucked my bottom lip into my mouth to staunch the small wound, struggling to find a good excuse to be in this state in the middle of the hallway. "Headache."

He nodded, as if that were a perfectly reasonable response, closing the space between us until he was a comfortable few feet away. Not too close to encroach on my personal space, but close enough that I couldn't avoid him. He was good at this. Playing the game. Where we pretended to be civil members of polite society instead of sharks in fancy clothes.

"My friends and I were going to play cards before dinner. Care to join?" The intelligence in his gaze told me I couldn't refuse him even if I wanted to. They would probably play some boring game of rummy that would last forever while they boasted about being masters of the universe or some horseshit.

"What are you playing?" I glanced up at him through the fringe of my lashes. The epitome of shy capitulation. I could play this game, too. It was just strategy, after all, and men were easily manipulated.

Not all of them.

The insidious reminder of Montana had me wavering on my feet, reluctant to go with Lucas.

"Poker," he said, grinning as my eyes lit up. "We like to lose money to each other, or favors. Are you up for some gambling?"

My father would be horrified, but I was delighted. Nodding, I took his arm and let him lead me away. All the while trying not to think of the dark corner of the library and how Montana's touch made me feel more alive than I ever had.

CHAPTER TWELVE

SAVANNAH

T EA SETTINGS FOR TWELVE?

I counted the carefully arranged dishes, my gaze sliding quickly across the three tables where Audrey's guests would sit in the parlor of Lee Manor. The room had been used only a handful of times in my tenure, and I was determined to make Audrey's brunch an event to remember. I folded back a napkin flapped up at the corner, smoothing its crisp edges.

Check.

Refreshments?

A black tablecloth adorned the rectangular buffet table against the wall, a gold fleur-de-lis pattern lining the fabric. Though *I* wanted to use the yellow one—bright, like the summer sun, and inviting—Mr. Lee's lovely assistant insisted on this one. Because, technically, this was *Audrey's* event. Not mine.

Audrey was a Lee.

Fleur-de-lis it was.

I'd carefully arranged an array of delightful sweets on trays made of real silver. The first time I'd seen them, I'd wondered whether Mr. Lee would notice they were gone before I could buy my way onto a riverboat.

Sweat beaded on the outside of the glass canister containing my personal recipe for mint julep—just sweet enough with a hint of mint. While, yes, it was a brunch, this was the south. You always had to have drinks on hand. Not that I'd partake.

Check.

Sandwiches?

A tiered serving tower sat in the center of the table. Thin, triangular finger sandwiches—cucumber, muffaletta, and peach preserve and cream cheese, with a layer of pecans—were carefully arranged with their edges crisp, not a crumb out of place. I'd spent hours this morning cutting each one exactly. Decadent sweets made delicate shapes on the spotless silver trays. Squares of almond cake drizzled with a light cinnamon-sugar icing. Slices of pecan pie. Still-warm croissants. Butter. Jam. Sugar. Syrup. All was in place.

To anyone else, it would be shameful, the amount of time I spent perfecting the party.

Everything *had* to be perfect.

Audrey struggled through social gatherings with these society sharks. The last thing she needed was something going horribly wrong.

And I couldn't get caught disobeying any more orders. That punishment wouldn't go well for me.

Matching teacups?

A smile perched on my lips as I moved about the room, turning each cup so the handle jutted perfectly to the right. I stood back, hands on my hips as I surveyed my hard work.

Perfect.

No. *Not* perfect. My expression fell as I realized what was missing from the refreshment table.

The tea. Jesus Christ, I'd forgotten the sweet tea!

How could I be *such* an idiot?

With a shake of my head, I strode into the corridor. My gaze darted up and down the hallway in search of someone strong enough to carry the gigantic batch of tea from the kitchen. My shoes echoed against the hardwood floors as I rounded a corner.

A few guards milled about, blocking my path to the kitchens. They chatted casually with one another, rifles slung over their shoulders as though they hadn't a care in the world. It would take precious time I didn't have to take the long way to the kitchens. I hesitated, then backed slowly away.

"Well, well," a male voice said. "Look who it is, boys."

My muscles coiled tight as I prepared to run. Their heavy, booted steps made the hair on the back of my neck lift. Metal clicked as they adjusted their guns. I'd have one chance to get away, and I had to make it count.

Sebastian led the other two, lip curling up and fire in his eyes.

"What do you think, Jimmy?" The man with the cross tattoo on his hand smiled in response, eyes darkening in a way that made my stomach thrash.

"I think Savannah forgets she doesn't belong in the back house," Jimmy said, his gaze rapt as he studied me. He took his time, letting his eyes slide down the curve of my neck, over my shoulders, my hips. It felt wrong, a violation. I crossed my arms over my chest.

"I'm going to the kitchen, I'll have you know." My voice sounded far stronger than I felt. "Now, if you'll excuse me—" I turned, sending up a silent prayer to whatever gods might be listening.

The gods, however, had no intention of answering me.

"What's wrong, *Savvy?*" Sebastian's fingers twisted around my wrist. "The kitchen is this way." He jerked his head in the opposite direction. Tension filled the air. I reached for the quiet spaces in my mind, willing the tightness to leech from my body as a smile crossed his face. It didn't reach his eyes. It never did. His fingers tightened, and he jerked forward, placing a rough hand on the small of my back as he ushered me down the corridor.

Heart pounding, I stared ahead, hoping that someone, *anyone*, would come along and distract the guards.

"Un*fuck*able, Savannah," Sebastian said. With a twist of his wrist, he spun me, using the momentum and his broad frame to shove me into the nearest wall. A cry escaped from my lips. He stepped back. I had a chance. I could run. Instead, the cruelty in his gaze stilled me.

Why do you hate me so much?

"I wonder, when you fuck, do you enjoy it? Or do you just lay there and take it like your whore mother?" Sebastian's shoulders slackened, the tension gone. As if tormenting me brought him peace. My jaw dropped, but even if I'd been able to think up a retort, my tongue didn't want to work.

Sebastian's gaze slid to Jimmy's. With a nod, the second guard lurched forward. He yanked me from the wall. I shouted, and a second later, his hand slapped over my mouth. The corridor spun. What were they going to do to me? They'd *never* been this brazen before.

The last thing I saw before plunging into darkness was Sebastian's cold, cruel smile.

The slam of a door. Muffled laughter. My knees crashed to the hardwood planks. Their bootsteps faded away. There wasn't even a sliver of light from the corridor. I reached tentative hands out, searching the small space. My fingertips brushed against shelves filled with linens and other things I couldn't make out.

Silence grew beyond the door. The men were gone, but I wasn't. My heart pounded. I closed my eyes, counted to ten, opened them. Still dark. A shuddering breath escaped me. I rocked my weight forward, wrapping my arms around my knees for a long time as I strained to listen.

I could be locked in here for minutes. For hours. For *days*.

Days.

Adrenaline surged through me as I imagined any number of demons coming to claim me in this darkness. This stillness.

For years, I was the perfect picture of a southern lady. I didn't raise my voice. I did as told. I never bucked authority.

I wasn't a lady anymore. Not in the darkness.

My fingers found purchase on smooth wood. I slid them along the surface, searching for a doorknob as my heart threatened to pound out of my chest. I couldn't breathe. I couldn't *think*. I needed to *get out*.

Cool metal. I let out a choked sob. It was flat. Because they didn't need a doorknob from *inside* a closet.

"Let me out," I whispered. Darkness encroached on me, stole my breath, sent my racing pulse skyward. I banged against the door with my palm. "Let me out! Let. Me. Out!"

Just as I balled my hands into fists and raised them to beat on the door, light flooded the small space. I pitched forward, fists landing hard against a male figure. I took in a sharp breath, shoving the man.

"*Let me go*."

Instead, long arms enveloped me. "Savvy."

I shouldn't have felt relief at his presence. If anything, I should have feared William Ellis because of the things he did. But somehow, he was the least intimidating man in this house. Instead, I melted into his warmth. I buried my face against his chest, shuddering as tears spilled over my cheeks.

"Are you okay?" Will asked.

What was I doing?

I pulled back, swiping at my cheeks as I left his comforting embrace.

"I'm fine." I hadn't seen Will since the night of the dinner. My face heated beneath his curious gaze.

Don't threaten me with a good time.

I'd wanted him to kiss me. *That* was dangerous. Not just because of the things I wanted him to do to me, but because the man who loved him despised me.

"I'm fine," I repeated, forcing a scowl. Before he could respond, I stalked away. I quickened my steps to put distance between us, making it to the kitchen at nearly a jog. I forced back the terror of being locked in the closet and focused on Audrey. She needed me. I could do this for her.

With Etty's help, the large carafe full of tea settled on top of a rolling cart. She plopped down a large, insulated bucket filled to the brim with ice chips. My eyes widened. How much money had Mr. Lee spent on this party?

Using my hip to leverage the door open, I pulled the cart behind me and into the corridor that led back to the main house.

"Savannah, there you are." Audrey wore a pretty pink gown adorned with lace at the sleeves and neckline. "I've been looking everywhere."

"Sorry, I had to get the parlor ready," I said. "What do you need?"

Audrey lifted her hands, motioning to her hair. It looked mussed from sleep, and the ends curled every which way. I frowned.

"Where are all of the maids?" I shoved the cart forward. It took more effort than it should have, and it only actually started moving when Audrey joined my effort.

"You know I'm hopeless without you," Audrey said.

A grin found its way to my mouth. "Isn't everyone?" The lingering edge of darkness faded away. "Grab a handful of pins and your brush." She sighed loudly and veered off toward the stairs. I slowed the cart and wheeled it through the parlor door, freezing the moment I entered.

A pair of mud-covered boots. On. My. White. Tablecloth.

William Ellis reclined in one of the hard-backed chairs, cigarette dangling from between his lips, feet propped up on a pristine tablecloth. As he caught sight of me, his mouth curled into a grin and his eyes crinkled in amusement. My heart skipped at the joyful expression on his face.

Why did he have to do this?

Wasn't it bad enough that he'd encroached on what was supposed to be an otherwise civilized dinner with houseguests the other night? That he'd purposefully antagonized me to the point of embarrassment and gotten me in trouble with Mr. Lee?

"Out," I ordered.

"What's wrong, Savvy?"

I'd had *enough*. Three years, I'd tolerated his sarcastic commentary and chaotic antics. I'd witnessed how flippantly he jumped from one staff member to the next, leaving a trail of shattered hearts in his wake. His brand of trouble was too much. Even if he'd just saved me from a dark closet. I was *done*.

"You," I growled, searching the room for a weapon.

Instead of acknowledging my anger, he relaxed into his chair. "You see, Savvy, I've been thinkin'. . ." As he prattled on, I moved toward the credenza. I wrapped my fingers around a thick crystal candlestick holder. ". . . maybe you should let me teach you to defend yourself."

"What?" I asked, loosening my grip on the weapon.

Will flashed a grin, pleased with himself as usual. "You wouldn't have ended up in that closet if you knew a thing or two about self-defense." My scowl deepened, even as my cheeks heated. "I've been training Audrey forever, but you never come along."

"It's not appropriate for a lady," I snapped.

"Not *appropriate*." He rolled his eyes and grinned at the same time. My knees weakened at the sight. "Don't you ever want to break the rules, Savvy?" He inhaled deeply from his cigarette. Smoke curled from between his soft lips. Lips I'd forgotten about until he'd nearly kissed me the other night.

"Don't you ever want to *follow* the rules, William?"

His eyes glimmered at me. I knew his answer without him saying it. Of course not. He wouldn't be William Ellis if he followed rules. I huffed, glaring at him once more.

"Just—get out!" I pointed to the open door.

"Is everything okay here?" I turned at the male voice, feeling confused yet pleasantly surprised. The young man who'd sat beside me at dinner the other night, Mr. Patrick MacNeil, lacking his coat and tie. His sleeves were rolled up to his elbows in an approximation of nonchalance. My cheeks flushed as I turned back to the intruder seated at the table.

"It's fine. Mr. Ellis was just leaving," I said, glaring at him.

Will's boots dropped to the floor. He shrugged as he stood, then reached across the table and dropped his cigarette into the rose-filled vase serving as the centerpiece. It hit the water with a faint hiss.

That was all it took. With a muffled scream, I grabbed the nearest thing I could find—a teacup—and lobbed it at Will's head. He moved effortlessly out of the way. The cup shattered as it crashed into the wall behind him. My expression fell.

"You have terrible aim, Savvy," Will remarked with a wink as he brushed past me. "I can teach you that, too."

My heart clutched. What had I done? I crossed to the shards of ceramic littering the floor, gathering the pieces as quickly as possible. My heart pounded in my chest. The tea set was an antique. Mr. Lee would kill me if he found out.

"Miss Beauregard?"

I bundled my skirt around the broken cup and turned to face him, adopting as pleasant an expression as I could. "Yes?"

"Was he bothering you?"

"Yes." I blew out a breath. "No. That's just who he is." My scowl dropped quickly at the concern on his face. "Was there something I could help with, Mr. MacNeil?" I'd been pleasantly engaging in small talk with him at dinner before William intruded. He opened his mouth to speak.

"Savannah," Audrey said as she reappeared in the doorway. "I need more hair pins. These are all bent."

"That's what happens when you use them for target practice," I murmured. "I apologize, Mr. MacNeil, but you must excuse me. I'm certain a butler or maid could assist with what you need."

With a brief curtsy, I deposited the ruined teacup in a wastebasket and shuffled toward my friend, hooking our elbows together as I steered Audrey upstairs.

A half-hour and many curses from Audrey later, we emerged from the bathroom between our bedrooms somewhat victorious. I'd tamed her unruly hair into a smooth bun against the nape of her neck. I'd powdered her nose and cheeks a little extra to help with what would no doubt be a trying afternoon.

Even as I dressed for the party, I spied Audrey twisting her fingers together from the corner of my eye.

"It's going to be fine." I hoped I could keep that promise.

"How can you know that?" She wheeled on me, but not in anger. In fear. Her eyes were wide, and her skin had lost most of its color beneath the cosmetics. Lines creased her forehead. "I wouldn't even be doing this if my father hadn't insisted. Why would anyone want to spend time with those miserable women?"

I secured the zipper of my dress at my neck, smoothing my hands across my skirts as I moved toward her. I clutched her upper arms, dipping my head to meet her haunted gaze.

"They wouldn't. That's why your father had to force you to do this." I gave her a half grin. "They're absolutely rotten, I have no doubt. But—" I squeezed her arm. "Since when does Audrey back down from a challenge?"

Slowly, her features slackened and the light returned to her eyes. I brushed a wayward strand of hair behind her ear.

"There," I said, then stepped back and turned to my own vanity. I sat heavily before it, unsure of what to make of myself. I tugged the pins from my hair, letting the long, dark tresses spill over my shoulders.

"You should wear it like that," Audrey said.

I glanced over my shoulder at her, horrified. "Like a rat's nest? I think not." I shook my head. Before I could turn back to my reflection and get to work, she crossed the room and began to smooth my hair down. She turned me back to the mirror.

"See how it frames your face? I hate that you never wear it down." She pouted adorably. I cocked my head to the side, staring at her with dull eyes.

"It's not . . . me." I lowered my eyes from my reflection, instead letting my fingers work their magic. I braided the long locks and wrapped them into a careful bun. I applied a little smoothing gel and used a comb to capture all of the wayward curls.

Audrey grimaced at me. I stuck my tongue out at her and climbed from the bench seat to find my shoes.

A loud bell rang through the house. My stomach jumped. It was time. Tension had found its way back to Audrey's shoulders.

"You stay here. I'll send for you when they've all arrived so you can avoid the awkward pleasantries." I tapped her cheek. She offered a grim smile. I walked briskly from our rooms, making my way to the parlor.

I didn't have a chance to marvel at the sweet tea carafe and ice bucket that *I* hadn't moved from the missing cart to the refreshment table before the women arrived.

The first two entered together. I greeted them warmly, only to find dismissive expressions as they marveled at the parlor. They said something about having never been in this particular room before sitting at the farthest tables. Even though there were name placards clearly above each setting. Placards I'd spent the better part of two hours writing by hand and sorting out the arrangement to seat those most likely to give Audrey a chance at her table, and by moving the nastiest of them—like the mayor's daughter—as far away as possible.

Before I could interject about the assigned seating, more guests arrived in silks and chiffons in varying shades of blue, green, and purple. The vague image of Easter eggs passed through my mind, but I didn't know where it came from.

"*Iced* tea?" one woman said, surprise crossing her face as she surveyed the refreshments. "How lush! We haven't had ice at an event in years." She leaned toward the nearest woman. "You'd think the Lees were trying to *buy* our affections."

Anger roiled inside of me, but I held my tongue. The last thing Audrey needed was for me to make a spectacle, even if I wanted to.

"Oh, I love that gown!"

"Do you? It's *vintage*. My mother's from *before* the Culling." The gown in question appeared to be made of some lightweight fabric—polyester, maybe?—and seemed to float around her ankles.

"I love *yours*, it's so—original!" The dress barely reached the woman's knees. The petticoats beneath made the sequined skirt flare out, and the strappy top was anything but modest.

While the women traded polite, bordering on terse, conversation, I sent the butler upstairs to retrieve Audrey.

The last of the guests arrived—Alice Devereaux. Society darling and the mayor's daughter, Alice was on the cusp of entering her first season as a debutante. With how the rest of the women stared, one would think she was the sun that the world revolved around. The women flocked toward her, unable to hide their excitement.

In truth, I hadn't expected her to come. The invitation was merely a show of respect—one that I would have preferred *not* to send, but Mr. Lee's assistant had insisted, of course.

Once the initial bustle of her arrival passed, Alice turned to me, tipping her chin the moment her eyes passed over the brand on my neck. I fought against scowling. Audrey didn't need me causing a scene. As I ignored the harsh dismissal, horror struck me.

The gown she wore was pale pink, not all that different from the shade Audrey wore. It had long sleeves made of lace, the fabric hugging her too-thin figure. She made a show of it as she walked about the room, barely gazing across the assortment of treats.

Why had I cared so much about this brunch?

The butler arrived. He cleared his throat, and the room stilled around us.

"Miss Audrey," he announced politely, then backed away.

My best friend's trepidation showed in the crease of her brow. I crossed to her, touching her wrist and offering a gentle smile. It was easy to smile when it came to Audrey. Even if she were wandering into a den of vipers.

Shocked whispers and stilted horror blanketed the room. We should have gone with another gown—any gown. Not because she didn't look beautiful, but because Alice Devereaux would make this as painful as possible.

Above the excited gossip, I cleared my throat. "Shall we?" I forced a brilliant smile onto my lips. None of them heard me, instead focusing on whispering behind their hands and shooting suspicious glances at Audrey. My eyes fluttered shut, and I took a deep breath.

This was for Audrey. And *only* Audrey.

I clapped my hands together. "Ladies!" Slowly, the chatter stopped. With a quick squeeze of my hand around my friend's wrist, I stepped forward. "Thank you all so much for coming today. Audrey and I are ecstatic to be hosting." A scowl crossed Alice's face. I fought against rolling my eyes. "Please, help yourselves to this lovely spread."

I didn't have to tell them twice. While society ladies pretended to worry about their figures, nearly every single one of them moved to the refreshments.

Alice Devereaux remained seated, arms crossed over her chest as she glared at Audrey.

"Savannah—"

The panic in her voice made my hackles rise. "This is fine," I whispered. "You're going to do wonderfully." I offered her a quiet smile, but she didn't buy it.

Instead of speaking, I moved about the room, making small talk about shoes or dresses. Audrey remained on the edge until I dragged her into a conversation about horses with one of the other ladies. Though she hadn't been allowed out to ride often, my best friend knew more about horses than anyone I'd ever met.

A sprinkle of relief coursed through me. At least she'd managed to find one friend amongst this bunch.

Eventually, I settled with a cup of tea and a plate of sweets. Though I should be mingling on Audrey's behalf, the purpose that drove me through preparations went out of me. My shoulders drooped as I poured cream into my tea. The temptation to retreat to my room and take a well-earned nap weighed heavily.

Unfortunately, I wouldn't have the chance today.

Once brunch ended, I had to oversee the clean-up. The very best I could hope for was the rest of this event to go without a hitch. Tonight, I'd sleep like a rock. At least, I hoped.

"Oh my *God*, I am *so* sorry!" The high-pitched voice echoed through the room above shocked gasps.

My gaze darted toward the refreshment table, where a dark stain bled into the front of Audrey's gown. Beside her, Alice Devereaux's false horror made my heart clench in my chest. The glass in her hand held the remnants of orange juice—probably from the mimosas.

Jesus Christ.

Audrey's lips pulled tight in a fake smile. "It's okay, Alice," she said. "Excuse me."

She turned from the room before I could get my feet beneath me. I blew out a long breath, mentally steeling myself for whatever would be waiting for me when I found her. I sipped hot tea as chatter started up again.

"I didn't know Mr. Lee even *had* a daughter until I got this invitation," one of the women said.

"Well, no one knew she existed before her father locked down the square a few years ago. Before that, there weren't any guards or searches or anything," another said, as though she were an expert on the topic.

"Why do you think I even came to this thing?" Alice asked, the malicious glint in her eye unsettling me. "It's no secret she's a recluse. I mean, what was she even talking to you about, Sarah?" She fixed her malicious stare on the woman who'd discussed horses with Audrey.

A flush rose into the woman's cheeks. She shrugged. "I mean, she could barely hold an intelligent conversation. Kept prattling on about God knows what."

"You don't know?" Alice asked, her eyes flickering back and forth. "Lucas Rutherford is here from Manhattan Island. Apparently, he's head over heels. He must not know about *Insane Audrey*."

Cruel laughter broke out. My fingers tightened around the teacup, knuckles blanching. A figure hovered near the doorway. *Montana.* I rolled my eyes, rising from my spot but keeping an ear on the conversation behind me.

"You can have your hour later." I glared at the man as he stalked off.

"Insane Audrey?" one of the younger women asked.

Montana's attention piqued. He turned back toward the door, but I stopped him with another glare. I crossed my arms over my chest, waiting until he disappeared around a corner before turning back.

"She's been locked up in this house for *years*. I can't believe you haven't heard the rumors." Alice fanned herself as she carried a fresh drink. "Staff members have whispered about her violent fits, and doctors come and go all the time." She twirled her finger near her temple.

"I heard she ran away from her father, got knocked up, and when he found her, her lover was shot and killed." My brows furrowed. They knew *nothing*.

Then again . . . neither did I.

I would never speculate, but the truth was, I knew nothing about Audrey from before. There were times I wondered about her past life, like when her accent slipped and she forgot her *gs* on certain words. Or when she got so happy when it rained the first time. She'd forced me to escort her down to the courtyard to feel the water on her skin.

"He dragged her back to New Orleans, and she went mad from the grief," the woman finished.

"That's so sad."

"Don't feel sorry for her," Alice snapped. "She's a menace. I heard she killed the baby in a fit of madness and *that* is why her father keeps her locked up. She's dangerous."

Movement from the doorway captured my attention. Audrey had returned in a fresh gown. Though I didn't have time to worry about what she wore. The color drained from her cheeks as she stared, gaping at the women as they crowded around Alice and her gossip.

"Audrey." I launched from the chair and in her direction. My friend shook her head and wheeled around. I barely managed to touch her arm before she rounded on me, unshed, angry tears brimming in her eyes.

"Get rid of them," she said to me in a harsh whisper. The anger flared anew. I recognized that glint in her eyes. She was close to losing herself.

"Audrey—"

She shook her head violently at me.

"Please, let me—"

"There's *nothing* you can do to fix this, Savannah. Stop trying." Her gaze darted to the room behind me, and she sprinted away.

Fires everywhere. And I had the only pail of water.

The women didn't even have the decency to look ashamed. I clenched my hands until my nails bit into my palms. These women didn't know Audrey, didn't even want to try. As much as I wanted to defend her, I saw in the defiant glint in Alice Devereaux's eyes that it didn't matter. It never would. She'd made up her mind about Audrey long ago.

"Thank you, ladies, for coming, but that will conclude brunch."

A couple of the women looked at me in protest, but I lifted my eyebrows in challenge. If they wanted to argue, I could argue. It wouldn't go well with Mr. Lee, but I'd do it. For Audrey.

"If this is what you call a brunch, I'd hate to see how the Lees hold a dinner," Alice said beneath her breath as she strolled past. I watched as they receded down the hall. The butler who'd announced Audrey earlier appeared at my side.

"Make sure they leave," I said. "I have to see to Audrey."

"Miss Savannah—" a new male voice said.

Jesus Christ, what was the deal with these men today? I pinched the bridge of my nose, slowly turning to face Lucas Rutherford.

"Is Miss Audrey alright? I saw her running up the stairs."

I forced a smile. "She's fine. I'll let her know you asked after her."

Without waiting for a response, I darted for the back staircase. It was the quickest way. I took the stairs two at a time, not even bothering to apologize to the staff members I crashed into at the top. They cursed me as I sprinted down the long corridor.

Audrey's door was already open when I reached it. Her chamber was eerily silent. The bed was cleanly made, the sheets tucked in perfectly, as they often were. The mess of cosmetics on her vanity was in its usual disarray, but everything else was perfectly put together.

"Audrey?"

A crash sounded through the open door of the bathroom. It sounded farther off, though. I hurried through and yanked open the one to my room.

Whereas Audrey's space had been perfectly put together, mine looked like a hurricane had blown through. The sheets were balled in the center of my slightly skewed mattress. Oil dripped from my bedside table, the lamp in fractured pieces on the floor. The drawers of the side table were open, revealing absolutely nothing inside.

Clothes were strewn about the room. I found her tossing boxes and shoes and anything she could get out of my wardrobe.

"Audrey?"

My friend wheeled around. The kohl I'd lined her eyes with trailed down her tear-stained cheeks. Her red-rimmed eyes were wild as she fixed them on me. Her chest heaved and her hands trembled. When she noticed my attention on them, she clasped them together.

"Where is it?!"

I flinched at the bite in her voice.

It had been a long time since the last fit. Audrey had recovered so well from the glowroot. With the help of bourbon and a few trusted doctors, we weaned her off in a matter of weeks. But when the cravings flared up, even years later, I didn't recognize her.

An echo of my past floated at the edge of my memory, but I shook it away. I couldn't get lost right now.

"I know you keep some on hand," Audrey said, chest heaving. "Just in case you have to . . . to dose me again." She fixed me with wide eyes; my heart clenched painfully. "I *need* it."

"Audrey, I—"

Clearly seeing my refusal, her expression fell, tears spilling over anew. *"Please."*

Rooted to the spot, I swallowed around the lump in my throat. I'd promised her father after the last time that I wouldn't give in to her addiction again. It was hard, knowing the troubles she'd been through. I wanted to help. I wanted to take away the grief in her eyes, aid her through this.

Mr. Lee wouldn't like it if I gave in.

"I—I can't."

Grief and desperation shifted to rage then. My jaw clenched and my eyes slammed shut as Audrey yanked open my bedroom door. It slammed against the wall, and I flinched. For a moment, I was six years old, hiding beneath our shared bed at the brothel.

"Savannah!"

Even years later, I heard the anger and desperation in her voice as clearly as if she stood before me.

I shook the memory away, somehow gathering my courage and striding from the room. I followed Audrey's stomping footsteps down the stairs and through the front house. As she darted across the courtyard, more than one staff member paused, eyes widening at the frazzled young woman.

Including William Ellis and Montana. I avoided them as I rushed toward the kitchen, but it was hard to ignore the flash of concern and recognition on Will's face. I felt his presence like a rolling wave as I shoved open the door to the kitchen.

"Now Miss Audrey—!" Etty's stern expression snapped tension into my back.

My friend stood on her tiptoes, flinging open the nearest cabinet. She shoved dishes to one side, running her fingers along the shelf in search of a vial.

"Audrey, please—" Before I could finish my sentence, she slammed the cabinet door and moved to the next. Emotion stuck thick in my throat as I watched her desperate, shaking hands. Etty ushered the kitchen staff out the exits, sparing a pitying glance in my direction.

"What happened." Will's voice was low in my ear as his warmth brushed against my skin.

"Society cunts," I ground out between my teeth.

Audrey opened the cabinet nearest the door. Glass clinked together as she reached between the bottles Etty kept there. Her fingers wrapped around the neck of one. Blue eyes flashed across the label before she thunked it down on the cabinet. She repeated the motion half a dozen times.

"I know you keep it in the house," she said, the words shaky.

"I know you have it, Savannah." My mother advanced on me across the small room furnished with a single bed and a rickety table with two spindly chairs. Her brown eyes were so dark they appeared black, like she was possessed.

Truthfully, she was. By glowroot.

Blue-tinged fingertips twisted the front of my smock dress. She yanked me from my hiding spot beneath the table. My head banged against the lip. I fought back the cry at my lips.

"Mama!"

"Where did you put it?" Her liquor-stained breath washed across my skin. A hot flush crept up my neck and into my cheeks as I stared into the eyes of a stranger.

"Nowhere!"

"You're lying!" She released me. My knees gave out, and I crumpled into a heap. Mama moved to the bed, ripping the threadbare comforter and searching its lining. I'd stopped hiding her stash after she found it last month. After throwing the blanket to the floor, she yanked up the thin sheet, desperate as she ran her fingers across the mattress.

"Mama, please." My bottom lip quivered as I climbed to my feet.

But she couldn't hear me, lost to the throes of glowroot. Horror froze me as my mother yanked the thin mattress from its frame, tossing it away as though it weighed nothing. She wheeled around and advanced on me, gripping my arm hard. She turned, dragging me behind her. I begged and pleaded with her as she pulled me across the small room, but she heard none of it.

"Have a client," she mumbled as she ripped open the closet door.

"No! Please!" I dug in my heels, but it did nothing. She shoved me inside and slammed the door, plunging the world into darkness. I pounded against the door, tears streaming down my cheeks. How long would I be locked in this time? A few hours? A few days?

"Savannah." Will's rumbling voice brought me back. I wasn't in St. Louis anymore. Hadn't been for a very long time.

Audrey sat against the cabinets, arms around her knees as she rocked, tears spilling across her skin as she whimpered.

I met Will's gaze, and an understanding passed between us. This wasn't the first time. I doubted it would be the last. He brushed a hand across my forearm before approaching Audrey as if advancing on a spooked horse.

"Audrey," he said gently.

Montana moved into my line of vision. My brows furrowed. Why the hell was *he* here?

As Will lowered to a knee, I crossed the room in broad strides. "Out," I ordered. Montana's blue eyes flashed at me, something more than worry in his eyes.

"I'm not going anywhere."

"Yes," I said. "You are." I didn't care that he was easily twice my size. I didn't care that he was some famed fighter. I wouldn't let him—or anyone else—see Audrey like this. I shoved against his shoulder, but he stood firm. My eyes hardened at him. "All it will take is *one* word from me to Mr. Lee and you're fired. Try me."

Montana regarded me, anger filling his features. His gaze flickered to Audrey. Will's voice, soothing and sweet, rumbled behind me.

"Get out."

A muscle twitched in his jaw, but he turned, allowing me to shepherd him to the door.

I felt like I had that first night. When Audrey'd finally settled into the glow-root haze, all of the energy sapped out of me. But I couldn't rest. Not yet.

Without words, I moved to the bottles dotting the counter. Once I found the bourbon, I grabbed a teacup and poured a measure. I walked to Audrey and Will with slow steps and knelt beside my friend.

"Here." I offered the teacup.

Red-rimmed blue eyes met mine. "But—"

I reached over, smoothing her hair. "You can get through this," I said gently. "You're stronger than the drug."

Words I wished I'd said to my mother. But I was ten the last time I'd seen her. I was ten, and I didn't understand then what I did now.

Reluctantly, I helped Audrey lift the cup to her lips. She swallowed the bourbon, slurping unattractively. Not that it mattered. Will and I had seen her in worse shape than this before.

I reached to refill the cup, but she stuck her arm out and snatched the bottle. I settled back on my knees, releasing a gentle sigh. I could give her that much, at least.

Will's gaze was on me. I felt it, familiar and gentle, as I always did in moments like this. When I dared to look at him, the stormy sea of memories and anxiety eased. Maybe this was why I wasn't afraid of him. Because I'd seen him *before*. Before Lee had turned him into what he was now.

Then again, maybe my demons scared me far more than Will Ellis ever could.

CHAPTER THIRTEEN

JESSE

M Y FEET WERE GOING to wear holes into Lee's fancy hardwood floor. Two hours had passed since Will carried Audrey past me, through the courtyard, and to the front house. Savannah paid me no attention. Instead, they moved in silent understanding, as though this wasn't the first time they'd done this.

Gone was the animosity in Savannah's eyes as she led the way upstairs. She barely noticed my presence as I trailed behind them.

I didn't know what the hell I'd witnessed in that kitchen. I had a million questions. What would I write to The Kid about this?

Hey, Kid. Bonnie's a glowroot addict. Fun times. Maybe you could give me a tip or two on how to win her back?

I swore beneath my breath, boots echoing against the hardwood.

The doorknob to Audrey's room rattled, and I wheeled toward it, hoping to see her like I had in the library. Kindness, compassion, and a flare of the woman I once knew.

Will walked out, snapping the door shut as he put his hat back on. When his eyes found mine, his grim expression only deepened.

"How is she?"

He walked past, letting out a breath. With long strides, I caught up with him.

"She's resting." He didn't elaborate. Instead, he lit a cigarette.

"How often does this happen?" I forced back the bitter edge in my tone. "How long was she on that stuff? And why would anyone purposefully dose someone with it?"

Will straightened his shoulders, fixing me with exhausted eyes. "Jesse—"

"I should talk to Savannah about this—" I turned, taking only two steps in the direction we'd come from before my friend's ironclad grip tightened around my arm.

"Don't," he warned.

"Why not? She's her companion. She could answer my questions."

"Listen to me, okay? You don't want to get on Savvy's bad side. I promise."

My mind flashed to the kitchen, when the younger woman had threatened to get me fired. I'd been more annoyed than anything.

"Maybe we should tell her," I said suddenly. "We tell her so she can understand why I'm here—"

Will shook his head, silencing my words. "We can't bring her in on this."

"Why the fuck not?" My brows furrowed as anger flared anew in my chest.

"Because I'm not putting her in danger."

"Danger? What danger?" As my friend loosed a long, smoke-filled breath, my patience grew even thinner. "I can help her. You know I can."

"I know," Will said. "But we're not involving Savvy. That's final." A flash of darkness passed across his face.

That seemed very un-Will-like. He wanted to get Bonnie back as badly as I did. Why wouldn't he go for something that might help us? I opened my mouth to protest, like a petulant child, but he fixed me with a hard glare.

"Get some sleep. It's been a long afternoon." He descended the staircase. I followed, argument after argument ruminating in my mind. He turned toward the front door of the manor, yanking it open.

"Where are you going?"

"Out." He disappeared into the night beyond.

What the fuck was I supposed to do? My gaze darted to the top of the stairs. The temptation to ignore everything Will had said tugged at me. What would he do if I *did* tell Savannah the truth?

The shiver that went down my spine told me I didn't want to find out.

Instead, I marched through the front house and to the back, eventually to my room. I picked up the sketchpad from the table next to the single bed and sat in the rickety chair. With a pencil in hand, I'd intended on sketching, but my mind went back to Audrey, hurriedly rifling through the cabinets, begging for a fix.

Kid, I wrote instead. *I'm in over my head. I don't know what to do. Before, we had time. We had space. Every single day feels like we're fighting against Sixgun and his men again, and I always lose.*

I thought back to the library, to the way she'd touched my cheek, to how that gentle caress set my skin on fire and reminded me that I could feel.

I'm still trying. I'll write again when I have more to tell you. -J

After securing it in an envelope, I made my way to the kitchen.

Etty leaned against the counter, nursing a mug in one hand. Her eyes were closed as she hummed along to some tune only she could hear.

"Etty?"

Her warm brown eyes flickered open. A lazy smile crossed her mouth. "Hey, Montana. Need somethin'?" With a nod, I handed over the letter. "Lord, you sure do like writing letters. Who is it? Some lover you left in another city?"

I couldn't help the smile that crossed my lips. The woman wouldn't believe me if I told her. "Not exactly." With a brief nod of thanks, I turned, intending to climb the stairs and put the day behind me.

Only, an image of Bonnie's face passed through my mind. *Bonnie*, not Audrey. In the early hours of the morning she'd been taken from me, when I'd sketched her stretched out across the bed beside me. My heart clenched in my chest. I missed her. I missed her and she was in this very house. We'd spent hours together, yet she was still a stranger.

I'd look in on her once. Just to check.

My feet led me toward the front house. I shoved my hands into my pockets, glancing across the courtyard to gain my bearings. Without Will here, I felt out of my element. I hadn't spent much time getting to know any of the other staff members, I'd been so focused on Bonnie.

"Montana?"

I stilled at the male voice. I'd barely entered the front house, yet there was Rutherford, a glass in hand. He hovered near the entry to the parlor.

"Mr. Rutherford." I gave a curt nod and headed toward the front staircase.

"Call me Luke. Have a drink with me."

My steps faltered. Much as I didn't like what I knew about him, that Mr. Lee was intent on a match with Audrey, I didn't think I could get away with blowing him off. I'd already angered one person with influence today. I couldn't really afford another enemy.

Lucas tipped his head into the parlor and disappeared inside. I steeled myself, letting out a long breath, and headed inside.

The remnants of Audrey's brunch lingered. The tablecloths remained, with most of the dishes still untouched. The pastries had been picked apart, and the giant canister that had been full earlier today was empty.

"What's your poison, Montana?" Lucas asked. He stood before a large credenza, an array of bottles spread in front of him.

"Whiskey."

"Good man." He lifted a bottle and poured a glass.

If he wasn't out to get my woman, I could see him as more than competition.

"I received word yesterday that Jersey is in for the match," Lucas said as he settled down onto a thick, plush couch shoved beneath the wide windows. I made a sound of half interest as I sipped the whiskey. The burn reminded me that he and I weren't friends. No matter how amiable he seemed. "You know, I saw you fight in Louisville a year or so ago."

I tried to remember Louisville. In truth, most of my matches blurred together, faded into memory.

"I heard the Colonel nearly lost an eye after you were done with him." There was a measure of respect in his voice.

The Colonel was a moniker like my own. Every good fighter had one. In truth, I couldn't give a shit less about the damage I left behind. All of it led me to Bonnie.

"I did what they paid me to do." I drained the rest of my glass.

Some of the rosiness in the man's cheeks dimmed. He narrowed his eyes. I felt the weight of his scrutiny. He wasn't buying my half-hearted attempt at humoring him. Without a word, he took the glass from my hand and moved across the room to refill it.

"What about the women?" he asked.

"What about them?"

A lazy grin crossed his face as he moved back to the couch and handed me the glass. "C'mon, Montana. Don't be coy. You've left dozens of broken hearts across the country."

My brows lifted at his words. "Not really."

Lucas settled beside me. "I find that difficult to believe. Women *have* to be fawning all over you."

Hands reaching out to me. Women throwing themselves in my space. More than one copping an unwanted feel.

"Just because they fawn doesn't mean I do." I shrugged.

"You *do* like women, don't you?"

I barked out a laugh. "Of course."

Mistaking my laugh for camaraderie, Lucas settled back against the couch. "So what is it? Why doesn't the biggest fighter in the circuit take advantage of his popularity?"

"Why do you care so much about the women I've fucked?"

"Just making conversation," Lucas said, some of his boyish swagger faltering beneath my disinterest. We sat in jilted silence before he turned to me once more. "What do you think of Audrey?"

A jolt of awareness went through me. I sat in the house of the man who most likely murdered my parents, drinking with someone out to get my woman. I sat straighter, forcing a shrug.

"What about her? She's the boss's daughter." I averted my gaze, sipping at my drink to keep from punching him.

"Right, but you know what happened earlier," he remarked casually, as though we were talking about horses or the price of liquor. "Lee wants to broker a match between us." My knuckles tightened around the glass. "If you were in my shoes, what would you do?"

The skin of my neck heated. What would I do in his shoes? I'd knock myself out, because I had no chance with Bonnie. Then again, that was probably the alcohol talking.

He's rich, not bad looking, and intelligent. He also doesn't spook easily, which I think will intrigue her.

Will's words from that first night banged around in my mind. Rutherford had some advantages. But he also had weaknesses. One of which was not knowing Bonnie. I adopted an easy smile, planting one of my ankles over my knee as I settled back into the couch.

I knew Bonnie. And Bonnie would never go for some pompous asshole flaunting himself in front of her.

"You should go for it." I hated every single word. "I mean, so what if she's a little crazy? It's not her mind you want. You know what I mean?"

For a moment, I wondered if I'd said the wrong thing. Lucas stared at me, wide-eyed, then relaxed, the glaze of alcohol in his eyes.

"It's settled then." He clapped a hand on my shoulder. I tensed against the brisk contact. "Montana, I'm going to show you how to live."

My brows lifted.

"You should come out with me and the guys sometime. I can introduce you to some of the finest women New Orleans has to offer." His words slurred at the edges.

With a shake of my head, I said, "I lost the woman I loved, Luke. I'm not ready to move on yet." I drained my glass and set it down on the short coffee table in front of me. "Thanks for the invite, though."

Rutherford protested as I rose to my feet, but I couldn't spend another minute with him. I couldn't pretend to be chummy with the man who viewed the woman I loved as little more than a conquest. But what I could do was sabotage any chance he had at winning her affection.

I just had to make her fall in love with me first.

CHAPTER FOURTEEN

AUDREY

I TILTED MY CHIN, eyes sliding over to peer at Montana in my periphery. His mountainous frame was strung tight and focused. His battered, calloused hands held the charcoal delicately, flicking the tip across the page faster than seemed possible. Talented hands. Noted.

"You moved again." Amusement hid in his words. Snapping my face back into profile with a sigh, I lowered my eyes to the book in my hands.

"I didn't think you were the type to torture innocent women." He'd posed me in a reading position on my window seat as the afternoon light spilled through the leaves of the crepe myrtle tree outside.

"You could *actually* read the book." He stifled a chuckle. I groaned in torment. Not being able to see him was worse than I'd imagined it would be. Since our last meeting, he was all I thought about. All I saw when I closed my eyes. I'd been afraid that after my relapse, he would cancel our obligatory hour, but when no word came, I met him like usual.

Instead of any awkwardness about the scene I'd made or stilted explanations for the strange way we'd left things the last time, he'd asked me to sit and, with two fingers, tilted my chin a certain way before sitting in creative silence. It wasn't necessarily uncomfortable; this was better than the mindless staring from before. Purposeful.

It was not knowing what he thought of me that grated against some raw nerve. I shouldn't care. I *couldn't* care about his opinion. It didn't change the fact that I did. Enough that after however long it'd been, sitting here quietly, I was finally losing the last shred of sanity I'd retained.

"At this rate all I'll be drawing is that scowl on your face." He was teasing me. Frustration broke within me, and I threw the book across the room at him heavily. It thunked his shoulder and fell to the ground in a heap of aged pages. That infuriating grin of his curled on his mouth, but horror had me scrambling up from my seat.

"Wait, I'm not done!"

I only had eyes for the poor book. It was one of my favorites, a book of poems that was old enough that I'd probably damaged it beyond repair.

"Oh, shove it." I crossed to pick up the small, tattered thing. It looked like a bird with a broken wing, the spine perilously separated from the binding, pages rumpled. I smoothed the paper as well as I could, pressing them back into place carefully.

He stood, peering over my shoulder and trying to read the faded title on the cover. *Great.* Just what I needed. For him to make fun of my obsession with poetry. Call it a useless, girlish whim as my father did. Closing the cover and pressing it to my chest, I rocked back on my heels and looked up at him from my spot on the ground.

Fuck.

He was so impossibly tall I had to tip my head back pretty far to meet his gaze. My throat bobbed, and I swallowed down the reckless urge to say something inappropriate as the erotic nature of our positions thudded into me. Like a spark igniting a blaze, desire flushed across my skin. He noticed it, too, eyes fixated on my mouth, probably imagining it wrapped around his cock.

"What did the poor book ever do to you?" His voice was strained as I rose to my knees and stood shakily. A poor attempt at glossing over the ripple of awareness threading the air between us. I felt each individual beat of my heart, my pulse thudding in my ears and throbbing between my thighs. I wanted to taste his skin, wanted to see him undone because of me, all of that carefully leashed impulse freed beneath my body.

"Nothing." I cleared my throat of the husky rasp that'd crept in. "I forgot this was the one I was holding."

"Are you going to make me ask?"

I arched an imperious eyebrow in his direction, my expression all derision.

"Fine. What book is it?"

"Nothin' important." My cheeks flushed hotter, and I stumbled over my words. Quicker than I thought possible, he snatched it from my grasp, and I lurched toward him in a foolish attempt to retrieve it. "Give it back!"

"I want to know what has the woman who blatantly propositioned me blushing like a virgin." He held the book above his head. *Fucking fuck.* Why was I so goddamned short? Even though it was impossible to reach, I raised on tiptoes and let my weight rest full on the hard planes of his chest as I stretched as far up as I could go. A half-foot of space made it clear that there was no retrieving the aged tome unless Montana chose to give it back.

"Fine!" I huffed, dropping onto the flats of my feet. "But if you make fun of me, I'm not coming back."

He blinked down at me slowly, shoulders stiffening. Instead of opening the book, he offered it to me without a second glance. "I would never make fun of you."

Such a simple statement, but it rang with earnest truth I realized was typical of him. Honesty was hard to come by, and each time he showed me these simple kindnesses, I was left feeling childish. And touched. I gripped the worn cover, pulling it gently from his grasp.

"So you do know about the other day." I dropped my eyes to the book. "You didn't say anything, so I wasn't sure if . . ."

I trailed off, shame choking the words from my lungs. It'd been bad this time. The need for numbness pounded through every cell in my body. Until desperation and grief overwhelmed my common sense. Then I'd given in and made a spectacle of myself, proving all those society bitches right.

"I was there."

Mortification filled me, hollowing out my chest and heating my eyes. I raised my hands to my face, half covering it with the book.

"Oh god," I groaned, horrified.

"Hey." His voice was soft. Softer than I'd ever heard it. Then his hands were on mine, pulling them gently from my face. My eyes fixed firmly on the floor, counting each slat between the wood planks. With his calloused hands, he tipped my chin up until I fell into the perilous blue of his eyes and the kindness wavering within them. "You don't have anything to be ashamed of."

A cynical bark of laughter bubbled from between my lips. Shame felt like my second skin. Images from the other day flitted through my mind. Slamming open the cabinets and running trembling fingers along the insides, tossing Savannah's belongings onto the floor without a thought, crumpling into a pile on the kitchen floor and sucking on the bourbon bottle like a lifeline. *Nothing to be ashamed of?*

"You're a bad liar," I spat, more in self-loathing than anything else. His thumb brushed the corner of my mouth, and a shaky inhalation leeched the animosity from between us. "Why aren't you steering clear of me? After all that, most men would be halfway out of town."

"I'm not most men." His eyes fell to my mouth as his thumb traced my bottom lip. *No, he certainly isn't.* The space between us, scant as it was, seemed electrified. His thumb passed over my mouth again, higher, tracing the seam. Instinctually, I parted my lips, and he pressed the digit between them until the pad of his thumb rested tremulously on my tongue.

The taste of his skin sang to my soul. Faintly I detected the charcoal dust from his sketching, but beneath that was hot flesh, slightly salty but an echo of his scent. *Leather, desert dust, and something warm. Something uniquely him.*

Before he could leash his control again, I closed my mouth around him, letting him feel the flexion of my lips as I sucked slightly. Was he remembering me on my knees before? Imagining what I had been as I stared up at his lust-heavy eyes? A deep rumble of pleasure sounded from the back of his throat. It urged me on, my heart pounding furiously as I flicked my tongue against the pad of his thumb. My teeth scraped over his knuckle as I pressed forward and took the rest of his finger deep. Staring up at him through the fringe of my lashes, I shivered at the carnal hunger fixated on his face.

How long had it been since he'd been with a woman? He'd said *years* when I asked before, but how many? I wanted to unravel him. As if he heard my thoughts, he pulled his hand back from my mouth, slipping his finger from between my lips, shining wet. With a ragged breath he cleared his throat, blue eyes shuttering as he hid the stark passion beneath that mask of civility once more.

"So what's the book about?" His voice was deep and gravelly in a way that had me stifling a grin.

"Sex."

His eyes widened. I bit my bottom lip hard to stop the wicked grin from spreading across my face.

"And love. Death. Loneliness. It's a book of poetry."

"Poetry?" A note of surprise crept into his voice. I sighed wearily, moving around him to the window seat.

"I know." I held up a hand to still whatever chastisement was certainly poised on his lips. "It's a useless, girlish whim. A waste of my time."

"I wasn't going to say that." He ran a hand through the long hair slicked back from his face, causing a stray piece to stick out endearingly.

"No?"

"No, I like poetry."

I laughed. I laughed until mirthful tears gathered in the corners of my eyes. A bare-fist brawler with a penchant for art and poetry? Had I *actually* lost the remaining shreds of my sanity?

"It's not that funny." He crossed his arms defensively over his chest and narrowed his eyes. Wiping at the corners of my own eyes, I stared up at his serious expression.

"You want to hear my favorite poem?"

He nodded slowly like he was trying to figure me out. Instead of cracking open the book, I faced him full-on, setting it gently to the side.

"'I want you to know one thing,'" I said, pressing my thighs together on the seat.

"'You know how this is: if I look at the crystal moon,'" I recited breathlessly, squirming beneath the intensity of his gaze.

"'At the red branch of the slow autumn at my window.'" I stood again, watching his fists clenching at his sides with my nearness.

"'If I touch near the fire,'" I whispered, hot breaths of poetry falling on his skin.

"'The impalpable ash or the wrinkled body of the log, everything carries me to *you.*'"

He shivered, gooseflesh rising on his skin.

"'As if everything that exists, aromas, light, metals, were little boats that sail towards those isles of yours that *wait for me.*'"

He turned his face, jaw tight with the same furious want that ran through my blood. I wanted to wake him up the way he'd woken me. Wanted his skin to buzz with my nearness and see the weakening of that steely restraint. His Adam's apple bobbed with his deep swallow. I still tasted him on my tongue.

"It's called 'If You Forget Me,'" I said softly. His eyes snapped to mine, searching my face for something. "What's yours?"

"I can show you." Those talented fingers lifted to the buttons on his shirt. With a dextrous flick, the first one popped open. My breath hitched, and I realized the teasing game I'd started had been turned around on me. Unable to look away, with each button, a shock of pleasure coursed down my spine. Until I was nearly a puddle of quivering flesh on the ground at his feet. He pulled the sides of his shirt open until the hard planes and dips of muscle were exposed, black lines of ink painting parts of his body.

"'Hope is the thing with feathers.'" He stepped forward to close the distance between us. "'That perches in the soul.'" My fingers were on his ribs, tracing hot inked flesh even as my eyes stayed trained on his. "'And sings the tune without the words—'"

Naked legs tangled together in a mess of sheets. A tiny yellow flower pressed between the pages of a small book. A heavy arm around my shoulders, tucked safely in the cage of strong arms. Poetry spoken sweet in my ear, breath catching on the tiny hairs near the base of my neck and my temples.

I gasped, tears flooding my eyes as panic trilled like a musical note inside me. "'And never stops,'" I said incredulously, eyes unfocused as I tried to bring the images back to the forefront of my mind. Trying to memorize each detail in case I couldn't summon them again. My chin tipped up, his eyes filled with incredulity, fixing on the image of his face.

"'At all.'"

"You've . . . read that one?" His chest heaved. I shook my head. I hadn't. I'd never heard the poem before today. Yet, I'd finished it. As if it were a bigger part of me than I realized. His hands tangled in my hair, thumbs brushing against my skin.

"Did you remember something?" The blue in his eyes grew bright with desperation. "Audrey, did you remember—"

"I—" But I couldn't finish the thought. Was it a memory? It *felt* like a memory. My body still felt the weight of that man's arm around my shoulders. "I—"

"Audrey, your hour's *been* up and—" Savannah's voice rang from the doorway behind Montana's shoulder, and when I turned to look at her, Savannah blushed furiously and averted her eyes. Blinking away my confusion, I realized what it must've looked like with Montana embracing me and only half-dressed.

"Jesus Christ!"

Montana dropped his hands and took a few bracing steps away, allowing me enough space to clear my thoughts. He began buttoning his shirt, brows knitting together.

"Always getting fucking interrupted," he muttered beneath his breath, but loudly enough that I still heard him. "I haven't missed *that.*"

"It's fine. It wasn't what it looked like—"

"I should hope *not!*" Savannah's voice cracked like a whip through the room. My shoulders tensed at her tone. I *hated* being chastised like a child. I was a goddamned adult, and even if Montana and I *had* been in the middle of something, it was still my decision to make. "Your father would—"

"Be even more disappointed in me than he already is?" She glanced warily at Montana, who was buttoned up now, which was a pity. "I was looking at his tattoos. I'm thinking about getting one on my face; what do you think my father would have to say about that?"

"Nothing good."

I didn't have the strength to fight with my best friend. Sighing, I crossed the room and looped my arm with hers.

"Why were you looking for me?" I dropped the hostility from my voice. With another wary glance at Montana, her eyes slid back to me, and she offered me a conciliatory smile.

"You have an . . . *appointment.*"

No, I didn't. I opened my mouth to say so, but Savannah shook her head, the motion so slight Montana might not have noticed it. A warning not to let him know the truth.

"Alright, lead the way." I let her drag me across the room and away from Montana.

"Wait! We need to finish talking about—"

"Your hour is up, *Montana.*" Savannah glared him into silence with her resolve. I shrugged. She was impossible to argue with when she got like this. The almost-memory would have to stay our secret for now. Until I figured out what it meant, if my memories were returning or if this was my overactive imagination at work. Maybe it was a sign that I was losing touch with reality and I'd *actually* gone crazy.

I struggled to leave the image of Montana behind as she led me out of the room and we walked down the staircase and through the first floor. As we entered the parlor where the brunch had been held, my feet faltered beneath me.

"Savannah—" I warned, hesitating to go any further.

"Do you trust me?"

Swallowing heavily, I looked over at her. How many times had she pieced me back together? She'd never asked for anything in return. I nodded, letting her drag me forward and into the parlor that was set up with a long antique dining table bisecting the room. Along the table were bottles of varying shapes, with liquids in all kinds of colors. Honeyed, amber, clear, murky brown, even one tinged slightly blue-green. Two place settings were laid across from each other, complete with gold-edged teacups and embroidered linen napkins.

"What—"

"I heard your last society function ended a little abruptly, so I threw one in your honor," Lucas Rutherford said from across the table. Savannah's arm slipped from mine and she exited, shutting the door behind her.

Lucas was perfect. As always. Chestnut hair shining in the light, flopped carefully over his forehead in the approximation of casual niceness. His shirt was white and buttoned at the wrists, glinting with cufflinks, the neck starched carefully. But today he wore jeans, instead of his usual slacks. I smiled as I realized he was making an effort to be casual, misguided as it was.

"What is this?" I trailed my fingertips along the table as I walked closer. Stopping at the place setting, I squared myself and faced him.

"What they did was cruel." He rubbed his palms on his pants. "I thought this might cheer you up. Besides, my version of brunch will be more fun anyway, like when we played cards the other night."

I remembered the card game. Lucas had been reserved, strategic, intelligence flaring in the dark depths of his eyes. For the first few hands I'd done as women normally did and observed, at his side, like a silent cheerleader. Then, after a few rounds, he leaned in and asked my opinion. Quietly, I guided him through the games, winning hand after hand as I read the tells on his friends' inebriated faces. He'd been impressed, that much was clear. But once dinner was called, the spell broke, and we barely made eye contact the rest of the night, his attention stolen by his rowdy friends while I made quiet conversation with my father.

He grinned, and I wavered on my feet. This side of Lucas was *unexpected*. I'd resigned myself to the calculating man who wanted to broker a deal with my father and might get me in the process. I hadn't expected to find him a little irreverent, even if he dressed like a goddamned choir boy. I certainly hadn't expected kindness.

"What did you have in mind?" I pulled out the chair and sat gingerly. His smile broadened, and he crossed to me, popping the cork from a bottle and pouring a generous helping into the teacup in front of me.

"Well, for one, there's a ton of alcohol." He chuckled when I picked up the dainty china cup, pinky extended. "For another, I thought we could use the alcohol to talk."

"You don't need alcohol to talk to me," I said, tipping the cup and fighting back reminders of Savannah pressing a china glass into my trembling hands, filled with bourbon and her fragile hope that one day I wouldn't be broken anymore.

"I disagree." He poured a generous helping into his own glass. "You are *really* beautiful." Licking the sting of alcohol off my bottom lip, I dipped my head slightly, acknowledging the compliment without fumbling over my words like an idiot.

"Do I make you nervous?" I watched carefully as he considered my question.

"Yes," he admitted finally, though it seemed to cost him some of his pride. "For a few different reasons."

"Oh, I see." I swallowed the rest of the alcohol in the cup and held it out for more. In an overly polite gesture, he bowed his head and poured.

"You know your father is trying to set a match between us." He cleared his throat uncomfortably. I nodded. It wasn't a secret, after all. I mean, it was why his father sent *him* here to broker the deal in the first place.

"I'm aware."

He swirled the liquor in his glass before downing it and pouring himself another. He sighed wearily and leaned back against his chair, slumping. I think it was the most un-put-together I'd ever seen him.

"That doesn't bother you?" The glaze of alcohol crept into his dark eyes. I shrugged, wondering where this conversation was going. "See, the thing is that I was dead set on *not* getting entangled in an arranged marriage. Or letting my father be right about anything."

"Then don't." I felt the warmth and relaxation of the liquor warming up my muscles and loosening them, making me feel good. *Too* good.

"Then I met you."

I didn't feel so relaxed anymore.

"This whole arrangement should seem absurd. But I—" He cut himself off, swallowing another glass of alcohol before abandoning the teacup for the bottle. Sucking in a steadying breath, he faced me.

"The truth is, I find you fascinating. You don't act like any of the society women I've ever known. There's something *magnetic* about how you don't care about what other people think."

A lump rose in my throat. "Those women were saying what everyone thinks about me, Lucas," I said. "It won't change. People will treat me differently everywhere I go. Is that really the kind of thing you want?"

"Fuck them," he said, words a little looser than before. "There's nothing wrong with you, Audrey."

I didn't know how badly I needed to hear those words until they'd come from his mouth. Blinking back the emotion, I ground my teeth together.

"You think you can handle me?" I set the teacup on the table with deliberate carefulness.

"I'd certainly like to try." His eyes turned molten as they roved over me. I wasn't wearing anything special, just another sundress that breathed in the hot weather. My hair fell down my back in tangled waves.

"I'd like to mess up your hair," I said in return. He blinked, confused.

"W-what?"

"Your stupid, perfect, swoopy hair. I want to mess it up."

He swallowed nervously as I stood. With a wicked grin and a drunken giggle, I crawled on top of the antique table, the teacup crashing to the floor in a shatter of delicate pieces. When I was before him, his eyes were deep in the view down the front of my dress. Naked lust filled his expression, dark intentions and lascivious thoughts splayed clear across his face. No asking me for more than I could give. No talking in circles or hiding his desire for me. With the almost-memory thrumming in the back of my mind, the uncertainty of the day heavy on my shoulders, and the lingering taste of Montana's skin on my tongue, I needed to make a mistake. Any mistake. Needed to fall into oblivion.

Glowroot wasn't an option, but Lucas was.

I buried my fingers in his hair and watched as his eyes dragged from my breasts up to my face. He reached out to my hips, tugging me into his lap. I could feel him hard and thick against my thigh.

"They say I'm crazy, Lucas," I said, my lips inches from his own.

"We're all a little crazy." He gripped the back of my neck and kissed me softly. Too softly. I nipped at his lips with my teeth, parted his mouth, and let my tongue dip inside. But no matter how I pressed him, he wouldn't kiss me harder. Maybe he didn't know how. We were like that for a while, his hands traveling the curve of my waist, cupping my ass, feathering over my breasts.

It all left me wanting more. For him to sink his fingers into my flesh, drag my bottom lip through his teeth, to make me breathless and begging. Instead, by the time we were finished, my mouth wasn't even sore.

Could I marry a man who didn't make my heart pound like furious hoofbeats? Who touched me like I would break?

When a staff member finally came knocking to tell us it was time for dinner, I couldn't have been more grateful for the interruption. Lucas looked up at me, eyes glazed in passion and drink, like I was his goddamned salvation. He waved the maid away impatiently and cupped my jaw. His hand was soft, no rough calluses or knotted knuckles from hard work and violence. I could still taste

Montana on my tongue through the haze of alcohol and sloppy kissing. He was going to drive me to insanity.

"Audrey, I—"

"My father will be waiting for us," I said, avoiding whatever sappy shit was poised on the tip of his tongue. Sliding from his lap, I smoothed down my dress and hair. He adjusted the front of his pants and settled an arm around my waist, keeping me tight against his side as he escorted me into the dining room. Our place settings were on opposite sides of the table, but after he walked me to my chair, he claimed the seat next to me. He didn't seem to care about my father's quick, calculating gaze fixated on us or the staff members scrambling to change the place setting.

Everything had changed in the blink of an eye.

Yet, it was still the same. Lucas's arm slung around the back of my chair, and he talked over me, reducing me to his silent companion. He and my father spoke animatedly while I avoided Savannah's gaze. I cut my food into smaller and smaller pieces, pushed it around my plate, but I didn't eat.

All I could think about was the almost-memory from before, how safe and cherished I'd felt in those fractured moments, hazy around the edges. It was at that moment that I realized I wanted *more*. It was time for me to learn about my past.

It was time for me to try to remember.

Chapter Fifteen

WILL

"T HERE'S A STORM COMING."

Coming? Fuck, it felt like it'd been here since Jesse reappeared. I tried to be patient, to keep the irritation at Lee's summons from showing on my face. Stoically, I stood in front of him, at his beck and call like always. The devil's puppet, choking on the sea of innocent blood I'd spilled at his command.

He didn't wait for a response, probably because he knew there wasn't one coming. I'd learned not to say every foolish thing that passed through my head in his presence. It only gave him leverage. And he was *never* shy about exerting pressure to get what he wanted. Usually, through me.

"I've already delegated tasks to the staff to prepare the house and grounds, but I'll need you to oversee it."

Now *that* caught my attention. Lee was as anal-retentive as a person could be. He didn't delegate. Well . . . not the shit that kept his hands clean, anyway.

"I have to cross the river to help with fortifying the levee system and the river channel. I won't be back until after the storm passes."

Smoke curled from my mouth as I let out a long exhale. "Isn't that the mayor's job?" The nicotine calmed the nervousness coiling in my gut.

He barked out a laugh, sliding his eyes over to me in such a cynical way that it felt like a sliver of Bonnie peeked out from within him. A shiver raced up my spine at the thought. I didn't like remembering their relation, that the same blood ran through both of their veins. Though, I didn't really have any room to talk, considering my own infamous parentage. Evil men had fucked-up children, I guess.

Since Audrey's relapse and the rumors swirling around about her hot make-out session with Rutherford, I didn't have much hope left that we'd ever get Bonnie back. Not that I would say that to Jesse. He'd settled into a sort of calm in the days since he arrived, peace muting the desperate edge in his expression after every hour spent with Audrey. Only the edge was back now, and everyone in the house was talking about it. My life was beginning to look more and more like the *telenovellas* my mother told me stories about as a child.

"That man doesn't run this city; he sits on his ass and lines his pockets with my bribes. You know that. Don't pretend to be ignorant about how things work, Ellis." Lee gathered several papers and shoved them into a worn leather briefcase. "Feigned ignorance does you no favors."

I exhaled another sour puff of smoke, listening to the wind whistling and rattling the shutters over the window. Lee finished packing and faced me, palms on the desktop and dark eyes glinting with malevolent intention.

"There's something else." He ran a weary hand over his jaw. "We've had a few problems with some of the boats on the far bank." Zachary didn't look up from his ledger as he wrote in perfect, looping lines. "A few shipments have been interrupted, and I'll need to take care of it before I return."

I knew what he wasn't saying. *Jones* was interrupting his shipments, hedging into Zachary's stream of smuggled contraband and boat-loads of slaves. He'd been getting bolder over the last year. With the partnership with Rutherford looming and negotiations still happening, Zachary would want to squash any hint of a problem with his shipping industry before word got back to the man.

"It's been a few days since you last reported your findings about Rutherford," he said, not missing how I sat straighter in my chair. "I still don't have the leverage I need, Ellis."

"I know." I raked in a long drag from my cigarette before putting it out in the bottom of my glass. "I've exhausted my contacts, but the prick is careful. I can get proof of what he's doing, but . . ." I opened my hands and exhaled.

"You want me to authorize you to use force." His jaw worked as he considered. Standing straight, he glared down at me for a long time. His eyes tracked over my unshaved jaw and rumpled clothes, nose turning up in derision. I was pretty sure I smelled like horse shit too, after spending a night on the floor of the stall.

"Keep eyes on Rutherford while I'm gone. Give me a report when I get back, and we'll re-visit the conversation then."

I nodded, standing as the meeting ended. At least with Rutherford here, I hadn't been tasked with my usual jobs. Even the prospect of using force on some of the people he'd contacted while in town wasn't as dark as my normal tasks. Keeping an eye on the *pendejo* was much preferable to the alternative.

"Oh, and Ellis?"

I turned, shoulders tense with anticipation. Had I tempted fate with my relief?

"You did good work bringing me Montana. His last fight went well." He tossed a pouch onto his desk, the metal bits inside clinking together. He motioned to it with his hand. "Consider it a finder's fee."

As the weight of the money settled against my hand, I tried not to like the swell of pride settling into my blood at his validation. Disgust and contentment warred within me as I dipped my head and headed back to the room I shared with Jesse. I'd been avoiding him, but probably needed to check in after what the staff said happened between Rutherford and Audrey. An idea formed as I passed the money back and forth between my hands. It was enough to throw one hell of a party while Lee was gone, and I didn't like the idea of using it for myself. Not the way I'd earned it.

As I made my way down the hall, I noted staff locking the storm shutters over the windows, blocking out the scant gray light filtering through the cloud cover. Passing through the courtyard, guards tied down the iron furniture and pulled it beneath the breezeways. Hurricanes came every year, the storms raging for a few days against the city as if trying to reclaim it, to raze it to the ground like a small culling of their own.

New Orleans always won.

Laughter trilled, a voice I didn't recognize. Following the sound to the corner of the courtyard, I saw Seb and one of the freckled maids he was friendly with, heads close together as an easy grin passed between them and she laughed again. The sting of sorrow made it hard to breathe. When was the last time I'd seen him like that? Seb's smile was soft and luminous, reminding me of sweet words he'd whispered to me late at night before I kissed that same smile from his lips.

When he caught sight of me, he straightened, his easy smile falling swiftly from his face. His eyes caught on the bag of money still resting in my hand, and disappointment soured his expression. It hung thick in the air as shame churned in the pit of my stomach. Snippets of arguments we'd had over the years laced through my mind, creating a tapestry of us. The yearning pull to be close to someone, his kind insistence of a future we could have together, and his absolute disgust at the things I did to stay here. To be with Bonnie. To keep her safe.

Look at yourself! You're covered in blood. This is killing you, Will. You're being taken advantage of. You'll never amount to anything like this. Maybe this is all you're good for, since you can't seem to stop. You're just like your father, only you're too scared to admit it.

My gaze dropped to the cobblestones, unwilling to let my self-loathing strangle me today. Not with the prospect of a party, letting loose, without Lee and his demands hovering over me like dark storm clouds. For once, just for once, I wanted to stop thinking about what a piece of shit I was. I wanted to drink until I couldn't feel my face and dance with anything that moved. Until I was so far out of my body that I couldn't remember who the *Beast of the Bridge* was. Or the parts of myself I'd carved out to make room for him.

"Will." Seb's voice was soft behind me. Cautious. He'd crossed the distance between us, that too-familiar tinge of disappointment glinting in the dark depths of his eyes. My stomach twisted beneath that expression. The hollowness inside of me spread, until I could barely breathe. He reached out, resting his hand just above my thundering heart, before it fell and he looked around us. Another reaction I was responsible for. I'd never wanted to be public with our *arrangement*, thinking it would give him unrealistic expectations. I saw the longing in the set of his shoulders. I opened my mouth to explain, to mask this pain with another ill-timed joke, anything.

"Ellis!" Jesse barked from across the courtyard. The heavy moment shattered as my attention shifted to my friend, charging toward me like an avenging angel ready to mete out justice. When I focused on Seb, jealousy flashed in his eyes, flared his nostrils. I shook my head.

"It's not what you think—" I tried to explain, but before I could finish, he'd turned his back and disappeared. It was so easy for him to think the worst of me. Too easy.

Jesse reached me, eyes full of desperate fury. "*Why* would she kiss him?!" His voice was loud, too loud, with too many pairs of eyes and gossiping workers for this kind of meltdown. I shoved him in the shoulder until I managed to corral him in the direction of our shared room. As we crossed the threshold, I slammed the door behind us.

"Maybe because all you've been doing is reading fucking books and talking." My words were dark and angry. Angry at myself, at all the ways I failed the people I cherished. Jesse's spine straightened, the fury in his eyes disappearing like smoke on the wind. He studied me, but I didn't like the scrutiny. I crossed to the wash basin, tossing my hat off and splashing water over my face and neck.

"What did I interrupt?" He sat on the bed in the center of the room, where pillows piled in a line between the two sides we'd occupied. A sketchbook and a jar of charcoal sticks lined the table on his half. I sighed, a long-suffering sound as I dragged wet fingers through my hair, dampening the curls at the base of my neck.

"I'm not talking about Seb." I spared a glance at my friend, who couldn't seem to reconcile this version of me with the one he knew. I didn't blame him. "There's not enough alcohol here for me to even start."

"Look, I know I can be self-absorbed. Especially when it comes to Bonnie. But I'm here, and I'm not going anywhere. You can tell me anything," he said, his voice low and comforting in a way I'd never heard before. No. That wasn't entirely true. I sucked in a sharp breath as memories flooded me.

You'll never be alone. I won't ever let you be alone. Do you hear me?

I did. I heard Bonnie's voice so clearly that the hollowness devoured me. Until there was barely anything left. All the breath whooshed from my lungs at the reminder of the friend I lost, the one that might never come back. I leaned against the dresser and slid down it until I sat on the floor, my long legs crooked in the space between the bed and the dresser. A dark laugh bubbled up from my throat, catching on the edge of my seemingly endless self-loathing.

"You don't understand," I said. "You *can't.*"

Jesse looked ready to argue until I dragged my eyes up to his. Whatever torture he saw in my face forced him to clamp his mouth shut.

"I'm fucked up, Jesse. I mean, I never really had a chance, did I?" I opened my arms wide. His brows furrowed in confusion, but I barreled ahead.

"Look at who my father is," I said, the words hard. "You know about the shit he does to women. But do you have any idea the ways he broke me?" Jesse shook his head. I barreled forward, reckless and cruel. "*He tried to cut my fuckin' face off.* The only reason he didn't is because Bonnie wasn't waking up, and he needed me to keep her alive long enough to get here."

A long silence stretched between us. "They call him *Sixgun*, like they call you *Montana.* Some sort of messed-up respect that he gets for being a monster." I stared at the ceiling, willing the chasm of hopelessness that'd cracked open in my chest to stitch back together again.

"They call me the *Beast of the Bridge.* I'm his legacy. Made in his image. And if this were just about him, or the shit he did to me . . . that'd be one thing. But I—" I cut myself off abruptly as blade-like pain twisted deep in my chest. "I've done *things.* Things I'm not proud of. Things that make me *no better than him.* In fact, I might be worse."

I tucked my arms close but opened my palms as I finally brought my eyes back to Jesse's. He sat there, so still, so quiet, as if he were letting my words sink into his skin. A kind of tattoo. My pain became a part of him as much as it'd become part of me.

"Seb wants me to be better than I'm capable of. Whole. Happy. But that's just not in the cards for me. Then there's Savvy—"

"Savannah?" Jesse asked, eyebrows knitting together. As if the thought of us together was the most ridiculous thing in the world. Maybe it was. She was so goddamned beautiful. Inside and out. A real fuckin' lady, like a flower that bloomed through the cracked asphalt highways. An anomaly nowadays.

I nodded, sucking my bottom lip between my teeth as I thought over how to explain my unhealthy obsession with her. How there were moments when I felt myself coming apart at the seams until I saw her, with all her strict rules and routines, making order out of the chaos, and it made me feel like I'd been put back in order too. Just watching her juggling it all, keeping it together, had me believing that my life didn't have to fall apart. Or the kindness she showed Audrey, through the tragedy and heartache of the last few years, reminded me of my mother. And I'd tried so *hard* to forget my mother. To forget her goodness, and how my father carved it from her piece by bloody piece.

"Yeah," I breathed, sighing at the inevitability of the two of us. She deserved so much more than me. Because the truth was, there was so much I *couldn't* give her. Impossible. "I've held a torch for her longer than I want to admit to."

Jesse folded his fingers together, leaning his elbows on his knees as he studied my strained expression.

"So, you and Sebastian have dated and care about each other." His eyes tracked over my face, searching for something. He was quiet for so long that I shifted uncomfortably beneath his scrutiny.

"Does Savannah even like you?" His brows rose as if he were afraid to ask. I shrugged, unsure. She yelled at me more often than not, and we worked well together keeping Audrey's episodes at bay, but . . . beyond that?

"Let me guess." I breathed a laugh as I reached near her hip. *"You dream about taming the beast."*

"I dream about stabbing you."

But we both knew it was a breathless, empty threat. Her pupils were blown wide, making her eyes dark with desire.

"Don't threaten me with a good time." I leaned close enough that her eyes fluttered shut.

"She's never given me an indication either way," I said after a minute.

"You're nothing like your father. No matter what you've done," he said, his voice lowering into a serious tone that I'd rarely heard. I let out a bitter bark of a laugh. If only he knew. "Bonnie murdered people, robbed them. She did plenty of things I'm sure would make her feel the same . . . if she remembered them." He ran a hand through the long hair at the top of his skull and slicked it back from his face. "It didn't make me love her any less."

Something about that admission caught and held in my chest. *It didn't make me love her any less.* She found redemption, through Jesse's acceptance. Did that mean it was possible for me too? Was there a world where *Will* and not the Beast of the Bridge could be worthy enough to deserve love?

"Seb and I had a . . . well . . . a few days ago, he sucked me off in the stables. But I fucked it up. Like I always do." I leaned my head back against the dresser. Water dripped from the ends of my hair onto my shirt, forcing a shiver down my spine. "And he thinks I'm screwing you."

He offered me a sheepish smile, and I couldn't help relaxing at the sight. "I haven't exactly helped in that regard."

"No." A grin curled on my mouth. "You haven't. But I'm pretty sure my reputation didn't either."

"So, Savannah—"

"*Mierda*," I swore, closing my eyes tight at the sound of her name. "She's going to be the death of me."

"I have to be honest." He opened his hands, and the corners of his mouth tightened. Like he was going to deliver bad news. "From what I've seen, it looks like she *hates* you. Like a lot."

I groaned, the sound smooth and tortured.

"I know," I responded, running weary hands down my face.

"Is it possible that you think you like her because you know it'll never happen?"

I took a moment to think that over. Like a self-fulfilling prophecy. I knew I'd never be good enough for her, that she was out of my league. And if Seb looked at me like I was a disappointment, I'd never be able to earn her respect. Was my obsession just another way to punish myself?

"If you think I'm that self-aware, *hermano*, you haven't been paying attention." I chuckled.

"From what you're telling me, Sebastian cares about you, and if you *let him*, maybe there's a chance you could find happiness. But you have to *try*. You can't just go after someone else when things get hard."

We sat in silence for a while after that, my mind swimming with Jesse's advice and a faint glimmer of hope for a way out of the darkness I'd been drowning in for so long. That I could regain parts of my humanity and stop hating myself so goddamn much.

"Alright." I sat up against the dresser. "Your turn."

Jesse looked at me like I was insane, but I'd be damned if I was the only one spilling my guts tonight. He'd been nearly unhinged in the courtyard, so I knew there was plenty of damage control I needed to do to keep him from doing something reckless.

"Audrey and Rutherford—" I started, piercing him with a knowing stare. That was all it took. He balled his fists and sat up straighter, jaw clenching so hard I thought his teeth might break.

"I could have *sworn* she remembered something the other day, but we got interrupted and—"

I cut him off with a sharp laugh, waving at his narrowed eyes to continue.

"The irony of that wasn't lost on me either," he remarked, smoothing his hair back again. "It's just . . . *infuriating*. Bonnie would never go for a guy throwing himself at her like that, and I never would have suggested Rutherford do it if I thought—"

I held up a hand to still his rambling thoughts, seeing how his eyes were widening in his desperation. "Wait." I readjusted in my seat, leaning forward to sling my arm over one of my knees. "Your *first* mistake"—I leveled my eyes at him—"is that she *isn't* Bonnie. She hasn't been for a long time. And *why the hell* are you giving Rutherford tips on how to win her over? That seems counterproductive."

"My plan backfired, okay?" He pressed his knuckles into his eyes. "I was *trying* to sabotage him."

"Clearly that worked out." My sarcasm earned a scathing glare. "Listen, Audrey doesn't have the same baggage that Bonnie did. Bonnie was used to guys throwing themselves at her. It was *literally* her job to make it happen. She saw it as a weakness. Audrey's been ignored, an outsider, seen as *crazy*. I'd bet my left testicle what she really wants is for someone to make her feel normal. Wanted."

"Which is *exactly* what Rutherford did," he finished, and I nodded in response. "Right after her relapse. Fuck!"

Silence descended heavily as the weight of my words settled on his shoulders. I stood, clapping a hand on his shoulder in a pathetic attempt at comfort. Sure, he screwed up, but it wasn't insurmountable . . . At least, I didn't think it was.

"In all these hours you spend with her, have you only been looking for the tiny slivers of Bonnie? Or have you started to like *Audrey*? Because, even if you somehow manage to return her memories, the last three years aren't going to disappear. Have you considered that, as much as you've grown and changed in all this time, she has too? And will you still love her if she's not the same take-no-shit outlaw you met in the desert?" I asked, wondering if he'd ever considered that *Bonnie* the way we knew her might never fully come back at all. Even if we regained bits and pieces, Audrey would still exist.

My mind took a darker turn, remembering a night filled with horrors of a different kind. The night that broke Audrey. The truth of it, the grief, sat poised on my tongue. I should tell him. I should've already told him. Only I couldn't form the words. Could barely get myself to think of the way Audrey had screamed, a keening sound that had echoed through the house for weeks. It still rattled me to my bones.

I couldn't look at him, so I dropped my hand and turned to the dresser, pulling the leather strap from my hair and raking it away from my face to re-tie it. He stood, walking to his side of the bed and fiddling with the ends of his charcoal sticks.

"Of course I will." He declared it with such conviction that it reminded me of how they talked in Jones's camp. Death sentences carried out in clear, unwavering voices. Verdicts given to condemn you as guilty or innocent. Looking over my shoulder, I offered him a nod.

"Then you should get to know Audrey and stop living in the past. I know you've chased after her for a long time, but she's here. Now. Right in front of you."

"How do I un-fuck this, Will?" His blue eyes held a powerless expression that made his obnoxious bulk seem suddenly small.

"Don't say I never did anything for you." I offered him a grin that spread across my whole face. "I'm gonna throw a party. Get the both of you out of that fucking library and drinking. Dancing."

"How is *that* supposed to make a difference? If she's already—"

"She's not *married, ¡maldita sea!* Rutherford played his hand, Jess; now it's time for you to ante up or fold. Which is it?"

His shrewd expression sharpened.

"That's what I thought." I smoothed down the front of my rumpled shirt and settled my hat on my head.

"Where are you going?"

"I think it's about time for me to ante up too."

Before I could open the door, Jesse stopped me as he said, "Hey, what does that mean?"

"What?"

"*Hermano.* Just wondering what you're swearing at me now. I just got used to *pendejo.*"

A grin rested on his mouth, and I chuckled softly. "It means *brother.*"

The grin slipped off his face, and his eyes warmed. "Oh."

"Don't read too much into it; you're still a *pendejo.*"

I took a bracing breath and left without a second glance back. My fingers twitched, an outward indication of my nervousness. With Jesse's advice whirling in my head, I forced all thoughts of Savannah from my mind. He was right. I'd been holding onto the possibility of something happening between us when I had someone *right here* who cared for me.

If he still did. If I hadn't pushed him too far. If we hadn't broken each other too many times with the on-again, off-again.

If.

When it came down to it, this was a leap of faith. I'd had very little in the way of faith in my life and even less trust in myself. I'd been branded from an early age as *troublesome*. Being told that often enough had me believing it was true. But what if it wasn't?

Jesse thought I could have a measure of happiness, if I tried for it. Bonnie and I hadn't been able to imagine happiness when we were fighting for survival one day at a time. Even after the last few years, out from under the threat of my father, I'd been too chicken-shit to make any choices that would help me live freely for the first time.

But Jesse believed I could change, so maybe it was about time I started believing it too.

People parted before me, as they always did, with fear muted on their faces. And it didn't take long to find myself standing hesitantly in front of Seb's door. He hadn't been wearing his uniform earlier, so chances were he'd be here. Hiding from me.

I raised my fist to knock, but it fell to my side after a few tense moments. What was I supposed to say? Nothing would make him believe I'd be different this time. It had been written all over his face earlier.

"I don't think he's home," a familiar voice said behind me. As I turned, I drank in the sight of him. My eyes caught on Seb's stony expression and crossed arms. "What do you want?"

I tipped the brim of my hat down to hide my eyes from his dark, piercing gaze. What was I doing? This was so fucking *stupid.*

"I made a mistake—" My shoulders ducked as I shoved my hands in my pockets and started past him.

Only he didn't let me walk away this time.

A hard hand gripped my elbow, turning me to face him. My breath shuddered as he reached out, pulling my hat off my head so he could see my wide, helpless eyes. His stony expression softened. That was the thing about Seb: he reserved that softness for me alone. To everyone else he was strict, efficient, reliable. But with us? He was able to shed that hard exterior a little at a time.

"Talk to me, Will." His voice was low as his hand dropped away. "Why were you coming to see me? Did you—" His expression screwed up in pain before he finally said, "Did you and *Montana* have a fight or something?"

"A fight?" He really did think Jesse and I were screwing. Wonderful. "What? No. That's not—"

"My business. I'm sorry I asked." He held up a palm in a gesture of peace.

"No," I breathed, grabbing his outstretched hand and lacing our fingers together. "What I was *going to say* is that Montana and I are friends. *Just* friends. He's infuriatingly straight."

His nostrils flared, his mouth opening and shutting. Before he could form a response, I cleared my throat and shuffled closer to him.

"He said something that I—" *Fuck.* This wasn't going well. "What I mean is—

"Fuck it," I finally managed to say between my ramblings. I gripped his face between my palms and kissed his surprised mouth. His mouth was soft and opened for me with a sigh I drank down. I kissed him until we were both breathless. Leaning my forehead against his as I dragged an inch of space between us and he clutched the back of my shirt like a lifeline.

"I'm tired of punishing myself, Seb," I admitted, eyes still closed and the taste of him lingering on my lips. "I want to try this. For *real* this time."

There. I'd said it.

Cracking my eyes open, I noticed the way his dark eyes shone. Brimming with joy that made them look less cold and mysterious, but soft like the tips of raven's feathers. Relief buoyed me forward, allowing me to swallow down the trepidation that'd been trying to strangle me moments before.

"No more hiding it from the staff or keeping it casual. I want you. I want *us.*"

He didn't answer me. Instead, he fisted his hands in the front of my shirt and dragged me towards his door. With a quick fumble behind him, it swung open, and a smile dawned on my face as I crossed the threshold with him.

"I guess this means you'll have me," I said with a quiet chuckle.

"Oh, shut up," he muttered, muffling my laugh with his mouth before I kicked the door shut behind us with the heel of my boot.

CHAPTER SIXTEEN

SAVANNAH

T HUNDER CRACKLED AND RAIN pounded against the garden window. The manor house had gone quiet with the storm raging outside. Normal work activities were suspended, because what was anyone supposed to do in a hurricane? It wasn't my first within these walls and most likely wouldn't be the last.

The staff and guests remained mostly in their rooms, giving me the perfect opportunity for a little quiet time.

I didn't have anything to do for Audrey or Mr. Lee, for once. My scheming with Lucas Rutherford to get Audrey to spend time with him had been successful. Will Ellis hadn't committed any atrocities that required my attendance either.

So I settled back into the plush pillows, cradling my new favorite novel between my hands as I tucked my feet daintily beneath me. I'd seen the novel at the bookstore weeks ago. Somehow, it had ended up here. I was already on my third read.

The man on the front cover had glistening, olive-toned skin. While most of his features were out of frame, I could make out the hard line of his jaw and the elegant slope of his nose. Long, dark locks spilled over the man's bare shoulder beneath a black cowboy hat. I was too ashamed to admit he'd starred in my dreams more than once.

I flipped open to the page I'd left bookmarked last night.

Noah's jaw set in a hard line, dark eyes unreadable across the dim space. He took a bracing step toward me, shoulders tense and spine straight.

"What makes you think that, Miss Everly?" he asked, a playful edge to his voice, though his features betrayed nothing.

My heart beat wildly as he crossed the space. I'd watched him for weeks. He got along well with the other hands, even if he preferred to spend his time in the barn with the horses.

My mind wandered to the countless mornings I'd found Will asleep in the stables. It had been a regular occurrence before he secured quarters outside of the manor. I shook thoughts of the man away and turned back to the page.

"Because you haven't said more than ten words to me in all the time you've been here," I said, too breathy. He paused before me, eyes trailing along the skin of my cheek and down the column of my throat. They paused on the swell of my breasts.

"There's a reason for that," he said, his deep voice rumbling down into my core. He reached up with a confident hand, calloused fingertips brushing against my cheek. "Your father warned me to stay away from you."

I took in a sharp breath as he cupped my face. "My father isn't the boss of me."

"No, but he is of me," Noah said. He tipped my head toward him. "Though, I think you're worth the risk." I took in a sharp breath, chest heaving as he leaned toward me slowly, so slowly.

"Miss Beauregard?"

Cheeks flushed, breath uneven, I snapped the book shut and turned toward the voice. Mr. MacNeil stood in the doorway, a pleasant smile on his face.

"Mr. MacNeil." The corners of my mouth turned upward even as my skin heated further.

"I apologize. Am I intruding?" Thunder boomed just beyond the window.

"Not at all." I averted my eyes and willed my heart to slow down. "Please, help yourself to whatever you like."

His pleasant smile expanded, and his dark eyes lit up. As he stepped into the room, I couldn't help but think about how *this* was the type of man I should want. Well off. Handsome. Got along well with others.

"What are you reading?" His eyes dropped to the half-naked man on the cover.

"A romance novel." I stared at him with a silent dare. He wouldn't be the first person to judge me for my taste in literature. "I have so little time to read. I was just taking advantage of a quiet morning." I folded my fingers around the book's spine "Do you read much, Mr. MacNeil?"

His attention went to the giant bookshelves lining the entire wall of the room. "Patrick."

My cheeks heated again. "Right."

"Not much, I'm afraid," he said, moving toward the bookshelves. "Too busy."

"That's right." I untucked my legs and flattened my feet on the floor. "What is it that you do? You mentioned you work for your father." Will's smug face as he'd baited me at dinner filled my mind. I blinked, forcing his image away. I'd been trying to better acquaint myself with Patrick when Will decided to implant himself in the conversation.

"I run the shop floor of my father's textile mill," Patrick said.

Another point for Mr. Lee's charming guest. He worked in industry on Manhattan Island. No doubt he had money.

"Oh? Are you going to take over the business for your father?"

A shadow passed across his face as the smile fell from his lips. "Not if my older brothers have anything to say about it. I'm the fifth son. I doubt I'll even have a job when my oldest brother inherits the business."

A flood of empathy washed through me. I'd never had any siblings, but if my friendship with Audrey was anything to go by, they could be difficult. "That's so cruel."

Patrick fixed me with wide eyes, brows lifted as if he couldn't fathom what I was saying. "Never you mind, Miss Beauregard."

"Savannah."

The hardness disappeared from his face, and he adopted a pleasant smile once more. "Savannah." There was a depth to his dark eyes and bright smile.

This was how my story was supposed to play out. An appropriate courtship culminating in a fortuitous marriage.

Lee had charged me with aiding the match between Audrey and Lucas. Maybe if Patrick and I got on well enough, I could go with them to Manhattan Island. I'd always wanted to see the world outside of this city.

But Mama . . .

Guilt filled my chest. I was supposed to go back, to find her, to save her. If I left New Orleans, I'd lose my chance of returning to St. Louis. I was supposed to leave after I stowed away the money from Audrey's glowroot. I'd even booked passage home.

Things rarely went to plan for me.

I cleared my throat, shoving away the guilt that wracked me even after all these years.

"Is that a phonograph?" he asked.

Patrick was already across the room, examining the old machine on a side table. "I wouldn't," I warned, setting my book on the window seat. "It's old. It might fall apart."

Instead of responding, he smiled and cranked the machine. In moments, a male voice crooned from the speaker to a slow melody. I'd never heard it before, but I loved it immediately. I wrapped my arms around myself, not realizing that I'd started swaying to the song. I'd loved music and dancing since I was very young.

"May I?" Patrick asked, extending a hand. I wasn't sure when he'd crossed the space between us. My heart beat erratically as I eyed his smooth hands.

The music swelled around us, dragging my focus to this singular moment. I hadn't expected a man to come along. In fact, for most of my formative years, I avoided men altogether. Not because I didn't find them attractive, but because trust didn't come easy. I'd grown up with a mother who fell into any number of addictive things: glowroot, alcohol, men.

A deep-rooted fear was that when I did fall in love, I'd fall so hard I'd lose myself, and that the person I fell for wouldn't feel the same.

Stop it, Savannah. It was just a dance. What was the worst thing that could happen in the course of a single dance?

With a gentle smile, I placed my hand in his. His soft fingers sent a chill across my arms as he pulled me toward him. They felt different, more feminine than I anticipated for someone who worked in a factory. Not at all like the calluses that lined Will's hands, how they'd felt against my cheek as he'd kissed me all that time ago.

I gripped Patrick's hand, placing my other on his shoulder, leaving several inches between us. We swayed to the tune, gently but stilted. Something about it felt wrong, a way I'd never felt about dancing, no matter the partner.

"You'll have to come closer, Savannah," he said in a low voice, a smile hovering around his words.

I cleared my throat, letting out a breathy chuckle. "Of course. It's been a while since I had a partner." I brushed a loose strand of hair out of my face.

Patrick took that as his shot, wrapping his arms around my waist as he pulled me gently against his chest. I let out a surprised gasp at the sudden closeness. That seemed to please him, though, because a smile lit up his face. My heart pounded beneath my breast as I wrapped my arms around his neck and forced the tension from my shoulders.

It's just a dance.

We settled into the rhythm. I hummed absentmindedly, keeping my eyes low. Patrick's gaze remained steady on me, but I couldn't bring myself to look at him.

"You're a wonderful dancer," he said to break the awkward silence between us.

"Mr. Lee was responsible for my education, including the best dance instructors in the city." I glanced at him once before averting my eyes. We were too close. Our nearly-matched height placed his face dangerously close to mine.

"So, is he your—"

"No." I shook my head, staring down at the lapel of his jacket. "I am his daughter's companion. I have all of the benefits of being Audrey, but none of the responsibility."

Patrick tightened his grip around my waist. I lifted my gaze to his, finding curious eyes staring back at me. "How did you manage such an arrangement?"

"That's a long story." I looked away. The room seemed to rock around me as I beat back my memories. It *was* a long story. One I'd rather not relive. The longer the silence grew, however, the easier it was for my past to drag me under, like a giant tidal wave bringing me back, back, back, to a day a decade ago in St. Louis.

"I can do whatever the hell I want with her, Reese. She's my *daughter!"*

"Lana told me you tried to sell her at the whorehouse last week, Stella. She's only fucking ten. You need help *to get clean, and I can—"*

"Don't you dare judge me like you've got room to talk!"

I hadn't anticipated the argument stirring at our front door between my mother and the closest thing I had to a brother. Reese Davidson brought us food or warm clothes at the boarding house. He usually had a scowl on his face, except with me. There were times he'd take me with him on jobs around the city. He always had peppermints. I headed for the door in search of candy.

"What's that supposed to mean?" he asked, his bulk filling most of the entryway. I froze, just out of sight.

"The profession doesn't seem to bother you. Lana's a whore. The woman you love is on her back raking in the bits. Now go away." The door slammed.

Mama turned with shaking hands, tear-filled eyes finding me. With the widest blue smile, she told me to put on my best dress. That she was taking me somewhere very special.

Gravel crunched beneath our feet as we rounded a giant, metal boxcar. My eyes widened at the sight before us. A steamboat, three stories high, docked nearby, a beautiful fleur-de-lis painted in gold on its smokestack.

"Stay here," Mama said.

While I gaped at the magnificent boat, wondering what it would be like to watch the city go by from its upper decks, my mother headed for the dock. She spoke quietly to a middle-aged man, who retreated into the boat. Minutes later, he returned with another man dressed in a fancy suit, the same fleur-de-lis from the boat on his breast pocket.

Mama spoke with her hands, gesturing to me as they conversed. His dark eyes found me, little more than vague interest passing through them.

The man handed something to my mother and snapped his fingers. A large man wearing a black cowboy hat and a pair of sunglasses appeared on the dock.

"Some people are just lucky, I suppose," Patrick said, dragging me from the memory.

That was the first time I'd met Sixgun Ellis. Will's father. When I refused to go quietly, he tossed me over his shoulder, carried me onto the boat, and locked me in a stateroom. My mother was gone when I reached the porthole window. I promised myself I would go back, I would find her, I would make sure those men didn't hurt her.

I nodded, unable to form words. Patrick flattened a palm against the small of my back as the music crested, guitar and cymbals and any other number of instruments crashing together to bring the song to its crescendo. As the song wound down, he dipped me slowly in time to the music. His breath washed across my lips. He was so incredibly close. I sucked in a sharp breath as he leaned closer, his mouth a hair's breadth from mine.

The last time I'd been kissed had felt different. When Will kissed me in the kitchen all that time ago, it felt warm and inviting. Wanted. I'd felt wanted. I didn't feel any of that now.

A slow clap sounded above the rain and thunder beyond the window.

Darkness flickered through Patrick's eyes as he straightened. I wobbled on my feet as I tugged out of his embrace, turning to the doorway.

William Ellis leaned too casually against the doorframe, a grin on his lips and mischief in his eyes.

"I love that song," he said, dropping his hands to his sides. "A word, Savvy?"

I lowered my gaze, busying myself with smoothing my skirt. "I'm busy."

As Patrick scowled, Will said, "It'll only take a minute. Promise." He flashed a dazzling, disarming grin. My knees weakened at the sight. It wasn't because of Will. No, it was because I had been close to Patrick and the dancing and the memory . . . Absolutely nothing to do with that grin of his.

"I'll be right back." I didn't bother to look Patrick's way as I brushed past Will and into the corridor.

The moment we were out of earshot, I wheeled on him, not bothering to hide my anger. Will's grin only widened.

"What do you want? I have things to do with my time *other* than clean up your messes, you know." I crossed my arms over my chest.

Will's gaze darted in the direction of the library, a shadow crossing his features. When he turned back to me, it was gone, replaced with the ridiculous amusement that always painted his face when I was around.

"I need a favor."

I rolled my eyes. "*Of course* you do."

Will took a moment, warm brown eyes studying my features. As they trailed down the column of my neck and across my dress, it felt like the gentle wash of the ocean on the beach, in and then out, calming, placating.

"I'm throwing a party for the staff tonight."

My brows lifted, and I rolled my eyes. "In the middle of a storm?"

Amusement flickered to life in his eyes once more. "Lee's gone. He won't be back until after the hurricane passes."

"What does that have to do with me?"

"Two things." He took a broad step in my direction. "Need some of your world-famous pastries. Cookies, cupcakes . . . Hey, what about that king cake? I heard it was delicious. I wouldn't know, considering I didn't get to eat my piece, but—"

"That is your own fault! I wouldn't have had to make it at all if Sebastian hadn't—" I cut myself off, mouth snapping shut.

"If Seb hadn't what?" Will asked, suspicion darkening his eyes and making him look more beastly.

I'd never mentioned Sebastian's behavior to anyone. It didn't seem to matter in the scheme of things.

"Nothing." I rolled my eyes, forcing my shoulders to relax. "Why would I spend the rest of my day in the kitchen baking for a bunch of people who hate me?"

"Because I asked nicely?" His grin turned impish, and my heart stuttered in my chest.

"Really?" Too breathless. Damn it, Savannah, get a hold of yourself.

"C'mon, Savvy. The boss is gonna be away. We can finally let loose." He quirked his brows at me, eyeing the high neckline of my dress. I scoffed at him.

"Because *I'm* going to this party." I rolled my eyes so hard they hurt.

"Well, yeah, Audrey needs her companion," he said, as though it were the most obvious thing in the world.

"Audrey isn't going—"

"Of course she is," Will said. "She hasn't given Montana all of his time this week."

"That isn't my problem," I said. "You heard Lee. I'm supposed to encourage Audrey toward Rutherford. Why would I do *anything* for Montana?"

Will narrowed his eyes, as though he were contemplating what tactic would best work to get me to agree. "Because all it would take is one word from Montana to get that lovesick guard back into the house?"

A new kind of horror filled my chest. I couldn't have that. It was bad enough trying to balance Audrey between Rutherford and her dedicated hours with Montana. I could *not* handle a third party pursuing my best friend.

And Will knew it. I could tell by the triumphant glint in his eyes.

"Fine."

"Good."

With a huff, I started past him, intent on returning to the library.

"Savvy." My eyes fluttered shut at the ridiculous nickname, but I stopped walking. I couldn't help myself. I couldn't just walk away. As if some small part of me held on to the hope that the next words from his mouth wouldn't be something absolutely ridiculous. "You should be careful."

"Careful? About what?"

Will's features darkened as he once more glanced toward the library. "Not everyone has good intentions."

A flush crept up my neck and into my cheeks. I remembered our argument in the hallway following dinner. How he'd spoken of Patrick. Of being jealous that I showed interest in another man.

I didn't understand his jealousy that night, and I didn't understand his unwanted warning now.

"What's it to *you?*"

Will blinked, confusion flitting across his face. "What?"

"What does it matter?"

Will balked, as if offended that I'd even think such a thing. "It matters because—"

"Don't you dare say it's because you *actually* care. You've made it *abundantly* clear that you don't." I crossed my arms over my chest once more, if only to keep them from quaking at my sides.

"What does *that* mean?"

My jaw clenched as he stared at me, a mixture of confusion and something else, something that made my stomach tighten and my body ache.

"That *means* . . . you had your chance," I finally said. Some of the color drained from his face.

"When did I have a chance with you?"

Unfuckable Savannah. The familiar taunt flashed through my mind, lighting up like a brothel sign on Bourbon. The staff didn't like me much before Audrey and Will came along, but it got much, much worse after that.

"When you kissed me," I said, forcing back the memory of that single kiss and how it still lingered in my mind all of this time later.

"When did I kiss you?"

Ouch. My chest tightened. Not only did he have no interest in me then, he didn't even remember a moment that had replayed in my dreams countless times over the last three years. It meant nothing.

I meant nothing.

"The night we met." Will opened his mouth to say something, but I cut him off. "I guess you can add *Forgettable Savannah* to the insults the guards throw at me."

The color drained from Will's face. "Oh. *Oh*, fuck. I thought you meant recently. Those first few weeks, I was a goddamn mess, Savvy."

"Clearly," I snapped. "But it doesn't matter, does it? You jumped Sebastian the next day. The rest is history."

Will balked, his mouth opening and closing. His hands twitched at his sides, something he seemed to do often, at least around me. "Why didn't you say anything?"

Why didn't I say anything? Was he serious?

I charged toward him, anger and hurt dragging me under. It was hard to catch my breath, but somehow, I managed to demand, "What would it have changed?"

Will gaped, staring at me with wide eyes. I stood close enough to see the silver flecks against his brown irises. As frustrated as I was with him, that helpless expression on his face made my stomach coil tighter. I battled against the raging need to close the space between us, to snap the hat from his head and run my fingers through his dark hair.

I'd never felt a pull toward anyone like I did with Will. It was part of the reason I couldn't tolerate him for long. Because I wanted to kiss the stupid smirk off of his face as much as I wanted to slap him.

"Everything," he whispered. I barely heard the word.

Had he felt the same way I had all of this time? The seemingly random times I came across him in the manor. The charming grins that made my knees quake. How his face lit up when I snapped at him anytime he antagonized me.

Looking at him now, the pale tint to his skin, tight lines between his brows, I couldn't control myself. I lurched toward him, cupping his face in the second before I pressed my lips against his.

They were just as soft and warm as I remembered, but this time felt different. As if a storm raged inside of me. I couldn't stop. Not as I had that night in the kitchen. A moment passed, and Will tangled his fingers in my hair, one arm wrapping around my waist. He pressed me against the wall, every lithe inch of him pinning us together. I ran my tongue along the seam of his lips.

Will froze. My eyes snapped open as he pulled back from me, something like shame in his eyes.

"Savvy." I didn't think that nickname could sound so painful. Yet, it did.

I nodded to myself as cool air rushed up in the space between us. I knew it. I knew he didn't have feelings for me, and I'd kissed him anyway. What sort of idiot did that make me? Without a word, I turned on my heel. I needed to be alone.

Instead, warm, calloused fingers wrapped around my wrist. "Savvy, wait—" He brushed his thumb across my skin. Goosebumps prickled along my arm, that ache inside of me intensifying. I lifted my gaze, waiting to hear what the hell else he wanted to say. "That Manhattanite—he's only interested in fucking you."

My brows furrowed, and anger flared anew in my chest, even as my heart clenched. "Not everyone is like *you*—"

"When he figures out he can't get between your legs or any of Lee's money from you, he'll leave."

"Whatever," I snapped.

"Don't believe me?" Shadows danced through his eyes. "Invite him to my party. See if he shows." His Adam's apple bobbed, any hint of the Beast gone. He looked almost innocent as he said, "He doesn't want you."

I barked out a bitter laugh and yanked my arm from his grip. "No one does. Right?"

I didn't wait to see the effect of my insult. If I stood there any longer, I'd do something even more idiotic than kiss William Ellis. A loud crack sounded behind me, followed by a murmured Spanish curse. I didn't turn around. I couldn't.

I bypassed the library, instead charging to my room. I ignored the curious stare of a maid I passed, barely breathing until I shoved open the door to my bedroom. After slamming it shut, I leaned back against the wood, hot tears stinging my eyes.

Most of my life felt like a stormy sea. I'd weathered the rises and falls for years. But this time, I was drowning, and I didn't know how to save myself.

"Savannah!" The bathroom door muffled Audrey's voice. I had two seconds to get myself together. I snapped to my feet, viciously swiping at my tear-stained cheeks. When the door opened, she practically floated into the room. "There you are! I've been looking everywhere."

"I'm right here," I said, swiping beneath my nose.

"What's wrong?"

With a steely breath, I turned to her, adopting the best smile I could manage. "Nothing." I waved a hand as I moved past her and into the bathroom. I ran the hot water and grabbed a washcloth from the cabinet.

Audrey didn't buy it. She leaned against the door and fixed me with a hard stare. "Uh huh."

I couldn't look at her. If I did, it would all come spilling out, and I wasn't going to burden her with this. She'd been through enough. She didn't need my issues weighing her down. I thrust my hands beneath the hot water. The burn, at least, numbed the pain in my chest.

"Um, what did you need?" I switched off the tap and wiped my face with the steaming cloth. She didn't respond. The hard expression in her blue eyes never wavered as I continued to hide my face.

A moment passed, and Audrey's gentle fingertips touched my hands. She tugged the cloth from them. A rush of cool air hit my skin, soothing the sting. As she set the rag down on the counter, she fixed me with wide, concerned eyes.

"What happened?"

"Nothing."

"Liar." I pursed my lips, lifting my eyebrows to adopt an unbothered expression. When Audrey didn't relent, I blew out a breath.

"I'm fine."

"You're not," Audrey said pointedly. "Was it one of the guards again?" She crossed her arms over her chest, squaring her shoulders.

"No."

The last time she'd discovered guards harassing me, Audrey had been furious. Before she got them fired, she punched the worst of them in the jaw. The momentary satisfaction didn't last long, because the teasing began in earnest the next day. The other staff just waited until she wasn't around to act as my shield.

"Savannah—"

"Listen." I cut her off and moved back into my bedroom. "Ellis is throwing a party tonight for the staff. He said because you didn't get all of your hours with Montana this week, you have to go."

Audrey followed me into my room. I sat on my vanity bench, somehow managing to keep myself together.

"He's lying."

Of course, he was.

"I had my last hour with Montana yesterday." Audrey settled on my bed. She didn't seem too perturbed by Will's treachery. In fact, a pretty flush filled her cheeks as she stared blankly at the wall across from my bed.

"Then we don't have to go," I said, shoulders sagging in relief.

"What? No! We have to!"

My brows shot up at her rather visceral reaction.

"What I mean is . . . it'll be fun. Dad's gone until after the storm blows over. Why should we stay locked up when the rest of the house is having a good time?" She fixed me with a grin. "Plus, I can dress you up for once." Audrey wiggled her eyebrows suggestively.

I groaned, putting my head in my hands. The last thing I wanted to do was face Will after the *incident* in the hallway. Was Audrey really going to make me relive it all over again?

I could see it now, Will holding court with a drink in his hand, blabbing about how *Forgettable* and *Unfuckable Savannah* kissed him in the hallway.

"What's going on with you?"

I blinked, finding Audrey kneeling before me, her skirt pooling around her. She took my hands in hers, raw concern written in the deep blue pools reflecting back at me.

"Nothing."

"Savannah, you're about as good at lyin' as I am at cross-stitching. Talk to me." She squeezed my hands, imploring me with her gaze.

"Will. He blackmailed me into spending the rest of my day baking and to get you to that party," I said, blowing out a hot breath.

Audrey's eyes narrowed. "So you were in here crying because Will was an ass to you?"

"Pretty much."

"That's all?"

"That's all."

She climbed to her feet and pivoted toward the door. "So if I go ask *him* if that's all that happened—"

"Audrey, *no!*" I shot up, gripping her arm hard enough that my nails dug into her skin.

Her brows lifted as she waited for me to get on with it. I dropped my hands to my sides and stepped back, horrified at my reaction. The backs of my knees hit the bench, and I lowered to my vanity, once again hanging my head in my hands.

For three years, I'd kept my feelings to myself. I never told Audrey about the kiss in the kitchen, never once even dreamed I would do it again. I'd seen William Ellis love and leave people countless times since. Why would I ever subject myself to the uncertainty that came with him? Never knowing if he actually cared about me or whether he was with someone else.

It was easier to pretend it never happened.

I needed it to have never happened.

"When are you goin' to admit you like Will?"

"When you stop forgetting the Gs at the ends of your words," I mumbled as I lifted my head.

Instead of amusement, her expression shifted. She settled on the narrow seat beside me, wrapping an arm around my shoulders. It was comical, really, to have a woman so much smaller comforting *me*. "You can tell me anything; you know that."

Several arguments bubbled to the tip of my tongue. I could deny it until I turned blue in the face, but it was true.

I *liked* Will. And I hated that I liked him.

"I've tried to ignore it, you know," I said, my voice low. "I thought maybe I was just being empathetic. He—" I bit my bottom lip, brow screwing up. "He was in bad shape that first night. After we got you settled." Audrey stiffened beside me. Though she hadn't been conscious, how could anyone forget what had happened that night?

I waited, in case she wanted to talk about it. When she didn't, I cleared my throat. The truth spilled out of me. With each word, I spoke faster and faster, as though if I didn't lay it all out before Audrey, I'd lose. She didn't balk at it, didn't tease. She listened with kind eyes while I bared my heart before her.

"So I kissed him," I said, finishing with my embarrassment on full display.

"What?" Audrey's blue eyes brightened, her back straightening.

"And he immediately pushed me away." I chuckled darkly. "My luck, huh?" I shoved to my feet, shaking my head as I walked to the door.

"Where are you going?"

"A man charmed me into making him baked goods."

Jesus Christ, that *charm* would be the death of me.

CHAPTER SEVENTEEN

JESSE

D ROPLETS OF WATER CASCADED along my skin. I toweled most of it from my hair in the communal staff bathroom. I'd spent nearly the entire day sparring with a trainer at the fighting pits in preparation for my upcoming headline fight in Baton Rouge. I'd be gone for nearly a week.

I was dreading it. Because it meant I'd be leaving the city, and Bonnie.

Audrey, I reminded myself as I buttoned the front of my shirt. Even though the hurricane raged outside, keeping temperatures relatively cool, inside the manor was swelteringly hot. The breeze from the storm didn't reach inside, because storm shutters and other preparations had been made throughout last night and this morning.

Rain misted against my heat-tinged skin as I shoved into the open breezeway overlooking the courtyard. Even though I was physically tired from training all day, my mind buzzed at the prospect of this party Will was hosting.

How long had I spent sleepless nights reliving what happened between me and Bonnie? How often had I longed for her touch, her kiss, her mind? I hadn't realized just how shitty of a job I was doing until I heard the news about her and Rutherford. Will was right. I needed to lay my hand before her. And I had to accept that I might never get her back. Not as who she was.

It was a challenge to reconcile the woman I'd only begun to know with the woman I'd lost.

Audrey had a tenderness to her that Bonnie only showed in rare moments. She still had that sharp mind and venomous tongue, but she lacked the shadows from her childhood. As if losing her memory had been somewhat of a blessing.

Even if I'd thought she almost remembered something before . . .

Smoke wafted out of the open door to my room. Brows furrowed, I walked in, finding Will seated on the bed, back pressed against the wall, head in his hands and a cigarette between his lips. When he hadn't returned to the room last night, I assumed he'd made good with Seb. Maybe I'd been wrong.

After setting my stuff to the side, I glanced over my shoulder. He hadn't budged an inch. "You alright?"

Will blinked, as if he'd suddenly realized I was there. From the moment I'd met him in New Orleans, I'd known he was different, but I didn't realize just how much.

Before, I always thought he didn't give a shit about anything. As it turned out, he cared too much about everything. I'd given him advice last night with the hope of his finding happiness. I didn't know what else *to* do, seeing the haunted expression in his eyes as he confessed that he'd done things that made him no better than his father.

While I didn't know everything, Will wasn't like his father. Sixgun preyed on the innocent, the helpless. He had no conscience. That the last three years weighed so heavily on my friend was further proof that he was *nothing* like the madman who'd attacked my brother and stole Bonnie.

A flash of his predatory smile as he'd hovered over Bonnie's prone form with a belt wrapped around her throat passed through my mind as Will lifted his eyes.

"I fucked up," Will said, a haunted edge to his quiet voice.

"What?" I lowered into a rickety chair, watching as he inhaled from his cigarette. He held the smoke for a moment before blowing it out in a burst of breath.

"Savvy."

I cocked my head to the side, narrowing my eyes at him. He stared blankly at the wall. "What about her?"

Will blinked hard, eyes wide as he stubbed his cigarette out on the table. He shook his head, as if he couldn't quite form the words. "I fucked up."

I'd never seen him like this, not before Fort Hood and certainly not here. I was used to Will's confidence, his swagger in pursuing people. There was never any hesitation. He saw what he wanted and he went for it. At least, that was the impression he'd given me.

"Talk to me," I said, resting my elbows on my knees and clasping my hands together.

"She kissed me."

"Savannah?" I asked, brows furrowed and confusion flitting through my mind. Didn't we discuss this very thing last night? That for all intents and purposes, she seemed to hate him? Will himself admitted she'd never given any indication that she liked him.

"Yes."

"How?"

Shadows darkened Will's eyes as he looked directly at me. "I thought—" He exhaled slowly, shaking his head. "I didn't—"

I'd truly *never* seen him like this.

After a few more tries, Will told me about reconciling with Sebastian and eventually managed to explain what had happened when he approached Savannah about the party. By the time he was finished, I sat back in my chair, brows lifted and guilt spilling into my chest.

"Fuck," I said.

"Yeah." Will lit another cigarette, banging his head back against the wall.

"What're you gonna do?"

"Fuck if I know." He ran a hand through his hair. I'd hoped the next time I saw him, he'd be more like the old Will. Not this strange shadow of himself. "I made a promise to Seb. I—" He inhaled from his cigarette. "I can't mess that up. It wouldn't be fair to him."

I remembered the way Will admitted he'd held on to the hope of something with Savannah. Clearly, I couldn't understand whatever there was between them, because I'd been convinced she hated him. I opened my mouth to agree, but he cut me off.

"But . . . it's Savvy." He lifted his gaze to mine. "I don't know if you've ever done drugs before, but it was like the first hit. I can still taste her, and if I don't get to again, I might—no. No, I *can't*."

I frowned, rubbing my forehead with a mixture of guilt and aggravation at myself.

"What would you do?"

"Nope," I said, rising and grabbing my boots. "I already gave you shit advice. Not doing it again."

After a moment, a grin split across Will's face as he regarded me, eyes narrowing slightly as he studied my shirt. "Is that what you're wearing?" Some of the tension went out of my shoulders. "I could give you some advice on how not to look like such a prick."

In a moment, he'd gone from the conflicted shell of himself back to regular old Will Ellis. He climbed from the mattress. "Wait until you see what I bought."

As Will rifled through a pile of stuff, I tied my boots. I hadn't thought anything was wrong with my shirt. Now I wasn't so sure. As I moved toward the dresser to see if I had anything else to wear, my friend let out a satisfied sound. When I peered over at him, he held a rectangular box with weird markings on it.

"A car battery. For the music. Pre-Culling." His grin widened, splitting his face into his usual cocky brilliance.

I had no doubt this party would be one for the ages, if Will had any say about it.

"I'll meet you down there. You should change." He pointed at my shirt with his cigarette. "It's gonna be *hot*"—his brows shot up suggestively—"down there."

Then he left, like a tornado that'd blown in and out in a matter of seconds. I stretched my shoulders to force the nervous energy from them.

I only had one shot at this, and if I fucked it up, I could lose her forever.

Fifteen minutes later, I made my way into the kitchen, opting for a plain white t-shirt instead of the button-down. Etty's features warmed as she took me in.

"Montana, just the man I was hoping to see." She slid a plate of cookies across the island as she pulled out a letter with *Montana* scribbled across the front. "This came today."

My heart sped up at the sight of my brother's untidy scrawl across the envelope. I offered Etty a grin, enjoying that her cheeks flushed and eyes glittered at me. I shoved the letter into my back pocket and snatched a warm cookie.

"Good luck," she called as I headed toward the short breezeway that led toward the staff's dining quarters.

How that woman just seemed to *know* things stumped me.

Rain sprayed across the cobblestones. Thunder boomed in the distance, reminding me that there was an actual hurricane going on outside. The courtyard was abandoned; all of the furniture had been removed, even the bulky cement planters that'd held bright purple hyacinths and other vibrant flowers I'd never seen before.

People brushed past, one winking in my direction as they moved through a set of double doors propped open by wooden crates. I hesitated at the entrance, noting the room was full of people milling about in cotton shirts and dresses. Most of them had foregone long pants in favor of something lighter. I suddenly regretted wearing my jeans, because I could nearly feel the heat sweltering beyond the threshold.

As I forced myself inside, humidity weighed down the air. Rain battered against the closed shutters. The giant dining table that usually split the room in half rested against one side of the room, filled with trays of cookies and cake squares. In the center of the table rested a giant king cake covered in purple and green frosting. Gold sprinkles glittered in the lamplight.

I finished my cookie and finally allowed myself to look for her. Will stood with a couple of the guards in a corner as they worked over the black box. Their mouths moved, but I couldn't hear them over the buzz of conversation.

At least that spark was back in his eyes. Some of my guilt eased.

Eyes followed me as I crossed the room. I was used to their stares by now, but it didn't make me feel any more comfortable. I knew that some of the women, and men, imagined peeling the shirt from my chest. I'd heard enough of the whispers as I walked through the house to know.

No one stood near the bar in the corner. I lost count of the bottles as I approached. There was no bartender. Instead, it looked like Will had managed to procure enough alcohol that each person could have one or two whole bottles to themselves.

"Good man," I murmured with a smirk to myself as I spied my favorite whiskey. I plucked the bottle from the table and poured a glass before allowing myself to peer back at the crowded room. More people had arrived. They spoke in excited voices. A handful danced together to the sound of the wind blowing against the boarded windows. I recognized even more of the guards hovering near Will, Sebastian included.

Guilt flared quickly in my chest. At least this time he didn't see me and think the worst. It was bad enough I'd given the impression Will and I were sleeping together. I made a mental note to avoid him at all costs tonight, especially given what Will had told me about Savannah.

Music banged to life from Will's corner of the room. My friend stood to his full height, tossing his hat into the air as he let out a gleeful shout. I smiled, even as several others eyed Will with caution. *Beast of the Bridge.* The strange treatment of my friend made sense, even if he didn't deserve it.

Will wrapped Sebastian in an embrace and kissed him hard. More than one person's jaw dropped at the sight. While some of the staff still eyed him distrustfully, there was also a measure of respect in their eyes. Or maybe it was the alcohol, as nearly everyone had their own bottle in hand.

I didn't recognize the slow, banging beat of the music. Low and heavy, reverberating off of the walls and filling the humid air with a sultry tang. I stood at the edge of the room, a spectator more than a participant as people began to pair off and dance in time with the music. Writhing bodies bumped against one another. My brows shot up.

Apparently, this was how they danced in New Orleans.

I swore silently at my parents for their traditional teachings. I could dance circles around these people, but not like this.

Then again, if I had the opportunity to get that close to Bonnie—*Audrey*—my cock twinged to life beneath the denim of my jeans. I shifted my weight and poured another drink, preferring the glass to the bottle as a means to distract myself. The whiskey went down easy, burning my throat and reminding me that I was very much alive.

I'd felt dead for so long. I wasn't going back to that.

One song shifted into another. Though the tempo was faster, the staff seemed to freeze. The crowded dance floor shifted, parting to one side. I spied Savannah, her spine snapped tight as she entered the room, eyeing the crowd warily. Her normally-pulled-back hair spilled over her shoulders in voluptuous curls, even though it was pinned away from her face. She wore a yellow sundress that came down to her knees, the color complimenting her pretty brown skin. I'd never really looked at her; I'd been so caught up in Bonnie. But, I acknowledged, she was quite pretty.

Scandalous whispers sounded, most mentioning the low neckline and short sleeves of her dress. Her eyes lowered to the floor. She seemed to shrink, even for a woman who was barely shorter than me. Her gaze landed on me a moment later, her eyes hardening. I offered her a kind smile, and some of the lines in her face eased.

She probably fucking hated me too.

Savannah turned, her attention going back to the entrance. That was when I saw *her*.

Audrey. The white dress she wore looked more like a nightgown. The fabric hugged her curvy hips, leaving very little to the imagination by way of her figure. The straight neckline allowed ample view of the swells of her breasts. My cock strained against my jeans, arousal snaking its way around me.

LEATHER & LACE

Most of our interactions had been relatively innocent. A time or two I'd purposefully tried to goad her, but I controlled myself.

I didn't want to control myself. Not when she looked like *that*.

I wasn't the only person studying the dips and curves of Audrey's body as she crossed the room, tangling her hand with Savannah's and tugging her along. She let out a high laugh. The sound made my heart swell in my chest. I didn't think I'd heard a genuine laugh from her in all the time I'd been here.

An echo of Bonnie, in those rare moments she'd let herself be free.

I stalked her with my gaze as she and Savannah stalled near the food. Audrey grinned at her friend, saying something that had the woman rolling her eyes. I couldn't help but watch her obsessively, as I always had, ever since Vegas.

Old habits and all.

As if sensing my gaze, dark blue eyes snapped toward me, lighting up as they met mine. I couldn't help the grin that crossed my face as Audrey headed in my direction. Amusement twinkled in her eyes as she moved toward me with confident steps. More than one of the other staff members glanced at her, something akin to longing in their expressions.

Old, familiar jealousy flared to life, reminding me that while I'd spent years pining over her, she'd been sampling the staff in this household.

I shoved it way down. She didn't know me, *know us*. If she did, she wouldn't have done it. Or at least, I hoped she wouldn't have.

An image from that long-ago train ride with the dark-haired bartender's face between her thighs flashed through my mind.

I swallowed around the lump in my throat, eyes fluttering shut. I couldn't lose myself to the past. Not tonight, and maybe not ever again. Will was right. I had to learn to accept her as Audrey. There was a chance I might get Bonnie back, but then again, I might not.

Something other than amusement tinged her blue eyes. Desire. Like when she'd wrapped her plump lips around my finger in the library. *Fuck*. It'd reminded me of Bonnie on her knees, lips wrapped around my cock.

My jeans grew impossibly tighter.

The soft cotton of her white dress clung to her figure, outlining her curves and revealing a tantalizing amount of cleavage. Her nipples peaked through the thin fabric. This was definitely something Bonnie would wear to run a con. The hem of the dress reached midway down her thighs, leaving too little to the imagination.

I knew what loomed beneath that dress. My mouth watered as I imagined trailing my tongue along her inner thigh; I could hear her moan my name breathlessly.

Fuck me.

I wasn't going to make it through tonight. I was certain of it.

Audrey stopped, planting a hand on one hip in a very un-Bonnie-like fashion.

"I'd like a drink," she said, her lips curling up. The blue of her eyes brightened as she lifted her brows. I grinned as I set my glass down on the bartop and waved my hand to the bottles.

She did like bartenders, after all.

"What'll it be?" I grabbed a glass.

Audrey worried her bottom lip between her teeth, contemplating the different bottles of alcohol before her. *Goddamnit*, I wanted to bite that lip. My cock twinged at the sight of it, the memory of how many times I'd tugged on that lip with my teeth, begging to be let loose. The woman didn't even have to touch me and I was ready to blow my load.

"Mint julep?" Her dark hair fell in a curtain around her face, making her look more like Bonnie than I'd seen her since my arrival.

Not Bonnie, dipshit.

"I think we're missing a few ingredients." I smiled at her. That elicited a sensuous curve of her lips.

"Then what about a hurricane?"

I grabbed my own bottle and poured a couple of fingers into the cup. She eyed me curiously as I extended the glass to her.

"We're in the middle of a storm," I said, tossing a cocky grin at her. "They're all hurricane drinks."

Audrey lifted the glass to her lips. Time moved in slow motion as she took a deep pull from it. As the drink filled her mouth and slid down her throat, her small body became pliant, as it had beneath my hands in the cab of that old truck, burned up all that time ago just outside of Fort Hood. A guttural moan came from deep within her. Tension snapped my spine straight as she regarded me with darkened eyes, glazed in passion, the expression burning all the way to my already aching cock.

Without a word, she tipped the glass back. Her throat bobbed around the remnants of the drink. A single drop escaped, sliding from the corner of her mouth, over her jaw, and all the way down her throat. I struggled against the urge to drag my tongue along her skin to where the whiskey dripped between her breasts.

For a moment, Bonnie stood before me. Like we were back in Fort Hood, the two of us alone behind a locked door for the first time. The fire inside of me blazed higher. I clenched my hands into fists to stop myself from kissing her senseless.

When her eyes refocused, Audrey wiped along the whiskey trail. I shifted at the thought of her fingers on my skin.

"God," she moaned. "More." She thunked the glass down on the bar. All I could do was smirk and pour her another.

"Yes, ma'am."

Her mouth curled into another sensuous grin as she lifted the glass to her lips.

"There you are," an airy female voice said. A woman with dark auburn hair and fuck-me-red lips stared at me.

"Here I am," I said, turning my attention back to Audrey. The woman sidled up to me, trailing a finger down my chest. I stood frozen, eyes tracking the movement until she pulled her hand away.

"Come back to my room with me," she murmured, voice full of sex. I couldn't look at Audrey, but it wasn't because of this woman. It was because I *wanted* to fuck. Just not this stranger.

"I'm good here," I said, finally dragging my eyes up to stare at the woman.

A sly smile crossed her ruby-red lips. "You sure?" she asked as she pointed to a woman standing on the far side of the crowd. Blonde, similarly painted lips. She brought her bottle to her mouth, eyes full of arousal. "My bunkmate and I thought we might share you." The woman's breath rushed against my skin, full of scintillating promise.

"I'm good," I repeated with a tight smile.

As the woman walked away, I turned back to Audrey. Her eyes were wide, and her mouth hung slightly open. "Well, it looks like there's nothing that can tempt you into bed if you turned those two down."

I shrugged. "She's not really my type. Most of the women here aren't."

"What *is* your type?"

A grin crossed my face as I moved closer to her. "I have a thing for women in positions of power," I said in a low voice. A muffled sound came from deep within her throat, making my grin widen. "Like the boss's daughter."

I could have sworn I saw goosebumps prickle along her skin. I moved back ever so slightly, if only to force myself to take a breath.

"You mean a crazy half-Korean woman?" The words came out breathy, even as she forced incredulity into her features. "You've got *questionable* tastes."

"What's that?" I asked. "Korean?"

Confusion flickered through her gaze. "It's a country?" She shifted, as though my naivete made her uncomfortable. "Or it was, before the Culling. I forget that people don't know about places on the other side of the world. My father's parents were from there. You can really see it in the shape of my eyes."

Huh. That made more sense than I realized. I'd never seen anyone like her before Vegas. That was why she'd stuck out so much to me. Having never seen someone with her features had ignited the artist in me, given me the desire to draw for the first time since my life burned to ash in Montana. My fingers twitched. I didn't want to draw right now.

"I need a drink." Will blew past me and moved around to the back of the bar. Darkness laced his words as he grabbed a bottle and twisted the cap off, letting it clatter to the floor. He turned the bottle up, taking a deep pull.

Audrey's brows lifted as she stared at my friend. *Our* friend, I reminded myself.

Seeming to notice our attention, Will glanced up, wiping his mouth with the back of his hand. "Savvy *and* Seb are here," he said. "What the hell do I do?"

My gaze shot out through the crowd. Sebastian stood near where the music boomed, while Savannah had been milling about by the food. Her eyes caught on me, then settled on Will. She squared her shoulders and headed in our direction, more determination in her posture than I'd ever seen.

"Whatever you do, you better think quick," I said. My brows shot up as I spied Seb looking our way. Will followed my gaze.

"Fuck my life," he said. The song shifted, and Will bounded away. He grabbed Etty by the hand and pulled her onto the dance floor. A smile crossed my face as I watched the woman's eyes light up. Whether it was from the green bottle in her hand or Will, I couldn't tell.

"The Beast of the Bridge asks *you* for advice?" Audrey questioned incredulously. The glass in her hand was empty, so I poured her another.

With a shrug, I said, "Even beasts need encouragement from time to time."

"Like William Ellis needs encouragement," Savannah said with a scowl. She tugged at her hair, pulling it back from her face.

"Stop that!" Audrey said, turning to Savannah. She grabbed her companion's hands and dragged them to the woman's sides. She *tsk*ed. "Your hair is beautiful, especially when you let it down like this. You need to show off those high cheekbones." There was a lightness to the moment; Audrey's teasing of her companion reminded me of Bonnie, of life on the road when there wasn't much to do other than poke fun at one another.

While Audrey and Savannah argued over hair, a man approached me. I glanced up. Sebastian moved beside me, crossing his arms casually over his chest as he widened his stance. Guilt at what I knew had transpired with Will and Savannah today crept up my neck.

"Will told me you convinced him to stop being an asshole," he said, giving a brief nod. "Thank you."

Fuck.

I gave a half-hearted murmur of assent. We watched as Will swung Etty across the dance floor, the latter's laughter booming from deep inside of her. I thought of Mom, then, rolling around on the living room floor with The Kid as a toddler.

My smile slipped. I hadn't thought of my parents. Though I'd managed to heal the trauma we'd gone through with the fire and fleeing for our lives, there were still so many unanswered questions. I missed them, more than I would ever say.

How would Pop handle this situation I'd found myself in?

The song shifted once more. Will pulled Etty close, and they swayed in time with the music. My gaze went to Audrey, but she wasn't the one who captured my attention.

Savannah stood on her other side, eyes full of open longing as she watched Will and Etty. But it wasn't even just Will and Etty. Her gaze lingered on the couples dancing along to the music. I cleared my throat as I set my glass down on the bar.

"Miss Savannah," I said. She snapped her attention to me. "Would you like to dance?"

Audrey's eyes widened, but I couldn't explain it. I wanted Savannah to like me, to trust me, and if I couldn't tell her the truth, maybe I could convince her that I cared about Audrey, show her that we had something in common. Savannah's eyes went to Audrey, as if asking for permission.

"Oh, go on," she said, smiling at her friend. "Don't do anything I wouldn't do." There was a forced playfulness in Audrey's tone, but something else tinged the words. Was she . . . jealous?

"That doesn't really limit anything," Savannah said, flashing a brilliant grin. Audrey stuck her tongue out petulantly, the lines of her face softening.

I offered the younger woman my hand. She stared at it for a moment, and her eyes shifted back to the dance floor, to Will and Etty. A hard mask came over her, and she took my hand. Her skin was soft against my calloused fingers. I led her onto the dance floor, swinging her out in a wide arc before pulling her toward me, keeping a respectable distance between us.

Uncertain at first, Savannah stiffened for a long moment as we swayed alongside the others. She eventually settled into the rhythm and relaxed against my touch. She was nearly as tall as I was and incredibly pretty. I could see why Will was so caught up on her.

"Thank you," she said in a low voice.

"For what?"

"Making me feel like I belong here." She ducked her head, lowering her eyes. I offered a quiet smile.

"We all belong here."

"No, Montana," she said quietly. "We don't."

In all the time I'd been in the manor, I'd only ever seen Savannah being tough. She had a sharp tongue and didn't shy away from people who were bigger than her, especially when Audrey needed her. Her eyes shifted toward her friend at the edge of the dance floor.

"I know you care about Audrey," I said in a low voice. Her hand tightened around mine as brown eyes snapped back to me. "I respect that. I admire it."

"I don't—"

"You don't know me. So I understand why you might think I'm not here with the best intentions. But I care about Audrey, too."

Something shifted in her eyes. Bitterness? Grief? Her gaze moved across the room, to where Will and Etty stood beside the refreshment table, the latter fanning herself with her hand.

"Sometimes, caring for someone isn't enough," she said, a bitter edge in her voice. I frowned, wishing more than anything I could tell her the truth. If she only knew that I was here to save Audrey, to get her out of this house, maybe she would understand. "It's hard *not* to care for her." She didn't know how deeply I felt those words. "Even when she's making my life hell, I'd rather have her here than not."

I opened my mouth to ask her about that statement, to mention a time when Audrey *wasn't* here, but the music changed and Will stole Savannah from my arms. The woman looked back at me with pleading eyes, but I just gave her a sheepish smile and watched as they disappeared into the crowd.

CHAPTER EIGHTEEN

WILL

S AVANNAH GLARED UP AT me like she was imagining separating my head from my shoulders. It should've probably made me wary, but instead I'd never wanted to kiss her more. It didn't help that I had my arms wrapped around her body, her soft curves fitting perfectly against me.

Mierda.

She was so goddamned beautiful with her eyes lit up in fury. I didn't even care that it was directed at me. Well, mostly.

She tugged and twisted in my arms, trying to get free, but I held her fast. "Let me go." Instead, I pulled her closer, until she was pressed flush against my body and there wasn't any space left between us.

"No."

Her pupils widened, and her lips parted unconsciously. *Fuck. Why was she so goddamned kissable?*

That small taste of her earlier was a kind of torture I wouldn't wish on my enemies. I hadn't been able to part her lips and kiss her until she begged me to stop. I didn't get a chance to ravage her mouth until it was swollen. I'd had the barest hint of her before my promises to Seb pulled me back. Forced me to live with the taste of her on my tongue. I'd felt the fire in her eyes as she came alive in my arms, blazing beneath her skin. Making her melt against me and rage for *more*.

Like a phantom, meant to haunt me and drive me to insanity.

She kept her face turned to the side, eyes on the other couples, and the song would be over too soon. Much too soon. I leaned closer, smelling the honeysuckle and lemon on her skin. She always smelled like that, or vanilla and flour, probably from all the time she spent in the kitchen.

"I wanted to thank you," I said quietly, glad that she raised her eyes back to mine. "For the food."

"You wanted to—" Her incredulous voice cut off, and she stifled whatever retort had been poised on her tongue. Instead, with a weary sigh, she said, "You probably shouldn't thank people for doing things you blackmailed them into. It's kind of tactless."

"I'm not exactly known for my *tact*," I said with a soft chuckle. The shadow of a smile relaxed the tension at the corners of her eyes.

"Look at her, and dancing with the *Beast*," someone drunkenly whispered not-so-quietly. Her cheeks flushed and her eyes lowered, the mask of her propriety slipping firmly back into place. It made me sick to see how the words of these unimportant assholes shackled her in self-doubt. My eyes raked over her dress and hair, how she'd peeled back one of the layers that kept her hidden away.

Clicking my tongue, I tilted her chin so I could dive into those eyes of hers again. I didn't want her ever looking down. "You're the most beautiful woman in this house," I told her quietly. Honestly. No cowering behind jokes this time, instead I let the sentiment hang in the air between us. "You hide away beneath those dresses, by keeping your hair back—"

I couldn't help it; I let one of my fingers twine around a curl that had come free from the pins attempting to hold her hair back. The way it wrapped around my finger, as if clutching onto me, made me want to bury all of them in the thick, dark tresses. Until I'd never be free of her again.

"But I see you," I whispered, my eyes dropping to her mouth before I dragged them back up to her face. Where I saw her conflict, dulling the warmth of them. She was struggling against what simmered undeniably between us and how I'd rejected her earlier. "I wish you'd let the world see you a little more."

You can't just go after someone else when things get hard.

Things hadn't even gotten hard yet, and here I was, my body aching to close the careful space between us. To kiss her into oblivion and make her gasp my name in pleasure. I let out a shuddered breath, my hand on her waist tightening as I fought to control those urges.

"Earlier," I said, clearing my throat and forcing my eyes away from the temptation of her mouth and her pretty face. "When you kissed me—"

"We don't have to talk about that," she said swiftly. "It was clearly a mistake."

"A mistake?" I asked, eyebrows knitting together and a pang of lonely hurt forcing its way beneath my skin. *Not good enough. Never good enough.*

"Of course it was," she said casually, as if it hadn't meant anything to her at all. "You didn't want to kiss me, and that's completely fine—"

"I've wanted to kiss you every moment of every single day I've been stuck in this fucking house."

Her jaw snapped shut at my words, her eyes wide.

"No, that's not entirely true," I admitted roughly. "I've wanted to do much more than kiss you. If you knew the things I've imagined . . . you'd run screaming."

"Then why didn't you?" She swallowed hard, her voice a husky whisper. I ran a hand through my hair before turning her in time to the music.

"I thought you hated me," I told her honestly. "Or at least that you didn't think about me in a romantic way."

"God, Will, I—"

Seb's eyes caught mine over her shoulder; there was trepidation and jealousy swirling in his expression, and my heart sank in my chest. If this had happened any earlier, perhaps tonight would end differently. Or maybe I would've been able to pour myself into her when she'd pressed her mouth to mine. But Jesse was *right*. I couldn't go back on my word to Seb. I wouldn't.

"It doesn't matter now," I said. My fingers twitched against the small of her back, itching for a cigarette between them. "Listen, the reason I pulled away earlier is because Seb and I decided to give things between us a real shot recently."

The spark of hope in her eyes faded. Until I was left with her showing nothing but neutral disinterest. Had her attraction to me only been some morbid fascination? Too damaged to actually consider as a partner, but damaged enough for some wild fun between the sheets. I hated to think about how often I'd taken them up on the prospect of casual sex. A small bandage on the wounds inflicted by my work for Lee.

"Good," she said, not unkindly but not warmly either.

"I just wanted you to know that it wasn't about *you*. I'm just . . . trying to be a better man. If Montana can be believed, I might even find redemption one day," I said with a bitter, self-deprecating laugh. Seb started to make his way through the crowd toward us just as the music ended and Savvy pulled out of my arms. I felt colder without the warmth of her skin seeping into mine.

"I truly hope you find it," she said, that goodness of hers leaching into every word.

"Mind if I cut in?" Seb said, smiling over at me. I watched as she ducked her head, nodding and turning away. My boyfriend took up her spot and ducked his head between my shoulder and my neck, wrapping his strong arms around my torso as she disappeared from sight, making me wonder for the millionth time today if I'd made a huge mistake.

CHAPTER NINETEEN

JESSE

W HEN I TURNED BACK to the bar, Audrey was gone. *Damnit*. Had I missed my chance?

With broad steps, I crossed to the bar to pour myself another drink. I drained the glass and poured another. My gaze shot out across the crowd, searching for her through my shaky vision. Alcohol flowed, and smoke hung thick in the air above the bodies merging together in time with the slow beat of the music. It thrummed inside of me, blending with the pounding of my heart in my ears.

I caught sight of a younger man near the food table. He was tall and lanky. He reminded me of The Kid.

Shit. My hand shot to my back pocket, and I pulled the letter out. I'd nearly forgotten about it. I set my drink aside and ripped open the envelope, eyes scouring the scribbled words across the page.

You're lucky I got your last letter. We intercepted the messenger at the state line. M sent riders ahead to scout out a place for us to stay. Hoping to arrive by the full moon. I'll let you know. -K

P.S. Stop being a dumbass. Get her back.

I couldn't help my barked laughter mixed with longing for my brother.

Suddenly, someone snatched the letter from my hand. My eyes zeroed in on Audrey's form before me as she smoothed out the letter. Panic gripped my chest. *Shit*. She couldn't read that.

"Who's *K*?" she asked, blue eyes glittering up at me. I tugged the letter from her and folded it, quickly tucking it into my back pocket. She narrowed her eyes playfully at me. "A long-lost lover?"

"Actually, no." I sipped my whiskey. "My younger brother. We call him The Kid."

"You call him *The Kid?* What's his real name?"

"Harry."

"What kind of name is that for a kid?" Her brow screwed up even as she spoke the words. Her chin tipped upward, much like in the library, when she'd finished citing the poem inked into my skin. Hope seized hold of me. She'd been so close to something that day. Maybe all it would take was a little nudge to push her past whatever boundary held her back.

"How do you know he's a kid?" I asked in a low voice.

For a moment, as her mouth opened, I expected her to call me a dumbass and say that of course she knew he was a kid. Her lips closed, and she crossed her arms over her chest.

"You did say *younger.*"

"Fair," I said, hope fading quickly into disappointment. "He isn't as much of a kid as he was when he got the nickname."

"How old is he?"

"Fourteen."

"You said *we.* Who's we?"

The blood drained from my face. I couldn't hide how my expression fell. I lowered my gaze and ran a shaky hand through my hair.

"Bonnie." She said her own name like a prayer. My tongue stuck heavy in my mouth. All I could do was nod. The moment hung between us as I remembered how she'd held me in the library, when we'd talked about her. As if she were dead and not right there. In a way, that was almost true.

I didn't know when she moved closer, but the next moment, Audrey's fingertips touched my chin. I lifted my gaze to hers, finding that tenderness in her eyes again. She shouldn't be looking at me like that. Not when this was my fault.

All of it was my fault. I hadn't taken note of the security at the base. I was more worried about fucking her than ensuring our safety. I wasn't there to stop them from taking The Kid.

And in those last, desperate moments, I couldn't convince her to stay.

Maybe I didn't deserve to get her back.

"Dance with me," Audrey said gently, blue eyes darkening. When I hesitated, she tugged the glass from my hand. I'd never imagined a time that those words would come from her mouth. Bonnie hated dancing.

But this wasn't Bonnie, I reminded myself for the hundredth time tonight.

Audrey lifted my glass to her mouth, lips wrapping around the rim as she drained the whiskey. A glint of mischief passed through her eyes as she deposited the empty glass on the bar, tangled her fingers with mine, and began to move backward toward the crowd.

She was so goddamn beautiful.

Like the day at that lake outside of Roswell, when she'd stripped to damn near nothing and slunk back into the water, beckoning me like a siren song. My cock sprang to life once more, remembering the heat of her in my arms against the cool water, the way I'd kissed her beneath the hot desert sun.

The world moved in slow motion, my pounding pulse drowning out everything else. The crowd flowed around her, blurry in the background as she remained constant. From that moment in Vegas, I'd only ever had eyes for her, and that hadn't changed even through distance and heartbreak. With each step, my body thrummed harder, building to the promised peak of pleasure in her gaze. I'd never needed anything so bad in my life as I needed her.

My gaze trailed the line of her cheek, her skin flushing. Whether it was from the heat or my scrutiny, I couldn't tell, but it sent a thrill through me. She might have kissed that asshole, but there was clearly something between us, something she couldn't deny even if she wanted to. I didn't hide my longing as my eyes roved lower, along the column of her throat and to the swell of her breasts.

I wanted her to know what she did to me. That without words, with little more than a gentle touch of her hand, I belonged to her implicitly, even if I couldn't tell her why.

As we reached the center of the crowd, Bonnie stopped walking. Instead, she moved toward me, flattening a palm over my pounding heart. She bit her bottom lip once more. *Goddamnit.* A challenge filled her eyes as she tipped her chin. I had to clench my jaw to stop myself from claiming her lips as mine.

"I don't know how to dance like this," I admitted, eyeing a nearby couple as they ground their pelvises together.

A wicked smile crossed her lips, sending my heart into the pit of my stomach. "It's just fucking standing up," she said, quirking an eyebrow suggestively at me. "You know how to do that, don't you?"

A deep rumble sounded from my chest. "I know how to do much more than that."

Audrey stared up at me through her lashes, once again biting her lip, as if she knew what that did to me. "Touch me."

I shuddered at her command, eyes blazing at her. "Where?" I growled, already itching to touch her in the ways I'd dreamt about over our lost years. She turned her back to me, her fingers wrapping around mine. She pressed against me, guiding my hands onto her hips. As she leaned into my chest, I gripped the soft flesh beneath her dress. A groan reverberated from her. She shuddered against me as I pressed my jean-clad cock against her supple ass. I bit back my own groan, nearly popping out of my jeans.

Bonnie swayed in time to the music, grinding her ass deliciously against me. *Goddamn*. She dragged her hair over one shoulder, brandishing the sweat-slickened skin of her neck to me. I leaned closer, bridging the gap in our heights, lips hovering above the sensitive skin over her pulse. Her scent enveloped me, sweet, tantalizing. Different. Not quite the bitter tang of ozone and sharp sting of pine I remembered, though it lingered beneath the sweetness of Audrey.

"You smell like rain," I said against her skin. I clutched the tender flesh of her thighs as she ground harder against me. *Goddamn it.* My tongue darted out, tracing the line of her pulse. She shuddered. I smiled against her skin. "You have no idea of the things I want to do to you."

With a flick of my wrist, I spun her to face me, tugging all of her soft curves intimately into my hard, unyielding body. I wrapped my arms tight around her, limbs tangling to the point that I didn't know where I ended and she began. I lifted a hand, my thumb sweeping across one of her nipples through the thin fabric. The gutteral sound that came from between her lips undid me.

My other hand slid down her side, pausing briefly at her hip as I pressed her against my cock. Dark blue eyes flashed up at me. I grinned. "Say the word. I'll have you bent over a table in seconds."

CHAPTER TWENTY

AUDREY

I THOUGHT HEARING HIM admit he wanted me would make me feel differently. That I would be less confused if things were purely physical. I wasn't. In fact, I felt more confused than ever. Memories, *real* memories, had been at the edge of my consciousness, yet I hadn't been able to grasp them. I'd been so terrified after the last one that I'd kissed Lucas Rutherford, and here I was, about to make yet another mistake.

I slid my hands to his shoulders and put some much-needed space between our bodies. Dragging in a breath that was thick with his scent, my chest strung too tight, I tried to ground myself through the haze of the whiskey.

"Why the sudden change of heart?" I asked, suspicious. "You've been pretty clear that you didn't want to *just* sleep with me. Why now?"

I already knew the answer, of course. The entire household had been buzzing with the news of Lucas and me. Enough that my father had commented on how proud he was to see me *holding up my end of our bargain.* Like my worth was in seducing a rich man, and none of the studying I'd done to this point had meant a goddamned thing.

Was Montana jealous of Lucas? Or just trying to bury his grief in my body?

"Because I couldn't let that Rutherford fucker steal you away from me." His deep voice rumbled beneath my skin. I leaned back, needing to let him feel the long curve of my spine as he dipped me low to the thick bass of the music. My breasts arched up, his strong hands keeping me aloft for a breathless moment before he dragged me back against the dizzying heat of his body. Inch by inch we came together, powerful and devastating, until my eyes met the striking desire in his own, thudding into me like the tip of a knife into my chest.

As our bodies writhed together, I knew that if I gave myself to him, he would know *exactly* what I wanted without words. That he would unravel me at the seams until I begged for more. One of his thumbs ran from my temple, along my jaw, to the pounding pulse in my neck.

"My father wants me to give him a chance." Yearning throbbed in time to my heartbeat, in every piece of me. Through my chest, tingling in my extremities, thudding between my legs where his thigh guided us to the thumping of the music.

"Is that what you want?" His deep baritone set my nerve endings aflame. The dark tone of his voice, the flash of his bright eyes, the tightening of his hands along my spine. He was *jealous*. But more than that, he was the first person who'd made any of this feel like *my* choice. The words turned to ash in my mouth, and I stilled, our bodies frozen amongst the writhing masses. I couldn't look away from his devastating eyes if I wanted to. Even if I wanted to lie, nothing came to mind. The truth spilled from me in a hot rush.

"I want *out*." I wouldn't apologize for being selfish. I'd spent so long stuck in the past or trying to get my father to see my worth. I *needed* to be selfish. If I wasn't, who else would look out for me? "I want to leave this house and see the world. Lucas can give me that."

His eyes flashed in the dim light, and he gripped me tight for a moment before loosening. A muscle ticked in his jaw. Violent yearning lurked in the set of his shoulders and the too-still way he held his body against me.

"What if I took you away from here?" His voice went dark again. I shook my head but didn't speak. This was *crazy*. But the possibility of having my freedom *and* Montana thrummed straight to my heart, and my lungs swelled with hope. When I still said nothing, he wrapped a strong arm behind me and hauled me against his body. His cock was hard against my thigh, and a gasp of pleasure fell from my open mouth.

"Did kissing him feel anything like this?" He tipped my chin up to inspect my expression. Too open, too lost in dark thoughts. I laughed at the question, blatantly. Shaking my head silently.

"No, it was . . ." What was it about this man that made me feel so *safe*? So comfortable saying all the things I would never dare tell anyone else. "Soft," I said, watching as a satisfied glint lit the blue of his eyes from within.

"That's because you weren't kissed by a *man*." His voice was so deep, it was almost hard to hear. His tone was pure sex. "Do you want to be?"

My hands traced the lines of his shirt and the hard planes of his chest to settle on his shoulders. No one paid us any mind. Frozen in the midst of swaying bodies, the scent of sweat and lust hanging heavy in the air. As I reached the skin of his neck, arms hooking around his shoulders, he inched closer. Waiting. Always waiting. For my permission.

If I kissed him, my entire world would shift beneath my feet, and nothing would make sense anymore. It radiated in the air around us, begging for release, like my body. Strung taut, waiting to snap. I opened my mouth, and his eyes were hot on my lips.

"Audrey!" a familiar, jarring voice called over the music. My eyes shifted as panic lanced down my spine, sending tendrils of cold dread down my legs. Luke's furious face locked on mine as he pushed through the crowded dance floor. I twisted from Montana's arms, feeling the absence of them immediately.

"What the hell do you think you're doing?" Lucas asked, his lip curled in disgust as he surveyed the room. He gripped my arm above my elbow and dragged me away. People stopped, music quieted, and whispers sounded in our wake as the scene unfolded. I tried to glance over my shoulder to see Montana, but Lucas yanked me forward, making it impossible to find his gaze before I plunged into the screaming wind and torrential rain.

CHAPTER TWENTY-ONE

SAVANNAH

WHY THE HELL WAS I even still here?

No one talked to me. No one spared me more than a second's glance. I shouldn't have come. If it hadn't been for Audrey's excitement at picking my outfit and fixing my hair, I wouldn't have. The sheer mortification of facing William Ellis after earlier today made me want to disappear.

I found him for at least the tenth time since I'd left him with Sebastian. His *boyfriend*. Officially.

I didn't realize how much that would hurt me. I didn't think I *could* be hurt by Will. He didn't owe me anything. There was *nothing* between us. That didn't ease the ache in my chest.

Will tossed back his head, laughing. There was a glimmer in his eyes as he spoke with Sebastian while they danced. Jealousy rose like bile in my throat. *Jesus Christ*, I swore at myself. *There was nothing there. Get over yourself.*

I'd spent most of the last three years avoiding my feelings, knowing that there would never be anything between us. And still, I'd kissed him. I'd come to this party. I'd done so many stupid things because a beautiful man asked me to.

I forced my eyes away, that jealousy easing only slightly when I found Audrey.

Then all hell broke loose.

Rutherford stormed in and out, taking her with him. I didn't like that possessive look in his eyes. The crowd milled about, tossing around the usual insults about Audrey's state of mind. A breath, and Montana headed for the exit. Nothing good would come of this. I darted after him, shoving past staff members as I marched toward the double doors. Beyond, standing in the breezeway, I thought I spied a familiar form. I wasn't the only one. Will had gone after Montana as well.

Only, he hovered at the open doors. I ducked behind an oversized vase.

Patrick MacNeil and Will were in a heated discussion. Some of the jealousy in my chest eased at the sight of Rutherford's friend. I'd sent him a brief note while I was in the kitchens, inviting him. He'd come. Maybe Will was wrong about him.

I strode toward the exit in time to spy Patrick stalk off through the courtyard. Will reset the switchblade in his hand as he turned around, freezing at the sight of me. Instantly, his cheeks flushed, and shame flooded his eyes. I folded my arms over my chest.

"What was that?"

"That? Nothing." He tucked the blade back into his boot.

My brows lifted as he attempted to brush past. I moved in front of him, denying him re-entrance to the party. "What did you say to him?"

Will's gaze darted toward the now-empty courtyard. He shrugged. "A few choice words. Just in case he forgot who I was."

"How could anyone forget who you—" I cut myself off, horrified. He *didn't*. The tense words they'd spoken as I'd watched them. The blade in Will's hand. He'd *threatened* Patrick. The very man he'd dared me to invite to see if he'd come to the party. He had. Yet Will intervened. *Again*. My face screwed up as furious tears stung my eyes. I shook my head, not allowing it to show.

At least Will had the decency to look guilty.

"Let me say this, just to be certain that I'm crystal clear," I said in a low voice, closing the space between us. "You're with someone else—" He opened his mouth to argue with me, but I held a hand up to silence him. "And you sabotage someone who *might* want to be with me."

"He just wants to *fuck* you—"

"So what!" I threw my hands up, dark laughter bubbling deep within me. "Have you ever thought for one second maybe *that*'s what I want?"

The color drained from his face. He looked at me as if I'd slapped him.

"Of course not, right? *Un*fuck*able* Savannah. That's what they all say. Just because I don't throw myself at people doesn't mean I can't want actual human connection once in a while."

I averted my gaze, unable to stomach this. "You have a twisted way of handling things that have *nothing* to do with you."

"Nothing to do with me?" Will asked, his voice rising in a way it never had at me. "You were kissing me a few hours ago!"

"Which would have *never* happened if you just minded your own damn business!"

"You kissed *me*. That makes you my goddamn business!"

"You are *delusional!*" Wasn't it bad enough that I'd embarrassed myself by kissing him? He just had to throw it in my face like it was some defense.

"No. You just don't want to admit that it's not that son of a bitch you want in your bed." He leaned close. Too close. "Say it, Savvy. Admit you want me to fuck you so hard you can't think straight." He was so close now that I felt his shuddering breath on my upturned face. My stomach plummeted at his crass words. But also . . . the truth in them.

Not that I'd admit it to *him*.

"I wouldn't *screw* you if you were the last man on earth, you arrogant prick!"

His face fell into a stony expression that I couldn't read.

"I don't have time to deal with whatever jealous bullshit this is, especially when you have *no right*." I turned on my heel, needing distance, even if that put me in the path of the storm. "I have to make sure everything's okay with my best friend."

"She's not *your* best friend!" he shouted. "She's mine!"

Something broke in him. He stared at me, but I could tell he didn't really see me. Will ran his hands through his hair, eyes shifting back and forth as panic set in. My brows furrowed as his shoulders slumped, making him appear smaller. He peered over at me, something like resignation in his eyes.

"What are you talking about?"

"Shit," he swore, tugging his hair near the scalp. "I said I wasn't going to involve you—"

"Involve me in what?" I crossed my arms, anger shifting to concern. The harsh lines of his face relaxed, even if there was still self-loathing in his gaze.

"For fuck's sake, I've known her my entire life, Savannah." He fixed me with dark eyes. "She's been my best friend since we were children." My lips parted, but I couldn't speak. My brow screwed up as I considered. How could that possibly be true? He and Audrey had a cordial acquaintance, but never once had he pushed beyond the boundaries of propriety.

"You never asked about *before*," he said, fixing me with a hard stare. "Never asked me why I was the one carrying her into this house. Why not?"

My throat went dry at the mention of *that* night. At the desperation and grief in his eyes.

"It wasn't my place." I suddenly felt small. My gaze fell to the damp stone as I remembered the crash outside my room, finding Will there alone, grief-stricken. "You'd already been through so much that night. I didn't think asking you about it would help. And when Mr. Lee gave us strict instructions on how to handle everything, I just—"

How did I miss it?

Had my hurt feelings blinded me to the gentle way Will spoke to Audrey when she was lost to her glowroot cravings? Had my pride kept me from realizing that he spent mornings training with Audrey not because *she* needed it, but *he* did?

"I'm sorry," I said, finally lifting my eyes. "I always assumed that if you wanted to talk about it, you would."

Will blew out a long breath, whiskey mixed with the bitter scent of tobacco. The sounds of the party were miles away as he stepped closer to me. My breath hitched as his warmth washed across my skin. *Jesus Christ, Savannah.*

"I made a deal with Lee. So I could stay with her. Protect her." His words settled heavily between us.

All the times he'd randomly poked his head into the kitchen to ask me how Audrey was doing. Even if he sometimes talked around it. It hadn't been to annoy me. I peered up at him. Well, maybe not *just* to annoy me.

"She's the only real family I've ever had. Every day, she looks right past me and remembers *nothing.*"

My fingers twitched at my side with the need to reach out, to comfort him, because I knew that feeling, losing everything important to you. I balled my hands into fists, my nails digging into my palms so hard they hurt.

"That woman . . . She's not some rich asshole's daughter. She's an outlaw. Like me. Like Jess—*Montana.*" Will paced away from me, once again tugging his hair.

Was I finally learning the truth about Audrey?

When Will advanced on me, I stood my ground. I wasn't afraid of him; I never had been. In fact, that crazed look in his eyes and the pale tint to his skin made me want to touch him. To comfort him. To lend him my shoulder, as he desperately needed it.

"No, fuck it. I've already told you this much." He blew out a breath. "*Montana's* real name is Jesse. He's the love of her life. My father ripped them apart when he gave her that head wound and tried to cut my fuckin' face off."

My gaze lifted to the scar that ran from his temple to the corner of his eye. I'd gotten used to it since seeing it that first night, even if he kept it concealed beneath his hat most of the time.

"He's been searching for her for three years, Savvy." He placed gentle hands on my upper arms. Warmth crept across my skin beneath his touch. "He's here to help her remember who she is. To get her back."

Deep down, I ached. While I understood Will's pain, the things he told me, what if the person she was *before* . . . the *outlaw* . . . what if, when she remembered who she was, she hated me?

After all, the night that broke Audrey was *my* fault. I still heard her inhuman wails of agony late at night. Her dead, lifeless eyes haunted me for months after. All this time, I'd coaxed her back into a semblance of normal. Just as much to absolve my guilt as to help her. What if, when she remembered, she realized I'd stolen everything from her?

Even if it meant she'd hate me, I would never forgive myself if I didn't do something. Will was an asshole, sure, but I knew he spoke true by the sincerity in his eyes. There was a chance that I could lose Audrey in the midst of all this, but it wasn't fair to her or Montana—*Jesse*.

It wasn't fair to Will.

So, I asked, "How can I help?"

CHAPTER TWENTY-TWO

AUDREY

C HILLY RAIN RAN OVER my skin, soaking my dress and plunging me back into reality. Luke didn't spare a glance at me as I stumbled behind him into the main house and up the stairs. It was when we arrived at my door that I found my voice again.

"Let me go." The words echoed without response. All the guards were at the party, and the house was stifled from the storm prep. I tried to wrench my arm from his grip. Instead, he spun me toward him, jaw hard and fury dulling his normally kind eyes. He pressed me against the wall, eyes running over my body, nothing hidden by my translucent dress.

Lightning flashed beyond the shuttered windows. He pressed his mouth to mine, swallowing my protest as I shoved against his chest.

A bright smile on a dark face, looming over me. "You'll pay for that, bitch." I sobbed, and the man above me grinned lasciviously. I tried to push against him, to fight, but his weight held me down.

"Stop!" I cried, hot tears streaking over my face. He fumbled with his belt buckle, pushing my jeans down and settling between my thighs.

Powerless. Dirty. Used.

Lucas tried to pry my lips open beneath his, and I twisted until my shoulder slammed into his chest, sending him sprawling against the railing. I wiped my mouth clean of his unwanted kiss, spitting at his feet.

"The next time you touch me without permission will be the last time you touch *anyone*." I didn't recognize my dangerous growl but felt it through my entire body. I stood tall and fisted my hands at my sides, muscles taut and ready to strike should he test me.

"You were down there practically fucking the help." His mouth twisted into a sneer. "Now you want to act shy?"

"Shy?" Rage simmered low and steady in my chest, ready to blaze forth at the slightest provocation.

"After the other day, I thought we had an *understanding*."

"We *kissed*. Under the influence of alcohol. If you think for one second that gives you some sort of ownership over me, you're wrong," I seethed. "I can dance with, kiss, or *fuck* anyone I want. I'm not your property. I don't owe you anything."

He ran frustrated hands through his hair and turned on me, glaring and stepping too close. I tensed at his nearness.

"It's not like you've given me a real chance! All I've done is try to get to know you. But nothing I do seems to matter."

"Why exactly have you been trying to get to know me, *Luke*?" My words turned cruel as my eyes flashed dark in the hallway. I felt the feral smile as it curled on my mouth, lips pulled back from my teeth like a wild beast scenting blood in the air. "You're here to make a deal with my father. You've given me no reason to trust you. No reason to think you aren't just interested in me because of this business deal. Be honest. You wouldn't look *twice* at me if it weren't for the goddamned contract."

He laughed, incredulous as he stared at me like he was seeing me for the first time. Maybe he was. The thrumming in my blood urged me to violence. Urged me to eliminate the threat of him before he could strike first.

"Stay the fuck away from me if you know what's good for you." I turned on my heel before I did something I'd regret. I slammed the door behind me, adrenaline rushing through my blood. With nothing to do to mute the swelling urge to run or slam my fist against something, I paced. Rainwater dripped from the ends of my hair, slicking my dress against each curve of my body like a second skin.

The settling heat was nearly unbearable, sticky and cloying against my flesh. I crossed to my vanity, planning to pull my hair back as my pulse slowed. My father wouldn't be happy with how I'd treated Luke tonight.

A rapid knocking sounded, and I gritted my teeth together at the prospect of round two with Lucas.

"What?!" I flung the door wide, stilling at the sight before me.

Montana.

There he was, arms stretched above him, his fingertips clenched along the top of the doorframe. He seemed impossibly taller when he stood that way, body stretched so long it exposed a line of flesh between the edge of his shirt and the waistband of his jeans. He was soaked too, having obviously walked through the torrents of rain to get here. His tattoos were visible beneath his see-through shirt, sticking in the hollows of his muscled chest and stomach.

He raised a curious eyebrow. The panic simmering below my skin cooled almost immediately. Now, I felt silly and childish. The scene Lucas made earlier forced a flush into my cheeks. I'd let him drag me out of there like a petulant toddler.

"Expecting someone else?" Sarcasm lilted the deep timbre of his voice. I breathed out a chuckle, my hand dropping away from the doorknob as I waved him in with a bored flick of my wrist.

"Yes." I crossed back to my vanity and fiddled nervously with my brush. The door clicked shut, and I noticed he'd walked into my room, gaze roving over the space with calculating interest. It lingered in places that made me feel vulnerable. Like my closet door, riddled with holes and hairpins from my throwing sessions. Or the desk in the corner, piled high with books. I twisted my hands together. He was too large in the expanse of my room, too tall, too *male*.

I didn't know what to say. So instead, I walked to the door, flicking the lock into place. The sound echoed between us. His gaze found mine in the darkness as lightning flashed beyond the windows. My heart thudded hard in my chest. His lusty promises from the dance floor weighed heavy in his eyes.

"Savannah," I said by way of explanation. "She has a tendency to walk in without knocking, and I don't want her to have to lie to my father."

He stayed silent, instead offering a half-drunk bottle of whiskey he'd brought with him. Being that close to him felt dangerous, but after my argument and the violence thrumming through my body, I needed to tempt the danger of him.

I took a swig, relishing the burn of the liquor as it slid down my throat and settled into my blood.

"She thinks I don't know that my father makes her spy on me." What did he think of *that*? He took the bottle, bringing it to his mouth quickly, a bead of the liquor lingering on his full bottom lip. "I don't want her to have to tell him about this."

"What is *this*?" His words came out in a hot rush. Too honest. Too raw. I shivered. Tension hung low in the air, roiling between us like storm clouds. He wanted me to admit that I wanted *more* from him. More than just sex. It might be true, but I wasn't ready to say it. Not yet.

"Why are you here?"

He shrugged. Neither of us wanted to answer direct questions tonight.

"I wanted to make sure you were okay." The words sounded false, a flimsy excuse. One that brought him into my bedroom after his declaration about bending me over and fucking the blush off my cheeks.

"I'm a big girl, Montana. I can take care of myself."

He dipped his head in understanding, eyes shuttering, like the windows of this expansive mansion. Locking away the hurricane inside his gaze.

He turned for the exit, lithe strides retreating from me. As he reached the door and placed a hand on the knob, he glanced at me from over his shoulder.

"I lied." The deep resonance of his voice shook the air between us. Thunderous and damaging. "I didn't come here to check on you." I sucked in a sharp breath, the sound whistling between my teeth.

"You never told me downstairs," he stated. "Would you leave with me if I asked?"

I couldn't answer that question. I didn't know how to handle anything that'd happened tonight. Closing my eyes for a long moment, I tried to settle my rapid pulse. When it didn't work, I opened my eyes to see he hadn't moved an inch. The longer we stared, the more charged the air became. He placed the whiskey bottle on an end table, eyes never leaving mine.

"I can't answer that."

"Why not?" His tongue flicked out to lick the whiskey from his bottom lip.

"You know why," I whispered. He shook his head, the motion tossing his hair over his eyes. I wanted to push the locks from his face. Wanted to bury my hands in his still-damp tresses.

"No, I don't." He moved toward me. Each step shifted the ground beneath my feet. The wind screamed beyond the windows, shaking them in their frames. "Tell me what you want."

As if it were that simple. As if I were allowed to want anything for myself. As long as I met my father's many expectations and pretended the darkness of my past didn't exist, I had a measure of peace, a sliver of life for myself. But *wanting* like this wasn't possible, it wasn't in the rules. *Wanting* like this would destroy me. My heart slammed against my ribs. My breath came in ragged bursts.

"Why do you comfort me in the library? Why do you look like you're going to murder any woman that gets close to me? Why did you dance with me like you wanted me to pull you into the nearest dark room and make you scream my name until you couldn't speak?" With every question, he closed the distance between us, the storm in his eyes threatening to break.

I opened my mouth, but no answer came. Because we both knew the truth. We knew what neither of us said aloud. That whatever was happening between us was *undeniable.*

So I crossed the room with fury in my gaze. I gripped his shirt and pulled him down to my mouth. As I pressed my lips hard to his, his spine snapped straight and his arms stiffened at his sides. My stomach lurched at his reaction. He'd talked a big game about wanting me tonight, but by his own admission, he hadn't been with a woman since Bonnie. What if this was too much? Too fast?

Stupid. He turned down a threesome tonight. Why the hell would he want you?

"I'm sorry." I wished I could be enough to lessen the sting of her loss. I ran my hands through my hair as I fought my humiliation, fingertips pressed to my lips.

"I shouldn't have done that," I said. "Forget it happened."

He hadn't moved. Instead, his blue eyes flashed in the darkness like a strike of lightning in the room. I opened my mouth to say something else, desperate to smooth things over between us.

"Are you drunk?" The deep timbre of his voice was gravelly in a way I'd never heard. Like water in a deep canyon, running over the rocks, vowels rounded pleasantly by the echo off of steep cliff faces.

"No," I said, clearly confused.

"Are you sure?" The same silent command remained in the timbre of his voice.

"Yes." I swallowed hard as the danger lurking in his lightning-strike eyes flashed bright and clear.

"Good. Because I want you to remember this." His words careened toward me before I could comprehend them. Then the hurricane trapped in the cage of his body broke and unleashed on me. In two long, graceful strides, he crossed the room. His large, calloused hands gripped my head, and he wrenched my face up to his own. The hard slant of his mouth slammed against mine with the might of a gale force wind.

My back banged against the wall, and he pried my lips open beneath his. A breath, a heartbeat, a muffled cry. That was how long it took to respond to the onslaught of him. A wolf was unchained within me. Pitch black, jaws snapping, rending through all my reservations. I clawed at his skin, needing him closer, harder. His tongue plunged into my mouth with ruthless intention, and I matched his fervor stroke for stroke.

Some hidden part of me unlocked, freed by the taste of him in my mouth. He wasn't gentle, and neither was I. His lips bruised mine, and my teeth bit down on his lip, every breath raked in as if it'd been a prize won in battle. Then his mouth was at my throat, stubble rasping against my neck as the heat of his kisses dipped lower.

"More." I plunged my fingers in his hair.

He didn't need further prompting. His hands lowered to my hips and gripped my ass, forcing me off my feet and carrying me the short distance to my desk. He shoved me onto it, books falling forgotten. My thighs fell open for him, my dress bunching up as he settled between them. His cock pressed punishingly against me. He caught my mouth again, and suddenly I was drowning in sensation.

I lifted my hips, grinding our bodies together, the friction sending sparks of pleasure racing down my spine until I could barely think. He slammed his palm against the top of the desk as he dragged his mouth from mine.

"If you do that again, I won't be able to hold back anymore."

"This is you holding back?" I asked, breathless and mindless. His gaze roved over me. I felt the path his eyes took like a brush of fingertips against my skin. He drank in my passion-glazed eyes, my flushed skin, my swollen lips. His eyes dipped to my pounding pulse and the hard points of my nipples straining against my dress.

"Yes." The word vibrated against my skin as his fingers tangled wildly in my hair. Then he kissed me like it was the last thing he would ever do. Until I forgot who I was, where I was, that there was anything but *this*. Time was meaningless. I was burning alive, lightning crackling along every nerve ending and turning me to ash, until my bones melted beneath the heat of our open mouths and I became pliant beneath him.

One of his hands fisted in my hair, and he pulled softly to angle my chin higher until I was completely at his mercy. His other hand wrapped tenderly around my throat, fingers tensing and stroking down the length of my neck until he slid the strap of my dress over my shoulder. The slick fabric shifted and rolled down, peeling from my skin until my breast was freed. A shiver ran down my spine, cool air washing over my still-damp skin.

"Fuck." He tugged off the other strap and folded the top beneath my breasts to bare them completely. "You are so fucking beautiful."

The rasp of his stubbled jaw and the hot, wet slide of his mouth down my neck made me whimper. It was too good. Too *fucking* good. As his mouth traveled lower, past my collarbone, I raked my nails through his hair and arched my back. My body wasn't my own anymore.

It was his now.

"I can taste the rain on your skin," he mumbled against the swell of my breast before his teeth scraped against the sensitive skin. I made a pitiful, desperate noise, eyes rolling in the back of my head when his tongue *finally* covered my hard nipple. He groaned, sucking the tender flesh into his mouth, arm snaking around to clutch me tight and keep me flush against him.

I couldn't move. Couldn't writhe or arch or wriggle, and I needed friction to relieve the swell of desperate frustration flooding between my thighs. Only, Montana took his time gorging himself on the taste of my breasts. I tugged his hair between my fingers, trying and failing to buck my hips beneath him.

"I need—" My words stuttered into nothing at a greedy flick of his talented tongue. "I need your skin against mine."

Finally, he lifted his head, licking his lips as if he could still taste me on them. He was so much more handsome like this. Eyes dark with lust, hair mussed, lips swollen. It was unfair how he looked better the more unraveled he became. I wanted to see him completely undone. Fisting my hands in his shirt, my nails raking his skin, I pulled it up. He tossed the wet fabric to the floor as I leaned forward, pressing my lips over his hammering heart and tracing my tongue over the hard lines of his chest.

The salt on his skin, how his muscles bunched and tensed as I mapped his body, drove me into a mindless frenzy. This wasn't like the others. Those had been distractions. I'd never been so connected to myself before. Every ragged beat of my heart, every throbbing pulse deafening my ears and spreading heat along each square inch of my skin, grounded me here. A storm raged outside, battering the walls of this ancient house, but the one in this room was tearing apart my defenses. Brick by hateful brick.

His fingers curled into the fabric of my underwear. He lowered to his knees, sliding the fabric along my thighs and sending a shiver of pleasure down my spine. My mouth dropped open at the sight of him, kneeling before me. His blue eyes were dark and possessive as he stared at me, glistening for him in the scant moonlight.

"I know what you need," he said, his voice gravelly with promised pleasure. His teeth raked against the inside of my thigh, tongue trailing closer.

"Touch me."

His eyes lifted to mine, and he stood to his full, towering height. Only it didn't make me feel small now; instead, knowing I could bring this mountain of a man to his knees made a reckless sort of power thrum in my chest. His hands, calloused and thick from the violence he'd inflicted, ran over my knees, streaking lines of quivering heat in his wake.

His fingers dug punishingly into my thighs as he bunched my skirt at my waist. For all the ways I'd witnessed him control himself, shutting down other women, walking away from anything too *intimate,* I saw none of that control now. His palm flattened against the skin of my lower belly, and his thumb reached the small bundle of nerves at the top of my sex.

I cried out, collapsing on top of the desk. With slow circles, he teased me, his thumb never quite reaching exactly where I needed the pressure. From the wicked glint in his eyes, he knew it too.

"Please." I jerked involuntarily beneath the ministrations of his hand.

"You beg so pretty for me." His words settled deep in my bones. Until I was being shaken apart by them, by *him.* Another maddening circle. He leaned his face down to take my earlobe between his teeth. "Beg me again*.* " It wasn't a question, but a command. One I was defenseless against.

"*Please,* I need—" But I couldn't quite form a coherent thought. He pressed his thumb down hard. A screaming gasp erupted from my mouth. "Yes!" He sank one of his thick fingers deep inside me. My hands scrambled for purchase, nails raking his skin as I arched my hips and tried to drag him deeper. I wanted him to give me *everything.*

"Tell me what you want."

My head tossed back and forth. I couldn't *think*, much less speak.

His other hand wrapped around my throat again, anchoring my writhing body. "*Beg me again.*"

My hips arched and bucked against him, until I was wild and lost to the intoxicating desire pulsing hot in my veins. I'd tell him anything. Give him *anything.* Give him all of myself. I was his anyway. I was ruined for anyone else.

"Please." I pleaded for the release I was so desperate to achieve. Another finger plunged deep, sliding, stretching. A strangled sound came from my throat. He raced me toward a precipice like none before. Eyes locked on my face as I succumbed to him, mapping every expression, memorizing each gasp and moan. *"Please, Montana, Please!"*

All it would take was a shudder of a breath or the whisper of his skin on mine. Instead, the hurricane in his eyes died. Like the wind falling out of the sails of a ship. In the next few moments, shame and humiliation blushed over my skin as his hands retreated from my body.

When he put space between us, his expression locked down. Cold seeped into the place he'd occupied before. I was left bare and open, sprawled on the desktop as he turned away. Furious tears pricked my eyes. At first, confusion swept over me, then anger. The shame came last, but of all the emotions, it remained.

He shoved his damp shirt on, rolling the fabric over his skin until he was covered. It put into perspective how naked I was. Frigid rejection dripped down my spine and left me bereft. I hooked the straps of my dress up and tugged my skirt down to cover my thighs. My knees squeezed together as I slid onto quaking legs.

One of his hands found my shoulder. I turned but couldn't look up at him. Not like this. This was *too much*. Just as I'd feared. At the edge of oblivion, he'd balked. As if realizing that it was only me, not his *Bonnie*, writhing beneath him.

All I wanted was to be *enough*.

Swiftly, I pushed his hand from my skin.

"Hey." His voice was soft and conciliatory. I shook my head, blinking back furious tears while keeping my gaze averted from his face. "Look at me."

Another command I couldn't ignore. With a steadying breath, feeling the tears settle back in my eyes, I tilted my chin. I wasn't sure what he saw. Or if he cared about how this only reinforced all the worst thoughts rolling around in my mind.

"It's just—"

"It's *fine*," I lied.

He reached for me, to drag me into the heat of his body. I held my arms out and refused him, unable to handle the friction of his skin on mine. Not knowing that while his fingers might have been inside of *me*, he'd been thinking of another woman. I couldn't compete with a ghost. I didn't want to. I was no stranger to loss and grief, but it was apparent to me now that unless he *wanted* to move on, he wouldn't.

And I wouldn't be the woman he used to piece himself back together.

A sick churning started in my gut. Was I the same? Stagnant. Unable to live life to its fullest because of my own grief? Biting the inside of my cheek hard, I waved a hand lackadaisically at the door.

"Audrey—"

I needed to be alone while I tried to untangle the knot of darkness in my mind. No, I needed *space*. Needed time and care. Not whatever fleeting pleasure I thought I could find with the beautiful man in front of me.

"Leave."

He ran frustrated hands through his hair, a muscle in his jaw feathering as he squared off against me. "I can explain—"

"I don't *want* an explanation." I wanted him to leave before the ghosts of my past caught up to me. "I want you to leave."

"But—"

"Whatever *this* was, it's over. I'm done letting you play games with me."

Ducking his head, he turned to the door, shoulders slumped in defeat. I'd done the impossible; I'd defeated Montana. I'd reduced him to slinking from my room in shame after *years* of abstinence.

When the door shut, I curled up beneath my duvet and cried until there were no tears left. It didn't matter that my dress was still damp or that my hair was a mess. All that mattered was the swell of sadness I couldn't quite shake and the nightmares that came for me when my eyes closed.

CHAPTER TWENTY-THREE

WILL

I *HAVE A JOB for you.*

It'd only been two weeks since the hurricane party. Two weeks of spending every night in Seb's room and avoiding Savannah at all costs. My guilt drove me into his arms again and again. And somehow, in making up for my transgressions, I began to find us again. Making him pretentious tea in the mornings and reading aloud to him while he rested his head in my lap. Kissing him when he got off shift until he was breathless. Letting him attempt to braid my hair and fail miserably.

But, of course, the relative peace I'd found wouldn't last. Zachary had too many enterprises, too many people to rule over. This was the bargain I made. In order to stay close to Bonnie, to try to piece her broken body back together, I became his weapon.

I shut down the way I always did, burying anything good or joyful so deep it wouldn't witness what I'd become. All the pieces of *Will* I'd gathered since Jesse had reappeared in my life vanished into a dark corner of my mind. Without words, I readied myself; the envelope in my back pocket had a name in Zachary's perfectly penned letters. As I loped through the house to Jesse's room, whatever tenuous warmth had begun seeping into the staff had clearly been sapped.

Everyone gave me a wide berth. Maybe it was the expression on my face. Or the soullessness in my eyes.

It didn't matter.

At least Jesse was out of town and not here to witness my descent back into madness.

I entered the room quietly, finding a black shirt and changing. Black hid the blood that would stain my clothes tonight. I strapped on my gun belt, checking the rounds of the black piece before pulling several knives of varying lengths from the bottom of my saddlebag. I hid them efficiently. One on my belt, one in my boot, two hidden by the fabric of my shirt. Finally, I tied my hair away from my face into a tight knot at the base of my neck, settling my hat on my head low enough to hide my eyes.

Thank God Jesse didn't get back until tonight. I wasn't sure I could explain this away. I'd alluded to the work I did, but he didn't know everything. I couldn't bring myself to tell him the truth of what I was. What I *did*. He'd been the only person in so long who knew me before I became *this*.

I'd almost made it to the alley when Seb called my name. My spine stiffened, and my feet froze to the cobblestones.

"Don't go." He hovered just behind my shoulder. He'd never begged me for anything before. "You don't have to do this anymore. Just tell him *no*." He pressed his face between my shoulder blades, wrapping his arms around my waist.

"I have to," I breathed in a harsh whisper, because I didn't trust my voice not to falter.

"You have a *choice*." He moved in front of me. Lifting my hands to cradle my jaw, he tried to comfort a part of me that'd long been carved away. "Just walk away. I'll walk with you."

My heart ached to accept his offer, to burn the name in my pocket. To feel the way I had since Jesse had returned. Like there was hope that I could one day find redemption. Hope that it hadn't been for nothing. That he would find a way to get Bonnie back and she could help me stitch together my shattered soul.

I clenched my teeth so tight they hurt. A muscle in my jaw ticked beneath his fingertips. His hands dropped, and he stepped away. I wasn't Will anymore.

I was Zachary's retribution, and he wouldn't be kept waiting.

"Tell Montana I'll be back by morning." I brushed past him, ignoring the hurt that flashed in his beautiful, dark eyes.

"Morning?" He stared at the midday sun around us.

"Zachary wants me to send a message. It'll probably take all night." Seb's shoulders stiffened, anger hardening his jaw. He knew what this would take from me. The pieces of myself that I would never get back.

I walked away without looking back. The alley opened up to the stables on the far side of the house. I didn't have to ask the groom to ready my horse. Zachary must have sent word ahead of me.

I guided my stallion out, black as pitch, making it easy to move unseen at night. Checking the long lengths of ropes carefully coiled over the saddle horn, I slowly retrieved my cigarette case to light one. I inhaled the nicotine deep, settling the raw edges of my nerves and resigning myself to my purpose. I looked up to the sky for a moment as I finished. Was there a God? What did he see if he looked down on me?

I flicked the cigarette, pulling out the envelope from my pocket and reading the tidy words several times as dread unfurled in my stomach.

The Melancon Brothers.

A dark chuckle escaped before I could stamp it down. Of *fucking* course. I headed out, mind whirring through plans to get the job done. Multiple targets, more opportunity for things to go wrong. It didn't matter to Zachary that he didn't provide me with *how many* brothers there were. Just that they were all taken care of.

I trotted toward the other end of the city, taking as many back alleys and side streets as I could. I was too recognizable in the open, and I would need the element of surprise on my side tonight. The humidity strangled me as the hours grew long and the sun dipped in the late afternoon. I stopped in front of a dark building marked with a white *X* on the door. I was in the fringes now. As long as I had coin or glowroot in hand, I'd get all the information I needed.

I shoved into the half-barricaded door, hand poised on my gun. Several undesirables slunk toward me, happy to see me for another unsavory transaction.

"The Melancon Brothers. Where and how many?" I fished a few copper bits out of my pocket and held them on my palm. One undesirable, a woman with red hair so dirty it reminded me of the color of dried blood, stepped forward. She placed her ruined hand, fingers fused together, on top of the coins and glared at me with green eyes that glowed in the darkness.

"Three. In the warehouse district near the river. The house with blue shutters." She clutched the money to her chest and slipped into the shadows. It was the only time I didn't see fear settle deep in someone's eyes, when I came here. Or when I looked at Savvy. But people on the fringes weren't scared of anything.

"*Gracias,*" I muttered softly.

"I hope they kill you." Her voice echoed in my mind as I exited the hovel and mounted my horse.

"Me too," I muttered darkly. The light was fading fast now, and I needed to make up for lost time. *Three*. I didn't like being outnumbered, and I hated the idea of my night's work even more. Just as the sun disappeared below the horizon and the last rays of light cast long shadows over the pockmarked street, I found the house.

Blue shutters, and wildflowers grew in boxes beneath the windows. Lace curtains drifted in the slight breeze through the open panes. This was a family's home. I looped my stallion's reins around the fence as I approached, stomach churning.

Instead of striding right up to the front door, I prowled around the side, sticking to the shadows. I peered in through the window to catch sight of my targets. They were all there. The eldest brother led the rest of the family in prayer as they sat around a large wooden table. The youngest brother couldn't have been more than twenty, and his irreverent grin hinted at a wild streak. A woman and four children sat around the table, clearly the eldest brother's family. He pressed a quick kiss to her temple.

I waited, the numbness of this night encroaching on me. Starting in my heels and creeping up my legs. I had to be detached. I couldn't feel it. If I felt it, I would have killed myself a long time ago. Just like my mother.

When the woman ushered the children upstairs and the brothers were alone, finishing off the last of the pie and a cheap bottle of whiskey, I struck. With a flick of my wrist, a knife sailed through the open window, pinning the sleeve of the gun hand of one brother to the table. In two strides, I kicked the door open, pistol drawn. The eldest brother rushed me, and I used his surprise against him, ducking beneath a hasty blow and wrapping an arm around his neck, knife at his throat.

The youngest brother got his gun, but mine was already leveled at him. I cocked the hammer back with an ominous *click*. His hands shook around his weapon, breathing hard in his fury.

"Don't make me kill you in front of them." The words were a smooth kind of dark, too practiced, too apathetic.

"Robert?" called a soft voice from upstairs. My captive swallowed hard, and his Adam's apple bobbed against my blade, which sliced gently into his skin.

"Tell her everything is fine," I whispered in his ear. He nodded frantically, cutting himself deeper.

"Everything's fine, honey. Just get the girls in bed." His voice was a strange, high-pitched tone that didn't sound natural at all.

"Tell her you love her." His eyes widened until I could see a ring of white around his irises. "It'll be your last chance. Tell her you love her."

"I love you, honey," he called up the stairs. I wasn't sure if she was still listening, only that it felt important. The youngest brother's control was hanging on by a thread. He was bolder because of the gun in his hand. I saw the moment his control snapped. As his eyes tracked the blood dribbling down the eldest's neck, he raised the gun, and the room exploded in a *bang!*

He was dead before he hit the floor, a hole blown clean through one of his eyes. I preferred shooting through an eye, so they couldn't stare up at me in death. It was easier to look at them that way. I shoved forward, forcing the man in my grip to stumble ahead before pressing the barrel of my gun to the middle brother's temple.

"Robert!"

"Don't come down here!"

Feminine sobbing echoed down to my ears. I sighed wearily.

"I told him not to make me do it." I dropped the knife from the man's neck and motioned to the dead man on the floor.

"*Please*," he begged me, dropping to his knees. The scent of urine filled the room. Piss dribbled to the floor next to the man I threatened with my gun.

"You stole from Zachary Lee," I said, my voice emotionless.

"I can pay it back! I can pay it all back! Just give me another week!" His cries fell from his lips and grew more frantic the longer I stared, unblinking.

"He doesn't send me to collect debts. He sends me to wipe the books clean. You have two options: walk out of here with your head high, or I can drag you behind my horse. Your choice." My usual offer. Dignity, if they accepted it. Usually, it wasn't enough to tempt them.

The man on his knees sobbed, face buried in his hands. I kicked him onto his side, hoping to break him out of his hysteria.

"Get up."

He rose on shaky feet.

"Pick him up." I motioned again to his youngest brother, ignoring the liquid leaking from his nose, slinging one limp arm over his shoulder and dragging the lifeless corpse outside. With a hard yank, I pulled my knife from the top of the table and forced the middle brother out at gunpoint as well.

It took no time at all to tie them to the back of my horse. The youngest brother dragged between them as I mounted and we rode into the night. This was part of the job. The pageantry. I learned early that Zachary wanted more than just someone who was quick and efficient to take over my father's debt. He expected what Jones had exploited in my father for so long: the incitement of fear. The creation of a dark, bloody legend. Until I became the specter that people feared in the night, and, by proximity, so did Zachary.

We clopped along as I forced my stomach to stop thrashing. The only sound was the sobbing of the men behind me and the occasional slick glide of their brother's body over the broken asphalt. People hid behind locked doors but peered through curtains to take us in as we passed. Another three lives lost to the phantom created in my father's stead.

I knew what they said about me.

He drags their souls to hell on the back of his black steed.

He hangs them to drain them of blood; it's easier to drink that way.

He wears that hat because you can tell he has no soul when you look in his eyes.

On and on and on. More and more outlandish, yet with a sliver of truth. I'd bartered away my soul a long time ago. I heard the whimpering of children and the hush of parents dampening lanterns as we passed for so long; it nearly drove me to madness. Images from over the years assaulted me as they were dragged through the city streets.

"Stay quiet this time, mi amor. *I won't let him hurt you." My mother's whispered words stoked terror in every part of me, trembling as I was forced to watch from across the room. He carved into her for hours, her blood inciting him into a frenzy. He licked it from the blade. Dragged his fingers through the fresh wounds. Moaned in ecstasy until she couldn't sit up anymore. Slumping to the floor, too still.*

She hadn't died that night. But years later, as I cut down her body swinging from the beam in our tent, I'd wished she had.

Finally, we made it to the bridge. My stallion pranced nervously at the sight. I hadn't been here in weeks. There had been no new bodies to feed to the crater beast living in the river below. He was smart to be nervous. I swung down and walked the horse the rest of the way up the incline until we'd made it to the top, then tied him off. This part was hard, but what came after would be harder.

"Don't give me any trouble and I'll make it quick." I stood behind them. Their brother was barely recognizable after being dragged across miles of crumbling roads. His skin had peeled away from the front of his body until there was no hint of that irreverent grin I'd noticed earlier.

"On your knees," I barked. They lowered to the ground, sniveling. "If you believe in a God, pray to them."

They didn't. I guess the grace they'd said before dinner was for the children's benefit.

Before I could think about it, two gunshots rang in the stagnant air, and bodies dropped with muffled thumps. I kept my grip on the pistol but rushed to the side of the bridge and heaved until my stomach was empty.

I pulled my canteen off the saddle horn and washed my mouth, spitting onto the concrete. How many times had I done this? Why didn't it get any easier? From the stories told by the mercenaries I'd run across in seedy New Orleans bars, it was supposed to.

Not for me. Never for me.

I pulled out another cigarette and lit it, closing my eyes for a few solitary moments to gather myself before the real work began.

It wasn't enough to kill them quickly. I had to brutalize them. Put them on display. A warning not to cross Zachary, or I'd come for them next. So even though I spared them pain, it was little comfort compared to what I did next.

I *carved* them. The way my father carved into me. And Bonnie and my mother and countless other victims. It was too easy after all the times I'd been forced to watch my father work.

I cut down the desiccated corpses that were already hanging, eyes pecked out by birds, skin shriveled against their bones. It wouldn't be much of a meal, but Pontchartrain Patty had never been particular before. They were light as I hefted them over the railing and watched Patty's tentacles drag them down below the dark surface of the water. Never to surface again.

I tied the nooses and began to haul my latest victims up, pulling and wrenching until my arms nearly gave out from the strain. My shirt was covered in blood and sweat, splattered on my face, sunk into every groove of my hands. I only had the youngest brother left. The other two were already hanging, swinging softly on the summer breeze like macabre wind chimes.

"You don't have to do this." The familiar voice came from behind me just as I started hauling the last brother up. The rope nearly slipped from my hands. It wasn't tender, like Seb's voice earlier, though the words were the same.

"Go *away*, Jesse," I forced between my teeth as I yanked the rope, the corpse's feet hovering above the concrete. He moved then, walking closer, until his hand rested over my forearm. An attempt to still me. I clenched the rope tighter, slick with blood. I couldn't tell how much was mine or theirs.

"I said *go away*, goddamnit!" I shoved him off and kept the brim of my hat low enough that I couldn't see his eyes. I couldn't handle him looking at me like a murderer. I couldn't let go of the rope now. The job had to be finished. I couldn't leave the body of the man I'd killed slumped on the ground or let him fall into the river, where Ponchartrain Patty's suckered tentacles lazily circled the concrete columns, always greedy for more no matter how well she was fed. So I pulled again, renewing my efforts as I kept my eyes trained away from my friend.

He reached out, as if to help me, but I shoved him back. A silent sentinel, marking each heaving yank that ripped the last shreds of my humanity from within me. Until I was nothing. Hand over hand, I raised the corpse over the bridge and secured him with his family. When I finished, all my strength crumbled into ash. I dropped to my knees, stomach thrashing again. Shame coated my skin along with the film of blood and sweat that lacquered me.

"I didn't want you to see me like this." I pressed my bloodstained fists into my eyes.

"This is the debt you paid for your father." No accusation or judgment. Too kind for someone like me. Someone who had done the kind of evil I had. Too forgiving. "For Bonnie."

I let out a long breath, pulling the hat from my head and tossing it to the ground. I rested against the railing and pulled out my cigarette case. This time, when I held the cigarette between two fingers, a crimson smear was left behind, near my lips. How appropriate.

"My father owed Zachary a debt. A big one. He called it in and told him to track Bonnie down and bring her to New Orleans. When we got here, he was going to call in the rest of the debt. My father swore him five years of *exclusive* service. I have *no idea* what the fuck Zachary Lee has on my dad to make him agree to that. But the bastard pays his debts." The words spilled out hot and ugly.

"Bonnie was in bad shape, sure, but I took the deal because I was more afraid of my father being that close to her than I was of what Zachary would make me do." I inhaled another long drag of the cigarette. "The son of a bitch is one hell of a businessman, I'll give him that. He countered my offer. See, five years of having *Sixgun* doing his dirty work wasn't the same as some no-name outlaw, rejected from his own gang, with a target on his back. It wasn't just about the work. It was about the *name*."

I flicked the ash from my cigarette and finally looked at Jesse. His face was unreadable, just a series of hard lines in the dim light. Seeing him so stoic in the face of what I'd done, what I continued to do, shattered something inside of me. The last ounce of defense I had against the parts of myself I'd tried to lock away in these moments.

"I'm his *indefinitely*. And with each job, each kill, it's *my name* that strikes fear into the hearts of the people here." A dark, hysterical chuckle caught on the edge of my mouth. He knew everything now. It was only a matter of time until he cut his losses. I was too broken, too damaged to be worth his friendship.

"I told you, Jesse." I forced the whisper from the back of my throat. "I'm Sixgun's legacy. I never had a chance to escape it."

He fisted a hand in my bloody shirt and pulled me toward him, his blue eyes a blade in the night. "That is *not* who you are." His words charged angrily between us.

"I've killed *so many* people." My shame laid bare before him. "There's no redemption for me now."

He pulled me to my feet, and I staggered to keep up with him. There was no hope. No light in the darkness. No flicker of life bringing me back from the abyss.

"You can't save me." The blood from my shirt smeared on his hands now too. He'd never forget tonight. Watching my execution. How I defiled them. How, with each senseless act of violence, I chipped away a little more of my soul until there was nothing left. Until I was empty. One day, it would get the better of me. One day, by Zachary's hands or my own, I'd hang on this cursed bridge.

"You didn't come here for me anyway. Just focus on Bonnie. She, at least, *can* be saved," I deflected, trying to turn the conversation to anyone, anything other than me and my gruesome work.

"Rule number seven, Will." He offered a grim smile. "No one gets left behind."

"Speaking of that." I leaned against the railing. "Our exit strategy needs to include one more person."

Jesse stilled, waiting for an explanation to follow my statement. *Fuck it*. It wasn't like he could think worse of me.

"I told Savvy."

He let out a breath, sighing wearily before he ran his fingers through the long hair at the top of his head. "I thought you said you didn't want to involve her."

"I fuck up everything, or haven't you noticed?" I turned my back to him as I headed toward my horse. His large head bent down as I approached him, his nose nudging against my shirt pocket greedily. Unsnapping it, I offered him a sugar cube on my blistered, bloodstained palm. "Keep away from the railings or Patty might pull you down. I keep her well fed, but she gets greedy."

Jesse peered over the edge warily before backing away from the railing and following me down the bridge. Neither of us spoke. He didn't try to convince me I was misunderstood or a good man, and I didn't try to justify murdering innocent people. At the base of the bridge, where No Name waited, we mounted and started the ride back to Lee's house. I led the way, taking as many back streets and alleyways as I could.

Jesse watched as I tipped the brim of my hat down and weathered the fear that followed me like a shadow. He bore witness to Will dying and the Beast taking his place. As block after block faded beneath the ominous echo of our horses' hooves on the crumbling asphalt streets, I tried not to think about the lace curtains in that house. Or the sounds of children splashing upstairs in the bath.

Tried, and failed.

In what felt like no time at all, Lee Square came into view, and I let out a ragged breath. My night's work weighed me down until I was crushed beneath it. Lee would want confirmation that the job was done. But it was late, and he'd find out first thing tomorrow anyway. All he had to do was ask how many bodies swung over the bridge.

Trotting into the alleyway, then the stables, I slid down my mount. I avoided Jesse, even though he stared at me the entire time I untacked my horse, washed him, brushed out his coat, and made sure all the blood was wiped clean from his hooves. This was my routine, gruesome and practical.

"Stop staring at me like that." I shut the stall door and retrieved my cigarette case to still my twitching fingers. It was smeared with blood, my hands sticky as it dried in thick streaks over my knuckles and palms. If it weren't for Jesse, I'd have gone back to my apartment. Taken a cold shower. Cold enough to make me feel something again.

I couldn't stop staring at my hands. The crimson faded into dark rust, settled into the lines of my skin, like a system of rivers. Everything brought me back to the fucking river and the bridge across it.

"Let's get you cleaned up." His voice was gruff. I shook my head as he started toward the back house. Seb would be waiting up for me, with dark circles under his disappointment-laced eyes. Just the thought of him seeing me like this, the things he would say . . . my chest tightened uncomfortably. Until I couldn't breathe.

"I can't—" I said, the words strangled from between my lips, tortured. Jesse seemed to understand, and he changed direction, leading me toward the kitchen instead. My feet were clumsier than they'd been earlier tonight, my exhaustion catching up with me all at once. Jesse glanced at me from the corner of his eye, brows furrowed in concern.

Not that I deserved it.

CHAPTER TWENTY-FOUR

SAVANNAH

T HE LAMPLIGHT DANCED ACROSS my book as the kettle screamed from the stove. I'd sat up with Audrey for a while tonight, trying to help her through her ever-changing emotions. After whatever happened with Jesse—she wouldn't tell me—following the hurricane party, she seemed less herself. As if he'd sapped some of her fire. And her nightmares returned. Full force. Leaving her exhausted, with dark circles beneath her eyes and a lingering, haunted expression dulling her eyes. She'd stopped their hourly sessions since the party. It was almost a relief when he left to fight out of town.

But with him returning, Audrey was on edge. Even if she didn't say anything, I could tell.

The knowledge I now held—the truth about Montana and *what* he was—weighed heavily on me. After tossing and turning for what felt like hours, I threw the blankets from my body and made the trek down to the kitchen. Like so many nights when I couldn't sleep, I lit the oil lamp, set the kettle to boil, and settled at the kitchen island.

I hadn't seen Will since the party. Since he confessed all of his secrets. Things he hadn't mentioned before. Whether I was avoiding him or he was avoiding me, I didn't know. My days dragged without my best friend's usual smile and without my—What *was* Will to me?

It didn't matter. Not really.

I'd always liked the house at night. When everyone was tucked into their dreams. When I could just be myself for a while. I didn't worry about anything, so I wore my robe and let my hair cascade in waves down my back. After pouring my tea, I settled back on the barstool, shoulders relaxing as I reopened my book to read more about Noah and Everly.

Murmured voices and shuffling footsteps stole my attention. At first, my shoulders tensed, and I readied myself to flee at a moment's notice. But, as Jesse wandered into the kitchen, William trailing behind him, I relaxed. At least it wasn't anyone who would report back to Lee that I was out so late.

Jesse looked road-weary, his jawline extra sharp as he stared at me. A muscle twitched in his face. Pain settled behind his blue eyes. I'd honestly never looked at him so closely before, but I saw it. As I set the book down on the island, my gaze shifted to Will. To the blood staining his hands and clothes. He lowered his head, using the brim of his hat to hide from me.

How many times had this very thing happened? I'd be alone at night in the kitchen and he'd wander in after a job. A combination of anger and sadness passed through me. My lips curved downward, but not in disgust or judgment. In grief. Because I knew what these nights did to him. Without a word, I rose from my stool.

"Sorry to bother you, Savannah," Jesse said.

"It's no bother," I said quietly. "I couldn't sleep." I moved toward the sink, retrieving a few linen napkins from the cabinet. I felt Jesse's intense stare on me the entire time.

"And . . . Audrey?" he asked. "How is she?"

"Spending a lot of time with Lucas Rutherford after his associates returned to Manhattan." I frowned at him. I'd encouraged her to talk about whatever had happened between them, to help her work through it, but Audrey seemed more inclined to throw herself into whatever distraction she could. I had to be careful in how I handled things. I tested the temperature of the water, my gaze darting toward Will. He looked ready to bolt at any second.

"Oh," Jesse said.

"Whatever happened between the two of you after the party, I suggest you try to fix it." I soaked one of the rags with water. I switched the faucet off and moved past him.

"How? She canceled our time together. She's avoiding me."

I shrugged at his desperate words.

"If she won't see me, how can I—"

A shrill scream pierced the night.

"Audrey," I said at the same time Jesse said, "Bonnie."

He bolted toward the front house before I could stop him, and I started after him. Slender, calloused fingers captured my wrist. I wheeled around, Will fixing me with an intense stare.

"Let him go to her."

I nodded, gently tugging my wrist away. I'd check in after a while to make sure she was okay. But if the screams started again . . .

Will regarded me for a moment and eyed the nearest exit. Before he had the chance to leave, I said, "Have a seat." He shook his head and tugged his hat off, running a hand through his hair. "William Ellis, if you don't sit down, I'll tie you to that chair." I gathered my napkins as he begrudgingly listened, lowering himself onto the stool beside the one I'd been sitting on.

I missed Will, I realized as I settled beside him. I missed his easy grin and running commentary.

I reached for one of his dirt- and blood-stained hands. This part never bothered me, the aftermath of what he did for Lee. He didn't have a choice any more than I did. I'd watched these jobs whittle him away, bit by bit, over the years. The least he could do was let me clean him up.

Will's gaze settled on my face as I took one of his overly large hands in both of mine. My fingertips brushed across his calloused palms, eliciting a reminder of how reverently he'd cradled my face when I'd kissed him. I forced it away, throat bobbing, and fell into the rhythmic motion of wiping away the stains I knew reached all the way to his soul.

"I'm thinking about going down to the river to make some inquiries about passage out of the city," I said quietly.

The amount of blood lining his hands and splattered across his clothes told me what I needed to know about how bad the job had been. If he wanted to talk about it, I'd listen. But I doubted he would. He never had before. I swapped to his other hand, cleaning the mess. In a way, I hoped it would soothe his frayed nerves, ease the missing pieces of him.

My mind trailed back to the party, to dancing with Will, to the things he'd said. To the way he'd built me up when the rest of them wanted to tear me down. I hadn't wanted to face him, hadn't wanted to talk about what had happened earlier that day.

In the last two weeks, I'd replayed every moment between us recently, every single time he'd poked and prodded at me, his jealous behavior in front of Patrick, his admission that he'd wanted to kiss me every single day that he'd been in this house. My realization that I wanted him in my bed.

I'd forced myself to accept the situation for what it was. After all, he was with Sebastian, and the last thing I needed was to stoke that fire.

But as we sat there, just the two of us in this quiet moment, I found it very hard to accept that he wasn't mine.

"Jesse's got his work cut out for him, though," I said, finally looking up at Will. "If we're going to get Audrey out of here, he needs to get back on her good side, and I don't know what more I can do to help." He stared at me so intently. The silence thickened around us, drowning out whatever was beyond these walls. He stared at me so long that I shifted uncomfortably on my seat. I focused on wiping the remnants of the blood from his hand instead, hoping it might still my trembling heart.

"She'll never know what you've done for her." My throat bobbed at the memory of his admission at the party. "What you've sacrificed. Thank you for keeping her safe." I squeezed his now-clean hand. His stare deepened, mouth parting with unspoken sentiment.

I'd never wanted to kiss him more.

Instead, I cleared my throat and rose from my stool, idly gathering up the soiled linens. Before I could move away, however, large, slender hands found my waist. My brows lifted as I turned back to Will. His dark eyes trailed along my face, and a tremor went through me. He reached up, gentle fingers caressing my curls as he tucked them behind my ear.

Will brushed a thumb across my cheek. My eyes fluttered shut at the contact. We should not be doing this. Anyone could see. Anyone could tell Sebastian.

But I didn't want to stop.

"Will," I whispered. His thumb brushed along my bottom lip.

Every single protest died as my lips parted. Regret rolled around inside of me as I cursed every time I thought that Will's jabs or insults meant he didn't like me. That all of the time I'd wanted him, wanted this sort of closeness, he'd wanted it, too.

I ran my fingers through his hair, not bothering to wonder what this made me. What encouraging this would do.

I hadn't been lying when I told him that I wanted human connection. I'd spent years starved of touch. Letting him touch me now, I couldn't stop.

"Will—" I started again but didn't finish. Instead, he swallowed my words, smooth lips pressed against mine and driving every raging thought away.

The sea inside of me quieted. The waters stilled, and the clouds opened up to reveal a bright, star-filled sky. I hadn't realized how badly my soul needed this. Needed *him*.

My eyes fluttered shut, my arms wrapping around his shoulders. He flattened a palm against my back, tugging me against his hard chest. A whimper came from between my lips. This time, when he ran his tongue along the seam of my mouth, I didn't stop him. He tipped my head back, tasting me more fully.

His hands found my hips. As he rose from his seat, he hefted me onto the island, planting himself between my thighs. He gripped my hips, eliciting another cry from deep inside me. My hands scrambled over his shoulders. I didn't know what to do with them. I'd never done this before, with anyone. But he didn't notice.

Our chests heaved together as Will trailed his lips along my cheek, my jaw. Calloused fingertips tugged the shoulder of my robe and nightgown to the side, and he pressed his mouth to a sensitive spot beneath my ear. His hand slipped into the fabric of my nightgown, his palm curling around the curve of my breast, his thumb circling my nipple until it tightened into a hard peak. I shuddered, biting my bottom lip to stifle my moan.

It was only when he pressed me back against the countertop, when one of us knocked the teacup over and it crashed to the floor, that I came to my senses.

I was kissing a man that was with someone else.

"Will," I gasped, tangling my hand in his hair. He slid the fabric of my robe upward, fingers brushing along my bare thigh. "Will, what are we doing?"

Suddenly, all sensation ceased. My eyes snapped open. Darkness consumed Will's features; self-loathing and shame coated his skin. He stepped backwards with wide eyes, running a hand through his hair as he lifted his hat from the island. Using my elbows, I sat up, legs dangling off the edge of the cold granite beneath me.

"*Lo siento, mi sol. Lo siento,*" he muttered.

I stared at him, wide-eyed, watching him retreat from me. Not just physically, but internally. His posture was rigid, and his hands clenched and unclenched at his sides.

"W-what does that mean?" I asked, trying to catch my breath.

"It means *I'm sorry*," he said, jaw tightening around the apology.

Shame coiled inside of me, licking up through my chest and spreading to my extremities. I lowered my head, biting my bottom lip to fight back against the warring desire and sadness and shame. Tears filled my eyes, threatening to spill onto my cheeks.

"You don't—"

"Don't ever forget *what* I am, Savannah." His words were gruff as he put on his hat and settled the brim low.

I huffed. He thought so poorly of himself, and I knew no matter how much I tried, he wouldn't listen. "Not *what*, William." I righted my clothes. "*Who*." I slid from the countertop and ran my hands through my hair, smoothing it back behind my ears.

"You know," he said, hands twitching at his sides. "It doesn't matter how many times you clean them; I'll always see the stain."

But when I opened my mouth to argue, he cut me off.

"I'm not a good man, or an honest one, or even a fucking loyal one, apparently."

I ignored the stab of pain in my chest.

"I'm a murderer, Savvy. Plain and simple. And if you knew what was good for you, you'd stay away from me." He tipped his hat down, fully cloaking his eyes from me. He walked toward the door.

"You wouldn't hurt me, William Ellis, and you know it," I growled at his back, chest heaving as he disappeared.

I let out a sharp breath. A scream threatened to choke me as I settled down on the stool he'd been seated on. I flattened a palm against my chest, my eyes fluttering shut as I tried to slow my pounding heart.

It had been a mistake. I knew it was a mistake.

But I didn't regret it.

Chapter Twenty-Five

JESSE

M Y HEART AND FEET pounded in rhythm together. Across the courtyard, through the door, up the giant staircase. I skidded across the hardwood floors, Audrey's cries growing closer as I scrambled to get to her. The cool metal of the doorknob. Locked. I kicked. Once. Twice. A third time. The frame splintered and cracked beneath my boot.

The moment the door swung open, I bolted across the space toward Audrey's writhing, jerking form, highlighted by a sliver of moonlight peeking in from the curtained window. Her screams sent my skin thrumming as I searched for an intruder, an attacker, someone hurting her. The stillness of the room made my nerves worsen. There was no present danger.

The danger was in her mind.

I rushed to the bed, not bothering to go around to her side. I shuffled across the mattress, untangling the sheets around her. She trembled beneath my grip as I found her shoulders.

"Audrey," I said, my voice a shaking quiver.

"Give her back! Give her *back*!"

The anguish in her voice stung my eyes.

"Miss Audrey!" I tried again. Another yowling wail pierced the night. "Bonnie!"

She stilled, slumping back against the rumpled sheets as her eyes fluttered open. Panic lingered as she blinked. The cloudy haze receded, desperation disappearing into slight recognition. Slowly, Audrey focused on me. Only me.

"You were screaming." I forced a steadiness into my voice that I didn't feel. I stared for a long moment, knuckles white, before I realized how hard I held her. I rocked back onto my knees, silently cursing myself for reacting so strongly.

I didn't want to spook her this time.

Audrey launched toward me, fingers desperate as she threw her arms around my waist and fisted the back of my shirt. She buried her face against my chest. Her warmth soothed my ragged edges. As her heat seeped into me, I relaxed, folding my arms around her and pressing my lips into her hair.

Audrey sobbed, her tears staining the front of my shirt. I ran my hand along the length of her spine, against her quivering shoulders. Her petite, trembling form wracked with sobs. I couldn't remember seeing her like this before.

As the night grew quieter, Audrey's crying eased, tension seeping out of her as she relaxed against me. I pressed my lips to the crown of her head, letting them linger there longer than I should have.

"It was a nightmare," she finally said, words shaky against my chest. "Just a nightmare."

I knew what she sounded like when she wasn't sure there was truth to her own words. She was trying to be strong, trying to convince herself more than she was trying to convince me. I kept my mouth shut, arms tight around her. The silence billowed between us, cloying and thick.

"I have them, too." My voice creaked against the silence.

Audrey shifted, pulling her head back just enough to peer up at me through her eyelashes. I brushed my fingers across her cheeks, her chin, wiping away the salt tracks.

"What are yours about?" Her voice was a whisper as she settled her cheek against the thundering of my heart.

"Lots of things." I held her tighter, my arms keeping her locked against me as my throat bobbed. "My parents were murdered in a fire about four years ago. My little brother and I barely escaped." I'd only managed to survive my grief because of Bonnie. When I'd lost her, I didn't have anything else to hold tight to, anything to keep me pushing through this new kind of grief. "It's gotten better with time . . . but it still haunts me."

Audrey's grip slackened, and she lifted her head from my chest. I tensed against the urge to pull her tight against me once more.

"And I relive the day that I lost . . ." My breath hitched, my eyes shutting tight at the memory. Cracking bones. Screams. My world turned upside down. ". . . *her*." My brows knit together as I railed against the grief and devastation that had consumed me for so long.

I lowered my head, trying to keep it hidden. Audrey had to think that my behavior the night of the hurricane party was driven by my loss of Bonnie, but it hadn't been.

Montana. That was who she knew. *Not* Jesse.

I couldn't keep going on like this, being someone else, when I wanted nothing more than for her to know *me*. The real me.

"It was my fault." I lifted a hand, rubbing it across my forehead as the truth spilled out in a harsh whisper. "It's why I fight. Because it's the only time I don't have nightmares about . . ."

Grief choked me, stole my voice.

Audrey fixed me with her beautiful blue eyes. My heart stuttered, aching with grief that felt all too fresh. Her fingertips brushed gently across my jaw. I leaned into her touch, my eyes fluttering shut as I let her feel *me*. Jesse. Not Montana. Not some nameless fighter.

"Bonnie," she whispered. My eyes fluttered open, and the empathy I saw in the soft lines of her face nearly undid me. I took in a shuddering breath. I covered her hand, tangling our fingers together. I'd forgotten what it was like to have this, to be vulnerable, to let someone see the deepest, darkest parts of my soul, the parts that threatened to shred me to pieces, the parts I wasn't proud of.

Even before Fort Hood, I think Bonnie had been so jaded by the world, by everything she'd been through. A moment like this wouldn't have been possible. Bonnie could empathize, knew how to reach me in tough moments, but I'd never seen her shoulder my burdens like the woman before me.

There was something so distinctly *Audrey* in this moment. And I realized, staring down at her, that whether I got Bonnie back or not, it didn't matter.

I was so hopelessly in love with this woman all over again, this new part of her.

I wouldn't have thought it possible to fall in love with two separate parts of the same person.

But could she love me back? Especially once she learned the truth? I wanted her to see me, to know me, to *love me*. Guilt struck like a viper in my stomach. I needed to tell her.

"I'm sorry." I dropped my hand, loosing a breath. "You don't need to hear all of this—" I shifted backward, sliding from the mattress and turning toward the door.

"Please don't leave me alone." Her whimpered words struck at the center of my chest, stilling me before I could reach the door. I whirled, taking in the sight of her on the bed. Small amidst the tangles of sheets and pillows, fear in her eyes.

How could I leave her now?

I crossed back to the mattress, pausing to fix her with an inquisitive gaze, asking permission. She gave a swift nod. I climbed into the bed and dragged her against my chest, locking her tight in the space against my shoulder where she belonged.

"It's worse when I'm alone," she whispered. I buried my fingers in her hair, inhaling her scent, letting it soothe my fractured pieces. I fixed her with a long stare, concern knitting my brows together.

"What is?" I tipped her chin toward me.

Audrey's throat bobbed as she stared up at me with such raw vulnerability that I thought my heart would shatter all over again. She didn't have the memories of before. The things Jones had done to her. Sixgun's cruelty. What haunted her now? What made her look like a shell of the woman I loved?

"I lost a baby."

Tears filled her eyes, wobbling on her lashes. I went deathly still at the revelation, a muscle feathering across my jaw as I forced myself to stay frozen. I clenched my teeth so hard I was sure they would crack, shatter into a million pieces.

A baby?

"I . . . " My gaze tracked Audrey's quivering bottom lip, the way her throat bobbed heavily.

I knew about her history over the last three years. About the staff she'd let into her bed in the time we'd been apart. Had it been one of them? Or—?

My mind raced as the silence dragged between us, a heavy fog blanketing the space.

"Say something," she pleaded, eyes wide and fearful. But I couldn't even think it.

"Does . . ." I stammered, my lips feeling clumsy. "Does the father know?"

Instead of answering immediately, she snorted derisively. "That's assuming I know who he is."

Which meant it couldn't have been one of the staff that'd shared her bed. But then—

"You know about my head injury, and the glowroot." Audrey's voice snapped me from my raging mind. "But what most people don't know is that the doctors found out I was pregnant a few weeks later."

My heart stopped at what could only be confirmation.

We had a baby.

Don't worry, farm boy, Bonnie had said that last night when she mentioned restocking her herbal tea. *There's plenty of time*.

But there hadn't been.

We'd taken the tentative peace we'd found in Fort Hood for granted. We thought we were safe. That we had time to be together, to make a life, to grow. Only for Sixgun to rip it all away.

We had a *baby*.

"That's when my father was sure I'd been raped," Audrey pressed forward. "He begged me to get rid of the child, but I just *couldn't*." I focused intently on her face, tracing each line and curve as I tried to decipher the emotion weighing down her words. "When I started showing, he was happier than I think I'd ever seen him before. He kept saying he was so sure I was having a boy because of how hard she kicked his hand. She was so tough, so *strong*, I just never thought—"

"She?" I asked, my voice thick and my tongue heavy.

A girl. A daughter. I had a daughter.

Audrey nodded, unable to form words as tears spilled onto her cheeks. "My daughter, Emma. I named her after my mom."

Silence settled once more, but it wasn't thick and uncomfortable. Instead, the air felt clean, refreshed, like after a thunderstorm. Like it'd washed away our sins. She swiped at her cheeks and tangled our hands together.

"I know it must seem stupid; you've lost so much and—"

"It's *not* stupid." The words came out in a hot rush. There were so many things I wanted to say. Things I wanted to tell her. I wanted to share with her every broken, shattered part of myself, so we could feel this. I wanted her to know *I* felt this. That she wasn't alone.

"The thing is, when I woke up without any memories, in the middle of a raging glowroot addiction . . . I was completely lost. There was nothing that mattered to me, nothing worth fighting for. There was just the *need* for glowroot." Her throat bobbed again, her gaze faltering. "Until Emma.

"I went from no one to someone's *mother* in the blink of an eye. I went from this lost, strung-out wretch who'd given up to fighting like hell to stay healthy.

She saved my life—" Her voice broke, chin wobbling as her gaze dropped to our entwined fingers once more. "And I couldn't save hers."

Guilt. Sticky, hot, all-consuming, it struck in my core. She'd had to deal with this by herself. All alone. I'd *left her* to do this alone.

"What happened?" I finally asked, cautiously. I didn't want to spook her with how vehemently I felt. But I had to know.

"She came early, probably because of the glowroot, but the doctors couldn't be sure." My eyes slammed shut as I fought against a newfound anger bubbling inside of me. Whoever started her on that shit was going to pay.

"After she was born, I got to hold her for one minute, just one, before they took her away. She never even cried." Audrey wiped at her face with the back of her hand, letting out a breathy, tear-filled laugh and offering me a strained smile. "She was so beautiful, with the tiniest fingers and pink skin that looked translucent in the morning light."

I silently begged her to keep talking, to keep telling me about Emma. My daughter. *Our* daughter.

Hadn't that been what had ripped us apart to begin with? That unyielding love Bonnie held within her.

He has The Kid, *Jesse.* My *Kid.* Our *Kid.*

"After," she said, dragging me from my self-loathing. "They just stopped talking about her. Like they weren't allowed to speak about what happened that night or that I'd been pregnant at all. My father started having parties, introducing me to rich men and the women who wanted to marry them. Savannah adjusted my clothes, all of Emma's things were packed away, and it was like she'd never existed. Like she hadn't mattered."

"She *mattered*," I said, so vehemently that I was sure to give myself away. A surprised gasp caught in her throat. She leaned back, propping herself up to look at me. I stared back, fighting every piece that wanted to scream the truth.

She was *mine.* She was *ours.*

"I guess I thought if I pretended it didn't happen, then maybe it would stop hurting so much. But it doesn't stop hurting. Not ever."

I knew that feeling so intimately that I couldn't find words to speak. When you experienced loss like that, only someone who'd felt it before could really, truly understand.

"And then I met you, and I see how you love Bonnie. How you grieve her." A line creased between her brows. "You don't hide your pain or pretend that it doesn't exist. And I think that's brave."

"I'm not brave." I let my head fall back against the upholstered headboard. I stared up at the ceiling, at the fancy crown molding, because I couldn't face her. How could she think I was brave? I was a fucking coward. If I were brave, I'd have fought off Sixgun and his men. I'd have figured out how to keep the people I loved from that bastard.

"I disappeared into the bottle. It didn't matter that my brother was hurt, that he needed me. All that mattered was drinking myself into oblivion every night, waking up, and doing it all again. Because I'd rather drink myself to death than face a single day without her."

I bore my shame openly before her, needing her to know the truth.

"It took an eleven-year-old kicking me in the ass to pull myself together." I released a breath and, with it, the tension in my shoulders. Somehow, telling her eased my burden. "Even then, I threw myself into the fighting pits. Anything to avoid how much it hurt."

Maybe this was what I'd needed, to find a way to grieve Bonnie, to let go of what might have been and could have been and stop fighting the loss of her.

We leaned against one another in companionable silence for a while, my arms wrapped around Audrey as she settled against me.

"It's alright to still love her, you know."

I turned toward her, brows screwing up in confusion. She cleared her throat, averting her gaze.

"I would never try to replace her, but the other night—" She pushed a few wayward strands of dark hair behind her ear. "I don't think it's asking too much to be the person you're thinking about when your fingers are inside of me."

"You're all I think about," I said, the words harsh. I fixed her with a heavy stare. It was the truth, even if I couldn't tell her why.

Audrey settled into my shoulder, a contented sigh escaping from her mouth as she became pliant against me. I wrapped my arm around her, tucking her in tight, feeling lighter. Sharing what pieces of my trauma I could eased my pain, if only a little. She slid an arm across my chest.

"I've never told anyone about Emma before," she whispered. I tangled my fingers in her long locks and leaned down to brush my lips across her temple. Audrey tilted her chin to meet my mouth, a feather-light kiss that sent shivers through me. I touched her jaw, my mouth opening hers beneath mine. She was the air I breathed, the light I needed to see. She was *everything*. And as tempting as it was to lean into this moment, to devour her in ways I'd longed to do, now wasn't the time. I pulled back just enough to take in a sharp breath, our foreheads pressed together as I inhaled her.

"I'm glad you told me." I relaxed against the pillows, tugging her tight against my chest. She molded against me.

"You make me want to remember."

Her scent captured me—rain mingling with lavender, like the two parts of her I loved combined to create a new person—as we tangled together in the silence.

My body slackened, and for the first time in years, I could find peace again. I wasn't there yet, but with Audrey in my arms, it was possible. Even if she never remembered.

That possibility was better than any certainty, as long as I had her.

CHAPTER TWENTY-SIX

AUDREY

T HERE WERE NO NIGHTMARES. No slivers of dark memories haunting me. Grief didn't swallow me whole. Instead, I woke softly, his rhythmic breath puffing hot against my neck. The world was hazy and sleep-addled, like I was still caught in the throes of a beautiful dream.

Last night came back to me as I sloughed off the last vestiges of sleep. How he'd wrenched me from my nightmare, like he was ready to do battle with all my demons. An avenging angel. Holding me through broken truths as they spilled from my lips like dark blood. He never even flinched.

Wriggling gently, until I turned in his arms to face him, I laid there and fought against the stupid smile on my face. He was so beautiful. Too beautiful. Even with his unshaven jaw and rumpled clothes, I'd never seen a man so devastating. Dark circles lined his eyes, as if he hadn't slept much either. It must have been late when he got back from Baton Rouge last night.

She mattered.

I hadn't thought it was possible to feel like this. So full of happiness I was sure it would crack my ribs and explode from my chest like a bright star. He shifted unconsciously, arm tightening around my waist like an iron band, dragging me into his heat. I scented the warmth and salt on his skin and felt his pulse pounding steadily against my cheek. Turning my mouth against his neck, I kissed him sweetly. Again and again. I slid my arms over his shoulders, eliciting sleepy sounds of pleasure from the back of his throat.

His hands woke before he did. Hard and uncompromising. Running down the ridge of my spine like it tethered him to the ground. A breathy groan, lazy and sleepy, sounded in the space between my neck and shoulder as his hands curved around my ass and dug into my thighs. Until every nerve ending in me was awake and electrified. He raised his head, stark blue eyes blinking into wakefulness and softening as they traced the lines of my face in recognition.

"Mornin', sunshine," I muttered, cupping his scratchy jaw and tilting my chin to kiss him softly. His answering smile made my stomach flip. He shifted slowly until his weight pressed more firmly into me.

"Am I still dreaming?" he asked with his lips against my shoulder. Dipping down to my collarbone as my heart raced in my chest. I shook my head, hair wild on the pillow, unable to speak. His hands never stopped, creeping beneath the cotton shirt I wore and cupping my breasts adoringly, eyes fixed on my face as my mouth parted with a sigh.

"I almost remember my dream from last night," I said breathlessly, filling the quiet with inconsequential words. His lips traced my jaw, my chin, my throat.

"What was it about?" he asked, teeth grazing and setting my skin ablaze.

I groaned, unable to remember, not with his hands and mouth and body all over mine. Making me feel new and alive. "Um . . . I don't . . . I remember the smell of fresh hay and baking bread." I laughed. At the ridiculousness of it. But he raised his head, hair mussed and lips swollen. Gazing down at me as if I'd gifted him the greatest thing he'd ever received. He traced my bottom lip, parting my mouth and no doubt noticing how I couldn't catch my breath.

"I'm definitely still dreaming," he said, nose brushing mine.

"Yes," I confirmed, my hands drifting over his chest. He was still fully dressed. It must've been uncomfortable, sleeping in his jeans. Only he hadn't complained once. Slowly I unbuttoned his shirt until, with his help and a little strategic shifting, the garment fell to the floor. His hard expanse of skin was above me, and I traced my fingers over the long muscles along his back. Pressed my lips to his chest.

"Then I don't want to stop," he said, husky as his fingers tangled in my hair. Tugging gently, he lifted my gaze back to his. Dark with lust, still clouded with lingering sleep. It was addictive. I longed for it like the numbing radiation of glowroot. Insistent, urging, always present.

"Then don't stop."

My words swelled, sultry and capitulating. Understanding passed between us, without words, hearts pounding in perfect time. He didn't have to ask me for permission, because I felt the rightness of this in my bones. I didn't have to ask if he was thinking about *me* instead of Bonnie, because he was so present in this moment there was no doubt in my mind. As if last night had shattered some boundary we'd been afraid to cross.

He kissed me. Slow and deep. He gripped my hips, tugging gently until I was fully beneath him and his hips separated my thighs. My arms slung loosely around his neck, my fingers running through his hair as the hard length of his cock pressed against me. Making it painfully clear that as slow and sweet as this was, his arousal was anything but. My hand drifted down, unbuckling his belt as he shifted to give me room.

I held his gaze as I popped the button on his jeans, slid the zipper down, and dipped my hand inside. He filled up my hand, and, as I wrapped my fingers around him, his eyes fluttered shut on a smooth groan. His fingers curled into the sides of my underwear, and I stroked him. Until his hips rocked with the motion, seeking sweet release. He gripped my wrist, pulling my hand away and locking it above my head, fingers entwined. He slid my underwear down my hips, and all I could think was that I'd waited *so long* to feel like this.

The door slammed, crashing against the wall as Savannah burst in without hesitation. The way she always did, my name half-poised on her lips.

"Oh!" she squeaked, seeing us tangled together, mostly undressed. "Well, I didn't mean to interrupt, but you can't spend *all day* in bed—"

Montana scrambled off of me, yanking his jeans up, as red flushed up his neck. A wicked smile curved on my mouth as I raised onto my elbows. He was *embarrassed*. And it was fucking adorable. I shot a quick look at Savannah, all deviousness and laughter, one she understood immediately.

"Can't you give me . . . hmm . . ." I peered over at Montana as he zipped his pants and blushed furiously. "Like *five* more minutes?" His gaze shot to mine, his brows furrowed over his bright eyes as he caught my expression.

"Five minutes?" he asked, clearly offended. I shrugged lazily, a smile unfurling on my mouth.

"You might be overestimating him," Savannah chimed in, studying her nails before settling a flat expression on her face. Montana's mouth dropped at our teasing.

"I'll have you know—"

"You said it's been *years*—"

We talked over each other as he lurched forward, his fingers digging into my ribs and tickling me until I howled in laughter, kicking beneath him with mirthful tears leaking from the corners of my eyes.

"You are such a brat!" he shouted good-naturedly, a reluctant smile lighting up his blue eyes.

"I tell her that all the time," Savannah said, chuckling at us.

"Okay," I breathed, pushing against his hands to still him. When he finally stopped tickling me and I'd caught my breath, I leveled him with an amused stare. "*Ten* minutes."

"I should spank you." His words fell heavy and lustful in the air. I sucked in a breath and bit my bottom lip hard. I never thought I might *like* that, until the possibility stuck suddenly between us.

"Alright, this is getting weird." Savannah's words cut through the tension. "I really do hate to break up this . . . *lovefest*, but Lucas is waiting for you in the parlor."

Shit.

I had forgotten about spending time with Lucas today, and guilt tumbled in my stomach as Montana stared at me in confusion. Over the last couple of weeks, I'd spent a lot of time with Lucas. After a clumsy apology that was, at the very least, sincere, he'd reached out. Without my time in the library with Montana, I'd been lonely. In need of a distraction so my thoughts didn't linger on how hopeless things were between us.

"Lucas Rutherford?" he asked. I didn't acknowledge his question, instead sliding off the opposite side of the mattress. We both knew exactly who Savannah was talking about.

She stared at me expectantly, arms crossed, as if she, too, were curious what I would say to the half-naked man still in my bed. Last night, something had changed. A new feeling, a significant one, snapped into place between Montana and me like it'd always been there. I couldn't ignore that.

I didn't know how to handle it.

"I completely forgot," I said, crossing the room to my wardrobe and pulling on a pair of cotton shorts. At least if I was fully clothed, I would feel less vulnerable.

"You aren't going." Montana's words forced me to turn and stare at him. "Are you?"

His shirt hung open, his hair still mussed, looking glorious in the early morning light. And more vulnerable than I'd thought possible.

"Of course she's going," Savannah said.

"Why? You don't even *like him*." He directed his comment at me after a quick glare at Savannah.

Awkward tension filled the air, suffocating me and making words impossible. "Well . . ."

He stepped forward, eating up the distance, making it even harder to speak with the tenderness of last night shimmering in the early morning light.

"Don't you have a fight or something to train for?" Savannah asked.

"Savannah," I chastised her softly. "That's not helpful."

"My job isn't to be helpful, it's to be sure you meet your social engagements." She checked the non-existent watch on her wrist. "Time's short."

"Just . . . calm down," I told her, turning back to Montana and running my hands through my hair. "The thing is, I made a promise—"

"After last night . . . How can you even think about entertaining him? He's a pompous, shallow piece of shit who wants to *buy you* from your father in that goddamned shipping contract. He doesn't deserve your promises." He trembled, and I placed my hands on his forearms in an effort to still him.

"I didn't promise Lucas; I made a promise to my father. That I'd *try*. And Lucas isn't the monster you think. He's funny, and kind, and he listens—"

"You're serious?" he asked, scoffing and taking a step back from me until my hands dropped away.

"*Please*, don't act like this—"

"How am I supposed to act? Grateful?" His blue eyes were cold now, his words cruel. My heart dropped to my ankles. "Thank you for deigning to stoop to my level for a while, Miss Audrey."

"That's not fair!" I said, hurt and angry now. "This isn't easy for me. I told you things last night I haven't told anyone. I just need some time to—"

"To what? String me along? Like I'm just a passing itch you need to scratch?"

"Damnit, it's not like that!" I saw, however, that despite my words, my actions spoke much louder in this moment. And in truth, I didn't really *want* to spend time with Lucas. But I wanted to make my father proud more than anything else. As fucked-up as that was. I let out a resigned breath that took the fight out of me. "I need to get ready."

I turned away, blinking a little too hard. Savannah ushered him out the door, taking all that giddy happiness I'd felt with her. Until I was alone again, feeling worse than before.

CHAPTER TWENTY-SEVEN

JESSE

THE DOOR SNAPPED SHUT, and I wheeled toward it, coming face-to-face with Savannah. The woman lifted her gaze, a warning written in her eyes.

"Leave it alone for now." Her voice was deep, an unspoken warning. Though there was a hint of the kind woman who'd spoken to me in the kitchen last night, there was something else in the hard line of her mouth, the tension in her shoulders.

"You were the one who told me to fix it." I pointed to the door behind her. "How the hell am I supposed to do that if you throw me out?"

"Time, Jesse," Savannah said. "I'm all for helping you as long as it's helping *her*. But right now, she needs time. Now go." Her eyes flickered down the corridor, a clear dismissal.

"So Will did tell you," I said. "You know who I am?" Savannah nodded, her mouth snapping shut. "Why didn't either of you tell me about Emma?"

Her eyes grew wide, and her features slackened. "It—I . . ." Her cheeks blanched beneath my anger as she averted her gaze. Guilt. It was all over her.

"Who was the doctor that prescribed her glowroot? I have a thing or two I'd like to say to him." My hands balled into fists.

A sharp, pained gasp came from Savannah. It was almost inaudible, but the sound captured my attention. Her brows knit together as she clutched the front of her robe and shuffled her weight from one foot to the other, gaze shifting as though preparing to flee. I'd seen a hundred fighters do the same thing when they realized they couldn't beat me.

"Savannah?"

Shame coated her cheeks as she blinked rapidly. "It wasn't the doctor," she said, her shoulders hunching as if she were trying to make herself smaller. She averted her gaze swiftly, shaking her head. "They needed to hold her still so the doctor . . ."

I blinked. *Savannah* had done it?

"*You?*"

"It—it was the only way." Her back flattened against the door to Audrey's room.

"She was *pregnant.*"

"Shh!" Savannah's attention darted up and down the corridor. "We didn't know," she said in a hushed voice.

I didn't give a shit if anyone heard our conversation. Not one.

I stepped back, shaking my head slowly. This woman, who claimed to care about Audrey, the person who intervened when Audrey needed her, who tossed vulgar gestures and insults at Will . . .

"You killed my daughter."

My heart had somehow mended itself over the weeks I'd been here. I didn't register the horror on Savannah's face, nor the tears filling her eyes. Instead, I wheeled around and strode off, not able to trust myself. My heart shattered as I stalked blindly through the halls. My feet carried me of their own accord, away from Audrey's room and toward the back house, as I muttered curses at Savannah, at Lucas *fucking* Rutherford, at myself.

We lost a baby.

I stopped short at the edge of the courtyard. Will knew. He and Savannah knew about Emma. Neither of them thought her important enough to tell me.

I'd forgiven him for not reaching out. For not sending word she was alive. But he *knew*.

He fucking knew she was pregnant and didn't even try to tell me.

My feet carried me across the cobblestones of the courtyard, still damp with morning dew. I stalked in the direction of Sebastian's room near the stables. As I rounded a corner, the man I'd considered my friend stormed out, slamming the door behind him.

Will lit a cigarette, leaning back against the wall as his eyes fluttered shut. I stomped toward him. He glanced at me, deep lines of exhaustion in his face.

"When were you going to tell me she was pregnant?" I snapped. Will's features shifted, from exhaustion to guilt and surprise.

"Wait, Jesse—"

"*No*," I said, pointing a finger in his face. "You *fucking* knew and you couldn't be bothered to tell me." I advanced on him at the same time Sebastian opened the door. He, too, appeared tired, and anger filled his eyes as he regarded me.

"What's going on?" he asked, hard gaze flickering between me and Will.

With a heavy sigh, Will said, "Just . . . give me a second?"

"Fuck you, Ellis!" I stormed off, blindly stalking away. I wanted a drink. I wanted to fight. I wanted to murder someone.

Footsteps slapped against the stones of the courtyard behind me. "Jesus, *wait!*"

I wheeled around, throwing my fist directly into Will's jaw. My knuckles cracked against his skin, pain lancing up my wrist and forearm. Will staggered back, rubbing his jaw. I squared off against him, white-hot rage the only thing I felt.

Because if I focused on what we'd lost, what'd been destroyed . . .

"Hit me," Will said, rolling up his sleeves and flicking his cigarette away.

My chest heaved as I glared at him, hot tears stinging my eyes.

"Hit me," he repeated, less than a foot between us. I balled my hands into fists at my sides, my jaw clenched and every muscle strung tight. I didn't think I could forgive him for this. For not telling me.

"You should have come for me," I growled.

Will stared at me steadily. He blinked, and his features returned to normal. "You're right. I should have." His back straightened. "Hit me."

"Did you hate me so much that you thought I'd be better off not knowing?" I demanded. "That *she'd* be better without *me*? Audrey matters, Will." The words rolled heavily from my tongue, dark and dangerous. The man lifted his chin, stoic, silent, jaw set. "Three goddamn years. While you're here living up the high life and—"

"Hit me."

So I did. I threw my elbow at him. He absorbed the contact with his shoulder and recovered quickly. With a left hook, I punched his cheek. Will didn't even stumble. Instead, he lifted his hands, egging me on.

I didn't know what to do. I didn't know how to process the lead ball of grief consuming me. I hit him. Again. And again. Until my knees shook and nearly gave out. I stumbled backward into a stone wall.

"*FUCK!*" My knuckles met stone, and sharp pain radiated up my wrist and all of the way to my shoulder. I cradled my hand against my chest. "Goddamnit!"

LEATHER & LACE

Tingling spread out from my knuckles. Pain pulsed in time with my pounding heart. I fell back against the wall and slid to the damp stone. My tears renewed, spilling onto my cheeks as I put my head in my hands.

"We lost a baby, Will," I said. "We lost a baby and Audrey doesn't even know she was ours."

My friend dropped to a knee in front of me. He reached out, his hand gripping my shoulder. I grabbed his wrist with my uninjured hand, focused on settling my uneven breath. I couldn't look at him.

"Why do you think I didn't come for you?" Will asked after a too-long moment. His words were quiet, gentle. If I hadn't let them take her from me, *none* of this would have happened. All I did was fail the people I loved. His voice cracked as he said, "I couldn't tell you that."

Will's grip tightened on my shoulder as I finally lifted my gaze. His eyes were full of grief, mirroring what I felt in my chest.

"Her name was Emma," I said, breaking all over again.

"She had blonde hair," Will whispered.

Hot tears streamed down my cheeks. I could see her. A little girl with Bonnie's dark blue eyes and a dusting of blonde hair. Like The Kid. A mischievous grin crossed her face. I ached at never knowing her, at never seeing her smiling face.

"I don't know what to do," I whispered. "She's got plans with *fucking* Rutherford today."

"You make her forget about him," Will said, dropping his hand. "I've known Bonnie my entire life. And I've never seen her at peace or happy like she was with you. Who cares if she's Audrey now? You saved her once. You can do it again."

Did he really believe that? Because I didn't.

"C'mon," Will said as he rose. He helped me up. I clutched my right hand to my chest; pain throbbed all the way to my elbow.

"Montana!"

When I turned, Zachary Lee strode into the courtyard, trailed by a guard.

"Sir," I said, turning away to compose myself.

"Good work in Baton Rouge." He tossed a purse at me. I caught it with my left hand. It was heavier than the others I'd received after my fights. I pulled open the drawstring, eyes widening as the morning sun flickered off of dozens of gold bits. *Gold* bits. I didn't even know the last time I'd seen *one*.

"Thank you," I said, finally looking up at him. He regarded me quietly, gaze darting to Will, then back to me.

"Be ready for next week. Jersey nearly ripped a man in two last night in Knoxville. He won't be easy to beat, but I know you're the man for the job." Lee regarded me quietly. "Ellis, meet me in my office in thirty minutes. I've got another job for you."

As soon as the man walked off, I turned toward Will. Already, his features screwed up into something far away, haunted. As he'd been when I found him on the bridge last night.

As suddenly as it appeared, it vanished. He turned to me, a grin spread across his face. "So how fucked up is your hand?"

CHAPTER TWENTY-EIGHT

AUDREY

S OMETIMES I THOUGHT THE walls of my room were shrinking. Closing in inch by inch until I couldn't breathe anymore. I'd imagined it enough over the years during long periods of confinement that it made my chest hurt. Still, I'd rather sequester myself in here for another three days than risk seeing Montana again.

I'd had too much time to think. About the tender moments shared between us in the library, the rare vulnerability he seemed only able to show me. Or the devastating attraction I had to him, drawn like a moth to flame, my body coming alive when he touched me. Even the fact that I'd been able to open up to him, no matter how disastrously that turned out, had me aching to find him and take it all back. Every word spoken in cowardice and uncertainty.

He's a pompous, shallow piece of shit who wants to buy *you from your father in that goddamned shipping contract. He doesn't deserve your promises.*

The truth was a dagger, twisting beneath my ribs until I couldn't ignore it. As angry as I was that my father dismissed me so easily, all I'd done was play the part of the perfect daughter with the tiniest hope he would *finally* acknowledge me. My mind, my capability, my goddamned fortitude. Instead, I entertained the affections of a man who didn't truly value me in a doomed attempt to be seen as worthy. By a man willing to sell my hand in marriage for the *business*. All at the expense of someone who never once made me feel like less. And I let it happen.

What the fuck did that say about me?

My father tried to visit, speaking in low tones through the door about keeping my word to try with Lucas. I never responded.

Because even though I knew I should refuse . . . I ached to see him proud of me. Just once.

Savannah poked her head through our shared door, expression careful as she noticed me atop my messy bed, staring up at the ceiling and fighting the urge to find the nearest bottle of glowroot to disappear into. So I didn't have to feel anything anymore. What I wouldn't give for a bottle of numb relief right now.

"How are you feeling?" she asked gently, the way she had each day since Montana left to meet with Lucas. Rolling my head to the side, I stared at her long enough that she finally shuffled into the room. "Dumb question?" she asked, cracking a smile.

Instead of answering, I rolled onto my stomach and pressed my face into the mattress, screaming in frustration.

"So, I'm assuming that means you *don't* want to leave your room today?" she asked, sounding closer now than she'd been a few moments before. Lifting my head from the tangled sheets, I glared in her direction.

"How could you tell?" I asked, deadpan. "What I don't understand is why either of them would even *want* to be with a mess like me. I'm just . . . overwhelmed, I guess."

"Maybe it's the two-day-old syrup on your shirt from breakfast?"

I didn't want to smile, but Savannah had a way of coaxing it out of me. "Damn those pancakes. That's it, Etty's fired." I chuckled softly. Savannah sat on the edge of the bed, her eyes crinkling at the corners.

"I'll leave you to give her notice."

"Never mind," I responded. We looked at each other and giggled ridiculously, until mirthful tears appeared in the corners of my eyes. When we settled into companionable silence once more, Savannah leaned closer, resting her head on my shoulder.

"Seriously, do you want to talk about it?" she asked gently. She always did that, I realized, blunting the edges of my bad moods and making it easier to think. I twisted one of my fingers around her curls, pulling it from her careful hairstyle as she scrunched her nose.

"It's like I woke up one day a complete disappointment," I said, voice cracking. "And I don't even remember what I did that was so wrong. I don't understand why I can't be enough."

When she didn't respond, I let out a weary sigh. "And maybe I'm tired of feeling that way. I've been running from my past for so long. Making myself small and agreeable and apologizing for things I can't even remember. Maybe I'm tired of pretending I fit in, when clearly I never have. I thought if I could get Lucas to propose to me, if I entertained him, then my father would finally see I'm not a screw-up he has to be ashamed of. And if he could accept me, I would feel like . . . *myself* again."

I sat up, and we shifted together on the bed. Turning to face her head-on, I pressed my lips together to order my thoughts before I finally said, "Don't you think it's weird? The more I've thought about it, the stranger it seems. I woke up after forgetting *everything* and was told who I was, how I was supposed to act, to feel, to *look*. Then, I did it." My brows knit together as I tried to figure out a way to articulate my chaotic musings. "I didn't question anything or try to find myself, and lately I feel like . . . maybe I got it all wrong. Maybe I'm not supposed to be *this*." I waved at myself, like it would make the tears wobbling on the edge of my vision disappear.

Savannah went unnaturally still; I didn't even think she was breathing until she said, "You're *not* supposed to be this."

Now *I* wasn't breathing. I didn't ask what she meant, because we both knew she was talking about *before.* Swallowing loudly, I gripped her arms tight, shuffling closer to her. "Tell me."

Something broke free in Savannah, like a dam burst wide and I could finally see past those careful lists and the starched dresses she used to hide from the world.

"You weren't here before your injury, not once since I was a child. They carried you in one night, bleeding, *dying*, and after the doctors left, Mr. Lee hired almost all new staff members, introducing you as his daughter and spinning a story about your *accident*. I don't know where you were before, but it wasn't here. It wasn't *this.*"

My heart thumped against my ribs until I thought they might crack.

"You aren't crazy, Audrey."

Tears welled in my eyes and streaked down my cheeks. My reality fractured in seconds. How many times had my father told me the story? About how I'd been so cock-sure I could make it on my own, the argument we had, how in the weeks that'd followed he'd searched for me until finally . . . he found me nearly dead. The victim of a brutal outlaw attack. Jones and his men. Vengeance because of their feud with my father.

It was all a *lie.*

One I'd swallowed down happily as long as it meant I could get more glowroot, and later because this was a refuge from my pain. Relief slammed into me like a tidal wave. If I'd been standing, my knees would've buckled at the weight lifted from my shoulders. The expectations I'd fought for so long finally disappeared, like smoke on a strong southern wind.

Shards of memories resurfaced in my mind, ones I'd dismissed because I feared my broken mind had made them up. *Naked legs entwined together in a tangle of sheets.* I stood, crossing to the mirror I'd avoided for so long. *A tiny yellow flower pressed between the pages of a small book.* Almost violently I tore my shirt off, standing in just my bra and some cotton sleep shorts. I touched the crisscross scars tracked over my ribs. *A heavy arm around my shoulders as I was tucked safely in the cage of strong arms.* I traced the gnarled letters falling from my shoulder to my forearm, spelling out Jones's name. *Poetry spoken sweet in my ear, breath catching on the tiny hairs near the base of my neck and my temples.* A pink gash on my hip that looked too neat, almost surgical as it healed.

Hope is the thing with feathers, that perches in the soul, and sings the tune without the words—

"—and never stops at all."

I buried my face in my hands, mopping my wet cheeks and trembling as a long-familiar ache flared anew. I'd thought it was fear, or desperation, a knee-jerk reaction after my attack. I awoke with this ache cracking wide inside of me for so long that it felt normal, expected.

Open your eyes.

"I'm not crazy." I turned to Savannah with all my scars on display and freedom singing in my veins. It set me on fire. Life bubbling up from the cracks I thought I could mend all on my own. "I'm not crazy," I said again, firmer this time.

I marched over to her, sitting small and afraid on the edge of my bed, and dragged her into my arms. A teary laugh caught on the edge of my mouth, and a wild smile lit up my face. "Thank you," I whispered into her hair, crushing her against me.

At first, she stiffened in my arms, but as she exhaled and her body relaxed, she clutched me back. For so long that my giddy elation hummed beneath my skin. I pulled away, tucking my wild hair behind my ears and wiping salt tracks from beneath eyes that felt like they could finally see the world clearly.

"You know," she said, blinking back emotion of her own. "If you *really* want to thank me, you'll go riding with Lucas Rutherford."

"Savannah—" I started, groaning. How could she think the first thing I'd want to do with this newfound possibility was waste it on an entitled prick like Lucas Rutherford? More than anything, I wanted to talk to Montana. To reassure him about the other night, what it meant to me, and how I felt about him.

"The truth is, *I really need you to do it,*" she said in a rush, sitting heavily back on the mattress. I knew why my father needed me to entertain Lucas and the farce of a courtship he'd arranged, but why would Savannah ask this of me? My eyebrows furrowed low in concern and confusion as I opened my mouth to ask.

"I need to get out of the house," she said before I could. "And if they're all watching *you*, they won't care what I'm doing."

I picked up my stained shirt and dragged it over my head while I thought. Savannah rarely left the house, and when she did, it was short, practical trips. Running errands or buying ingredients for one of her confections. Like she was bound to the bricks that kept us both caged here. In many ways, especially in those early weeks when I'd been known to try to run away, I'd taken a lot of my cues from her.

Sitting next to her, I gripped her hand. "Wh—"

"I almost had sex with Will the other night!" She covered her face and inhaled in humiliation.

A surprised laugh bubbled from my lips. She constantly said she hated him, but I'd always thought there was something *more* between them.

After blinking in shock a few times, I smiled softly and peeled her hands away. She kept her eyes averted before relenting and staring at me, cheeks flushed in embarrassment. I didn't ask for an explanation. Honestly, after all the times she'd covered for me when I picked less-than-stellar bed partners, this was child's play.

"I was going to say, 'What do you need me to do?'" I said quietly, watching as the words registered and she blinked at me in quiet gratitude. "Do you need to talk about it?"

"There's nothing to talk about," she said, straightening her spine and shifting into a primmer position as she adjusted her skirt. "He's with Sebastian."

"Men don't just *almost* have sex with someone if they're blissfully happy in a relationship. *Please* tell me I don't have to explain that—"

"It was a *fluke*—" She interrupted me as she sliced her hand definitively through the air. "Just a . . . moment of weakness. We were both feeling vulnerable an-and . . . nothing happened. It's done."

I arched an eyebrow at her, and she rolled her eyes in response, sniffing primly to indicate she was finished with the subject. If I pushed the issue, she'd leave in a huff. Instead, I changed the subject like she wanted. Begrudgingly.

"So how do we get everyone's attention?" I asked, narrowing my eyes enough that she was aware this subject *would* be revisited later.

She pursed her lips and stood, pacing as she pondered. "I have the perfect idea!"

Her face lit up, and she rushed through the door that connected our rooms. Curious, I followed as her shoes clattered along the tile floor in the bathroom, and she flung her bedroom door wide. She dropped to her knees when she got to a corner and pulled up a small area rug, fitting her fingers between two wooden slats until one of them lifted.

"How many secrets have you been hiding?" I asked with a breathy laugh. She grunted as she pulled the board up and shuffled around to peer into the floor.

"Way too many," she muttered as her arms disappeared inside. Pulling out a worn cardboard box faded with time, she brushed some dirt and dust off the top as she set it on the floor. Her fingers clenched the edges, and she hesitated before she pushed it toward me.

"What is it?" I asked, sitting cross-legged on the floor in front of her.

"Everything you had with you, from *before*," she said, biting the corner of her cheek. My eyes fell to the box, a vice around my heart. "Your father isn't going to be happy that I gave this to you—"

"Fuck him," I said vehemently. "He's a liar."

"I was supposed to burn this. He won't like that I disobeyed him . . ." As her words faded, real fear clouded her eyes. Catching her gaze with mine, I unclenched my jaw to tell her what I should have a long time ago.

"When I leave this house, you're coming with me," I said. "I promise."

Before she could respond or I thought too hard about it, I flipped the top off of the box and peered inside. There wasn't much inside. If I thought the memories of my past would come rushing back, I was wrong. A pair of muddy boots. A black shirt, caked with dried blood and ripped beyond repair.

A pair of the shortest shorts I'd ever seen.

Something about them gave me pause. So, without thinking, I shuffled out of my sleep shorts and slipped my feet into them, pulling them up over my hips.

They fit perfectly. Worn in all the right places. As I buttoned them, my entire body released a sigh of relief. I shuddered at the feeling unfurling inside of me.

It was like coming home.

My hands dipped into the pockets. In one, I found a tiny yellow flower, pressed and preserved by time. Just like the one from my rememberings. My hands curled over something metal in the other. A ring rolled on my palm. Heavy and large, with a purple stone and words etched into it. *Jeff. Class of 2020.*

I'll come for you. I don't care what I have to do or how long it takes.

Tearful words whispered harshly on heavy, shared breaths, calloused hands wiping away my tears. I clenched the ring in my fist, stifling the urge to cry again. A piece. It was a piece of my heart back.

I didn't know what it meant, or who'd said it, but it was important. Vital.

I'll come for you.

It'd never been a threat, but a promise. One filled with suffering and regret. That sliver of myself slid back into place easily. As if it'd never been missing at all.

"Are you alright?" Savannah asked. Leaving the ruined boots and shirt in the box, I walked back into my room, Savannah on my heels. Gripping the ring in my palm tight enough to cause marks, I caught sight of myself in the mirror.

My eyes were bright, my cheeks flushed, and even though my hair was a mess of wild tangles falling haphazardly down my back . . . something about how untamed I was felt more right than anything ever had until now.

There I was.

Not whole, but healing.

And I was through letting other people make decisions for me. Setting my shoulders in determination, I crossed to my vanity, pulling a large opal pendant off the chain and tossing it onto the floor. Threading the ring onto the long chain and clasping it around my neck so it rested just above my heart. *Right.* That was right. Before Savannah could question me, I pulled open my wardrobe and threw the dresses and skirts to the floor in a heap.

"Hey, wait! What on earth—"

With a devilish grin, I emerged with one of the tight black tops I used to train with Will, changing quickly. Whirling back to the mirror, the woman I saw before me was confident. Self-assured. She didn't shy away from her scars or her body. She didn't hide her flaws; she *embraced* them. She used them as weapons.

Shoving my feet into a pair of boots haphazardly, I stumbled towards the door before Savannah stopped me with a frantic hand on my wrist.

"Wait a second, we have to do your hair and—"

"No," I said with a smile. She shook her head, eyes wide.

"But—"

"Savannah," I said, resting my palms on her shoulders. "Look at me."

She did. Her eyes roved over me, nose scrunching at my exposed skin. She'd never been a fan of my dipping necklines or short hems, and those were *conservative* compared to this.

"I'm *enough*," I said, meaning it more than I ever had before.

"Is this what it feels like to have a stroke? I think I'm having a stroke—"

I laughed, shaking my head and waving a hand at her as I spilled into the corridor.

"He said he'd meet you in the stables!" she called after me.

The guard in the hallway turned to see what the commotion was about and stumbled. He wasn't even walking anywhere, but I felt his eyes on my ass the entire way down the hall as I reached the back staircase.

Tossing my hair and tilting my chin up, I didn't let the scandalized and lascivious stares from the staff members bother me as I strolled through the courtyard toward the stables. In fact, if anything, their reactions gave me even more confidence. I needed to cause a scene and turn heads. Well, I was definitely accomplishing my goal. Who knew all it took was a pair of shorts to topple the fragile ecosystem of the house? I should have done this *years* ago.

I'd nearly made it to the stables when my steps faltered, pinned to the spot by blue eyes that'd sharpened into blades and cut straight through my swell of brazenness. There he stood, across the courtyard, leaning against a column in front of the fountain. Montana. He drank me in like I was a fine vintage he wanted to savor. As his gaze tracked every clearly-displayed curve of my body, I swore I felt the phantom of his touch grazing my skin. I remembered the heat from my room the night of the hurricane party, the air muggy and sticking to our skin, heightening the friction of his calloused hands on every part of me.

Wrestling my attraction, I shut those thoughts down hard. Savannah needed me to distract everyone, including Lucas and my father. Even though all I wanted was to go to him and explain, I didn't have time. Not now. I turned sharply on my heel and walked quickly towards the stables, unable to keep looking at him. Because if I did, I'd forget all about helping Savannah and fall into him. Like I always seemed to.

Lucas was waiting for me, impatiently, letting the groom tack the horses while he glanced at the watch in his palm. He wore jeans again, clearly trying his hand at casual attire. They molded against his thighs nicely as he shifted his weight back and forth. He had one of those infuriating button-down shirts on, the elbows rolled up, top two buttons undone. It was adorable how even when he tried *not* to be so put-together, he still tucked his shirt in.

"Audrey!" My name rang across the courtyard, Montana's deep voice boomed through the space like a clap of thunder. *Shit.* Maybe I could just let him know this wasn't what it seemed before—

At the sound of my name, Lucas lifted his eyes and noticed me in the doorway. His jaw dropped, and his watch clattered to the straw at his feet. I smiled, wide and wicked, and it was a lie. It was all a *lie.* From my periphery, Montana approached, a determined march across the courtyard, his long legs eating up the space between us too quickly.

"Did I keep you waiting long?" I asked, letting the words drip from my mouth like honey. Slow and husky. Lucas shook his head, Adam's apple bobbing with a nervous swallow.

"I didn't know if you'd—I mean, I'm *glad* you—"

Ten feet.

Too close, much too close, and, by the expression in his eyes, Montana wasn't going to let me go easily if he caught up. The need to run thrummed through my blood, making my heart stutter in my chest. My eyes caught Lucas's once more, his stammered words falling into silence as I sauntered right up to him, until there were only a couple inches between our bodies. The hitch in his breath wavered in the air.

Five feet.

Montana turned the corner, skidding to a stop when he noticed Lucas and how close we stood. His blue eyes went wide, a thread of betrayal lacing into his expression. His jaw clenched hard enough for a muscle to feather beneath his skin, and I stared at him with wide, desperate eyes.

It's just a distraction! I wanted to scream. *It isn't what it looks like. It's you I care about. The other night meant something to me. Please.*

My fingers went to Lucas's waistband, and he let out a shocked gasp. "Miss Audrey! I—What are—"

Tugging swiftly, I untucked Lucas's shirt from his jeans, freeing the tails of the fabric and trying to ignore Montana, who looked like he wanted to burn this whole fucking house to the ground. Every muscle in his body tensed, practically vibrating as he held himself back.

I'm sorry.

"Get comfortable, Lucas. It's going to be a long afternoon," I said. "Have you done a lot of horseback riding?"

Lucas cleared his throat as I pulled away, taking the reins from the groom and swinging my leg over to settle into the saddle. Lucas scrambled onto his own horse a moment later, after searching the straw for his watch. He sat stiffly, arms raised in front of him with the reins in his hands. I stifled a laugh, biting my bottom lip to keep the grin from stretching over my mouth.

He flicked the reins and trotted precariously into the side street that led to the square. Wrapping the leather reins around my hand and clicking my tongue, I tugged hard to steer my mount after him, turning to Montana for one last look. Only, he was gone.

Digging my heels in, letting my body rock with the rhythmic bouncing clop of the horse beneath me, I caught up to Lucas quickly. He looked like he was trying with all his might not to unseat himself. We turned the corner together, my stallion taking the lead and hedging his into a smoother gait that wouldn't jostle him quite so hard.

"Audrey Lee!" My father's angry voice shouted across the square toward us from the front steps of the house. I waved at him, a mischievous grin plastered on my face as I pulled the reins to turn farther away.

"We'll be back later, Dad! Don't wait up!"

"Get back here *right now*!"

"Sorry! Can't hear you!" I shouted back, leaning over to take one of Lucas's reins in my hands. "Hang tight."

With a swift kick to my horse's ribs, we were off. The echo of clattered hoofbeats matched my thrumming pulse as we raced from the square. Lucas gripped the saddle horn for dear life, face pale in the moments before he adjusted to the swift pace. I could've let him go, pushed my stallion faster, until we were racing the wind and disappearing into the wilderness. The urge to open my hand and let him go pounded right alongside the freedom singing in my heart. A melody of wild abandon that set my soul alight.

Instead, I pulled on the reins, slowing us incrementally until we were at a lively trot, and Lucas grasped the leads. He looked over at me, gulping in ragged breaths like it'd been him and not the horses that'd sprinted us into the bustling city. His eyes were wide and a little fearful, like he hadn't seen me until this very moment. Not really.

I didn't want to admit how much I liked surprising him.

"Did I just kidnap you?" he asked once he'd caught his breath. I laughed, a full-bodied sound that had me clutching my stomach and wiping tears from the corners of my eyes.

"If anything, I kidnapped *you*," I said between fits of laughter. An honest smile crossed his face as we fell into a comfortable silence.

"I didn't think you were going to come," he said after a while, his arms up in that ridiculous pose again, elbows akimbo like it might ground him in the saddle. I tried to stifle a giggle but failed.

"I think if you relax, it might kill you," I said, my eyes sliding over his arms again.

"I've never been riding before." He tried to adjust in the saddle and looked even more ridiculous than before.

"I hadn't noticed," I drawled sarcastically, earning a huff as he shifted again.

"Just drop your arms and sit upright, heels in the stirrups and back straight—" As I instructed him, he listened without complaint, until finally he relaxed enough that his horse fell into the rhythm of the stride. "There. Better."

"Why did you?" he asked, daring a glance over at me. "Come today."

"I almost didn't, but I *really* wanted to get out of the house. It can be . . . stifling sometimes," I answered carefully. No way in hell would I confide in him that I wanted to give Savannah enough room to sneak out to do God knows what.

An awkward silence stretched between us, both of us avoiding talking about the unpleasantness of the card game the other day. Montana had left, taking my self-confidence with him, and I'd been stiff. Unable to carry a conversation if my life depended on it. It swelled in the peace of the afternoon, making me wonder if we'd avoid talking for the rest of the outing. Honestly, that might be more enjoyable.

"Listen, I—" he started, but I didn't give him a chance to finish the thought.

"You don't have to—" Only he cut *me* off this time.

"Yes. I do." His eyes were dark. It was the first time I'd noticed them. There was no hint of the playful dimple so often present on his cheek when he laughed or joked with his friends. "You don't have to pretend to like things when we're together. The other day, I felt bad because it was clear that you weren't having a good time. I don't want you to think you have to be some perfect socialite. I just . . . want to get to know you."

I twisted my hands until the leather creaked, my eyes wide and my bottom lip clamped so tight between my teeth I might actually draw blood. Lucas peered over at me, his dark eyes raking over my expression as if he were reading a ledger. Taking note of every line and shift.

"The truth is, I like you. A *lot*. I thought after we kissed that it meant the same thing to you that it did to me. That it meant we were *together*. I realize now, you didn't see it that way, and my jealousy was really out of place." He let out a ragged sigh, flicking his head to toss the hair out of his eyes.

I scoffed before I realized it. His eyebrows lifted in response, clearly offended. "I just don't get what you like about me. I'm a *mess*."

"I like that you're a mess," he answered sincerely. "And I like that you don't care what other people think about you. That you're not afraid to call me out on my bullshit. I like the wild streak you have, kidnapping unsuspecting Manhattanites, drinking whiskey out of teacups, challenging your father's expectations for you—"

"That's not—" I shook my head, closing my eyes briefly as I sucked in a breath. All I could think about was how much of myself I'd compromised to have a relationship with my father. "I care about what people think of me. Too much, sometimes."

"I *wish* I had the courage to stand up to my father the way you do," he said, surprising me, his eyes falling to the saddle horn.

I like you. A lot.

I'd be lying to myself if I didn't admit how good it felt for someone to be so clear about their feelings for me. To know for sure that it was *me* and not some ghost from the past occupying his thoughts. It was really nice to have someone like *me*, not just the lure of my body.

It's not like you've given me a real chance! I've done nothing but try to get to know you. But nothing I do seems to matter.

He was right. I'd been so consumed by my feelings for Montana and convinced that Lucas would only use me to get closer to my father and the shipping deal. Montana had said as much himself. Only, Lucas *hadn't* done that. When I really thought about it, he hadn't actually talked about the contract. Other than acknowledging that my father was trying to set us up because of it. Which was the *truth*.

Maybe it was time I started trying. Started trying *anything*. Stopped living in the past and seeking approval where I would find none. Maybe I should stop avoiding the mess my life had become. Instead, I could figure out what I wanted.

"I still kind of wish I could mess up your stupid hair," I said, glancing slyly at him from the corner of my eye. He smiled so wide it reached all the way to his eyes.

"What *exactly* is so stupid about my hair?" he asked, his words edged in humor.

"Exactly?"

"Yes. *Exactly.*"

"Okay, well, first of all . . . it's always flopped so perfectly to the side. Like you wake up that way. Which is stupid. It takes forever to fix my hair and you get to just roll out of bed and have it look like *that*." I waved my hand at his face.

"It takes hours," he said, deadpan. "I have to wake up before dawn, wear a special bonnet, and don't get me started on the hot oil treatments. It takes *great pains* to get my hair to look this stupid."

I laughed. *Really* laughed. From all the way down in my belly. Until water prickled at the corners of my eyes. It felt good to laugh this much. To smile.

"It's not *that* funny," he grumbled.

"I'm imagining you in a *bonnet*." I snorted, sending him into his own fit of laughter. It was a good laugh. Full-bodied, easy, like he laughed a lot. When we finally calmed down, the silence between us grew warm and personal.

"So, where are you taking us?" I asked, excited about spending the afternoon with him now. In fact, I wanted to know *more* about him.

"You feel like breaking the rules?" he asked, a playful glint in his eyes as his dimple stood out clearly on his cheek.

"Always," I said, remembering the restlessness inside me that'd solidified into something strong. Something I recognized. I bit my lip to contain the smile spreading wildly across my face. "Aren't you afraid of my father?"

"No," he said, sitting back in the saddle as he led us down a paved street. "I know what it's like, having a father who casts a long shadow. Feeling like nothing you can do will help you step out from underneath it." He ran a hand through his *stupid* hair, and pieces of it stuck at odd angles. How oddly endearing.

"What's it like? Manhattan Island?" I asked, genuinely curious. He came from so far away, it almost seemed like another world.

"It's *magnetic*. The city never sleeps. Literally. At any time, day or night, there's something to do, somewhere to go. The buildings are so tall they almost block out the sun. People from all over the world live there. Speaking every language known to man. Small farms and gardens are grown on the roofs so high up in the air, it's like they're floating in a world all their own." He kept going, and I realized quickly that he talked with hands. I hung on every word, every description. Realizing for what felt like the millionth time that the world was so much bigger than I ever could've imagined.

I was intoxicated by the new streets we explored, the ugliness, the decay I'd been so sheltered from. Captivated by the knowledge that out here there were no guards, no overprotective fathers, just me and the surprisingly playful man I'd underestimated. Telling me stories about a world I wanted to explore to its fullest. The restlessness within me rose again, making me feel giddy and child-like.

"Do you really not remember anything before three years ago?" he asked after a long silence. I shrugged, not sure that was entirely accurate anymore. And I was surprised that I didn't want to lie to him.

"I know we talked about it before, but I guess I can't imagine it," he pressed, and I sighed deeply.

"Some things are natural. Others are just *gone*. Like my mother. I don't re-member her. My father has photographs in his study, and sometimes he'll drink too much and talk about her for hours. But it's not the same as *remembering*," I said by way of explanation.

A mournful saxophone called out a melody that danced in the air. We shared another easy smile. It was almost too perfect, not feeling any walls caging me in. I leaned back, inhaling deep the scent of chicory coffee on the air as my hair splayed out behind me and the sun beat down on my skin.

"I didn't think you could look more beautiful," he said from beside me. I opened my eyes to see him staring at me with awestruck wonder. Heavy tension hung in the air. I averted my eyes quickly, unsure how to respond. How was it that I could feel like *this* when just a few nights ago I had been in Montana's arms, spilling my heart out to him? Was it possible to care for two people at once?

"Where do you want to go? I've never been able to explore this far and—"

He held up a finger to silence me. "I want to show you something," he said, turning us down a side street. He stopped in front of a dilapidated shop with dark windows. One of my eyebrows rose in question.

"Is this the part where you hack me into pieces and hide my body?" I asked, watching him shake his head before holding out a hand to help me dismount.

"You've been reading too many novels," he said jovially. I took his hand and dismounted, Lucas squeezing my fingers before leading me inside. The shop was lined with masks. Every kind imaginable. Feathered, full-faced, porcelain, gauzy, jewel-encrusted, masks on decorated rods you held up to your face, some that were secured with pins or with ribbons you tied on.

"Masks?" I asked, trailing my fingers over a particularly elaborate one with peacock feathers framing the eye holes.

"What better way to be yourself, even in a crowded room?" he responded softly. "Beneath a mask, you can be whoever you want. Whoever you are. Put one on and suddenly no one else's expectations matter. You can just *be*." He regarded one with a wicked smile in red leather before moving on through the rows.

"I know what that feels like," I said beneath my breath, thinking of how relieved I'd been with Savannah's admission. As if the weight of a mountain had lifted with those expectations. Luke tried on a particularly clown-esque mask that made me scream so loud the shop owner glared at us from behind the counter. I tried on some of the most ridiculous ones, batting my eyes wildly at him until he grappled with me over one particularly gaudy mask to reveal my face. His arm wrapped around my waist, and we were so close that if I leaned forward an inch, our lips would touch. Strangely, the idea of kissing him wasn't as repulsive as before.

Then, as if called, I spied a mask beneath a glass case. The pattern on it whirled in artistic swoops, deep blue gemstones making it glitter like sunlight on the surface of water. The color was a blue so dark it was nearly black. I pressed my palms against the glass, watching it fog with the heat of my hands. Something about it, about the color and the design, raged toward me in the silence.

To remember me by, or trade if you're in a pinch.

Peace. A child's laughter. Water splashing. Campfire flames crackling as I danced beneath the stars. Another sliver of memory surfacing from the dark recesses of my mind.

"Try it," Luke said, startling me back to the present. I looked down again, a little sorrowfully, shaking my head.

"No, that's alright." I plastered a smile on my face as we finally made our way out of the shop. Luke bought me a beignet from a seller on the corner, and we ate the sweet, messy confection as we walked our horses back home. Until all that was left was the powdered sugar on our fingers that we licked away.

When the square came into view again, several of my father's and Lucas's men took the reins of the horses from us. We wavered before the front door, neither wanting the day to end. I hadn't thought it possible, but I had *fun* with Lucas. A chuckle stole my attention as his eyes fell to my chin.

"You have powdered sugar on your face," he said. I tried to wipe it away, but he shook his head, sending his perfect hair over his forehead. "Here."

His thumb brushed down my jaw and over my chin. Suddenly, with his fingers on my face, my chin tilted to him, and the way his eyes darkened as they settled on my lips, I realized I *wanted* to kiss him. I would never figure out what I wanted if I didn't gather the courage to *try*. Not for my father or anyone else, just me.

So I closed the space between us, and he brushed his mouth over mine reverently. Gently, he mapped my lips with his own. I wrapped my arms around his neck, and we shuffled together into the foyer, our mouths parting, then coming back together as he backed me into the wall. He never pressed himself too close to me; his hands never gripped me like I was his lifeline back to earth. His lips were never hard on mine. Even when I nipped at his mouth with my teeth, I couldn't tempt his passions to flare any hotter.

He pulled away.

And I was left there, wanting more. Wanting the desperate rush of mouths slicking together as you devoured and were devoured in equal measure.

"Let me get to know you," he begged into my mouth. "Let me show you who I *really* am."

Thoughts whirled in my mind, dizzying and conflicting. The way I still felt about Montana, if I hadn't ruined that. My father's lies. The contract. Savannah. Needing a way out of this house, out of this city. Laughing with Lucas. It all came together, culminating into one word.

"Okay."

CHAPTER TWENTY-NINE

SAVANNAH

I F ANYONE HAD ASKED why I left the manor, I'd have told them I was scheduling an appointment for Audrey with the seamstress. Blessedly, they hadn't. I'd escaped, if only for a few hours. I made the appointment as instructed but didn't stick around.

The air flowed into my lungs easier. I could breathe for the first time in too long. It didn't help that everywhere I went, I felt Will's eyes on me, even if he was nowhere around. After the confrontation with Jesse the other morning, I couldn't handle the stifling walls of the house much longer.

I strolled down the Riverwalk, scouring the boats as I passed. I'd mentioned to Will that I would inquire about passage out of the city, and I intended on doing just that with the opportunity Audrey had given me. Jesse and Will seemed to be focused on getting *Bonnie* back, but they didn't appear to have plans on what to do when that happened. That responsibility fell to me. As usual.

Nearly every single riverboat had a gold or black fleur-de-lis painted on its sides, smokestack, or above the rudders on the rear.

It'd been difficult to find that single boat without it years ago. It felt impossible now.

Armed men strode past me as I neared the Riverwalk ruins, an old mall that had been mostly lost to time. Changing climates had caused the river to rise, and over the past two decades, the Mississippi had begun to reclaim its banks, starting with the concrete and glass building hovering near the water's edge.

My skin prickled in warning as a uniformed guard milled about, assault rifle in hand. I turned sharply as his attention found me. I was too far from the house, the square. If he recognized me or saw the brand on my neck, no doubt I'd be in worse trouble than I already was after letting Aud—Bonnie out of the house in those incredibly inappropriate shorts.

My heart had squeezed at the joy in my friend's eyes. I'd do it all over again.

Most of Audrey's lingering trauma and pain was my fault. Jesse's words haunted me even days later.

You killed my daughter.

It wouldn't have hurt if it'd been a baseless accusation. But it wasn't. I *was* responsible for the loss of the child that'd brought life back into Audrey's eyes. It still hurt to think of the happiness I'd witnessed for that short time. Too short.

As I pretended to stare longingly over the muddy river waters, boots marched toward me. *Shit.* I was busted. I clasped my fingers together in front of me, the delicate purse hanging around my wrist swinging back and forth. How was I going to get out of this?

"Miss, this is a restricted area," the guard said brusquely.

I looked over at the man with wide eyes, feigning shock. I let out an airy laugh. He was young, younger than me. His loose posture indicated he wasn't one of Lee's men, or at least he hadn't been shaped as one just yet. I tugged the neckline of my gown up and folded my long curls over my left shoulder to hide my brand.

"Is it? Well, I'll be. I just wanted to see the old ruins." I flattened a palm against the soldier's chest. His pale cheeks flushed, and he eyed me with reluctant curiosity. After a moment, I stepped closer, lowering my voice in the same way I'd heard Audrey over the years. "There's a rumor that the crater beast Ponchartrain Patty frequents these waters." I spoke to him as if we were in confidence. "Can you blame a girl for wanting to get a closer look?"

The guard's shoulders slackened as he let out a sharp exhale, his lips twisting upward. "I suppose not."

I flashed a brilliant smile in his direction and swirled a curl around my index finger. His eyes marked the movement, a flash of desire passing through them. Good.

This was far easier than I'd imagined. I wasn't some seductress. But if I could get my best friend to safety, I had to take a chance, for her.

"You wouldn't be able to get me . . . closer, would you?" I asked, feeling his pulse pound through his uniform shirt. His throat bobbed, eyes flashing to mine in a move that reminded me of when Will had me pressed against the door to Lee's office, when I thought he'd kiss me.

Had his interest in me then been genuine?

"She sometimes circles the bridge," the guard said, glancing toward the hulking mass of metal and concrete looming above the muddy waters. "But mostly at night. When the *Beast* rides."

My heart stuttered at the mention of Will. Would it stop hurting? That desperation inside of me ached worse than anything I'd experienced before. Kissing him in the hallway before the hurricane party had been bad enough. His admission haunted me for days after.

I've wanted to kiss you every moment of every single day I've been stuck in this fucking house.

He should have never said that. I could live with him not wanting me. I could manage it, heal. What I couldn't do was live in the past, wondering what might have been if I'd been honest about my feelings with him. With myself.

I've wanted to do much more than kiss you.

I let him kiss me in the kitchen knowing he'd made a commitment to someone else. Because all I could think about since the party was letting him do *more* than kiss me. I'd let him touch me in ways I'd never been touched before, let him lay me down on the island because, for some stupid reason, I couldn't say no to him. I didn't want to. Even if that made me a terrible person.

"Could you"—I trailed my index finger down the breast pocket of his uniform shirt—"maybe show me around? I'm only in town visiting my sick grandmother for a few days before I have to leave."

He stared at my hand for a long moment. "I'm really not supposed to, Miss." The guard's gaze lifted to mine. I poked out my bottom lip in an approximation of a pout, something I'd witnessed Audrey do many times.

"That's too bad," I said, lowering my voice. "I was going to say, I'll be back in a month and maybe we could have dinner or something." His lips parted, and a muffled sound came from deep within his chest. His desire overpowered his sense of duty. He offered me his arm, and I took it, giving a small squeal of false delight.

Was manipulating men really this easy?

As he escorted me on top of the ruins, I asked pointed questions about his work, even if I didn't bother to listen to the answers. Instead, I scoured my surroundings, searching for something I hoped would deliver us to safety. He was an absolute gentleman the entire way, helping me climb the decrepit concrete pillars that led to the upper levels of what was once a shopping center.

The bridge loomed ahead. Bodies swung from the highest point. A warning. I'd heard about them but never gotten close enough to see for myself. Nausea roiled inside of me. *Will* had done that.

No. The *Beast of the Bridge* had done that. I couldn't accept they were the same, much less acknowledge it openly. The man I knew . . .

I knew monsters. And William Ellis wasn't one.

A series of wood and rope bridges crossed from the ruins to the nearest overpass that led to *the* bridge. The guard stopped, eyeing me with curiosity.

"See enough?"

"I think so," I said, nodding. "But, if you'll give me a moment, I'm afraid I have the bladder of a toddler." I couldn't force my cheeks to pinken beneath his gaze, so I averted my eyes to approximate some semblance of shame.

After murmuring that he'd be just behind a concrete wall, I counted to five. Once ensuring the coast was clear, I loosed a breath and stepped toward the rope bridge. My pulse quickened as it rocked on the breeze. Aside from the way I'd come, it was the only way off of this blasted ruin, and I'd come too far to go back.

I inhaled deeply, forcing my eyes ahead as my fingers curled around the rope. If the men patrolling on top of the bridge could walk across this, I had no doubt it could carry me.

It probably wasn't a good time to admit my fear of heights.

"Are you ready, Miss?"

Shit.

I didn't have time to think. I rushed forward, reminding myself not to look down with each step. The bridge listed to one side, and I froze, eyes snapping shut. I'd barely made it ten feet. It was far windier than I'd expected. Another gust shot up, knocking my hair from its careful style.

"Savvy!"

I opened my eyes. Twenty feet ahead of me, looming just on the other side of the concrete wall of the bridge, Will stood, staring at me with wide eyes. What was he doing here? He extended an arm in my direction.

"Don't just stand there! Come on!" Will leaned over the concrete barrier.

A shot rang out, and I ducked. It ricocheted off of concrete. I glanced over my shoulder to the guard as he held his rifle. He lowered the gun, trepidation in his eyes. "I have to ask you to come down from there!" His voice was barely audible over the raging wind.

This was insanity. I was so, *so* stupid to think I could do this.

"Savvy, to me!" Will had a gun in one hand, the other still reaching for me. If I went back to the guard, Lee would definitely find out what I'd been up to. But the thought of climbing farther on this rickety bridge made me want to vomit.

A second shot came from behind me, and that spurred me into action. No one else decided my fate.

Not today.

I rushed forward, nearly losing my footing as the wood beneath me inclined toward the concrete bridge ahead. I cursed myself silently, hands burning on the fraying rope as I climbed.

Vaguely, I registered shouting. I could focus only on the path in front of me, on Will's hand that was only a matter of feet away, on his eyes as they begged me to hurry.

My arms burned as I climbed, breath ragged as the distance closed. Ten feet. Five. I slipped, my knee banging against the wooden planks and the rope ripping at my palms as I bit out a cry. The bridge shook beneath me. I looked down.

Suspended above the ground by nearly fifty feet, my heart plummeted into my stomach. A few more guards milled about. One glanced up. *Shit.*

Warm hands grabbed my arms. Will had come over the concrete barrier. He lifted me to my feet, scanning me quickly before he took me by the hand and dragged me after him. Without a word, he hoisted me up before him. I cursed my heavy skirts as my fingers found purchase on the concrete. This would have been *much* easier if I'd worn pants.

"Hurry!" Will's breath washed across my brand. I stifled my groan as I lifted myself up an inch. Large hands found my hips, and he gave me a boost.

A moment later, I was up and over, skirts pillowing around my knees as I fell to the hard concrete. Panting, I found my footing just as Will hurled himself over. Another shot rang out, concrete dust whipping in the wind.

"Fuck," Will said, turning back to the guard. He aimed and fired in the span of a heartbeat.

"No!"

It was too late. The guard crumpled to the bridge. His body suspended for a moment before another gust of wind rushed forward. He toppled to the ground. I turned on Will, shoving his shoulder hard. "Why did you do that?!"

"Because if he didn't shoot you, he would've identified you." Will shook his head. Beads of sweat formed on his forehead, and frustration lined his eyes. "What are you doing?"

I glared up at him, blinking back the mixture of anger, exhaustion, and fear. I stomped past him to the far side of the bridge and pointed to the north. Will blew out an exasperated breath but crossed to my side. His gaze shot out to the single steamboat docked past the bridge in the bend of the river.

"It's the only one Lee doesn't own."

Some of the anger evaporated from him. He shook his head, staring at me with incredulity. "Lead the way, then."

Will ended up taking point most of the way. He knew the bridge better than anyone else, after all. The thought made me shudder as I tried to forget the bodies swinging above it. Not that I'd say anything. I knew the guilt that ate at him intimately without pointing it out.

"Why were you—"

"Not yet," Will said, words tight. A shadow passed across his face as he glanced toward the bodies swinging on the breeze. I noted a bruise on his jaw. Where had that come from?

We walked in silence until we cleared the bridge. Even then, he was on edge, hand resting on his holstered pistol until we were far from the patrols.

"Why were you following me?" I asked. His gaze found mine, but it didn't linger.

"I knew you were up to something back at the house," he said. My cheeks heated. "You never leave from the side entrance, and you've never gone to this part of the city before."

"H-how would you know that?" Deep lines formed on my face as confusion swirled through me. If he knew my patterns, that meant he'd spent a long time watching me.

Will didn't respond. Instead, he rubbed the back of his neck and averted his gaze.

"You've been following me?" He lifted panicked eyes to mine, confirming it. I breathed out a laugh, shaking my head. "You've been following me."

"Only when you leave the house," he said too quickly. "To make sure you're safe. And not that often . . . really."

I crossed my arms over my chest. "How often?"

Once again, he averted his gaze, lowering his head to hide his eyes beneath the brim of his hat, even though his cheeks darkened.

"Once or twice a month. You—you don't go out a lot." He shuffled his weight back and forth. "You could have told me what you planned to do."

I'd thought I was clever, convincing Audrey to cause a distraction so I could get out unnoticed.

Of course, Will hadn't been fooled. He had always been more perceptive than the others, always seeming to be just around the corner when I was in a tight spot, like when the guards had locked me in that closet.

I snapped my mouth shut against the arguments that rose in my mind. It wasn't like I could ask him for help. Not when I'd find him with Sebastian. My pride couldn't stand it. "I told you what I planned to do," I said with a shrug. It was a shotty defense, but it was the only one I had.

"I could have gone for you. You didn't need to put yourself at risk like this," he said, the words kind but still edged with frustration.

"I did have to." I shook my head at him.

"Why?"

Warmth coursed through me at his inquisitive gaze. Normally, I would have told him to shove off. Explaining myself seemed pointless. I sighed, grimacing as my boot rubbed against a sore spot on my ankle. "To prove that I'm useful. Just sitting in that house all day, doing nothing . . . it drives me crazy."

Will didn't respond. Instead, he guided me through dilapidated buildings. The ground sloped toward the river past an old warehouse, its smokestacks long dormant. Once we moved past, the steamboat came into focus. It was painted brown with no name on its side.

"How do you know it's not owned by Lee?" Will tossed his cigarette to the ground and crushed it beneath his boot.

"Etty made some inquiries for me a few years ago." I tried to ignore my aching feet and hands. "One of her sons found this couple that runs a legitimate shipping business up and down the Mississippi. They smuggle slaves out of the city." A lump formed in my throat as I remembered the day I'd booked passage from the city. "I'd been looking for a way home."

I felt Will's eyes on me before I looked at him. We hadn't talked about my past any more than his, I realized. He'd asked me where I'd been before New Orleans, but confiding about what I'd lost in St. Louis hurt too much.

It still hurt, but the least I could do was answer his questions after he saved me.

"Lee found me in St. Louis ten years ago. He . . . took me from my mom," I said on a hot breath. "I've been trying to get back to her. I only had a handful of bits squandered away, and anytime I approached someone about it, one look at the brand on my neck and they turned me away like I was a leper.

"You don't mess with Zachary Lee's property." A bitter tang filled my mouth. While the mark kept me safe from outside dangers, it trapped me. "So," I said. "When Etty's son found these people, I knew it was my way out. I sold things—things that weren't mine, trying to get enough money to pay for a way out." My throat constricted as I remembered the night that changed everything.

"When Lee gave me the money to buy glowroot for Audrey—" I cleared my throat, my voice scratchy. "I didn't spend it all. I kept some. It was enough."

We walked silently, the boat getting closer. Men moved back and forth across the dock, loading crates and barrels.

"But you're still here," Will finally said. I stopped, facing him fully and nodding.

"Because when I finally had my chance, we found out Audrey was pregnant." I let the words linger as something unreadable passed through his eyes, darkening those silver flecks I'd come to like so much. I averted my gaze as guilt clawed up the back of my throat, reminding me yet again of Jesse's accusation.

"How could I leave after what I did to her? To Emma?" It felt wrong to say her name, even though it wasn't. Lee had given the entire staff a strict lecture about not reminding Audrey of her trauma, to move forward and be *normal*. I bit my bottom lip to hide its wobble. If I hadn't given her glowroot, it wouldn't have happened.

"What you *did*," he said, fixing me with a hard stare, "saved her life, Savannah." There was no easy grin or sparkle in his eye. No bullshit whatsoever. A trill ran down my spine.

"Tell that to Jesse," I said bitterly.

"What?" Will asked, eyes narrowing.

Shit. It wasn't like me to expose someone when they'd been cruel. I exhaled sharply. "He found out about Emma. Told me I . . . killed his daughter."

Shadows drifted into Will's eyes. "He shouldn't have said that."

"That doesn't make it any less true," I said, averting my gaze.

"Jesse didn't mean it, not really," Will said. "He beat the shit out of me for not telling him sooner, but it's all his grief." Some of the tension in me eased. I *knew* that, but hearing Will speak it made it feel real. And explained the bruise on his jaw. "It makes monsters out of all of us. Give him time. If he doesn't come around, I'll put a bullet in his shoulder. I owe him anyway."

I gaped at Will. "What?"

"Long story," he said. "Anyway, it's a miracle that the doctor was able to drill the burr holes precisely enough not to penetrate past the dural layer and—"

He cut himself off, eyes shifting awkwardly. "It's a miracle the doctor didn't kill Audrey during the procedure. If she hadn't stayed still, she could have wound up a vegetable." The ache in my chest eased at the seriousness with which he spoke. "Able to think and hear, but not move or speak. All day lying in bed, not being able to really live in the world. Could you imagine that for her?"

That would have been horrifying.

"No," I admitted, unconsciously rubbing my arm. I hissed at the stinging pain in my palms, having forgotten how the frayed rope of the bridge had ripped my skin.

"I'll clean that when we get back." Will ducked his head so his hat covered his eyes.

"I can take care of it," I said, not unkindly.

As if the matter were settled, we made our way to the steamboat.

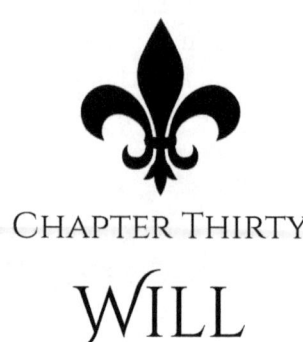

CHAPTER THIRTY

WILL

S HADOWS DANCED ACROSS THE cobblestones of Lee Square as we returned. The steamboat would leave at the same time as Jesse's big fight in a few days. The captain promised Savannah a place, but only if we made it before launch. The boat would be held for no one.

My pulse hadn't slowed since I'd caught sight of Savannah earlier. Between the danger she'd been in, the unspoken words poised on my tongue from the other night when she'd been spread beneath me on the kitchen counter, and the shadows of swinging bodies that'd fallen across her sunny face, I didn't know that my heart would ever beat normally again.

I'd needed to see her, I realized, walking in companionable silence next to her. After going back to Seb's room the other night only to spend the rest of the evening being torn to pieces by his disgust at my continued actions on Zachary's behalf, I felt too whittled away. Too much like the beast everyone saw each time they looked at me with fear in their eyes. Until now, I hadn't realized Savannah was the only person who'd never been afraid of me.

As the house came into sight, Savannah sighed wearily and started toward the front steps. I gripped her wrist, and when her eyes fixed on mine, suddenly I couldn't speak. Instead, I shook my head and motioned toward the alleyway on the side of the house. We walked silently through the darkening streets. The lamps were being lit as we pushed into the stable.

She strolled past me, and the easy camaraderie we'd shared beneath the open sky would soon be replaced by walls made of stone and blood. Within this house, she was a lady, and I was just . . . the Beast.

"Savvy, hang on."

She stilled, shoulders tense, as I moved into a stall. Quickly finding one of my saddlebags, I rifled through it for the small leather kit inside, motioning for her to move into the house. Confusion and curiosity lit those honeyed eyes into a dark liquid gold that had my knees weak. "It's a medical kit."

"Why do you have a medical kit?" she asked, walking ahead of me.

"The Beast still bleeds," I replied dryly, blowing out a tense breath as we headed down one of the side corridors into the front house. No one would bother us this far from the staff quarters. *Seb* wouldn't. "Here."

I brought her into the parlor, a place I'd seen her entertain society ladies many times on Audrey's behalf. She was comfortable here, so maybe she would stop looking so nervous being alone with me. She entered silently, and I shut the door. Suddenly, the air thickened, like I couldn't quite take a full breath. Every time I drank in the air, it tasted like she had the other night. Sweet. So *fucking* sweet. Addictive. Like if I wasn't careful, I could die kissing her.

"Have a seat." I forced myself not to clear my throat of the desire clawing its way up from my chest. Motioning casually toward the plush couch shoved against the windows. *Fuck.* If I sat that close to her, she would see the effect she still had on me. She'd see the fragile threads of my self-control threatening to snap in her presence.

I took one of her hands, soft and elegant like the rest of her, between mine and gently turned it over until her palm faced me. I hated that the same hands I held her with now were the hands of a murderer. She should recoil from my touch, but she relaxed into it instead.

"Be sure to keep these clean." I managed to choke the instructions out, pouring alcohol onto small bandage squares. I lost myself in the work, letting my twitching fingers skim over the shallow wounds, debriding the area before cleaning it through. I felt her staring at the side of my face, but for once, it didn't make me hate myself. In fact, it was comfortable letting her see me this way. As a man who could do more than kill.

"I can't stress enough how dangerous that was." My eyes never left her palms. Glancing up was a mistake, because she sucked her full bottom lip between her teeth and my cock stirred to life in my jeans.

"I know."

"I don't think you do," I said, feeling dissatisfaction that I'd killed the guard so quickly. "When I told you about Jesse, about how he's trying to get Bonnie back, I didn't mean for you to go off like that."

"I told you I wanted to help—"

"I know." I turned my attention back to her hand. She hissed as the alcohol stung her wound, and I leaned my lips down to blow gently and soothe the ache. "But you're an outlaw now. And outlaws always stick with their crew."

"I'm not an outlaw." She rolled her eyes.

"Aren't you?" I asked, fixing her with a deep stare that pieced something together inside my chest. Something that'd been broken for too long. "You just escaped a gunfight after conning a guy. That makes you an outlaw."

A soft smile curled on her mouth, her eyes softening at the edges. Like the idea of being an outlaw, part of *my* crew, gave her comfort. How was it that a smile like that could make me feel my heart pound in my throat?

"You don't have to do anything alone," I said as I wrapped a bandage around her hand. *I'll always be here for you*, I almost said. "Ever."

She didn't respond. Instead, she watched as I worked on her other palm, deft fingers moving with a purpose I'd nearly forgotten about. There had been a time in my life when I'd imagined doing *this*. Putting people back together, instead of taking them apart. A time, not so long ago, when I'd imagined atoning for my father's sins. What had happened to that man? How had I gotten here? And more importantly, could I atone for *my* sins?

"About the other night . . ." she started. My hands faltered as my stomach dropped to my boots. The other night I'd taken liberties; in my fractured state, I'd reached for her goodness like the bridge over the Mississippi reached for the moon's luminescence in the dead of night. As if she could redeem me with the heat of her body and the sweet taste of her on my tongue. If she wanted me to apologize, or forget about it, I couldn't. I *wouldn't*.

Even if that made me a fucking monster.

It certainly didn't make me a good boyfriend to Seb, and guilt twisted in my gut until I forced my fingers to start working against her palm once more.

"I could have stopped you, so don't beat yourself up over it."

I let out a low breath, trying and failing to come up with something to say to her that wouldn't tear both of our lives apart. Everything that came to mind would have her beneath me again, my tongue in her mouth and fingers tangled in her dark curls. The way she looked at me, like she was imagining the same thing, didn't help.

I swallowed the admission threatening to choke me, that the other night had been a salve to my bedraggled soul. That when she looked up at me with no fear or disgust coloring the clear warmth of her bright eyes, it made me long to be a better man. A man that she wouldn't have to survive, the way my mother had tried to survive my father. A man she could be *proud* of.

And the certainty that I was too broken to live up to the task.

My fingertips stilled against her skin, the bandages tied, but they didn't break contact from the warmth of her pulse at her wrist, pounding in perfect time to my racing heart. It was like being doused in sunlight, pooling hot between my fingers. How would it feel to touch every inch of her body as my name fell husky from between her full lips?

Just as I thought I might cross the line and tempt fate, damn the consequences, the door creaked open. She jolted, wrenching her hands away and leaving me cold. She stood, her shoulders hiked up toward her ears and her eyes wide, darkening with the fear she'd never shown me before. I turned, seeing Seb standing there, the dark lines of his face tight with anger, like gathering storm clouds.

Fuck me.

"Boss wants to see you," he said, voice devoid of emotion as he addressed Savvy. *Double fuck.* "I'm supposed to bring you, but do you mind giving me a moment with my *boyfriend*?"

The possessive jealousy coloring his words promised another screaming match like the many that'd become our every conversation lately. It was my fault. For failing his expectations, as he'd reminded me at every opportunity, and for how I'd been avoiding him. My heart hadn't been as fully invested in *us* the way I'd promised, and there was no denying it was entirely my fault. Savannah dropped her eyes to the floor and shuffled out of the room. I couldn't look at her, even though I wanted to.

As soon as we were alone, I turned my attention to putting the medical kit back together. If he wanted to do this *here*, instead of the relative privacy of his room, he'd have to initiate it. Because I was so goddamn *tired*. Tired of the constant fighting. Tired of being conflicted. Tired of never being *enough*.

"You went on another job, and you didn't tell me about it—"

"I didn't realize I had to report to you."

"—and now, here you are with Savannah, *again*. After being gone *all fucking day*, and don't think I haven't noticed that you've been *lying*!" His voice rose until he towered over me, screaming. "What was happening with Montana the other night? How many people are you *screwing*, Will? Huh?"

I stood stiffly, crossing to the mantelpiece and setting the medical kit down, fingers twitching toward my cigarette case at his accusations.

"I'm not screwing anyone." I tried to keep my voice calm and put some distance between us. But the truth was that I *had* been lying to him, for years. I hadn't told him about Bonnie, about the deal I'd made, about any of it. How could I? Seb always had a selfish streak, a cruel streak, one that would have had him begging me to leave her. And in my weakest moments, after a fresh kill, I might've listened. "You *know* that when Lee orders me to do a job, I have to—"

"Have to what? Be at his beck and call? You're *pathetic*, Will. You act so broken when you have to kill them, but you don't stop doing it. Either you're going to be Lee's little *bitch* and keep executing people, or you won't. Just make up your mind and be a fucking man about it."

The arguments were on repeat. The words broke me apart the way they always did, hitting too close to the truths that I was too cowardly to face. Swallowing hard, I shoved my hands into my pockets, tilting my hat down to hide my eyes.

"It's not that simple." I tried to keep my voice from sounding so small, but like a predator scenting blood in the air, he detected the slight waver in my voice and crowded me, his face dipping low enough to see my tortured expression.

"At least your father has conviction," he said as my shoulders slumped forward. "You said you were ready for this, for *us*, but you're a goddamn mess—"

"Seb, *please*—"

"Why were you in here alone with her? Where were you all day?" He fisted a hand in the front of my shirt. Irrational anger thrummed to the surface of my skin as memories of beatings at the hands of my father surfaced in my mind. Shoving his fists off of me, I tried again to put space between us. He didn't let me. With every step I took, he cut me off, caged me in.

"I know you've been fucking her!" Spittle hit my cheek from his hysteria, his eyes widening in manic desperation. I couldn't take it anymore. Couldn't deal with the constant battle our relationship had become. It didn't matter that I cared about him, that we'd shared so much. I didn't want to feel like the bad guy anymore, didn't want to *be* the bad guy anymore.

"Did you ever think that maybe what I love about her is the fact that she doesn't treat me like a *monster!*"

The words fell stagnant, echoing in my ears as Seb's face fell into resigned violence. Silent rage was worse than the desperate anger from before. Because I couldn't tell what he would do next. My eyes widened at the admission, something I'd sworn to keep locked tight inside the confines of the jagged corners of my heart.

"Seb—" I tried, begging for resolution, but as I extended my hand toward him, he slapped it away.

"You'll regret this, Will Ellis," he said quietly.

"I can't do this anymore." I wished it wasn't true. Wished he hadn't pushed me when I made it clear I wasn't ready.

But when did any wish of mine come true?

Without another word, I crossed the room, wrenching the door open to find Savannah staring like she could see every broken splinter of my heart. Shame and revulsion twisted my guts until I couldn't stand it. Stalking away, I tried to remember the man I'd been in Fort Hood all those years ago.

The one who, though not whole, had a chance to be.

CHAPTER THIRTY-ONE

SAVANNAH

As Will's footsteps receded, I fought against going after him. Lee wanted to see me. That was what Sebastian had claimed before he'd booted me from the room. I wasn't sure if my hearing their argument was intentional or not as he stomped into the hallway.

If looks could kill, I'd have been dead.

Sebastian didn't speak. Instead, his jaw set in a hard line, his eyes blazing angrily as he moved past me. His boots drowned out all other sounds as I followed down the corridor, twisting my fingers together.

The things he'd said to Will . . . They weren't okay. I didn't know if the man knew the truth about Audrey and Will and their past, but even if he did, it wasn't okay to speak to someone like that. No, I didn't like the things that Will did. But I understood them. I understood doing things because you *had* to.

Maybe Sebastian had never had to do anything he didn't want to.

Or maybe he just wanted to control Will, who everyone knew wasn't a beast to be tamed.

Sebastian moved to the side, motioning to the staircase that led up to the second level and Lee's study. My heart pounded. Lee hadn't called me to his office for a private meeting in weeks. He knew I'd gone down to the river. He had to know. Why else would he be calling now?

If he knew, I was screwed, because I couldn't explain my presence that far away from the house.

Guards bracketed the doors to the study, their imposing figures making my already-thundering heart pound harder. I lifted my head, forcing the appearance of confidence as I walked between them.

Lee sat behind his desk, never lifting his eyes from the thick book spread before him. Blood thrummed in my veins as dread coiled in my gut. Sebastian shut the study door and positioned himself against the back wall. I clasped my hands together, knuckles blanching as I lowered my head as expected.

I should have felt guilty, telling Audrey the truth. Should have been ashamed that I'd burst the precarious bubble around my friend's sanity. But I wasn't. I was tired of seeing her struggle so badly. I figured maybe if she knew at least a sliver of the truth, it could help her with the rest.

It was better than telling her the whole story. About Jesse. Emma's *father*.

Did Lee know?

He left me to stand awkwardly before him. I shifted my weight back and forth, waiting for a long time. Eventually, he set down his pen and closed the thick tome. He rose from his desk and swung out the giant map on the wall behind him, revealing a safe built into the wall. His hands moved quickly over the dial. With a click, he pulled it open and deposited the large book within. I didn't have a chance to spy what else he might be keeping in there.

Once he finished, Lee turned, buttoning his suit jacket. The moment his eyes fell on me, I lowered my gaze, clasping my hands together more tightly. He moved around the desk to his decanter, taking his time pouring a glass. Only after he sampled his drink did he perch on the front edge of his desk.

"Report."

Prior to Rutherford's arrival at the manor, I had weekly meetings with Mr. Lee to keep him updated on Audrey. At first, the reports regarded her health. Over time, as Audrey healed and got better, he requested details about her day-to-day interactions. Who she spent time with. What she liked to do. Eventually, that turned into who shared her bed.

I'd seen what he did to people who lost their value. Even though spilling Audrey's secrets filled me with self-loathing, the threat of punishment for disobeying outweighed my guilt. I'd always told him everything.

In the weeks since Rutherford's arrival, Lee hadn't called me, and I'd been relieved. There were far too many things going on in Audrey's life that I *couldn't* tell him. I wouldn't. Because it would hurt the people I cared about.

"I did as requested and made an appointment for the seamstress to come later this week."

Lee studied me, eyes settling on my bandages. I curved my spine slightly, to appear smaller, unclasping my hands and clasping them again behind my back.

"And what of the careful instruction regarding the Rutherford party?" He brought the glass to his lips and sipped, the appearance of a proper gentleman.

"I have encouraged Audrey to entertain Mr. Rutherford, as you wished," I said. "At times, she's agreeable to the possibility."

"And when she's not?"

I gulped around the lump in my throat. "I continue to press the importance of a match. I *did* convince her to go riding today." Lee scrutinized me silently, draining his glass and moving back to the decanter to refill it.

"And where, I wonder, did my daughter get those clothes?" My blood ran cold. The weight of Lee's icy, dead eyes on me sent chills through my veins.

"I—"

"Think very carefully before you reply, Savannah," he said, returning to his perch on the desk.

How could I explain to this man the look in his daughter's eyes when she put them on? That she'd never seemed so open . . . so happy?

"Miss Audrey hasn't been well lately, sir," I began, measuring every single word. "She wanted to feel like herself. I thought if she had something from before—"

"Your second mistake is that you *thought*," he said. My mouth snapped shut. "Your first was that you didn't burn those items as ordered."

I couldn't. I wouldn't. If it had been me instead of Audrey, I would have wanted someone to do the same.

"As pleased as I am that she is entertaining Lucas's affections, rumors have surfaced of a party held while I was away," Lee said. *Shit.* I was dead. I was *so* dead. "Report."

For three years, I'd witnessed Audrey's suffering. I'd done what I could to help, when I could. But I remembered the way she'd looked at Jesse, remembered how the two of them seemed inextricably linked, even before Will told me the truth. Knowing how much Jesse loved my best friend, how hard this was on Will . . .

"There's nothing to report, sir," I said, remembering the tender look in Jesse's eyes as he and Audrey bantered when I'd found him in her room.

I'd always longed for someone to look at me that way.

"Are you certain?"

"Yes, sir," I said, tipping my chin forward ever so slightly.

I'd made my choice. I wouldn't stray from it.

The tension broke as Lee pushed off the front of his desk. If he believed me, he gave no indication as he settled back in his chair. Without looking up, Lee said, "Sebastian, I'll leave Savannah to you to dole out her punishment as you see fit."

It only took until Sebastian gripped my upper arm and dragged me from the room that I realized what Lee meant. He was giving Sebastian free reign to punish me. From the cold expression in Lee's eyes, he knew *exactly* what he was doing.

"M-Mr. Lee—" The man faced me, black eyes angry. "*Please.*"

"Should I call for the *Beast?*"

The blood drained from my cheeks. Would it be worse if Will was forced to hurt me?

Sebastian took my hesitation as acquiescence and dragged me from the room. A second guard fell in line with us, clutching a long-handled key.

Sebastian's fingers bit into my skin as we rounded the corner to the front corridor. A figure leaned casually back against the nearest wall, using a Bowie knife to clean beneath his fingernails. He glanced up at us, brows lifting above his sunglasses. He shoved from the wall, attention immediately on Sebastian.

My stomach flipped as the man lowered his sunglasses on his nose. Cruel, dull brown eyes roved over my face. Sixgun Ellis smiled and snatched the toothpick from between his teeth.

"Well, look at you. You have such *pretty* skin." A shiver ran down my spine. He lifted the knife, but Sebastian shoved me roughly away. The man turned to him. "Boss has a message for you."

"Go on ahead," Sebastian said to the other guard, and he fixed me with a hard glare. "Wait here." He and Sixgun walked down the corridor, just far enough to be out of earshot. While I couldn't hear them, it was clearly something important. Sebastian's eyes widened, and he looked at the older man with lifted brows. Even as his lips pursed, a glimmer flashed in his eyes. With a nod, he headed in my direction.

My brows furrowed as Sebastian's features shifted and he resumed his usual stoic facade. I turned as he reached toward me, stalking toward my room.

"Does Will know you're friends with his father?" I asked, brows furrowed.

"Shut the fuck up," he replied, venom in his words. The second guard exited my bedroom and passed the key to Sebastian as he left.

I shouldn't have prodded him, but I just couldn't help myself. "I'd be curious to know what he thinks about that. Maybe we should ask him?" As I neared the open door to my room, I made to turn toward him, but before I could, his boot slammed into the base of my spine. I stumbled forward, crashing into the door before landing in a heap on the hard floor of my bedroom.

"I *said*, shut the *fuck* up," Sebastian said through gritted teeth as he slammed my bedroom door shut.

Taking quick stock of my body, I realized the only thing hurting was my elbow. I scrambled, hauling myself up. He advanced on me, and I backed away.

"You shouldn't have that door closed if you're in here," I said, the words coming out in a rush. "If anyone catches you in here—"

Sebastian gripped my face in one hand, shoving me back against the nearest wall. He bared his teeth at me. "They'll what? Think I fucked you?" He barked out a cruel laugh, disgust curling his lip. Storms and shadows danced across his features.

"No one would believe you, anyway," he said. "Not just because you're *Un*fuck*able*, but because you aren't exactly *my type*." He slammed my head against the wall but released his grip on my face. I bit back a groan as pain blossomed at the base of my skull. "But you are *his* type."

I leaned heavily against the wall, steadying my head with a hand. "What?"

"*Will*," he said, advancing again. I flinched, and that seemed to still him. "He thinks I don't notice. The way his eyes find you the second you walk into the room. How he's memorized your schedule to find ways to bump into you." The blood drained from my face. Hadn't Will himself admitted to following me? At the time, I'd only thought he did it for my safety. But what if it was more than that?

"Or the fucking romance novels." Sebastian rolled his eyes and spat at my feet. "He has them delivered as if Lee bought them. You're a spoiled little bitch, just like Audrey." He regarded me coldly for a long moment. "Maybe I *should* give you to Sixgun. At least then you'd be out of my way."

"No," I whispered.

"No, you're right." Sebastian stepped backward. "If Will found out, he'd never forgive me, and I can't have that."

"You'll be lucky if he forgives you for how you treat him," I said. "Honestly, how can you speak to someone like that and claim that you *care* about them?"

Sebastian barked out a bitter laugh. "You couldn't possibly understand what's between me and Will. Tomorrow, we'll be back together. You'll see." His gaze darted about my bedroom. He shrugged and headed toward the door. He stopped with his hand on the knob.

"How long have you been fucking him?" The words seemed to pain him. As if accepting that something happening between me and Will was such a horrible thing.

"I've never had sex with Will," I snapped. Some of the tension released from his jaw. "But I almost did, the other night in the kitchen. He was moments away from stripping me naked on top of the island."

Even as fury filled his eyes, there was a sort of sick satisfaction inside of me. Being able to hurt him after he'd so grievously tortured me made me far happier than I had any right to be.

Sebastian snapped. In seconds, he lurched toward me as he retrieved something from his belt. He bared his teeth as he flicked his wrist, the cylinder in his hand extending to nearly two feet long.

"You're lying," he ground out between his teeth.

Fear filled me, but I couldn't let him win. Not this time. He'd won too many times before.

"I'm not." I tilted my head toward him. "And if I could go back, I wouldn't stop him. I see Will for who he is, and I want *him*. I'm not trying to change him into something he isn't."

I honestly didn't think I could see whatever it was that Will liked enough about him to agree to a commitment. Sebastian was cold and cruel. That wasn't love. Love wasn't pain and heartbreak and anger.

The blow came before I saw it. The club crashed against the side of my head. I careened sideways into my wardrobe. Before I could recover, Sebastian kicked the back of my knee, and I crashed to the floor again. I cried out as pain exploded in my leg. I curled in on myself, clasping my leg to my chest.

"How *dare* you." Sebastian stood over me. The club clattered to the floor as he delivered a swift kick to my gut. I gasped for air, even as he forced me onto my back and drove his knee into my belly.

Cool steel pressed to my forehead. My eyes widened as I stared up at him. Sebastian's hand shook, his finger hovering just over the trigger.

"I could do it, you know," he said, the low whisper of his voice deadly. He clicked the safety off, licking his lips like a madman. "Then I'd never have to hear the name *Savvy* again."

Cold sweat slid across my skin, and my throat went dry. I didn't doubt he *could*. Knowing Sebastian, it would be all too easy for him to pull the trigger. I didn't dare speak. I barely breathed as I stared up at him through tear-filled eyes. I wasn't ready to die. There were so many things I'd never done, never seen.

"I want to make something very, *very* clear to you," Sebastian whispered, leaning down. "Will Ellis is *mine*. If I so much as catch you looking at him, I won't hesitate next time." He flicked the safety back on. My chest heaved, and a sob wrenched its way from between my lips. His weight lifted from my chest, and I gasped sharply.

Sebastian cocked his arm back and brought the butt of his gun down hard across my jaw. Stars erupted in my vision, blurring everything around me. A copper tang filled my mouth.

"Enjoy your books, Savannah. It's as close to Will as you'll ever get again," Sebastian said.

The door snapped shut, and, a moment later, the lock clicked.

I curled in on myself again, tucking my knees to my chest and slamming my eyes shut.

Powerless and alone, like I always would be.

CHAPTER THIRTY-TWO

JESSE

M Y OPPONENT'S FIST SLAMMED into my jaw. I reeled backward, bouncing against the ropes of the ring. Sunlight streamed from the concrete crater above. The fighting pits were closed to the public until tonight, but that didn't stop curious onlookers from peering down curiously.

I spat blood on the floor of the pit and advanced on the man, lifting my hands. Will had wrapped my right hand in white tape, as tight as he could. It throbbed with each passing heartbeat. I'd hoped the tape would help, but, honestly, my hand was broken. I ducked, narrowly avoiding another blow, and backed away from the man.

"What's up with you?" he asked. My opponent was the main trainer for the New Orleans fighting pits. I'd been working with him for weeks between fights. He'd offered himself as a sparring partner when I showed up this morning.

Tonight was my big match with Jersey, and I had no clue how to fight with my right hand. It didn't help that yesterday, I'd watched Audrey ride off with that piece of shit Rutherford. In those *fucking* shorts. Back in the desert, she wore them to drive me crazy. Even if she didn't remember, that glimmer of Bonnie made my heart ache.

"Nothing," I said between short breaths. I advanced, faking a throw with my left hand, only to hook him in the nose with my right. Instead of the satisfactory crunch of a broken nose, shooting pain ran through my hand. I wheeled away from him, my curse echoing in the cavernous pit.

"C'mon, Montana. What's wrong with you?"

"You need to fake with the right," Will said, seated on a metal folding chair just beyond the ropes. He'd come to help me figure out how to compensate for my broken hand. But, also, I'd invited him with me to get him out of that damn house.

He'd spent the last three nights in my room. Not Sebastian's. Something must have happened, though when I asked, Will changed the subject.

Mixed with Will's surly mood, feeling the loss of Emma, and seeing Audrey with Lucas Rutherford in those *fucking* shorts, I'd wanted nothing more than to lose myself in the bottle. Instead, I lost myself in training. Sketching didn't help. The lines were too rough, the pain pulsing with each stroke.

I turned back to my sparring partner.

"Never thought I'd see the day someone had to pull punches for Montana."

"Fuck you."

The fingertips of my right hand had turned purple. I ducked between the ropes. Will met me, his physician's hands immediately unwrapping the dressings. I watched the deep concentration in his eyes. He dropped the tape to the ground and took my hand in both of his. He put pressure on the back with his thumb. I hissed and jerked in an attempt to pull back, but he held fast.

"It's probably fractured," he said around the cigarette dangling from his mouth. "Again." I frowned at the lackluster color of his eyes. He'd been struggling. With the jobs. With his relationship. With everything. Why wouldn't he talk to me?

"Stop that." He pulled the cigarette from his mouth and flicked it into the darkness of the pit.

"What?"

"Staring at me like a creep." He grabbed a thick, taupe bandage and wound it around my hand.

"I know you're used to keeping it to yourself, but you can talk to me."

His eyes flashed to mine and then back to his work.

"I'm worried about you."

"Don't be," he said gruffly as he took a step back and lit another cigarette. "Flex your hand."

Smoke curled in the air between us. I attempted to flex, cringing at the pain shooting up my arm.

"You know that's what family does, right?" I asked. He stared at me blankly as he inhaled his cigarette.

"Not mine." He turned his back, strolling toward the exit. "You better figure out how to fight with that hand. Or Jersey's gonna murder you." A moment later, he was gone.

"I can't believe you're friends with that guy," my sparring partner said as he moved beside me.

"Why not?" I asked, face screwing up as I flexed my hand.

"Well, he's . . . you know." He lifted his eyebrows.

My spine straightened at his tone. "He's what?"

A mixture of fear and intrigue passed across his face as he looked to the spot where Will'd disappeared. "They call him the *Beast of the Bridge.*"

I tilted my chin forward. I was sick of the looks from the staff at the house, how people in the street gave him a wide berth, thinking about the bodies that swung from the bridge. They all thought him a monster. Will was nothing of the sort.

"I know exactly who he is."

"I knew you had connections, but that guy . . . he's a goddamn psycho."

I wheeled toward him, throwing my right fist at the man's face without another thought. My knuckles connected with teeth. I recoiled, hissing and clutching my fist to my chest. "*Fuck!*"

The man stared at me with a bloody mouth, eyes wide. I gathered my bag and secured Selene at my side before glaring at the man.

"Watch your fucking mouth." I pointed at him with my good hand. "That's my brother you're talking about."

Pain jolted up my arm, worse than before. I clambered into the bright afternoon sunlight of New Orleans. I needed a drink and a doctor. After retrieving No Name from the nearby stables, I headed back in the direction of the square. I was glad, at least, that I could give my horse an opportunity to stretch his legs, even if it was a short ride.

Once No Name was secured, I passed by my room; it was empty. The stale air told me that Will hadn't come back here. I made my way to the kitchen, seeking Etty. She'd know if he was in the house.

"Etty."

The woman gave me a warm smile and wiped her hands on her apron.

"Have you seen Will?"

"Sorry, I haven't," she said. "You look like you need something stiff." She grabbed an unmarked bottle from the back of a cabinet and a glass. She poured a light green liquid into it. I took the glass and sniffed it. The liquor overtook my sense of smell. I cleared my throat as the fumes burned. "Just a little Nouvelle-Orleans Absinthe Superieure." She chuckled, a deep booming sound. "Just knock it back, baby; you'll be fine."

I did. The liquor was spicy and sweet as it blazed down my throat. I set the glass down, fighting back tears.

"Damn." I blew out a breath.

"That's my secret stash." She winked, and her gaze caught on my wrapped hand. "What happened to you?"

"Punched a wall." I shrugged. "That's why I was looking for Will. I have a fight, and I'm gonna lose if I can't use it."

"If Savannah wasn't under the weather, I'd suggest letting her look at it. She probably can't fix it, but I bet she'd know a way to numb it." The woman shrugged.

"Under the weather?" I hadn't seen her after accusing her of killing Emma. Guilt wracked my chest.

"Haven't seen her in a few days." Etty returned to chopping vegetables, dismissing me.

If Will wasn't back, I'd have to find Savannah. Pain jolted through me as I crossed the courtyard and made for the front staircase. Secretly, I hoped I'd catch sight of Audrey. I climbed the stairs and turned left. My eyes roved across the door to Audrey's room. Someone had already fixed the broken frame from when I'd kicked it in.

I moved directly for the door at the end. As I lifted my fist to knock, a familiar tune sounded from down the hallway. I paused, pivoting toward it. There was something oddly familiar about the gentle humming. My feet carried me toward the library. With each step, the humming grew louder.

An image of Bonnie, seated beside me in my old truck, smirking and singing along to a song I didn't know, passed through my mind.

The humming came from beyond the half-open door to the library. My feet slowed, but my heart raced. I knew that song. I knew that voice. *Bonnie.*

I caught sight of her immediately as I peered around the doorway. Audrey leaned back against a plush pillow, a book in her hand and legs stretched out in front of her. Clearly lost in her reading, her fingers toying with a chain around her neck. But it wasn't just a chain. There was something *on* the chain.

My heart stuttered.

You can't lose me, she'd said in Fort Hood as she desperately placed Selene in my hands. *I'm yours.*

I'd given her my father's ring. Something for her to remember me by until I could find her. Until I could bring her home. She ran the chain over her lips with one hand and flipped the page of her book with the other.

Did she remember? I didn't dare to hope, but I couldn't just walk away this time. I took a step forward but froze in the doorway.

Audrey's legs were slung across Lucas Rutherford's lap. He focused intently on rubbing her bare feet.

Feral rage consumed me. I envisioned it, storming into the library and punching that asshole. Maybe I'd throw him through the window and see how he fared against the concrete street below. My hand balled into a fist as my gaze flickered back to Audrey. She'd frozen, her eyes wide as she saw me. She was really entertaining this man. By the flush that filled her cheeks and the guilt in her blue eyes, there was no other explanation for the scene before me.

I released my fist and stalked back down the corridor. I had enough going on. Starting an unnecessary pissing match with the Manhattanite wouldn't benefit me right now. Not when I was hours away from getting my ass kicked by Jersey.

"Montana, wait!"

I stilled. I should just walk away, leave it, come back to it after the fight. But I couldn't. I turned toward her slowly, schooling my features. I didn't want to fight with her. But, it seemed, Audrey just wanted to stare at me. Her lips parted, but she didn't speak.

"I don't get it," I said.

"Don't get what?"

"Are you just trying to make me jealous?" I thought back to her riding away with Rutherford wearing those *fucking* shorts. "Or do you actually have feelings for that asshole?"

Audrey's cheeks flushed further. It would have been satisfying to see her in such a way before, but I was too upset. As she opened her mouth to respond, I cut her off.

"Because I know *he* doesn't have feelings for you. You're just another conquest. Another deal." I kept my words low, even, hoping that she could understand that this wasn't some jealous bullshit. He couldn't care for her. Not like I did.

"And?" She crossed her arms over her chest.

The single word hit me straight in the heart. "And?" I echoed. "Why would you ever settle for someone that you don't care about? When you have a man in front of you who sets your soul on fire?" Her gaze lowered from mine. She bit her bottom lip as her fingers fiddled with the ring again. "I'm serious, Audrey. He can't make you happy. You know it."

"Maybe," she said, her eyes flickering up to mine. "But how will I ever know for sure if I don't at least try? I've tried to explain, but you haven't let me. I'm tired of letting other people tell me what to do, what's good for me. I want to figure that out on my own. Are you really that threatened by him? Or is it the fact that I want to make my own choices that you can't handle?"

I raked my hands through my hair, blowing out an exasperated breath. I was so close to losing my temper, to screaming at her, to telling her *everything*.

"I would never try to control you!" My eyes slammed shut, and I tugged at my hair, willing my temper to cool. "God, Audrey, if you really knew me, the *real* me, you'd know I would never tell you what to do. Hell, I don't even think that's possible, but—"

"So who's the real you?" Audrey asked, dropping her hands to her sides, almost in resignation.

Who was the real me? Was I the farmer's son, wishing desperately for a way out? Was I an outlaw, running from dangerous men and crater beasts? Was I a fighter with a score to settle?

Or was I just a man, staring at the woman I loved, wishing I could bare my soul to her?

I dared a step forward, fixing her with a hard stare. "I'm the man that's in love with you, Audrey Lee. The guy who would go to the edge of this world just to see you smile. I'd sacrifice anything and everything, if only to make you happy." She tilted her head back slightly, fixing me with a tense stare. My hands twitched at my sides as I fought against the animal inside of me that wanted to grab her and kiss her until she remembered.

"I *love* you. Can you say the same for him?"

The space between us had disappeared. She was within reach now, and it would be so easy to pull her against my chest and kiss her, to remind her of all of the ways she was *mine*. But I couldn't force her. She had to make her choice.

"Are you okay, Audrey?" Lucas's voice echoed in the corridor. I lifted my eyebrows pointedly at her. She turned toward the man, but I didn't spare him a look. She seemed torn as her gaze flickered back to me.

"Miss Audrey," I said, bowing my head slightly.

I wheeled around and stalked away. I had a match to worry about. Even if I wanted nothing more than to throw down with Rutherford right here.

CHAPTER THIRTY-THREE

AUDREY

D AMN HIM STRAIGHT TO hell! Lucas's arm slid around my waist as I tracked Montana's retreating form. How dare he leave me here in pieces. How *dare* he say he loved me and then walk away. Like I don't matter. Like his words didn't matter. When it was all I could hear, echoing on repeat.

"What did he want?" Lucas asked, suspicion heavy in his words. I wasn't in any state to walk the tightrope between these two men right now, but if I wasn't careful, Lucas would see the conflict raging inside of me after Montana's wild declarations.

I'm the man that's in love with you, Audrey. The one who would go to the edge of this world just to see you smile. I'd sacrifice anything and everything, if only to make you happy.

His words burned like a brand on my skin. They lived inside of me now, a permanent part of me, braided into my blood and knotted around my ribs. He couldn't have known how much I'd ached to hear his declaration. Yet, it was as if he'd peeled back all my layers and stared straight into my mangled heart, making sense of the mess. He'd turned my turmoil into poetry.

I'd almost made my decision, goddamnit!

The burgeoning friendship with Lucas could lead to a life of contentment, of that I was sure. There wouldn't be the frenetic ups and downs, the fighting and making up, the agony of never knowing where I stood. But Montana was right: there would never be any of the passion either.

"Oh, I was just wishing him well in the fight tonight," I said, blinking up at Lucas as if a thought had just occurred to me. "God, you organized the showcase! How could I forget that?"

He smiled at my acknowledgement, suspicion fading from his dark gaze. He tugged me closer, brushing a wayward strand of hair over my shoulder and looking like he wanted to—

"I've been keeping you so busy today," I said, running my hands over his arms and leaning against his chest. It distracted him from the intention that had been in his eyes a moment before, at least. "You must have so much to do."

He shrugged, vanity stroked enough that he couldn't refute the claim outright without giving up a piece of his all-too-valued pride. "You sure you can't come?" he asked, tightening his grip around me. I laughed, letting my fingers trail over his shoulders and play with the back of his hair.

"After our great escape attempt? My father would rather skin me alive than let me out of the house again so soon."

Lucas's face lit up at the reminder of our afternoon together, his smile earning me a glimpse of that good-natured dimple I'd come to appreciate at the corner of his mouth. It should be so *easy* to let go of Montana and embrace Lucas. Lucas was intelligent, playful, kind when he wasn't being misguided or influenced by his friends. He was interested in me despite my horrible reputation and looked at me like he was the luckiest guy in the world just to share the same space with me.

So why didn't I *feel* anything?

"I should probably go find my friends and make sure they haven't cracked open any of your father's good liquor before the fight. I don't relish the thought of having them slobbering drunk around the mayor and his family," he said with a sardonic twist of his mouth.

"Another reason to be glad to miss this fight," I said sarcastically. He lifted an eyebrow as he stared down at me expectantly, and I realized he didn't know about my struggles with the society women. Not really. "The mayor's daughter isn't my biggest fan." I left it there, and he opened his mouth in an *ah* gesture as he released his grip.

"I doubt she'll be attending tonight anyway. These showcases can get a bit . . . *rowdy*."

He didn't elaborate, and I didn't want to keep the conversation going while my mind still buzzed with Montana's words. So I let him give me a chaste kiss before he twisted away, and I watched as the *second* man disappeared down that set of stairs.

Finally alone with my thoughts, I sank against the wall, letting it hold me since my legs didn't seem up to the task. With every day that passed without being able to speak with Montana after our argument the other morning and his misinterpretation in the stables, I'd been sure that things were over. How was I supposed to move on if Montana wouldn't let me?

Each ragged beat of my heart thumped hollowly in my chest. It was so *easy* to imagine what it would be like if I gave in to Montana. We'd fight with teeth and nails and biting words, and he'd ravish me like a man possessed and make the world shift beneath my feet. My days would be filled with poetry and witty banter; he'd challenge me and push my boundaries. Even if it infuriated me, I would become braver for it.

And each night, I could find peace in the strength of his arms. Peace I'd never known before.

Savannah had locked herself in her room. As soon as I came back from my afternoon with Lucas, I'd tried to find her to ask how her adventure outside the house had gone, only to find the door locked. Each time I called her, I was met with silence. I'd tried to give her space, considering her humiliated confession about nearly sleeping with a known murderer. Not that I judged her. I didn't care who she invited to her bed as long as they treated her with respect.

Though, after she'd cut the conversation off so abruptly, I thought giving her space would allow her time to sort out her feelings. Hell, I knew what it was like to be twisted into knots over a man.

Only now I *needed* her. Not to clean up my mess or to take for granted, the way I did too often, but because I needed to talk to my best friend. I needed her to let me cry and to tell me what a mess I'd made. I needed her to make me laugh when it was the absolute last thing I felt like doing. I needed her to hold the jagged pieces of my heart together until they were strong enough to mend themselves. The way she always did. So I made my way down the hall to her door, jiggling it to find it still locked.

"Savannah!" I called, knocking softly. "Savannah, *please* open the door."

Silence greeted me.

Was she angry? It seemed like everyone was angry with me lately, like I couldn't do *anything* right. Furious tears rose in my eyes as I shuffled dejectedly back to my bedroom. Alone. Feeling like the world was falling apart around me. I stood there for too long, the echo of Montana declaring his love for me burning the air from my lungs, until my feet were halfway to the door between mine and Savannah's rooms.

I should be less selfish, more considerate of her need for space. I knew that, but my chest felt like it was caving in, and Savannah wasn't just my best friend.

She was my tether back to the world. My anchor to reality. Lips trembling, I tried our shared door only to find it locked fast. I smacked my palm against the wood, making the door rattle in the frame.

"Damnit, Savannah! I know I'm the worst friend in the world; all I do is ask for more when you give so much. I'm selfish and messy and get us both into so much trouble. But I—"

I was talking to a wall. No, I was sobbing into the wood grain of a door like it would have all the answers of the universe written on it. This was the stuff *Insane Audrey* was infamous for. I knelt, resting my forehead against the hard surface.

"I don't have anyone else." The words caught on my tears, ripped from somewhere small and vulnerable inside me. "Not anyone that I trust. Not anyone that really knows me. Not like *you*."

A muffled thump sounded from the other side of the door, followed by a low groan. It sounded strange, *wrong*. Too slow. Savannah was nothing if not punctual and practical. She didn't do *anything* slowly, flitting from task to task like it was her personal mission to organize and straighten and delegate every detail of this house within an inch of its life.

"Savannah?" I called, to again be met with silence. I peered through the keyhole, finding I couldn't see much through it at all, even when I craned my neck to the side. Just shafts of late afternoon sunlight streaking across her ugly floral rug and—

My heart plummeted to my feet. "Savannah!" I called again, as loudly as I could, banging my fist rapidly on the door.

With fear suffocating me, I slammed my hand against the door again, straining to catch sight of her through the small keyhole. "Savannah! Answer me!"

There. A hand and lump of tangled sheets slumped on the rug near her bed. Her elbow was bent at a strange angle, and she wasn't moving. She *wasn't moving*! With frantic yanks, I tried to pry the door open to no avail. The lock held fast.

Was she sick? What if she was so sick that she couldn't breathe? What if she was *dying*?

I couldn't face the rest of my life without her. I couldn't face a few days without her, and the thought of her absence stretching into eternity forced me onto clumsy bare feet, nearly slipping as I barreled into the hallway, searching the corridor for the guards that were nearly always present.

Empty.

The *one* fucking time I needed my father's obsession with my safety to work for me and there was *no one*. Slamming my eyes shut, I sucked in a sharp inhalation as the realization rocked through me. I'd been with *Lucas* earlier. Of course my father would call off the staff; he wanted to give us enough privacy that I could secure a proposal. *Motherfucker!*

My hands trembled, my pulse hammering so hard that it was like a musical note vibrating in the air as it hung suspended in the midst of a song. *Think, Audrey, think!*

I scanned the room, searching for anything to ram the door down. Books. Curtains. The chaise? No, I couldn't lift that on my own. *Stupid. So fucking stupid.* Bottles of perfume on my vanity. Oil lanterns with hand-painted flowers. *Stupid, vain, useless shit!*

My eyes caught on the hairpins sticking out of my closet door. The ones I used for target practice, instead of the tight updos my father intended them for. I wasn't strong enough to burst through the door. But I was smart enough to pick the lock.

In seconds, I crossed the room and ripped a couple of them from the closet door, my feet slapping against the bathroom tiles as I dropped to my knees and shoved them into the lock. *Breathe, Audrey, slow down. Think.*

I'd never picked a lock before, but it couldn't be that hard, could it?

"Hang on, Savannah! I'm coming!" The edges of my words were high and a little panicked. *Just like she taught you. In . . . two . . . three . . . four . . . out . . . two . . . three . . . four . . .*

Twisting the pins, my fingers never wavered, and after a second, I put my ear to the lock, listening to the tinny clicks barely audible through the mechanism, as if on instinct. With a deft twist, a loud click sounded, thumping in my ear canal, and with baited breath, I reached for the knob.

It swung free. Open.

How the fuck had I done that?

My shock took a backseat as concern flooded through me. I swung the door open and rushed to Savannah, crumpled on the floor. I untangled her from the mess of her sheets, the pain in my heart easing as I saw her chest rising and falling, her eyes opening weakly to stare up at me in bafflement.

Alive.

Tears welled in my eyes, and I sniffed hard to keep them in check.

"How did you—"

I shushed her, helping to get her fully untangled before the state she was in took hold of me. Blood caked the side of her mouth, her face a map of mottled bruises. Like dark flowers blooming against her warm brown skin. Purple, red, green, yellow, a kaleidoscope of violence that extended down to her exposed arms.

Everything inside of me stilled. Because if it didn't, I would have exploded into a thousand tiny pieces, chaos in every direction. I couldn't form coherent thoughts, couldn't speak, couldn't even breathe. All at once I wanted to know everything, and I wanted *revenge*. Dark purple fingerprints spread along her arm. This wasn't some unfortunate fall or accident.

It was intentional.

"I didn't—" she tried to say, though her voice was weak. A dry croak, and in that moment, my eyes flitted over her room. There was no water beside her bed, no empty food trays. Disgust roiled inside of me. How long had it been? Three days?

"Wait here." I pulled a pillow from her mattress to rest beneath her head. Even the slight adjustment forced a groan of pain from her battered body. "I'll be right back."

In moments, I returned with my own carafe of water and a glass. It took a long time to find where I could touch that wouldn't cause her more pain as I lifted her onto my lap, tucking limp curls behind her ears and swinging wildly between murderous rage and breaking into heart-aching sobs.

"Slowly," I whispered, tilting the glass to her lips. Her eyes became more alert, her lips not nearly as chapped. Without words, her gaze slid to her bed, and I nodded, bracing myself for the next part. With her help, we settled her back on the bed, her body relaxing once I'd gotten her half upright and the pillows cushioning the worst of her wounds. At least the ones that I could see.

Your father isn't going to be happy that I gave this to you—

I didn't want to think my father was capable of this. The truth was, I'd turned a blind eye to a lot of my father's shortcomings. Because if I didn't acknowledge the oddities in his shipments, or what *everyone* knew Will Ellis did for him, then maybe I could still let him love me. Maybe it wouldn't matter.

Only . . . it *did* matter.

He'd lied to me for years, and *that* I could forgive eventually. I didn't care if he hurt me, if he was thoughtlessly cruel, if he didn't acknowledge my accomplishments or defend me from ruthless gossip. But *this* . . .

I could never forgive him for this.

"I'm sorry I didn't answer you," she said quietly, eyes averted and chin wobbling. I put my hand over hers gently, and she squeezed it tight. "I didn't want you to see me like this."

Leaning my face down, I kissed the back of her hand and blinked back hard tears. Shame was thick in her voice, as if she'd done something wrong instead of someone having wronged *her*. I couldn't let that stand.

"This is *my* fault. I shouldn't have worn those shorts, I shouldn't have pissed off my father or—"

"No," she said, wearily. "I refused to report on you. To tell him about Montana."

Montana.

Hearing his name made all the fragile strength I'd gathered crumble once more. Until I was blinking back tears furiously.

"We have to get out. I have to get *you* out. Montana doesn't matter anymore. It doesn't matter that he loves me; I'm going to find Lucas tonight and—"

"Wait." She squeezed my hand hard again. "What do you mean?"

I couldn't take her wide-eyed expression, couldn't remember the stark honesty in Montana's blue gaze as he'd stared me down earlier in the hallway. Standing swiftly, I tugged my fingers sharply through my hair.

"H-he told me he loved me," I admitted, pressing my lips into a tight line. "And I thought—I don't know what I thought. But it doesn't matter, because we're out of time. I can't . . . Savannah." I stopped, staring down at her, bruised and broken. "I would do *anything* for you. You know that, right? You know that you aren't just my best friend . . . you're my family. The only family I think I've ever known. I have to get you *out of here*, and it doesn't matter that—"

"How do you feel about *him*?" she asked, her voice stronger than I'd heard it in a long time. I opened my mouth to tell her that I didn't feel the same. That it would be fine. More than fine. I could just move on. But the words stuck in the back of my throat and threatened to choke me. The tears I'd fought all night tumbled down my cheeks.

"I don't know," I whispered. The words rang false between us, and I dragged my fingers over my cheeks.

"Yes, you do." Her dark eyes were always so wise. But she could always see me more clearly than anyone else.

"It doesn't matter—"

"It's the *only* thing that matters," she retorted sharply. "Do you love him?"

I wanted to deny it. More than anything. I *hated* him, and that thought pulsed clear at the forefront of my mind. I hated him for forcing me to face my failings. Hated him for making me feel alive again, because feeling alive meant feeling pain. Hated him for giving me hope when at every turn there were people ready to stamp it out. Mostly I hated him for making me love him so desperately that the thought of losing him felt like dying. Slowly. One inch at a time.

"Yes," I confessed, the word hot on my tongue. Horrible. Because Savannah needed *me*, and admitting that I loved a man I couldn't have might just be the thing that killed me. "But Lucas can get us both out of here and—"

"There's a steamboat." She cleared her throat. "It's leaving tonight. Will and I bribed the captain to book us passage and smuggle us all out of the city."

My mind went blank. Shock and confusion warring for control.

"What?"

"When I left the house, Will and I went to the river and found a boat," she said, offering me a soft smile. "We can leave. All of us. Tonight."

"No," I said, shaking my head. "No, Savannah, he's at the showcase fight tonight across the city and—"

"Then what are you still doing here?" Her smile widened across her face. "Go *get* him."

"But—"

"Audrey Lee, if you love that man, let's go *get* him." She tried to toss her covers off and rise from her bed. Her body protested sharply, and she groaned, her face screwing up in pain.

"You can't go anywhere like that, and I'm not leaving you," I argued, arms crossing defiantly over my chest.

"Then go find Will," she said. "Get him to bring you to the fight and send him back for me."

Was this happening? Was *Savannah* telling me to do something reckless? How the fuck did I end up as the voice of reason?

"I've spent every single day with you since you came to this house. Until he came here, I don't know that I'd ever seen you smile. *Really* smile. You can't keep punishing yourself for things outside of your control. You deserve to be happy. We all do."

I swallowed hard as a thick silence descended between us. Life was a series of decisions. It boiled down to the memories you made and the chances you took. I'd already lost so much of mine, even more swallowed by grief. If

Savannah was willing to take this risk, then didn't I owe it to myself to be brave enough to try?

"I'll send Will. I won't leave without you," I said, breathless as a wild sort of adrenaline took hold of my limbs and woke my body up.

"You need to change out of that dress. You'll be a dead giveaway in that," she said as I turned my back and started toward my room with a devilish smile twisting on my lips.

I had *just* the thing.

Minutes later, in the shorts that felt like home and a tight top with a hood, I snuck down the back stairs of the house. It was quiet, but that was probably because almost everyone was at the fight. No need for extra staff tonight, thank God. I kept to the shadows, careful to make sure my footfalls were silent. If Will Ellis wasn't in the stables, then I had no idea where to look for him.

The animal and hay scent clung heavily to the air, soft nickering blanketing my approach. Will's massive horse was always housed in a stall near the end of the row, the largest since he needed the head room. When I was almost there, a stallion the color of burnished copper chuffed loudly near my ear, yanking the hood from my head. I put my palm on his nose, but he butted my hand with his snout.

Giving him an appreciative scratch, I looked over at him, vague recognition lighting in the back of my mind. "Not now, pretty boy," I said soothingly.

"Who's there?" *Thank God.* Will's voice grunted from the stall on the end, his tall frame appearing as he stood.

"I need your help," I said, swallowing hard as I stepped closer. When he recognized me, his eyebrows rose so high that they disappeared beneath the brim of his hat.

"What the hell are you doing out so late? Your father'll—"

"I need you to take me to Montana," I said, words falling out in a rush. "Now."

He sighed, leaning against the stall door and lazily perusing my appearance. Quiet resignation etched the lines of his face. His answer written in his eyes. Savannah had been sure that he would help me, help *us.*

"He's on the other side of the city at the fight tonight. Whatever *this* is, it can wait until morning. I don't need your father—"

"I have to see him tonight, Will; we have to get to the steamboat."

My words fell like stones in the air between us. It took a moment for his mind to catch up to my implications. Something wild lit the darkness of his eyes. Something that made my stomach flip and reminded me what it felt like to *hope*.

"Savannah?" he asked, and all I had to do was nod.

"Can you get me there?"

He took a moment, fingers running under the stubble on his chin as he considered. "Yeah, I think I can." A reckless grin twisted at the corner of his mouth. "For the record, this is a *really bad idea.*"

I chuckled. "I know."

"Lucky for you, those are my favorite kind."

Excitement thrummed inside of me, heating my blood and lighting up every nerve ending. Strangely, I felt more myself in these frantic moments than I ever had. Both of us tacking our horses as quickly as we could, speaking in soft whispers about steps in the plan as it began to unfold between us. Routes we should or shouldn't take. This felt too *easy*. As if Will and I had been planning wild escapes our whole lives, instead of just the last few minutes. In fact, it was kind of *nice*.

As we led our horses out, he motioned for me to pull my hood up again. As we crossed the threshold into the alleyway, a guard in a pristine uniform stopped us, and I ducked my head close to my saddle, attempting to stay as small and unrecognizable as possible.

"Will," the guard said, his voice thick with emotion. *Oh.* Well, at least I hadn't been noticed yet.

"Seb, this isn't the time for—"

"I'm *sorry*, can we just talk for a few minutes?" He reached out to clench the front of Will's shirt. It was then that he noticed the second horse, and me hiding beside it. "What are you—"

"I need a favor," Will said, cutting him off. "We can talk as soon as I get back, but can you cover for us?"

The guard peered over Will's shoulder, catching sight of me. His eyes widened, and his jaw clenched tight.

"Will," he warned, voice low and dangerous.

"We're just going to the fight; we'll only be a couple of hours. I *promise.*"

I wasn't breathing. Each second of silent deliberation stretched into eternity, and my lungs felt like they were going to burst.

"Hurry," he said finally, and I exhaled in relief. Though his eyes, almost pitch-black in the darkness of the alleyway as the last of the fading evening light seeped from the horizon, caught and held on me. It was a calculating glare, one that set my nerves on edge and raised the hair on the back of my neck.

Without hesitation, Will ushered me forward, and I trusted him. Trusted his judgment in this guard, whoever he was. Swinging into the saddle, Will led us at a brutal pace. We galloped through the darkened city, careening through back alleys and streets, and even though I could barely see, Will's relaxed shoulders gave me a point to fix on. Will spurred his horse faster as we came to a straight-away and I leaned low over my stallion's back as we raced across the streets, bathed in moonlight, hurtling faster and faster as the earth crashed beneath their powerful hooves. Wild abandon tore from my throat, and I bit back a shout of glee that threatened to rip from me. Finally, the lights from the fighting pits appeared, reaching into the darkness from below, and we slowed. My heart echoed the rapid gallop from before as we tied the horses down and slipped off of them.

"Keep close to me. It'll be crowded down there." He led me to the narrow staircase that descended deep into the earth. Like a stairway straight to hell. I pressed in close as we descended. With each step, the roars of the crowd deafened me in a cacophony of riotous sound, until we were crammed flush in a sea of bodies, the smell of sweat and stale alcohol thick in the air. I was so much shorter than everyone here that elbows knocked into me, and a few times I was almost battered off my feet. Will twisted through the crowd, men parting as they recognized him.

Another roar lit the night as we inched closer to the ring obscured by shouting men with betting tickets clenched tight in their fists. Someone's beer sloshed from their cup, soaking the shoulder of my shirt.

"Kill him!"

"Make him bleed!"

"Hit him again! Hit the bastard again!"

Shouting of all kinds erupted around me, growing more violent the longer we stood there, trying to trace a path toward the ring in the thick crush of bodies.

"*Fuck.*" Will looked out above the crowd. The stricken expression on his face made my stomach lurch. Something was *wrong*. I elbowed past the bodies, fighting toward the front, shoving until I broke through the line of people to see the well-lit ring. Two men grappled together, sweat-slickened muscles bunching and jolting with every violent blow.

There he was, *Montana*, as the other man's fist slammed into his face. Again and again and again. He fell. He clutched his right hand to his chest as his opponent brought his knee down against his ribs.

Incredulous blue eyes found mine somehow in the crowd. For a moment, the roar of the spectators faded into silence and it was just the two of us.

He was losing. Badly. And if he didn't get up soon . . . he might not get up at all.

Chapter Thirty-Four

JESSE

THE FLOOR OF THE ring flew up to smack against my body. Or maybe I smacked against it. I couldn't be sure. All I knew was that I was on the ground, right hand clutched to my chest.

Jersey was an ugly son of a bitch. His dark, cropped hair looked like dirt beneath the tall spotlights that highlighted the fight from above. A thick, single brow hooded his eyes. His skin reminded me of tanned leather, as if he'd spent too much time in the sun. When he smiled, several gaps were where his teeth should have been.

I curled around my broken hand as he delivered a swift kick to my ribs.

Fuck. Me.

Blood trailed down my chin from my split lip at the beginning of this round. My skin would be mottled with bruises by sunrise, if the aches in my back were any indication. Jersey let out a booming laugh. He turned his back, raising his arms and sending the crowd into more of a frenzy. I pressed my forehead to the mat, lifting my hips off the floor.

Get up.

If I didn't, I'd forfeit round two and this son of a bitch would be closer to stealing the biggest fight of my life.

I lifted my head, bracing myself with my good hand. The world narrowed to a single point as a pair of dark blue eyes captured mine through the crowd. Buzzing in my ears silenced the shouts and cheers. Bright lights blared, but all I could see was her. Wild-eyed, pin-straight black hair caressing her smooth skin and cascading over her shoulders. Light highlighted the smooth curve of her chest, where her breasts were nearly on display.

And those shorts. Those *fucking* shorts.

Bonnie?

Was I dead? I almost wanted to be. That would be better than this hell, watching those I loved suffer, missing Mom and Pop. Emma. *Emma.*

Suddenly, everything snapped back as Jersey's boot made contact with my ribs yet again. The jeers from the crowd, the bright industrial lights shining down on the ring from above, the taste of copper on my tongue, all of it, in one swift moment. People wolf-whistled, calling for my head, for blood and destruction. I splayed out across the floor.

Jersey! Jersey! Jersey!

They sure as hell had been chanting my name after the first round. Blood-thirsty cocksuckers.

Bodies pressed toward the ring as the referee called for me to get up or yield. A bell dinged from somewhere. I blinked, and I didn't see her anymore. I must have imagined her. I forced my forehead against the ring again, biting back against the pain. How the fuck was I going to get through this? If I lost this fight, no doubt I'd be out at Lee's. Then what? What would I even do? Go back to Fort Hood? Where I had to see nothing but disappointment and disgust in The Kid's eyes when I told him I'd found her but she was gone? Back to Montana? Where nothing more than charred ruins of life remained?

Where did I even belong anymore?

I'd laid myself bare with Audrey. Admitting my feelings had been the easiest thing in the world. But now? Hours later, when I'd had nothing but time to stew over my grief and sorrow, I felt like the dumbest asshole in the world.

Even more when I spied Rutherford in the crowd next to Lee.

"Three!" The crowd joined in on the referee's count.

"Get up!" a voice snapped near the edge of the ring, a fist pounding a foot away from my head. I looked over.

"Audrey?" I whispered. She'd come.

"Two!"

I flattened my left palm against the mat, using every ounce of strength I had left to climb to my knees. She *was* here. I hadn't hallucinated her. The world spun as I lifted my torso, focusing on nothing but her. Using my good hand, I balanced my weight and pushed onto unsteady feet.

The countdown stopped, and a bell rang above the savage crowd, much to their dismay.

"Round two, Jersey!" The referee eyed me, lifting a brow to ask if I was sure I wanted to go through to the third round. I glanced at Jersey, finding a disgusted sneer on his face. He was *ugly*. No wonder people called him the Devil of Jersey. Rage reflected back in his gaze. He was just pissed I beat him in the first round by kicking him in the nuts and kneeing him in the face.

No one said we had to fight clean.

While most of my fights had been only one round, tonight's was three. With each round, money swapped hands and the spectators became more bloodthirsty. Those who'd placed bets on me at the beginning of the match now swapped bits to the other side. One more round. I only had to survive one more.

Audrey stood near the edge of the ring. I staggered toward her as Will shoved a couple of guys away.

"You suck, *hermano*," he said.

"Yeah, nice of you to come tonight, fucker." Audrey's eyes narrowed as her gaze shot across the ring. I saw that calculating glint her gaze, reminiscent of Bonnie when she was planning a con. She took my injured hand in both of hers. I hissed at the pressure, jerking it out of her grip.

"You're a fuckin' idiot." Her blue eyes captured me the way they had in Vegas all those years ago. Her gaze was wild, but even then, I could tell she was formulating a plan in her head. She bit her bottom lip, and I had to stop myself from yanking her to me so I could bite it.

"Yeah, tell me something I don't know." I grabbed my water and swished some of the blood from my mouth. I spit it on the mat.

"Left shoulder." The words came out in a rush. "He's swinging too far back during the wind-up. He's tired and his shoulder's hurt. If you get one good hit in, you can go for the knockout while he recovers."

I glanced toward Jersey, watching his movements. The dude was huge. His mother must have fucked a giant, because he was easily a head taller than even Will. Light gleamed off of his sweat-slickened head. He had a stocky build, but what he lacked in muscle he made up by using his body weight. The man flexed his shoulders, making a pained face and flinching as he did so.

Suddenly, I knew how I was going to win.

I turned back to Audrey, eyes bright. "You're brilliant, you know that?" Adrenaline surged in my veins, and I saw it reflected back at me in her eyes. She felt it too. The electricity in the air, between us, all of it. I could have remained staring at her wild expression for hours.

With my left hand, I reached over and tucked her dark hair behind her ear. Heart pounding and blood humming beneath my skin, I swept her against me with my good arm, covering her mouth with mine in a searing kiss. She cupped my cheek, melting against me. Goddamn, she tasted sweet.

A seconds passed, and I released her, turning my back. Because if I didn't, I'd strip her bare and fuck her in front of the crowd. I adjusted the front of my fighting shorts and narrowed my attention on Jersey.

The bell sounded, and I circled him. Because he was my prey. Only one of us could win, and it had to be me.

After all, my woman was here. I couldn't look like a jackass in front of her.

Jersey stomped toward me, and I leaned into it, bringing my left fist up into his already-injured shoulder. The man staggered back, gasping against the pain. His nostrils flared with rage, and he leaned forward, allowing his bulk to lead his movements. I ducked beneath his outstretched arms, side-stepping just enough to bring my knee up into his gut. Even through the din of the crowd, I heard air whoosh out of his lungs.

Before he could recover, I dealt an uppercut to the underside of his jaw, hitting that sweet spot beneath his chin. His eyes rolled back, and he crashed onto the mat.

The world erupted. People booed, but most of them shouted my name. The referee grabbed my arm, lifting it in victory. Fireworks shot high above Canal Street, brilliant reds and greens and blues casting across the people in the pit. The crowd began to move, mistaking the bright flashing lights for gunfire.

Audrey climbed between the ropes. Will shouted something, but I couldn't hear it. No. All I could think about was her.

A surge of people followed them into the ring, crowding us. We needed to get out of here before this became a riot. I clenched Audrey's hand, dragging her from the ring and through the crowd, intent on getting inside of my locker room. I shoved people out of the way with my shoulder, heart pounding. I squeezed her hand to remind myself that she was still here. I yanked open the door to the locker room and pulled her inside behind me.

Audrey tugged her hand out of mine as the door closed, silencing the noise outside. Suddenly, we were alone, and I didn't know what to do or say. Not with the wild look in her eyes, her mouth slightly open. Her eyes flared bright. She advanced on me and delivered a swift punch to my chest.

"You are so *fucking* stupid!" She shoved me, forcing me to falter back a step. "You could have gotten yourself killed, asshole!" She raised her fists once more, but I caught them deftly. That look in her eyes was like the night we'd escaped the crater beast, when she'd hit me for putting us all in danger. Something snapped tight within me. Maybe it was that leash she'd secured around my heart all that time ago.

"I can't lose anyone else that I love," Audrey said, chest heaving, eyes wide and vulnerable.

Cold shock swarmed through my veins, but it was quickly replaced by keen warmth. Love. She *loved* me. I thought I knew what love was. It was warm and beautiful. But those were the feelings of a boy.

Love was deeper than that. It was all-consuming. It was seeing the person you loved and just knowing in your soul that they were meant for you. It wasn't always pretty or easy, but it was worth it.

Staring at her now, knowing that I'd desperately fallen for her all over again sent a stark jolt through me. This feeling between us wasn't some average infatuation. Most people could live a lifetime and never experience the raging, all-consuming need to be close to another person, no matter whether you knew why.

My soul called out, and hers answered.

Everything that I'd lost three years ago was suddenly before me. In the span of a breath, I closed the distance. I clutched her hips, a smile curling over my lips at the little gasp she let out as her back met the steel door and my mouth covered hers. I reached behind her, flicking the lock. Too many times we'd been interrupted. I'd be damned if I let it happen now. Not when she loved me again.

Audrey loved me.

I pinned her against the wall, letting her feel each hard inch of my body. Her breasts pressed deliciously against my sweat- and blood-slickened bare skin. My hands slid down, cupping her ass in my palms. A keening moan came from her lips, the rush of air just what I needed to deepen the kiss. Her head tipped back as my tongue met hers in a dangerous dance.

In one fluid movement, I yanked her off of her feet. Audrey's legs wrapped around my waist as if it were the most natural thing in the world. I ground my pelvis against hers, wanting—no, *needing*—her more than I ever had before.

Audrey's hands raked across my shoulders and back, skin catching beneath her fingernails. I smiled against her lips at the thought of the scratches that would mottle my skin alongside the injuries from the fight. My fingertips dipped above the hem of her shorts, brushing against the smooth skin of her ass. She shuddered, her body tensing and releasing beneath my ministrations.

When Audrey ground back against my stiff cock through the layers between us, I unleashed a growl I didn't think I was capable of.

I'd been through too much and waited too long to have her in my arms like this. I had to have her. I had to have her *now*.

The table across the room was a fleeting thought that passed through my mind. I should lay her down on top of it and fuck her senseless over there, but I wouldn't make it. I braced her against the wall, lowering her legs so she could stand on them again. She whimpered in protest as my lips moved across her cheek. I ran my tongue along the column of her throat.

My good hand slid over the swell of her breast, brushing against the cool metal of the chain she wore. The chain that held my father's ring. A grin curled across my mouth.

Even if she didn't remember me, even if she *never* remembered me, she knew me. She knew my soul just as I knew hers.

My fingers slid beneath the fabric of her bra, cupping her breast and gripping harder than I should have. Audrey bowed into the touch.

"Montana!"

The last time we'd been in a similar situation, this had happened, too. She'd called me by my false name. That was the night I'd realized that I wanted—no, *needed*—her to know the truth. *My* truth. The night of the hurricane party, I hadn't stopped because I didn't want her. I wanted her to know me, *not* Montana.

As I teased her nipple into a hard peak, I lifted my head from her shoulder, brushing my nose along the side of her face. My lips hovered above hers long enough that her blue eyes snapped open, stealing my breath at how beautiful she looked when she was like this. Lost to me.

"Jesse," I said as I brushed my lips across hers.

"What?" She curled a hand into the hair at the back of my neck.

"My real name," I said, gasping for breath as she gripped my hard cock through the front of my shorts. "It's Jesse."

A smile curled across her lips, and her eyes lit up as if I'd given her the world.

That was who she was, though. Bonnie had never liked fancy, trivial things. I wasn't surprised that Audrey didn't either.

"Jesse," she whispered, caressing my cheek.

Hearing my name on her tongue unleashed me. Some carnal part of me that'd been holding back for so long. I didn't think it was possible to love her more. But, somehow, I did.

I reached between us, popping the button on those fucking shorts. In a perfect world, I'd have taken my time. I'd have savored every inch of her skin, elicited every single sound I remembered and more, but my need to be inside of her was too great to ignore. I would take my time later.

Audrey bucked against me and ripped at my hair. I slipped my fingers across the plane of her belly, dipping beneath the waistband of her shorts and lacy underwear. I couldn't contain my moan as I felt the molten heat between her thighs.

"Fuck," she whimpered as I pressed down on that one delicious spot. Her head slammed back against the steel door, eyes fluttering shut.

My hand stilled against her. "Audrey, look at me," I whispered. As her eyes opened, I began again, slower, agonizingly slow. "I want to watch you."

Something flickered through her eyes—a hint of recognition?—before that lustful glaze overtook them once more. As her breaths came shorter and her whimpers grew louder, I cupped her cheek.

"What do you want?" I ground out.

"More," she gasped.

As always, I obliged. I followed the bucking of her hips, her short gasps of breath, the way her fingers dug into my skin. Her eyes fluttered shut, and I pressed hard against her so she'd open them again. There was nothing I loved more than having her like this, beneath me, her every pleasure at my whim. Her mouth gaped open as her body tightened. I didn't slow, didn't stop. I raced her to the edge of pleasure and over it, until the only sound in the locker room was her screaming my name.

My name.

Only when her breath began to even and she cradled my face in her hands did I retreat from her shorts. After a moment, I made quick work of them. In a perfect world, I'd have knelt before her, feasted on her, relished every single sound and pleasurable shudder of her body, but I needed her now in a way I'd never needed her before.

In a flurry of motion, her shorts were discarded to the floor. Audrey reached between us, shoving against my waistband. She grasped my aching cock in her hand, stroking me once, twice, a third time. I shuddered and jerked against her. My good hand slid down her back, cupping her ass for a moment, before I tugged her leg up and around my waist.

As I positioned my cock between her thighs, Audrey's eyes flashed up at me. She cupped my face, kissing me slowly, sweetly. The moment suspended between us. I didn't want to go another day of my life without *this*, without her *like* this. In my arms, pliant, fierce, and full of love.

Audrey's arms wrapped around my waist as I eased into her. I didn't want to go too fast, didn't want to ruin this moment for either of us. She bucked her hips against me, and I slid in further, the sensation forcing my eyes closed and staggering my breath.

Goddamnit, this woman would be the death of me.

She didn't give me a chance to think before her nails dug into the skin of my ass, encouraging me. My self-control snapped, and I unleashed.

There wasn't time to relish in this moment, in each other, because the feral need inside of me took over. Flesh met in a cacophony of moans, grunts, and whimpers. I wasn't going to last long even though I desperately wanted to go all night. I gripped her thighs, keeping them splayed open beneath me as my rhythm increased.

"I fucking love you," I whispered into the crook where her neck met her shoulder.

Audrey wrapped her arms around my neck, holding me tight against her as I raced faster and faster to that peak. She ripped my head back to hers, tugging my bottom lip with her teeth, her hands scratching along my skin in the best way possible.

"Jesse!"

That undid me. Completely. I was no longer in control of myself. My pace quickened, our bodies slapping against each other. Sweat poured across our skin, mingling. I bit down on her shoulder, and she cried out again.

Her body tightened, and she cried out. Her release pulled me faster, harder, until my teeth clamped harder on her shoulder and I let out a muffled groan.

Fireworks went off in my head, my knees weakened, and I knew that all of the pain, all of the trauma and heartbreak had been worth it. Because it brought me here. Back to her.

Audrey clung to me, our breaths mingling together in the humid air. I cradled her cheek, brushing her hair behind her ear as I eased out of her.

"Give me a few minutes," I whispered before feathering my lips across hers. "And then I'm going to do that again." I shook against her, willing my heart to slow down and my breathing to even.

"W-we don't have time," she said, breathless.

"We'll fucking make time," I growled. I was tired of being apart from her. The back and forth, never knowing where I stood from one moment to the next.

I'd treated her like she was some fragile doll all this time, but that wasn't the woman I loved. She was immovable, strong, and she could handle me. My teeth grazed against her jaw and my fingers tangled in her hair as that ember of desire in my belly caught and flickered to life once more.

"No." Her chest heaved against mine. "There's a steamboat." Even as she spoke, her nails scraped along my back. "It's leaving tonight out of the city. We . . . we have to . . ." I smiled against her skin. The words faded as I rolled my hips against her. The shudder of her body sent the flames higher inside of me.

"We have to leave," she tried again, even as her body arched against mine. "Will and Savannah." Why were we talking about our friends right now? I lifted my head, intent on kissing the words from her lips and reminding her of what was important. "They bribed the captain to smuggle us out of the city." I stilled, brows tightening. Her blue eyes caught mine. "Together."

Together. Like we did everything.

Audrey wanted to leave New Orleans. She wanted to go. With me.

How was it possible I could love her more?

As I opened my mouth to speak, a rapid knock came at the door. Will called my name. My eyes fluttered shut as I pressed my forehead against hers.

"Lee's looking for you," Will said through the steel door.

"Fuck me," I murmured.

If Lee caught us together, there'd be hell to pay. I'd have to play the part of the fighter for a while longer.

"Your father's a dick," I said, regretfully disentangling myself from her. We righted our clothes quickly, even as Will's fist hit the door again. "I hear you!"

"He's coming," Will said. I flicked the lock, and my friend stormed into the locker room. He assessed the two of us quickly, a hint of amusement in his eyes.

Regretfully, I turned toward Audrey, taking in the sight of her swollen lips and mussed hair. I wrapped my arms around her, pressing my lips quickly to hers. As I tried to pull away, she gripped me tightly.

"We don't have time for this," Will said, peering out of the two-inch gap in the open door.

Our lips parted, and I gripped her tightly. "I'll distract him, give you enough time to get out of here," I said and turned to my friend. "Where's this steamboat?"

"Half mile north of the bridge," Will said.

"Good. I'll get Lee out of here and then swing that way." I gave my friend a nod, retrieved my shirt from my bag, and moved toward the door.

"Wait, Savannah—" Audrey said, grabbing my hand. Her gaze flickered between me and Will. "She's still at the house. I was supposed to send Will—"

"I'll get her," I said, nodding curtly. Confliction filled her blue eyes. I pulled her toward me once more, covering her lips with a searing kiss. "I promise."

"Don't you fucking show up without her, *pendejo*," Will said, his words firm.

I gave my friend a curt nod and pulled away from Audrey before I got lost in her all over again. "I love you," I said, fixing her with a stare. I brushed past Will and moved out into the madness beyond.

While people walked to and fro, there seemed to be an audience waiting just for me. Lee and Rutherford stood off to one side. The former seemed quite pleased to see me. The latter, however, eyed me with suspicion. Had he noticed Audrey in the ring?

"There's my prized fighter," Lee said. I tugged my shirt over my head, flashing a fake smile that was all teeth. I wasn't his anything. Audrey's father clapped me on the shoulder. "Let's have a drink. I want to talk to you about Nashville."

As he steered me through the crowd, I dared to glance over my shoulder. I spied Audrey and Will, peering from the opening in the door.

We were leaving the city. Tonight. No matter what happened, as long as we were together, I knew it'd be fine. We just had to make it to the boat. Then our lives could begin again.

CHAPTER THIRTY-FIVE

WILL

ACHARY BARELY SPARED ME a cursory glance as I slid out the door behind his prized fighter, looking like he'd gone another three rounds with a raging crater beast. One with *claws*, by the look of the scratch marks running over his shoulders and down his spine.

"Who was the woman you kissed in the ring?" Zachary asked. I ducked my hat lower to hide the expression on my face as I watched them.

"Just a fan," Jesse said, shrugging. *Damn*, he was a good liar. A real natural. "A pretty one."

Zachary guffawed and clapped a hand on Jesse's shoulder before introducing him to several of his associates that'd been waiting for a chance to see the victor up close. Sex-mussed hair and swollen lips aside, Jesse kept his composure long enough to steer Zachary and his friends toward the exit. Investors looking to set up even more lucrative fights, if their excited chattering could be believed.

As soon as they were far enough away, distracted by Jesse's mangled hand and whatever story he told them, I rapped on the door twice with my knuckles. A clear signal to get the hell out of the locker room. Audrey peeked out, and I jerked my head until she twisted from the room, keeping her head low as I hid her from view. In minutes, we were up the stairs and in the open expanse of Canal Street. I chuckled low as I took in the sight of her swollen mouth and flushed skin.

"What?" she said, with all the sharp challenge I expected from my friend.

"Oh, nothing, just wondering how you can still walk." I offered Audrey an irreverent grin that made her blush like a whore in church. "I mean, after all the *noises* coming from behind that door—"

She punched me in the shoulder, glaring at me in an all-too-familiar way that forced warm recognition through my chest; that spark of the woman I knew flared bright in her blue eyes. She grumbled a quick "shut up" before we made it down the street. I peered around the corner, seeing that Zachary's horse-drawn carriage was gone.

"Let's get to the horses. We need to find the boat and stall the captain until they can meet us," I said as we rushed toward where we'd tied them out front.

We mounted swiftly, setting off at a rushed pace. For the first time in what felt like an eternity, hope lit like a beacon inside of me. We were *leaving*. New Orleans. The deal with Lee. That *fucking* bridge. I could start over, become someone that Savvy could be proud of. That *I* could be proud of. Somewhere they'd never heard about the Beast of the Bridge, where no one knew I was a monster.

"I'm not getting on that boat without them," Audrey said as we turned down an unfamiliar alleyway. I looked over at her, noting how she held her shoulders back, chin tilted in defiance. She looked so much like Bonnie tonight that it hurt.

"We won't."

It was an easy promise to make. Easy because I couldn't either. If Jesse or Savannah were left behind, I'd never be able to go without them. Perhaps this part of Bonnie was still alive inside of the woman she was now. The little orphaned girl, at the mercy of evil men, always searching for someone to call family. We were the same that way. We always had been. Clinging to each other like a lifeline in the darkness. Until Jesse. Until *Savannah*.

"After all, what will you do on the boat ride if you aren't locked in your cabin with the bloodied-up *gringo*, screeching like a wet cat." I chuckled at the horrified look in her eyes. It faded quickly into steely anger. That, if nothing else, was such a *Bonnie* expression it made me feel giddy. Like she was close to the surface. A reflection of her former self, but *here*.

I winked over my shoulder at her. She scowled as we picked up our pace and crossed into a twisting back street I vaguely recognized. I could smell it now: the river. The wind picked up, and the air was wet and muggy. It was a sweet sort of decaying scent. Like death and cypress. That scent, that *river*, had been the instrument of my demise for so long. Strange to think after everything, it would become my salvation.

"I do not screech like a *wet cat*," Audrey said as we trotted on for another twenty minutes. The farther we got into the back streets, the freer I felt.

I stopped after a few turns, to reorient myself. A foghorn cried too close to us over the muffled quiet of the night. It was there. *Right there.* Relief trickled down my spine, my shoulders relaxing as I drew in a full breath for the first time in forever. Audrey's eyes flickered to mine, freedom turning them luminous in the moonlight.

I swung down from the back of my stallion and watched as she smiled widely before doing the same. The alleyway was too narrow to ride on horseback. I wanted to laugh. To shout. To cry. I hadn't realized just how many parts of myself had died. Just how much I'd grown to hate myself. Not until the chance to escape it all threatened to burst me open wide, happiness swelling in my chest until my ribs hurt.

"I can't let you leave, Will," a familiar voice said from the other end of the alley. I froze, feet cemented to the cobblestones beneath my boots. What was he doing here? We'd left him at the house more than an hour ago. His guard uniform was gone; instead, he was dressed in black, a gun belt slung around his hips. One I'd never seen before.

Something was wrong. A warning trilled up my spine, a sensation that'd kept me alive enough times to ignore. He started toward us, the thunk of his boots echoing in the stillness of the night.

Seb stared me down once he'd made it halfway up the alley, stance taut. A lone streetlamp filtered light into the alley, reflecting up from the too-smooth cobblestones at our feet, enhancing the long shadows surrounding us. That wasn't what gave me pause.

It was the expression on his face, one I'd never seen before. I thought I knew every part of him from the years we'd spent together. His face slackened in passion, twisted in anger, jealousy and disappointment turning down the corners of his mouth. All of that was replaced by firm resolve. Dark purpose shrouded his shoulders. He neared me, standing tall with firm resolve in his gait. The warning clanged louder in my ears.

"What is this, Seb?" I pushed the brim of my hat up to see him more clearly. It had to be some mistake of the light, some sort of trick my eyes were playing on me. I knew Seb, I knew him better than anyone. Had kissed him breathless and broken his heart. Had let him tear me apart too many times to count. "Why are you here?"

Audrey went too still beside me, sucking in a trembling breath. He stopped, only a few feet away. Determination hardened his jaw as he widened his stance, every muscle pulled tight. He pulled out his gun and leveled it at me. With an ominous *click*, he cocked the hammer back. Disbelief slammed into me, stealing my senses. I shoved Audrey behind me, letting the reins of my horse loose so I could have both hands free.

A loud rushing started in my ears as my heart thundered against my ribs. Every throb of my pulse sent a cold numbness through my body. *What was he doing?*

"He's not going to let her leave the city, Will," he said, his hands steady on the gun. Not a waver in his eyes or his stance. As if it were the easiest thing in the world for him to see me as an enemy and not the man he'd laid next to many nights over the years. I couldn't stop staring at his hand gripping the gun. Hands that'd set my skin on fire, tangled in my hair, made lazy circles over my ribs as we lay naked in sated bliss. I shook my head, refusing to understand what was right in front of me. "I can't let you and Bonnie get on the steamboat."

Bonnie.

I sucked a sharp breath between my teeth. My past raged forward, shattering my hard-won self-control. Betrayal twisted beneath my skin like tiny shards of glass, slicing through my veins, cutting deep enough to kill. I'd never called her Bonnie in front of him before, never told him about her past, about *mine*. There was only one way he would know who she *really* was, only one person who would do all of this to get her back.

Jones.

"That's not possible," I whispered, begging him to tell me it wasn't true. "You don't have a Hanged Man tattoo."

"Jones isn't stupid enough to mark his *spies*, Will." His answer was too easy. Too logical. I couldn't have been that blind. *Three years.* Longer, even, since he'd been working for Zachary when I got to New Orleans. The pause between us grew heavy with all the things we hadn't said to each other yet. All the broken promises of time we were supposed to have together. All the lies tangling like thorns in the empty space between us, keeping us from each other, pitting us against each other as opponents.

"I tried to get you to leave," he said, as if that were an explanation. His hard gaze faltered the longer he stared at me. "So many times." His words broke in the stagnant air. The first hint of emotion he'd shown. I wanted so desperately to believe in it, that he didn't *want* to do this. Didn't want to stand across from me as an enemy. Not after everything. "I know how much you want a family. A *real* family. Come back to the crew. *We can be together; we can be a family.*"

Heat gathered in my eyes, and my palm found the handle of my gun, cocking the hammer in its holster on my hip. I closed my eyes tight, thinking of how *alone* I'd been these years. How lonely. How Seb made me feel like *maybe* I didn't have to be alone anymore. I'd finally thought I could be worthy of someone. That I could live through the horror of my nighttime work, if only I had him to come home to. I remembered the fighting, the breakups, the cruel words, how he'd never tried to understand. How he'd compared me to my father. So many hints.

"Don't make me do this," I begged. *Please. Please, no. Don't make me be the monster I fear I am inside.*

"We were supposed to do this at the house earlier, with most of the guards gone to the fight, but your little detour fucked that up. It's time to bring her back," he ground between his teeth, his words landing like a blow. "For *both* of you to come back."

"Will?" Audrey said my name like a question and a prayer. Her voice was small and scared, reminding me of the broken little girl who'd found something worthy in me once. Who'd found me lost in the darkness of my life and walked in to lead me out of it. How she climbed into my bed nearly ten years ago now. When a mark got too close and she was terrified that one day, Jones would let them have her before springing his trap. How she told me that she didn't want to give that piece of herself to them. How she only trusted me with that. We'd been barely more than kids then, but she'd given herself to me because she knew she was safe with me. Seb's next words stole my attention from the memories crowding in.

"After everything you've done here, the name you've made for yourself, Jones will welcome you back into the crew. You'll have a place of *honor*. Your father is proud of you, Will. Isn't that what you always wanted?"

I didn't want to be tempted. I didn't want to admit that it sounded so *good* to have a place where I belonged. I didn't want to imagine the ease with which I could step right into that role. How I *knew* I would excel at it. That I wasn't useless. I would never have to feel powerless again. How a part of me *did* want my father's approval. Even if it made disgust roil beneath my skin.

"Think about it. You could be his right hand . . . and we could be *together*."

A gunshot rang into the night. I'd made my choice.

Seb swore, dropping the pistol and clutching his bloody hand before rushing toward me with wild eyes. I pulled my gun up again, but he was too fast. And I was too broken. He slammed me against a crumbling wall, elbow at my throat and the other hand grappling for my gun. I leaned in, slamming my shoulder against his chest as we crashed to the cobblestone street. The pistol skittered away from us as we lurched together, a tangle of limbs reaching for pressure points and advantages.

He was fast and well-trained, landing a swift blow to my ribs that stole my breath before I could slam him against the ground. He shifted his weight, and I toppled from above him. He reached for the large knife strapped on my belt, but I twisted my hips away from his reach. I grunted as another blow landed on my shoulder but forced him off with all the strength in my arms. My shoulders burned with the effort, and my biceps trembled.

Suddenly, with a thud, his knee caught me in the temple, and I slumped to the side, ears ringing. My vision blurred, black spots receding slowly. She screamed then. Audrey. Bonnie. A brave, broken little girl. A wild-eyed outlaw on the run. A prisoner in a gilded cage. Two pairs of feet shuffled past me as he jerked her forward.

"Stop it! Will!" Her voice was terrified as it echoed off the walls.

Her scream reverberated in my mind, catching on too many memories to count. *My father carving Jones's name into her skin. Jones with a bloody belt dangling from his fist. Her blood on my hands as I dragged a needle back and forth over an open wound.*

El dolor es fugaz.

Pain is fleeting.

It wasn't fleeting. It was endless. Everyone I tried to keep safe, I failed. The pain of loss and grief and horror never subsided. I saw all my victims when I closed my eyes. Hanging. Swinging with dead eyes and open mouths, cursing me silently. My mother had been the first one, but so many joined her. I stood shakily, blinking to clear my eyes as they focused on Seb, dragging Audrey away with a dagger pressed against her throat. Tears shimmered in her eyes. Eyes that *always* saw me for exactly who I was and loved me anyway. I wouldn't fail her. Not again.

Never again.

I pushed my doubts away and let the Beast of the Bridge free. With practiced ease, I knew exactly how to disarm him. In two long strides, I grabbed Seb's wrist and twisted. He cried out at the wrenching pain, and I kept twisting until there was enough space to shove Bonnie out from the cage of his arms. She fell heavily, a line of red on her collarbone, hitting the ground with a muffled *thump*.

"Don't!" Seb cried. Fear made the air thick around us as we struggled for the knife in his hand. He forced his knee up to thud into the outside of my thigh and tried to shove me. Catching my balance, my arms moved without thought. I thrust forward on instinct until I felt the blade glide through my fingers, ending in a sickening *crunch*. Warmth flooded over my hand and down my wrist. Neither of us moved. Instead, we stared, mouths open, breathing rapidly. As if we were locked in a familiar lover's embrace. Cold dread unfurled within me as the Beast retreated and it was just Will, alone in the aftermath.

Seb's eyes widened, and a strained whimper escaped his closed lips. Jagged realization crashed over me. The warmth seeped over my shirt and down my pants as he slackened against me. Tears spilled over my cheeks, and I shouted into the still night, a sound more animal than human. The knife was buried deep in his chest, too deep. I'd read so many medical books. Discovered so many ways to put people back together.

But I couldn't fix this.

"No!" I roared at his face as his legs no longer held his weight. He coughed. A slick, wet sound that ended in a horrific gurgling noise. I dropped with him, arms tight around his body, hoping I could keep him together. Maybe if I could just hold him together for a while longer, I could . . . I could . . .

He raised his bloody fingertips to my cheek. The warmth that I used to love so much returned briefly into the depths of his dark eyes. A grim smile played on the lips I'd kissed a thousand times. He coughed, a line of crimson leaking from the corner of his mouth. His hand fell away, and I cradled him in my lap, trembling fingers feathering over the elegant length of his nose and the smooth line of his jaw. He was always so clean-shaven, so neat.

"I-I'm cold," he whispered. Hot tears dripped from the bridge of my nose and beneath my chin, splattering against the dark beauty of his skin.

"No," I sobbed. Another gurgling breath. Another. Another. Another. "Stay with me," I begged, pressing my hands against the wet stain on the front of his shirt around the hilt of the knife. "Don't . . . don't close your eyes. *Please*, Seb."

Another breath, with too long between. His mouth opened as if he wanted to say something. I pressed my forehead against his, hoping to catch the words but unable to make out any of them. Another breath.

Until there weren't any more.

His dark eyes went dim and unseeing. It was so much worse than the disappointment that'd tortured me for so long. Silently I begged for that disappointment, for anger, for hate, for *anything* but this. I pressed a kiss to his still-warm mouth, memorizing the feel of them, the taste of them. So I could carry it with me. With shaking, bloody fingers, I closed his eyelids so that he could rest. So I could hide the horrible truth of what I'd done. What was gone.

I rocked back, unable to reconcile the limp, lifeless body on the ground with the man who'd loved to run his fingers through my hair when it was wet. The man who'd hidden my clothes once to keep me from leaving in the middle of the night so that he could hold me. The crimson stain grew around him, nearly black in the night. What did I do now?

I couldn't leave him here, in this alleyway, alone.

A soft gasp of horror sounded behind me, and I remembered that Audrey was here. I turned, wrenching my eyes from Seb's lifeless body to focus on my friend. She'd sat up, clutching her collarbone. I shuffled closer, and she pulled away, her blue eyes wide and afraid. Her eyes trailed over the blood staining my hands, soaked into my shirt and sticking to my skin. I looked at her now and saw none of the girl who'd once been my friend. All I saw was her fear.

Fear of *me*.

Bonnie would never be afraid of me. But she was gone. I killed the spark of her that'd been there before. Just like I killed Seb. And my mother. The last of my humanity drained from my skull as I realized it.

I killed everything I loved.

Because I *was* the Beast of the Bridge. There were no monsters in the dark for me, because *I* was the monster. Will was dead. He had been all along. I'd clung to death, and it'd reached back, clinging to me.

"We need to get you home," I said, my voice a dark growl. I pulled her up by her elbow and helped her onto the back of her horse. I cradled Seb gently in my arms. I carried him to my mount and draped him over the saddle. His arms lay in an unnatural angle that made my stomach thrash. I couldn't leave him.

I led my stallion forward as blood rolled down his flanks and Audrey cried softly. As we made our way through the city tonight, the Beast of the Bridge set off alarms. Shutters closed. Cries of horror lit the night. Guards on Lee Square scrambled to aim weapons. Shouted orders wafted toward me on the breeze.

But I didn't stop.

Not until the job was done.

CHAPTER THIRTY-SIX

SAVANNAH

I WAS SUPPOSED TO have time. Time to pack, to prepare to leave. *Leave*. The thought of getting out of this town, out of this *house*, propelled me through the lists running in my mind. I'd gotten myself into the bath after Audrey left, and it helped with some of the soreness in my aching muscles. Enough that I felt renewed.

With nearly everyone out of the house for the fight, I didn't worry about being caught out of my room. I moved between mine and Audrey's, figuring out what we would need, what we would *want*.

As I'd stared around my room, I realized there truly wasn't anything within these walls I wanted to take with me. I'd come to New Orleans with nothing. I was leaving far richer.

For the first time in years, true hope blossomed within me. Hours. *Hours* left. I could taste freedom on my tongue. Oddly enough, it tasted like tobacco and whiskey. My heart fluttered as an image of Will passed through my mind. How he'd stared at me in the kitchen in the seconds before he laid me down on that counter.

An unfamiliar warmth pooled low in my belly. *Maybe*, I dared to think, *maybe when we got out of New Orleans. Maybe when we escaped Sebastian.*

Afternoon turned to night. I'd packed and repacked the small bag I'd take when Will came for me, filled to the brim mostly with clothes and personal effects. I had stashed away a couple of personal things of Audrey's—a tiny music box her father had said belonged to her mother and a copy of *The Art of War*—that weren't necessary but that I thought might ease this transition.

I had no idea where we would go. But, for the first time in my life, I was filled with possibility, with *hope* so bright nothing could dampen my spirits. Not even Sebastian.

A commotion sounded from beyond my windows. Brow furrowed, I moved past the now-empty tray Etty'd brought me earlier—broth and toast, tea and water—and ripped the curtains away from the barred window.

In the lamplight, I spied a dark figure walking toward the house, leading a jet-black stallion.

My chest swelled with bright hope. Will had come for me.

But why was he using the front entrance? Wouldn't it be smarter to use one of the—

A second horse carried Audrey's familiar form. Something was wrong. She shouldn't be here.

Without another thought, I moved through our rooms blindly, ripping open the door. I peered out, searching for any guards that might be posted to keep me in place.

Empty.

On harried feet, I rushed to the staircase, gripping the railing as I descended. A few guards spilled through the entry hall and outside into the night. Far fewer than normal. I shoved between the uniformed men and women. A couple tried to stop me, but I pushed forward.

At the head of the group, soldiers held their rifles up, pointed at a tall, shadowed figure hovering just outside of a circle of lamplight. I'd know that figure anywhere.

"Put your guns down!" I shoved the nearest one to point toward the ground. "It's Audrey and Will!"

Instead of the normal derision, confusion crossed the faces of the guards. I turned my back on them, rushing toward my friends. Audrey approached me on shaky legs. Before I could speak, she threw her arms around me, burying her face against my chest.

"What happened?" I whispered. She didn't speak. All she did was shake her head.

I lifted my gaze to the man six feet away. He clutched the reins of his black horse. *Harbinger of Death.* His eyes were shadowed beneath the brim of his hat. His entire body was tense; he stood taller than usual. A flicker of lamplight highlighted pursed lips.

I hadn't thought it possible that he could look like his father. But at that moment, I saw it.

The *Beast of the Bridge*.

Placing fear into the hearts of men and women. His presence leant to the tense hush shrouding the square. I shifted Audrey from my arms. In all of the times I'd seen Will *after* he'd done a job, he'd been a shadow of himself, but this was different. Something had happened, something far worse than usual.

I crossed toward him, my steps steady even though my heart pounded erratically.

"Will—" I reached for him. He shook his head, shifting backward. Enough that the light illuminated his face. He looked at me, but he didn't see me. His usually-warm brown eyes were cold, dead. His jaw clenched. My gaze followed the line of the reins in his hand to his stallion.

To the figure slung across his saddle.

My eyes adjusted, and I took in a sharp breath.

Sebastian.

"What happened?" I lifted my gaze as a muscle feathered across his jaw, but he remained silent. "Will—"

"He was working for Jones," Audrey said behind me.

Jones. A man whose name had locked down the entirety of Lee Manor five years ago when the Hanged Men were in New Orleans, searching for someone. The name carved into Audrey's arm. The only person I'd ever seen Lee fear.

I should have been shocked. Should have feared this moment like the others. Only, I didn't. Because, I realized, I'd known. I didn't know that I knew, but I did.

Sixgun, the other day. Word from the *boss*. Only, it was a different boss. Not Lee. *Jones.*

My gaze settled on Sebastian's still form. Confliction struck in the center of my chest. This was someone Will had cared for enough to *try* to be a better man.

And Sebastian hadn't deserved it. At all. He'd torn Will apart for his dirty deeds, and all along . . . he'd been no better.

I moved toward Will slowly. His hard eyes looked at me—through me, really. I cared nothing for the dead man on the horse. But the man that stood before me . . . Sorrow filled my chest at what he had to do. To protect Audrey. *Bonnie.* His only family. I reached for him, not sure what to expect. My fingers touched his shoulder, and I thought I heard his teeth crack from how hard he clenched his jaw.

"*Don't.*"

But I didn't listen. Not when he was hurting. I was the only person in this city who didn't fear him. He wasn't the monster everyone else made him out to be. He did terrible things, but he did those things to protect the people he cared about. I would never fault him.

Will's muscles bunched beneath my touch.

"Will," I said, his name full of deep sorrow and pain. I wanted to comfort him, to help him, even if he wouldn't look at me.

Dead eyes lifted to mine. His voice was emotionless as he said, "Leave me alone."

"But—"

Sensing my resolve, Will wrenched from my grip. Cool night air filled the space between us.

"Get the fuck away from me."

The words smacked me in the center of my chest. This wasn't the man I knew, cared for. He was a shell of the William Ellis that infuriated and amused me in the same breath.

That William is gone.

"I'm sorry," I said, my resolve stiffening. "I'm sorry that you—" My gaze went to the corpse once more. I shook my head.

Realizing I could do nothing more, I turned to Audrey, cradling her head as I scanned her for injuries. She trembled beneath my inspection. Aside from a shallow cut at her neck, she appeared unharmed. I wrapped my arm around her and ushered her toward the house.

"Tell Lee," I announced to the guards. "Jones had a spy on staff." The guards stared at me, incredulous. "*Now!*"

I didn't have time to sit around and order them into motion. I guided Audrey through the front doors and up the stairs. Once inside our rooms, I locked the door.

Lockdown would be initiated. Bar the doors. Lock the windows. Staff off duty except for Lee's most trusted.

After settling Audrey in the small chair near her window, I retrieved a towel from the washroom and some ointment from the packed bag. I snatched a bottle of liquor from her bedside table. I returned to my friend, her skin understandably pale. I worked silently, cleaning the cut before spreading ointment across it.

"Doesn't need stitches." After setting aside the supplies, I brushed her hair behind her ears and cradled her head gently. Her eyes were glossed over, far away. "Audrey." She blinked, and her eyes settled on me. "What happened?"

"I—I don't—" When she'd left earlier, she'd been alive with hope and possibility. Those feelings propelled me forward, sent me into the flurry of preparations to leave. With *Montana*.

"Where's Montana?"

Audrey's brows lifted. "He—he distracted my father at the pits. He said he'd get you and bring you to meet us on the boat."

Relief washed over me. At least he wasn't involved with Sebastian.

Audrey's expression crumpled. Her bottom lip wavered as a tear slid down her cheek. "Savannah," she said, blue eyes desperate. "We were *so* close."

I let out a slow breath, taking her hands in my own. I squeezed them tight, nodding.

"We'll figure this out," I said, fighting back against my own rising sorrow. "You're my family, too." She squeezed my hands, nodding through the tears cascading over her cheeks. "I promise, we'll find another way."

I wrapped her in my aching arms, holding her tight against my heart. This couldn't be how everything ended. I refused to accept it. I would find another way.

For all of us.

CHAPTER THIRTY-SEVEN

AUDREY

S ECONDS TICKED BY LIKE years as Savannah peered through the keyhole. It'd been an eternity since I heard boots in the corridor. I held my breath, listening for any sound of the watch on our floor only to be deafened by my pulse hammering in my ears.

"Is he still there?" I asked in a whispered hiss. Savannah waved her hand at me in annoyance.

"It's a different one, at the end of the hall." She slumped away from the door with a weary sigh. I dragged my pencil across my meticulous notes, groaning.

"Well, there goes that pattern." I crumpled the paper into a ball and threw it violently against my closet door. For once, completely hairpin-less. Mostly because my plan of escape needed them intact so I could pick the lock on the door.

"We've never been locked down for this long before." Savannah rested against the wall as she stared at me. It'd been two days already, with no sign of my father letting up on security protocols. So far, I'd counted ten regular guards on rotation in the corridors. The bars on my window felt more like a cage than protection. "What if he never lets up?"

I snorted derisively, looking over my hand-drawn blueprints of the house and grounds, my notes on shift change, the number of guards, and their positions. There was always a flaw, always a weakness to exploit, I just had to *find* it.

"He won't keep this up indefinitely. It costs too much money, and the optics aren't great. You know he likes to pretend he's respectable." I rolled my eyes in bored irritation.

"I don't know. There isn't anyone that scares him as badly as Jones," she said, concern coloring her voice, making it high-pitched enough to raise the hairs on my neck. I stared at the papers scattered on my desk, gaze tracking back and forth across the space without finding anything to catch onto. "I'm sorry, I shouldn't have mentioned . . ."

Jones.

The man whose name was carved into my skin and *attacked* me. Bloodthirsty leader of the Hanged Men, a crew of vicious outlaws who trafficked in drugs, people, and murder.

Sebastian's boss.

I'd known Sebastian. Granted, not as well as Will or the other staff members, but he'd always smiled at me over the years. Comforted me after losing Emma. Held me down when I had a particularly vicious glowroot relapse to keep me from clawing my own face.

I can't let you and Bonnie get on that steamboat.

These words weren't part of my fractured memories; they were raw and recent. Spoken by a man I watched die. With the echo of Montana's lips and hands on my skin, it'd felt like I'd swallowed sunlight. Until he'd spoken those words. Until he mentioned *her.*

Bonnie.

Montana's Bonnie. *No.* Not Montana.

Jesse.

My mind had been racing ever since. Questions without answers threatened to spill from inside me like dark blood, coating my tongue. Why did Sebastian care about Bonnie? Who was she? Was she mixed up with Jones? How was Jesse involved in all of this? But most importantly . . .

Was she alive?

That thought kept me from finding any sort of peace. Because if Bonnie was alive, was in the city, would Jesse try to find her? Did he already know? What if he was out there right now, looking for her, and the heady promises we'd made were already forgotten?

I clenched my jaw and pressed the heels of my hands into my eyes until they hurt. Why did I always find myself competing against a ghost? I'd only tasted the kind of love worth waiting a lifetime for. I wasn't ready to give it up, to give *him* up.

Savannah touched my shoulder. I hadn't heard her cross the room. Even though her bruises were healing, she could still hardly move without groaning.

"At least you have a while without needing to deal with all the men chasing after you now," she said, and a sad giggle forced its way between my lips. If *that* wasn't the truth, I didn't know what was. She offered a small smile, tilting her head to the side as I dropped my hands. "You'll figure it out; I know you will."

Her unwavering faith was just the balm I needed for my frantic thoughts. Thoughts of not measuring up to a dead woman. Thoughts of Will and how wrecked he looked after . . . everything he'd done for me. Thoughts of being trapped in this house. Trapped within the confines of my own mind. Clinging to the tiny pieces I'd gathered from my life *before.*

I put my hand over hers and squeezed, grateful that if I had to be locked away in here, at least I wasn't alone. If I had Savannah, I wouldn't turn into *Insane Audrey*. She would keep me from falling over the edge into madness. She always did.

"You still haven't told me about you and Montana—"

"Jesse," I said firmly, liking the way it rolled off my tongue. His name. His *real* name. A piece of his heart that belonged to me now. She sucked in a sharp breath. "He told me his real name is Jesse."

Her exhalation wavered against my shoulder before I turned in my chair to face her. This, at least, was something to cling to. How I'd felt in that locker room with him, how he'd breathed his feelings against my neck as we shattered together. The smile that crept onto my face was bright and only a little sad. I wouldn't think about how he could be chasing after another woman right now. Not while remembering the taste of him in my mouth, blood and sweat, desperation and passion mingling into a dizzying cocktail of euphoric bliss.

"I told him," I said as she sat on the edge of my mattress, attention rapt. "That I loved him. It was all so *fast*. Both of us clinging to each other, like we were trying to crawl into each other's skin. I've never felt so *alive*."

She stared at me, wide-eyed and dumbstruck. Maybe because I wasn't the type to wax poetic about feelings. Or maybe because she'd tasted a bit of that same drug, more addictive than glowroot, more vicious than any crater beast. Love was a twisted, ugly thing sometimes. When it sank its claws into you, it never let go; you were damned and saved all at once. Even now, I wouldn't take it back. Not a second of it.

"I'm probably not explaining it very well." A flush crept into my cheeks. I pressed my fingertips into them, trying to dispel the heat radiating beneath my skin.

"But did you . . ." She flicked her wrist, eyebrows wagging suggestively. I bit the inside of my cheek, but the devilish smile that cracked over my face was a dead giveaway. She grabbed a pillow and tossed it at me. I twisted away to avoid it.

"What!" I felt lighter than I had in days. "He was all . . . sweaty and half-naked and kissing me. I couldn't help it!"

"Uh huh, sure," she said, laughing at me. "You've been dying to get in his pants since the moment you met him."

"It was standing up against a door, actually," I said wickedly, enjoying the flash of shock and reluctant curiosity that dawned across her face.

"How—No, no, I don't want to know!" She pinched the bridge of her nose. "That's so . . . *dirty*!"

I stood, a teasing glint in my eyes as I stalked toward her. "Yes, it was. Dirty and hot and *hard* and perfect." I wrapped her in my arms and squeezed tight. She squealed before we fell back against the mattress together, laughing for the first time in days.

As our laughter subsided into a comfortable silence, I turned to stare at her profile, outlined by the morning light. Her smile faded into sorrowful concern. The same look she'd leveled at Will when he'd brought me back to the house that fateful night. Memories flooded my mind, and I fixed my gaze on the ceiling.

"It was horrible," I said, knowing that she needed to hear it. Because her thoughts were fixed on him. In every quiet moment these last two days, when her eyes glazed over in deep, pensive silence, I knew her mind wandered down the corridors to where he slept. "We were close enough to hear the foghorn of the boat. I'd never seen him look so . . ." I swallowed loudly. "*Free.*"

Savannah's breath caught as the word landed in the air between us. She reached over, grasping my palm in a grateful squeeze.

"Then he came from the shadows," I told her. "And leveled a gun at Will."

I blinked back tears as I remembered how Will's voice broke in the muggy night air, how his hands clawed at the front of Seb's blood-soaked shirt.

"They fought, Sebastian got Will's knife, and they scrambled together and . . . I don't know if he meant to do it. Or if it was instinct. But afterwards—"

I cleared my throat. Unable to give voice to what I'd witnessed. How did you put the sound of his wails and pleading into words? How did you describe watching as a person fell irreparably apart?

"It was horrible."

Savannah sniffed, and I kept my eyes shut tight. I wasn't strong enough to handle her tears. Not when I'd shed so many of my own after I returned home. How did we find ourselves here? Trapped by circumstance, ripped apart from the people we cared about, succumbing to the unfairness rotting the world?

A knock sounded against the door. Booming and authoritative. The lock clicked, and we scrambled off the bed. Was this it? Was the lockdown *finally* lifted?

The door swung open, revealing a guard, fully strapped with an automatic rifle. No. I studied the details of the gun. An M16, military issue, semi-automatic rifle. How *the fuck* did he get equipped with a gun like that? Did my father trade in weapons? Was this another of the secrets he kept from me?

How did I recognize that gun? It was like the lock, instinctual, terrifying. But I didn't have time to focus on that now. Instead, I focused on our escape plans, how the weapons changed things. These guns weren't a joke. They were magazine-fed, meaning the guards had more than enough ammunition to gun us down if we ran for it, even if we split up. Three-round bursts made the likelihood of a grievous wound rocket skyward.

Fuck my life.

"Your father wants to see you in his study," the guard said as Savannah and I exchanged wary glances. Each second we held eye contact was part of a silent conversation.

Should we make a run for it?

Don't do anything stupid.

What if this is our only chance?

I said, don't do anything stupid.

Savannah's concerned glare won, and I followed behind the guard on bare feet, my shoulders drooping at the missed opportunity. In moments, we arrived at my father's study door. It was closed.

It was always closed.

To me, at least.

Muffled voices inside made memories of the last few years surface. How many times had I stood here, waiting for him to conclude business meetings that excluded me? How many times had I imagined being invited into those conversations? The nights I'd spent awake, studying business and economics, until my eyes ached and I couldn't keep up the pace. He'd seen none of it. Any time I attempted to show him what an asset I could be, he brushed it off. Given me dancing lessons that I abhorred. Or brought books back from his travels, poetry and gardening, classic novels, nothing too hard or too educational.

Until the prospect of marrying me off for the shipping contract, he'd never once given me the slightest indication he would *ever* bring me into the family business. I was such a fucking idiot. I'd been so eager to win his approval that I didn't stop to think about if he should have *mine.*

Frantic sobbing wrenched me from my thoughts. The door opened, and two guards dragged out a woman in a Lee uniform, her black pinafore embroidered with the gold fleur-de-lis my father was so fond of.

"*Please!* Mr. Lee, I only spent a night with that guy, I never saw him again. I had no idea he was a Hanged Man. I didn't tell him *anything*! I swear!"

The guards dragged her away, one of them taking a pistol from the holster of his hip as she clawed and twisted, nearly breaking their hold. He put the gun to the back of her head, and before I could call out to him, a shot resounded. She slumped lifelessly to the ground before the guard barked at the maids standing sentry to *clean it up.* Then they dragged her, leaving crimson streaks on the hardwood, until they disappeared around a corner.

With wide eyes and a hammering heart, my feet moved before my brain could catch up when my father called out to me. My eyes didn't leave the crimson streaks. Would he do the same to me when I tried to escape? Would he have us all killed for defying him?

"Audrey, stop gawking." My father sighed, wearily, as if dealing with me gave him a constant headache. Like he didn't just have a woman murdered in the halls of the house I once thought was *safe.*

He looked tired but calm. Too calm. How many times had he done this that it'd become second nature? There was a single metal chair, complete with handcuffs still swinging, where the woman had clearly been restrained *before.*

He walked around from behind his desk, crossing the room towards me. When he was a few feet away, my mind snapped back into focus. I flinched as he reached for me. Irritation flashed in his dark eyes before he busied himself with the crystal decanter on the sideboard.

"Don't look at me like that," he snapped. "I'm just doing what's necessary."

"Hasn't there been enough death?" My words came out in an unattractive croak.

He finished pouring the amber liquid into a glass and capped the decanter again with a *clink.* He pointed at me, his nostrils flaring in annoyance.

"You don't get to judge me. This is *your fault*." His voice never rose, but his words thudded into me like the points of knives. I was numb. My mind went blank in shock.

"*My* fault?" I questioned clumsily.

"If you hadn't snuck out of the house, if you'd stayed put like I told you to—"

"*Fuck you*." The numbness in my body shifted to hot rage. He blinked in shock at my foul language and possibly how I trembled. "I'm not a dog you can order around. I'm sure as hell not some animal you can cage. Though, I suppose you've never quite seen me as a human being, have you?"

His mouth gaped, and he sputtered as I took an enraged step closer. "I have given you *everything*!"

"Yes," I said, nodding. "You've given me a beautiful, comfortable cage. You've given me lies. You've given me the assurance that I am an *asset*, to be traded in a shipping contract at your whim. Not a daughter. Not a *person*. You've shown me who you are, what's important to you, and the lengths you'll go to in order to amass power."

My gaze flickered to the fleur-de-lis tie pin he was so fond of wearing. Gold and diamonds. A symbol of his status. Of the stranglehold he had on this city. On everyone in it.

Including me.

"You want your own little kingdom, and God help anyone who gets in the way. Right, Dad?" His brows lowered on his forehead. "The saddest part is . . . you got it. The world ended and you had an opportunity to make this city *anything*. To start over. To be *better*. And instead, you tried to *literally* take us back in time with a classist social hierarchy that puts you at the very top. It must hurt your pride that I'm such a fuck-up."

Hurt flashed in his dark eyes as he set his glass down. He gripped my arm and pulled me closer, his gaze tracking over my face. Like he was memorizing the shape of my eyes, exactly like his. Furious tears welled in them, the image of his face wavering.

This was what I'd clung to. These human moments. The times when he looked at me like he would do anything to keep me safe. To give me the world. When I wanted nothing more than to be his little girl forever.

A little girl I didn't remember being in the first place.

"Audrey." He said my name like a prayer, and it broke my heart.

"I'm never going to be enough for you, am I?" I whispered, a tear tracking down my cheek. "All this time, I've tried to be what you wanted. Tried to win your approval. The only thing I couldn't change was *me.* No matter how hard I tried."

My lips trembled, and he let out a sigh. I was inconveniencing him again with my emotions. Like I had when I lost Emma. When he couldn't understand why I couldn't get out of bed or spent all my time alone in the library staring out at the world. He'd never known how to handle me when I was like this. Hurting. Flawed. *Human.*

"Where was I before?" I asked him, the words thick in my throat. His hands fell away, and he picked up his glass, taking a nervous swallow.

"I've already told you all this—"

"I want the truth," I said, my words hard. "I've remembered things, and I thought I was going crazy, but I'm not. I wasn't here before my head injury, was I?" Which, of course, was a lie. Or a partial lie. I had begun remembering things, but it was Savannah, not my memories, who'd confirmed his deception. But I would never put Savannah at risk again, so in my head that truth would stay, like an ugly sin.

He looked away from me. I'd never seen him so guilty before. Not once. Not ever. I'd always seen him strong, decisive. But now, all I saw was a man who'd made mistakes. One who wouldn't own up to them. Not even if it meant losing me.

That, more than anything, confirmed what I said next.

"I'm going to leave," I said, sounding calm and confident for the first time since I'd stepped foot in this office. His eyes snapped up to mine.

"It's not safe—"

"Not right now. Not today. But soon, I will leave this house, and when I do . . . I want you to forget you ever had a daughter." I folded my hands together to keep from fidgeting.

"Audrey, don't be rash—"

"Because I plan to forget about you." I could feel my heart splintering into a thousand pieces. "Don't worry, Daddy. I won't be a Lee anymore. I won't tarnish your good name again."

I turned but paused and glanced over my shoulder. "Oh? And this little kingdom of yours . . . it won't last. The problem with forcing us to live in this fucked-up shadow of history, with all its debutantes and arranged marriages, isn't that it's fucking archaic. Which it is, by the way. But you've forgotten the first tenet of history . . . it's doomed to repeat itself."

Without another word, I left him there. Stunned silent. And even though it hurt, it was a *good* hurt. The kind that meant that I would heal in time. The guard outside the door was eavesdropping, and instead of following me like I'm sure he was supposed to, he peered at my father. I didn't want to return to my room, so I wandered down the back stairs and crossed into the stables. The warm animal and hay scent grounded me when my heart felt too tender to stay whole.

The same copper horse from the other night tossed his head when he saw me. I reached for his nose, and he pressed it into my hand and nuzzled my hair. Almost like he knew I needed to feel warm again. God, horses deserved more credit. Gentle giants with hearts rivaling even the most ferocious crater beasts. I stroked his neck for a few long minutes.

Until I heard it.

Haggard breathing, the slosh of water, soft cursing. Soft *Spanish* cursing.

Turning the corner hesitantly, I caught my breath and held it. Will scrubbed his horse's back flank, his eyes rimmed red, his hands scrambling. I stared for too long. Unsure if I should approach or leave. Who was I to step into his grief?

But I couldn't leave him like that.

There was a pull toward him, from deep inside, and I followed it. Without words, I padded closer, ignoring his glare when I approached. The one meant to scare me off. It probably scared everyone else, now that I thought about it. Instead of turning around, I covered his hand on the brush, which clattered to the ground. He shoved me a few steps away, and I came back, my hands dragging him away from his horse. Until he had to stop.

"The water is still red, I have to . . . I have to . . ." The water in the bucket was a little dirty, but there was no red. No hint of blood.

"The water is clean, Will," I said softly. A tremor wracked his body, and he sat against one of the stall doors, fishing his cigarette case out of his pocket with trembling fingers. He struck a match on his boot and inhaled raggedly. I sat beside him, motioning after a minute for him to pass the cigarette.

I put it to my lips, inhaling the harsh tobacco into my lungs and trying not to let the irritation make me cough. Then I handed it back. We sat like that, passing his cigarette until it was a nub nearly burning our knuckles. With a rough exhalation, he flicked it into the bucket of water.

"What do you want, Audrey?" he asked. "Another training session? You want me to sneak you out again?" He laughed, dark and bitter. It hurt me to hear.

"No." I leaned my head against the stall behind me. "I want to thank you, but I don't think I'll ever be able to repay you for what you did for me."

"You were afraid of me," he said. His eyes cut over at me in accusation. I nodded. Not denying it.

"I've never seen someone . . ."

"Murder a person in cold blood."

"No," I said, eyebrows furrowing. "Not that. I've never seen someone break apart like I did. Brought up some old shit, you know?"

He stared at me, eyes dull and uncaring. No spark of life. I hoped Savannah could reach him. Because when I'd felt like this after Emma, numb and dead and shut down, it would've been so easy to just . . . stop *being*. I didn't want that for Will. I wanted him to pull out of it. I found myself rooting for him at that moment.

"Anyway, I wanted to ask you about something," I said, changing the subject. He didn't acknowledge me. "Sebastian mentioned Bonnie that night."

He ran a hand down his face wearily, clearly not wanting to talk about it.

"I have to know. Is she alive?"

He stared at me for a long time, then said, "No. She's dead and gone."

He rose and began toweling off his horse, ignoring me. I still had questions, so many questions. If she was dead, *why* had Sebastian mentioned her? Had he just lost his mind? Or what if Will was lying because he was angry with me?

Sighing, I stood and brushed the hay off my skirt, and when I looked up, the guard from earlier shifted his weight nervously at the entrance. He'd obviously come looking for me but wouldn't risk being the Beast's next victim. After Sebastian, I was sure the staff thought no one was safe. He didn't have to escort me back, but his boots thunking behind me stopped me from veering toward the back house. Toward Jesse.

I wanted to feel his arms around me, wanted to sink into his embrace. To tell him I was through being a Lee. That I was *his*. Only his. If he'd have me.

But that would have to wait until I escaped. For now, I needed them to think I was comfortable in my cage. Then, when they least expected it, I'd slip my shackles for good. Disappear with a new name and a new lease on life. Audrey Lee would die here.

Then, I'd *finally* be free.

CHAPTER THIRTY-EIGHT

SAVANNAH

T HE SUN WAS SINKING on the other side of the Mississippi when the guard came for me. Every member of the staff was to be interrogated; a means for Lee to root out any other spies. Everyone would be thoroughly questioned, and if he wasn't satisfied . . . they would fly above the bridge, too.

At the knock on my door, I stood, smoothing my dark purple dress. I glanced at my reflection in the mirror, noting the faded bruises on my arms, the healing cut on my lip. I'd chosen the dress with capped sleeves and a low neckline for a specific reason: I wanted to show the bruises on my arms. I wanted them to see what they'd done to me.

My hair fell in soft waves over my shoulders, pinned back to keep it from my face. When the door opened, warm surprise flooded my chest.

William Ellis stood in the hallway.

"Come with me," he said emotionlessly as he avoided my gaze. I rose from the chair and followed him into the corridor, matching his slow, even pace as his boots thumped against the floor. His spine was ramrod-straight, his muscles bunched beneath his shirt.

The corridors were eerily silent. All I heard other than our footsteps was my pounding heart. What was I about to walk into in Lee's study?

Each silent step coiled the tension further in my gut. My friends were suffering, and I was useless. I couldn't soothe their pain, as much as I wanted to. As we rounded a corner, Will glanced over his shoulder. It was the first glimpse of him, the *real* him, I'd seen since *before*.

I yanked on that small thread.

"William." He didn't respond, keeping his back to me. "Will, look at me." Still nothing. I quickened my pace, touching his shoulder. He froze. I didn't think he was breathing. He stood so still. I stepped in front of him.

The same cold, dead eyes from the square stared back. My brows furrowed as he tipped his head forward to hide from me, a habit I hadn't recognized until that night in the kitchen when he'd retreated into himself.

"You're not the beast everyone thinks you are." A muscle feathered across his jaw. "Lee makes you do things. I know what that's like." He lifted his head. A shift happened then. His distant, cold expression wavered as our eyes met. Pain and anguish filled his gaze. His jaw tightened as he fought against it, lines creasing his face. Like he could only show this pain to me.

"I'm sorry." I touched his forearm. His muscles shifted beneath my fingers. His other hand twitched at his side, and he balled it into a fist. "You shouldn't have had to—" I bit my bottom lip, unsure how to articulate my confliction.

Sorry you had to kill your ex-boyfriend seemed inappropriate. And I *wasn't* sorry that Sebastian was dead. I was sorry that *Will* had to kill him.

"I see you, William Ellis."

I squeezed his arm, then pivoted away, because I wouldn't let my empathy turn me into a blubbering mess before my interrogation. I walked confidently through the open door of the study, bracketed by armed guards I didn't recognize.

Lee stood to one side of his desk, pouring a glass of scotch. The leather armchair normally across from him had been replaced by a single metal chair in the center of the room, handcuffs dangling from either arm. Without hesitation, I sat, placing my hands in my lap before I finally lifted my gaze. His shirt was ruffled, as though he'd been wearing it too long. He lacked his usual fleur-de-lis pin and jacket. His hair was skewed as though he'd run his fingers through it over and over again. The door snapped shut, and Will moved behind me.

Most people would fear his presence during this meeting. Instead, my shoulders relaxed in his proximity.

Lee drained his glass as he moved in front of the desk, setting it down roughly on the polished top. "How well did you know Sebastian?"

"I didn't." What was this doing to Will? Overseeing interrogations about that man.

Oddly fitting, of course. Zachary Lee had a particular brand of cruelty.

"That's not quite true," he said. "As I understand, there have been many altercations between you two over the years."

The barrage of insults and cruelty incited by Sebastian ran together in my mind. I turned slightly, just enough to notice tension snapping Will's spine.

"Sebastian didn't like me very much." I kept my voice even. "I avoided him at all costs."

Lee snapped his fingers. A guard opened the door and shoved a woman with blonde hair inside. She stumbled, sobbing as she collapsed into a heap near my feet. When she looked up at me, tears sprung anew in her eyes, spilling over onto her dirty cheeks. I recognized her. She was one of the maids.

One of *my* maids.

I turned my attention back to Lee, brow screwed up.

"What about this woman? Do you know *her?*"

My lips parted, but I couldn't form words. What was he getting at?

He walked a few steps forward, peering down at the woman sniveling incoherently on the floor with no emotion in his dark eyes. "Tell her what you said to me, Mary." His tone was soft but commanding, and the woman glanced up at him with tremulous hope in her eyes.

"I-I . . . She . . ."

"We don't have all day."

"I saw Savannah sneak out of the house. To that riverboat she went to three years ago. She hides things, but I know she was lookin' to escape. I heard her talkin' to Etty once, and Miss Etty hushed her, tried to calm her down, but Savannah says she wants to go *home* a lot when she thinks the maids aren't payin' attention."

The warmth seeped from my cheeks, brows twitching as I fought against showing the emotion I knew he wanted to see.

How could I have been so careless? *Of course* Lee knew. He knew then and he knew now. But why hadn't he done anything about it?

"Sir—" I didn't know how to spin this.

"Shut your mouth." He didn't raise his voice but the hair on the back of my neck stood at attention all the same. Cold dread filled the room. "Thank you, Mary, you've been *very* helpful."

He looked past me, to the corner where Will leaned against a bookshelf half in shadow. "Ellis," he snapped, as if he were calling a hound to heel. Will straightened and walked forward, every thunk of his boots an ominous toll in the silence of the room.

"No! Mr. Lee, *please*, don't let that devil near me. I told you everything I know, I swear it!" Mary sobbed, grabbing at Mr. Lee's pant legs.

"Take care of it." Lee commanded.

Will's eyes were blank. Emotionless. No hint of the *William* I thought I knew living within them. He drew his pistol from the holster without hesitation and the room exploded with the gunshot, ringing terribly in my ears. She slumped to the floor, silent and still.

Somehow, I didn't scream. I didn't even flinch. I schooled my features carefully, snapping my mouth shut and narrowing my eyes to hide the shock surging in my chest. Lee snapped his fingers again, and the guard returned. A moment later, all that remained of my maid was a pool of her blood staining the hardwood.

As Lee returned to his perch, Will retreated to the same corner as before.

"Where were you going?" Lee asked.

I hesitated. Didn't he already know after the maid's confession? When I dared meet his gaze, his eyes hardened with each passing second.

"St. Louis," I finally said.

"Running back to your glowroot-addled whore of a mother?"

My jaw clenched.

Lee snorted as I averted my eyes. "Why would you return to the woman who sold you to me?"

Sold you. I'd been slapped. I gaped as unfettered shock coursed through me. I shook my head almost imperceptibly. My mother didn't *sell* me. *They* took me.

"You didn't know?" Cruel amusement curled his mouth. "Your own mother, selling you for a temporary high."

"You're lying," I whispered.

Even as the words escaped my lips, I remembered that day in St. Louis. How she'd told me to stay back. She'd spoken quietly with Lee. Something had changed hands. Then, she'd just . . . been gone.

All of these years, I thought they'd hurt her when Sixgun dragged me away.

"Would you like to know how much I paid?" His words dragged me from my hostile thoughts. "What your mother thought you were worth?"

I averted my gaze, my heart pounding, heat building behind my eyes.

He moved forward, jerking my chin to force me to look at him. "Would you?"

I turned my head, yanking from his grasp. He wanted a reaction. He wanted me to give him a reason to punish me.

"Your mother was a seasoned junkie, wasn't she?" He crossed to the desk to retrieve his glass and moved back to the decanter for another drink. "That's how you knew what dose to give Audrey to keep her sedated and how to wean her off of it."

My mother was sick, even before I was born. But she loved me. She wouldn't—

I sucked in a sharp breath. I'd been nearly eleven that day. She'd taken me to the brothel a week before. To *sell* me. My skin chilled. I didn't want to believe him, but . . .

"Haven't I been good to you? Provided you with every comfort?"

The bitter tang of disgust filled my mouth. He was no better. Worse, really, because he was stone-cold sober.

Lee held his glass to the light, focused on the liquid. "How could my dear, darling Savannah want to leave me after all I've done?"

He believed he did me a *favor* by buying me from a desperate, ill woman.

"All you've *done?*" My ironclad grip on my tongue slipped. "Years of captivity? Forcing me to spy on Audrey and report back to you? Locking me away in my rooms and letting your guards *beat* me?"

His dark eyes flashed to Will. I tensed. Would Mary's fate become my own? *William won't hurt me.*

"I think you planned to find my worst enemy when you left. You would go to Jones and tell him everything you knew," Lee said, ignoring my accusations to finally get to the point.

"I don't know Jones. Other than his name, what I've learned in this house."

"Are you certain?"

"Yes."

"You've lied to me before."

"To protect Audrey." I shook my head. "Do you really think as a little girl I was trained as a spy?"

Lee turned to Will behind me. "Use the knife."

Will had just killed a woman without hesitation in front of me on Lee's orders. My heart beat wildly. I closed my eyes, gripping my fingers together as I tried to steady my breathing.

He won't hurt me.

I had to believe it, that the man I knew wasn't truly gone. But would he have a choice?

The silence stretched for an incredibly long moment.

"No," Will said, the word gruff. Lee glared at him, opening his mouth to protest. For three years, he'd followed every order. Three long years of handling Lee's bloody business. Why would he stop now?

"She has no connection to Jones. She's too weak-willed for that kind of work."

Ouch.

"And Audrey won't take kindly to her being harmed. You need her compliant to secure Rutherford's contract."

Lee straightened, anger fading beneath Will's cold logic. He ran a hand through his hair, sitting behind the desk. "Fine. Dismissed." He fixed me with a hard stare as I stood. I didn't speak. I turned from the room, Will's footsteps behind me as we left.

Once out of earshot, I glared over my shoulder at him. "I can make it back to my room. I'm not too weak for *that.*"

My mind raced out of control, buzzing like bees.

She sold you. She didn't love you. Worthless. Forgettable.

"You aren't weak."

I stopped suddenly, wheeling to face him. He stared, his eyes unreadable beneath furrowed brows. I bit my bottom lip, forcing back the surging grief and destruction threatening to drag me under. My stomach fluttered at the sight of him, at his words. Some of the warmth returned to his eyes.

He lied to Lee. For me. If he was only the Beast and no hint of *William* remained, why would he protect me?

"And you wouldn't hurt me." I crossed my arms over my chest to hide my quaking hands. "If you really were the monster you think you are, you'd have followed his order."

Will stalked forward. My breath hitched as he filled my space, pinning me against the wall.

"Monsters come in all forms, Savvy. They hide behind pretty faces and kind words." He took in a breath, inhaling deeply. "Don't try to make a hero out of me."

He stood so close I saw the silver flecks in his eyes, a glimmer of the man I knew. Not the Beast. *William.* His gaze caressed my cheeks, following the line of my nose, before settling on my lips. They parted on their own. He balled his hands into the fabric at my hips and leaned close.

I fought against the urge to let my eyes flutter shut and kiss him. It took more strength than I cared to admit as I pressed my fingers to his mouth, stopping him. His eyes flashed up at me.

"No."

Each time he'd kissed me, something *else* was going on. Either he was upset over Audrey or his job or because of Sebastian.

"The next time you kiss me, William Ellis, I want it to be because you *want* to kiss me. Not because you need a distraction." His hands tensed at my hips, and I tipped my head toward him defiantly.

Will hovered for a long moment, his eyes lit up. The darkness had receded, but I wasn't fooled. I knew that grief fueled him now, and I couldn't feed it. I *wanted* him in a way I'd never wanted anyone before. But I wouldn't be a placeholder. I wouldn't be someone he only turned to when he needed comfort.

He leaned back, his eyes scanning my face for a long time, then twisted his fingers in my hair, his mouth covering mine in an unyielding kiss.

"Wanting will be the death of me," he said against my lips.

He backed away, disappearing down the hall.

I released a breath, my heart pounding as I inhaled sharply. The air still smelled like tobacco and whiskey. Like him.

Will instilled fear in the bravest of men. While I should have feared the darkness that shrouded him, I would walk into it. Give in to my darker desires. Let him *see* me in ways no one ever had before.

And save him from himself.

CHAPTER THIRTY-NINE

JESSE

I RELAXED AGAINST THE metal chair, propping an ankle on my knee. Lee crossed the room, handing me a glass with a small amount of scotch. I'd heard about the interrogations, how hard Lee came down on staff who had even a hint of interaction with Hanged Men.

He sat behind his desk, eyeing me with respect. As near as he could come.

"How well did you know Sebastian?"

How many times had Will suffered through the same questions?

"I don't think I ever spoke more than a handful of words to him."

Lee nodded. "Well, since my man here"—he motioned to Will near the door—"vouched for you, I don't have any other questions. You were with me during the attack, so I know you weren't plotting to steal my daughter."

Oh, if only he knew.

When word reached me, Lee, and his investors at a bar off of Canal Street that Audrey'd been attacked, we raced across the city. By the time we returned, she'd been locked in her room, and Will was nowhere to be found. I'd wanted to see her, to make sure she was okay.

Will was avoiding me, opting to spend his time with his stallion instead of me. After learning from Etty that he killed Sebastian, I gave him a wide berth and hoped he would seek me out when he was ready.

"We're done," Lee said, draining his glass. I knocked back my drink and headed for the door. "And Montana, good work the other night. Take care of that hand. My doctors will know if you don't."

My gaze fell to the cast fitted around my hand, extending halfway to my elbow. In the midst of the attack fallout, Lee had summoned his best physicians to tend to me. Most of the damage was to my knuckles. He'd chastised me, almost like a friend, saying I should have come to him sooner and they would have helped me before the fight. One of the doctors said it was possible I had a hairline fracture, but with time and keeping it immobile, it should heal.

It itched like a motherfucker, but I was grateful I wouldn't have any long-term damage. My next fight pended how quickly I healed. While I didn't know much about his plans for me, Lee had mentioned taking a riverboat to Tennessee after we'd left the fighting pits that night.

The only sound was our boots as Will and I descended the main staircase side-by-side.

"This can't be easy for you," I commented as we crossed the courtyard.

"It's fine." His words were tight, quiet. He didn't look at me, even as I stared at him.

"It's not, Will. You're—"

"I'm fine. Seriously." The lack of emotion in his face unnerved me. We continued toward the back house, pausing to greet Etty before we climbed to the second floor.

"I know how hard it must have been," I said as we reached my room. The only indication he heard me was the tense set to his shoulders. "Have you seen her?"

"Yeah, yesterday."

"She okay?"

"As okay as she can be." His gaze darted over the empty courtyard below.

Every night for almost a week, I'd tried to sneak into the front house. Guards kept watch at every entrance and exit. I didn't know or recognize most of them, so there was little chance they'd take a bribe. I had to lie one night after getting caught, saying that I was on my way back from a training session. The guard eyed my cast but didn't press further.

"Do you think Jones has other spies here?"

"I think Jones has spies everywhere," Will said, the words bland. I couldn't imagine what it felt like to be betrayed by someone you cared about, someone you would do anything for. The idea that Audrey could turn on me as Sebastian had turned on him was impossible. Will lit a cigarette as I shoved open the door.

"I'm sorry, really."

"It's fine." The hard set of his jaw told me he definitely *wasn't* fine. He took a long drag from his cigarette. "Have you heard anything from The Kid lately?"

Signature Will. Deflect.

"No, actually," I said. "I wrote to him when I went to Baton Rouge, but he didn't respond. He's probably still pissed at me for telling them to stay out of the city until we called for them." My heart ached with how much I missed my younger brother. The first few weeks here had been a flurry of activity, where I didn't have the opportunity to think about him much, but after this lockdown, I'd have given all of my money to talk to him.

He, at least, would keep me on the right track. The Kid always did. He'd tell me to buck up and find a way to get to Audrey instead of sitting on my ass pining like an idiot. He'd also remind me Lee might be responsible for our parents' murder, and I should probably use the head on my shoulders to look into it.

It was easy for me to obsess over Audrey. Normal. Ever since Vegas. Even as a crass outlaw instead of a polished lady, holding me up at gunpoint, I'd been hooked.

"You should get some rest." My gaze darted about, at the two dozen sketches I'd hung above the bed. I'd filled an entire sketchbook this week. While they weren't my best, the walls would be covered with them if we didn't get out of lockdown soon.

Will remained near the door. "Can't. Have a job." He pulled a folded envelope from his back pocket. Inside, I knew, was the name of his next target. I frowned.

"I'll go with you." I rifled in the bureau for a dark shirt.

"No," Will said, cold. I furrowed my brows as I looked at him, at the shift in his demeanor. His shoulders set back, and he stood straight. Almost like he physically changed to become the Beast. "If you try to fight me, I'll break your other hand." I opened my mouth to argue, but he cut me off. "I'm serious. If you come after me, I will put you down."

Darkness filled his eyes. He wasn't my friend anymore. Will pulled the cigarette from his lips and flicked it over the railing. Then he left.

Would facing his anger be smart? I wanted to support him, take on some of his burden, but he refused to let me. I understood. I'd kept our parents' deaths from my brother for months. I didn't like it, but I wouldn't push Will too far.

I sat in the rickety chair and pulled out a clean piece of paper, determined to capture Audrey's eyes from the locker room, lost in ecstasy. I'd relived it a thousand times over the last week, and I couldn't wait to do it again.

Before my pencil touched the page, a knock sounded. I set the sketchbook down and crossed to the door. When it opened, a mixture of surprise and pleasure coursed through me. In the week since I'd seen her, she'd only grown more beautiful. Her hair hung down around her face, pin-straight and tangled, and she wore a simple outfit of pants and a shirt instead of one of those frilly dresses.

Audrey opened her mouth to speak, but before she could, I wrapped her in my arms and covered her lips with mine.

CHAPTER FORTY

AUDREY

THE TASTE OF HIS mouth was familiar now, like coming home.

He crushed me against him, and I loved every second. I wasn't fragile, ready to break at the slightest pressure. With my breasts flattened against the hard planes of his chest, it was clear he knew it.

Our lips slid together, a desperate rush, greedy and insistent, like we'd been apart for years, not days. I'd imagined a thousand things to say when I finally stood here, but the moment he swept me into his arms, they'd faded away.

Wisps of smoke caught in a hurricane.

With our foreheads pressed together, we broke apart slowly, lingering in the inches between our mouths.

I felt drunk on him, his taste, his scent, his strong hand splayed against the small of my back and wandering lower. What was the purpose of my visit? My irrational jealousy and need for reassurance. All the unanswered questions. Though they remained, crowding my mind to taint our happy reunion.

"I missed you, too," I whispered against his open lips. He tucked my hair behind my ear with a hand covered in a plaster cast I hadn't noticed before.

"I tried every day, to see if you were okay, but the guards—"

I kissed him again to silence him. It didn't matter. Not anymore. We were together now. In all the hours of agonizing over Bonnie, I'd forgotten *this*. How we worked, the way we *fit*. Undeniable. Unstoppable. Since that first day in the library, with his false charm and witty retorts.

"Are you gonna invite me in, or do you prefer sweaty locker rooms?"

A sensual smile curled onto his chiseled mouth that stole my breath. It reminded me of how he'd ravaged me when we were last alone. Like I was a musical instrument and he knew every string to pluck and note to strike. I'd been with my fair share of lovers, but none that *claimed* me the way he had.

"Wait, how did you get out?" His arm tensed around my waist, keeping me firmly against the strong cage of his body.

I offered a wicked smile. "Easy. I memorized the guards' schedules and snuck out during shift change." I shrugged, but his blue eyes lit at my confession. He pulled me inside, my body pinned against his as he shut the door and flicked the lock with a *click.*

"Of course you did." He let out a soft chuckle. "Because you're *brilliant.*" His gaze was hot on my mouth, his thumb brushing my jaw in a dizzying friction.

"Not brilliant enough to keep everything from falling apart. It happened so fast, I thought—" His mouth came down on my neck as I spoke. His lips were full and soft, but his stubble rasped along my skin. The contrast of sensations made my eyes flutter shut as I struggled to remember what had been so important to say before.

"I met with my father and I—" But before I could finish my thought, his lips reached a spot below my ear that sent pleasure down my spine in a shivering tingle. I moaned, the sound deep and guttural. The nip of his teeth against my too-sensitive flesh forced me to bite my lip hard.

"Goddamnit, I wanna bite that lip," he said in a voice so deep I couldn't be sure if I'd heard him at all or if the words just vibrated into my skin.

Oh, fuck it.

We didn't need words. Not now, not when my thighs quivered and couldn't hold me upright. He flicked open the buttons of my shirt as his teeth took my bottom lip hostage. He dragged the swollen flesh between them, his tongue soothing the sting left behind.

I loved every second of blissful torture. How he wasn't gentle, and the flex of his stomach when I scraped my nails across his shoulders. When my shirt hung nearly open, he wasted no time trying to remove it.

"Wait," I breathed against his mouth. This should be simple. Only it never was. Never had been. His grip loosened, and he stared at me with a mix of confusion and concern. "I'm sorry, I just . . ."

My hands rose to the fabric of my open shirt, pulling it together and buttoning it lazily. With his broken hand, he tipped my chin up, and I offered him a shaky smile.

"I . . . I want to see your room," I lied. Even though it was painfully obvious, his expression softened, and he waved me forward.

The room was small and sparsely furnished, but everything in it had a place. Each book and pencil, every stick of charcoal or pad of paper was meticulously organized. A far cry from the chaotic state of my room. It was so neat and utilitarian, it barely felt lived in.

Until my eyes landed on the wall next to his dresser.

That was where he hung his sketches. Scenes from a world I'd never seen, images of a life filled with adventure. I moved closer, the sketches coming to life with pieces of him that felt all at once too personal and not personal enough.

An old rusted truck, hood up, in a field of wildflowers. A man who looked so much like Jesse, but with deeper lines around his mouth and the corners of his eyes. He held a glass of liquor and his eyes were crinkled with tears of laughter, a wide smile on his mouth. Will, with smoke curling around his face, making a rude gesture with his hand. The familiar depiction of a stallion. The affectionate one in the stables. But my gaze lingered on one in the center, with more detail than all the others combined.

For some reason, the image stung my eyes. I didn't understand why. There was nothing I recognized about it. A simple farmhouse, outlined by mountains in the distance. It was nighttime, and the lights of the house were on. As if the people inside were waiting for someone to come home.

"Audrey." He stared as I blinked back the glassiness and raked in a steadying breath. "What happened?"

I let out a bitter chuckle and offered what barely passed for a smile. What hadn't? But of all the places my mind had lingered in the last week, the only face I saw was my father's. Standing in that study, where I wasn't allowed, *refusing* to admit he was wrong. Even if it meant losing me.

"This one"—I pointed to the farmhouse sketch—"is exceptional."

"It's where I grew up," he said. Dragging my eyes from the image, I noticed everything about him at that moment. How his eyes dulled in memory, the slight downward tilt of his mouth, a silent resignation hanging around his broad shoulders. Sorrow put definition in the shape of him in my mind. The urge to soften those edges, to comfort him, welled inside my chest.

"You were lucky." I sighed wearily. "At least you knew they loved you."

His eyes cut through the room like twin blades; it was nearly painful to hold his gaze. He approached slowly, cautiously, hands sliding along my arms. Letting me feel the friction of his calloused hands, reminding me I was *here* in this room with him. Not in that study with my father, having my heart broken.

"Talk to me," he breathed against my temple. The heat from his skin sunk into my own and warmed me from the inside. My eyes closed as his lips pressed into my hair, letting him hold me together.

"I told my father I was leaving." I tried to ignore his hands tensing against my arms. "It turns out that he's been lying to me this whole time." His breath was hot in my ear, ruffling the small hairs on my temple and unsettling my nerves. I didn't want to care what he thought about that.

"He isn't a good man," I said, stepping from the safety of his arms. I ran my fingertips over the points of pencils in a cup resting atop his bedside table. "You'd have to be blind not to notice."

My gaze slid over his neatly made bed, the corners tucked tightly, almost militaristic in how exacting it was. Odd. The pillows, however, were aligned down the center of it instead of lying at the head. Odder still.

"It's easy to make excuses for the people we love. Every time he sent Will out on another job, I thought he had to have a really good reason. Every shipment of contraband that was impossible to ignore, I chalked up to his business acumen. Every moment he kept me trapped here, suffocating in this house . . . I thought it was because he was scared of losing me. That he needed to protect me, because I was *precious* to him. Turns out he just didn't want to lose a business asset."

My brows furrowed, thoughts lining up as I spoke them. I pointed to the row of pillows, needing a change of subject, and raised an inquisitive eyebrow. He gifted me with a crooked smile.

"Will likes to cuddle."

I chuckled in surprise, remembering them laughing together and wondering if I'd ever seen Will as Jesse did. As fully *human*. Flawed and contradictory. How he saw me too. In my entirety.

"You know you can tell me anything."

I nodded, stepping tentatively toward him, watching as his arms fell to his sides the moment I came close. I ran my palms over the planes of his chest, resting one over his thundering heart.

"Do you know why I fell in love with you?" I peered at him through my eyelashes. He shook his head, Adam's apple bobbing as he swallowed heavily.

"You were the first person who didn't treat me like I would break." I lifted onto my tiptoes to tease my lips over his hard jawline. "The only person who's never lied to me." I brushed my nose against his and his mouth dropped open, until I tasted his breath on my tongue. "I never felt like I had to hide my flaws from you—"

"Because you're fucking flawless." He grasped my hips hard. Like he needed something to anchor himself to. "Audrey, I—"

He sounded hesitant, uncertain, but I didn't want what had happened with my father to ruin this. Fisting his shirt in my hands to silence him, I dragged it up until, with a sharp tug between his shoulders, he pulled it smoothly over his head and dropped it to the floor.

My fingertips trailed the tattoos swirling on his skin. Pictures I now recognized, words and names that were slivers of the past that'd shaped him into the man I loved. His parents, wildflowers, an affectionate stallion, poetry; he was a work of art. His chest heaved under my exploring fingers.

The thick ridge of his cock pressed tight against his jeans. He pressed the heel of his hand down against the length of it, as if his arousal were an annoyance. His hair was mussed from its normal slicked-back style, long pieces slipping over his brow to hang in his eyes. With barely any pressure, I guided him toward the bed, until the backs of his knees were flush with the edge of the mattress.

"Sit." He didn't even hesitate at my barely audible command. The early morning light played over his shifting muscles. My tongue flicked from my open mouth to wet my lips, and that simple act forced a shudder down his spine.

"Audrey—"

My name was a strangled prayer on the chiseled bow of his lips, half-agony, half-hope, and all sex. My palms slid over his shoulders as I squeezed myself between his open thighs. His tilted chin illuminated the hard angles of his face, blue eyes glowing in the golden haze of morning. He looked like the future. My future.

One I was no longer afraid of.

"Tell me you want me—"

"I want you," he said swiftly, hands splaying wide against my waist, tugging me closer millimeter by millimeter.

"Let me finish," I teased against his mouth. He swallowed hard again, a muscle feathering in his jaw.

"Sorry."

"Tell me you want me to take off your pants."

His mouth dropped, jaw hanging wordlessly open. I kissed the abrasive line of his throat. My teeth tugged his earlobe. The rapid pounding of his pulse heated against the flat of my tongue as I traced the line of his neck.

"God. *Fuck*. Yes. Anything. *Everything.*" He stuttered out the words until it became incoherent rambling. My lips and tongue traced further onto his chest, and I lowered to my knees before him.

I raked my nails down the sparse dark hair that trailed beneath the waistband of his jeans. His abdominal muscles clenched and flexed in a staccato rhythm, matching his jagged breaths.

"What if what I want is to taste you? To feel you in the back of my throat?" I slid open his belt, and the clink of his buckle echoed in the room.

What he said next was gibberish and grunts of enthusiastic approval as I hooked my fingers in his waistband and he lifted his hips so I could drag the fabric down.

I hadn't had time to appreciate his naked form before. We'd been too rushed, too frantic, clawing our way inside one another so we could never be parted again. Now, I stared at him, thick and proud. I wrapped my fist around the base of his cock, barely able to reach all the way around.

"*Fuck.*" The curse dragged long from him, rumbling in that deep baritone that reminded me of gathering storm clouds. I caught the wildness of his eyes and held the hurricane of them as my lips parted and I sucked him down. Deep.

He hissed, his fingers clenching his pristinely folded quilt. As I stroked and sucked him, he came undone. It was the most beautiful thing I'd ever seen. His eyes blazing down at me, his hands raking my hair into a knot at the base of my neck to watch me. The sounds billowed in the sticky air; his desperate, animalistic cries of pleasure throbbed between my thighs.

"I can't—fuck! *Please*—"

His hips jerked beneath me, driving his cock deeper, faster, until, with a strangled cry, every muscle in his body tensed and he shattered beneath me. I marveled at him, his face flushed, his eyes dark and deeply satisfied.

As I stood, he reached for me, struggling up from his half-collapsed position on his elbows. Until he dragged me forward, his lips burying between my neck and shoulder.

"You're wearing too many clothes," he murmured sultrily against my skin. He reached toward the buttons on my shirt again. Cold dread trickled down my spine.

"Wait, please." I covered his hands with mine. He squeezed my fingers softly, pulling back to catch my eye. "I . . ."

He tilted my chin until I couldn't avoid his piercing gaze anymore. His eyes drew me in, drowned me, until my chest hurt.

"I should warn you about my scars," I breathed out in a flimsy approximation of confidence I was sure he saw through.

"No, you don't—"

"Yes," I cut him off sharply. "I do." I took a shaky breath and swallowed my trepidation. "There are a lot of them, and they're . . . not attractive. They're violent and ugly and until recently I couldn't look at myself in the mirror, so you might want me to keep my clothes on, and that's fine—"

As soon as I started speaking, the words slipped out faster and faster in a rambling mess. Until he buried thick fingers in my hair and pulled my mouth to his to muffle the words. Roughly, he ripped my shirt open with little effort. The buttons pinged around the room as he pulled the fabric over my shoulders.

I cried out in protest, but instead of hesitating, he unclasped my bra with a twist of his hand until I was bared to him. His mouth descended on me, hungry and explorative, his lips tracing my collarbone, his teeth scraping the swell of my breast, sucking my nipple into the wet heat of his mouth. He groaned around my tender flesh, and my fingers buried in his hair, my back arching against his strong hands.

"You're the most beautiful woman in the world, scars or not," he said, hot against my skin. "I want every inch of you bare before me."

He knelt, this mountain of a man, gingerly lifting my ankles in his plaster-covered hand. With calloused fingers that shouldn't have felt so gentle, he slid my shoe off and tossed it carelessly away. He moved to the other one. Gliding his palms over my legs and up my thighs until his fingers hooked in my waistband, he lifted his blue eyes to mine.

He paused, mouth agape with an unasked question hanging on his swollen lips. *Permission*. Asking for permission. If I wasn't already in love with him, I'd have fallen all over again.

"Yes."

His fingers unbuttoned my pants, and he stared at me like I was a miracle. As if with every exposed inch of flesh, I'd righted every wrong in his life. I drowned in his adoration, cupping the hard angle of his jaw as he slid my pants and underwear over my hips to pool at my feet.

I should have felt vulnerable being naked in front of him with my ugly past on clear display. Yet, there was no awkwardness, no shame. Instead, as his eyes roved over my flesh, the air thinned. My breath came quickly, my lungs unable to expand fully as he rose to his full height. My chin tipped back so far that I reached out to steady myself against his body.

He was hard again. The length of him jutted greedily between us. He stroked himself lazily, distractedly, almost an afterthought. A distraction from his true purpose of luxuriating in my naked body. He reached for me with his plaster-free hand. My pulse banged in my temple as he touched the gnarled flesh of my arm.

He traced the scar delicately, memorizing each knot and pucker in my ruined flesh. Forcing back a shiver of disgust, I pressed my lips together in a tight line. How could he stand to look at it, much less touch me with such adoration?

He gripped my chin in his thick fingers and tilted my head up until my eyes found his. "Every single part of you is beautiful, Audrey. Every line—"

He guided the tip of his finger down my neck. "Every curve—"

His hand folded around the swell of my breast, the weight and shape fitting perfectly in his palm.

"Every scar—"

He mapped the crisscrossing lines adorning my ribs, a violent checkerboard pattern, and my heart thumped louder, each ragged beat throbbing down to my toes.

"They're proof of what I love most about you. Your strength. Your bravery. Your goddamned force of will. You're a *survivor*, and that is beautiful.*"

I'll survive. I always do.

Sad words I recognized. In my bones. In my blood. In the dark, secret parts that never quite fit my life here. How did he do that? How did he *keep* doing it? Digging out slivers of my past, like splinters from beneath layers of my skin.

"And if I have to worship every inch of you to make you believe it, I will. Every single day. Until you have to see yourself the way I do." Each word was breathed against my skin, his fingertips tracing my scars like whimsical drawings.

"Every day?" I teased. "Someone has an unrealistic opinion of his own stamina."

He grumbled, the displeased hum more akin to the sound of a disgruntled bear than a man. Instead of a witty retort, he hauled me into his arms with so little effort that a girlish squeal slipped from my mouth. His lips crushed against mine. He parted my mouth and slid his tongue inside as my back hit the mattress, and he kissed me so furiously that my every thought shattered beneath the intensity of sensation.

"I'm going to make you come so many times, the only thing your smartass mouth will be doing is screaming my name or begging me to stop." The hard length of his cock brushed my thigh. I couldn't breathe normally; the bulk of him made it difficult to move, unable to claw closer to him. To relieve the building pressure flooding between my legs.

"Jesse," I gasped, my nails scoring deep along his shoulders as his tongue traced lower. His teeth scraped my ribs, lips moving down the midline of my body until it became obvious he wouldn't stop until he'd tasted every single inch of me.

"*Please.*"

He stilled, his lips curling over my hip bone into a self-satisfied smirk. I wriggled beneath his scrutiny, tossed my head, bucked my hips in encouragement. Anything. It felt like there were bees buzzing underneath my skin. Like if he didn't touch me, taste me, fill me, *right now*, I would burst.

"You beg so fucking pretty," he muttered, before standing at the end of the bed to stare down at me. Sin and mischief filled his eyes. He knelt, wasting no time and hooking my legs over his shoulders. With those strong, prize-fighting hands, he gripped my waist and yanked me to the edge of the mattress.

"I've dreamt of tasting you for *so* long." He buried his face against my glistening sex. I cried out, back arching, fingers tangled in his hair, and dragged him closer. He made love like he fought. Giving pleasure with such directness it was like he was landing a striking blow. With every flick of his tongue and satisfied groan, my heart pounded faster. When he reached up to cup my breasts and tease my nipples, I thought I might die.

What a sweet death.

He sucked and teased and devoured me with the enthusiasm of a dying man. In what felt like no time, I screamed his name, gripping his hair and riding his face like my life depended on it. Until fireworks broke along every inch of my skin. Like a gentle wave, my orgasm rolled through me, my toes curling and my eyes rolling back in ecstasy.

Throughout it all, he never stopped. He allowed me to collapse into a breathless heap as he kissed the insides of my thighs. He found the knotted pink scar on my left hip and traced it languidly. Before I could recover, he buried his face against me again.

"Jesse!" I cried out, halfway between a breathless laugh and a squeal of pleasure. If I thought that would deter him, I was sadly mistaken. He was even more fervent this time, his teeth scraping against the bundle of nerves at the top of my sex until I cried out for gods I didn't even believe in. This time, my orgasm didn't build so much as it broke against me, my muscles spasming involuntarily, my thighs quaking, my back arching so far off the bed that it might have broken in half. He rode me through it, wringing every drop of pleasure from my body. When I collapsed, I could do nothing but lie there in a puddle.

"Enough," I whispered, stroking his hair gently as he lifted his head. "I'll never tease you about your stamina again."

He crawled over me, careful to balance his weight on his forearms and not crush me. His lips were swollen, his chin glistening from devouring me. How he looked at me, as he used his plaster-covered hand to tuck a strand of hair clinging to the sweat on the side of my neck behind my ear, made me want to sink even further into him. To bask in the adoration of those cornflower-blue pools of desire.

"I love seeing you like this." He wiped the moisture from his chin with the back of his hand.

"What? A boneless, sweaty mess?" I asked with a soft chuckle.

"No," he replied, in that deep baritone that rolled through me like thunder. "Mine."

My chest felt like it would burst, swollen tight with happiness. Brushing my nose against his, I kissed him. Deep. He tasted like the best of us both. When I pulled back, our foreheads pressed together, I smiled shakily.

"Yours," I breathed, a vow of sorts. I wanted to be his. Always. Wanted us to be indistinguishable from each other. "Yours," I said again, more firmly. He smiled, and it was like the sun appearing from behind thick clouds. Like light suddenly spilled into the room and made everything more beautiful. Made *us* beautiful.

With very little pressure on his chest, I pushed him onto his back until I hovered over him. As I straddled his hips on quaking thighs, the curtain of my hair fell around us both. Reaching between us, I lined up our bodies, lowering myself until, with slick friction, I was fully seated with him inside me. He swore, scrambling to hold onto me. Fingers bit into my hips. My head tipped back as our joining sent tingles of delight in a shiver down my spine. Then, because I needed to *move*, needed friction and heat, I rocked my hips, and Jesse swore beneath me. My gaze fell to his face, his blue eyes glazed in mindless pleasure, his cheeks flushed and his lips dropped open in a wordless scream.

Holding his gaze, I decided I wanted to watch every second of *him* unraveling beneath me. So I rocked my hips again, harder, until he couldn't hold my stare and he bowed beneath me, his fingers bruising the tender flesh of my hips.

"Come here," I demanded. He didn't hesitate. Rising, he wrapped his strong arms like iron bands around me, our naked chests pressed together. Slinging my arms around his shoulders, I drank his breath into my lungs. "Tell me you love me."

We were moving again, gasping for air, clinging to the warmth of our joined skin. "I love you," he choked out. "Only you. Always you."

"Jesse! I need—"

Only I couldn't speak, couldn't do anything but *feel*. Feel the erratic thump of his heart. Feel his jagged breath. Feel the world shifting around us, until those slivers of my past tumbled together through a dark sky. Until there was no separation between us.

"Yes, yes, *yes*!"

With a strangled cry, he rolled me beneath him and thrust like a man possessed. My legs hooked over his hips, open wide to cradle his body with mine, and as he raced us both towards a screaming peak, I knew in the depths of my soul I would never feel this with another person.

"*Fuck*, I'm going to—"

I'd never believed in fate until our bodies aligned perfectly to the secret wishes of our mangled hearts. Until we became a beautiful, violent catastrophe. Desperate and clinging. As we cried out together, bodies shuddering in sweet release. I'd never been so deeply satisfied.

Not just the bone-deep relaxation in every part of my body, but how he pressed his jaw against my chest as he caught his breath. How when I trailed my fingers through his hair, he closed his eyes and sighed in relief. I acknowledged my hold on him, the comfort I brought him. Before then, I never knew how him needing me could heal me. Or how much it satisfied my heart.

We could have laid that way for hours. Time was immaterial. It stretched and stuttered to a standstill. We didn't speak. There was no need. Instead, we luxuriated in each other's skin. He gave me scratchy kisses and folded me into his arms so tight that I felt just how small I was in comparison. But small wasn't scary; it was safe. He drew lines and traced scars. His fingertips ran up the pink skin on my thigh, and the pad of his thumb brushed over the large burn on my shoulder. Tickling softly sometimes until I squirmed with discomfort. I outlined the curve of his upper lip and cradled the hard angle of his jaw.

"That one must be your favorite," I said, breaking our comfortable silence. He traced the knotted pink scar on my hip for the umpteenth time, seemingly fascinated by the puckering skin. He glanced down at his hand on my hip, blinking himself into awareness. "What are you thinking about?"

A line folded between his brows as they furrowed. It wasn't the way he should look right now, unbothered by the happenings of the outside world as we enjoyed each other. Slight panic trilled up my spine, forcing my fingers to play nervously with the hair at the back of his neck. Should I not have asked that?

"What you said, about your father—"

"You want to talk about my father while you're still inside me?" I arched an eyebrow so sarcastically that his serious expression faded beneath amusement. But it was short-lived. He turned until we were separated, space gaping wide between us and making me feel more than just a few inches of distance. I felt my nakedness for the first time and scooped his shirt off the floor.

"I realize you probably didn't have the privilege of these kinds of growing pains with your parents, and this might seem like a really selfish decision on my part," I said, shoving his shirt on and watching it fall past my thighs. "And while yes, his lies hurt me, I don't regret cutting him from my life. It's not just the lying, though. If he'd been honest with me, maybe we could have gotten past some of the other issues."

He pressed his lips together to stifle a smile that twisted onto his mouth anyway. "I think my shirt is longer than most of your dresses."

Looking down, I realized he might be right. His shirt swallowed me. Rolling my eyes, I let him pull me down on the bed beside him. He tucked me into the crook of his shoulder, where I seemed to fit so well.

"My parents had secrets," he admitted with a weary sigh. "Secrets I didn't even know to uncover until after they were dead and couldn't explain." He frowned, and I hated it. I kissed him softly, dragging my nails over his stubbled jaw. Inhaling a steadying breath, he pressed his forehead to mine. "One reason I came to New Orleans was to track down some clues to their past."

"Then you met me," I said, putting some of the puzzle pieces together in my mind. Why such a notorious fighter would want a sponsor when he'd been doing just fine all those years traveling in the circuits without one. Why he would want to be here, stay *here*, when he'd been out exploring the world for years before. He brushed his mouth over my temple.

"Then I met you," he confirmed. "But, if I'm being honest, I've had plenty of opportunities to dig into the past. I just . . . didn't. I think part of me was afraid of what I'd find. And another part just wanted to let go of it and find a way to finally be *happy*."

"Prioritizing yourself over your dead parents isn't something to be ashamed of. Life is for the living. And if they were here, they'd probably tell you the same." I tried to ignore how he blinked a little too hard and fast and the sudden glassiness in his eyes. In an effort to steer him from the darkness in his past, I offered a mischievous smile.

"I disowned my dad," I said matter-of-factly.

"What?!" he spluttered, half shocked, half amused. I nodded, leaning my chin on my hands, which were crossed together on his chest.

"Yup," I confirmed, popping the 'p' at the end of the word and reveling in the wicked glee that filled my chest as I remembered the look on my father's face. "I told him when I left this house, I would no longer be a Lee and wouldn't sully his family legacy anymore."

"Good for you." He ran his fingers through my hair.

"So, I guess I'm just . . . *Audrey* now. No last name. Like one of those outlaws in the tall tales." I looked up at the ceiling and bit my lower lip as I wondered what it would be like to be part of an adventure like that. "It's so strange to think about. I know it's just a name, but it's odd having just *nothing* in place of it, you know?"

"You could use my last name."

The room fell deathly silent.

I didn't think either of us was breathing anymore. My entire body froze in place, and my mind went blank. Then, as if someone restarted the world, we were both scrambling to face each other. My eyes were wide in shock, and his weren't able to focus on anything for more than a millisecond before moving on.

"W-what did you just—"

"I, uh, I think—"

Pressing my fingers to his mouth to quiet him, I took a deep breath before trying again.

"Did you just . . . ask me to marry you?" I failed to keep my expression as blank and neutral as possible. My fingers fell away. *One heartbeat.* He said nothing. *Five heartbeats.* He dragged his bottom lip between his teeth. *Twelve heartbeats.* He sighed.

"Very, very badly, it seems . . . I *did* just ask you to marry me."

"Did you mean it?" I asked, my heart in my throat.

He stared at me unblinking, with a look of abject terror on his face. Slowly, he nodded. But I wasn't afraid. Not of this. I'd imagined it a thousand times, how we would be together. Challenging and cherishing each other. Being careful with one another's hearts while allowing us both the room to open them up completely.

"Well," I said, and he swallowed hard. "There's a problem."

"What?" His fingers curled along my arms. Like he needed to feel the heat of my skin but couldn't bring himself to grab me.

"I don't know your last name." A smile widened my mouth as he let out a ragged sigh.

"It's James." He cradled my face. "Does that mean . . ."

"Yes," I breathed against his mouth. "I'll marry you."

CHAPTER FORTY-ONE

SAVANNAH

L OCKDOWN ENDED. WORD SPREAD like wildfire through the house hours after I distracted the guards and allowed Audrey to slip through unseen.

It was late, and I tried to sleep, but the silence floating between our rooms gave me time to think. Too much time.

At least I'd had Audrey to distract me during lockdown. Helping her craft a plan of escape, tracking the guards, that had taken any time I might have had to obsess over the things Lee had said.

About my mother.

The house had quieted some time ago, the news breaking when most of the staff were already preparing for bed. I stared at the ornate medallion in the center of the ceiling.

Even your own mother didn't want you; why the hell would Will? Or anyone else, for that matter?

After hours of self-torture, I could no longer stand it. I needed to do something, anything, to get my mind off of it. I tugged on my robe and padded out of my room. Guards still patrolled the halls, but their large guns were slung over their shoulders instead of in their hands. They eyed me but said nothing.

I crossed the cool stones of the courtyard, my gaze flickering up to the night sky. Even through the city's light pollution, hundreds of stars glittered down. I remembered the first time I'd seen it, the night sky outside of a city. Millions of shining, glimmering lights far away. Each one felt like a new possibility, a new hope, a new chance.

Or maybe that was my childish brain dealing with the trauma of being dragged from my mother by a monster and locked away until we were too far from St. Louis for me to escape.

With a shake of my head, I crossed the rest of the courtyard and shoved open the door to the kitchen.

"—But *he*'s still in the stables." Two maids stood side-by-side. They froze at my appearance. Clearly, I'd interrupted this scandalous conversation, because they shared a glance and headed toward the other exit.

"Who's in the stables?" I asked.

The one nearest me turned. "The *Beast*." With a shudder, the woman left.

I'd lost count how many times I'd found Will asleep in his horse's stall over the years. I'd never questioned it, but maybe I should have. Because if he was in the stables, that meant he was avoiding—well, everyone.

Before entering the kitchen, I thought I might have a cup of tea. Instead, I pulled things down from the cabinets and got to work.

No one disturbed me as I mixed the ingredients. Muscle memory led me along. Flour. Salt. Knead. Rest. Rise. I lost myself in the simplicity of baking, the one thing I was actually good at. It felt right using my hands, instead of sitting idly behind locked doors.

It was midnight before I stopped, judging by the distant bells from St. Louis Cathedral. I tucked the loaf of bread into a linen-lined basket. I retrieved a small jar of honey from the pantry and snagged one of Etty's better bottles of whiskey. I tucked a handful of apple slices in the pocket of my robe. After wrapping everything up, I left the kitchen, basket hanging in the crook of my arm.

I stopped at a linen closet. Summer was swiftly turning to autumn, and the stable was drafty even in the warmest weather. I grabbed a folded blanket and continued on bare feet through the silent corridors.

The closer I got to the stables, the quieter it was. As if Will's presence deterred everyone. That made me angry.

Did they think he would start killing indiscriminately? Or that was what happened to Sebastian?

Rumors spread like wildfire in this place, and I had no doubt it would take very little for such a thing to start.

The scent of hay and horses filled my nose. I'd never been particularly fond of them. When I'd asked Lee if I could learn to ride, he'd made it abundantly clear that I was to do no such thing. It wasn't until much later I realized he wanted to limit my options of escape. It resulted in my nerves pooling in my belly as I entered the narrow stables.

The horse in the first stall huffed at my appearance, and I flinched, not realizing how close he was to the stall door until he lifted his head over it. I pressed a palm to my chest, willing my heart to slow down at the abrupt intrusion.

Sensing I wasn't here to give it attention, the horse chuffed and turned away from me.

"Well, forget you too," I murmured and rolled my eyes.

Will's stall was the last one on the left. The first when you entered, the last before exiting. The stall door was closed, if the moonlight filtering in from the stable doors wasn't playing tricks on me.

"Will?" I'd rather not startle him if he was awake. If he was here.

I wouldn't have put it past one of the guards to claim he was here to keep people from trying to leave. No doubt there would be a mass exodus tomorrow from the staff needing to stretch their legs and get fresh air.

When only silence greeted me, I pressed forward.

Even if he didn't want my comfort or my help, that didn't mean I was going to give up. In the early days, when we couldn't tell if Audrey was going to make it, I never allowed myself to lose hope. I didn't give up on her then.

And I wouldn't give up on him now.

I caught sight of him as I peered over the stall door. His stallion lay against the back wall, and Will was asleep, his back against the horse. I imagined he'd probably drifted off with his hat on, as it rested in the hay off to one side. The horse lifted its head at my presence. I stilled, my hand on the latch.

Everyone in the house had some nickname or other for the jet-black stallion. *Hellbeast. Biter. Harbinger of Death.* But since Will had brought him here, I'd been in close proximity with him many times, and he'd never tried to hurt me. I unlatched the stall door and slipped inside, setting the basket in the corner.

The horse exhaled loudly, and I stared at him with lifted brows, giving a silent warning. He turned away, acting as though he no longer saw me. I chuckled beneath my breath and retrieved the apple slices from my pocket. *That* caught his attention. He shifted, as though he intended to come to me, but I put a hand up and moved silently across the hay-strewn floor.

He took each piece from my hand greedily, crunching on the fruit.

Satisfied, I unfolded the blanket and spread it over Will's sleeping form. From my vantage point, he seemed like the same old William Ellis. But I knew he'd be forever changed.

Audrey told me they'd talked. Even if he didn't say much. That he could still see blood on his stallion.

I didn't know how to help him, but I did know how to take care of people. Even if they didn't want it. He seemed peaceful as he rested, unlike our last interaction. When he'd kissed me in the hallway and stalked away. I longed to reach across the space, to hold him against me until he realized I wouldn't let him lose himself in his grief.

Instead, I pivoted toward the stall door.

"What do you want?"

I stilled. There was an exhausted note to his voice. When I turned back to him, Will peered at me, his face expressionless.

"Who said I wanted anything from you?" I asked, annoyed.

"Everyone always does. Whether it's a job, my help, or absolution of their own guilt." My brows furrowed at the bitter edge in his voice. At his words. As if I were here to use him. He lifted his hat and placed it back onto his head, tugging the brim low over his eyes. "Get out."

"Forgive me for ensuring you didn't *starve*." If he truly thought that I came here for myself, he didn't really know me at all. Maybe I didn't know him. I reached over the stall door, fumbling with the latch.

"Is that fresh bread?"

When I turned back to face him, his features had softened. He tilted his head toward me. The ghost of my friend reflected back at me.

A peace offering.

My gaze dropped to the basket near my feet. Without breaking eye contact, I lifted it and moved toward him. He sat up, focused on the basket. I unfolded the linen covering and set it beside him. His eyes widened hungrily. I'd been right. He hadn't been eating. As he reached for the basket, I headed for the stall door again.

"Eat with me."

This was a bad idea. A very, *very* bad idea.

"Please, Savvy."

I couldn't walk away.

I didn't *want* to walk away.

He didn't know it, but I needed his presence, too. I needed his sarcastic commentary and disarming grin. I needed that familiarity, to remind myself that the horrors I endured wouldn't last forever.

Even as I repeated how bad of an idea this was in my head, I lowered myself into the hay next to him. His hands stilled in the basket, his eyes darting between me and his horse.

"He didn't try to bite you." He tore a piece of bread. Steam rose up from it. "He likes me."

"He doesn't like anybody."

I watched his deft hands retrieve the jar of honey. "He likes apples."

As if sensing we spoke of him, the stallion lowered his snout toward me. He sniffed my hair, and my eyes fluttered shut as I bit back the panic in my chest. The horse's sniffs grew more persistent as he moved to my empty pocket.

"Sorry, boy," I said. "I'm fresh out."

Will reached into the pocket of his shirt and retrieved a handful of sugar cubes. The stallion whinnied in excitement, inhaling the treats in seconds. Visibly pleased, the horse gave me a final sniff before turning away.

We sat in a comfortable silence. Will passed me a piece of bread. I took a bite but found myself staring at him. He shoved the honey-covered bread into his mouth. One by one, he brought his fingers to his lips and licked the dredges of honey from them. My skin heated as I remembered how his deft fingers traced the tender flesh of my breast in the kitchen. Only when Will met my eyes did I realize I was staring.

I lowered my gaze to the bread in my hands quickly. Too quickly. I thought I saw a grin tug at his mouth, but I couldn't be sure.

As I chewed the last of my bread, Will unscrewed the whiskey bottle. I forced tension from my shoulders, allowing myself to lean against the stallion. His warmth seeped through my clothes, staving off the chill.

"How do you sleep in here?" I crossed my arms over my chest. "I swear, I've never seen someone who can fall asleep anywhere or as fast as you do."

Will offered the bottle of whiskey, but I shook my head. "Why don't you ever drink?"

The question disarmed me. He'd taunted me about not drinking in the past. I was certain more than a few comments were made about my need to loosen up, live a little. But he never pressed beyond the casual joke. I worried my lip between my teeth, untying and retying the sash of my robe to keep my hands busy.

I'd seen what could happen when one was lost to substance. My throat bobbed as an image of my mother with her blue-stained lips passed through my mind.

I was quiet for so long that surely, Will would let it go. But when I dared to look at him, he stared back in quiet contemplation.

Why would you return to the woman who sold you?

That single question threatened to unravel every fiber stitching me together for the last decade. I lowered my gaze to my fingernails, picking beneath them as I said, "My mother." I'd never spoken to anyone in this house about her. It hurt too much. "You heard how Lee spoke of her. She . . ." I sucked in a breath and blew it out with more force than necessary. "Glowroot. Alcohol." I lifted my eyes to his. "*Men.*"

My face heated. I should stop. I should just shut up, but once I started talking, I found it difficult to stop. "I've seen what addiction does to a person. I've witnessed how it makes one forget themselves. Lose control." I cleared my throat. "I can't afford to lose control."

Will's fingers twitched around the neck of the bottle. My heart stuttered at the thought that he might reach for me. Instead, he fished a cigarette out and lit it. As smoke curled on the cool evening air, he said, "Lee lies, you know." He lifted his head, staring at me until I met his gaze. "What he said about your mom—"

Nope. I wasn't doing this.

I snatched the bottle from him and brought it to my lips. The whiskey burned as I took a too-large gulp. I coughed, sputtering on the drink. In a heartbeat, his hands found me, helping me to sit up straighter and rubbing my back gently as I gasped for a breath that didn't burn.

"Maybe try a sip next time," he whispered in my ear. His breath washed across the sensitive skin of my neck. Goosebumps prickled along my arms. It wasn't until he plucked the bottle from me and his hand stilled on the small of my back that I realized just how close we were.

Too close.

Will's gaze darted between my eyes and my lips. I leaned into his embrace, into his warmth. His arm curled further around me. I shouldn't have let him, shouldn't have encouraged it, but I *needed* to feel him, needed to know that hope wasn't completely lost.

I reached across him, snagging the bottle back. My nose curled as I lifted it to my lips and took a tentative sip of whiskey. It burned, but not as bad as before. I felt Will's gaze on me the entire time, unsure if amusement or concern lined his eyes. I lifted the bottle again, daring to take a bigger sip.

When I finished, he grabbed the bottle and took a long pull from it.

Warmth pooled low in my belly, coursing through my veins and settling deep in my bloodstream. I lowered my head onto his shoulder, limbs loosening beneath the effect of the whiskey. Will leaned back, resting us against his stallion.

The silence that stretched between us was peaceful. For the first time in days, my mind relaxed, and my body became pliant.

"Growing up," Will said, the deep inflection of his voice reverberating through each part of me pressed against him, "every waking moment was a nightmare. The only place I wasn't afraid, where I could find peace, was escaping into sleep."

My father ripped them apart when he gave her that head wound and tried to cut my fuckin' face off.

I shuddered at the thought of Sixgun's cruelty. I'd never witnessed it, but I'd heard plenty of stories from Etty and the others over the years.

"That's how I can fall asleep anywhere." He lifted the bottle to his lips. He offered it to me after he drank, and I took it. I liked the heavy, relaxed feeling in my limbs. It should scare me. But I was safe. With him.

"I can see why people drink." I felt lazy, but in a good way.

My troubles didn't matter so much.

"I didn't understand back . . . home," I said, brows pinching together. The word felt wrong. St. Louis had never been home. A lump formed in my throat. "Lee was right about . . . *her*." My eyes slammed shut against the building heat. "We only had each other. I was born in the brothel where she worked. She . . ." I blew out a breath. Absentmindedly, Will ran his fingers in a gentle circle along the small of my back. It grounded me. "She'd send me down the street to the glowroot dens for her supply. Her hands shook as she drank it. Then followed it with whatever cheap liquor the brothel had on hand."

I bit my bottom lip to still its trembling. "It was like she had to be out of her mind to . . . to . . ." My cheeks heated, a sliver of embarrassment through my tipsy state. "It only got worse when the madam threw us out. There were days I thought she wouldn't wake up."

I took a long pull from the bottle, cringing slightly as the whiskey burned. As I passed it back to him, Will captured my wrist in one hand. His thumb brushed across the nearly faded bruises, sending a prickle of goosebumps across my arm. They'd clearly been finger imprints, but now it was hard to make out the shapes.

"Which guard did this?"

I averted my eyes. Instead of answering, I brought the whiskey back to my mouth and sipped. Drinking was easier than telling him the truth. And I *wanted* to tell him. But if he didn't believe me, I couldn't handle it. So I kept silent.

Will tangled his fingers with mine, lowering our joined hands to rest across his stomach. My eyes fluttered shut, and I tucked in close against his side. His arm tightened around me, his hand resting on the curve of my waist. His soft lips fluttered across my forehead, sending my heart into my throat.

It hurt. Holding back from him. I wanted nothing more than to let him kiss me, let him have me, as long as he didn't look at me the way he had that night, as long as he didn't pull away from me.

As long as I didn't lose him, too.

What a foolish thought. He wasn't mine to lose.

With flushed cheeks, I tipped my head back to look at him. His eyelids were low, hooded, hiding what he thought and felt from my gaze. Not that I thought I'd be able to read it. My vision wavered around the edges. He tipped his head toward mine. Our foreheads pressed together, whiskey-tinged breaths mingling on the cool night air, though I was anything but cold anymore.

"Will—"

He cradled my cheek, brushing a calloused thumb across my skin. I trembled against that touch, against how much I wanted him to do it again. I tipped my chin toward his. Our lips brushed for less than a heartbeat before my eyes slammed shut, and I shook my head, our foreheads still pressed together.

"Savvy," he whispered. I continued to shake my head. "Look at me."

"I can't."

"Why not?"

"Because I want you," I whispered, even as he leaned closer and whispered his lips across mine once more. Tempting me. He made me want to forget my rules.

All of my rules.

"I can't give you what you want," he said, voice low, solemn. "Seb didn't understand that either." His voice cracked on the man's name. My eyes fluttered open, noting the dim, dead expression in his. "I'll only disappoint you."

He truly believed that. My heart ached.

I bit my bottom lip, brows furrowing as I tried to make sense of my tipsy mind. "I don't want to be some mask you only wear to hide your grief, William."

"I'm not masking anything, Savvy. All I have left is grief." Lines creased across his forehead as he fought back against the sorrow shining in his eyes.

"You have me," I whispered.

Will brushed his thumb across my bottom lip. My mouth parted on a sigh. He was so close. So damn close. All it would take was a little—I tipped my chin up. Our lips met. He kissed me slowly, languidly, just the press of our mouths together. The hand cradling my cheek slid down the side of my throat, over my shoulder, across my arm, leaving heat in its wake.

Through my drunken haze, I felt his hand on my hip. He flexed his fingers, gripping my flesh. I shuddered at the contact. It felt so good to have his hands on me. Too good. Like the devil tempting Eve with the forbidden fruit. I was weak for him.

"What do you want from me? *Really?*"

"I—"

At my hesitation, Will pulled back. I tangled my fingers in his hair, tugging him to me, covering his lips with mine in a searing kiss.

Desire throbbed deep within me. I hadn't known what I was feeling before, when we'd kissed in the kitchen. But I understood now. How at the most basic level, my body reacted to his kiss, his touch.

"Savvy—"

I'd already let this go too far. He tugged the hem of my robe upward, his fingers grazing along my bare thigh. My mind raged like a stormy sea swirling out of control. It was too easy to fall into him like this. I didn't want to be someone he only kissed because he needed a distraction.

But the truth was . . . I needed one, too.

I'd left my room because I couldn't sit alone with my thoughts, couldn't relive my past.

How was that any different?

It wasn't.

It could have been the whiskey. It could have been my own grief. It could have been a million little things.

I couldn't deny him.

I couldn't deny *myself.*

He tugged the shoulder of my robe and nightgown away and leaned over me, sweeping his lips across the swell of my breast. I arched into him, desperate to feel his skin against mine.

The horse chuffed behind me, as if in admonishment.

Will pulled back as ridiculous laughter bubbled inside of me. His brown eyes lit up at the sound. Warm, calloused fingertips brushed across my bare shoulder as he stared down at me, the corners of his mouth turned upward.

"There he is." I cradled his cheek.

"Who?" A shadow of confusion darkened the warmth in his eyes.

"William." A smile curled on my mouth. I blinked, eyelids drooping lazily and lifting once more. I ran my thumb along his stubble-lined jaw. His eyes closed, and he lifted a hand, tangling his fingers with mine.

"You're drunk," he said, though his features remained soft.

"'S your fault," I slurred.

"Yeah, everything usually is," he mumbled.

Shifting, Will moved to my side, curling his arms around me and tugging me against his chest. He kissed my shoulder, arms tightening around my waist. As my eyes fluttered shut, he righted my clothes and covered me with the blanket I'd brought for him.

The whiskey lulled me into the most peaceful sleep I'd ever had.

The morning sun angled into the barn, casting across my eyes. I grumbled and rolled over, surprised to find the solid, warm body curled around me. My eyes fluttered open. Will was deep in sleep.

My head pounded in time with my heart.

I ran my hand through his dark brown hair. He inhaled sharply, and I snatched it back, fearing that I'd woken him.

Boots thumped against the floor, headed in our direction. My gaze darted back to his face, to how his brows knit together. If I hadn't woken him up, whatever was coming certainly would.

"Check every single stall," one of the guards barked. I recognized that voice.

I needed to extract myself from Will, before they found me. Only, my limbs were heavy, sluggish. I sat up as a guard I didn't recognize poked his head over the stall door.

"Found Savannah," he said to someone on the far end of the stable. Heavy boots trudged toward us.

A cruel grin spread across the man's mouth. Jimmy. Sebastian's buddy. The one who'd locked me in the closet. How did he survive his interrogation unscathed?

"Well, well." He sneered at me as Will sat up. "You're not where you're supposed to be."

I rolled my eyes at him and stood, swiping the dirt and hay from my robe. The guard's eyes trailed my bare legs, something dark passing in them.

"Lockdown was lifted last night, asshole," Will said, bringing a match to the cigarette hanging between his lips. "Last I checked, it's not your job to police where the staff goes."

"No," he said, eyeing Will with hatred. "But it is my job to make sure the *ladies* of the house are safe." As if Will were a danger.

"Oh, fuck off." I moved to the stall door. The guard unlatched it, and I shoved it open hard enough to make him grunt and glare at me.

"Where's Audrey?"

"I'm not her keeper." I glanced at Will one last time. "If you're so concerned about the ladies' wellbeing, maybe *you* should know where she is."

I stormed into the house, mortified, frustrated, and, strangely, at peace with whatever was between me and Will. Even if I wouldn't admit it.

CHAPTER FORTY-TWO

AUDREY

THE HAZE OF MORNING washed over me like warm water, stirring me from the most peaceful sleep I'd ever had. Strong arms wrapped around my waist, sealing me into the cradle of his body. When I cracked my eyes open and drank in the softened lines of his face, I remembered the last day.

My brother and uncle are outside the city, I'll write to them, and we'll figure a way out together.

A way out. Together. So we could leave this place behind and be married in Fort Hood. A safe place he'd made a home in. We'd made love so many times yesterday, exploring each other in every position, on every surface, over and over again. Until we fell into exhausted bliss. Whispering dreams for the future in the quiet moments between. How many children we wanted, the kind of house he would build for us, my nervousness about meeting his family, and his breathy confession that they would love me. Like *he* loved me.

The sheets were tangled around us, but as I began to kiss his neck to wake him, they didn't stop his hands from wandering along my spine. They folded over the curves of my ass, and he grunted sleepily, eyes cracking open.

"You have the most glorious ass," he muttered into my hair, squeezing again. I squirmed, letting my fingers trail through his hair as he yawned himself into wakefulness.

"You may have mentioned that once or twice last night." I grinned. He buried his face in my shoulder, kissing my neck and rolling me underneath him as his hands traced my body, mapping me.

"Are you complaining?" Amusement tinged his words. I shook my head, and he pulled back to stare down at me. The raw carnality in his eyes sucked the breath from my lungs. I would never tire of him looking at me like I was the best thing that ever happened to him. "Good."

With a soft giggle bubbling from my lips, he resumed his exploration. Until I was breathless and quivering beneath him, desperate to have him inside me. Low voices and heavy boots sounded on the stairs, and we stilled as fear burned in the space between us.

"Montana!" someone called from the balcony outside the room. Rapid knocking echoed. "Savannah and Audrey are missing from their rooms."

"I'll get rid of them." He pushed me softly into the mattress and shuffled to the edge, where he picked up his clothes, which were strewn haphazardly around the room. "I'm coming!" He turned around with his shirt falling from his arms. I pressed my lips together to keep from laughing at how discombobulated he was. "I can't find . . . oh, fuck it."

He shoved his jeans on, without boxers, and zipped them quickly. Then he settled his shirt over his head, inside out. I dragged my bottom lip between my teeth, smiling so wide it hurt.

"If you keep looking at me like that, I'm going to say to hell with it and let the whole house know *exactly* what we were doing all night." He leaned down to press his lips hard against mine. He groaned, body wavering closer to mine on the bed before he pulled away, sighing. "Stay here, I'll be back in a few minutes to finish what we started."

He made his way carefully outside, the door clicking shut as the men's voices rose in conversation. I sucked in ragged breaths to still my furiously beating heart, willing my pulse to slow.

His voice was low and muffled as he moved away from the door to speak with the guards. I rolled onto my side and stood, stretching languidly before I crossed to his dresser and opened the top drawer. Finding a clean shirt that smelled like him, I shoved it over my shoulders. Just like the other one, it dwarfed me. Then, just as I went to close the drawer, something metallic glinted in the early morning light. Moving one of his shirts to the side, I revealed a small ivory-handled gun carefully tucked into a holster. I brushed my fingertips over the handle, each worn ridge of the carvings as familiar to me as the planes of my own face. I jerked away as if stung, unwilling to acknowledge the secrets it may unlock.

Already, slivers of my past welled up within me like a tidal wave. Images of brandishing that gun, tucking it into the waistband of my shorts, firing it while being chased out of some unknown town, holding it steady against someone's temple. A familiar temple. Blue eyes.

My head ached as a name bubbled to the surface of my mind: *Selene.*

Her name was Selene. And she was *mine.* Why did Jesse have a gun from my past? My stomach thrashed wildly as I slid her out of the holster, her weight familiar in my hand. Like an extension of my arm. Small and deadly.

Shock and recognition clashed together inside of me. I looked wildly around the room for something, anything to explain this. It couldn't be a coincidence, but if it wasn't, then that meant . . .

My gaze landed on his sketchbook. Discarded like he'd been working in it moments before I arrived yesterday. His latest sketch was half uncovered, and I recognized the sharp slant of my eyebrows. I opened the book to see my face, eyes glazed in passion, mouth swollen and lost in ecstasy. I knew immediately this was an image of me from the night after the fight by the angle of the perspective. He'd taken such care with the deep curve of my eyes as he sketched. There was reverence in the lines of my face that made me realize this was how he saw me.

And in his eyes, I was *beautiful.*

A kind of beauty I never saw. My skin flushed as the memory of his hard hands and his wicked mouth rushed to the surface. It burned all the way from my cheeks to the deep longing swallowing me whole in my chest. I wasn't thinking right. There was no way this was the same gun. It had to be my broken mind playing tricks.

I flipped the page. Another image of me, knees tucked tight against my chest as sunlight spilled over my hair in the window seat of the library, completely engrossed in my book. When I turned the page this time, I didn't recognize the image. I didn't recognize myself in this sketch, yet something about it called to a part of me that felt like it'd been missing for too long. It was just a sketch of my face, staring straight at him, with a derisive arch of my eyebrow and a teasing smile on my lips. Another unfamiliar sketch came after this one.

My hair was wet and wild, breasts bared to the night as moonlight spilled over the planes of my stomach, nipples peaked in pleasure or cold . . . I couldn't be sure which. My dress bunched around my middle, thighs shining and splayed open. The arch of my neck and the curve of my spine displayed my body in a way I never imagined I would see myself. It was *intimate*, and I wondered if this was a fantasy he'd sketched to life. My heart hammered in my ears as I gazed at it.

With a perverse fascination, I needed to see more. To see them all. So I turned the page to find a young boy, eyes lit in curiosity, hair at odd angles. The thud of recognition slammed into me, stealing my breath. I raked my eyes over every detail of his face. I could feel my mind screaming at me, begging me to remember. Because I felt the softness of his hair running through my fingers. I couldn't breathe. Why couldn't I breathe?

I flipped to the next page.

There I was again, naked, the sun peeking over my shoulder as my hair whipped behind me, my body bowed as calloused hands gripped my hips. I drank in every line, every detail, every single stroke of his talented hands. My hands trembled as I spied the scars along my ribs, the fresh bandage on my hip. My mind whirled as suspicion and doubt bloomed like a flower in my chest. I ripped the image from the sketchbook, holding it in both hands so tight it crinkled at the edges.

The more I studied the image, the sharper my suspicion became. Snippets of conversation since Montana had arrived, odd reactions to normal situations, glances that lasted too long, too loaded with emotions I didn't understand, rained down in a torrent. Messy and out of order.

I'd known on some level from the beginning that things hadn't added up. I'd known the entire time, but I ignored it. Because his harsh beauty and soft attention had snuck past my defenses and into my heart.

Something cracked wide in my chest as the instances flooded through me of each moment, each doubt solidifying into a thorn that pierced my skin. They overwhelmed me like deep water closing over my head and filling my lungs until I couldn't breathe.

The door creaked open, but my eyes were glued on the sketch. Silence stretched for a moment too long before I looked up, schooling my features into an expression of careful curiosity. Jesse looked between me and the sketches falling from the pages of his book. So many of them were of me.

Then, his gaze fell to the gun gripped tight in my hand. As if it were glued to my palm.

"What is this?" I asked, the sketch still fisted tight. His shoulders tensed, and those blue eyes that always said so much shuttered until I couldn't read them. A sheepish smile crossed his mouth but didn't reach his eyes. He rubbed the back of his neck as he moved forward. I marked each movement, studying every expression so carefully it was hard to make sense of all of them at once.

"What can I say? I have a vivid imagination," he said in an easy tone. Too easy, too practiced. I closed my eyes briefly to disguise the hurt that would've undoubtedly flashed across my expressive face.

I wanted him to confess, I realized. I wanted him to explain. I wanted him to do *anything* other than lie. I opened my eyes to see him staring too intensely at me. I moved, footsteps even as I rounded the bed and crossed closer to him but kept out of reach.

"Yes," I breathed out. "Incredibly vivid. You have a real eye for detail."

It took so much effort to keep the sorrow and strain from my words as my gaze dropped to the sketch again. My vision blurred, and I blinked rapidly to clear my eyes of the emotion I wanted so desperately to hide.

"I thought this part was a nice touch." I brandished the sketch, pointing to the scars etched in a perfect map of crisscrossing violence along my ribs. "Considering you only saw these scars for the first time yesterday."

His eyes snapped to mine, wide and suddenly fearful. He stepped forward, but I lurched away from him, raising Selene between us instinctively. Tension snapped tight in the room, delicate and wavering in the air, neither knowing how to move forward or how to go back. He *lied*. The realization sliced through the confusion of the moment. He lied to me. What else had he lied about?

"Say something," I commanded, watching as he swallowed hard. I tracked his Adam's apple as it bobbed. Never once did his eyes even dip towards the gun leveled at his chest.

"It's not what it looks like," he finally choked out. Reckless tears built in the corners of my eyes as a hysterical laugh bubbled out of my mouth. Incredulous and painful. I placed the gun on the small table. I didn't need that in my hand right now, not feeling as frantic as I did.

"I'm such a *fuckin' idiot*." I dragged a hand through my hair and pulled hard at my scalp. "I'm so *stupid*." I tried to quiet the rushing pulse in my ears. He stepped forward again, once, twice, but I leveled him with a glare that stopped him in his tracks.

"*Who are you?!*" Water wobbled low in my vision, distorting his handsome features into something horrific. "Are you another spy, like Sebastian? Will used to work for Jones, and you knew him before he worked here—"

"No!" The word held so much disgust and offense that I wanted to believe him. His blue eyes turned desperate and liquescent, and he held out open palms as he inched forward. As if afraid of spooking me, though he desperately needed to touch me. To feel the warmth of my skin. The need for that kind of comfort surged forward from me, too.

But he'd already fooled me once.

"You know who I am." The words were so raw it hurt to hear them. "You just have to remember."

"I know who you are," I forced between my teeth, the words tinged with cruelty. "You're a *liar*."

"I have *never* lied to you." The words struck like lightning in a storm, cracking through the air and stealing my anger for a moment. "You know me. You know me better than anyone. We were—" He glanced away, his chest heaving. When he finally looked at me again, his eyes were glassy with emotion.

"We were in love."

I shook my head, tears spilling over my cheeks as he crossed the distance between us. His trembling hands grasped my arms, trying to pull me into the warm cage of his body as he had a dozen times before. I shook my head again, pulling from his grasp as the blade of his words twisted deep in my chest. I thought I was safe with him. Now it felt like nothing more than a cheap trick. My lip wobbled as I sucked in a ragged breath.

"You've never lied to me?"

He swallowed again, shaking his head and breathing so hard I couldn't hear my words over his ragged breaths. "Never," he confirmed with steely resolve.

"Then answer this: were you there when I was attacked three years ago?" The words tumbled out in a hot rush. Silence stretched long between us. One heartbeat. Three. Five. Fifteen. In that silence, my worst fears were confirmed.

"Yes." His admission rolled through me like a tidal wave. "But I would never hurt you." Not the denial I so desperately wanted.

"How about this: who's Emma's father?" The question burned as it passed through my throat. Like acid. Like shards of glass. Ready to destroy me.

His eyes never left mine, but they shifted, filling with unshed tears I didn't know how to interpret. Pain that mirrored my own suffering reached me, raking claws deep in my chest and slicing so deep that I didn't know if I'd be able to stand upright much longer.

"*Please*, I—"

"I *trusted* you." I wrenched from his grasp. Devastation rocked through me as I leaned against the door of his room. *No. No, it couldn't be.* But I felt it in the secret part of me that'd always been so connected to her. His blonde hair, so like hers, and the perfect cupid bow of his upper lip was *exactly* the same.

"Goddamnit, if you'll just let me explain—" he tried again, but tears rolled hard over my cheeks.

"I know that boy in your sketches! Selene. And sometimes you say things that—it's . . . I *can't*." My fingers dove into my hair, pulling hard as pieces of who I used to be fit together and shattered all over again. "I can't hear more of your half-truths and pretty lies. Even if you did start telling me the truth now, how could I ever believe you? Don't you get it? You've *ruined* us." I mopped at my eyes with the back of my hands before reaching for the knob behind my back. Slamming the sketch to his chest in my clenched fist, I opened the door behind me.

"I'm not this . . . this fantasy woman you've drawn, and you aren't who I thought you were either." I retreated onto the breezeway. "I want you to stay away from me."

I turned, rushing through the door and catching myself on the railing, not caring anymore if anyone caught me. I gasped as the dark pit in my stomach reserved for my grief yawned wide and threatened to swallow me whole. Jesse was right on my heels, but I jerked away, swiping unruly tears as I marched down the stairs and toward the main house. I didn't get far before his hands were on my arms again, turning me to him.

Without thought, my hand flew through the air. The crack of my open palm against his face echoed in the courtyard as his head jerked to the side. My palm stung, but I clenched my teeth together against the furious words clawing to the surface.

"*I said stay the* fuck *away from me!*" I shouted, catching on the edge of my hysterical sorrow. I clenched my throbbing hand into a fist and backed away from him until I was sure he wouldn't follow me again. I ran toward my room.

Run.

It pulsed inside of me, like it had on restless days. Like it had for so long. I heeded the urge now. I ran. Knocking into Etty as I hurtled through the kitchen, wild, gasping tears on my breath. She called to me, but I didn't listen. Instead, my bare feet slapped against the oak plank floor as I reached my room. The guards were so surprised by my sudden appearance, they didn't even question when I stormed inside. Savannah leapt at the violence of my entrance but didn't ask when I threw myself on the bed and curled around one of my pillows.

She took a moment, then climbed behind me and let me wail into the feathers of my pillow, stroking my hair. Until my eyes were sore. Until nothing made sense anymore. The way nothing had made sense ever since Jesse had arrived here. Until now.

He knew me *before*. And while I didn't know the specifics, I knew he was involved in both my pregnancy and the attack that nearly killed me. The storm of my sorrow raged until my eyes were so sore I couldn't cry anymore if I tried.

"Do you want to talk about it?" Savannah's hand made gentle circles on my back. I still wore his shirt, his scent clinging to my skin. A whimper escaped my throat, and my lips trembled as I looked up at her.

"H-he lied," I said. "He knew me. This whole time, he *knew* me. He's . . ." I couldn't say the words. Couldn't say *Emma's father*. Savannah stiffened, her hand falling away from me. Her warm, concerned eyes turned dark and dull with guilt. My stomach fell to the floor.

"You *knew*?" The words came out in an accusatory hiss. "You knew who he was this whole time?"

"Just since the hurricane party," she said in a hot rush. My mind spun. My reality fractured. That chasm of pain that'd been knitting together in her presence wrenched open again.

"Get out," I whispered.

"Audrey—"

"Is there *anyone* that hasn't been lying to me?" My sorrow flared into impotent rage more quickly than I'd thought possible. "Just . . ." I shook my head, standing swiftly from the bed and crossing to our shared door. "Get out."

She shuffled onto her feet, shoulders bowed, and left. I was alone with betrayal twisting in my gut and all the broken dreams of a future born from beautiful lies. All I was left with now was the ugly truth. That I'd given my heart to a man that hadn't deserved it.

My body shut down. To protect me from the harsh reality I wasn't strong enough to withstand. Maybe I was fragile, after all. I locked the doors from the inside and pulled his shirt off to lie crumpled on the floor. Then I curled into my bed and stayed there. Hiding from the pain that came in waves to break me apart, time and time again.

The first day was uneventful.

The second, Savannah knocked and tried to convince me to eat.

The third, my father attempted to get me to leave the room.

By the fourth, I made up my mind. I wanted to leave. Wanted to get away from the lies rotting me from the inside. So I stood on shaky legs and made my way dizzily into the bathroom, where I scrubbed my skin raw, trying to erase every touch and kiss, every place he'd loved me. Then, I ate. The food tasted like ash, but I swallowed it down anyway to regain my strength. When that was done, I dressed. I used my clothes like armor, to protect my heart from being vulnerable again. With mechanical movements, I readied myself into the picture of southern perfection, hair curled and resting gently over my shoulders. Pink sundress complimenting my skin tone.

When I finally emerged, guards stared at me in disbelief. With silent resignation. I made my way down the stairs and into one of my father's parlors, where Lucas usually played cards with his friends before dinner. And there he was, looking more solemn than I remembered ever seeing him before.

How the hell would I smile for him when it felt like I was dying? When he caught my eye across the room, he dismissed his friends and stood swiftly. I met him halfway, letting him fold me into his arms. He sighed deep against my hair, as if he'd been worried.

"Audrey, I'm so happy to see you. After everything, God, it's just not safe for you here anymore." He pulled back to look at me.

"That's what I came here to talk to you about." I offered him the barest hint of a smile. "I think you should marry me, Lucas."

His breath caught in his throat.

"I finalized my contract with your father this morning." His smile widened as shock from the news flashed across my face.

"So, you don't need me anymore," I said, sucking my bottom lip between my teeth.

"No, that's not what I meant! I've thought about what you said the night of the hurricane every day since."

My cheeks burned as I remembered my angry, ugly words. The threats I'd made. How I barely recognized my own voice. Or the ferocity humming in my blood. I accused him of only wanting me as a stipulation in that damned contract. Sorrow threatened to overwhelm me again, so I shook the thoughts away, offering an apologetic smile.

"God, I should never have said—"

"No." His thumb circled lazily on the back of my hand. "I'm glad you did. You were *right*. About everything. How could you ever know if my interest in you was real with the business negotiations hanging overhead? So, I finalized the contract, because I wanted you to know that what happens between us *isn't* about business."

Oh God. He wanted us to be in love. He wanted me to feel things for him that I didn't know I'd ever be able to feel again. I felt sick all over looking into his sweet, earnest face.

"I—" I had no idea what to say. The betrayal from earlier twisted in my gut, my heartbreak strangling me with a never-ending well of tears too close to the surface.

"Let me try to do this right." He breathed out nervously before dropping my hand to smooth the front of his shirt. "I wanted to finish the deal first, because I want you to know that how I feel about you has nothing to do with contracts or negotiations. We haven't known each other for long. Or made any passionate declarations of love."

I noticed his clothes then. I'd barely glanced at him when I walked in, overwhelmed by everything. Jeans, molded to his thighs, perfectly fitted. A white button-down shirt, top two undone and sleeves rolled at the elbows. He knew how much better I liked it when he wasn't so pristine and put together.

"But I know we could have a good life together. I think the best romances in history have started with a foundation of respect and friendship. And I know what it's like to feel trapped by circumstance. I can take you out of here, away from the people who want to hurt you. I can show you the world, or what's left of it, if you'll let me."

He knelt before me as tears began to roll down my cheeks. Every word was perfect. He was handsome and kind, patient and forgiving. He considered me at every turn, even in business matters, which he didn't try to hide like my father always had. Marrying him would be my escape.

From New Orleans. From my father. From *him.*

"Why me?" I had to know why he wanted me so much. He reached for my hand, squeezing it gently.

"Because you aren't afraid to be brutal with me. Because you don't give a shit about my money or my success. You challenge me to be a better man. To remember to stop and enjoy my life. Because you're smart and beautiful and *devious*, and that is sexy as hell. And I could keep going for days—"

"Yes." The word tasted bitter on my tongue as tears rolled unhindered down my cheeks.

"I haven't asked you yet." He let out a shuddering laugh. The tenuous moment grew taut as he pulled a ring from his front pocket. The stone was brilliant and clear in the light. He slid it onto my finger with a smile that was soft and reserved just for me. "It was modeled after my mother's." I stared at the large stone engulfing my hand. "Will you, Audrey Lee, do me the honor of becoming my wife?"

With every fiber of my body rebelling against me, screaming at me to pull away, to force my feet to move, I nodded.

He laughed, a joyful sound that echoed in my ears as he scooped me into his arms. Gathering me against him, he kissed me swiftly. He buried his hands in my hair and leaned his forehead against mine.

"I'm going to spend the rest of my life making you happy." He brushed the tears from my cheeks. I sniffled and nodded again, afraid to speak. Afraid to move. Afraid that if I did anything, the truth would spill from me like dark rivulets of blood.

That even through his lies and betrayal, there was only one man I'd ever love. And it wasn't my fiancé.

CHAPTER FORTY-THREE

JESSE

"I T'S A MIRACLE YOU didn't break it a second time," the doctor admonished from over his spectacles.

The day after Audrey looked at me like I was a monster, I tried to get to her room. Though lockdown was over, guards patrolled day and night, as if Lee expected an attack at any moment.

The second day, I didn't even try.

By the third, I stockpiled enough whiskey to send myself into sweet oblivion.

On the fourth, I punched a wall. Again. Shattering my cast.

"Do I need another cast?" Day five. My foot tapped impatiently against the floor, eyes darting to the open doorway. I forced my gaze to focus against my pounding headache, hoping, *praying*, I could catch her as she walked through the corridors.

"No, it's mostly healed." The doctor gathered the pieces of plaster and shook his head at me.

With my left hand, I pressed on the broken one, only feeling a slight twinge of pain. Good enough. I flexed my fingers, oddly rubbery after no real use in weeks.

"Do you need anything else, Mr. Montana?" The doctor stared at me exasperatedly.

I shook my head, rose, and strolled out of the room without another word. My gaze darted up and down the first-floor corridor as I contemplated whether it would be a good idea to check Audrey's room again.

The ache in my head cautioned against it.

I'd probably break something else.

Swearing beneath my breath at myself for being a dumbass, I headed for the back house. I checked in with Etty for news from The Kid or Mickey.

Instead, there was a letter from Gabriela, Mickey's girlfriend.

All is well to the west, if a little stir-crazy. You better send word soon. K's been spending too much time at target practice. Says he's gonna use those knives on Jones. Talk soon.

I wanted nothing more than to give my family good news. Unfortunately, I had none.

Everything was up in the air, and I had no idea how to fix it. Lee was under the impression I'd be traveling to Memphis for my next big fight. I had no intention of going, but I couldn't tell him that.

That single night with Audrey hadn't been nearly enough, and it had ended horribly. I'd allowed myself a momentary reprieve from everything. I fell into her, allowed myself to dream beyond the walls of this house.

I'd fucking *proposed*.

But that wasn't the worst of it. The worst part was . . . she accepted.

My mind rattled as I climbed to the second floor of the back house, so much that I missed the other staff members passing. The house seemed more alive today. But all I could do was drown in my misery.

The late-summer air blasted against my skin. I glanced over the courtyard, brows furrowing at the activity below. Men and women moved tables, chairs, floral arrangements . . . What in the world?

I glanced up at the sound of soft footsteps, my heart stuttering.

Savannah carried a bundle of dark fabric in her hands as she strolled toward me. It'd been a while since I'd seen her. Well before the lockdown.

"Savannah," I said by way of greeting.

Dark eyes flashed to me, widening as she froze ten feet away. She often seemed uncomfortable in my presence.

"Jesse." She lowered her gaze and continued walking.

"What's going on?" I asked as she neared me. Her gaze shifted from me to the courtyard and back. An approximation of guilt deepened the color of her cheeks. She looked down at the fabric in her hands, bunching it together as if to make it smaller. It was so dark it looked black, but as the sunlight washed over it, the fabric reflected a brilliant midnight blue.

There was only one person that could be for.

Audrey. It would match her eyes, accentuate her pale, smooth skin. Another blue dress flashed through my mind, and I *almost* smiled. What I wouldn't give to go back to that night. When things were simpler and our only worry was surviving the fall and clinging to each other.

The door to my room opened. Will appeared, shirt unbuttoned as usual and a cigarette dangling from his mouth. His eyes went to Savannah, curious but guarded. He'd been that way since everything with Sebastian. He hadn't pushed me about Audrey, even though he knew something was wrong.

I turned back to Savannah, waiting for her to answer, but she wasn't looking at me. Her attention had gone to Will, eyes dipping down the muscles of his stomach. The brown of her gaze darkened. She'd kissed him, Will told me.

Was it possible that he had, in fact, gotten her to fall for the *Ellis* charm?

I cleared my throat, and Savannah's attention snapped back to me. Her throat bobbed, and she blinked rapidly, confused. I motioned to the courtyard.

"Right." Her eyes darted to Will and back again. "An engagement party."

I lifted a brow at her in question. "Who?"

"Audrey." She clenched the fabric together. "And . . . Lucas Rutherford."

Her words struck me like a runaway train. Surely, I'd misheard her.

Will let out an incredulous laugh. "What?"

Savannah sighed, exasperated. "If you want me to explain, I can't. Audrey's not talking to me either." She glared at me.

"What did I do?"

"You and"—she turned her hard eyes to Will—"*him*. She found out that I knew the truth. Told me to get out and hasn't spoken to me since."

"Shit, Savannah, I'm sorry. I didn't mean for this to involve you—"

"What *did* you mean?" She advanced on me. She seemed much larger all of a sudden, because I felt like I should shrink away from her hard expression.

"I—well, I mean—"

"That's what I thought," Savannah snapped. "You know, you've wanted to get her back so bad, yet what have you *actually* done?" She advanced, forcing me back a step. "*I* secured passage on a river boat. I actually tried to get her out of the city. But *no*, Jesse, who's been looking for her for *years*, just sits on his ass and toys with her feelings—"

"Enough," Will said firmly.

Savannah turned her hard gaze to Will but snapped her mouth shut. "Right. I'm off. Audrey needs some last-minute alterations, and apparently I'm the only person in this house who knows her measurements." I narrowed my eyes at her as she took one last, long look at Will and barreled between us down the breezeway.

"That was weird."

"What was?" Will asked, taking a drag from his cigarette. I tipped my head toward Savannah's receding form.

"She was mean to *me*. Not you."

His gaze trailed after, watching as she disappeared around a corner. His brows furrowed in thought.

"I got her drunk."

"You got her drunk and . . . what?"

He shrugged. "I just got her drunk."

"You two are strange."

He shrugged again and turned back into the room.

I didn't have time to sort out whatever might be going on between them. There were more pressing matters to deal with.

Like Audrey marrying fucking Rutherford.

Even if I wanted to question *why* she'd done it, I already knew. I hadn't lied to her, not really. But I hadn't told her the truth. After learning that her father had lied to her for years, that everyone in the household had, I couldn't blame her for being angry.

Though she wasn't Bonnie, this was a very Bonnie thing to do.

Run. As far and as fast as she could.

I needed to talk to her. To explain myself. She wouldn't let me the other night, but I had to find a way to corner her, a way that she couldn't just brush me off.

"What's our move?" Will asked, settling in a chair.

"*Our* move?" I lifted an eyebrow at him.

"Yeah, I see that look on your face. You're plannin' on gettin' her back, aren't you, *pendejo*?" He stumped his cigarette out on the table.

"Of course, but I'll figure it out. You have enough—"

"C'mon." His eyes were bright and enthusiastic. He looked more himself than he had since before Sebastian. It was the first sign of life I'd seen in him in weeks. "I want to help. Remember, me and Bonnie were runnin' cons *long* before your violent ass came along."

When Will grinned, I remembered shooting him in the desert. How he'd smirked at me when Bonnie tended to his wound.

I guess I *had* been pretty violent then.

"Only if you're up for it." I wanted to be considerate of what he was dealing with. Even if he didn't want to talk, in the quiet moments, I watched the shadows creep in on him.

"Duh, asshole. That's what friends do."

"I'll have to get her attention at the party. If I can get her alone, I can tell her the truth."

He blinked, the expression fading from his face.

"That's it?" Doubt filled his eyes. I exhaled sharply, holding my palms out.

"What do *you* suggest?"

A brilliant grin crossed his face, lighting up his brown eyes like the man I'd first met. "Lee had me look into Lucas after he showed up. There were rumors of him getting into the slave trade behind his father's back. I confirmed it by putting a little *pressure* on some of his contacts in the city, but I couldn't find any hard evidence." He paused to light another cigarette. "How much do you wanna bet there's proof in his room?"

A grin crossed my face to mirror his. "That's brilliant."

Maybe I was getting Will back, even if he wasn't completely himself yet.

Not long after, we set out together, weaving through the busy courtyard to the front house, toward Lucas's room near the main entrance. As we entered through the double doors leading into the oak-laden hallway, the man himself walked our way. His gaze lifted to us. He regarded Will carefully, as most people did in the house. A flicker of concern passed across his face before he took me in and stopped short.

"Montana," he said. I stilled. There was something in his gaze, suspicion and animosity. An ugly sneer wrinkled his nose. "I—"

Will tipped his hat back, and Lucas flinched. I fought against grinning at the satisfaction in my chest from the fear in the man's eyes.

"I look forward to your next fight," he said.

He started to walk off when Will said, "If you're not careful, it'll be against *you*."

"What?" Lucas asked.

"What?" Will echoed sarcastically.

I smacked my hands onto Will's shoulders. "We should get going. My friend here has a *job* to do."

Rutherford visibly shuddered. I shoved Will down the hallway.

Once Rutherford was out of sight, we headed directly for his room. I kept an eye out while Will picked the lock. We entered silently. As expected, everything was neat and in order. The bed made, the desk organized. Will opened the wardrobe.

I grabbed one of the books from the desk and flipped the pages. It looked like a journal. Tidy scrawl lined the pages, detailing meetings with Lee and their trade deal, but nothing incriminating. I slammed it shut.

"Shit, are these Cubans?" Will asked, flipping open the lid of a wooden box. Sure enough, he pulled a cigar out and ran it beneath his nose, inhaling deeply. He tucked five or six into his pockets and slammed the lid shut. I rolled my eyes and picked up the second book. It was a list of numbers that didn't make sense to me. I set it down and turned my attention to the desk.

"Honestly, what kinda man drinks wine?" Will asked.

"A pompous fuck," I remarked, watching as he took a large pull from a fancy bottle. He made a face and spit the red liquid back into it.

"Expensive mouthwash, if you ask me."

I chuckled as I pulled out the drawers, rifling through them for anything suspicious. All I found were paper and pens.

"Hey, do you need a pocket watch?"

This time, my friend held a gold watch dangling from an expensive-looking chain. When I shook my head, he shrugged and tucked it into his pocket as well.

After a few more minutes of rifling through the wardrobe, he crossed to me and picked up one of the discarded books. I slammed the last drawer shut and moved to the bed, lifting the mattress to see if anything was under it.

Sure enough, there was a thick envelope with Lucas's name scrawled across it.

Will let out a low whistle as I retrieved the letter inside and unfolded it. My gaze roved over a map of the country. Lines in varying colors and consistency crossed the page. Across water, land, all over the place. Were these trade routes?

With the book from the desk in his hands, Will moved beside me. He scanned the map I held. "It's a ledger." He flipped to a page near the back. "But it doesn't match the register." A piece of paper fell out of the pages of the book. Will retrieved and unfolded it: a letter in a messy hand. But we both saw the signature at the bottom.

A hanged man singed on the page instead of a name.

"Lucas, you bad, bad boy." Will let out a low whistle.

"I need to show this to Audrey." Hope swelled in my chest. Would this be enough?

Will took the map from me and stuck it within the pages of the ledger before closing its cover and tucking it into the back of his jeans.

"Now what?"

Will turned to me, grinning. "It's time to spend some of your hard-earned gold. Let's go buy you a suit."

The midday sun was already high in the sky by the time Will steered me down Magazine Street. Like Bourbon, people flowed along the crumbling sidewalks, but, unlike Bourbon, these people dressed in what I assumed was the peak of fashion. I felt more out of place than I had since coming to the city. The streets were devoid of the usual litter, and the air smelled fresh.

One thing that wasn't different was the eyes that found Will and quickly moved away. A mere glimpse of him sent people from our path as he led me toward a row of boutiques. Mannequins lined the windows of one in particular, in pressed suits and glittering gowns.

From the moment we stepped inside, we knew we didn't belong.

It could have been the seamstress flinching every time that Will spoke, or how the manager kept shakily questioning whether we needed any more help. Once the woman went off to find something in my size, I turned to my friend. Will leaned casually against a wall, smoking as usual.

"Your turn."

Will lifted a brow at me, taking his time to pull from his cigarette.

"My turn for what?"

The seamstress returned, carrying a black suit. I took it, eyes searching the black coat, black vest, black shirt. It would be perfect.

"You can't wear *that* to the party." I stared at his blood-speckled jeans and worn button-down.

Will barked out a genuine, *Will Ellis* laugh. I stared, grinning but silent. The smirk fell from his face. "I'm not going to the party."

"I thought you were helping me." I passed my suit to the boutique manager so they could bag it.

"I already did, *hermano*." Will dropped his cigarette to the polished marble floor and stamped it out, not seeming to notice the scandalized look on the manager's face.

"Savannah will be there, I'm sure." I shrugged. "Doesn't she have a thing for pompous dicks in suits?"

Will's expression fell, and he groaned. "You don't think she'd go with that *pendejo*, do you?"

My smirk widened into a grin. "You won't know if you don't go."

"I fuckin' hate you sometimes." He climbed on the pedestal and let the seamstress get to work.

It was entirely too amusing, watching as the woman flinched or let out a frightened squeak when Will moved. He flipped me off when he caught me smirking, which only made my amusement grow.

For the first time in weeks, I had my best friend back. My *brother*. He wasn't the shell of a man that had returned to the house with Sebastian's body.

Once the seamstress stopped shaking enough to get Will's measurements, we were able to pay for our suits and leave. While I told the manager that he didn't have to give us any sort of discount, he insisted.

A smug smirk stayed on Will's face until we wandered back onto the street. The moment a woman caught sight of it, his features shifted into a grimace.

"Haven't you thought that if you looked a little friendlier, people wouldn't scurry away from you?"

Instead of responding, Will shrugged and lit a cigarette. Typical. Never one to answer personal questions. I didn't push. Instead, I tried to keep my jovial mood as we passed other shops.

"I hope you know I'm going to look ridiculous," he said, tossing the bag over his shoulder.

I chuckled, not bothering to hide my amusement. "You'll make me look better by comparison. Goal accomplished."

Sunlight glittered off of a store display. I stopped, eyeing the rows of jewelry glinting in the afternoon sun. There were rings in various shades and shapes. Necklaces. Bracelets. Watches like the one Will stole from Rutherford. But then, *there*. My heart stuttered and nearly stopped.

On the top row of the display, a comb nestled against black velvet. The teeth were made of silver. Dark blue stones lined the top, a spattering of diamonds and pearls interspersed between the sapphires.

Bonnie had lost hers in the river the night we jumped off a cliff. Maybe if I gave her something that reminded her of that night . . . Something I knew she once valued. Even if she wasn't upset over losing it then, I'd felt terrible because it was the last thing she'd had of Emma. The woman whose name she gave to our child.

"Does that one look like her mother's?" I pointed through the glass and turned to Will. "Do you think she'd like it?"

"How the fuck should I know?" he asked, elbowing me with a grin. "It's nicer than that piece of shit mask Lucas got her, though."

With a smile, I opened the shop door and disappeared inside. Hope flared anew in my chest.

Chapter Forty-Four

AUDREY

B LOOD SLICKED BETWEEN US, drying on our skin as he gripped me tight and tried to pull me from the darkness dragging me under. It was so cold. His skin felt like flames licking against my body. With each step, I fell further into nothingness.

Muffled words tinged with an edge of desperation and fear clouded his voice. The thudding footsteps stilled, and he held me tighter. Like his strength could somehow keep me tethered to the world as the radiating pain faded into an afterthought. "C'mon. Wake up."

But I couldn't open my eyes, couldn't speak. Not with the numbness that spread through my body and seeped out of me. Hot tears fell like rain on my cheeks, a choked sob echoing within me. It would be so easy to let go. I wanted to. I wanted to stop hurting. I wanted to rest. To stop fighting so hard all the time.

I struggled towards the surface and his words, until they cleared into recognition. "Don't leave me. Please." His lips feathered a tender kiss to my forehead. "I love you."

I wrestled toward him, fighting and clawing with everything inside of me. He needed me. We needed each other. It had to be enough. I couldn't drift away, not now.

I woke in a cold sweat, gasping into the darkness that still held the world tight in its grip. I didn't call for Savannah's comfort this time. Instead, I wrapped my arms around myself to still my trembling and bit my lip to hold back the whimper building in the back of my throat. The cold specter of death lingered after I woke. I felt it so starkly that it was a long few moments before I realized I wasn't dead. I was *here*.

Find things you remember.

That was what Savannah always said to help me find my way back. But now, what I remembered was blurred and distorted. Memories and flashes of a life I didn't recognize swam in my head, gauzy and ephemeral, alongside the stark reality of the last three years. Could I trust my own mind? Or had the damage from my injury finally plunged me into madness?

I looked around this room now, ostentatious and wasteful, and found nothing that made me feel like I had solid ground beneath my feet anymore. Silver-handled brushes, lavishly appointed furniture, hand-painted hurricane lanterns. None of this felt like me. None of this felt like *home.*

My gaze caught on a half-drunk bottle of whiskey, sitting sentry on my vanity, mocking me as a shaft of hazy morning light reflected off of it. I remembered the bead of liquor lingering on Jesse's full bottom lip as the storm raged both inside of me and beyond the windows. I remembered how I fit into his arms, tucked tight, in a spot that seemed made for me. How I'd felt so safe and at peace with his arms around me.

We were in love.

I'd read enough novels to know people believed love could conquer all, but that was fiction. And I didn't know if I'd ever forgive Jesse. For whatever part he'd played in the events that tangled somehow with Emma and my injury. Or for hiding his true intentions from me. I thought I'd cried all the tears out, but they reappeared. Painful this time. My eyes ached from crying.

Instead of waking Savannah, I slid out of bed quietly and crossed to my vanity as I did when the nightmares were bad. I studied my face for a long while. What I saw there was different than I expected. It was the same face, the same fierce beauty, but through my heartbreak, or because of it, there was strength I didn't have before. Sucking in a steady breath and holding it for a few moments, I wiped the salt tracks from my cheeks. Through the bars on my window, the sun climbed over the buildings of the square.

It was a new dawn, the first day of the rest of my life. I'd made my choices, and I would honor my promises. No matter how much it hurt. I entered the bathroom and ran a bath in the expansive tub, choosing peony as the scent for the water today. Delicate and feminine, something Lucas might like.

You smell like rain.

Stripping quickly, I stepped into the hot bath and relaxed into the encompassing heat. I slipped beneath the surface and let the water close over my head. Here, the rest of the world was muffled, except for the thump of my own heartbeat. I stayed under so long that by the time I re-emerged, I was gasping for air in a desperate rush, clutching the side of the tub as I finished quickly.

Tugging a soft robe over my shoulders, I brushed my wet hair. It was nearly to my waist now, spilling over my shoulders in thick, gleaming strands.

An eternity later, a soft knock came at my door, and Savannah bustled in. She carried a tray of food and a dress folded over one arm. She studied me carefully, as if worried at any moment I may break beyond repair. Or maybe she was waiting for me to throw her out again.

"What's all this?" I forced happiness into my words. From the look on her face, I hadn't fooled her. I sighed, wishing we hadn't fought. That I'd had her to bounce my macabre thoughts off of. "I'm trying."

"Etty put together a special breakfast for you. She's enjoying getting to cater an event like this." She set the tray on my desk, and I moved toward it. Strawberries and cream, sweet sticky buns, and crispy strips of bacon. The tray held fine china, a freshly-cut flower in a narrow vase, and a flute of champagne. A small yellow wildflower that reminded me of the ones tattooed on Jesse's arm.

"Champagne? For breakfast?" I blinked back furious tears and pretended to be happy. Savannah gazed over at me in agony, averting her eyes as I wiped away my tears.

"She doesn't know if she'll be able to cook for your wedding, so she's going a little overboard." Savannah plucked a strawberry off the tray and popped it into her mouth.

"That's really . . ." I swallowed the lump in my throat. "*Etty*," I finished lamely, but Savannah knew what I meant. How thoughtfulness was her constant state of being. How she made you feel loved without ever even speaking to you.

Savannah hung the dress on the bathroom door, and I watched the fabric flow like dark water across the wood grain. I bit into a strawberry, willing the ache in my heart to soften. It was beautiful and would go perfectly with the blue mask that Lucas had gifted me yesterday when the plans for this party began in earnest. He'd been so happy at my shock and delight when he confided that he'd requested a masked party.

After our day in the mask shop and our conversations about being free beneath them, the thoughtful detail endeared him to me even more. I ate mechanically, silently, as Savannah lowered into a spindly chair beside me. She covered my hand with hers. With eyebrows knitted together and concern in her warm brown eyes, she stilled my motions.

"I'm *sorry.*" Her words hung heavy in the air. She'd apologized several times now, but I hadn't been ready to hear it. I finished the strawberry and wiped my fingertips on the linen napkin resting gently on the tray.

"I forgive you." I offered her a gentle squeeze, and we laughed and blinked back tears. Until neither of us could take it anymore and we clutched each other tight. "Don't lie to me again, okay?" She nodded, mopping her cheeks. We ate in a comfortable silence together. I took a large swallow of the champagne to steel my nerves for the day ahead.

"Is *this* what you really want? To marry a man you don't love?"

I closed my eyes against her rush of questions before facing her and sighing deeply.

"Yes," I said plainly. "I know that I don't have *intense* feelings for Lucas. But feelings like that can be intensely good and intensely *bad.* I don't want to feel bad anymore. Lucas and I, we may not be some great love story, but he'll be kind to me. We'll be friends, and I know if I let him, that friendship might grow into love. He's *good* for me. And Lucas won't have the ability to hurt me the way *he* did."

She opened her mouth as if to argue, to convince me of something reckless and romantic, but after studying my face, the words died on her tongue. The worst part was that it was the truth. A future with Luke wouldn't be passionate and all-consuming. But feelings like that, how could you ever sustain them? They burned too bright and too fast. Like a shooting star racing across the night sky. Lucas wasn't a shooting star; he was Polaris. Constant and steady, a star you navigated by. He would care for me, and I cared for him, too, in my own way.

I turned back to my breakfast, picking up a slice of bacon before it clattered back to the fine china plate.

"Do you really think I'm stupid?" I asked, as the darkness of the night cocooned us in an embrace that for once didn't suffocate me. The warmth of his skin beat away the chill in the night air.

"No," he croaked, "I think you're the smartest person I've ever met."

And I believed him without a doubt. Because conviction laced his deep words, the kind of conviction that you could have faith in. The kind that would not fail when tested.

"Did you really climb into my bed because you thought I was upset about the train?" he asked, vulnerable now if the waver in his breath against my neck was any indication. Embarrassed, I buried my face against his dirty shirt. Enveloped by the scent of him. Soothed by the steady beat of his heart.

"No," I admitted. And it cost me something to admit it. "I don't have nightmares when you hold me."

"I don't have nightmares when I hold you either."

So I let him.

My chest ached with longing as I clutched my hand to my heart for a long moment. Grief swept over me as I remembered how safe I'd felt in his arms. I *remembered* it. It wasn't a dream or a flash of something insubstantial. I breathed slowly through trembling lips until the pain receded. Savannah was moments away from demanding to know what was wrong with me when a knock sounded at the door. Insistent and brash.

Without waiting to be invited inside, my father marched in confidently, appraising my appearance and the dress hanging on the door behind me. His dark eyes were lit with pride, an easy smile on his face.

"What do you want?" I didn't hide the cool hostility in my words. He raised one of the dark eyebrows I inherited from him, a harsh slant over the lines of his face.

"I came to congratulate you, and to talk for a few moments." He sat on the settee across the room. I sighed wearily, motioning to the copious amount of cosmetics and the last remnants of my breakfast.

"I have a lot to do to get ready. Can we make this quick?" I thought I saw a measure of hurt in his eyes before he hid his emotions behind a careful mask of indifference.

"Audrey." His voice was soft, like it always was when he'd spoken to me in the past. Before I saw him for who he really was. When I leaned on him to help me through the last few years. It hurt to imagine I might have been wrong about how much he cared for me. It hurt to reconcile my *father* with the man who'd done horrible things to people I care about.

"I—" he started, palms open. "I'm proud of you."

The words shocked me. I wasn't sure why. But they were so earnest, and his expression was open again. Genuine. It hurt more than I'd imagined possible.

"I know this arrangement hasn't been easy for you, that you've fought to find your place. Lucas is a good man, and you have no idea how important this will be for our family," he said. "My methods can seem harsh, but everything I've done has been to protect you."

"I want to be married in Manhattan Island. As soon as Lucas and I arrive. I expect you to be there for the event and to wrap up any outstanding business with Luke and his family. After that, I never want to see you again."

The softness in his eyes blinked away beneath his shock.

"Savannah." He addressed my friend, who stilled next to me. "I'm sure you have questions about your role in the house once Audrey is gone. The truth is, I took you on as her companion, and once she is no longer in residence, your primary function will no longer exist. When she prepares to leave for Manhattan, I'll provide you with enough money to start a life anywhere you wish. You'll be free to leave here with no conditions. I hope for your sake you'll have better fortune than your mother did." She flinched. With those parting words, he stood, smoothing his hands over his impeccably tailored waistcoat, touching his fingertips to his gold fleur-de-lis tie pin before leaving.

We didn't speak about him once he'd gone. We didn't talk about how much I wanted Savannah to stay with me, to come with me to Manhattan Island. It wouldn't have been fair of me to ask. Not after everything she suffered in this house. Not after the last few days. Instead, we fell into a routine that we knew well when my father had one of his extravagant parties.

Conversation turned to the guests attending and planning our outfits and accessories like we were preparing for battle. In a way, we were. New Orleans society had never been particularly kind to me. I was too damaged, too unstable, too hardened by tragedy to fit in with the gentlemen's daughters, with their soft smiles and effortless charm.

I was sure most of them agreed to the invitation expecting me to make a fool of myself. I had to be perfect. Above reproach. The gossips were in full force since the proposal yesterday. More than one shocked mother wrote to my father in the hours after to confirm that *the* Lucas Rutherford was officially off the marriage market.

With the help of a couple of maids, I lined my eyes and lengthened my lashes with kohl, accentuating their color. Faint pink rouge was dusted over my cheekbones to highlight the angles. My lips were painted the color of blood. Savannah, for once, allowed me to apply a soft layer of makeup on her that accentuated what was already beautiful about her. It took hours to curl her hair, leaving the strands long and twisting around her face before I pinned in tiny white flowers.

I couldn't decide if I wanted my hair up to show off the elegant length of my neck or down in sensuous, tousled curls. I asked Savannah for maybe the thirtieth time, earning a playful glare that forced a genuine laugh from deep in my throat.

A knock came at the door. Eyes wide, I turned to Savannah with a question on my lips. She shrugged, padding over in her bare feet and clutching her robe tight against the base of her throat as she opened the door a crack.

Will Ellis stood there, in a suit, shirt untucked and tie hanging loose around his neck. Half-dressed, as he usually was. He cleared his throat, and, with a wave of my hand, I dismissed the maids who'd been helping us get ready.

"I have something for Miss Audrey," he said, with no hint of his easy smile or the shadows that followed him like a dark cloud. "He wanted you to wear it tonight."

I didn't have to ask who he was talking about. My gaze fell to the floor as my heart lurched in my chest at the reminder. Savannah took a velvet box from Will and a folded piece of paper, promptly shutting the door in his face. My hands shook as she brought it over.

"I shouldn't open it," I said quietly. Savannah sat beside me and placed the box carefully in front of me. "I made my choice. I shouldn't entertain this."

"What harm could it do?" She twisted one of the careful curls that'd taken ages to force my pin-straight hair into. What harm? I felt my heart trying to beat out of my chest already. Felt my careful control slipping away, like water through my fingertips.

With a shuddering breath, I reached for the box. Cracking it open, I was stunned at the sight before me. A hair comb. It had blue stones and pearls in a pattern that reminded me of cascading water. Set in silver that gleamed in the light. It must've cost a fortune. Savannah's sharp inhale beside me only reinforced the awe in my chest. It felt *significant* in a way I couldn't explain. I swallowed hard, blinking away the sudden emotion that filled my eyes.

"Will you help me?" I croaked around the lump that'd formed in my throat. Savannah moved behind me, pulling my curls to fall down one shoulder as she secured the comb in place. I *felt* beautiful wearing this. Felt more myself than I ever had before. I closed my eyes and imagined my mother's hands were Savannah's, her fingers in the long tresses of my hair.

When I opened them, I unfolded the note.

Save me a dance. -J

I pulled the long silver chain and the ring it held over my head. I secured it to the bedpost before stepping into my dress. Savannah had done wonders with it. The neckline was so low I couldn't wear anything beneath the bodice, and the fabric flowed like cool water. The sleeves she'd added hid the raised ridges of my scar. They were lace, studded with silver beads that caught the light, reminding me of stars twinkling in the night sky. The bodice was tight until the curve of my hips, where the fabric hung like a waterfall to the floor. A scandalous slit on one side showed my leg all the way to the bottom of my thigh when I walked. Staring at myself in the mirror, I looked like a completely different woman. Elegant. Composed. Dignified.

I turned to Savannah to see that she'd changed, too. Her dress was white, contrasting beautifully against the dark shade of her skin. The top was reminiscent of a corset, with no straps or high neckline as she usually wore. Instead, the expanse of her shoulders and the swell of her breasts were exposed to the night air. It cinched in at her waist and showed each of the curves that she normally hid from the world. The top had a floral design stitched in silver thread before the gauzy waves of her skirt folded in layers to the floor. She was luminous as she tied the white lace mask over her eyes. Another way she refused to hide tonight.

"You're breathtaking." She turned to me, beaming so brightly that I felt her smile's warmth across the room.

"Don't forget your mask," she said. "As if anyone would miss you in that dress."

I laughed, rolling my eyes. "Yeah, well, I had a good seamstress." I let out a shaky breath as I secured the mask over my eyes. Suddenly, I was nervous, stomach fluttering with anticipation. I didn't like that people would be staring at me tonight, but I couldn't avoid it.

"Come on, you can't be late to your own party." Savannah ushered me toward the door, whether I was ready or not.

CHAPTER FORTY-FIVE

JESSE

"**T**HIS IS HOPELESS." IT was my fourth attempt at knotting my tie. The man at the shop had shown me how, but suddenly, I couldn't remember where it went under or over. I'd never worn a suit before. Pop said he'd show me one day, but the chance never presented itself.

Will shoved open the door, tugging at his collar.

"How the fuck do you do this?" I asked. He mumbled something beneath his breath. I smirked at the scowl on his face. He wore a suit, too. Where mine was black on black, he looked more like a penguin, in a black suit with long coattails. At his neck was a secure bowtie.

"How am I supposed to know?" He tugged at his collar again. "Etty stopped me on my way up and made me tuck my shirt in and tied this damn thing. This is your fault."

I loosened my terribly-tied knot, pulled it over my head, and threw it across the room. I unbuttoned the top two buttons on my shirt, letting the collar splay open at my neck. Better. I leaned in toward the mirror and smoothed my hair back. It had to look perfect if I had a lick of a chance at getting Audrey to talk to me.

When I turned to Will, he too had removed his tie and was deciding between securing his hair back or leaving it loose.

"What did she say?"

He spared me a withering glance before turning about the room. "About what?"

"The comb, idiot."

"What was I supposed to do? Storm in there and interrogate her?" He rolled his eyes. "No, I handed it to Savvy and she slammed the door in my face."

Something had clearly happened between them.

"What's going on with you two?"

"Who?"

I secured the laces of my too-polished shoes. Nothing about this damn suit felt right. It wasn't me. "You. Savannah."

"Nothing."

"Sure." I stood to my full height. Will reached for his cowboy hat. "Nope. No hats. This is a formal affair." He scowled but left the hat on the dresser.

After securing my simple black mask on my face, we headed out. Will opted out of the mask requirement, to no one's surprise. I scanned the party already in full swing a level below, sighing in relief. Audrey hadn't arrived yet. We weren't late. We walked silently together down the normal path, though nothing about tonight felt normal.

It felt like I stood on the precipice of the rest of my life, and I didn't know whether I would hit water or rocks when I jumped. It was terrifying. It was exhilarating.

Music trilled on the air as we approached. Lanterns strung on ropes cast a warm summer glow over the courtyard. Intricate dishes weighed down the tables; giant floral arrangements rested on them as centerpieces. A few dozen tables with seating lined the space, leaving most of the area around the fountain for dancing.

A handful of couples moved in time to the music. I searched their faces, all of these people invited to celebrate the engagement of Zachary Lee's daughter. Rich, pompous assholes. I recognized more than one of them from the crowds at my fights. Raving madmen, screaming at me like an animal. Now, with their wives on their arms, they appeared as perfect, polished gentlemen.

"How much do you think her father had to pay Rutherford to secure a match?" a woman whispered to her three companions as I walked past. My brows furrowed.

"You don't think—"

"Why *else* would a man like Lucas Rutherford marry *Insane Audrey*?"

My back straightened. I turned toward them, mouth open and ready to eviscerate them with my words, when one of the women's attention found me.

"I don't care," she said, undressing me with her eyes. I snapped my jaw shut. "I just want to meet his friends. Rich, handsome friends." She quirked her eyebrows at me lasciviously, and I turned away.

I let out a low breath as I found the bar. I needed something to steel my nerves. If I did this wrong, I could mess it up worse than I already had. I had to calm down; otherwise I would spew everything at her at once, and that would only make her run again.

Tonight, I would either get her back or lose her forever.

As I drained my glass of whiskey, a man moved to my side. I peered over, finding Lucas Rutherford. For the first time, I actually looked at him. He was about my height, slightly built. He scanned the crowd before he turned to me with a dark expression behind his mask. His vest was the same blue fabric Savannah'd been holding yesterday morning.

"I know she was with you the night of the match," he said, fiddling with his cufflinks. "As a gentleman, I'm respectfully asking you to back off of Audrey."

I grinned, slapping a hand on his shoulder jovially. "As a gentleman, you can go fuck yourself." A pained expression crossed his face before he schooled his features.

"She made her choice." He leveled me with a hard glare. "She chose me."

"That's the thing about choices, Luke. She chose me first." I grinned around the rim of my glass. "If the multiple orgasms are an indication."

Lucas sniffed derisively, fiddling with his cufflinks once more. "Good. I'm glad to know she got you out of her system."

I raised my glass, a mocking salute. "I wish you nothing but luck in your engagement. I hope nothing happens to make her change her mind . . . again."

He glared a second time before moving into the crowd. I watched him easily make small talk and accept congratulations from the guests.

What would he think if he knew she'd agreed to marry me first?

Before I could ask, Etty crossed the courtyard. She wore a pretty yellow dress, for once not covered in flour. She smiled at me. "You look mighty handsome." She smoothed her hands over my shoulders. "Who knew you cleaned up so well?"

I offered a genuine smile. "Thank you."

"Look at all these posh bastards," Will said, moving between me and Etty. He held a full bottle of champagne in his hand. "My party was better." He shot a grin at the woman, who murmured agreement beneath her breath.

"Montana." She leaned around Will to look at me. "What did you do to my girl?"

"Jesse," I said.

"What?"

"My name is Jesse. And I screwed up. But I'm getting her back." I had to believe I would get Audrey back, to convince her that I loved her and that I wanted to be with her. Whatever that looked like to her. If she wanted to stay in New Orleans, or if she wanted to leave like we'd talked about, I'd follow.

I'd gone to the edges of the world for her, and I would do it again in a heartbeat.

The music changed, and the crowd turned toward the second-level breezeway. I took in a sharp breath. If I didn't know Audrey, if I wasn't already in love with her, I'd have fallen all over again at the sight of her.

Dark hair curled and rested over one shoulder, highlighting the neck I'd kissed countless times. A mask so dark blue it looked almost black was tied around her face. It highlighted her beautiful eyes, eyes that I'd drawn a million times over the last three years. The fabric of her dress flowed like the rush of that river in the canyon, one we'd jumped into together. I thought I caught sight of her leg as she disappeared from view with her father. Seconds passed before they reappeared at the entrance to the courtyard. She looked absolutely radiant.

But she didn't look like a happy bride-to-be.

The low neckline revealed she no longer wore my father's ring on a chain. As she turned her head to the side, I spied the comb I'd bought for her. My heart soared in my chest. She'd worn it, when she could have very well tossed it out. Like a beacon, it called to me. She still wanted me. Even if she wouldn't say it. Even if she wouldn't look at me.

I took an unconscious step forward as she reached the edge of the crowd, only stopping when Rutherford offered his arm. A moment later, they moved onto the dance floor. Almost immediately, she stomped on his foot. The man grimaced, and I didn't even try to hide my chuckle.

A pretty woman wearing a white dress and a matching mask wandered over. I couldn't look away from Audrey, so I ignored the woman, instead opting to watch as Audrey crushed Lucas's other foot. It wasn't until I heard a low whistle from Will beside me that I dragged my eyes off of the dance floor.

"I see you left your neckline at home tonight, Savvy," Will said. I followed his gaze to the woman. Or rather, to her exposed cleavage. Savannah glared past me to Will from behind a white lace mask. "Can't say that I mind." He winked, dragging his eyes up to her face before flashing his signature grin.

"Jesse," Savannah said, the word clipped. "Dance with me."

When I looked over, she glared at Will again, then grabbed my arm and dragged me to the dance floor. It was hard *not* to notice the change in her as she put us in proper form, her features steely. We fell in line with the other dancers, but her gaze kept wandering to Will as he knocked back the bottle of champagne.

"Maybe you should ask him to dance," I suggested in a quiet voice. Her attention snapped to me.

"No," she said too quickly. My friend tipped the bottle back for several long seconds. He was hitting it hard tonight. Savannah stared at him as well. "How's he doing?" Her tone turned serious, concern in her eyes.

"It's hard to tell." I spun Savannah in time with the music before tugging her back. "He acts like he's okay, but I know him. He never lets anyone know what's bothering him." She worried her bottom lip between her teeth.

"You didn't see him that night." Her voice was quiet. "It was like he was someone completely different. I worry about him."

I chuckled beneath my breath. "Enough to get drunk with him?" I grinned.

Savannah's mouth gaped, and she gasped in shock. "That *ass*," she said. "I'll have you know *nothing* happened in the stables. We slept. That's all."

"You slept with Will in the stables?" My grin widened further. I could see why Will liked to poke at her. It was too easy to rile her up.

"*Sleeping*. That's it."

"Mm hmm," I said, twirling her out again. The moment she was back in my arms, her gaze darted to Will yet again. "Really, you should ask him to dance."

Savannah's brown eyes found mine, and for the first time, I saw something in them I didn't think she intended me to see: fear. Instead of pressuring her further, I switched topics.

"Did he ever tell you that the first time we met, I kicked his ass, and the second time, I shot him?"

Savannah's eyes widened in horror, her mouth opening in shock. "And now you're friends?" When my gaze found Will, he had his arm slung over Etty's shoulders and whispered something in her ear. The woman roared in laughter.

"That damn charm got me." I chuckled. I searched the crowd until I found Audrey, cringing as she stepped on Lucas's foot again. "How's our girl doing?" Savannah followed my gaze.

"She won't talk about you."

I ducked my head at her words. Though I expected it, it stung just the same. I watched her, just yards between us, yet she was far away. I needed to talk to her, if only for a moment. The song ended, and most of the couples paused to clap or walked from the floor. Lucas wrapped an arm around Audrey, guiding her through the crowd.

"Oh, go get her, idiot." Savannah smacked my arm. I smiled, murmuring my thanks, before stalking after Audrey, ready to leap off of the cliff that would lead to the rest of my life.

CHAPTER FORTY-SIX

AUDREY

H UMILIATION COATED ME LIKE a dark film, sticky on my skin. The repressed laughter and feral smiles of New Orleans society followed me like a bad dream. Passing judgment from every corner, every table. My cheeks burned as Lucas led me off the dance floor. What a disaster.

Almost immediately, gentlemen in fine suits toting cut crystal glasses filled with amber liquid and elegantly dressed ladies approached us. Most of them didn't spare me a glance, instead talking over me to ask Lucas about Manhattan or spouting tidbits about business. The women were more interested in getting introductions to the men who'd traveled with him from New York. I smiled as he held me at his side but felt more invisible than ever.

"I'm going to get a drink," I whispered. He turned from the man in front of him and pressed a kiss to my temple, squeezing me tight before allowing me to step out of his arms. As soon as I was free, I inhaled a deep, steadying breath. The tension building in my shoulders and the pit of my stomach eased the farther I walked away. As I twisted through couples and crowded tables, people called their congratulations after me.

My smile ached, and I kept my gaze lowered to stop anyone from capturing my attention. At the corner of the dance floor and only a few feet from the bar, a calloused hand gripped mine. Before I could look up, with a practiced pull, someone spun me roughly onto the dance floor, and I crashed against the hard planes of a familiar chest. My eyes rose slowly to drink in the intoxicating sight of him.

He looks like sin. The thought came unbidden, drawing my attention to the sharp angle of his clean-shaven jaw and his full, chiseled lips, which were visible beneath the dark slant of his mask. His eyes held the same hurricane within them that I'd glimpsed the night of the storm. Striking fast into my skin and setting my nerve endings ablaze. It felt so good to be in his arms, *too good*.

"I'm a terrible dancer." I stepped back to pull away from him. He moved with me, keeping me in the steel cage of his body. Confusion muted the barely-leashed hurricane in his eyes. He dipped down to place his lips close to my ear.

"You're a wonderful dancer," he said in that deep canyon timbre that shivered down my spine. "I can prove it."

My gaze fell to his bare throat, watching his nervous swallow as silence pulled between us for a heady moment. I noticed how impeccably he was dressed. The suit accentuated his broad shoulders and trim hips. He unbuttoned his jacket, letting it hang open over the ebony shirt tucked neatly into his pants. An innocent motion, necessary to move freely during the dance, but something in the slow, practiced way he'd flicked his fingers felt sensual. Forbidden.

"Fine." I forced any warmth from my words. "One dance. I hope you enjoy walking with a limp."

His answering smile was predatory, and I shouldn't have liked it. He led me further onto the dance floor, settling one powerful hand on my waist. With his fingers splayed, they reached my ribs, and my entire world narrowed to the contact of his hand on my body.

The music began and an awkward silence descended as he led us through the song. My mind was chaos, my heart was war. There were so many things I wanted to know, but pride wouldn't let me give voice to the questions running rampant through my head. The quiet stretched on for too long.

"You look beautiful tonight," he said, breaking the mounting tension rippling beneath his fine suit. Small talk? Compliments? My fury flared to life at the placating tone of his voice.

"What are you *doing here*?" I asked, each word a dagger. "I thought I made it clear I wanted you to stay away from me."

He turned in time to the music, twisting me just as I tried to stomp his foot. I'd driven my heel down to crush his toes. Instead, the anger pulsing within me fueled a deviation from the regular steps that he compensated for too easily. Was there *anything* he wasn't good at? He spun me, then pulled me in until my back pressed against his chest. He breathed his next words against my neck.

"You never gave me a chance to explain—"

I scoffed derisively, stepping away from him. I spun again, and Jesse trapped me once more against his dizzying heat, our bodies too close to be considered appropriate.

"You mean, I didn't give you another opportunity to lie to me," I spat, the hurt of his betrayal on display. His gaze shuttered, and he dragged me impossibly closer before his hand slid up the line of my body to splay on the small of my back. He dipped me low, as he had at the hurricane party. For a breathless moment, I was suspended in the air, at his mercy.

It was thrilling and disastrous.

As he shifted me to stand on my feet once more, my legs quaked beneath my skirts. I hated how my pulse pounded at the electrifying contact. I hated that he knew he affected me like this. That he'd used it to manipulate me all this time. I hated liking how alive I felt when he touched me.

"Did it *ever* occur to you that treating me like some fragile broken thing made me feel like one? No, you looked at me and saw what they *all* do." I jutted my chin out to indicate the people fawning over Lucas. "Not strong enough to handle the whole truth. Or was manipulating me just too much *fun* to pass up?" With every angry word, I danced, advancing toward him and ducking beneath his arm as the music crested at the end of the first verse.

His eyes flashed bright, a strike of lightning lurking within them, anger flaring beneath his mask.

"Exactly how the fuck would *that* conversation have gone?" His hands were hard on me. He lifted me easily, setting me down a little too hard. "I may not have told you everything, but I've *never* been dishonest with you. Can you say the same about your *fiancé*?"

My gaze snapped up to his. There was something unyielding in them, a certainty that I felt echoed in my soul. "Don't," I warned, but of course he didn't listen.

"Did you tell him you were engaged to me less than a week ago?" Each word thudded into me like the tip of a knife.

"Fuck you," I spat.

"You already did, sweetheart. Something else you neglected to tell Lucas. Not that it matters, since it seems the only thing the two of you have in common is keeping things from each other."

"What are you talking about?"

"Have you asked *Lucas* about the specifics of the deal he made with your father?"

I hadn't. But Lucas wasn't hiding anything. He couldn't be. It just hadn't come up after the events of the last few weeks.

"It's a shipping contract."

"Shipping *what*?"

I didn't know. I'd never even considered asking. He was goading me, I knew that. A part of me wanted to rise to the challenge. Another feared falling into whatever trap he laid. When I didn't respond, he barreled forward.

"People. They're shipping *people*. Stolen and sold into slavery. I found trade routes and ledgers—"

"Luke wouldn't do that," I interrupted, the denial feeling weak as it dropped from my mouth. "He—he's not that kind of person."

The music crescendoed, and we felt the dance rapidly ending. This was it: after this song ended, we'd never speak to each other again. My chest heaved, and so did his. With each ragged breath, my breasts pressed against his torso, and the friction set my skin on fire.

"Even if it meant making a name for himself separate from his father's?" he asked, the words ruthless. I thought of the conversations I'd had with Lucas. How he spoke of being himself beneath a mask. How hard he found it to be his own person with such an overpowering figure in his life. Doubt made my stomach plummet. Without his arms, I may have lost my footing, as my world tilted on its axis. The last few notes crooned from the musicians on the stage.

"After everything that's happened between us, why should I believe you?" I tilted my chin in silent challenge. The music slipped away, and silence descended in its aftermath. I retreated from his embrace, sucking in air that wasn't thick with his dizzying scent. I needed to clear my head.

"Give me one more dance, and I'll prove that you can," he vowed in a deep baritone I felt all the way to my toes. I shouldn't. I knew that. But the moment his hands dropped away from my skin, I yearned for his touch again. My body reacted to his nearness so forcefully, it dragged me under. But it was more than attraction now. There were things I *needed* to know. I'd been hiding for so long, running from my past, from the things I didn't want to accept happening right in front of me. He had answers, and he was offering them to me.

The decision wavered in the air between us. I swallowed my trepidation and let out a shaky breath. The music began again, sweet and lilting, and he extended a hand to me, a desperate unspoken plea. I bit my bottom lip, placing my hand in his and closing the space between us. He touched me differently this time. As if our anger before had faded with the music, and all that remained were two people who longed to be close to each other.

For all his declarations, he didn't speak. Instead, he buried his nose in my hair, inhaling deep. My eyes closed as contentment spread from my shoulders. We swayed together, my hand resting above his furiously pounding heart. I realized that he didn't *know* how to prove it. He swallowed nervously as our eyes met.

"You knew me before my accident?" I wanted to know desperately about what had led to my injury. I wanted to know so much about the life I lost.

"Yes," he breathed against my hair. "I know you better than anyone."

"Tell me."

"Tell you what?" He pulled back to rake his eyes over every inch of my face.

"*Everything*," I begged. He regarded me carefully, eyes sliding down the curve of my neck like a feather-light touch against my skin. They dropped to my chest for a moment but didn't linger. Instead, they crept across my collarbone to my lace-covered arm. Beneath the midnight-blue lace hid the most horrific of my scars. His fingers found it without challenge, mapping the knotted ridges like he'd memorized every raised hook and curve.

"I remember when you couldn't read this scar," he said with such tenderness, my heart throbbed at the sound. He couldn't know how I'd struggled to make sense of words when I emerged from my glowroot haze. It took Savannah a long time to teach me, not realizing until weeks later that I had a tendency to mix up the letters. "I was surprised to see you in the library that first day."

"They said it was from my head injury." He shook his head, and as we swayed, the heat that always burned between us licked across every inch of exposed skin.

"You never learned," he explained. "You may have been born Audrey, but before coming here, that's not how you lived."

My mouth felt dry, and I licked my lips. His eyes fell to them, the hurricane reigniting in his eyes as he touched my ribs. He traced along the frenzied criss-crossing lines there. Stroking with long elegant fingers, calloused by violence. Artist's fingers.

"Something bad happened to you and your mother when you were a child. You were stolen. Most of your scars are from years of abuse. They're proof." The words vibrated against my skin. *My mother.* The loss of her disappeared beneath the grief in my father's eyes anytime I asked about her. I'd thought of her often when I was pregnant. In the aftermath of losing Emma. I wondered if not remembering her at all was better than to know her and break beneath her loss, too.

"Proof of what?" I turned the subject from another tragedy I didn't know if I was strong enough to withstand.

"That you're a survivor. That you're the strongest person I know," he whispered in the inches between our mouths. Those *wicked* hands slid over my body so confidently that every touch felt like an extension of myself. One flat palm rose to the small of my back again, and I knew before he shifted that he would dip me in that breathless move that sent my world spinning.

This time, I hooked my leg around his powerful thigh. The slit in my dress opened, baring the pale expanse of my calf and knee. He dragged his other hand up my leg, the friction forcing me to shudder. He didn't stop where the slit ended. His hand dipped under the fabric, fingers skimming the laced edge of my panties until they found the angry pink knot of scar tissue just above the waistband. His favorite scar.

"I was there when you got this," he breathed. The words fell millimeters over the base of my throat. His hand moved away as he dragged me back against him. "It happened the night I knew without a doubt I would never love anyone else." He put space between us now, too much space. He glanced around the room, aware of those around us. They'd faded into smoke when he touched me.

"Tell me more."

"You wore a comb like that," he said, eyes trailing to my hair. Unconsciously I touched the comb that'd felt so *significant* the moment I'd seen it. "We were running from people with guns and found ourselves on the top of a cliff."

I felt the adrenaline coursing in my blood, the frantic thundering of my heart, the fear lancing down my spine, as if I were there.

"What happened?"

"We jumped." He studied my expression so closely that I swore hope flickered to life in the depths of those hurricane eyes. "Together. The way we do everything."

I heard the roar of the wind as we fell. The crash of the impact, like slamming into concrete, breaking our hands apart as we were torn from each other in the water.

"It wasn't until we reached the riverbank that we realized you'd been shot." His words were strained, as if talking about it still pained him. "I thought I was going to lose you and—"

"You told me to wake up." The words rushed out before I could think about the meaning behind them. Shock stole his senses, and he missed a step in the dance. I looked past him, through him, gripping onto the tendrils of the dream from last night. "I couldn't open my eyes, but I heard you. I was cold and numb and it was so *dark*—"

He trembled. This powerful, dangerous man *trembled*, eyes turning glassy. His fingers twisted into my hair as he dragged my gaze back to his. Asking a question I didn't have the answer to. Not yet.

"You said you loved me." Heat gathered in my eyes. I saw the truth when I looked at him now. The chasm he'd tried to close all these weeks. All these *years*. Just a flash, just one half-formed memory. I still didn't remember so many things. I wasn't the person he wanted me to be. I didn't know if I would ever be her again.

"Yes." The word was a sob and a prayer.

The music swelled before falling silent again. This time, we lingered, dragging our bodies away from each other against their screaming protests.

"Audrey!" Lucas called from over Jesse's shoulder. He glared, twisting through the couples. I looked at Jesse, wondering how to make sense of this. He spoke his next words in a rush.

"I promised that I would come for you, and I'm here. If you let me, I'll help you get back everything you've lost. Meet me in the front house." He leaned over my hand, kissing the back of it swiftly. He turned and, before I could think to track his departure, disappeared.

Lucas crossed the distance moments later, glaring over my shoulder before settling his gaze on me. I offered a brilliant smile to mask the screaming within my mind.

"What did he want?" He gripped my hand a little too tight as he led me off the dance floor and toward the bar. To get that drink I'd never managed to acquire earlier.

I'll come for you. Open your eyes. Wake up.

Realization slammed into me, twisting my insides into a tangle of swelling emotion. *Jesse* was the voice from my dreams. All this time I'd misunderstood what my fractured mind had been telling me.

He'd been telling me to open my eyes. To *wake up.*

Lucas stared at me expectantly. "What?" I fanned myself with a free hand and attempted to regain my senses. Remembering his question, I curled into his side briefly and let him wrap an arm around me.

"Oh, nothing. He was congratulating us and asking questions about Manhattan Island and the wedding. I think he mentioned some investors in his fighting matches." I lied so easily, so naturally. I didn't even feel bad about it. The bartender offered two flutes of champagne, and, when Lucas tapped his glass with mine, I fumbled it in my hand. The champagne spilled down my dress, and the flute crashed with a pretty tinkle, shattering on the cobblestone. Lucas patted the front of my dress with tiny cocktail napkins.

"I'm so sorry," I breathed in an approximation of embarrassment. "I get nervous and turn into such a klutz." Derisive laughter sounded from one of the tables nearby. Alice Devereaux's snide condemnation rang clear across the space. Lucas's eyebrows furrowed as he noted their derision.

"You were right, she *really* doesn't like you," he muttered. He must've remembered the last society function and how horribly that'd gone. He looked at me, eyes softening at my strained expression. How could someone so understanding be trafficking people?

"I need to put soda on this and clean up." I squeezed his hand tight. His kind eyes warmed, and he pressed one of those too-soft kisses swiftly to my mouth.

"Of course. Take your time, just be back for the toast." I twisted away from him, ambling away from the party. Once I was out of sight, I gripped the front of my long skirts and *ran*.

The rightness of running *toward* Jesse, instead of away from him, thrummed in my blood. As if my body had been telling me all along what I needed. I turned a corner and stopped short, the tall expanse of him drinking in the light of the corridor. His hair was mussed, as if he'd run nervous fingers through the careful style. He lifted his eyes to me, and with a ragged exhale, relief poured over him, running along his muscles until the distance between us disappeared. He ripped his mask off to stare at me without obstruction.

With trembling fingers, he loosened the ribbons tied at the back of my mask until it fell away. He lifted it from my face with reverence.

"You remembered—"

"Only that moment. Maybe pieces of other things, but I'm not . . . I haven't—"

Voices and laughter sounded on the other end of the corridor. Fear pulsed cold through my veins. We couldn't be discovered together. I didn't know what my father or Lucas would do, and the thought of hurting Lucas thrashed in my stomach. Panic sparked, and before I could voice my concerns, he dragged me behind him.

In my heeled shoes, I couldn't keep up with his long gait, stumbling as he rushed us down the corridor. The voices grew louder, drunken giggling and a roar of laughter. We twisted through an archway, but the voices lingered behind us. We spilled into another corridor, hands clasped tightly, my heart slammed against my ribs. What would happen if we were caught together? Would my father order Will to hurt Jesse?

"Fuck." He scanned the corridor. They were getting closer. He jiggled a doorknob that remained locked and moved to the next one. This one opened, and we tumbled inside. The space was small and dark. As the door clicked shut, we were plunged into blackness. His calloused hand covered my mouth, even though I wouldn't give our location away. The voices moved past, but neither of us budged when they faded into the distance. Our breathing echoed, heightening the intimacy of being pressed so close to him. My hands fumbled, feeling folded linens on the shelves. It must've been a closet.

His fingers fell away from my mouth, dragging along my skin reluctantly. Dim light from the one yellow bulb at the top of the closet flooded the space. Jesse lowered his arm from the cord, his artist's hands twitching toward me as I shifted on my feet. I reached trembling fingertips out to land on his chest, letting my hands splay wide and feel the erratic thump of his heart.

Then something happened. I laughed. It started as a hysterical giggle, but before I knew it, I could barely breathe. He stared at me for a moment before the boom of his laughter joined mine, echoing in the tiny closet. It took a few long seconds to steady myself, wiping at the tears on the edges of my eyes.

We fell into silence. Thick, heady silence.

"You wore the comb. You came to the house. You remembered," he said in that tone of voice that shook me to my core. The one that said he would burn this house to the ground to keep me safe. To keep me *his.* "You believe me."

"I believe you." His hands were in my hair then, his thumbs dragging along my jaw, his forehead pressing into mine until all I saw was the hurricane unleashed in the devastation of his eyes.

"Who are you?" His eyes flashed in equal parts hope and agony. He leaned down, bending to me. The power I held over him was apparent in the strain of every muscle of his body.

"I'm your farm boy." The words dragged out of some small, secret place within him.

Farm boy.

The term of endearment rocked into me. The reality was that it was only a few seconds, a few heartbeats, but this moment stretched into infinity as all the missing pieces of myself slid into place. Jagged and colorful, like the shattered pieces of a stained-glass window.

My eyes burned as I gulped in ragged breaths. In the years I'd longed for my memories to return, in the myriad of ways I'd imagined it happening, I couldn't have fathomed it would feel like this. I shook so hard I had to fist my hands in the front of his finely tailored shirt.

The pain, the loss, the grief and horror swept me away first. My mother. Jones. Sixgun. The times I'd been beaten, burned, starved, tortured. The feral violence that'd grown in the darkest places within me. A weapon I'd learned to wield to survive.

Tears rolled down my cheeks, hot and unhindered as they tracked my makeup in rivulets. Along with the pain of my past came something so much greater, swelling in my chest until it hurt. So painful and bright and full that I could barely take it. In that brightness was Jesse. A man who walked beside me in the darkness and banished it with his love. The same love that was so apparent in his desperate eyes.

There wasn't a flood of images. My life didn't flash before my eyes. I wasn't jarred out of my current reality. Instead, it was like putting on an old pair of shorts, worn in all the right places. They slid into place seamlessly. The memories were mine, had been there just below the surface, waiting for someone to put them in the right order.

Waiting for Jesse.

"It was me?" I questioned shakily, my voice small and filled with tears. All this time, fighting a ghost that didn't exist. Jealous of myself. Watching his heart break and wondering if I'd ever be *enough* for him when all the while, it was *me* he'd been mourning. The recognition in my voice forced a choked sob from his chest. Tears filled his eyes now, too, shining in the dim light. "It was me," I said more confidently. He pressed his forehead harder against mine as his tears fell, and he brushed his thumbs over my cheeks to rid me of mine.

"*Who are you?*" he grumbled from between his teeth. I slid my hands up his chest, hooked them around his neck, and pressed as close to him as I could.

"Bonnie," I sobbed. "I'm Bonnie." I cried out the words, but he swallowed them in a searing kiss. The taste and feel of him both familiar and new at the same time. He wrenched his mouth from mine, as if he were too afraid to believe that I'd finally remembered myself.

"What are you?" His words were raw.

"I'm yours, Jesse James. I've *always* been yours," I snapped in a tone that was harsher than any I'd used in this house, with its false compliments and passive criticism.

I shoved against his chest until his back hit the shelves. Before he could question me further, I shoved the jacket off his shoulders and let it fall forgotten to the floor.

"I remember. I remember *us*. Everything." His hands were on me a moment later, in my hair, over my breasts, running down my ribs, grasping handfuls of my ass.

The storm had been shuttered away for too long, and like all the times when we folded together like this, it roiled between us low and ominous until finally—

The storm broke.

CHAPTER FORTY-SEVEN

JESSE

THE PRECARIOUS LEASH HOLDING me back snapped. All of these weeks, these *years*, shutting myself away, losing myself in whiskey, in the search, in the pits . . . I didn't realize how much I'd held back. Not until she said her own name. Remembered who she was. What *we* were.

My fingers twisted into her carefully styled hair, tugging until her neck arched long and exposed. I dragged my lips and tongue and teeth along her humming pulse, the sounds coming from deep within her feral. I needed her. Needed her now more than ever.

Bonnie's fingers scrambled with my shirt, snapping the buttons open at frenzied speeds as I dragged my teeth across her collarbone.

"*Please*," she begged, arching her body into mine.

A hum of pleasure thundered from deep within me, the animal set loose.

I'd always loved her like this: lost to me, begging. Like she was starving and only I could sate her hunger. Her nails raked over my shoulders, and I gripped her hips, lifting her into my arms as I spun and slammed her back into the shelves, barely setting her on the edge of one before finding my place between her already open thighs.

I ground my cock against her sweet spot, that place meant for me—and *only* me. Her head fell back, eyes slamming shut at the sensation.

"Open your eyes," I growled. She complied, lifting her pleasure-glazed eyes to mine. A savage grin found its way to my mouth, my fingers moving on their own as I slipped the lace sleeves over her shoulders, tugging the top of her gown down until her breasts were bare to me in the dim light. "*Fuck*. You're so beautiful."

Bonnie arched her back, and I cupped her breast, rolling her nipple between my fingers, pinching it just enough to make her whimper. I lowered my head, wrapping my lips around the stiff peak. Her fingers yanked my hair, encouraging me.

"You taste like champagne," I whispered.

"I spilled my drink." She moaned, hips bucking up to mine.

With a grin, I slid my tongue along the swell of her breast, the curve of it, reaching for the fabric of her skirt tangled between us. My tongue flicked out across her chest, her collarbone, before moving to her other nipple. I grazed my teeth across the tender flesh until the glorious symphony of her cries was all I could hear. It was all I ever wanted to hear again.

Bonnie reached between us. The clink of my belt was loud and echoing in the small space. Before I could take another breath, her hand was deep in the fabric, wrapped around my cock. I pressed my forehead to the curve of her shoulder as she stroked me. My fingers tightened on the edge of the shelf on either side of her. I panted, knuckles bleached white as she took full control of me, the way only Bonnie ever had, until I was fucking her hand.

I wouldn't last. Not like this.

My fingers slipped across her bare thigh, sliding along her smooth curves until I reached the soaked fabric of her underwear. I didn't bother with the delicate silk, instead twisting it in my fingers until it shredded into useless scraps. I touched the slick heat of her then. I dragged my teeth across her shoulder, the only tether keeping me together.

My fingers wrapped around her wrist, tugging her hand from my cock as I slid her roughly along the shelf. Her hips tilted toward me, baring her to me, giving me everything.

Bonnie was everything. She always had been.

"I can't be gentle this time," I growled, shoving my forehead against hers as I gripped the tender flesh of her hips.

"Good." Her lips met mine at the same moment her hips jerked toward me. She was always so impatient. I'd have to remind her of that later, when *I* wasn't so desperate.

With a hard thrust, our bodies joined. My mouth hovered over hers. We drank in each other's ragged breath as my hips set a rhythm all their own. I swallowed her screams of pleasure, her nails digging into my flesh.

I knew I didn't have to be gentle. Not with her. She wasn't some simpering southern belle in a ballgown. She was an *outlaw*. She gave as good as she got. There was nothing gentle about her. She could take it.

Her arms tight around me, Bonnie's breaths came shorter and shorter, little gasps I got lost in, drunk on. She pressed her body into mine, our frenzied fucking breaking me and piecing me together at once.

When she cried out in victory, I plunged over that edge alongside her, teeth digging into her shoulder as I stifled my roar of pleasure.

For a second, there was nothing but the rapid pounding of my heart, the harried breaths between us. I let out a long breath and pressed my lips sweetly to the curve of her neck. Neither of us moved. As if the moment we parted, the trauma and pain would come back. I rested my cheek against her chest, eyes closing as I listened to her racing heart, its rhythm slowing with each breath.

Bonnie threaded her fingers through my hair, over and over, easing the tension in my shoulders.

Peace. A peace I hadn't known in years.

"I thought I lost you," I said.

"You almost did, you fuckin' idiot. You should've just told me." I lifted my head to look at her. Her eyes creased at the edges, a small smile finding its way to her perfect lips. I kissed her, slow, sweet, gentle. The opposite of moments before.

"The truth is," I said, "I don't care if you're Bonnie or Audrey or have no name. I will love you until the day I die." I cradled her cheek, brushing my thumb along her skin. I meant every single word.

A declaration. A promise. A vow.

Our mouths slid against each other lazily, basking in the taste of one another.

"Promise me we'll never be separated again," I said, the words heavy on my tongue. "It almost killed me, Bon. I can't—"

"I promise, Jesse James, wherever we go in this life. We go *together*." The truth in her eyes sent my heart soaring. I kissed her again, unable to verbalize this feeling inside of me. Our kisses lengthened, her arms tightening around my neck. "I love you."

My cock stiffened. I kissed her again. Maybe we had time for one more before we had to get back.

A knock sounded on the door, and it swung open. Will stood on the other side, a cigarette dangling from his mouth.

"Alright. Stop fuckin'. Lee's looking for her."

I blinked, brows furrowing as I focused on the light spilling into the room.

"Did I stutter or did you literally screw each other's brains out?" Will asked, taking a drag of his cigarette and arching a brow. I shifted, shoving my cock into my pants. I helped Bonnie to her feet and moved between them to give her some privacy as I buttoned my shirt.

"Would you close the door? Jesus!" I turned to Bonnie, helping her adjust the top of her gown and settling her breasts back into her bodice.

"Are you suddenly shy or something?" Will grinned at me and earned a glare in return. Bonnie and I shuffled together, redressing quickly. Which apparently wasn't quick enough. "I mean, you weren't shy when you were screeching like strangled cats. Did you forget this is an old house? Sound travels."

"Shut up, Will," I grumbled, zipping my pants and fixing my belt.

"*Shut up, Will. Close the door, Will.*" His high-pitched mocking sounded nothing like me, or Bonnie for that matter. Maybe more like Savannah. "How about *thank you for scaring off anyone who could hear us fucking in a linen closet?*"

Bonnie ignored him. I fumbled with her comb, straightening it in her hair.

"Imagine if it'd been Zachary that caught you," he continued ranting. "Or your fiancé?"

A grimace crossed her face.

"¡*Vete a la mierda*!" A cruel grin slid onto Bonnie's lips. I reached up, wiping the smeared lipstick as best I could.

"Fuck me? That's not very ladylike language, Miss Audrey," Will said.

"Wow, Ellis, you've gone soft. No *you've already done that, Bonnie,* or *alright, alright, stop beggin' me already?*"

I snorted, gratitude swelling in my chest. I tucked my shirt in and righted my jacket.

Will's face turned to stone, shock snatching his grin. A wide smile crossed his face, though his eyes seemed to darken. He clapped a hand on my shoulder, eyes still on Bonnie.

"Well, look at that. You didn't screw up this time. Congrats," Will said, even as the stare between them deepened into discomfort. "Now. Did either of you hear me about your father looking for you?"

"Shit." Bonnie swiped her mask from its place on the floor and tied it hastily over her eyes. She snatched the ruined underwear and tucked it neatly into my jacket pocket, her dark eyes glittering with the promise of pleasure later.

"Well, what am I gonna do with those?" She quirked her eyebrows suggestively at me, shrugging as a brilliant smile crossed her face.

"Hurry," Will said before either of us could shut him out of the closet.

Together, we moved into the hallway, the cool evening air washing across our skin. I tangled my fingers with hers, walking in sated silence until we reached the edge of the courtyard, just out of sight. Music and voices twined together, unsettling my nerves. I didn't want to let her go. Not again. Not back to *him*.

Bonnie started forward, her face a careful mask, as though she had to shift back into being Audrey for the sake of her father and fiancé.

But I couldn't let her go. I tugged her back, crushing her against my chest. I covered her mouth with mine *hard*, reminding her just what she was leaving behind while she went to play the part of the perfect daughter.

"We don't have time for this. They'll come looking for her soon." Will's harsh whisper cut into the moment, and I pulled back an inch. I brushed my thumb beneath her lip.

"Don't forget me by the time I come to your room tonight." I grinned at her, earning a half-hearted glare. "What? Too soon?"

Bonnie shoved my shoulder, and I chuckled, enjoying the sway of her hips too much as she walked away. I watched her the entire time as she twisted through the couples and staff until she reached Rutherford's side. My smile faded as the fucker wrapped an arm around her and leaned in close to whisper something.

I only made it a half step before Will held out an arm to stop me. I glanced up at him, a silent question on my mouth.

"Give it a minute."

Right. Because if I entered on her heels, people might get suspicious. I ran a hand through my hair, shuffling as nervous energy fluttered in my gut.

"I'm proud of you, Jess."

I turned to Will, my brows knitting together in confusion. My gaze, though, sought out Bonnie across the courtyard. "You never gave up. Unlike me. I knew you'd bring her back."

My mouth curved into a grin. I clapped a hand on his shoulder. "I couldn't have done it without you."

"What's family for?"

I beamed at him, unable to hide my joy. I wrapped an arm around his shoulders and yanked him in for a quick hug.

"Alright, alright. Don't get your panties in a twist. Go on. I know you'd rather be stalking your girl."

CHAPTER FORTY-EIGHT

SAVANNAH

M Y FACE ITCHED. I knew that choosing such a scratchy fabric for my mask was a bad idea. Even though it made for quite the statement, as the party continued, I wanted to toss it into the trash. But I wouldn't. Not until this night finished.

A boisterous laugh sounded over the stringed instruments, and I found Mr. Lee across the courtyard, surrounded by half a dozen men and clutching a glass of scotch. I bristled at him, seemingly unbothered by this ridiculous transaction taking place. And . . . because of what he'd said to me earlier.

I hope for your sake that you'll have better fortune than your mother did.

Whether he released me from service remained to be seen. What was clear was he felt like he held power over me by digging at my mother.

"Miss Savannah?"

Patrick MacNeil stood before me, dressed in a flawless navy blue suit. His eyes shifted behind his mask as though searching for something. I hadn't seen him since the hurricane party, when Will scared him off. I bristled again.

"Are you . . . alright?" Patrick asked.

"Yes, thank you."

Considering he'd disappeared for weeks following the party, and I'd been rather *preoccupied* with other things, his presence wasn't exactly welcome. I'd been angry at Will that night, sure, but the days and weeks following proved him right. Patrick MacNeil didn't want me.

I turned back to the party, staring at the couples dancing and laughing and drinking without a care in the world.

"Would you like to dance?" he asked.

This was the fourth invitation I'd gotten to take to the floor tonight. And the fourth I would decline. A waiter bustled by, carrying a tray of half-filled champagne flutes. I snatched one and stared pointedly at Patrick.

"No, thank you."

His features hardened. He stepped closer, and I tensed as anger flashed through his eyes. "You know, if you weren't interested, all you had to do was say so," he said quietly. "You didn't have to sic your dog on me."

I stood straighter, facing him directly and narrowing my eyes. "I did wonder, Mr. MacNeil, whether your interest was genuine. It seems it was not."

"Excuse me?"

My brows lifted, a cruel smile taking over my lips. "If a man is truly interested in a woman, sir, nothing would stop them," I said pointedly. "Furthermore, William Ellis isn't a *dog*, he's the *Beast*, and you would do well to learn the difference."

Fear flashed through his eyes, and mirth tingled down my spine. I laughed. Blatantly.

"Enjoy your evening, sir." I tipped my glass to him.

As he left, my gaze shot across the crowd once more. Audrey appeared near the edge of the crowd. She and Jesse had disappeared some time earlier, hopefully to talk out their problems. Her eyes were guarded as she approached her fiance. I hadn't seen Will since much earlier, not that I was looking for him.

I crossed an arm over my abdomen, clutching the glass with my other hand as I contemplated drinking it. Drinking whiskey with Will had been . . . *fun*.

But I couldn't afford that. Not tonight. Not with everyone here.

"I suppose we can't call you *Unfuckable* anymore, can we?" a deep, menacing voice said in my ear. I wheeled around, facing the guard, Jimmy, who'd discovered me in the stables.

"Go away."

"But we're having so much fun." He eyed my bare neck. His gaze slithered over me, skimming across the swell of my breasts.

I opened my mouth to curse him, but, suddenly, his eyes widened and he backed away slowly, disappearing into the crowd.

As I turned to find what'd spooked him, someone snatched the champagne from my hand. My eyes widened at the sight of Will towering over me. Too close and not close enough. I gaped at him, questions perched on my tongue.

All night, I'd longed for him to look at me and *see* me. Instead, all he gave was sarcastic commentary about my dress.

Instead of speaking, Will drained the champagne, discarded the glass, and held out a hand to me. I stared at it, remembering the feel of his calluses on my bare skin. The moment elongated, and he snatched my hand and pulled me into the fray. My heart fluttered, until we reached the center of the floor and Will turned to me. He glanced around at the dancing couples and snorted, eyes glimmering with amusement. He enveloped me, folding me against his hard chest. Close. I took in a sharp breath, unable to think about anything but his touch as he led us in a gentle sway. Ignoring the music, as if dancing to a song only we could hear.

"You're too beautiful to sit on the sidelines." The note of honesty in his voice made my heart race.

That was the second time he'd called me that. Beautiful. I stared at him, wide-eyed and mouth gaping because I didn't know *what* to say.

He seemed more himself tonight. That was a comfort. I forced the tension from my shoulders, squaring them and standing taller as we fell into our own rhythm. There were things I wanted to say to him. That I was sorry. I cared about him. I was here for him. That he didn't have to go through this alone.

But I didn't.

Another couple neared us, a woman eyeing me with disdain as her gaze darted between us. I lowered my chin, releasing a sigh. I didn't belong. I'd tried for years to fit with these people. Perhaps it would be a relief when Lee allowed me to leave.

Calloused fingertips touched my chin, gently lifting my face until I stared up into the warmth of Will's eyes.

"Don't lower your eyes for *anyone*." His hard voice made me shiver.

He pulled me closer, *too* close, until my hands slipped to his shoulders and his arms wrapped around my waist. I forgot my steps. Instead, we swayed in a circle over and over. There was something different about this embrace. Before, there was a rush of heat, of *need*, but something in me begged to pull away. It felt *wrong* in a way that his arms never had.

"I know I make a lot of jokes, and I'm an asshole . . . on the good days." He let out a dark chuckle. "But, I want to say something you'll resent. Because you need to hear it."

My mouth opened, a poisoned barb on my tongue, but he didn't give me the chance to speak.

"Stop living for other people. Stop putting yourself last. Stop trying to fix broken people. It won't bring your mother back to you." I took in a sharp breath. How dare he? "You can't *save* her. All you can do is forgive her."

Though his words were gentle, they ripped my skin, the claws of the Beast shredding me apart.

"You have no right to—"

"I don't," he said. "You're right." I glanced to either side, looking for an exit. I didn't like this conversation, and no good could come of it. Instead, his arms tightened. "My mother was the same way. I've only talked about her to one other person, and I have *no idea* why I'm telling you this now." He let out another dark chuckle, one that raised the hair on my arms. "She gave *everything* of herself for me, and it left her with nothing. Until she couldn't see a way out."

My breath caught in my throat. I'd known about the monster that was his father. But . . .

"Until she couldn't take it anymore." Will glanced away, lines creasing his face.

"Will." I didn't know what to say but wanted to reach out to him just the same. He shook his head and let out a long breath.

"*Live*, Savannah. Live recklessly. Live like your life is on *fire*. Because our time here is short. Make a mark."

Why did this sound like goodbye?

Will's hands tangled in my curls. I clung to him, my bottom lip trembling because I didn't understand, didn't know what to do. "Burn *bright*. Don't ask for permission, not *ever* again. Do you hear me?" His gaze met mine, imploring me to listen.

"Why are you telling me this?" My words were a harsh whisper as I searched desperately for something in his eyes. Will brushed a curl behind my ear and cradled my cheek. He ran his calloused thumb across my cheek, sending shivers across my skin.

"You are worth so much more than you know." He leaned close, lips touching mine in a chaste kiss, more chaste than any other. Before I could reach for his stubbled cheek, he pulled his lips from mine, his arms tight around me as he leaned closer. His breath fell hot against the skin of my neck, and his words tumbled haphazardly from his lips.

"Thank you." He sighed. "For seeing me when no one else even tried."

Heat stung my eyes.

This *was* goodbye.

Before I could stop him, Will retreated and left me standing there, shocked, on the dance floor. My mouth hung open as he stalked off, stealing a bottle from the bar and strolling out of the courtyard.

What did any of that mean? I shook my head, stunted for a long moment. Only when a couple bumped into me did I snap out of it. I didn't just move from the dance floor, though. My feet took me in the direction Will had disappeared.

If he was leaving the city, that was one thing, but something darker, something dangerous lingered in his words. Eventually, I found the stables. The last stall was empty. I stared at the place where we'd slept, shaking my head.

"He's gone, miss," the stable hand said.

"Which way did he go?"

He pointed up the alleyway, toward the square. I strode off.

"Miss, where are you going?"

I paused, turning toward the young man with determination guiding me. "To save the Beast."

CHAPTER FORTY-NINE

WILL

N OTHING MATTERED ANYMORE.

I said my piece, fulfilled my promises. Now it was time to go.

I swayed in the saddle and lazily walked my stallion through the dark city streets. Sweet cigar smoke curled in the night air. I cracked the bottle open and drank heavily, letting the humidity stick to my skin as languid fire coursed through my blood.

The alcohol was smooth as it slipped down my throat, reminding me of how easy it'd been. All of it. Taking on my father's debt. The killing. Helping Jesse get Bonnie back. *Kissing Savvy.* How the knife slipped between Seb's ribs. His eyes wide with shock and betrayal. Hearing so many people talk about how little they knew him. How isolated he'd been from everyone.

Everyone except me.

I swallowed hard as the horse trotted along, past crumbling buildings and dim streetlights. Until the scenery opened up, and the towering tombs of long-dead people blanketed the moonlight in shadow. I didn't know what I would've done if Zachary asked me to mutilate and hang Seb too. Instead, I buried him. With the money I'd earned leeching lives beneath my gun and blade. I hadn't had the courage to come here since the undertaker had carted him away, beneath a dirty cloth, on the back of a horse-drawn cart.

I tugged the reins, and the stallion obeyed, walking steadily through mausoleums, past plaques with names faded by time and the elements. I wondered if the souls left behind in this place watched. I traveled through the winding pathways until I found it: Seb's grave marker. I slid from the saddle, bottle in hand, not bothering to secure my horse. Better that he escape Lee the same night I did.

The gravestone rested on top of a hill, and the steep incline was bracing. As I finally mounted it, I found him, his name etched into a simple, jagged headstone. *Sebastian Jones.* I put the mouth of the bottle to my lips, drinking deep at the name carved there.

Jones.

Even in death, Jones owned him. The way he'd owned me and Bonnie all this time. He may not have paid for me, but by proximity, I'd been his. It was Jones's bloody mark Zachary had tried to burn away from my neck. I thought of the pleading deal Seb offered that night, the life he begged for us to have. I wished I could go back and make a different choice. Any other choice. Was any of it even real?

I tipped the bottle over and poured some of the liquid onto the freshly turned earth. The grass on this hill hadn't reclaimed the ground blanketing him yet.

"You would've appreciated the quality more than I would," I said. Tears caught in my voice. "You were kind of a snob that way." I walked closer, wishing the night wasn't so clear or the moon so bright. Wishing the silence here didn't feel so comfortable and inviting.

"This is the kind of thing you would've liked, too," I said to no one. "You always said you wanted a *big romantic gesture.*" No one answered me. Of course not. I was talking to a dead man.

"I keep thinking *how could you do it?* But I know, Seb. It's too easy to let them own you. To believe they'll care and keep you safe. Too easy to feel like you belong. I know why you'd do it. I even know why you never told me. I mean, it's not like I gave you much reason to trust me over the years . . . " I sat, picking at a blade of grass as I placed the bottle on the ground beside me. While I pulled out my cigarette case and lit a match, I thought of all the times he'd begged me to open my heart. How many times I refused him. I'd been so focused on Bonnie. Solely on helping her, on being there even as she looked through me. I didn't want to drag him into it. That felt like *defeat,* and I wasn't ready to admit I wasn't enough to get my best friend back. I never had been.

But Jesse was.

I'd been right about that all along. Inhaling the tobacco smoke deep into my lungs, I thought of earlier. The two of them gazed at one another like they'd found gold in each other's eyes.

"I might have been able to love you," I whispered at the headstone, taking a long drag and enjoying the bitterness of the tobacco on my tongue. A hysterical laugh bubbled up from my throat, and I sucked down another pull of harsh smoke. I could still feel the warm blood slicking over my hands. It'd been so *easy*. That was what I remembered the most. What hollowed me out until I was nothing. How *easy* it'd been to slide my knife between his ribs with practiced hands. "All I needed was for you to accept me. But maybe that's why it never would have worked. You couldn't *see* me.

"Damnit, Seb," I croaked. "A little acceptance. Not much, just a little. You used to look at me with that *goddamned* disappointment in your eyes whenever I pushed you away. Whenever I told you I didn't have a heart to give you. Like I was lying. Like I didn't wish I were different. Like I wouldn't give *anything* to feel something good. Anything good."

I dragged the bottle back to my mouth again, tears gathering in my eyes. I drank enough that it muted the sorrow that held me so tightly in its grip. When I finally lowered the bottle, gasping at the burn in my chest, I raised my eyes to the night sky.

It shouldn't look so beautiful here.

The heat from the alcohol in my blood was the only thing that made me feel alive at this moment. The quiet beauty and the still, silent night settled whatever reservations had been lingering from earlier at the party. Jesse would be alright. Bonnie was back. Savannah . . .

Well, I'd done my damned best, hadn't I?

"Now, I don't feel anything at all. I killed you, but I died in that alleyway, too, Seb. Nothing touches me. Not fear or anger or joy. The only time I feel anything, it's just . . . *pain*. The kind that doesn't have a beginning or an end. The kind that's always just *there*. Sucking me under until I can't breathe anymore." I paused, thinking I might've heard something rustling nearby. *Fuck it*. What was I worried about? Crater beasts? Grave robbers?

The truth clanged through me like a streetcar bell. *I* was the most dangerous thing here. I'd carved out all my humanity, piece by piece, and set it swinging like a rotting flag over the Mississippi. A dark laugh echoed around me that I barely recognized. And I had the nerve to wonder why I was hollow.

I pulled my pistol from its holster, studied it in the clear moonlight. Black grip. Black steel. Drinking in the light around it, like everything in my life. An aching absence of light and life and goodness. I checked the rounds, my hands steady, and cocked the hammer back. Lazily dragging the barrel over my jaw as the tears that clung to my lashes finally fell.

"I'm so *tired*, Seb. I'm tired of holding onto what little humanity I have left with both hands and still losing my grip. I'm tired and I want to stop. I just want to *stop*." I sniffed, stubbing the cigarette in the damp grass. With heaving breaths and a pounding heart, I dragged the barrel down, hovering on my lips before I wrapped my mouth around it.

The metallic tang and stinging taste of gunpowder residue on my tongue warred with the lingering sweetness of the alcohol. I squeezed my eyes shut, thinking of the happiness I'd seen on Bonnie and Jesse's faces tonight as they looked at each other. I'd done *one* good thing at least. *One good thing.*

It would have to be enough.

Warm hands covered mine on the grip of the pistol. My eyes snapped open in shock. Savannah knelt before me, her white dress stained with earth and grass. Her hands were gentle, but her chest heaved as she pulled the gun from my mouth and out of my grip. Worry folded deep in the lines around her dark eyes.

I couldn't think. Or move. Or do anything other than stare at her through the tears that hadn't fallen from my eyes yet. She tossed the gun away, movements slow, like she was trying to calm a spooked horse. Why was she *here*? How much had she heard? Why wasn't she saying anything?

My chest heaved, harder and harder, as if I couldn't fill my lungs all the way anymore. It grew tight, and pain blossomed beneath my ribs. Blackness crowded the edges of my vision. Was I dying? Was this what it felt like to die?

"Breathe, Will," she said, crossing the distance between us and cradling my face. Her hands were warm against my skin. "It's okay, just *breathe*."

I clutched my shirt, fisting it tight. "I can't—I can't—"

Her fingers buried in my hair, and she breathed, slow and deep. All I could see was her face in the moonlight, the way the light caught her cheekbones and made her eyes glow. The more I drank her in, the less frantic I became. I studied the full curve of her mouth and the long, elegant bridge of her nose. I watched moonlight dance through the haphazard curls framing her face. Some places were so dark it blended into the night, others bleached white, and some as brown as chicory coffee from the square. My chest didn't hurt anymore, I realized. She looked like an angel, only I wasn't sure if she'd come to redeem me or damn me to hell.

"You aren't supposed to be here," I said finally, the words harsh in the night. I pulled her hands away, needing to distance myself from her warmth.

"No, *you* aren't supposed to be here." The softness in her eyes turned steely. "I knew you weren't alright, but I didn't think you would—"

"Just *leave*, Savannah. Pretend you never came here." I lifted the bottle to my lips. She lurched forward, knocking it from my mouth until it rolled down the incline, the amber liquid soaking into the ground.

"If you think I'm going to leave you here *alone,* then you're stupider than I thought." I couldn't decipher her tone, and honestly, I didn't want to. Her words forced the last few tears to tumble down my cheeks. *Alone.* She didn't want me to be alone.

Something broke inside me.

A barrier I hadn't known was there, protecting me from the full weight of my sorrow. Or maybe it was because Savannah was here to watch me fall apart that I was able to do it so completely. Maybe all I really needed was an audience.

Her harshness melted away like wax from a lit candle, until she stared at me with that *goodness* I hated and envied so much. Her hand raised as if to swipe the tears from my cheek, but she dropped it, uncertainty twisting up the kind pity in her eyes. I didn't think; I just reached for her hand, pressing her palm to my skin. I held mine over it so she couldn't pull away, the softness of her touch an anchor to reality.

She shuffled closer, not caring about the stains on the fine fabric of her gown, until she was so close, I felt her breath on my cheeks. Until all I saw was her face lit in moonlight, crowding out the endless darkness.

"You aren't done yet, William." My thumb ran over her hand, the friction of the touch thudding into me with every beat of my heart. "I see you," she said more confidently. "I've *always* seen you."

I didn't know why it felt like I'd never seen *her* before now. Before this moment. When the pieces of her suddenly made sense. Like her words lifted a veil I didn't know had blinded me. Her eyes weren't dark honey like I'd thought. Sweet and pure. They were burnt umber lit with an edge of intelligence. They held a spark of rebellion now, searing straight into every shadowed corner of my black heart. Her eyes were like sunlight through whiskey; they were destruction, and redemption, and sweet numbing bliss.

"I'm going to kiss you." The words fell harsher than I intended. A small gasp came from her throat, her eyes widening. "If you don't want me to, push me away. Right now. Tell me no."

I touched her moonlit cheek, thinking I could feel the warmth of the light on her skin. Like a beacon, it called to me, leading me out of the swallowing dark. She didn't speak, but her breath came shorter, and I didn't know if it was fear or anticipation. I never knew if it was fear anymore. I'd grown so numb to people being afraid of me.

"Tell me no, Savannah," I said through gritted teeth. My fingers tangled in her curls. I loved how they clutched around my hand, grasping tight to me. Three heartbeats later, each one punctuated by the painful thud of my pulse, she hadn't pushed me away. Instead, she brushed her nose against mine, her lips parting in a sigh.

"Yes," she whispered.

My hand at the base of her neck tightened, and I pulled her hard to me. I crushed her mouth beneath mine in a bruising kiss, groaning as the taste of her lips obliterated whatever wayward thoughts I had left. *Goddamnit,* she was so sweet. I muffled the sound of her surprise against my mouth. I was so desperate to devour her, to touch the goodness inside of her, to be worthy of just one taste. Fuck, but I'd thought that before, and one taste was never enough. She whimpered, and I parted her lips with mine.

As our tongues tangled, any shred of self-control I had left was gone. She tasted bright like summer and sunlight. And I'd spent too long in the dark. I wanted to taste her skin, to feel her body shudder against mine, to see her bliss as she *finally* lost that unwavering self-control.

I *wanted* and I *felt* and for the first time in too long . . . I could breathe again.

I pulled away slowly, regretfully, to drink in the pretty flush on her cheeks and the glaze over those whiskey eyes. I took a ragged breath and realized that I needed *more.*

"*Fuck.*" I stared at her swollen mouth before kissing her again. Her lips were soft and eager, her body bowing into mine and snapping whatever tiny thread of self-control had hung on this long.

Every time I'd gotten too close to her, I'd leashed the wild impulses raging inside me. Careful to be gentle with her. Patient. Slow. So she knew without a doubt that everything was her choice. Not one of my wild, selfish whims.

But now?

There was nothing but the sweet taste of honey and champagne on her lips, reminding me of the first time I'd seen her. All wrapped up in her flouncy dress and high neckline, smelling like vanilla, with a fine dusting of flour in her hair and smeared on her cheek. I'd wanted to taste her then.

Now, I would devour her until there was nothing left of either of us.

I fisted my hands in the fabric of her skirts, because I needed *something* to hold onto. Something to prove this was real and not just another excuse for delaying the inevitable. She gasped into my mouth and pressed closer to my chest, eager and pliant. *Fuck*, she would be the death of me. Without thinking, my hands spanned her waist and I lifted her up, settling her directly on my lap so that she straddled me.

Mierda, this was torture.

Her mouth broke from mine, her dark curls framing our faces, millimeters apart. Like a moth drawn to flame, I reached out to bask in the warmth of her skin, reminding me that I was still alive. That being alive was full of *this*. Heat. Light. Pleasure. There was an end to the pain and darkness, and on the other side of that was *her*.

My fingers, stained with the blood of so many, skimmed along her jaw and traced the elegant length of her neck. Her pulse hammered against my fingertips, eyelids drooping into a heady expression. She was so unapologetically full of desire, it was fucking addictive. Her lips were swollen and red, making them look even more pillowy than before. I leaned forward, desperate to taste them again.

She rocked her hips and my world fell apart.

"Savvy." Her name dragged long from my throat. A plea and a warning. I shuddered beneath her, and she wriggled on my lap. I wasn't sure if it was an effort to put distance between us or to get closer. My cock was so hard that it rubbed painfully against the seam of my pants. Her wriggling, whatever the reason, made her slip further down until my cock was pressed against the searing heat between her thighs.

Her mouth dropped open, a little gasp catching in the back of her throat as her eyes blazed up at me. They were mindless, pupils blown wide, with an incredulous glaze about them that mirrored every sensation rolling down my spine. In this moment, my fingers digging into her hips as I bucked against her, I'd never felt more connected to anyone.

Every time I breathed in, I drank down her exhalations. My whole soul was anchored to here and now because of the grip I had on her full hips and her fingers tangled desperately in my hair. And when she looked at me, with those passion-glazed eyes, it wasn't the Beast she saw. Or a sarcastic outlaw. The son of notorious serial killer Sixgun Ellis.

It was me. *William.*

Through the swell of pleasure building with every rocking motion, like the push and pull of a strong tide, the edge of oblivion faded away. I knew every freckle on her nose, no matter how faint. I'd counted her eyelashes a thousand times. I dreamt about the curves of her full lips and the way her hands moved when she baked. It was like watching someone compose music. Confident and beautiful and artistic.

"Do you want this?" My words were barely audible above our haggard breathing. This couldn't be just about tonight. No. I couldn't use her to drown my own grief. I wouldn't. If she said no, it might kill me. But more than I wanted to lay her down and make her scream my name in ecstasy, I needed her to want *this*.

To want *me*.

She nodded, but the motion was timid, and even though every cell in my body screamed to ravage her like the beast I was, that timidness stopped me. Held me back. As if she saw the thoughts as they passed through my mind, Savannah pressed her mouth insistently against my lips. Her nails raked against my scalp as she gripped my hair like handles to drag me closer. It was so fucking hot I nearly died.

This time when she pulled her mouth away, she spoke in the scant space between our lips.

"*Please*, William."

Before she finished speaking my name, I pressed her into the soft turned earth. I didn't care if her dress was ruined, or the stupid expensive suit Jesse bought me for tonight. Her hands slid underneath the jacket lapels, shoving it over my shoulders as my lips wandered. Over her jaw, stopping to nibble on her earlobe and elicit a mewling moan I would hear in my sleep tonight. Down her neck, scraping my teeth between the base of her neck and her shoulder until she arched beneath me, guiding my mouth lower.

As I reached her cleavage, I dragged her skirts up, until my palms slid over her calves and knees. At the same time, I found the hard point of her nipple through the fabric of her dress with my mouth, my hand wrapped around the hot flesh of her bare thigh. The accompanying sound as she writhed beneath me echoed in the still night, encasing me in nothing but *her*.

This was heaven.

"*God*, you know your way around a woman's body." She groaned as I lifted my mouth from her skin. The grin that curled over my lips was obscene and hedonistic.

"I'm God now?"

Familiar irritation flashed through those whiskey-colored eyes and sharpened them. My fingers trailed along the edge of her silk panties, in the crease of her thigh. Just as she was about to cut me down, I pressed my palm against her hot cunt. The heel of my hand put pressure in a place that made her lips part, and a strangled noise clawed its way up her throat. She was *soaked*. The fabric of her panties was so damp that my teeth clacked with how quickly I clenched my jaw.

Any restraint I had left was gone. I needed her. I needed to feel her. *Right fucking now*.

With deliberate slowness, allowing enough time for her to protest, I pushed the fabric aside and mapped every slippery inch of her with my fingers. Discovering every place that made her breath hitch and her hips squirm. Until she begged incoherently for more, without fully formed words. When her nails scraped against my forearm, I curled my finger inside her.

Only one.

"*Mierda!*" I swore as she clenched around me.

"What?" Insecurity weighed down the rasp of her voice. "What is it?"

Brushing a curl from her forehead and feathering my lips over her mouth, I stared deep into her eyes. If this was the best my life ever got, it was enough. *She* was enough.

"You're so tight, *mi sol*," I breathed against her skin. I stroked her, soft, paying special attention to the small bundle of nerves at the top of her sex that made her whiskey eyes a color that intoxicated me. "You're so fucking *perfect.*"

I could do this for hours. Watch as every flick of my fingers faded all those layers of insecurity and sacrifice. Until her control was barely a memory and she tossed her head in the graveyard dirt beneath her. Her cries of pleasure echoed loud enough to shake the moon from the sky.

"That's it." When my thumb pressed down against that spot she loved, she screamed her pleasure, shedding the last of her self-control as she shuddered in my arms. It was the most beautiful sight I'd ever seen. I didn't stop. Not until I'd wrung every drop of pleasure from her, until she tapped against my hand and her mouth found mine.

She kissed me sweetly, breath jagged in my mouth. Shifting on top of her, I slid my finger from inside her and undid my belt between our bodies. This felt right. Right in a way nothing ever had before. As I dragged my zipper down, I took a moment to bask in the expression on her face.

Calm. Peaceful. Sure.

"You want this?" I needed her affirmation in the deepest parts of me. She slid her fingers over my jaw as I settled between her thighs. Pressing close so she could feel how badly I wanted her.

"You won't hurt me, William." She trusted me. Implicitly. And I'd be damned if I didn't make sure I deserved that trust.

I pressed forward slowly, rocking gently as I worked my way inside of her. Her mouth dropped open, her chin tipping back as we came together. She whimpered, and her gaze dipped down between us. With my thumb, I guided her chin until she was looking at me again.

"It's just you and me." I shackled every animalistic urge raging through my body. She was just so fucking tight.

"You're too . . ." She swallowed, unable to talk with another rock of my hips. "Too big. You won't fit."

I traced my nose over her cheek, inhaling the scent of her skin as I dragged one of her legs around my hip. I sank deeper, and she gasped at the friction. My hair fell into my eyes, but I didn't care.

Nothing mattered anymore.

Nothing but *us*.

"You can take it, *mi sol*." With another gentle press of my hips, I was buried fully inside of her. She groaned, and I thought this was *exactly* how I wanted to die. Just like this. With Savannah beneath me, wrapped around me, all her rules shattered and her soul on clear display through those intoxicating eyes staring up at every broken piece of my battered soul with complete trust.

She wriggled, and I fisted my hand in the graveyard dirt beneath us.

"Fuck! Don't move." I sucked in deep breaths through my nose, jaw clenched so tight I thought my teeth might crack.

"*Will.*" Every last shred of control I'd painstakingly gathered snapped.

Hiking her other leg up until her heeled feet were crossed behind me, I dragged my hips back and thrust deep. Her nails bit into my shoulders, scrambling down my back until she found purchase. I couldn't make sense of anything; sparks of bliss spiked along my skin in moments of perfect clarity. Like stars shining through the deepest, darkest pleasure sinking deep into my body. With every thrust, I came apart at the seams. More and more.

Moments of agonizing beauty reeled through my mind, mirroring every detail of us coming together. Savannah screaming at me, her cheeks flushed in rage as I tore down all her careful plans. Just like she screamed my name now, into the night air. Flushed and fucking gorgeous. The sweet taste of her lips that first night and the sinful taste of them now as I dragged her bottom lip between my teeth. How her skin always smelled like vanilla and honey from the kitchens, and now she smelled like graveyard dirt and sex. Musky, heady, and sweet.

Sinking my fingers deep into the thick flesh of her thigh, I tipped toward the edge. I had no idea what would be on the other side. For me. For *us*. All I knew was I needed to make her come so hard she'd feel me for *days* afterward.

"That's it," I groaned. "Let go, baby."

Fingers buried in her curls, the pounding slap of our bodies audible above the cries of passion riding the sweet summer breeze, she came apart beneath me. It was a sight to behold. She arched off the ground, grinding against me as her eyes rolled back. I couldn't hold on even if I tried. When she clenched around me, it felt like I'd touched the source of the universe. Something too beautiful to understand.

As I spilled myself deep inside her, she rode every last drop from me. Then her tongue was in my mouth. Both of us breathing hard through our noses. Neither willing to be finished. Not yet. Just not *yet*.

Fuck.

I'd come as quickly as I had when I was a lusty teenager, like it'd been my first time with a woman. As my heart slowed and our kissing became sweeter, my lips traveled to her sweaty temple and the side of her throat. The moments after our frenzied fucking, reality sank back in slowly. Guilt roiled in my gut as I stared at her. Though her eyes were bright and her body relaxed, I couldn't miss her ruined dress, stained with graveyard dirt where I'd been planning to kill myself.

I was a monster.

Carefully, we separated and I tucked myself back into my pants. As I righted my clothes, thoughts of how much more Savannah deserved intruded into the rightness from moments ago. After all this time, in all the ways I'd imagined this, it'd never been me screwing the common sense out of her in a graveyard. What the hell was wrong with me?

She sat up, sliding her arm around my waist as she pressed a kiss to the side of my neck. It was sweet, and so fucking *Savannah* it hurt. She tucked a wayward lock of hair behind my ear, and I finally turned to look at her.

"Well, that was . . ." A satisfied smile curled on her swollen mouth.

"Not even remotely *enough*." Before I could stop myself, even to think, I gripped her chin and stared determinedly into her eyes. "I'm going to give you so much more."

And I meant it. In every way that mattered. I might not be the man she deserved *now*. I was too selfish, too impulsive, too broken. But for her, I'd kill the devil inside of me. Until the only part left alive was the sliver of *William* she saw so clearly, even when I couldn't. Roughly, I pulled her forward, my mouth bruising hers. Now that I'd had her, now that I knew what it was to be seen by her, I couldn't go back. I wouldn't.

Pulling away, I rested my forehead against hers and smiled. "So don't compare me to anyone else you've been with. Not yet. Not until I've had a chance to lock you away for *days*, worshiping every inch of your body until you can't speak, or think, or *breathe.*"

She curled her fingers into my shirt, and my self-loathing melted away again. I brushed her nose with mine and wrapped my arms around her, dragging her closer, desperate for the heat of her skin on mine. To have her completely bare and at my mercy. *Fuck.* I was hard again.

She breathed a laugh against my mouth. "That won't be hard. There hasn't been anyone else."

My heart stopped beating.

Every muscle in my body froze, and I forgot how to breathe.

"Will?" she asked, timid. But I couldn't speak.

"What do you mean?" I said clumsily, my brain finally remembering how to form words.

"I've never *been* with anyone else." Her eyebrows furrowed at my gaping mouth and clear shock. There was no way. *No possible way.* She couldn't have been a—

"You're a virgin?" My throat was suddenly dry. She leaned back, the space between us sending a shiver down my spine.

"Not anymore." Her eyes dulled in confusion. I couldn't understand it. She was beautiful, smart, and kind. There had to be plenty of men who'd wanted to sleep with her. I knew Savannah. Knew her in my *bones.* Like she was a part of me. Even though she was a private person, and selective about who she got close to, how was it possible *tonight* was her first time?

Or that the man she'd chosen . . . was *me.*

In all my fucked-up glory. Ruining an important moment with my selfish bullshit that should have been all about her. That should have been so much more than what I gave her. My self-loathing returned in full force, and those disgusted thoughts turned to irrational anger. And I *hated* myself all over again.

I'd robbed her of something she could never get back.

"Fucking hell, Savannah." I recoiled from her. I couldn't touch her. "Why didn't you *tell me?*"

Hurt flashed across her face, and she scrambled to her feet, shaking dirt from her dress. *Goddamnit!* Why did I mess everything up? I reached for her, but her answering glare stopped me.

"Just because I haven't *fucked* half of New Orleans doesn't mean I can't make decisions for myself—"

"That's not what I meant!" Even as I climbed to my feet, she was already searching the ground around us, nostrils flaring and shoulders hiked up. Preparing for a fight of epic proportions. "*¡Maldita sea!* I didn't even take my pants off. I would have done things *differently.*"

"Differently?"

I nodded, swallowing down the rambling thoughts crowding my mind.

"If I hadn't been here tonight, you'd have blown your head off."

Her words dropped between us like the bombs that ended the world.

Then, as if proving her point, she found my gun and picked it up, scoffing incredulously. I'd never seen her like this. Every time we argued, there was a hint of flirtation, irritation, but beneath it all there was warmth. An echo of kinship. Now, her eyes were cold and hard, a grimace making her teeth flash in the night.

"What was that?" I couldn't form words. "You were going to do what? Join Sebastian in whatever afterlife you believe in?" When I didn't answer, she pinched the bridge of her nose. "There are people who would be left to mourn you. Who would be left with unanswered questions. People who would blame themselves when you were gone. Because whether or not you deserve it, people care about you. Like Bonnie, and Jesse, and me."

I swallowed hard, blinking back the rapidly rising emotion flooding my chest. The weight of my actions fell heavy on my shoulders. I'd had my finger on that trigger. I'd been ready to pull it. I almost had. Every word she spoke was a bullet, ripping through muscle and sinew with the hard truth.

"You care about me?" I whispered. Wondering if that was still true now. Even through this terrifying new anger. She straightened her shoulders and stared in disbelief.

"You're an idiot, William Ellis." Then, before she saw my face fall, she turned on her heel and strode down the hill. It was only when she was walking away from me that the world snapped into focus. I chased after her without realizing it, reaching out to grip her elbow and spin her back around.

"Don't leave. Not like this," I pleaded.

She ripped her arm out of my grip, like she couldn't bear my touch. "I need to get back before Lee lets another guard beat me." She rolled her eyes.

Her words pounded into my skull, and I snapped. The beast inside my chest raged forward, demanding I find the son of a bitch who put his hands on her and make him pay. Torture and death flooded my mind until I tasted metallic blood on my tongue. I grabbed her again, rougher this time. By both arms.

"Which one." It wasn't a question so much as a command. Her eyes widened, and for the first time, with absolute certainty, I saw her fear. Scented it in the air like a wild animal. "Which. One." I ground the words through my teeth.

"I wasn't supposed to—"

"You'll tell me now, Savannah, or I'll kill every single one of them." It was no idle threat. Her lips trembled, and silence stretched between us. Tears shimmered in her eyes as she opened and closed her mouth soundlessly. Her gaze drifted over my shoulder to land on the tombstone at the top of the hill. Sebastian's grave marker.

Fractured memories knit together: hard glances across the courtyard, snide comments and accusations. Dread unfurled, cold horror spiking down my spine all the way through my arms and legs until I felt numb.

"Say it," I demanded.

My heart pounded once, twice, a third time before . . .

"Sebastian."

I dropped her arms and stumbled back. Every bruise imprinted in the back of my eyelids. Stark against her warm skin, black and violent, on display during the interrogation. Yellowing as they healed. The shadows in her eyes as she wore them, creeping into the dark corners of my heart to promise retribution.

Thick silence choked me. My mind raced with all the ways I'd already failed her. But staring at her now, there was only one thing I could see clearly: the startling lack of disappointment in her whiskey eyes. Sweet relief buoyed me forward.

So, I raked in a shuddering breath and closed my eyes to regain my composure. When I opened them, she was still standing there. Waiting for me.

With steady hands, I ran my palms up her bare arms and cradled her face, watching her relax against my touch.

"No one will touch you again," I vowed, my words hard and murderous. "No one but me. If anyone tries, I'll nail their hands to the motherfucking bridge."

"Will—"

"No." I shook my head, kissing her hard on the mouth to silence her. "I should have killed him sooner. Slower. I won't make that mistake again."

Her eyes were wide, but she didn't protest again. "Wait here." I climbed the hill, retrieving my jacket from the ground and staring down at Seb's grave. It was the last time I would come here. The last time I would mourn for him.

"I never really knew you at all, did I?" I asked quietly. "Goodbye, Seb."

With every step down that hill, I felt lighter than I had in a long time. And when I reached Savannah, I wrapped my jacket around her shoulders and led her to my stallion, lifting her onto the saddle delicately before swinging on behind her.

I tucked her into my arms, and as I led us back onto the street, the slamming of windows sounded. This would ruin her. Riding with the Beast. I shifted on my saddle and tilted her chin to look at me.

"Are you ready for this?" I asked tenderly.

Without missing a beat, she kissed me full on the mouth.

"I'm ready."

CHAPTER FIFTY

BONNIE

LUCAS KEPT HIS HANDS on me all night. I'd run a lot of cons in my life, killed more men than he would believe. If he knew of the murderous thoughts running through my head every time he touched me, he'd run screaming. Instead, I kept a pleasant yet absent expression plastered on my face, and that suited him just fine.

My head throbbed. Pain bloomed at the base of my skull and pounded with each individual beat of my heart. Remembering was agony. In more ways than one.

My father arched an exacting eyebrow at me, taking a deep swallow of the liquor in his glass. Pinching the bridge of my nose to relieve some of the pressure, I tried not to let out an audible gasp as a long-buried memory rushed to the surface.

My mother's hands lifted from the rhythmic running of her fingers through my hair. I was nearly asleep when the pressure of her weight lifted from the edge of my bed. Even with my eyes closed, I heard her harsh whisper as the door opened.

"Zach, it's nearly midnight, and the landlord came earlier. Why haven't you paid this month?"

"I just walked in the fucking door." His voice was harsh and loud. I'd heard him this way so many times, but it always startled me. I'd learned to keep my breathing even, not to attract his notice, so that's what I did. Pretending to be asleep while peeking through my eyelashes as he scraped a chair away from the table and sat heavily, pouring a cloudy amber liquid into a dirty glass.

"Please, Zach, tell me it's not another one of your get-rich-quick schemes. We can't afford—"

"I used to fucking be somebody!" he shouted, finishing the liquid in his glass in one gulp before slamming it on the table. My mother approached him, shushing and holding her hands out.

"Audrey's asleep, don't wake her—"

"I don't fucking care! You don't understand what it's like for me. How could you? You were nobody before the Culling. Some washed-up actress waiting tables." My mother mopped at her cheeks; I realized she was crying. Silent tears pooled beneath her eyes and ran down her face. Then my father's expression changed, softened by her tears. "Fuck, I'm sorry, Em." He opened his arms, and she sat in his lap, letting him gather her against his chest. "I'm not built for this. You know? Working with my hands, in a field, barely enough to feed us . . . that wasn't what my life was supposed to be. But I have an opportunity, a real one; I just need a little more money."

"We don't have any money," Mom said, words careful and calm.

"We have that hair comb; those are real stones and we could—"

"No." The word fell heavy between them. My eyes opened wide, shocked that Mama dared to stand up to Daddy. She'd never done that before. "My brother gave that to me. I won't sell it . . . I can't."

He shoved her off his lap, anger hiking his shoulders up as he fisted his hands at his sides. She hit the floor with a heavy thump that forced a worried shout from me. When his eyes settled on me, lying petrified on our one shared bed across the small, shabby room we lived in, they darkened and turned calculating.

"Fine! You want to be a selfish bitch, there's still something of mine I can use as collateral for the loan."

Her face screwed up in confusion as she struggled to sit up on the floor, holding the arm she'd landed on as her eyes tracked between us. Until horror filled the dark blue of them. Everything dissolved then, into shouts and protestations. I clapped my hands over my ears because it was too loud. Why were they so angry?

I'd never remembered my childhood before. Any recollections revolved around the night my mother died. Now, I remembered how afraid I'd been of my father. How my mother gave me the last of our food more times than I could count, often watching me eat over her empty plate. And with the memory came a sinking feeling in my chest. One that shook the foundation of my life.

Jesse.

He was still here, on the edges of the party, eyes locked on me. Could he read the tension in my shoulders? See the flare of panic in my eyes? He tilted his glass at me from across the room, expression tight with concern. A silent acknowledgement. That he was here, and I wasn't that scared little girl.

Sucking in a deep breath to steady myself, I sipped the water I'd asked for, praying my headache would subside soon.

A loud clinking echoed over the din of conversation, and the music faded. The high pitch set my teeth on edge. Lucas dragged me forward, and I almost bit him. His grip on my elbow made me wild with rage. I wanted to hurt him. All of them. But before I could act on those impulses, I was leveled with dozens of stares. My hands were suddenly clammy.

"In case any of you weren't aware," Lee said, his voice strong, powerful. Ever the charismatic businessman. "I'm Zachary Lee, and this is my home." He motioned to the crowd with his half-filled scotch glass. A smattering of laughter sounded as the high-society pricks turned to one another, congratulating themselves for existing in the first place.

"I'd like to start by welcoming you today," he continued. "And ask that you raise your glasses to my late wife, Audrey's mother, Emma Lee."

Fury the likes of which I'd never felt before thrummed through my veins. And as quickly as rage burned my body, my mind plummeted into another memory.

A soft shaking woke me from a deep sleep, and when my eyes opened blearily, my mother's face swam in front of it. "Mama?" She held a finger to her lips and beckoned me forward.

I slid quietly off the mattress where my father slept next to me, smelling of sweat and whiskey.

Something was strange. The sun hadn't risen yet, and Mama always told me that when the moon was awake it was time for rest. When I swayed, rubbing my eyes, she lifted one of my feet and shoved me into my shoes before picking me up in her arms. She tucked her coat around me, and I settled my tired head against the crook of her shoulder, sleep dragging me under again.

"She would have loved to be here," Lee said, awkwardly clearing his throat and turning his gaze to the floor for a moment. He inhaled deeply before squaring his shoulders. "And to thank you for coming on behalf of the Rutherfords, who couldn't make it on such short notice from Manhattan Island."

The *fucking* audacity! To use her name and memory as a plea for sympathy. I should've hidden my intentions, but my face wouldn't cooperate. Instead, I stared incredulously at his gall. *She left him!* I wanted to scream into the crowd.

She was brave enough not to take his shit, to get out. No matter what it meant for us. Lucas gripped me tighter around my waist and leaned close.

"Are you alright?" he whispered in my ear. "You're pale."

"Headache," I muttered, finding Jesse's gaze across the room. A silent plea for help wavered in my eyes. He shook his head softly, and I breathed through the swell of disgust.

"Audrey is unlike other daughters," Lee continued, turning back to the crowd. "Even as a child, everything was a challenge. She always had to run faster, climb higher, fight harder than any other kid on our block."

As if he'd been there when I was a child. Even when we'd all lived together, he was always gone. Always drunk. Always distant.

"It was exhausting on the best of days, and terrifying on the worst of them." Some of the crowd chuckled uneasily. I disposed of my glass and crossed my arms, digging my nails into the meat of my palms to refrain from strangling him.

Had he ever actually thought of me as a daughter at all?

"But her tenacity has always amazed me." He looked at me, the harsh lines of his face softening, eyes glistening.

I hated him.

And I hated that he reserved that softness, however rare, for me alone. It fucked me up.

Then I remembered something else, something worse.

Our new house was even smaller than the last. But this time it was just me and Mama. Twice a week we paid a man to take letters that Mama wrote on any paper she could afford. We worked in the garden, and she told me fairy stories. She sang while she cooked, and she taught me to be wary of strangers. Especially Daddy.

The first time I saw Mama scared was when the letter man came a third time one week. She let me play with blocks in the corner as they spoke at the table. Mama cried into her tea.

"I just don't understand. Anna and Jeff—"

"We thought we knew where they were, but they left a long time ago. One of your letters was intercepted, and I only just found out. Please tell me you have weapons, some kind of protection."

Mama nodded and pulled down a tin from the cabinet. When she opened it, she pulled out a pretty gun with an ivory handle. It was like Mama's hair comb. Intricate. Beautiful.

"We can give you enough food and supplies for a little while, but you'll have to leave. Tomorrow."

Mama nodded, and after he left, she lifted me into her lap. Burying her nose against my neck and squeezing me tight. Her fingers shook as she dragged them through my hair.

"It's okay, Mama."

She gifted me a shaky smile.

That night we both lost our lives. She died and Audrey did, too.

I blinked hard, my expression tightening as I stood on display with my heart shattering once more. Because the realization was immediate and horrible.

This wasn't the first time my father sold me.

He was the reason the slavers came after us. He was the reason my mother died.

He turned me into *this*.

"It's no secret that Audrey has had to withstand her share of troubles. But the woman she's become in spite of them would make any father proud."

A murderer. The woman I'd become to survive in spite of him was a murderer. An outlaw. Relentless and exacting. And he was going to find out *exactly* who he'd made me into.

A moment passed before Lee turned to Rutherford. "Lucas, on the other hand, is one lucky son of a bitch. There's no denying it, he's marrying up."

Several snickers and chuckles came from the crowd.

"In all seriousness," Lee said. "I couldn't be happier to call him my son-in-law. He's an ambitious young man, and ambition I understand. I admire. Both in business and in life."

The crowd broke into polite laughter as Lucas tucked me tighter to his side. I spared a half-second glance at him before my gaze shot toward Jesse. He lifted his brows, the small gesture confirming he knew something was wrong. I clenched my jaw and Jesse tensed, his shoulders hiked up and his glass forgotten as he moved toward the far edge of the party. A message. That he was coming for me. We'd be together again in moments. I just had to hold on.

"To the both of you, I hope you learn that together, your ambition and tenacity will serve you well. But only if it's tempered with tenderness and patience. Enjoy every moment, because you never know when it might be your last." Lee turned to the crowd. "And never pass up an opportunity to tell each other how much you love the other."

Enjoy tonight, Daddy. You never know when it might be your last.

"Without further ado, raise your glasses to Audrey and Lucas!"

Cheers resounded and glasses clinked. Lucas pressed a soft, slimy kiss to my mouth that lasted three seconds too long. When he released me, his brows furrowed, and I offered a pained expression to indicate my headache. He brushed some hair from my temple and opened his mouth to say something before my father interrupted and pulled him away.

Run.

I had to get the fuck out of here. Now. Or I would do something to get myself hung in the middle of Lee Square. Slinking away as quietly as I could, I skirted the edges of the party and made a beeline for Jesse across the room.

He knew something was wrong, because I'd taught him how to look for danger, and he did just that. Head on a swivel as he assessed the room. To an onlooker, it may seem like casual interest, but I knew my farm boy. The protective glint in his eyes promised violence if anyone so much as touched me.

Sliding behind a column beneath the breezeway, I dipped into the shadows as naturally as breathing. Until he reached for me and we tangled together in an embrace that could get us killed. He traced my arms and shoulders, searching for wounds that existed in the deepest, darkest parts of my heart.

"What is it?"

"Not here; we need a safe place to talk." My urgency set him on edge. "Now, farm boy."

Hands clenched, I led him away. As we rounded a corner, familiar voices made my heart plummet to the ground. With a hard yank on Jesse's hand, we folded together. He pressed me tight against a brick wall, our bodies hidden in shadow. The voices crept closer, and Jesse squeezed tighter against the wall.

"She's more unstable tonight than I'd like, Zachary," Lucas said, words hard.

My father hummed his displeasure, but it wasn't a disagreement. "You might be right."

"I want the wedding to happen quickly. So she isn't tempted to break the engagement."

A pause, then my father heaved a sigh and said, "I can't argue with that. It will be a challenge curbing her wild spirit."

Lucas chuckled cruelly. "Oh, don't worry about that. I'll make sure she learns her place. Let's say two weeks, here at the manor?"

"That's fine. Plenty of time to arrange everything. Afterwards, we'll begin the new shipping route. Your friend, Patrick, can he smuggle them through the mill into the city? I heard there were concerns with an older brother—"

Lucas's glass clinked as the ice moved against the rim. "Actually, I wanted to talk to you about having your *Beast* join the first shipment. That should take care of our problem quite neatly." Their voices began to fade as they walked toward the party.

"I hate to be without him, but I'll consider it."

Then someone called them over, and they were gone.

Jesse gripped my chin hard, fingers digging into my cheeks. He kissed me brutally, and I knew it was his way of showing me what he couldn't say. I shoved him away and jerked my head, indicating we didn't have *time* for this. He followed without protest. We barely made it into the front house when the sound of guards' boots on the floor echoed around us. I motioned with two fingers toward the stairs. Second floor. Less chance of discovery.

We moved together as fluidly as we'd danced, ducking up the stairs before the guards rounded the corner. His hand splayed on the small of my back as we made it to the second floor. His warm touch steadied me in ways I couldn't explain. When everything fell apart around me, I could always count on Jesse.

The corridor was too open, too exposed. "C'mon." My heels clicked against the plank floor eerily in the darkness. My father's study loomed before us, and I turned the knob only to find it locked. Like always.

My nostrils flared, and I yanked the comb from my hair, bending one of the tines until I could insert it into the lock. Jesse grunted in disapproval, and when I looked up at him, he scowled at the comb in my hand. In seconds, a click sounded and the door swung open.

"Don't get offended; it'll bend right back into place. I wouldn't dream of breaking it." I shut the door behind us with a soft *click*. He kissed the crown of my head. "We don't have time."

"What's going on? Is it about what that motherfucker was saying?" he asked, his words on edge. "You haven't looked like that since—"

"I remembered *everything*, Jesse."

He sighed, running his hands through his hair as he paced further into my father's study. A hurricane lamp flickered dimly in the corner, either because my father was working until the party or planned to work after. Which meant we didn't have much time.

LAUREN SEVIER & ABBIE LYNN SMITH

"I know, I was there." He opened his palms toward me. I scowled at his sarcasm.

"No." I shook my head. "I remember my childhood. Things I didn't remember even before my head injury. I must have blocked it out before but—"

"You remember Lee?" he asked, his curiosity piqued.

"Yes!" I paced in agitation, trying to put things in order. In perspective. How did I explain this? My eyes caught on a picture of my mother, and it hurt to see her here. Frozen in time like it erased all he'd done. I marched toward it and smacked it over, hiding her discerning eyes from the truth.

Behind it, two familiar faces came into focus in another picture: Anna and Jeffrey James, Jesse's parents. Shaking hands with my father. With unsteady fingers, I picked up the picture. There was a large symbol behind them, and there were some very serious-looking people in smart clothes standing together. Clenching the frame so hard my knuckles went white, I cried out as pain rocketed through my skull once more. Jesse called my name, but all I heard was my thundering pulse.

I hadn't eaten in three days and my father was furious about it. But I couldn't bring myself to hear his frustrated pleas. Instead, I rocked in the rocking chair and stared out of the window in the library, clutching my empty belly. What was the point? Of anything. Of living.

I wanted to fall asleep and never wake up.

A knock sounded, and my father's aggravated sigh scraped against something raw in me. His shoes clicked against the oak slat floors as he opened the door and waved someone inside. Sitting again on the chaise, I didn't turn to look at the guest. I knew who it was from the glimpse in my periphery. Black cowboy hat. Sunglasses. Cruel smile.

Sixgun wasn't an uncommon sight in the house, though my father rarely let him near me. I suppose because he didn't want me to hear them talking about whatever business they had together. Though, a near-catatonic state did wonders for my inclusion, it seemed.

I closed my eyes, resting my head back on the chair, trying to block out everything. All the pain, all the grief, all of this interruption.

"How was the last trip to Montana? Did the locals know anything?"

"Uh . . ." Sixgun cleared his throat, the jingle of his spurs a testament to his nervous shifting.

"It's fine. She isn't listening. Even if she were, she doesn't know anything about it." My father ignored my presence. Anger and hurt thrashed in my

stomach. He dismissed me easily. Too easily. But I wouldn't let him do that forever.

No, I would learn everything about business. I would pull out of this, if only to prove him wrong. To prove I was worthy of his consideration.

"No. Nothing. They kept to themselves. Lived quiet lives. Got close to very few people and only in passing."

My father stood abruptly, slamming his hands on the coffee table before him, rattling the china plates he'd brought up to tempt me to eat. My eyes opened in surprise at his outburst. He so rarely showed emotion like this. Seldom did he lose control in any aspect of our lives.

"This is your fucking fault! You had clear orders to keep Anna alive so she could tell us where she hid them." His words were venom, and I sucked in a sharp breath. He looked at me, peering curiously at him. Then, he smoothed his shirt, tapping the fleur-de-lis pin on his tie as if it steadied him. "What of her sons?"

"No one knows what happened to them. Probably dead. They were so sheltered they couldn't have survived on the street." Sixgun grunted, head tilting in admonishment.

"We'll just have to keep looking, won't we?" my father asked. Sixgun nodded, mouth slanted into a grim, murderous scowl.

After that, I excused myself to be alone once more. I didn't care what they were looking for. I didn't care about Sixgun and his horrors. All I cared about was trying to stop feeling like I was drowning. To ease the pressure in my chest and my head. So I searched for Savannah. She, at least, knew how to steady the chaos of my grief.

"Bonnie! Goddamnit, Bonnie!" Jesse gripped my arms tight, shouting in my face as tears filled my eyes.

"Oh God," I moaned, unsure how to say any of this. How to tell the man I loved that I'd solved the mystery that ruined his life.

"I swear to God, if you don't start talking—"

I wrenched out of his grip, covering my mouth with trembling fingers. Walking a few paces forward, I tried to puzzle it all together. Anna hid something from Lee. Something dangerous. Something he wanted enough to kill and burn a town to the ground.

But it'd been *years* since he burned Jesse's home down.

He knew Jesse's parents before the Culling.

I stared blankly at the map behind his desk as my mind whirred, more questions arising with every answer. Jesse slid his hand onto my waist then, and the friction of his fingers on my body cleared my mind the way it always did.

My eyes drifted over the crater sites. The lines of the borderlands. But my gaze stuck on a small inscription at the bottom right corner. And a new horror dawned over me, forcing me to tremble violently on my feet.

"Bonnie, *please*, talk to me. You're scaring me." Jesse's words were tinted with concern.

January 17th, 2020.

"It was him." I gulped. My mind emptied, but my mouth kept moving. "All of it."

"Who? What? I don't understand."

"He sold me as a child. Collateral for a loan. My mother found out, and we ran in the middle of the night, but they found us. He killed her. My *father* killed her, Jesse."

His blue eyes darkened, his jaw tightening to hold in whatever angry words hung on his lips.

"That's not all. He killed your parents, too." I swallowed hard, pressing my hands to his chest. Letting him feel me. That I was here with him. His heart raced beneath my palm. "He said as much in front of me, thinking I wouldn't put it together."

Jesse let out a harsh sigh, his breath shuddering with rage.

"That's not even the worst part," I said, so quietly I wondered if he heard me. His hands covered mine, squeezing tightly. Urging me on.

"Look at the date on the map." His brows screwed up in confusion, and I pulled one shaking hand out from beneath his. Pointing to the date in the corner. The lines of Jesse's face deepened. Solidified into something dark and violent.

"That doesn't make sense. My father was just coming out of school in 2020. The Culling didn't happen until years later—"

Silence descended on us both then at the implication hanging ominous between us. How could my father have a map of the crater sites *before* the bombs dropped? Years before. When his breath caught, I knew he'd pieced it together.

"It has to be a mistake, right?" he asked, but neither of us really believed that.

"He planned it." The truth dangled freely as resolve settled into my bones. "He planned how to reshape the world and killed millions of people to make it happen."

Everything I knew was wrong. Broken.

His hands slid into my hair, cradling my face and tilting my chin until our eyes met. In his, I saw the fires of hell, promising revenge. Mirroring the dark retribution that sank into my chest.

"Who are you?" he asked, the way he'd always done.

"I'm his daughter *and* an outlaw."

"*What* are you?" His voice was a dangerous growl.

"I'm his worst nightmare."

"What are you going to do?"

Staring into Jesse's blue eyes, burning hot with loathing and pain, the answer came to me and dragged me down with purpose. Purpose I hadn't felt in a *long* time. It spurred me to action. I crossed the study in a few short strides, lifting the hurricane lantern. Hand-painted with a delicate fleur-de-lis pattern, clearly expensive.

Without a second thought, I threw it through the air, glass shattering against the map on the wall. The oil spread, and flames rippled from the center, crackling and smoking as the aged paper curled and blackened beneath it.

"I'm going to burn it all to the fucking ground."

As the flames caught and consumed the eastern seaboard, I buried my face in the crook of Jesse's shoulder. His hand came up to the base of my neck, and he tucked his nose into my hair.

Just like a night from so long ago, we leaned against each other to make it through. His breath was hot in my ear, ragged. Time moved differently now. It was more urgent, yet the crackle of the fire made it tick by slowly. The flames reflected in Jesse's bright eyes.

It was a fire that had brought him to me and stole his entire world away. We'd buried too many of the people we loved already, and they may not be the last before this was done. But as the flames blazed against the encroaching night, I still had hope. Something was hidden in Montana. Something secret, something dangerous, the key to ending this war. We were going to find it.

And the next person who burned wouldn't be anyone I loved.

ACKNOWLEDGMENTS

Last July, with suffocating humidity ruining our hairstyles and slicking against our skin, Abbie Lynn Smith and I launched *Guns & Smoke*. It was the culmination of a dream come true, and with every new reader, every excited review, and small win our outlaw gang grew stronger and more fierce than either of us could imagine. To say that I was terrified to write the sequel after such a great welcome of the first book in the series is an epic understatement.

But life is for taking risks and rising to challenges, and challenge ourselves we did. With adding two new characters in the mix, things could have gone horribly wrong. However, through the new character perspectives I found myself learning and growing so much more than I ever thought possible.

Will Ellis, in particular, terrified me the most to write. I knew from the time he came on the page in *Guns & Smoke* that the witty, sarcastic, carefree outlaw we met was only skimming the surface of who he really is. And *boy howdy* wasn't that the truth! William Ellis taught me a lot about life and perseverance, and the importance of letting other people in. Will and I are similar in a lot of ways, I always try to be the problem-solver in life, to take care of others (sometimes with little thought for myself), and I care about everything so deeply... even if I'm not always good at showing it. Will's journey in this book is dark and heavy, it's meant to make you uncomfortable at times. Too often the people who are suffering the most are some of the funniest, most charismatic people we know. And with the help of Savannah, Bonnie, and Jesse, we'll get to see Will claw his way back as the series continues. It's my fervent hope that you stick around to see him become the hero he claims not to be.

LAUREN SEVIER & ABBIE LYNN SMITH

Three months before *Guns & Smoke* was set to release, Lauren and I took a retreat to a cabin in the middle of nowhere to begin writing *Leather & Lace*. I'd known for months exactly how this novel would begin: showing how time and distance had changed Jesse James from the naïve farm boy we met in book one to an outlaw in book two. Jumping back into Jesse was one of the most natural things in the world, and I really enjoyed his growth in this novel.

Adding two character perspectives to an established plotline is risky. The early versions of The Fool's Adventure series introduced a new character to the fold: Savannah Beauregard. The difference between adding Will's perspective and Savannah's was that Savannah was a blank slate. Readers knew nothing about her. It was such a challenge, because after finishing that first draft, she definitely needed the most work. Even though I know that is natural, I can't tell you how many times I beat myself up over it. That's because Savannah has so many parts of me in her. I worried readers wouldn't like her, and that if they didn't, it meant they didn't like me, but I know that's not the case. That's literally just my brain being mean to me.

The final version of Savannah in the novel (and the rest of the series, as you will see), is a strong woman who, despite her trials, conducts her life out of kindness and compassion for others. It has been an honor to bring her to life.

We want to thank you, dear readers, for caring so much about our ragtag band of misfits and the broken world they inherited. But, of course, no outlaw can go it alone and we had *so many* wonderful people to help us along the way. A special thanks to:

Our wonderful beta readers for providing invaluable feedback: Joshua Guillory, Ashley Nelson, Emily S. Hurricane, David Folz, Nicole York, Angel Casillo, & Heather Welch.

Alexandra Ott, for her incredible line editing services.

Goddess Fish blog tours and Silver Dagger tours for their amazing promotional opportunities.

Jonathan Sevier for being our biggest cheerleader, bringer of coffee & snacks, and world-class toddler wrangler. Paw Paw Wayne for being an avid fan and source of inspiration for the series. And many countless friends, co-workers, and family members for their support and encouragement.]

Michelle & John Cavalier of Cavalier House Books for being the best indie bookstore in the world!

The Independent Book Review and Prairies Book Review for their fantastic editorial services.

Sign up for our newsletters or follow us on socials to get the latest teasers, exclusive content, and updates for the next books to come in the series!

Laissez les bon temps rouler!

Also by Lauren Sevier

Songs Series

Songs of Autumn

Songs of Winter

The Fool's Adventure Series

Guns & Smoke

Leather & Lace

ABOUT LAUREN SEVIER

Lauren Sevier lives a simple life in small town Central, Louisiana with her family and sweet Border Collie. She's a proud firefighter wife and mother to her miracle son, born through IVF after an eight-year battle with infertility. She works for a non-profit hospital in Cardiology. Writing and being in the service of helping others are her two passions in life.

She started writing song lyrics and poems on the front porch swing of her family home. She and her best friend get most of their inspiration on girl's night, after a glass of wine, or after watching movies from the early 2000's. They have plans to publish many series in the future together. However her passion is derived mostly from being a mother to her adventurous, imaginative, and affectionate son who ceases to amaze her every single day.

For more information, go to www.laurensever.com.

Also by
Abbie Lynn Smith

The Fool's Adventure Series
Guns & Smoke
Leather & Lace

ABOUT
ABBIE LYNN SMITH

 Abbie Lynn Smith is an author of romance novels. She holds a Bachelor's degree in theatre, where she learned the art of storytelling. A lifelong resident of southern Louisiana, she is a lover of coffee, naps, and animals.

When not writing, she can be found spending time with her rescue dogs, Klaus and Mama.

Abbie is passionate about mental healthcare and believes that helping others with their own mental health battles is her small way of changing the world. Abbie grew up watching westerns with her grandfather, which partially inspired the setting of her co-authored debut novel, Guns & Smoke.

For more information, go to
www.abbielynnsmith.com

www.ingramcontent.com/pod-product-compliance
Lightning Source LLC
Chambersburg PA
CBHW050844210726
48290CB00004B/1068